Tamamo
the Fox Maiden
and Other Asian Stories

a Cautionary Fables & Fairytales book

editors
C. Spike Trotman, Kate Ashwin, Kel McDonald

cover artist
Sabrina Cotugno

book designer
Matt Sheridan

proofreader
Abby Lehrke

Other Books in the *Cautionary Fables and Fairytales* Series:
THE GIRL WHO MARRIED A SKULL AND OTHER AFRICAN STORIES

Publisher's Cataloging-In-Publication Data
(Prepared by The Donohue Group, Inc.)

Names: Spike, 1978- editor. | Ashwin, Kate, editor. | McDonald, Kel, editor. | Sheridan, Matt, 1978- designer.
Title: Tamamo the fox maiden, and other Asian stories / editors, C. Spike Trotman, Kate Ashwin, Kel McDonald ; book design, Matt Sheridan ; cover art, Sabrina Cotugno ; print technician, Rhiannon Rasmussen-Silverstein.
Description: [Chicago, Illinois] : Iron Circus Comics, [2019] | Series: A cautionary fables & fairytales book ; [2] | Interest age level: 012-014. | Summary: "A collection of Asian folktales retold as comics include vengeful spirits, flying ogres, and trickster tigers from Japan, China, Tibet, India, Indonesia and beyond."--Provided by publisher.
Identifiers: ISBN 9781945820342
Subjects: LCSH: Fables, Oriental--Comic books, strips, etc. | Fairy tales--Asia--Comic books, strips, etc. | Asians--Folklore--Comic books, strips, etc. | CYAC: Fables, Oriental--Cartoons and comics. | Fairy tales--Asia--Cartoons and comics. | Asians--Folklore--Cartoons and comics. | LCGFT: Fables. | Fairy tales. | Graphic novels.
Classification: LCC PZ7.7 .T357 2019 | DDC [Fic] 398.2095--dc23

inquiry@ironcircus.com   www.ironcircus.com

s t r a n g e   a n d   a m a z i n g

first printing: December 2018   Printed in China   ISBN: 978-1-945820-34-2

Table of Contents

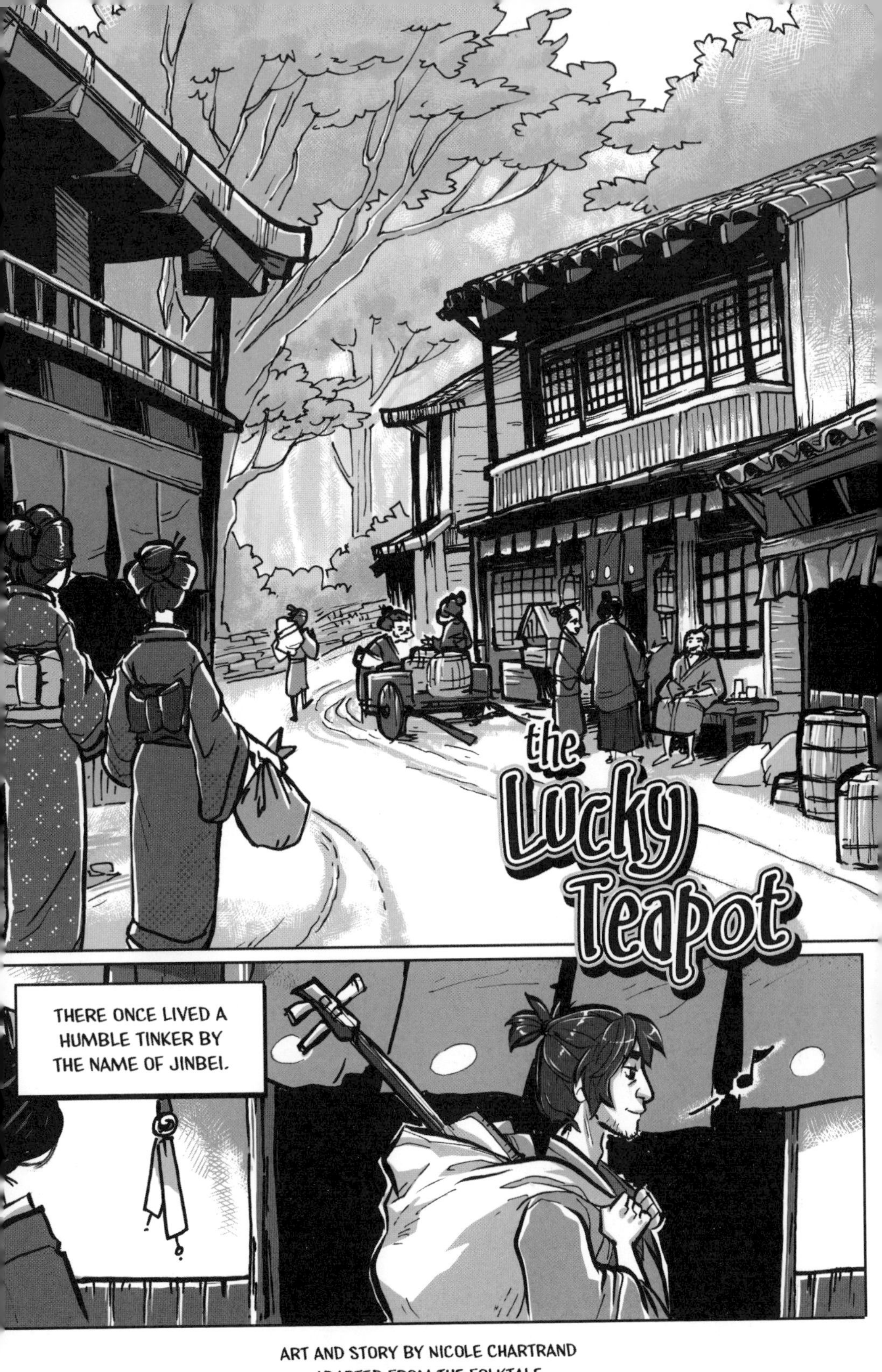
the Lucky Teapot
THERE ONCE LIVED A HUMBLE TINKER BY THE NAME OF JINBEI.

ART AND STORY BY NICOLE CHARTRAND
ADAPTED FROM THE FOLKTALE
BUNBUKU CHAGAMA

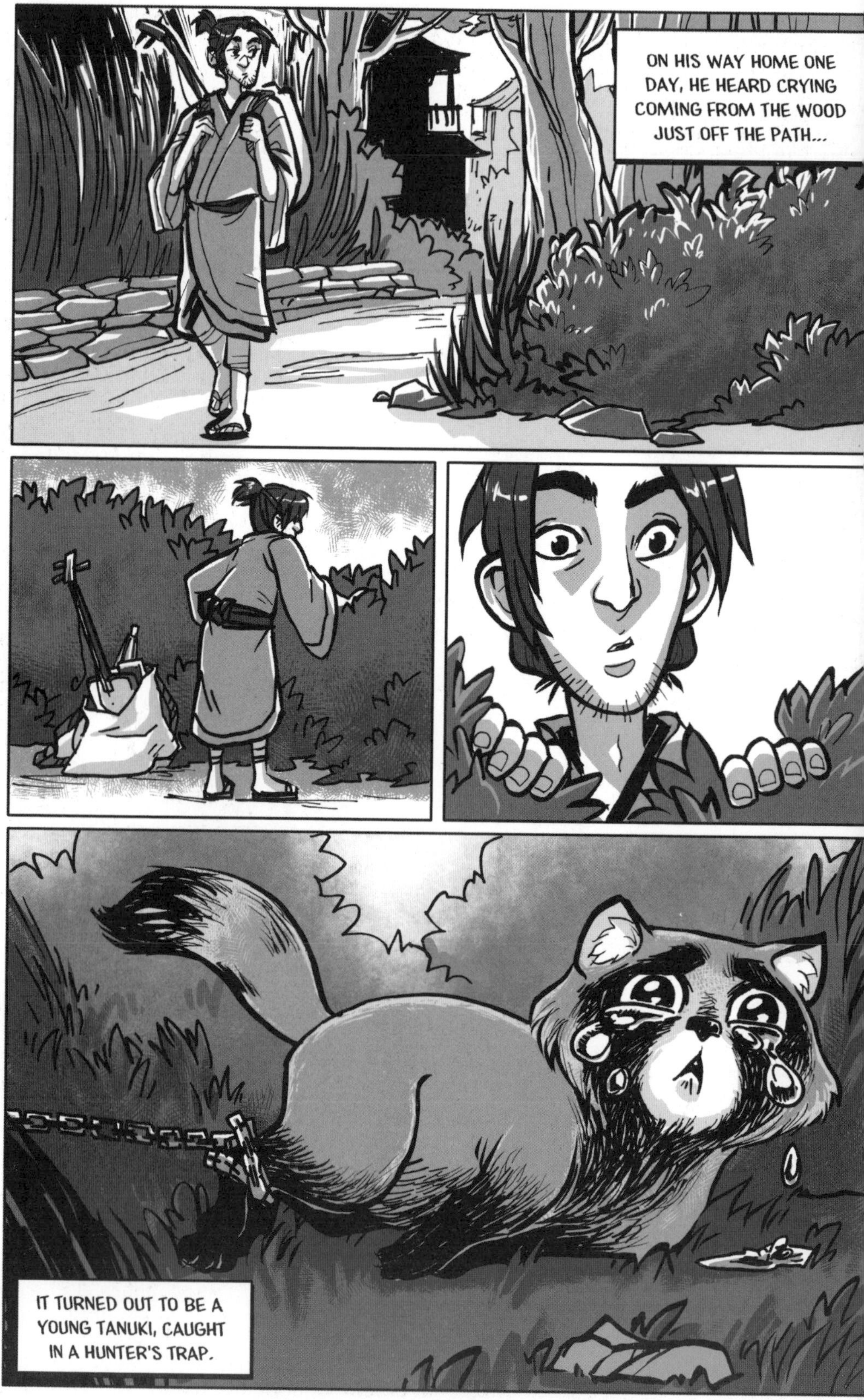
ON HIS WAY HOME ONE DAY, HE HEARD CRYING COMING FROM THE WOOD JUST OFF THE PATH...
IT TURNED OUT TO BE A YOUNG TANUKI, CAUGHT IN A HUNTER'S TRAP.

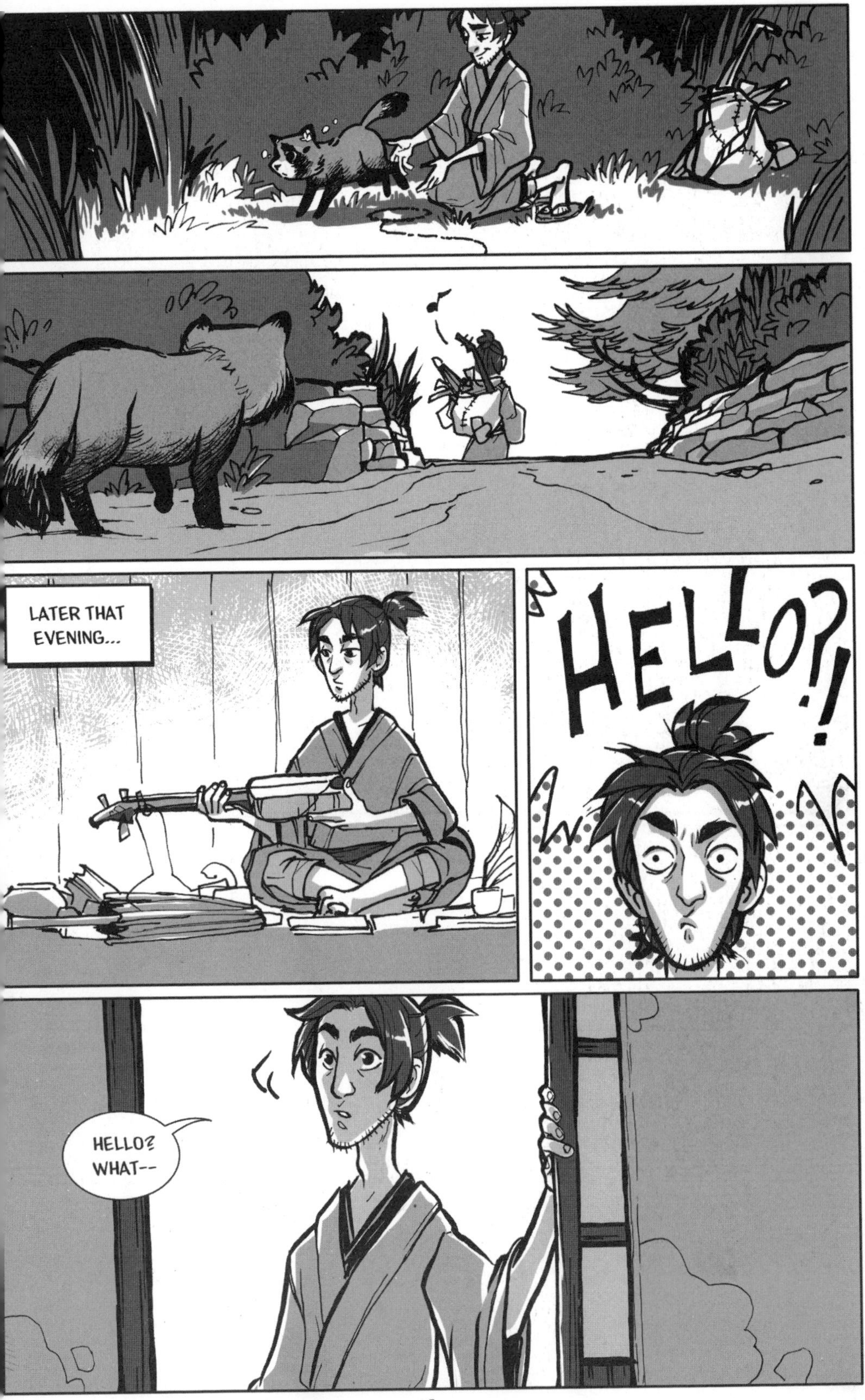
LATER THAT EVENING...
HELLO?!
HELLO? WHAT--

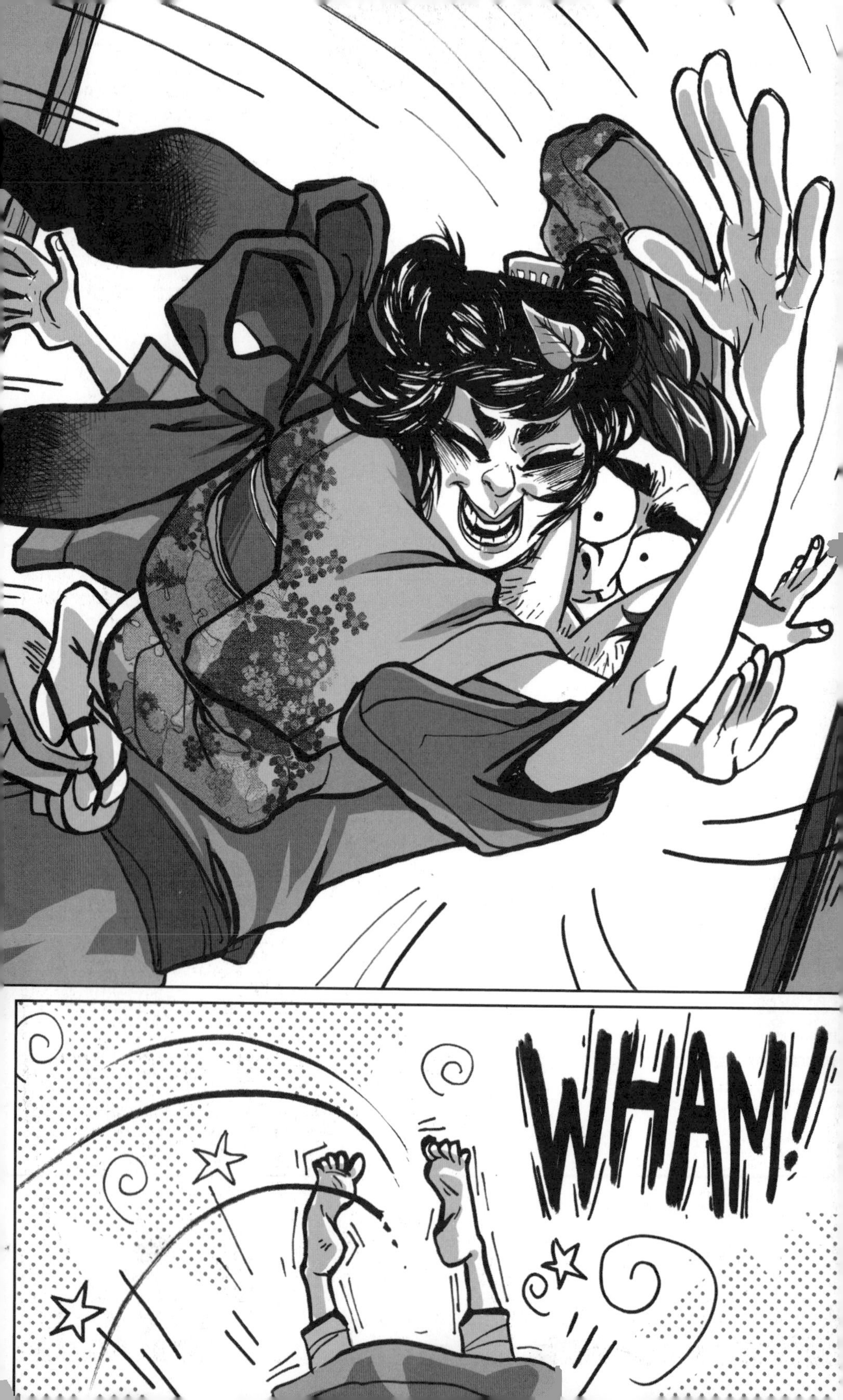
WHAM!

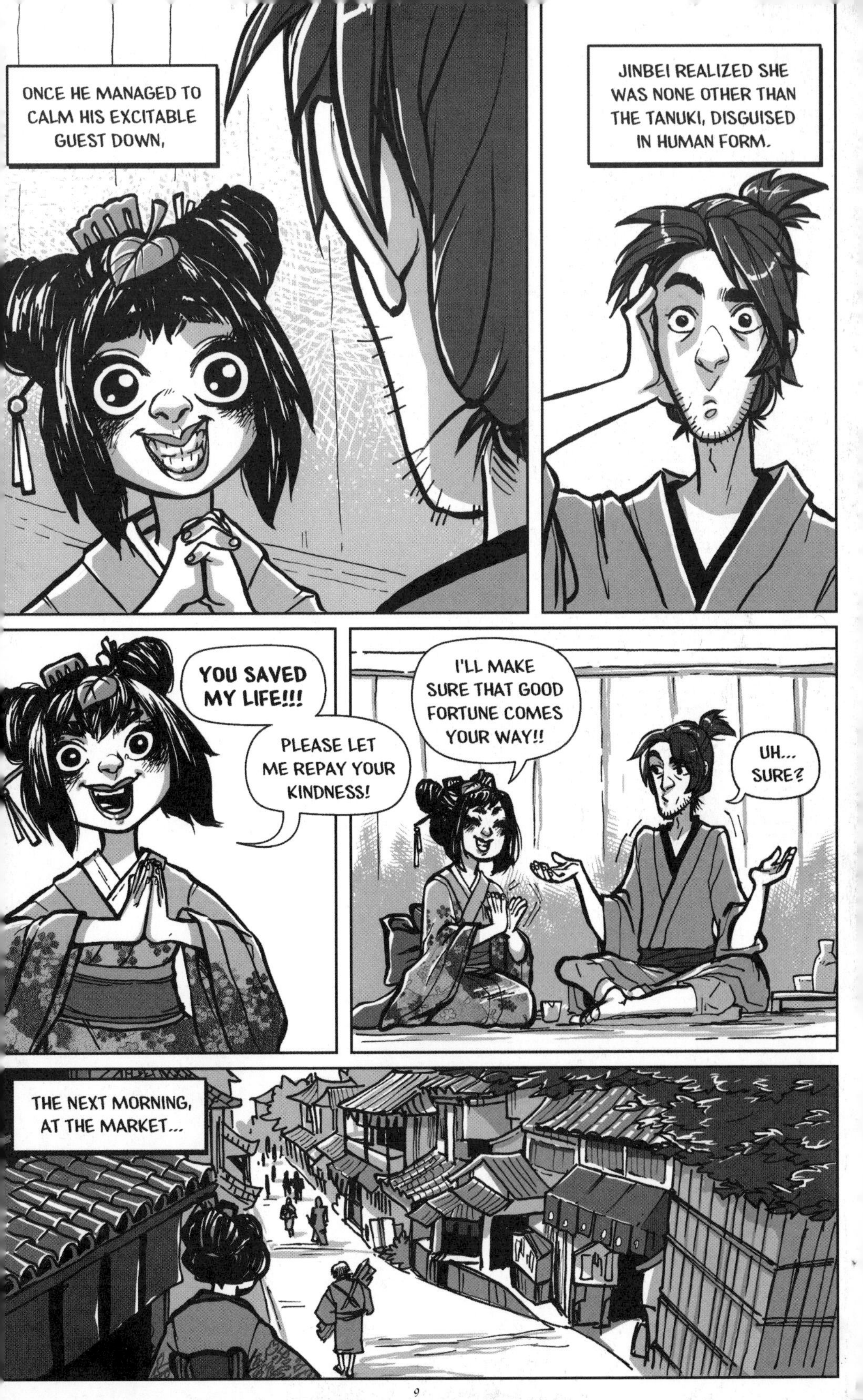
ONCE HE MANAGED TO CALM HIS EXCITABLE GUEST DOWN,
JINBEI REALIZED SHE WAS NONE OTHER THAN THE TANUKI, DISGUISED IN HUMAN FORM.
YOU SAVED MY LIFE!!!
PLEASE LET ME REPAY YOUR KINDNESS!
I'LL MAKE SURE THAT GOOD FORTUNE COMES YOUR WAY!!
UH... SURE?
THE NEXT MORNING, AT THE MARKET...

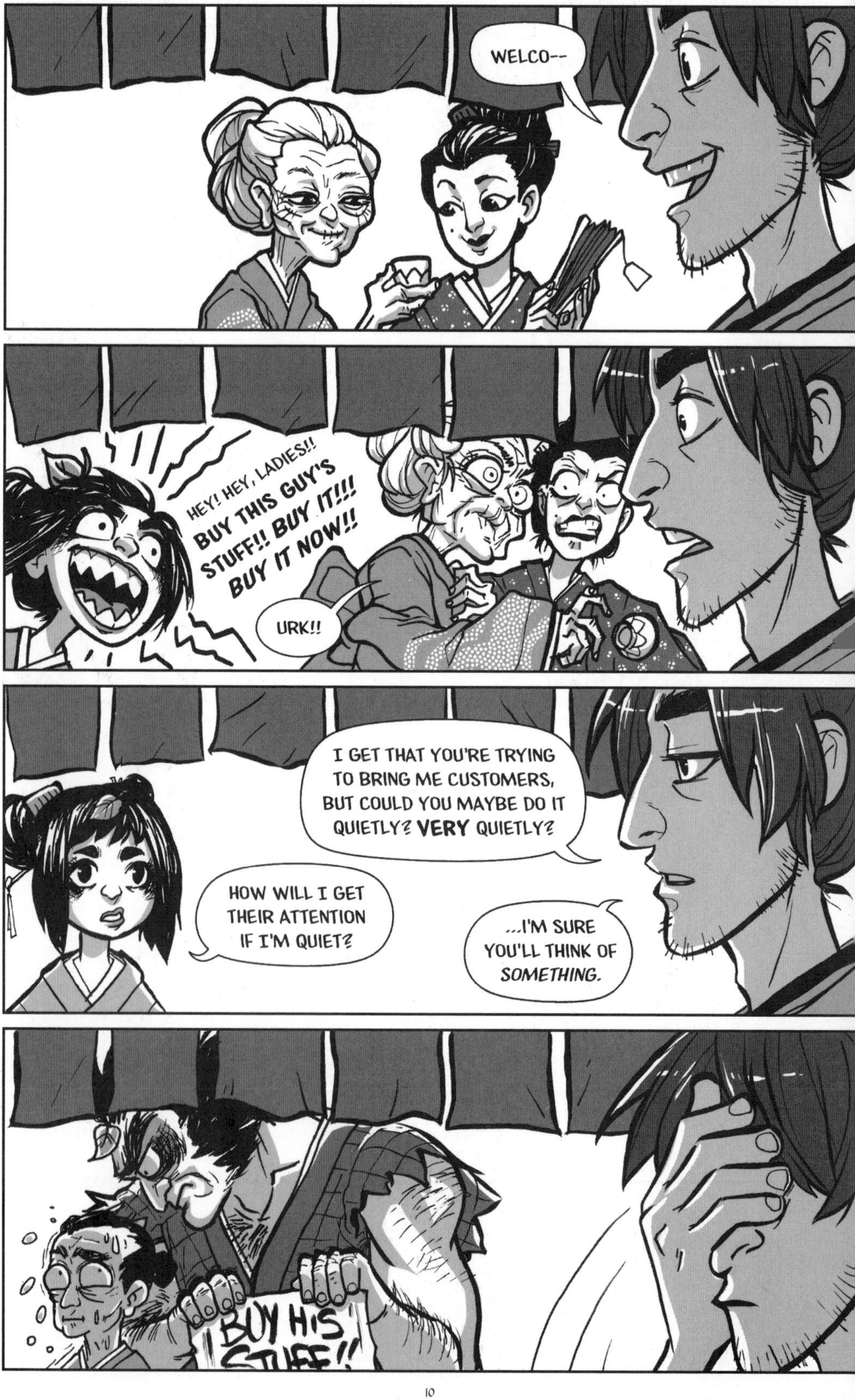
WELCO--
HEY! HEY, LADIES!! BUY THIS GUY'S STUFF!! BUY IT!!! BUY IT NOW!!
URK!!
I GET THAT YOU'RE TRYING TO BRING ME CUSTOMERS, BUT COULD YOU MAYBE DO IT QUIETLY? VERY QUIETLY?
HOW WILL I GET THEIR ATTENTION IF I'M QUIET?
...I'M SURE YOU'LL THINK OF SOMETHING.
BUY HIS

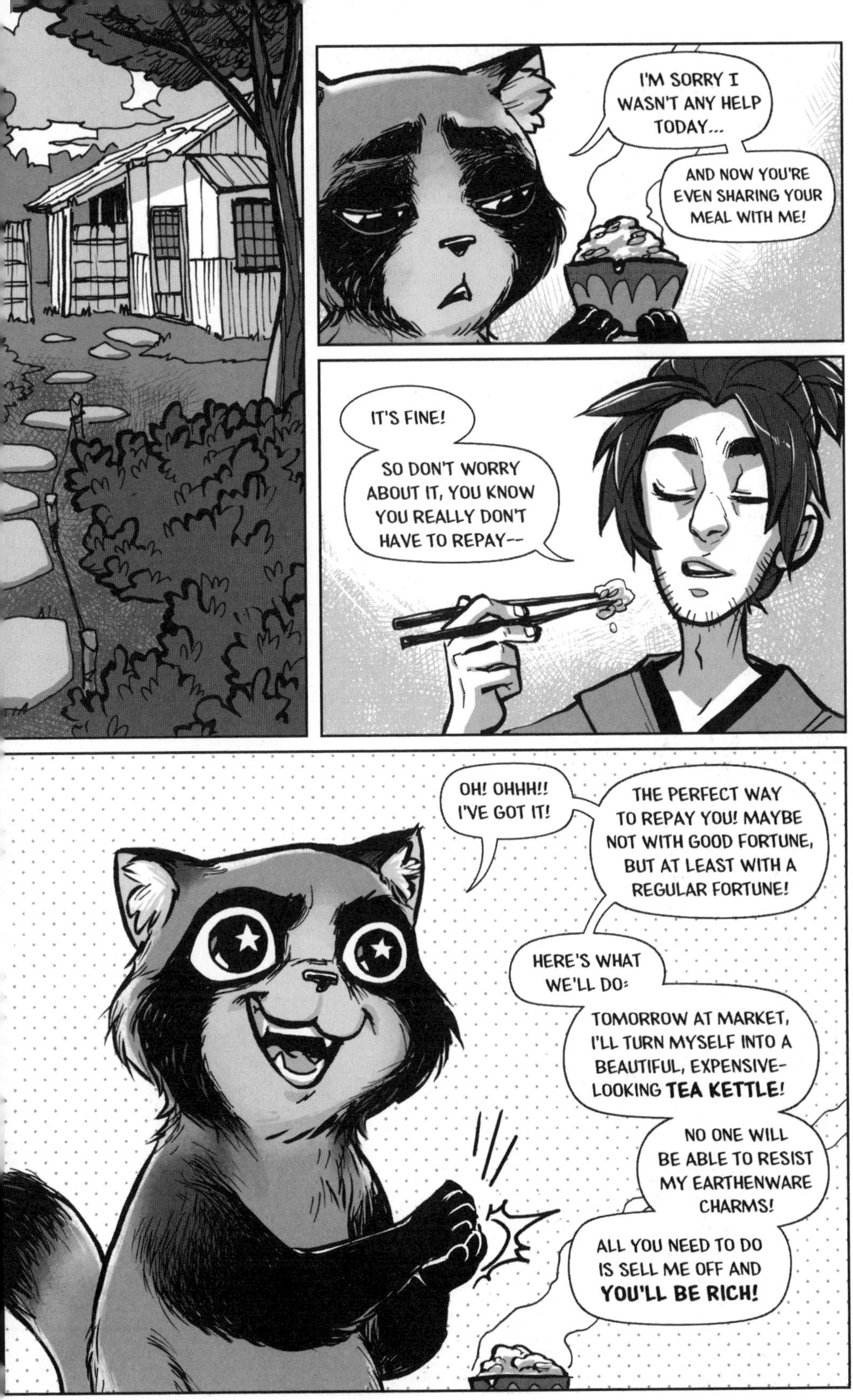
I'M SORRY I WASN'T ANY HELP TODAY...
AND NOW YOU'RE EVEN SHARING YOUR MEAL WITH ME!
IT'S FINE!
SO DON'T WORRY ABOUT IT, YOU KNOW YOU REALLY DON'T HAVE TO REPAY--
OH! OHHH!! I'VE GOT IT!
THE PERFECT WAY TO REPAY YOU! MAYBE NOT WITH GOOD FORTUNE, BUT AT LEAST WITH A REGULAR FORTUNE!
HERE'S WHAT WE'LL DO:
TOMORROW AT MARKET, I'LL TURN MYSELF INTO A BEAUTIFUL, EXPENSIVE-LOOKING TEA KETTLE!
NO ONE WILL BE ABLE TO RESIST MY EARTHENWARE CHARMS!
ALL YOU NEED TO DO IS SELL ME OFF AND YOU'LL BE RICH!

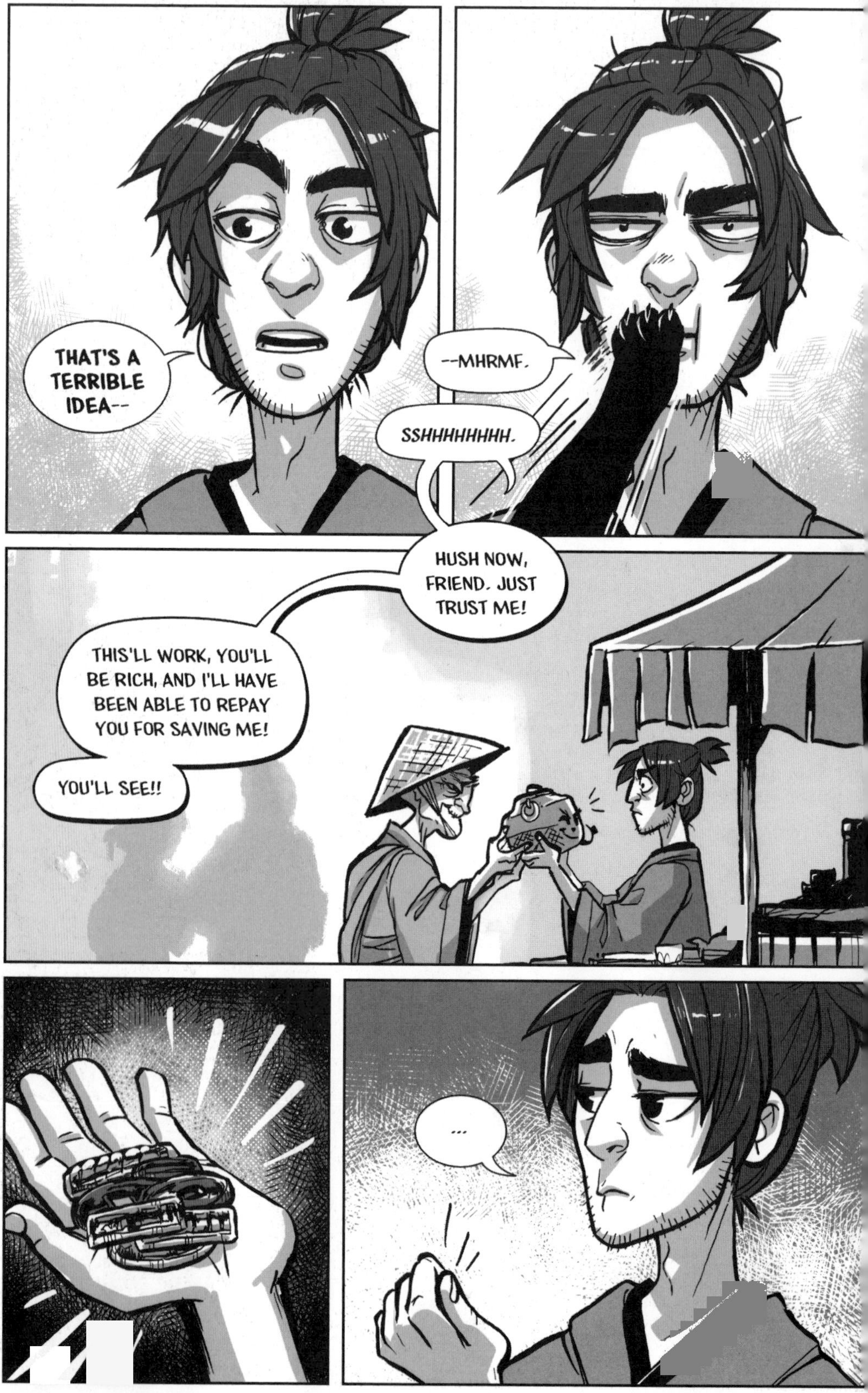
THAT'S A TERRIBLE IDEA--
--MHRMF.
SSHHHHHHHH.
HUSH NOW, FRIEND. JUST TRUST ME!
THIS'LL WORK, YOU'LL BE RICH, AND I'LL HAVE BEEN ABLE TO REPAY YOU FOR SAVING ME!
YOU'LL SEE!!
...

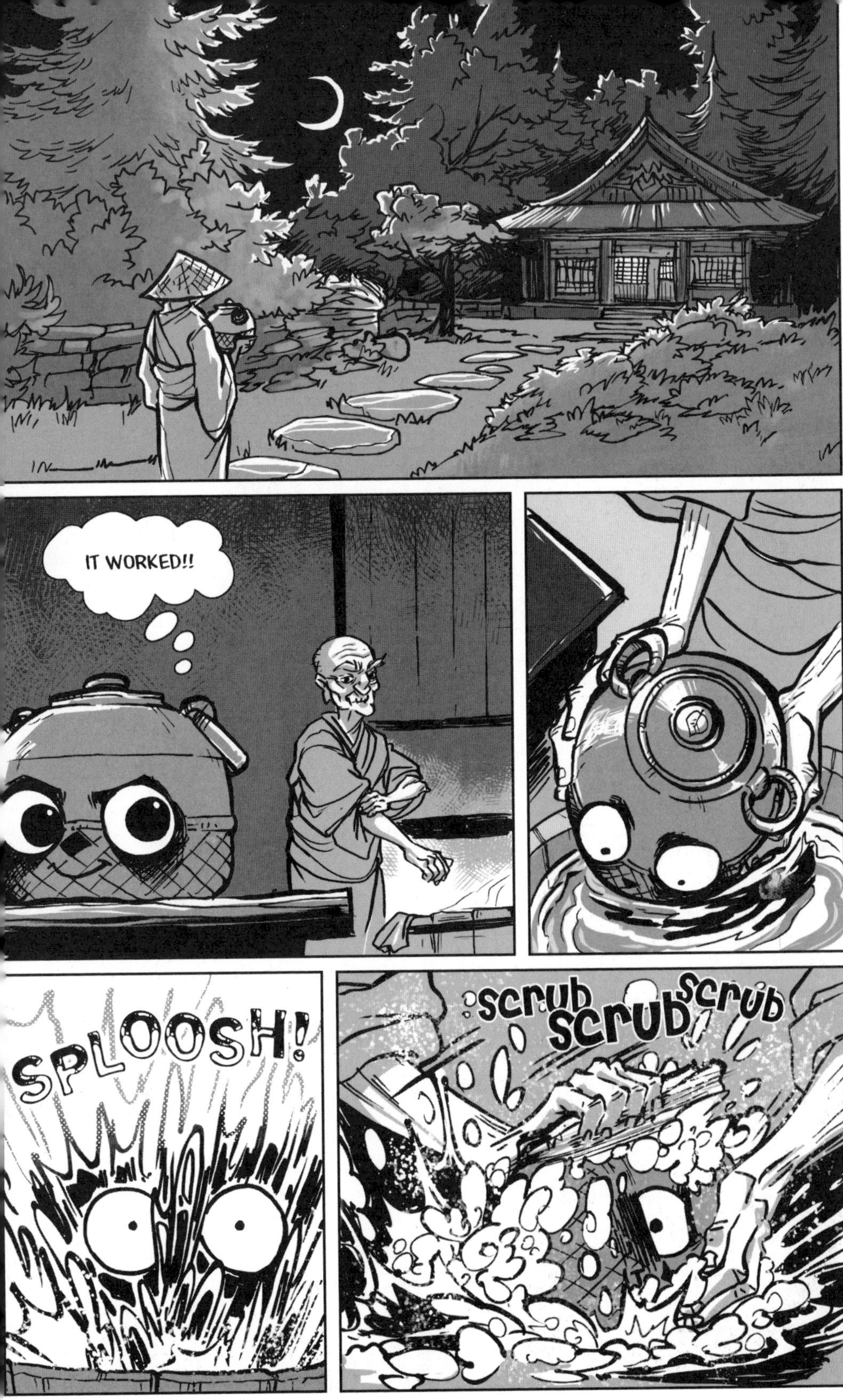
IT WORKED!!
SPLOOSH!
scrub
scrub
scrub

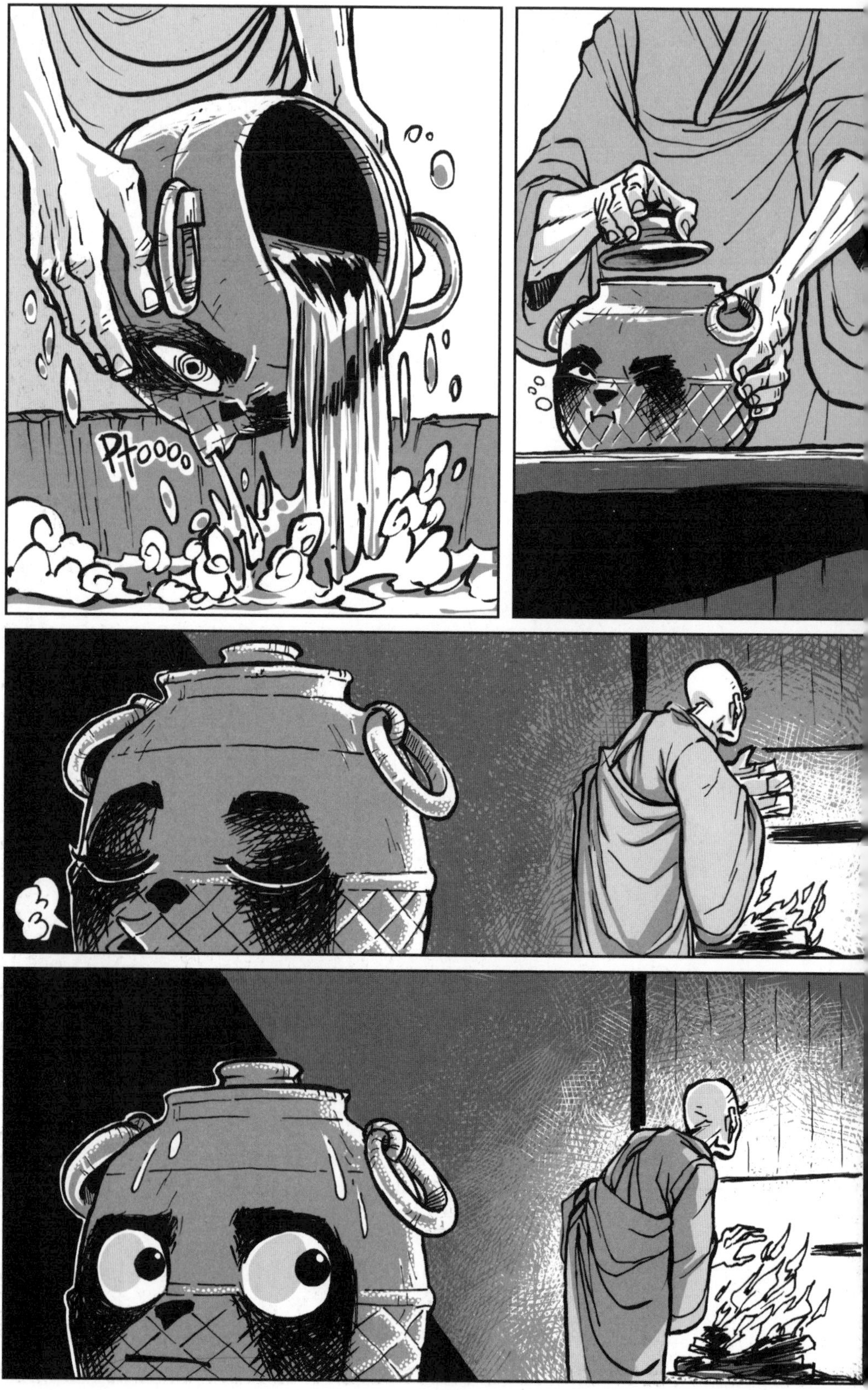
Ptoooo

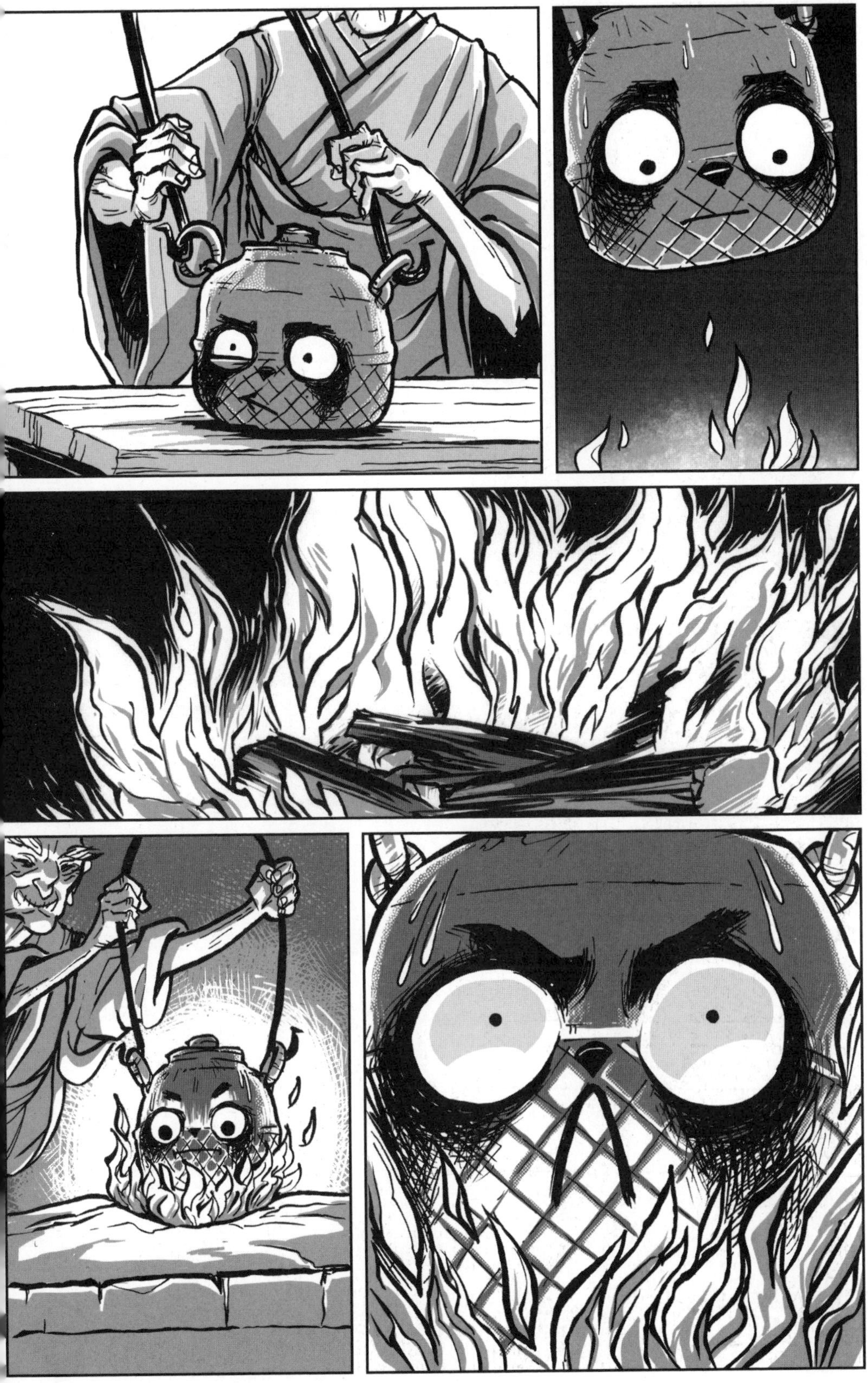

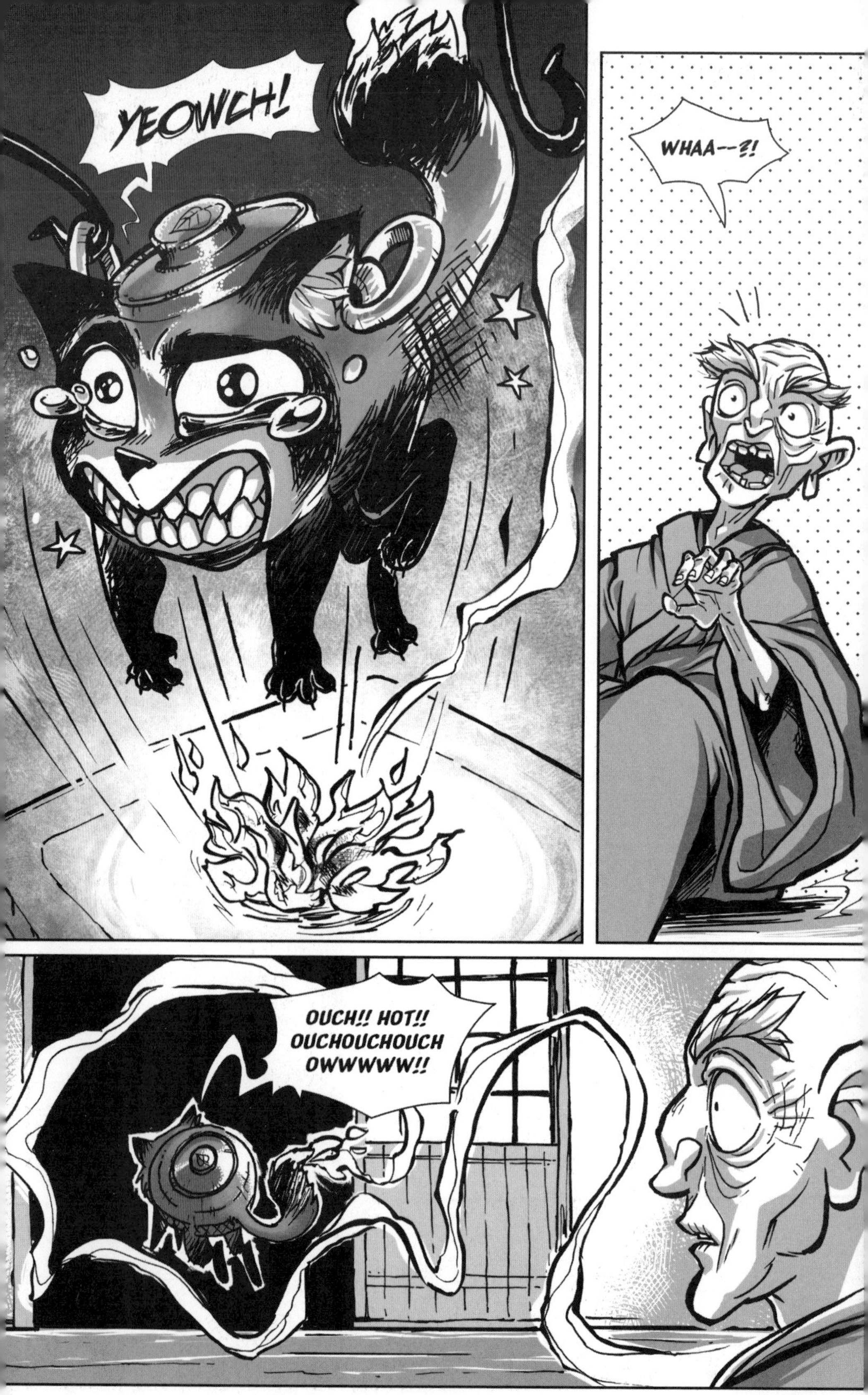
YEOWCH!
WHAA--?!
OUCH!! HOT!! OUCHOUCHOUCH OWWWWW!!

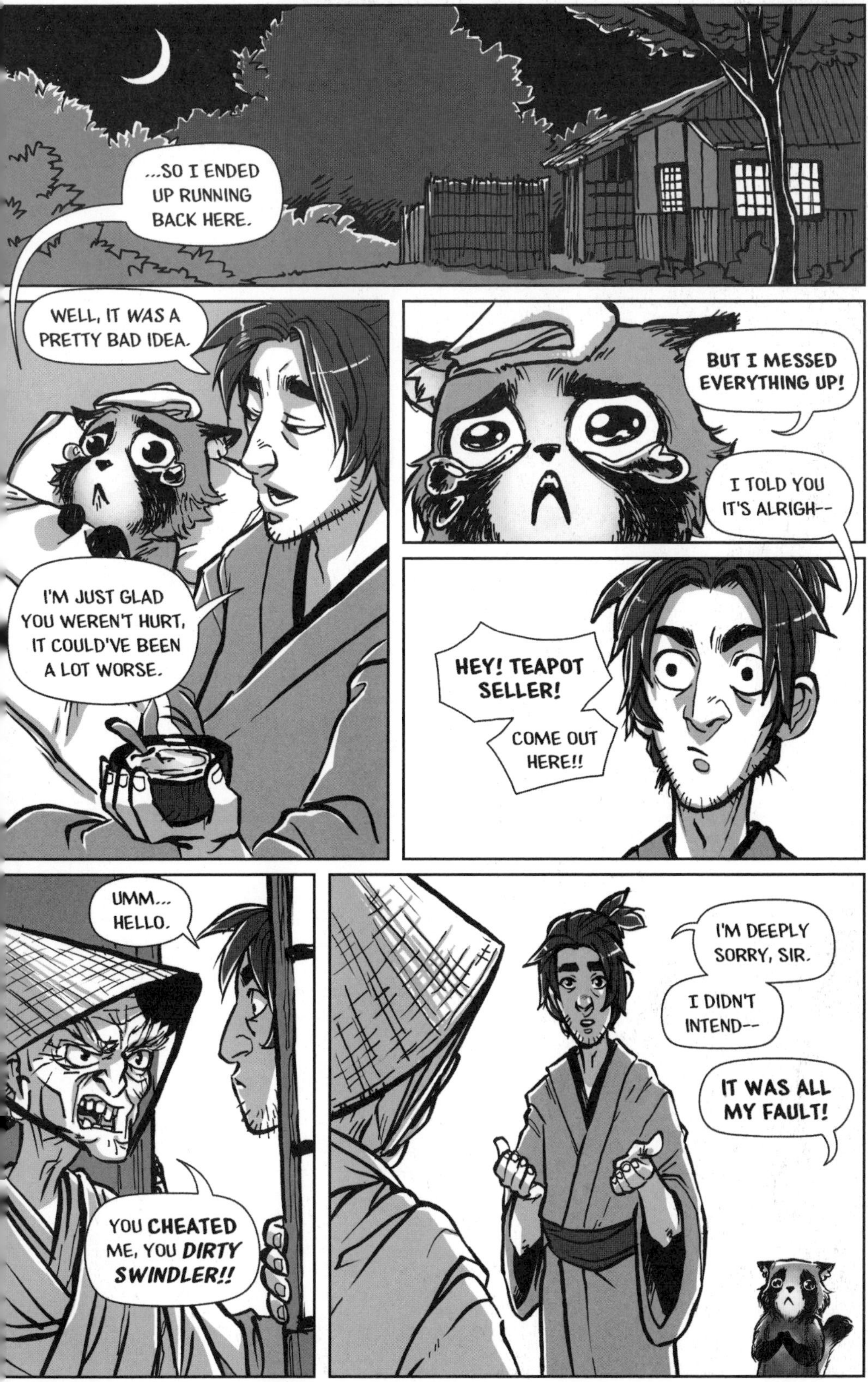

...SO I ENDED UP RUNNING BACK HERE.
WELL, IT *WAS* A PRETTY BAD IDEA.
BUT I MESSED EVERYTHING UP!
I TOLD YOU IT'S ALRIGH--
I'M JUST GLAD YOU WEREN'T HURT, IT COULD'VE BEEN A LOT WORSE.
HEY! TEAPOT SELLER!
COME OUT HERE!!
UMM... HELLO.
YOU **CHEATED** ME, YOU ***DIRTY SWINDLER!!***
I'M DEEPLY SORRY, SIR.
I DIDN'T INTEND--
IT WAS ALL MY FAULT!

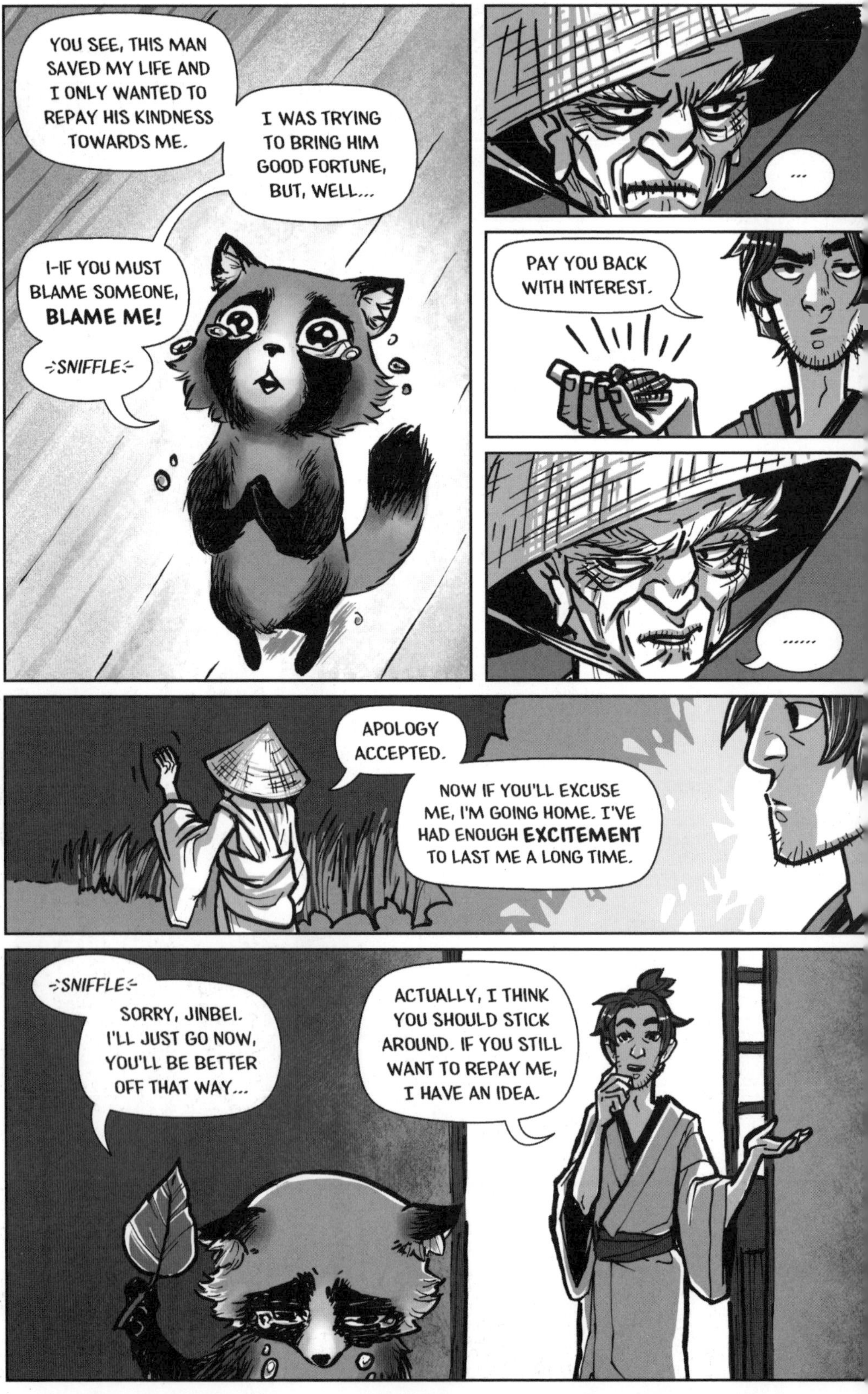
YOU SEE, THIS MAN SAVED MY LIFE AND I ONLY WANTED TO REPAY HIS KINDNESS TOWARDS ME.
I WAS TRYING TO BRING HIM GOOD FORTUNE, BUT, WELL...
I-IF YOU MUST BLAME SOMEONE, BLAME ME!
SNIFFLE
...
PAY YOU BACK WITH INTEREST.
......
APOLOGY ACCEPTED.
NOW IF YOU'LL EXCUSE ME, I'M GOING HOME. I'VE HAD ENOUGH EXCITEMENT TO LAST ME A LONG TIME.
SNIFFLE
SORRY, JINBEI. I'LL JUST GO NOW, YOU'LL BE BETTER OFF THAT WAY...
ACTUALLY, I THINK YOU SHOULD STICK AROUND. IF YOU STILL WANT TO REPAY ME, I HAVE AN IDEA.

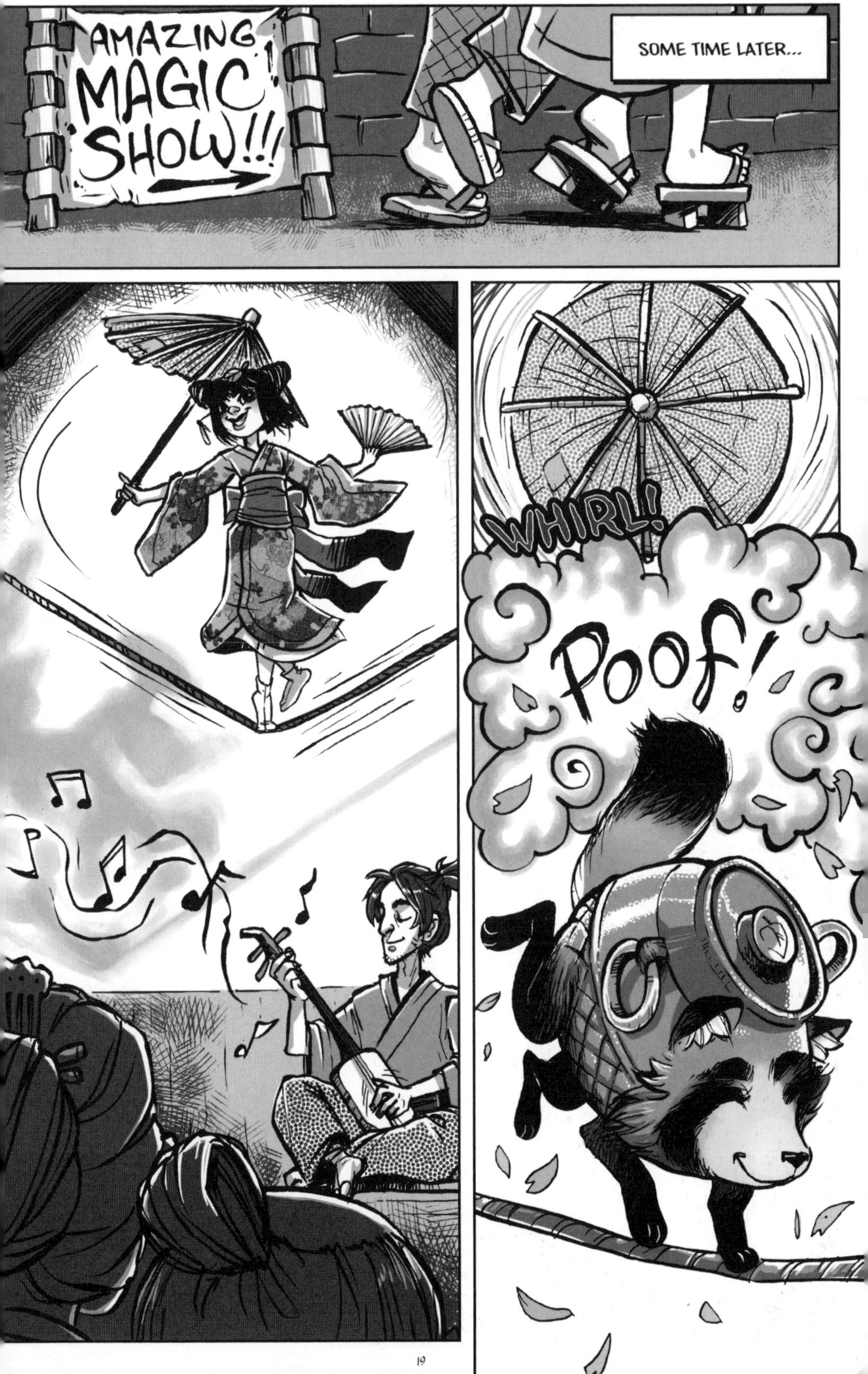
AMAZING MAGIC SHOW!!!
SOME TIME LATER...
WHIRL!
Poof!

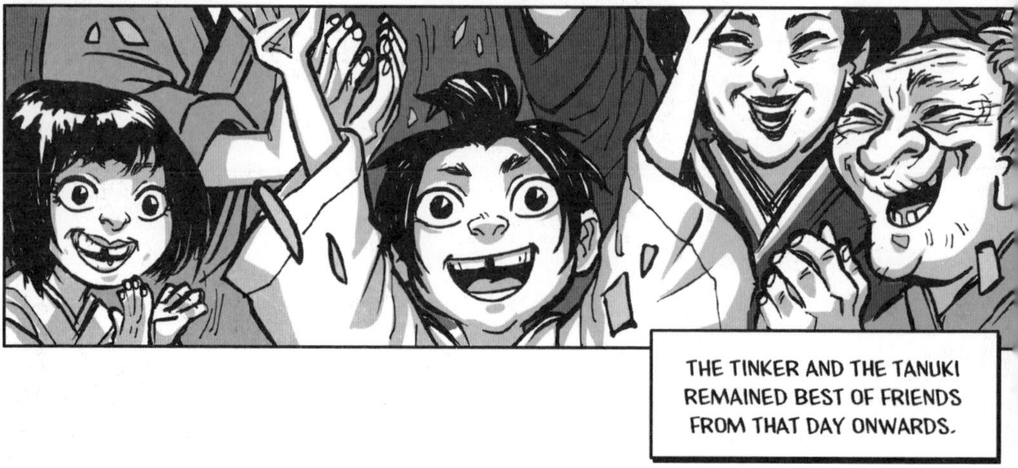
THE TINKER AND THE TANUKI REMAINED BEST OF FRIENDS FROM THAT DAY ONWARDS.

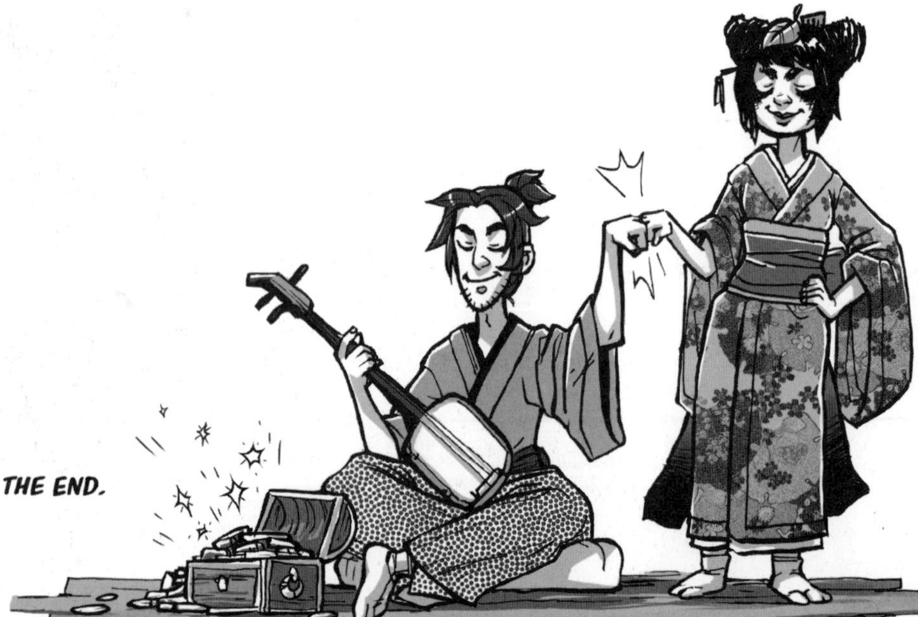
THE END.

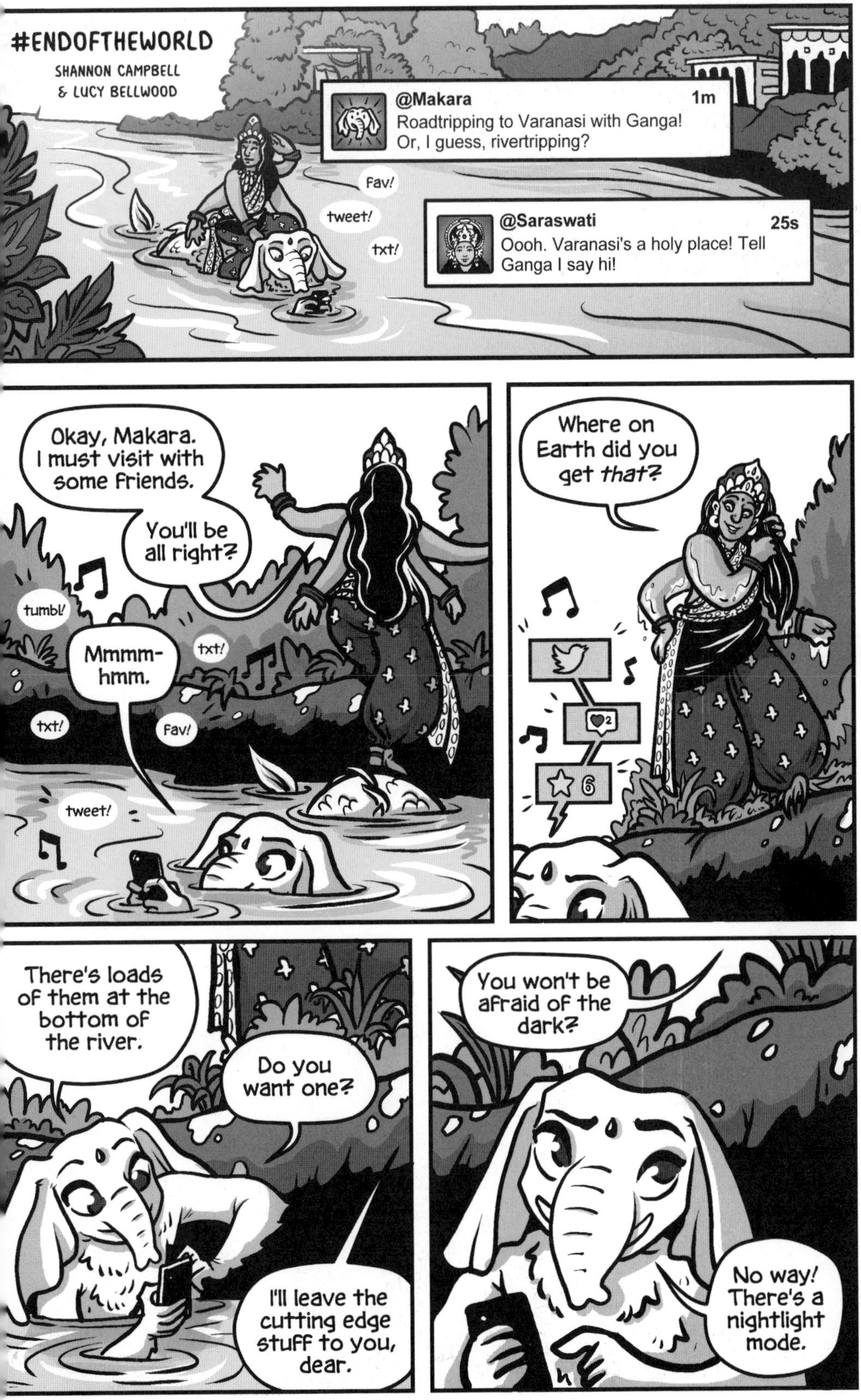

#ENDOFTHEWORLD
SHANNON CAMPBELL
& LUCY BELLWOOD
@Makara 1m
Roadtripping to Varanasi with Ganga! Or, I guess, rivertripping?
Fav!
tweet!
txt!
@Saraswati 25s
Oooh. Varanasi's a holy place! Tell Ganga I say hi!
Okay, Makara. I must visit with some friends.
You'll be all right?
tumbl!
Mmmm-hmm.
txt!
txt!
Fav!
tweet!
Where on Earth did you get *that*?
2
6
There's loads of them at the bottom of the river.
Do you want one?
I'll leave the cutting edge stuff to you, dear.
You won't be afraid of the dark?
No way! There's a nightlight mode.

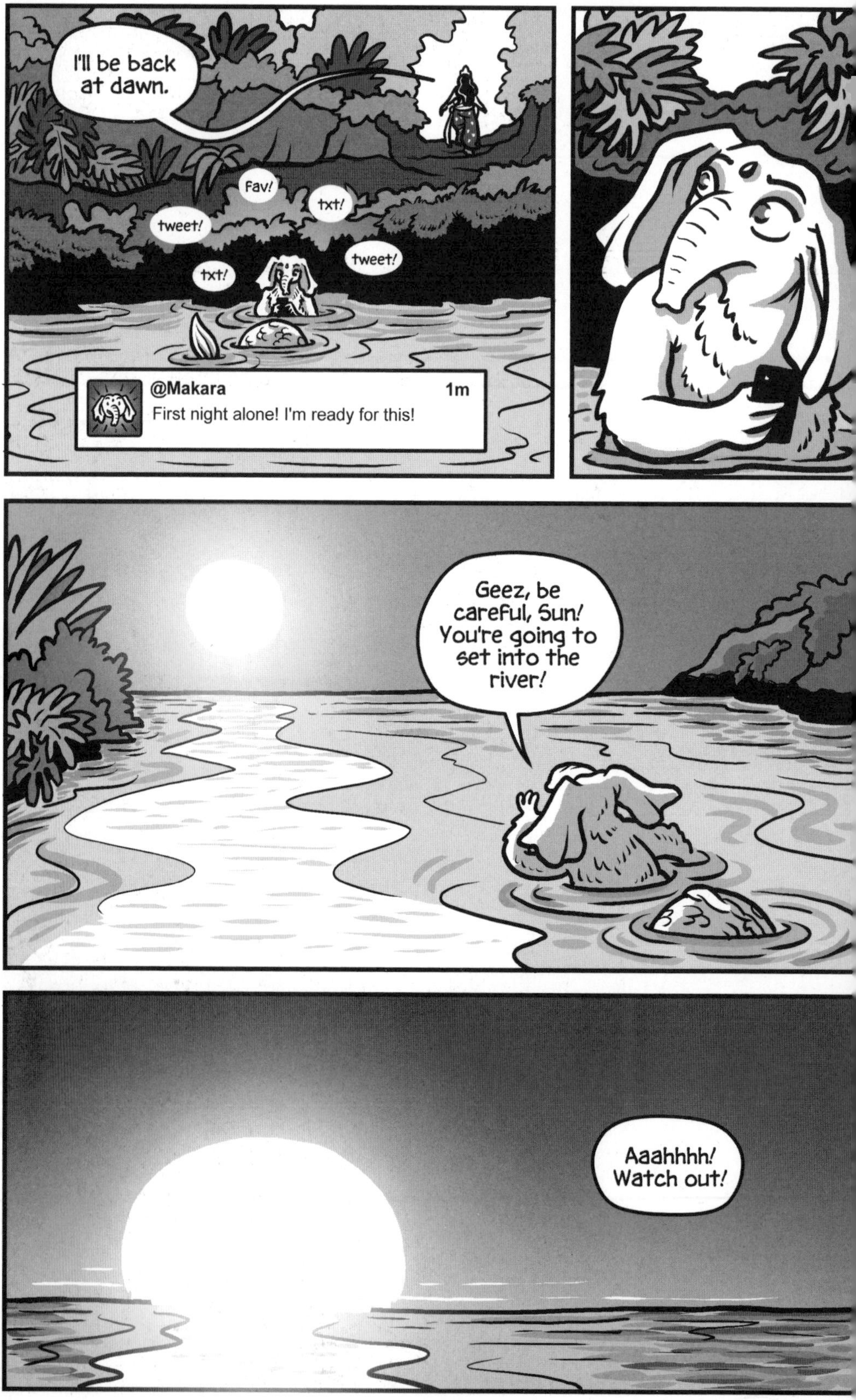
I'll be back at dawn.
fav!
txt!
tweet!
tweet!
txt!
@Makara
1m
First night alone! I'm ready for this!
Geez, be careful, Sun! You're going to set into the river!
Aaahhhh! Watch out!

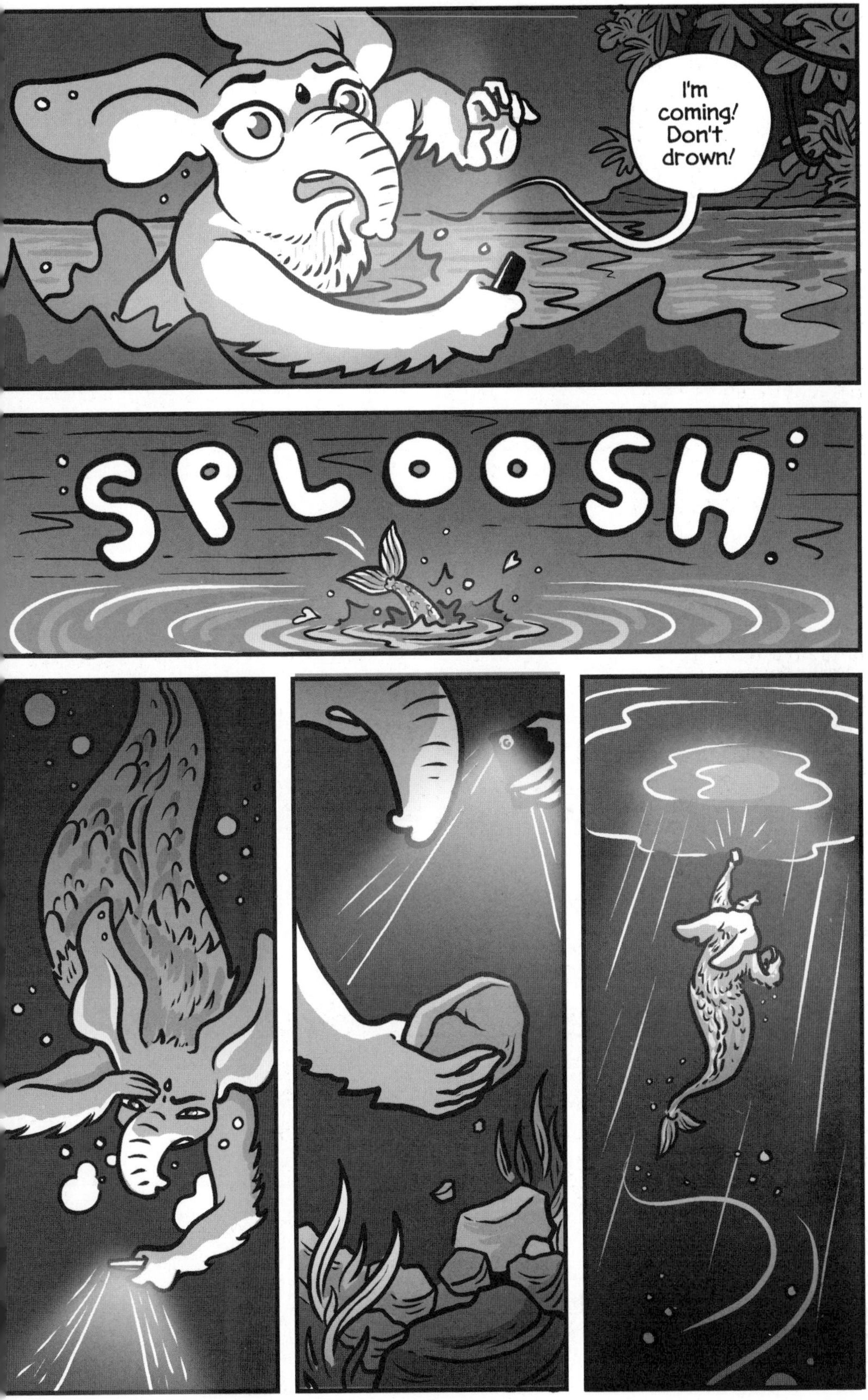
I'm coming! Don't drown!
SPLOOSH

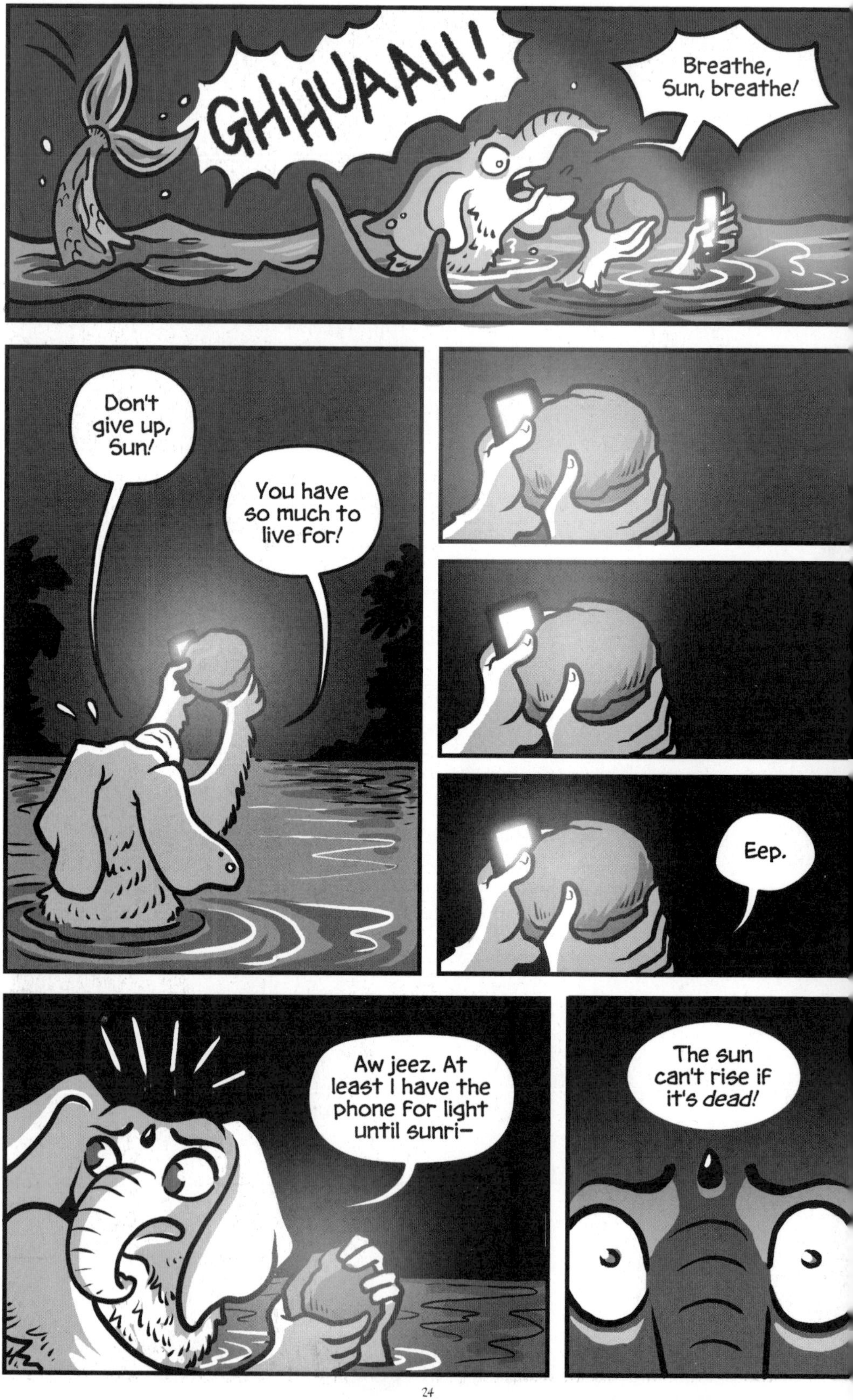
GHUAAH!
Breathe, Sun, breathe!
Don't give up, Sun!
You have so much to live for!
Eep.
Aw jeez. At least I have the phone for light until sunri–
The sun can't rise if it's *dead!*

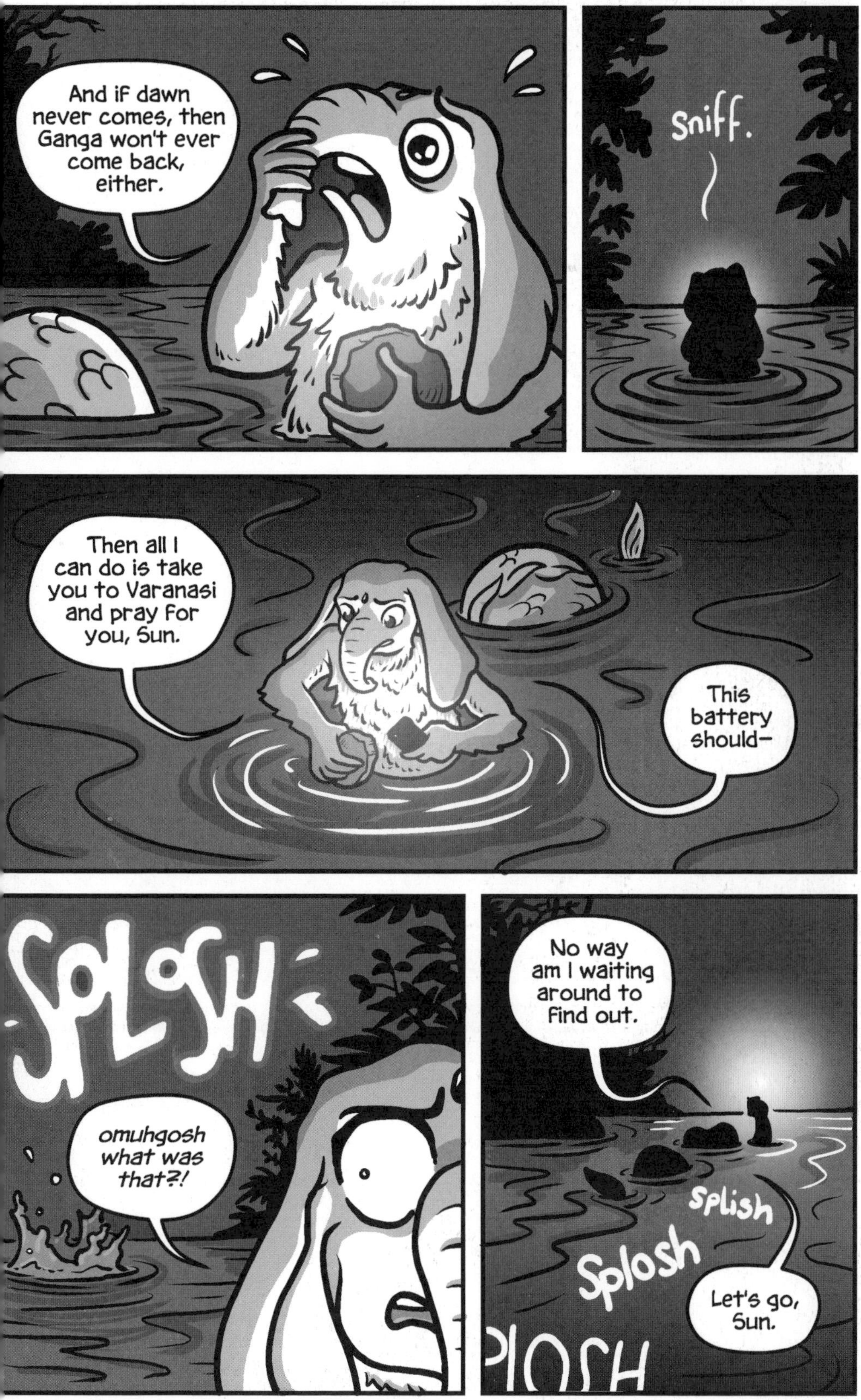
And if dawn never comes, then Ganga won't ever come back, either.
Sniff.
Then all I can do is take you to Varanasi and pray for you, Sun.
This battery should—
SPLOSH
omuhgosh what was that?!
No way am I waiting around to find out.
Splish
Splosh
Let's go, Sun.
SPLOSH

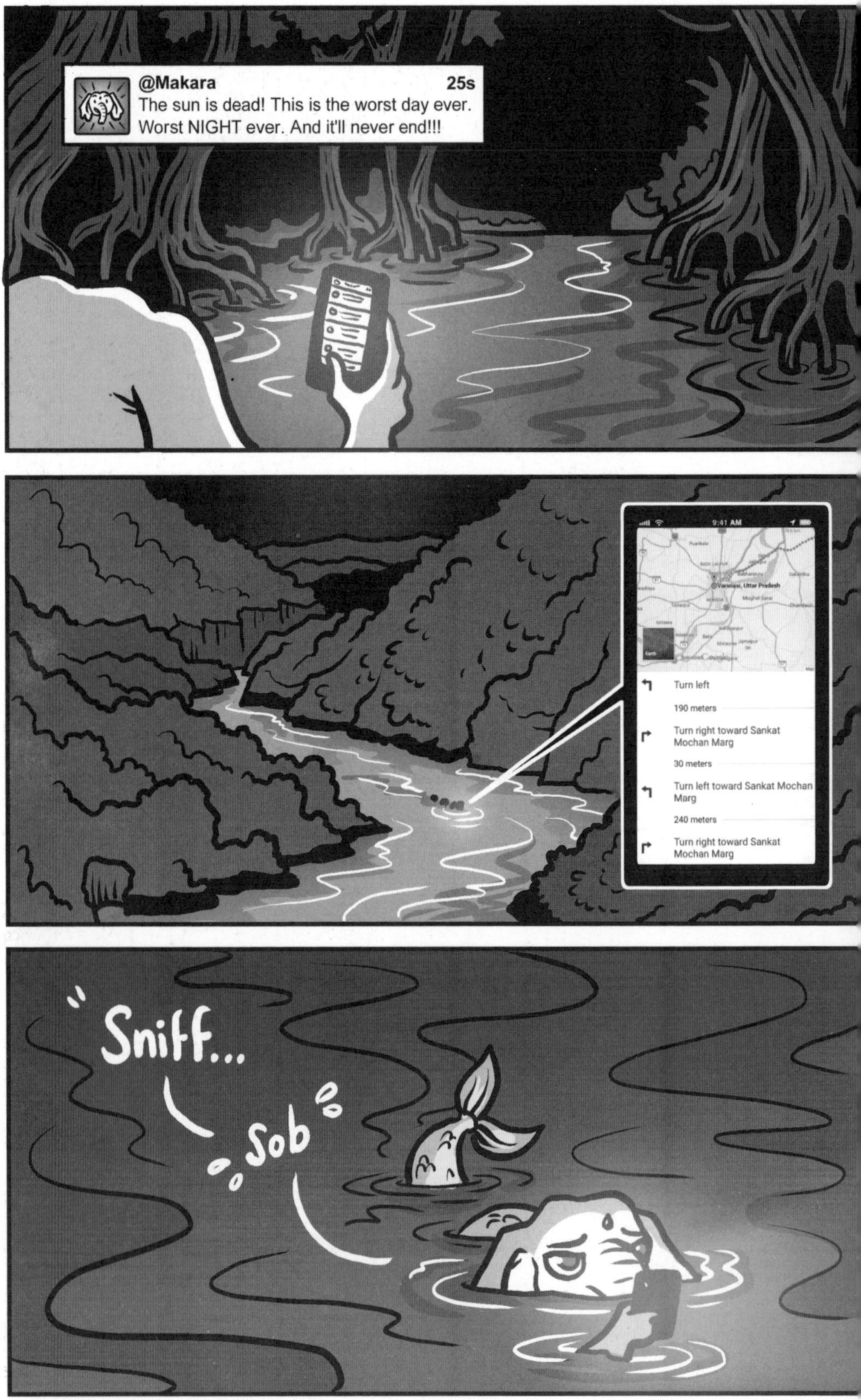
@Makara 25s
The sun is dead! This is the worst day ever. Worst NIGHT ever. And it'll never end!!!
9:41 AM
Varanasi, Uttar Pradesh
Turn left
190 meters
Turn right toward Sankat Mochan Marg
30 meters
Turn left toward Sankat Mochan Marg
240 meters
Turn right toward Sankat Mochan Marg
Sniff...
Sob

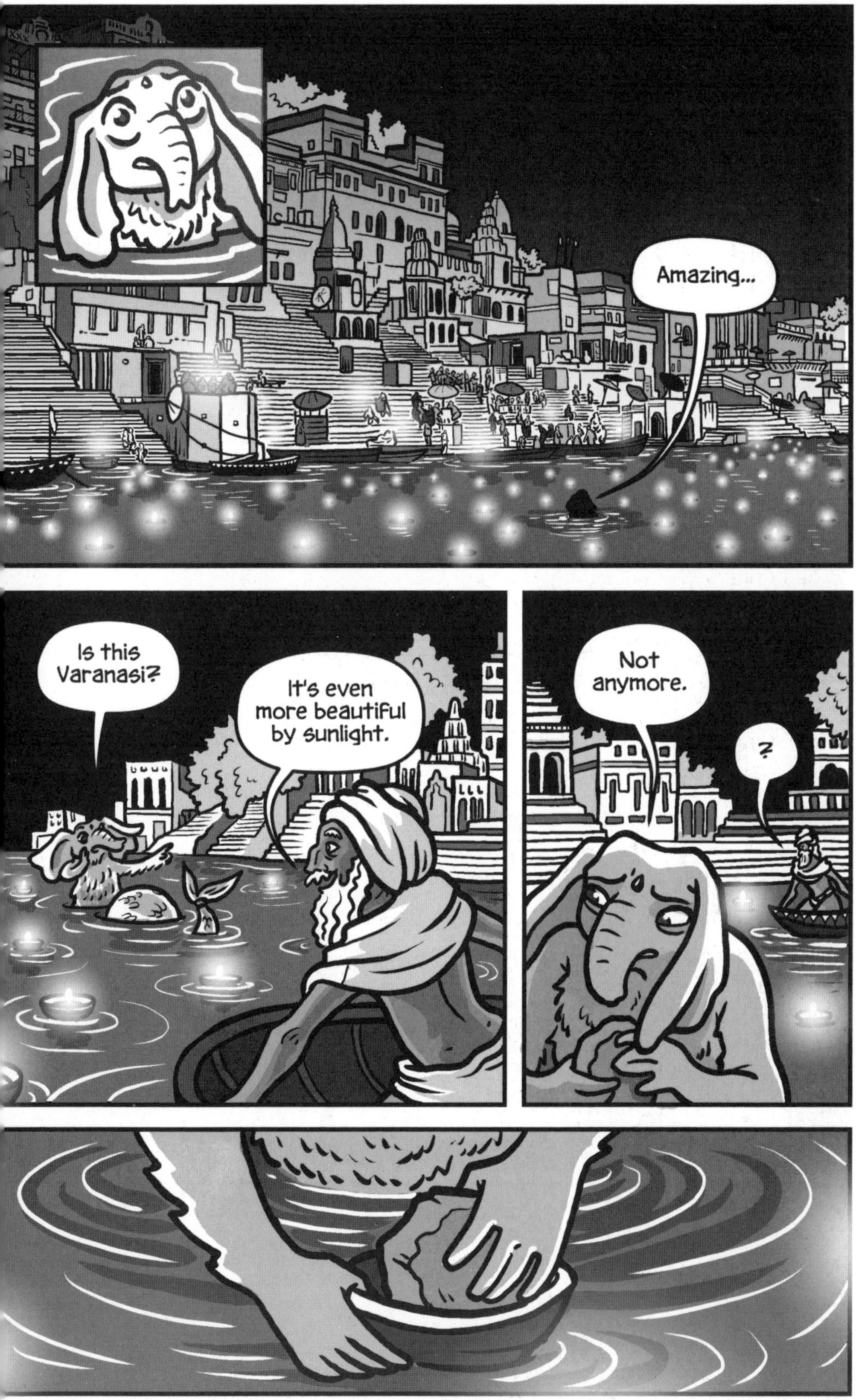
Amazing...
Is this Varanasi?
It's even more beautiful by sunlight.
Not anymore.
?

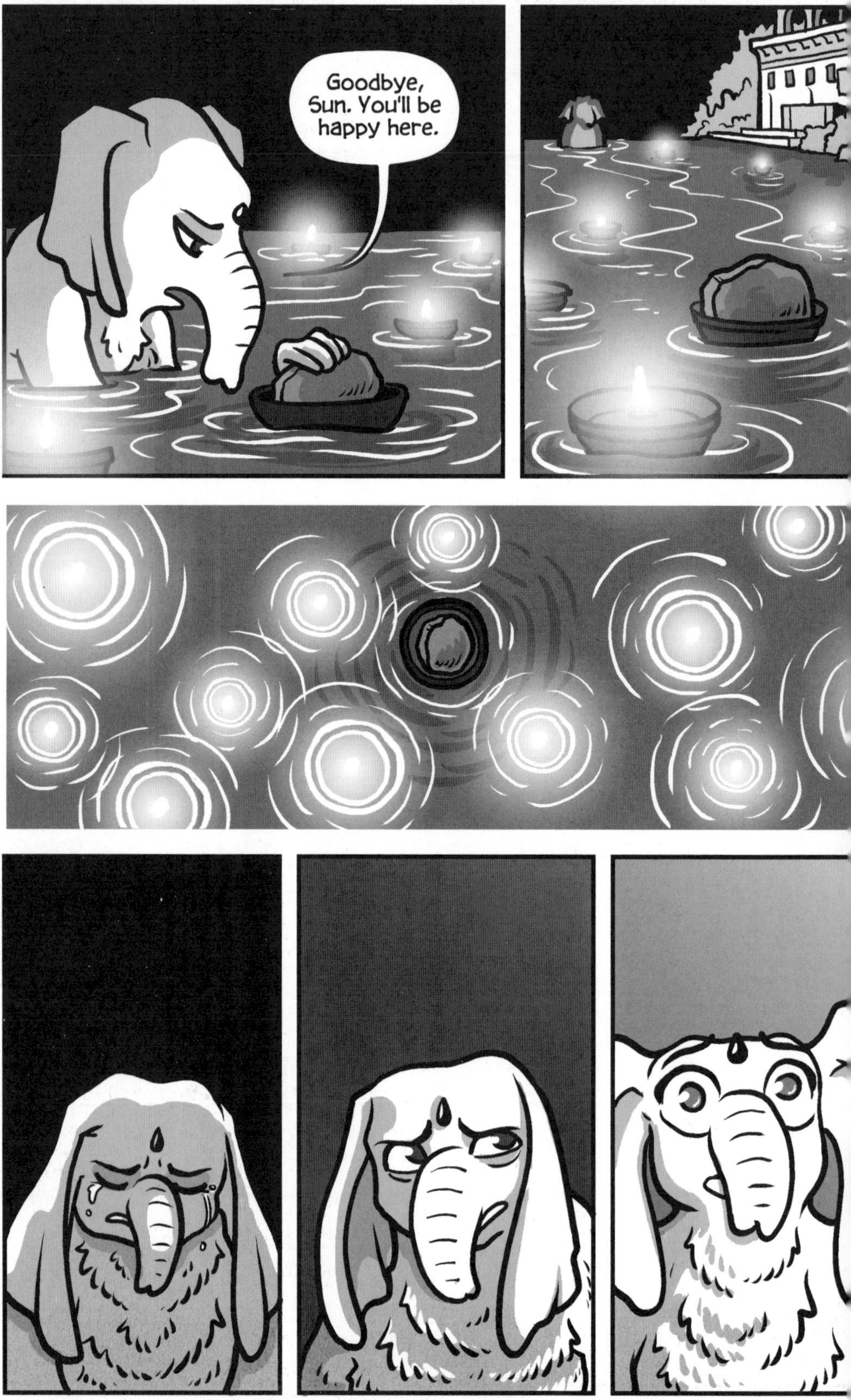
Goodbye, Sun. You'll be happy here.

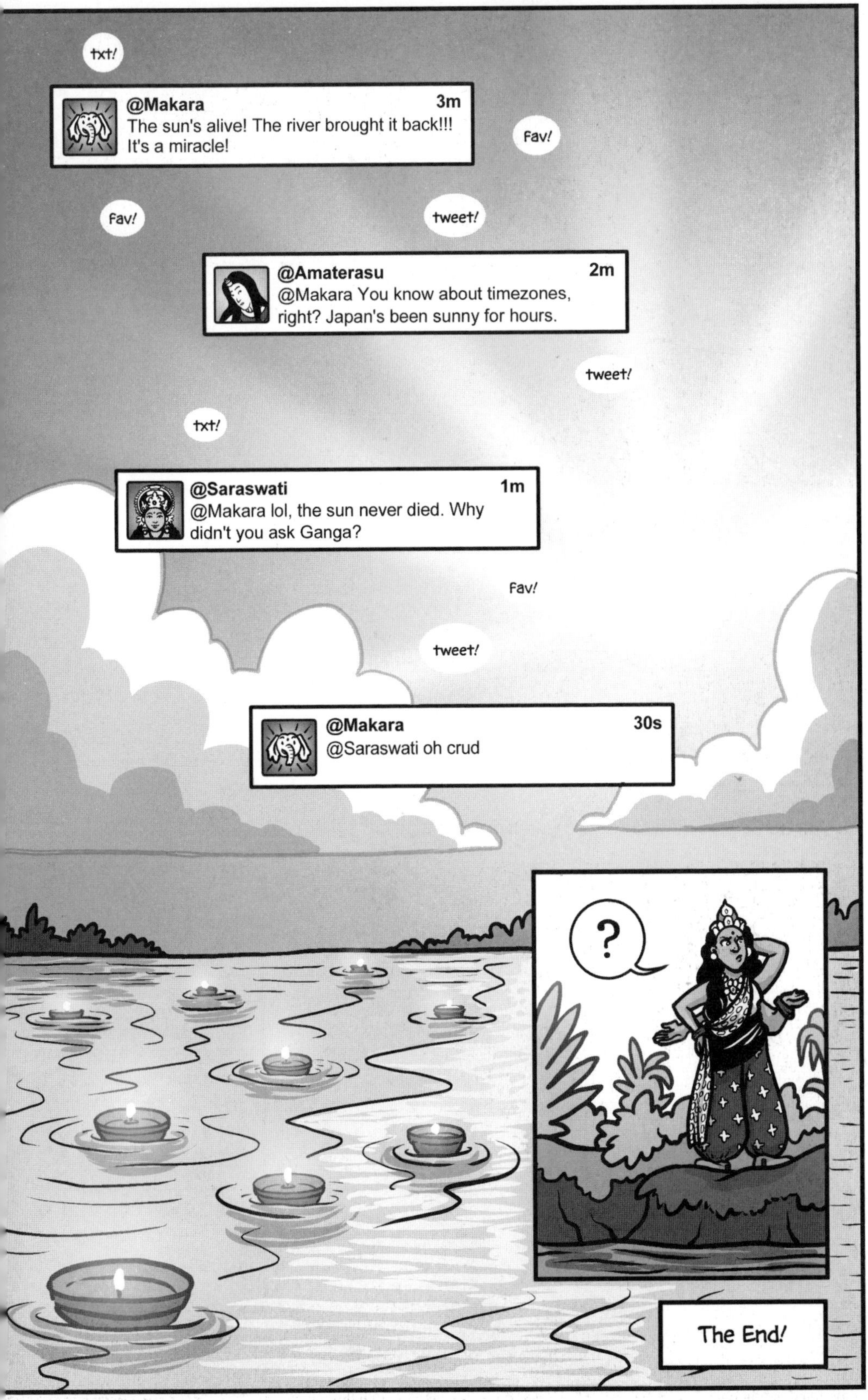
txt!
@Makara 3m
The sun's alive! The river brought it back!!! It's a miracle!
Fav!
Fav!
tweet!
@Amaterasu 2m
@Makara You know about timezones, right? Japan's been sunny for hours.
tweet!
txt!
@Saraswati 1m
@Makara lol, the sun never died. Why didn't you ask Ganga?
Fav!
tweet!
@Makara 30s
@Saraswati oh crud
?
The End!

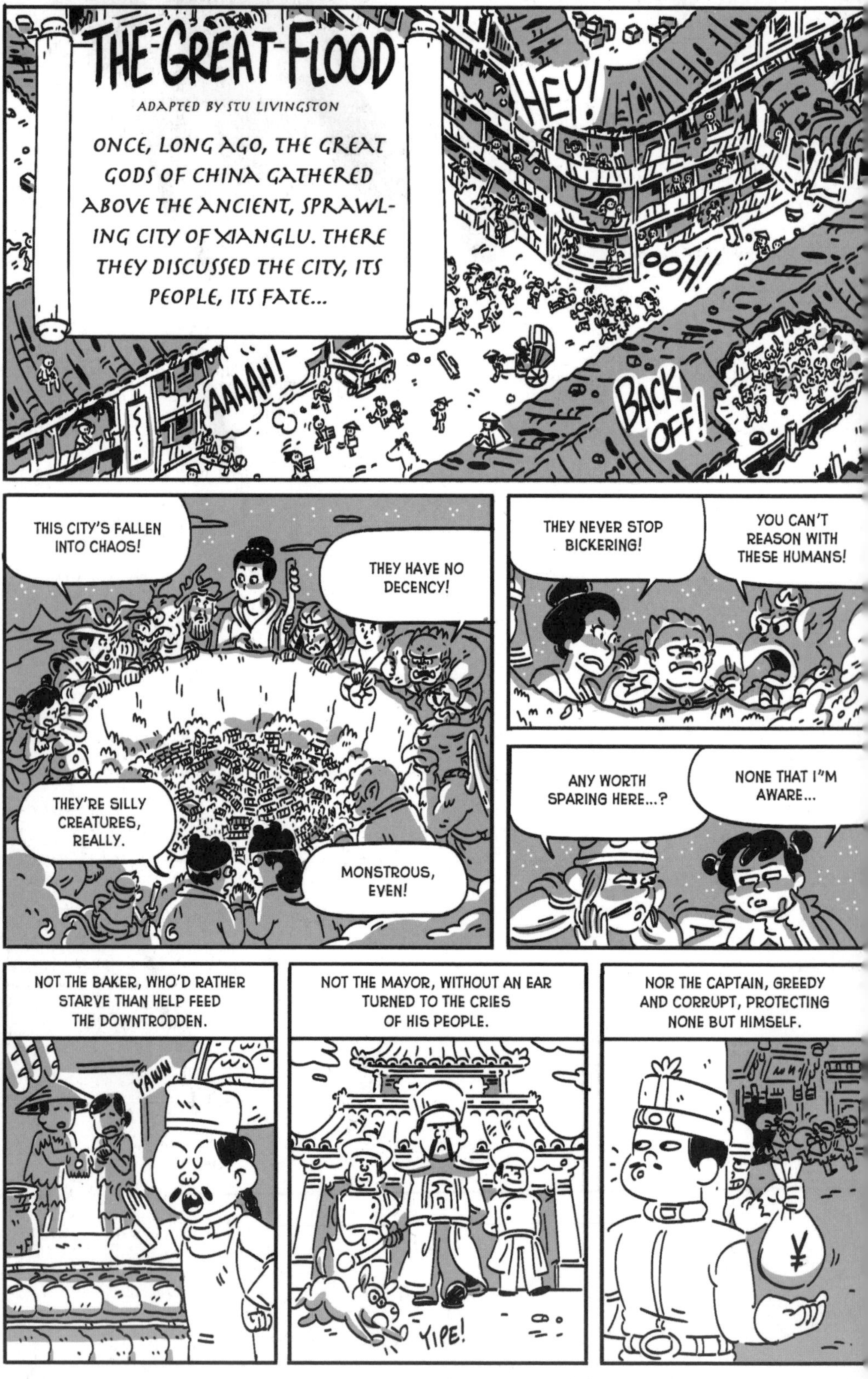
THE GREAT FLOOD
ADAPTED BY STU LIVINGSTON
ONCE, LONG AGO, THE GREAT GODS OF CHINA GATHERED ABOVE THE ANCIENT, SPRAWLING CITY OF XIANGLU. THERE THEY DISCUSSED THE CITY, ITS PEOPLE, ITS FATE...
HEY!
OOH!
AAAAH!
BACK OFF!
THIS CITY'S FALLEN INTO CHAOS!
THEY HAVE NO DECENCY!
THEY'RE SILLY CREATURES, REALLY.
MONSTROUS, EVEN!
THEY NEVER STOP BICKERING!
YOU CAN'T REASON WITH THESE HUMANS!
ANY WORTH SPARING HERE...?
NONE THAT I"M AWARE...
NOT THE BAKER, WHO'D RATHER STARVE THAN HELP FEED THE DOWNTRODDEN.
YAWN
NOT THE MAYOR, WITHOUT AN EAR TURNED TO THE CRIES OF HIS PEOPLE.
YIPE!
NOR THE CAPTAIN, GREEDY AND CORRUPT, PROTECTING NONE BUT HIMSELF.
¥

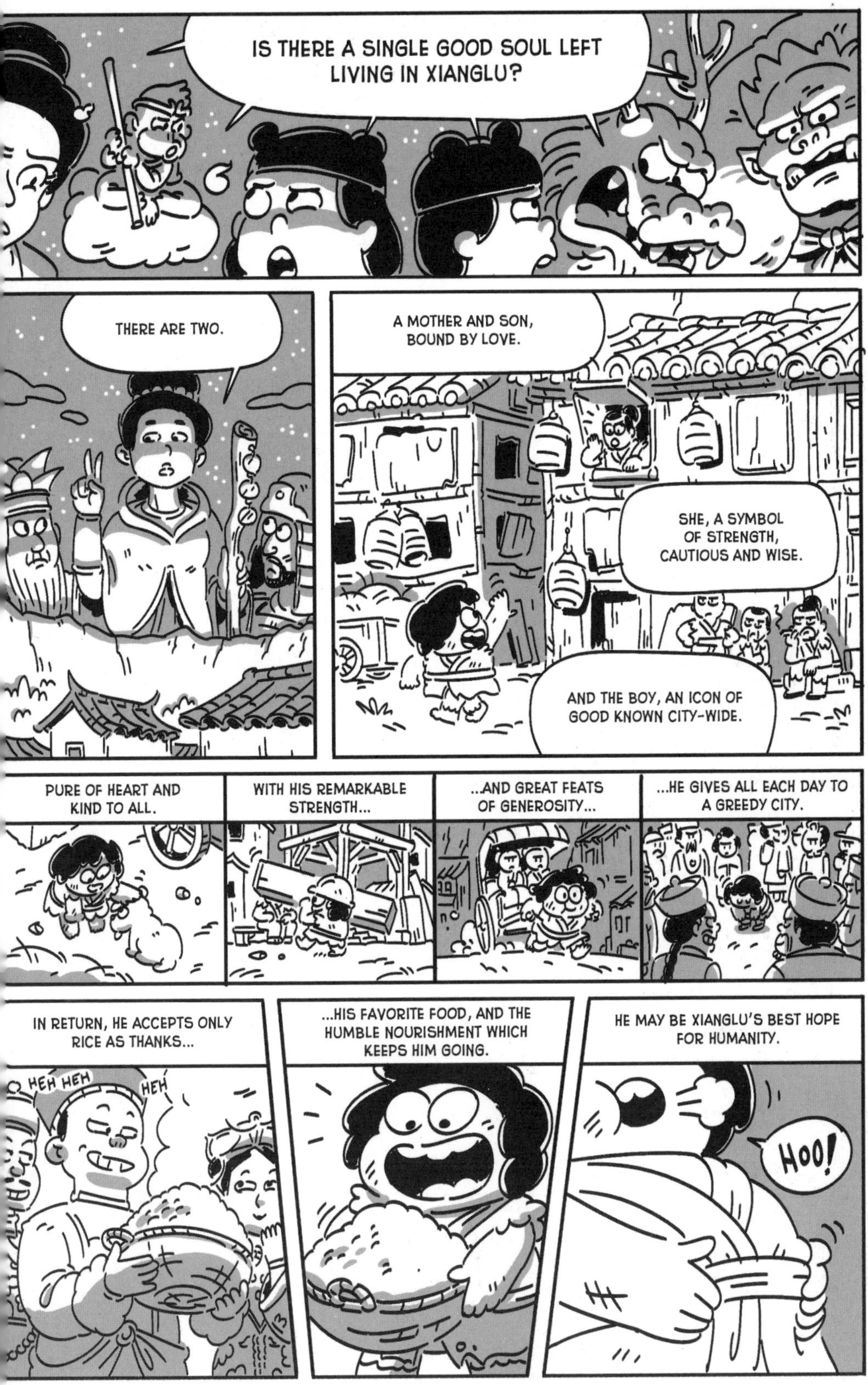

IS THERE A SINGLE GOOD SOUL LEFT LIVING IN XIANGLU?
THERE ARE TWO.
A MOTHER AND SON, BOUND BY LOVE.
SHE, A SYMBOL OF STRENGTH, CAUTIOUS AND WISE.
AND THE BOY, AN ICON OF GOOD KNOWN CITY-WIDE.
PURE OF HEART AND KIND TO ALL.
WITH HIS REMARKABLE STRENGTH...
...AND GREAT FEATS OF GENEROSITY...
...HE GIVES ALL EACH DAY TO A GREEDY CITY.
IN RETURN, HE ACCEPTS ONLY RICE AS THANKS...
HEH HEH
HEH
...HIS FAVORITE FOOD, AND THE HUMBLE NOURISHMENT WHICH KEEPS HIM GOING.
HE MAY BE XIANGLU'S BEST HOPE FOR HUMANITY.
HOO!

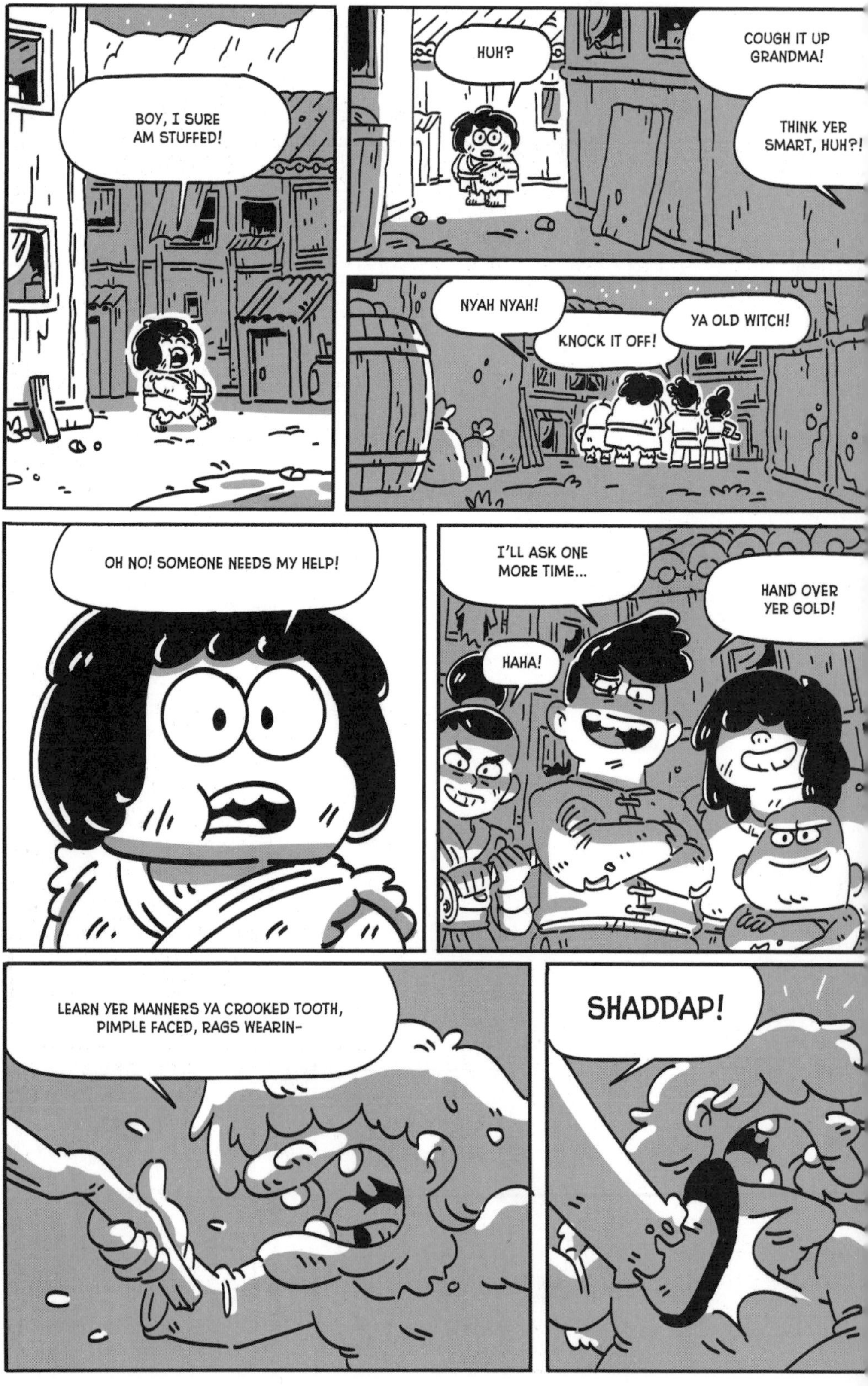
BOY, I SURE AM STUFFED!
HUH?
COUGH IT UP GRANDMA!
THINK YER SMART, HUH?!
NYAH NYAH!
KNOCK IT OFF!
YA OLD WITCH!
OH NO! SOMEONE NEEDS MY HELP!
I'LL ASK ONE MORE TIME...
HAND OVER YER GOLD!
HAHA!
LEARN YER MANNERS YA CROOKED TOOTH, PIMPLE FACED, RAGS WEARIN-
SHADDAP!

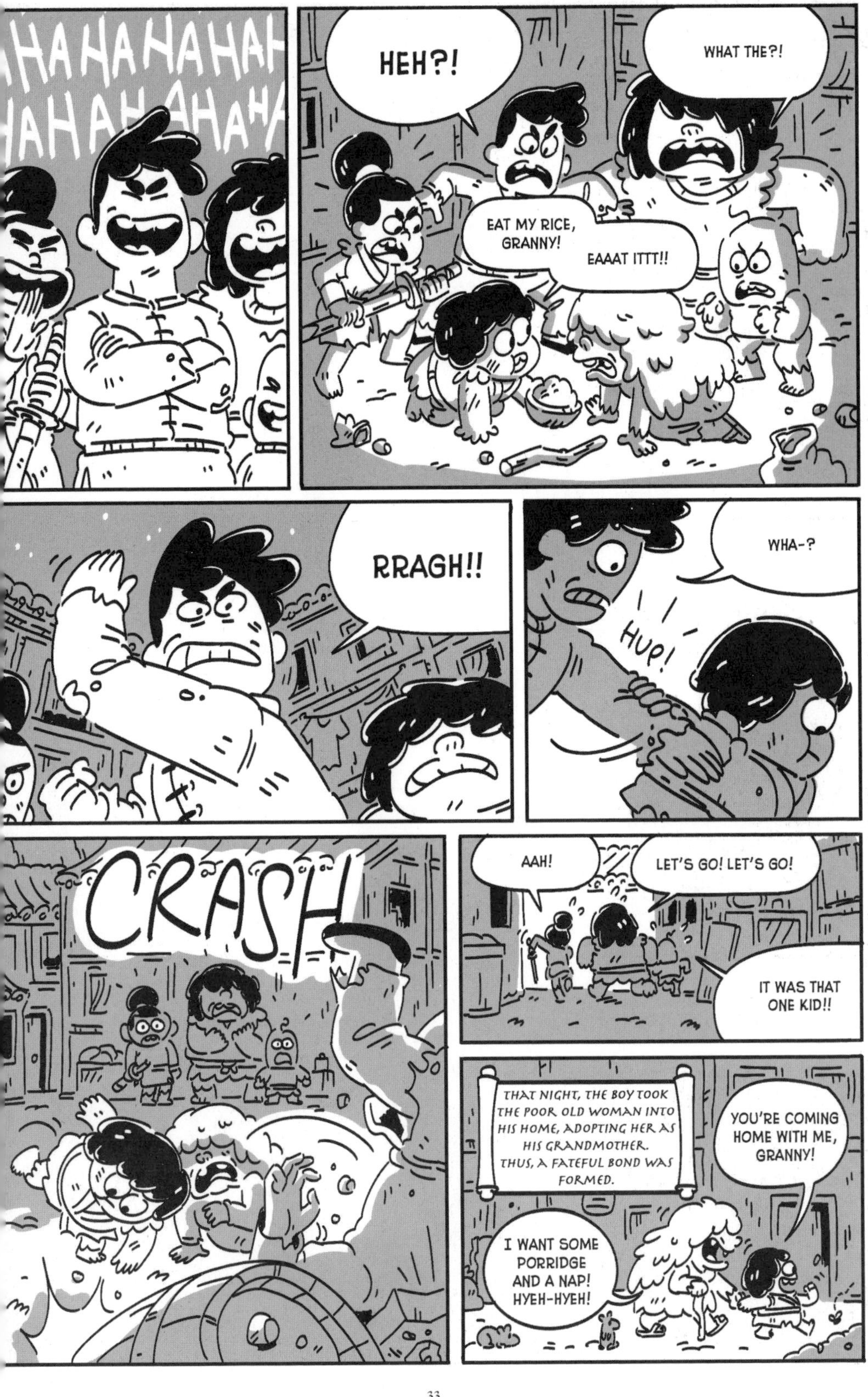
HAHAHAHAH
AHAHAHAHA
HEH?!
WHAT THE?!
EAT MY RICE, GRANNY!
EAAAT ITTT!!
RRAGH!!
WHA-?
HUP!
CRASH
AAH!
LET'S GO! LET'S GO!
IT WAS THAT ONE KID!!
THAT NIGHT, THE BOY TOOK THE POOR OLD WOMAN INTO HIS HOME, ADOPTING HER AS HIS GRANDMOTHER. THUS, A FATEFUL BOND WAS FORMED.
YOU'RE COMING HOME WITH ME, GRANNY!
I WANT SOME PORRIDGE AND A NAP! HYEH-HYEH!

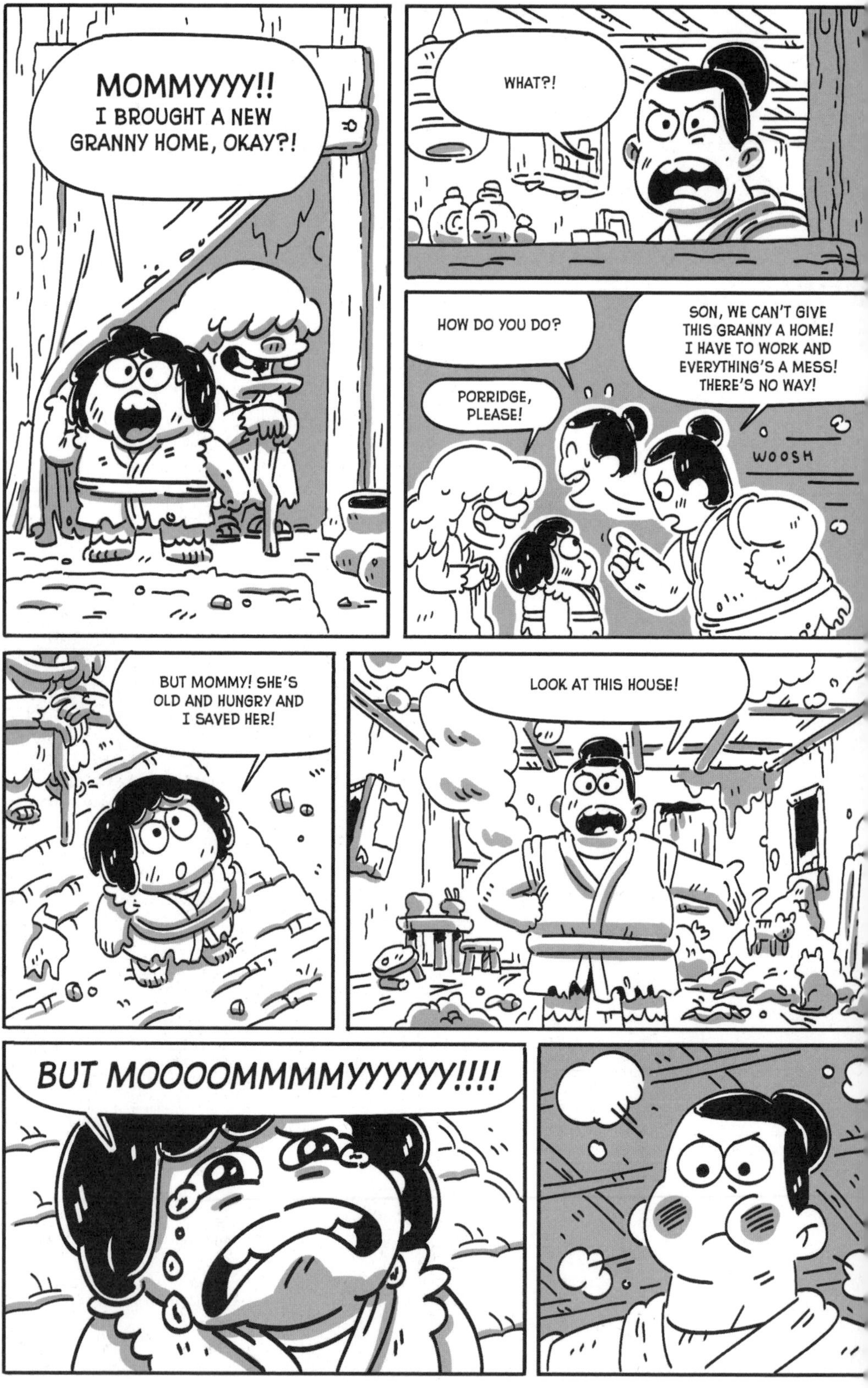
MOMMYYYY!!
I BROUGHT A NEW
GRANNY HOME, OKAY?!
WHAT?!
HOW DO YOU DO?
PORRIDGE,
PLEASE!
SON, WE CAN'T GIVE
THIS GRANNY A HOME!
I HAVE TO WORK AND
EVERYTHING'S A MESS!
THERE'S NO WAY!
WOOSH
BUT MOMMY! SHE'S
OLD AND HUNGRY AND
I SAVED HER!
LOOK AT THIS HOUSE!
BUT MOOOOMMMMYYYYYY!!!!

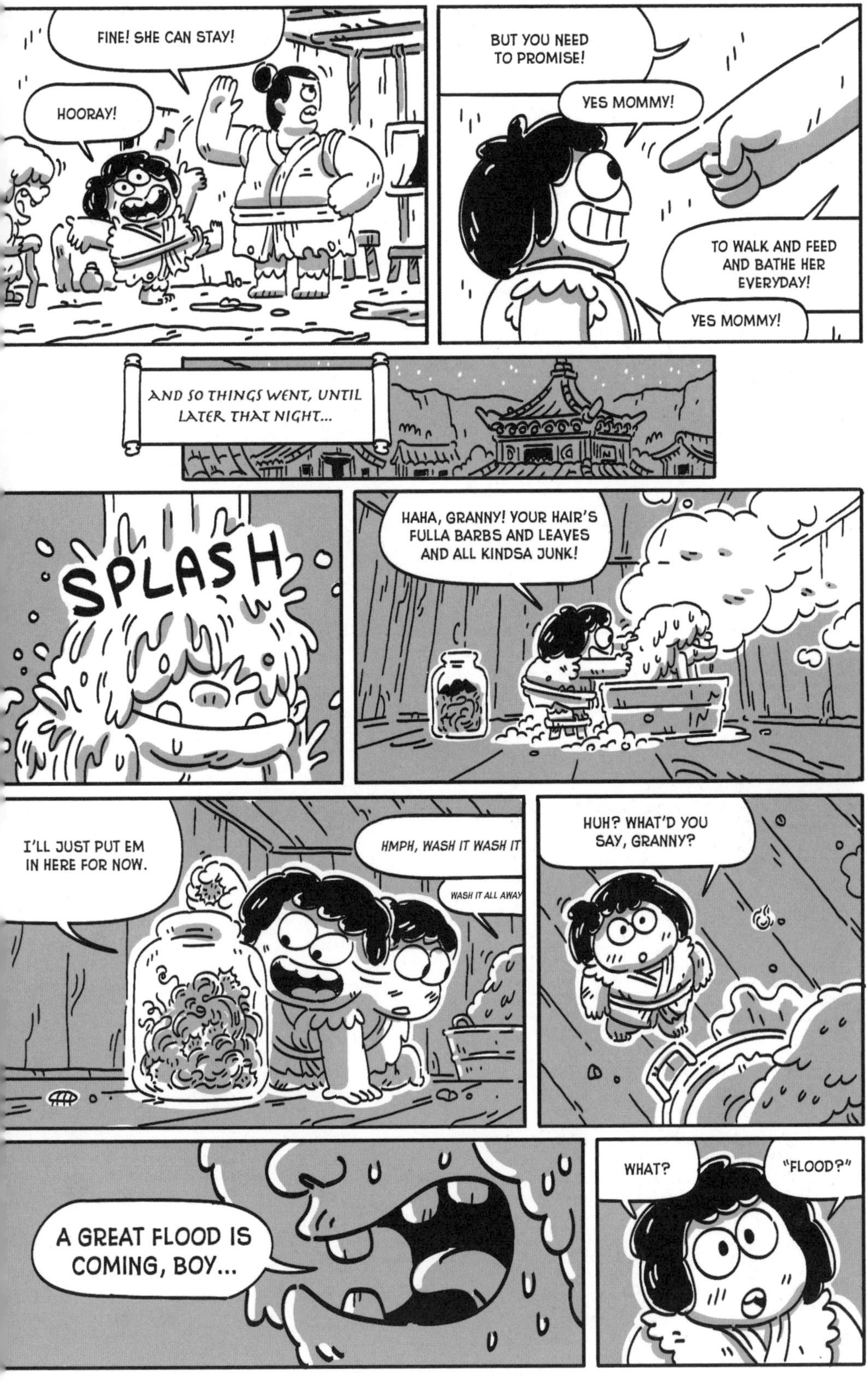

FINE! SHE CAN STAY!
HOORAY!
BUT YOU NEED TO PROMISE!
YES MOMMY!
TO WALK AND FEED AND BATHE HER EVERYDAY!
YES MOMMY!
AND SO THINGS WENT, UNTIL LATER THAT NIGHT...
SPLASH
HAHA, GRANNY! YOUR HAIR'S FULLA BARBS AND LEAVES AND ALL KINDSA JUNK!
I'LL JUST PUT EM IN HERE FOR NOW.
HMPH, WASH IT WASH IT
WASH IT ALL AWAY
HUH? WHAT'D YOU SAY, GRANNY?
A GREAT FLOOD IS COMING, BOY...
WHAT?
"FLOOD?"

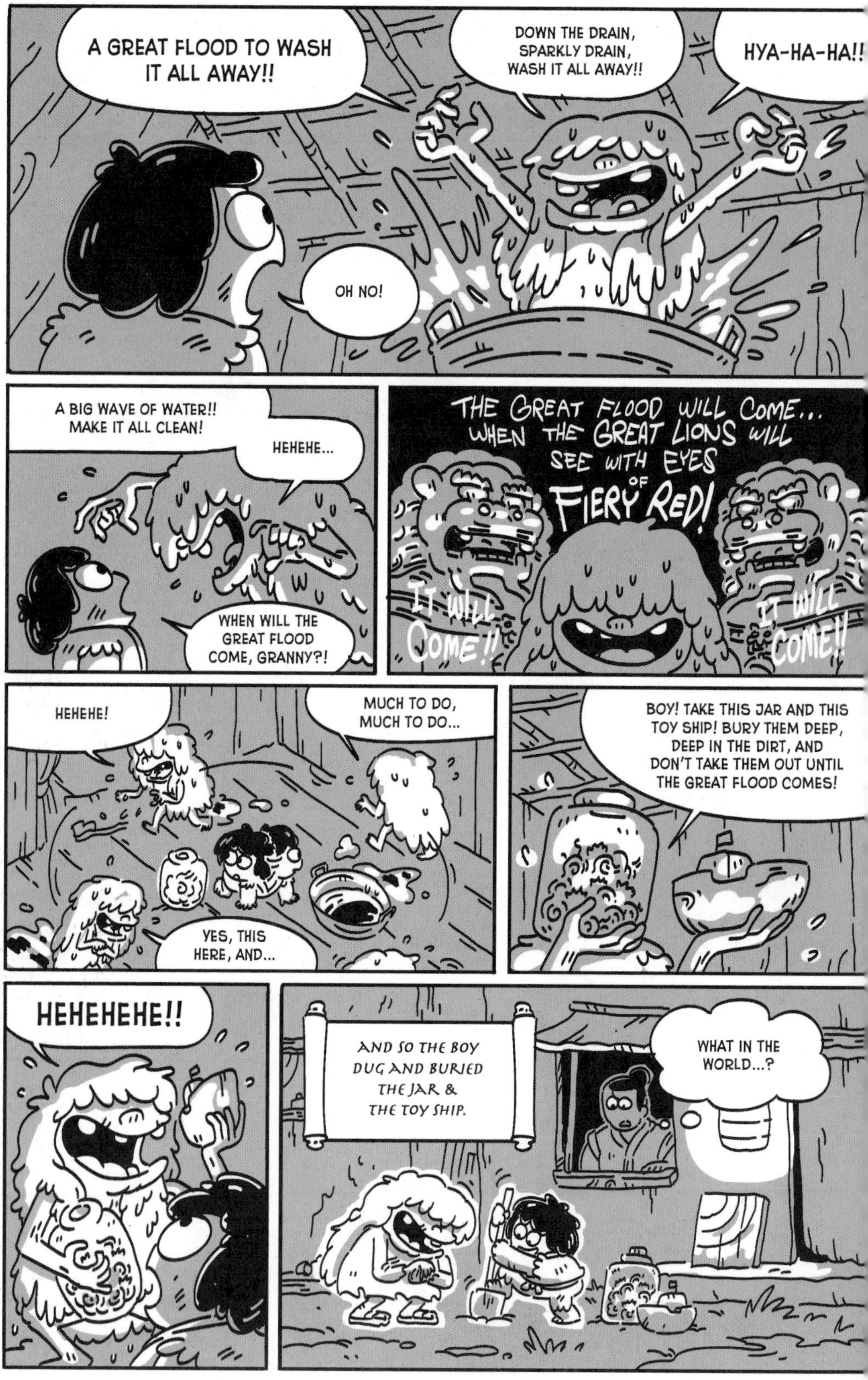
A GREAT FLOOD TO WASH IT ALL AWAY!!
DOWN THE DRAIN, SPARKLY DRAIN, WASH IT ALL AWAY!!
HYA-HA-HA!!
OH NO!
A BIG WAVE OF WATER!! MAKE IT ALL CLEAN!
HEHEHE...
WHEN WILL THE GREAT FLOOD COME, GRANNY?!
THE GREAT FLOOD WILL COME... WHEN THE GREAT LIONS WILL SEE WITH EYES OF FIERY RED!
IT WILL COME!!
IT WILL COME!!
HEHEHE!
MUCH TO DO, MUCH TO DO...
YES, THIS HERE, AND...
BOY! TAKE THIS JAR AND THIS TOY SHIP! BURY THEM DEEP, DEEP IN THE DIRT, AND DON'T TAKE THEM OUT UNTIL THE GREAT FLOOD COMES!
HEHEHEHE!!
AND SO THE BOY DUG AND BURIED THE JAR & THE TOY SHIP.
WHAT IN THE WORLD...?

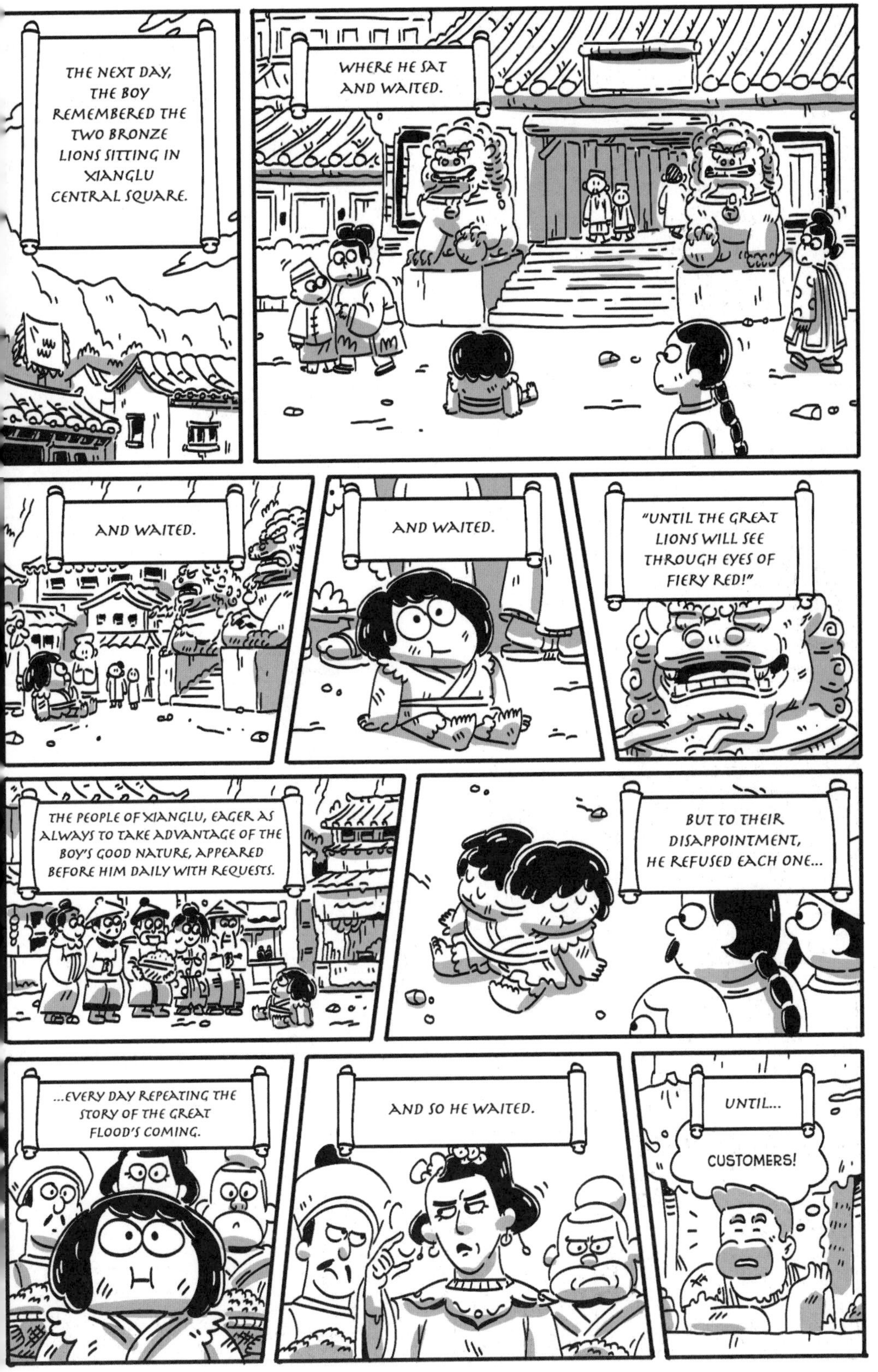
THE NEXT DAY, THE BOY REMEMBERED THE TWO BRONZE LIONS SITTING IN XIANGLU CENTRAL SQUARE.
WHERE HE SAT AND WAITED.
AND WAITED.
AND WAITED.
"UNTIL THE GREAT LIONS WILL SEE THROUGH EYES OF FIERY RED!"
THE PEOPLE OF XIANGLU, EAGER AS ALWAYS TO TAKE ADVANTAGE OF THE BOY'S GOOD NATURE, APPEARED BEFORE HIM DAILY WITH REQUESTS.
BUT TO THEIR DISAPPOINTMENT, HE REFUSED EACH ONE...
...EVERY DAY REPEATING THE STORY OF THE GREAT FLOOD'S COMING.
AND SO HE WAITED.
UNTIL...
CUSTOMERS!

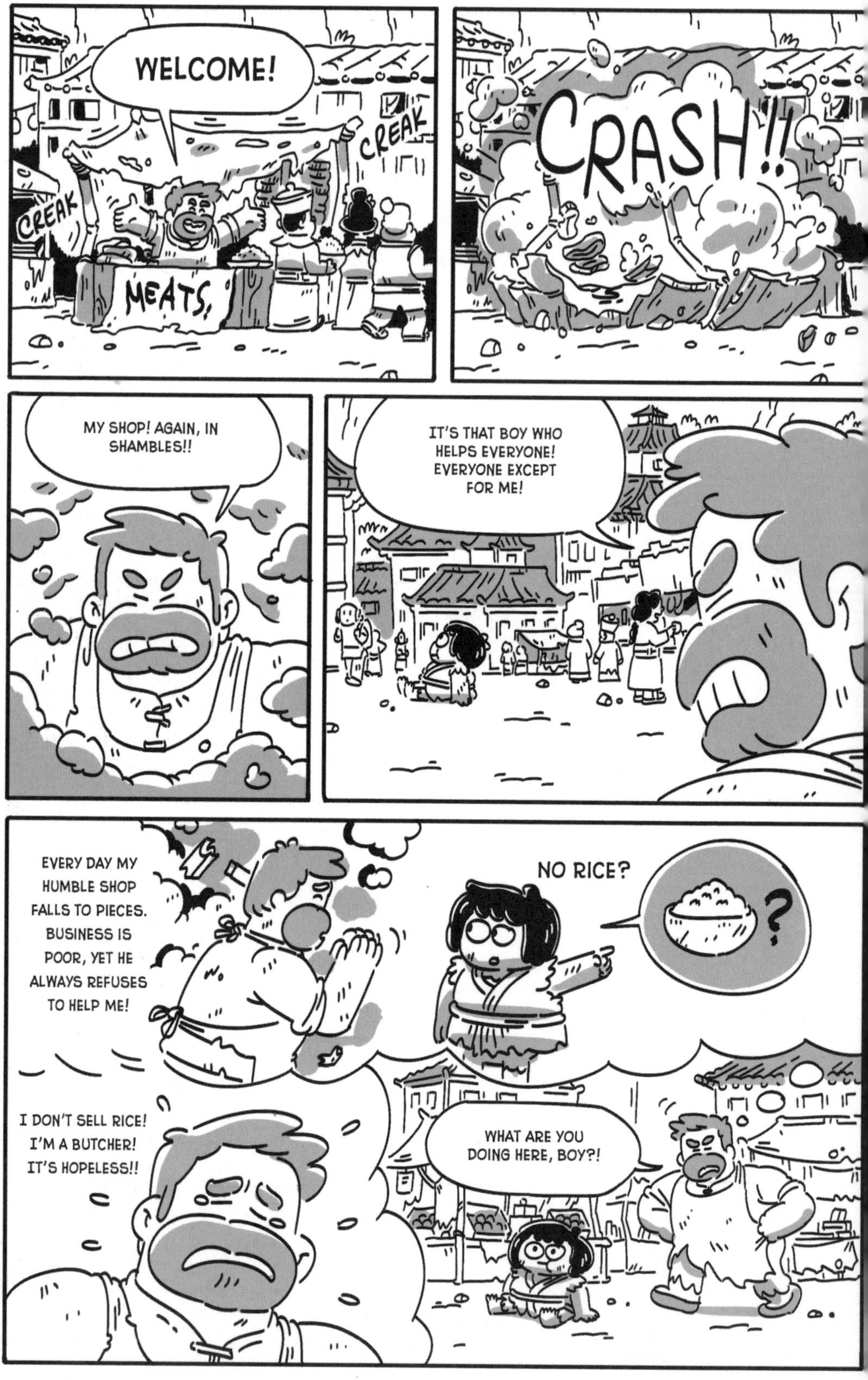
WELCOME!
CREAK
CREAK
MEATS
CRASH!!
MY SHOP! AGAIN, IN SHAMBLES!!
IT'S THAT BOY WHO HELPS EVERYONE! EVERYONE EXCEPT FOR ME!
EVERY DAY MY HUMBLE SHOP FALLS TO PIECES. BUSINESS IS POOR, YET HE ALWAYS REFUSES TO HELP ME!
NO RICE?
?
I DON'T SELL RICE! I'M A BUTCHER! IT'S HOPELESS!!
WHAT ARE YOU DOING HERE, BOY?!

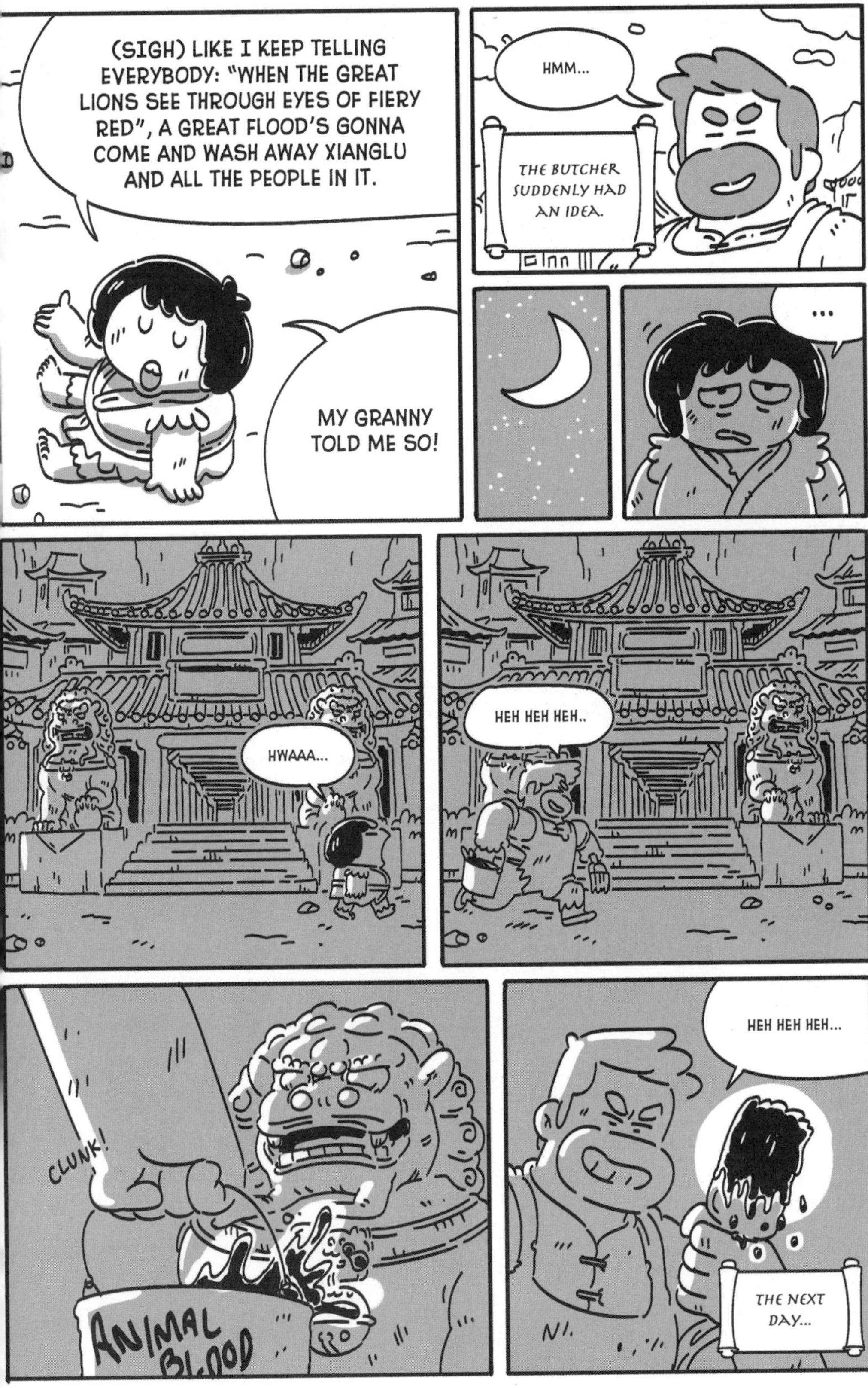
(SIGH) LIKE I KEEP TELLING EVERYBODY: "WHEN THE GREAT LIONS SEE THROUGH EYES OF FIERY RED", A GREAT FLOOD'S GONNA COME AND WASH AWAY XIANGLU AND ALL THE PEOPLE IN IT.
MY GRANNY TOLD ME SO!
HMM...
THE BUTCHER SUDDENLY HAD AN IDEA.
...
HWAAA...
HEH HEH HEH..
CLUNK!
ANIMAL BLOOD
HEH HEH HEH...
THE NEXT DAY...

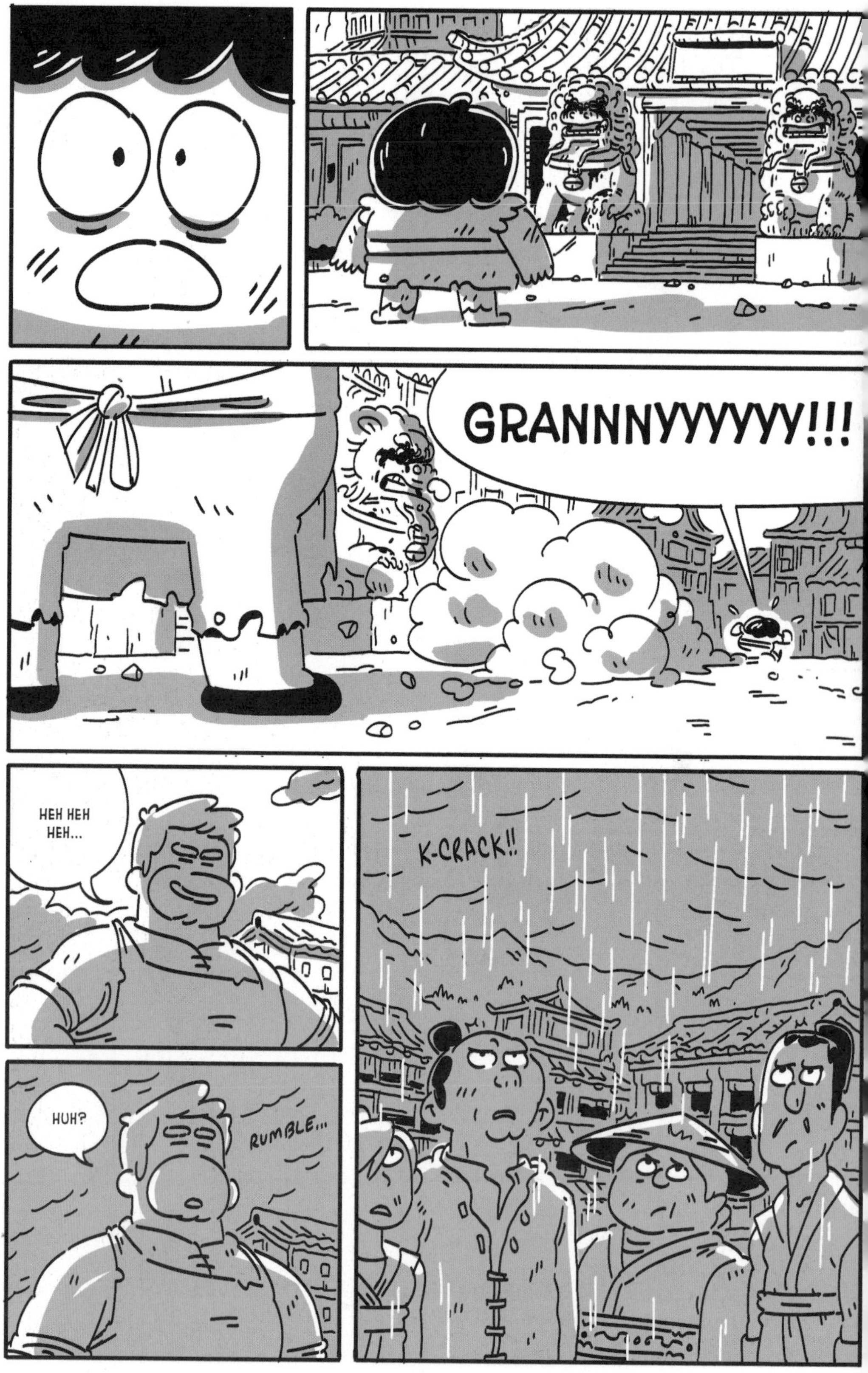
GRANNNYYYYYY!!!
HEH HEH HEH...
K-CRACK!!
HUH?
RUMBLE...

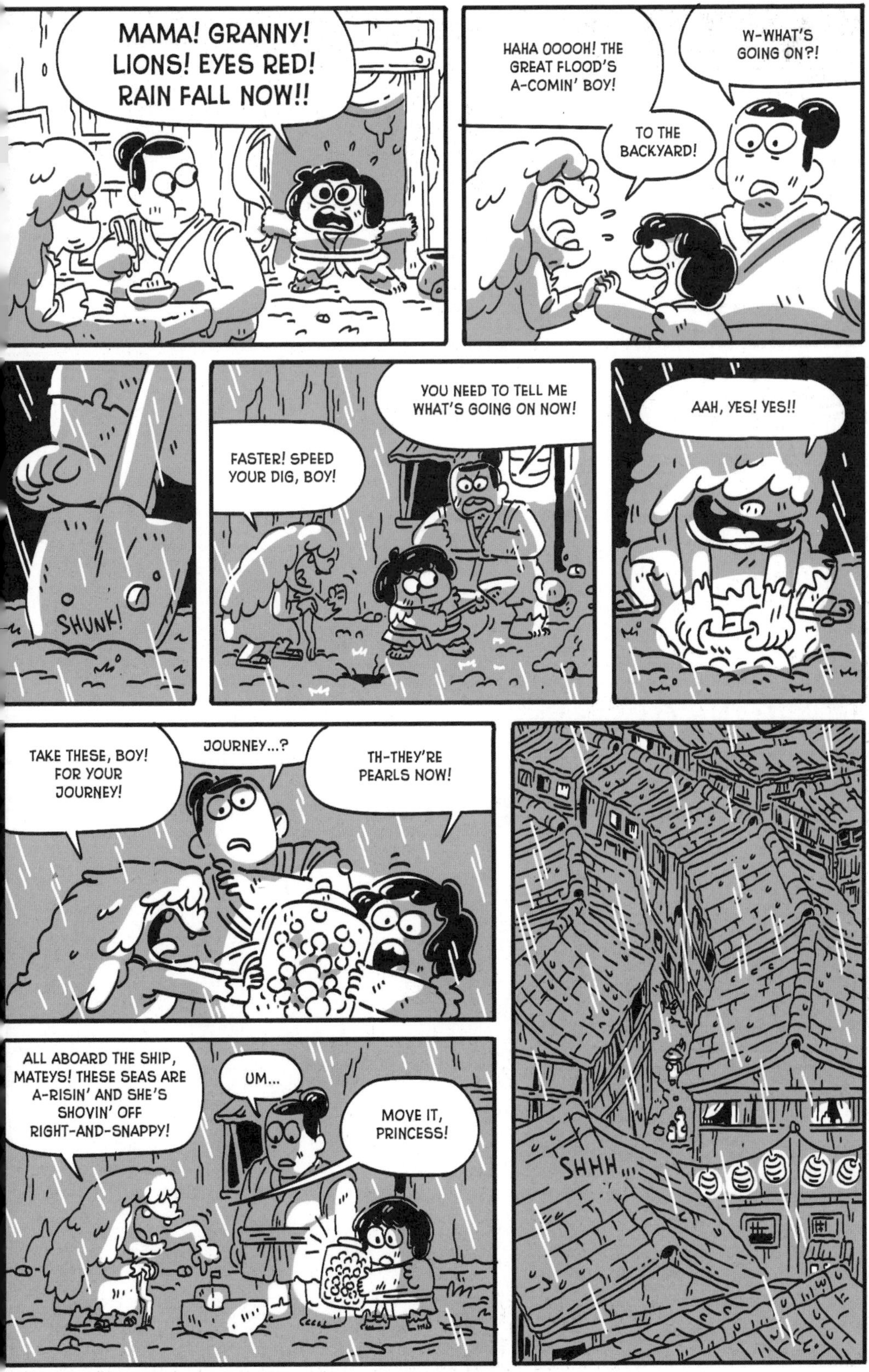
MAMA! GRANNY! LIONS! EYES RED! RAIN FALL NOW!!
HAHA OOOOH! THE GREAT FLOOD'S A-COMIN' BOY!
W-WHAT'S GOING ON?!
TO THE BACKYARD!
SHUNK!
YOU NEED TO TELL ME WHAT'S GOING ON NOW!
FASTER! SPEED YOUR DIG, BOY!
AAH, YES! YES!!
TAKE THESE, BOY! FOR YOUR JOURNEY!
JOURNEY...?
TH-THEY'RE PEARLS NOW!
ALL ABOARD THE SHIP, MATEYS! THESE SEAS ARE A-RISIN' AND SHE'S SHOVIN' OFF RIGHT-AND-SNAPPY!
UM...
MOVE IT, PRINCESS!
SHHH...

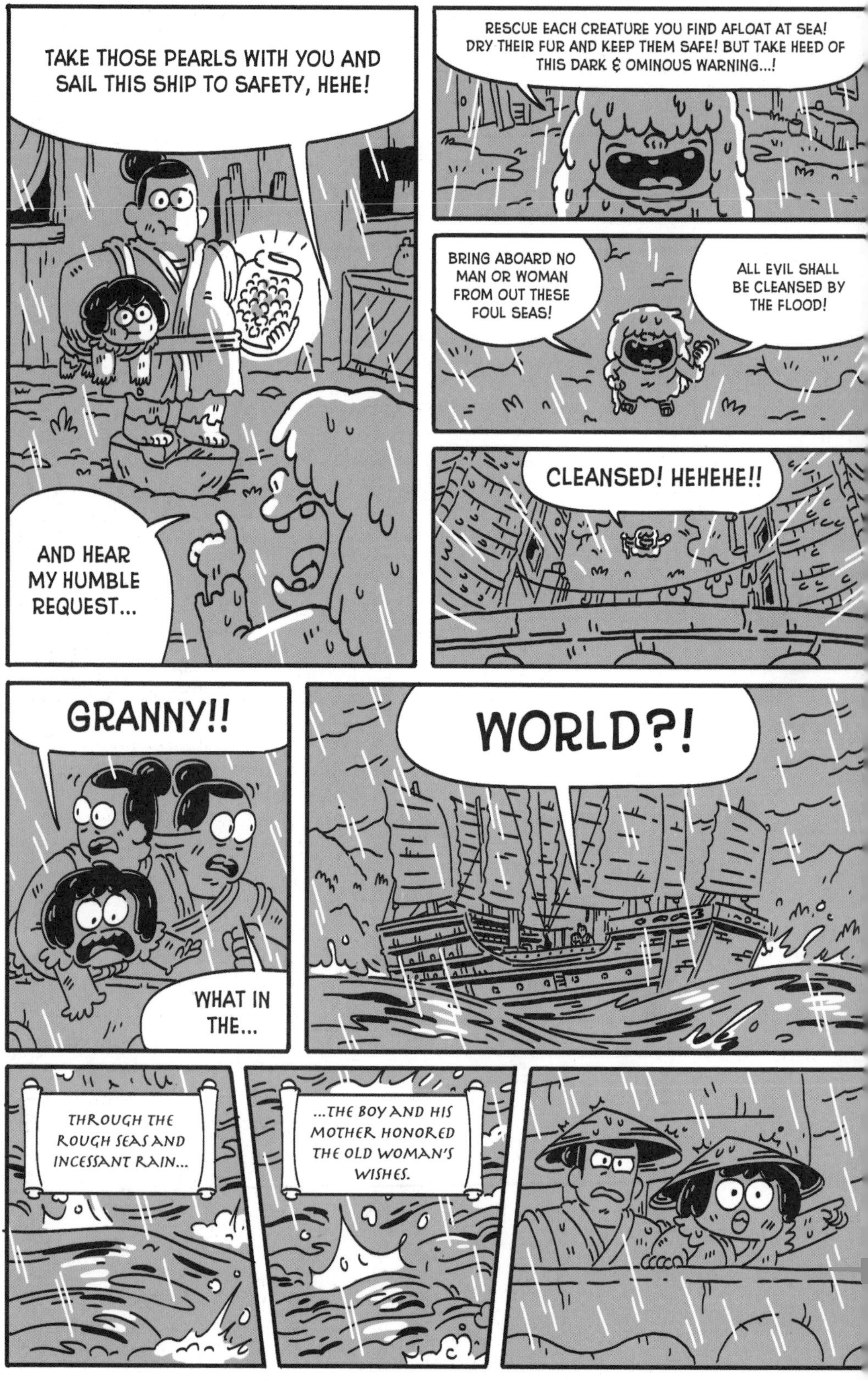
TAKE THOSE PEARLS WITH YOU AND SAIL THIS SHIP TO SAFETY, HEHE!
AND HEAR MY HUMBLE REQUEST...
RESCUE EACH CREATURE YOU FIND AFLOAT AT SEA! DRY THEIR FUR AND KEEP THEM SAFE! BUT TAKE HEED OF THIS DARK & OMINOUS WARNING...!
BRING ABOARD NO MAN OR WOMAN FROM OUT THESE FOUL SEAS!
ALL EVIL SHALL BE CLEANSED BY THE FLOOD!
CLEANSED! HEHEHE!!
GRANNY!!
WHAT IN THE...
WORLD?!
THROUGH THE ROUGH SEAS AND INCESSANT RAIN...
...THE BOY AND HIS MOTHER HONORED THE OLD WOMAN'S WISHES.

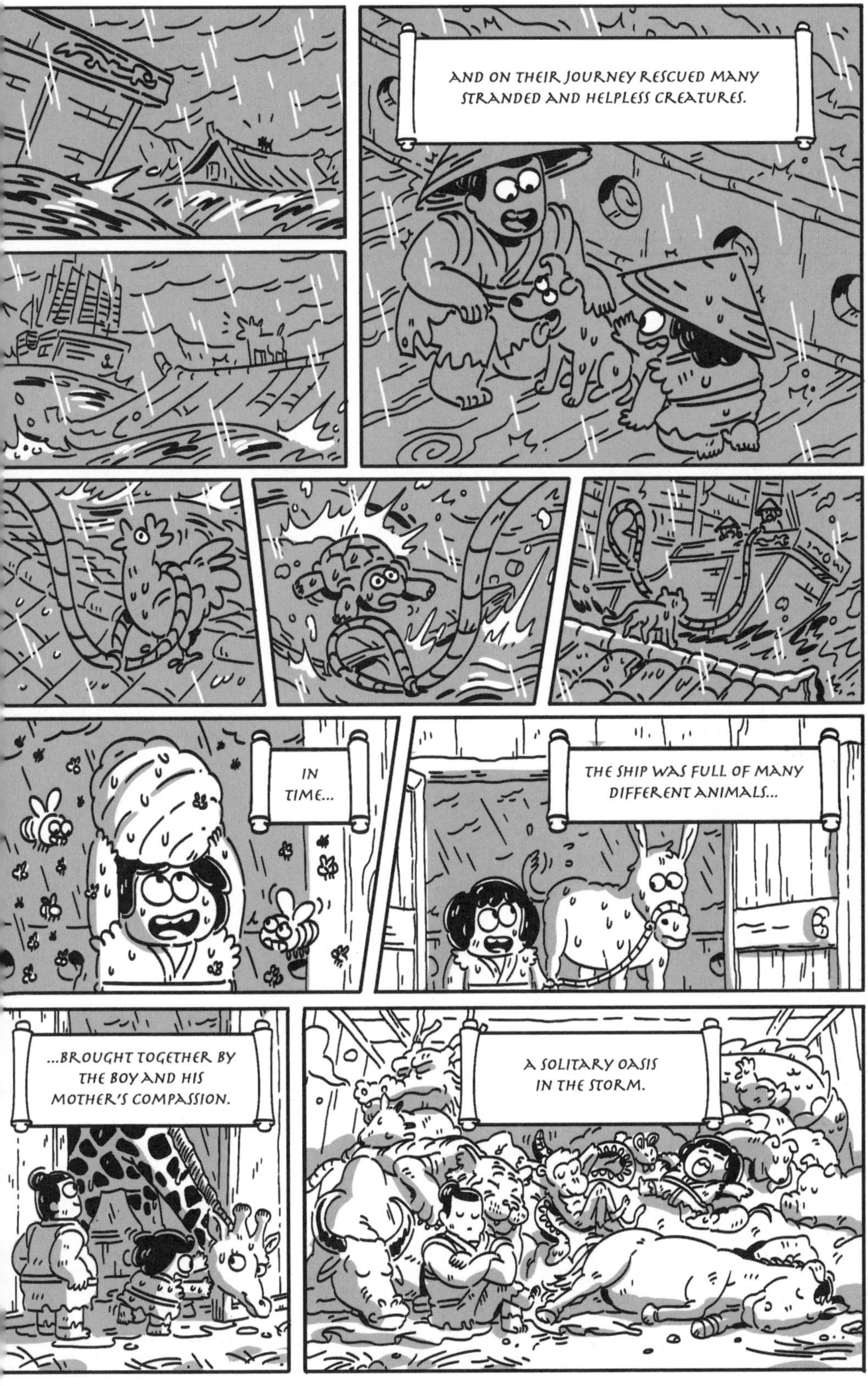
AND ON THEIR JOURNEY RESCUED MANY STRANDED AND HELPLESS CREATURES.
IN TIME...
THE SHIP WAS FULL OF MANY DIFFERENT ANIMALS...
...BROUGHT TOGETHER BY THE BOY AND HIS MOTHER'S COMPASSION.
A SOLITARY OASIS IN THE STORM.

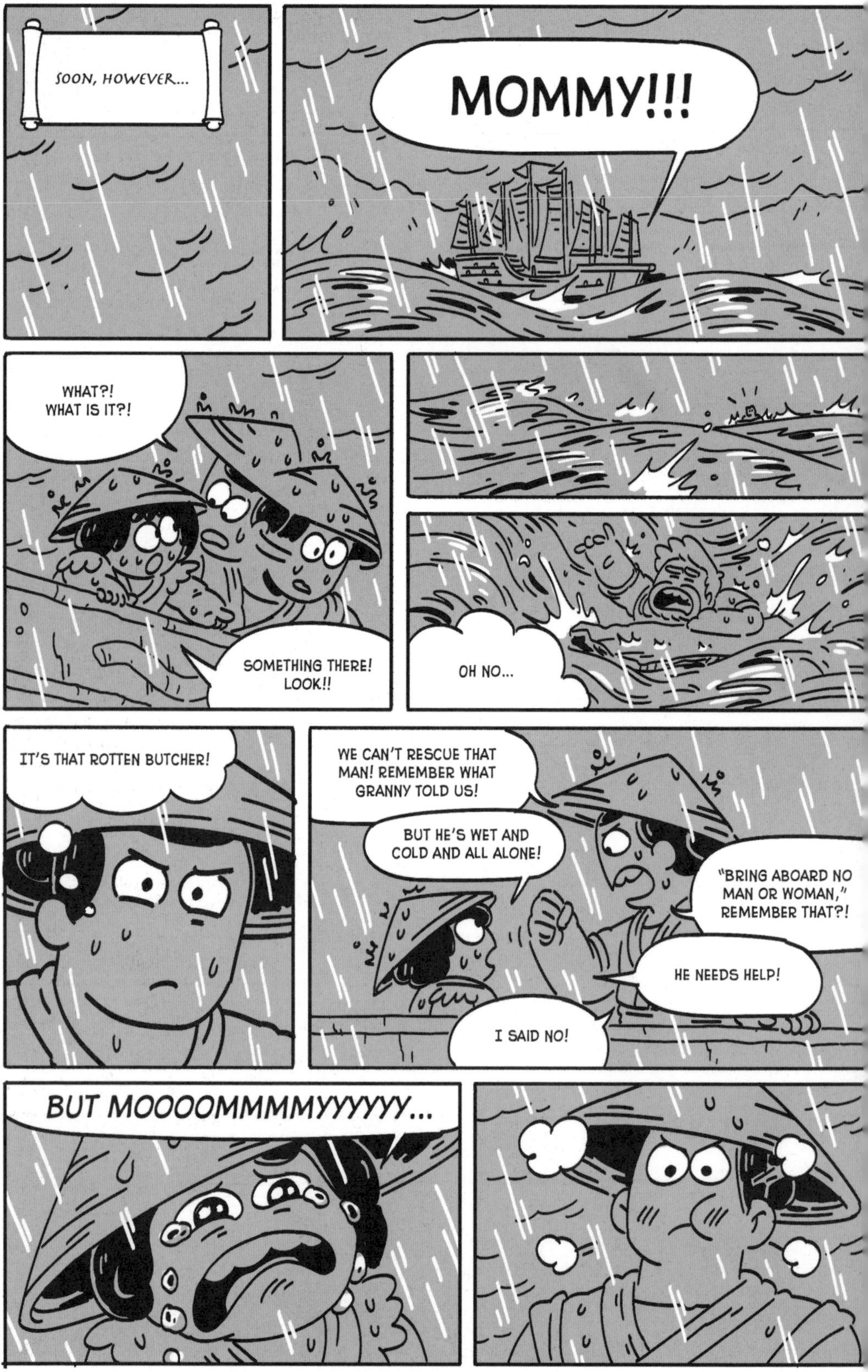
SOON, HOWEVER...
MOMMY!!!
WHAT?! WHAT IS IT?!
SOMETHING THERE! LOOK!!
OH NO...
IT'S THAT ROTTEN BUTCHER!
WE CAN'T RESCUE THAT MAN! REMEMBER WHAT GRANNY TOLD US!
BUT HE'S WET AND COLD AND ALL ALONE!
"BRING ABOARD NO MAN OR WOMAN," REMEMBER THAT?!
HE NEEDS HELP!
I SAID NO!
BUT MOOOOMMMMYYYYYY...

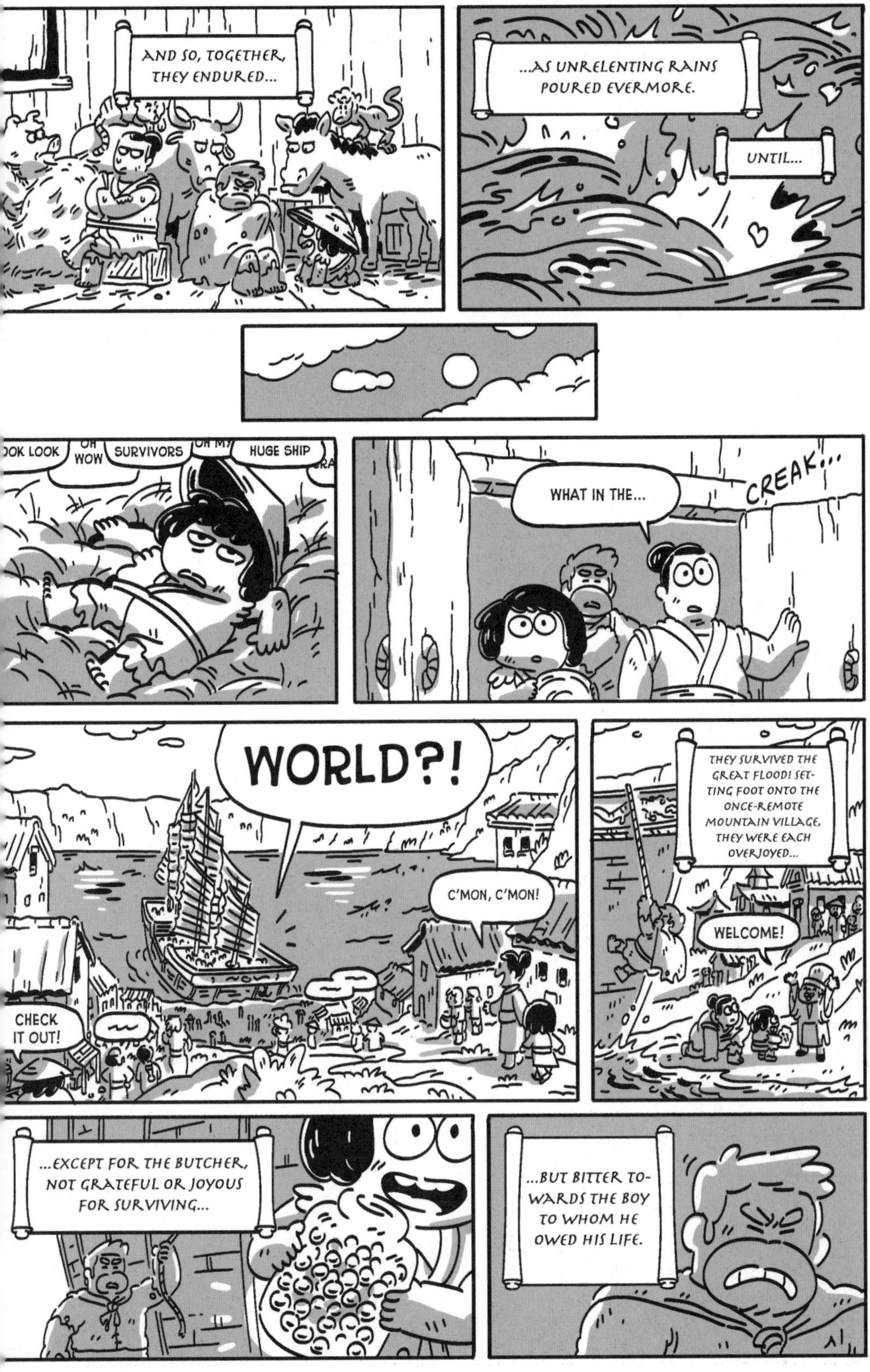
AND SO, TOGETHER, THEY ENDURED...
...AS UNRELENTING RAINS POURED EVERMORE.
UNTIL...
LOOK LOOK
OH WOW
SURVIVORS
OH MY
HUGE SHIP
WHAT IN THE...
CREAK...
WORLD?!
C'MON, C'MON!
CHECK IT OUT!
THEY SURVIVED THE GREAT FLOOD! SETTING FOOT ONTO THE ONCE-REMOTE MOUNTAIN VILLAGE, THEY WERE EACH OVERJOYED...
WELCOME!
...EXCEPT FOR THE BUTCHER, NOT GRATEFUL OR JOYOUS FOR SURVIVING...
...BUT BITTER TOWARDS THE BOY TO WHOM HE OWED HIS LIFE.

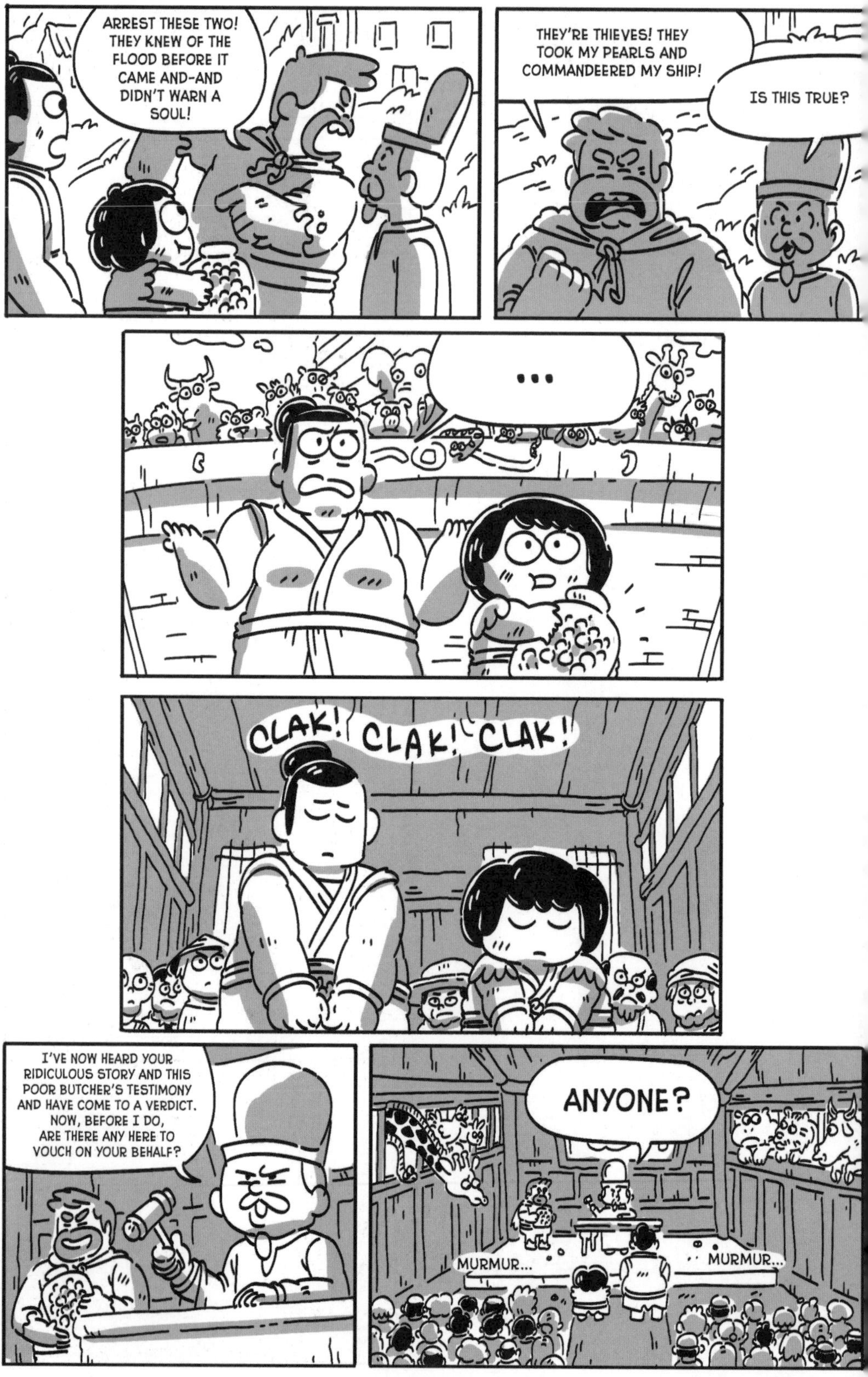
ARREST THESE TWO! THEY KNEW OF THE FLOOD BEFORE IT CAME AND-AND DIDN'T WARN A SOUL!
THEY'RE THIEVES! THEY TOOK MY PEARLS AND COMMANDEERED MY SHIP!
IS THIS TRUE?
...
CLAK! CLAK! CLAK!
I'VE NOW HEARD YOUR RIDICULOUS STORY AND THIS POOR BUTCHER'S TESTIMONY AND HAVE COME TO A VERDICT. NOW, BEFORE I DO, ARE THERE ANY HERE TO VOUCH ON YOUR BEHALF?
ANYONE?
MURMUR...
MURMUR...

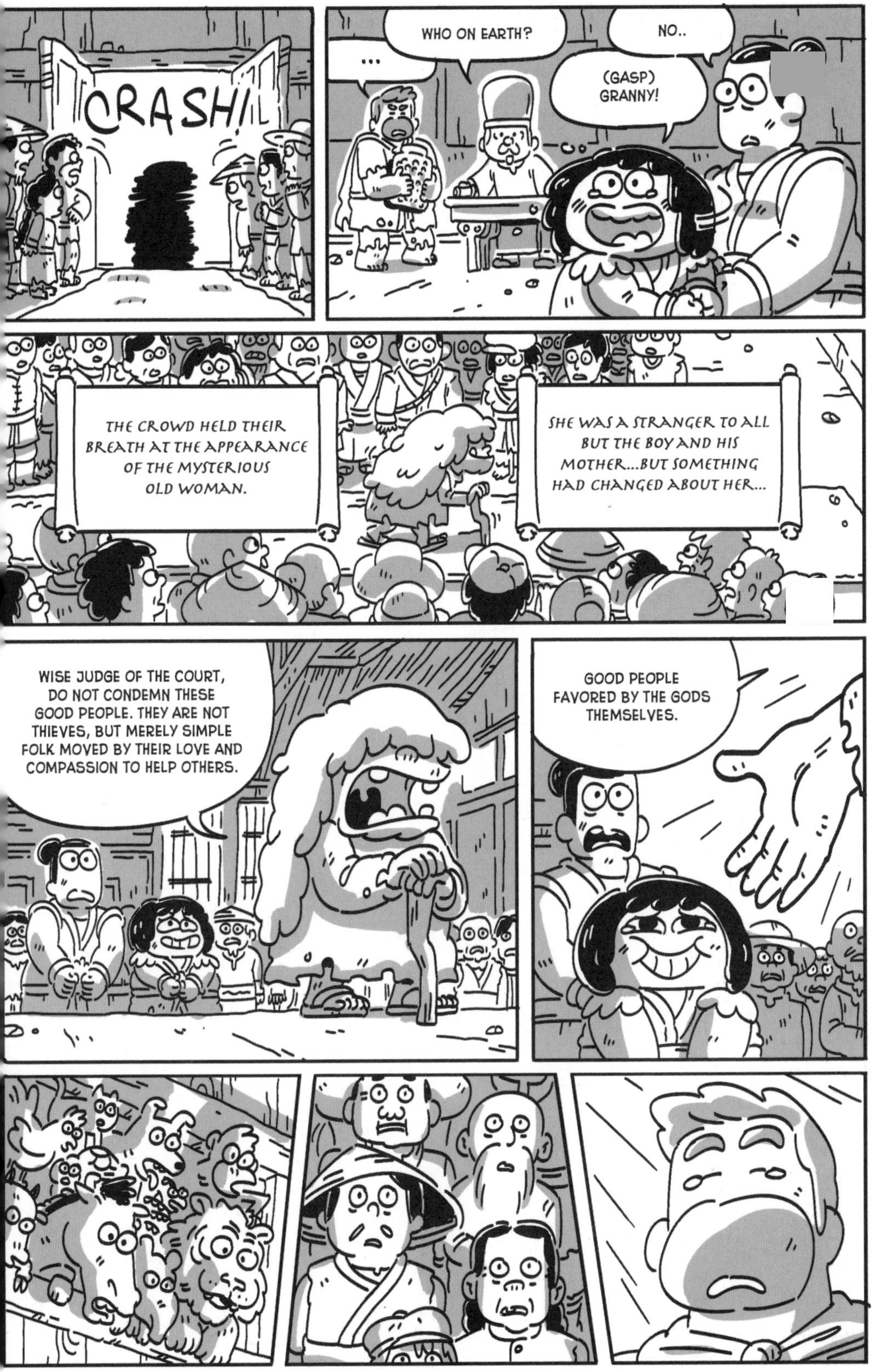
CRASH!
...
WHO ON EARTH?
NO..
(GASP) GRANNY!
THE CROWD HELD THEIR BREATH AT THE APPEARANCE OF THE MYSTERIOUS OLD WOMAN.
SHE WAS A STRANGER TO ALL BUT THE BOY AND HIS MOTHER...BUT SOMETHING HAD CHANGED ABOUT HER...
WISE JUDGE OF THE COURT, DO NOT CONDEMN THESE GOOD PEOPLE. THEY ARE NOT THIEVES, BUT MERELY SIMPLE FOLK MOVED BY THEIR LOVE AND COMPASSION TO HELP OTHERS.
GOOD PEOPLE FAVORED BY THE GODS THEMSELVES.

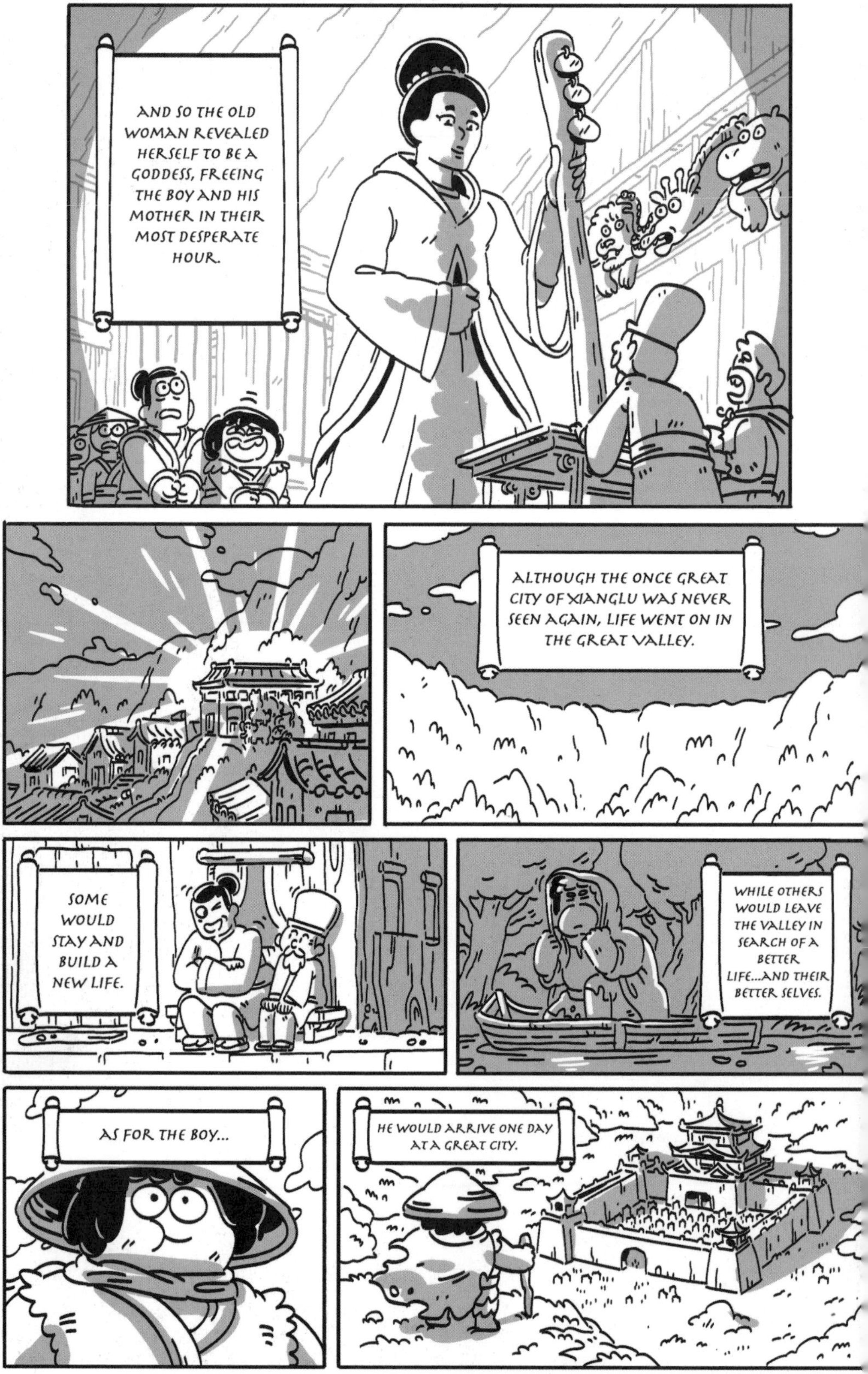
AND SO THE OLD WOMAN REVEALED HERSELF TO BE A GODDESS, FREEING THE BOY AND HIS MOTHER IN THEIR MOST DESPERATE HOUR.
ALTHOUGH THE ONCE GREAT CITY OF XIANGLU WAS NEVER SEEN AGAIN, LIFE WENT ON IN THE GREAT VALLEY.
SOME WOULD STAY AND BUILD A NEW LIFE.
WHILE OTHERS WOULD LEAVE THE VALLEY IN SEARCH OF A BETTER LIFE...AND THEIR BETTER SELVES.
AS FOR THE BOY...
HE WOULD ARRIVE ONE DAY AT A GREAT CITY.

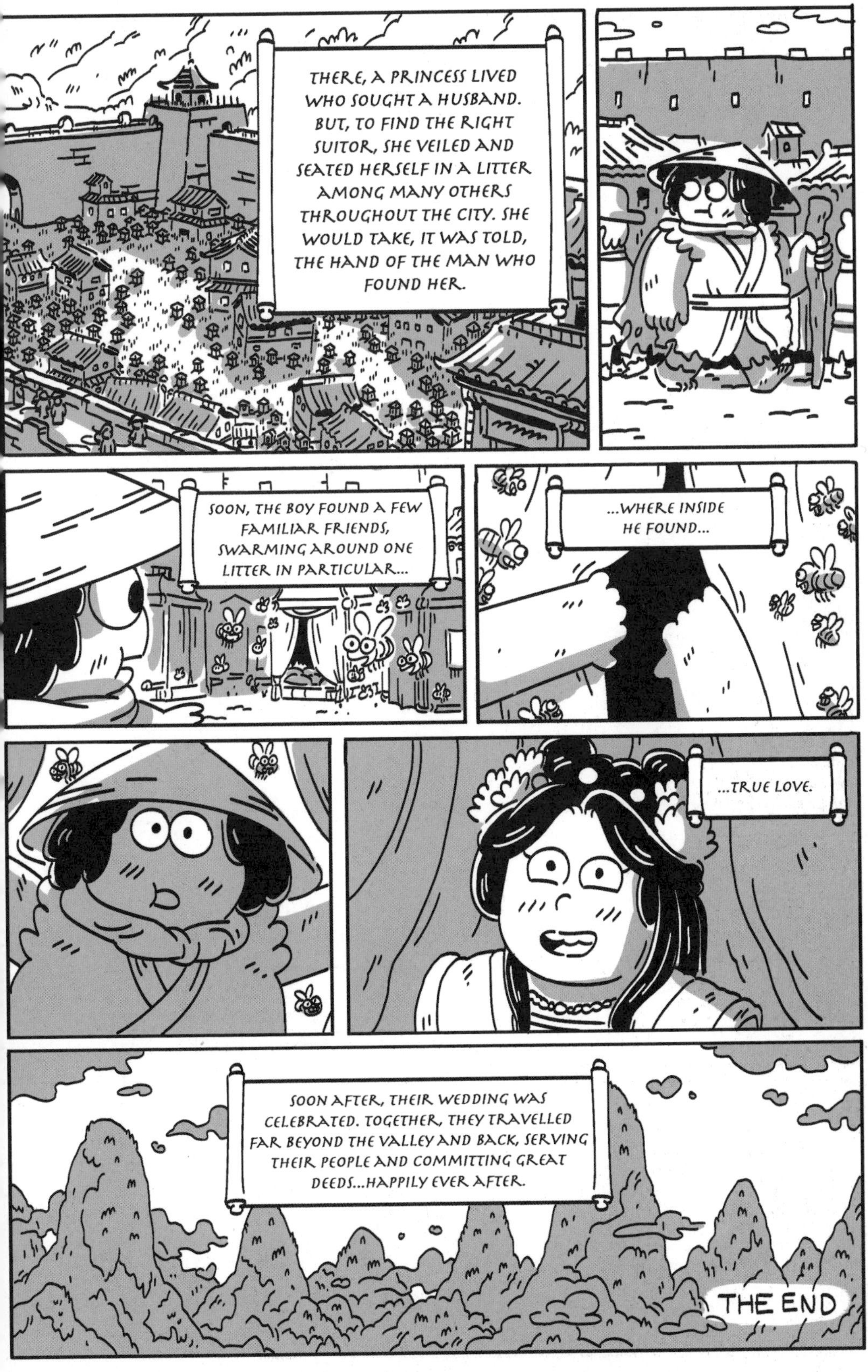
THERE, A PRINCESS LIVED WHO SOUGHT A HUSBAND. BUT, TO FIND THE RIGHT SUITOR, SHE VEILED AND SEATED HERSELF IN A LITTER AMONG MANY OTHERS THROUGHOUT THE CITY. SHE WOULD TAKE, IT WAS TOLD, THE HAND OF THE MAN WHO FOUND HER.
SOON, THE BOY FOUND A FEW FAMILIAR FRIENDS, SWARMING AROUND ONE LITTER IN PARTICULAR...
...WHERE INSIDE HE FOUND...
...TRUE LOVE.
SOON AFTER, THEIR WEDDING WAS CELEBRATED. TOGETHER, THEY TRAVELLED FAR BEYOND THE VALLEY AND BACK, SERVING THEIR PEOPLE AND COMMITTING GREAT DEEDS...HAPPILY EVER AFTER.
THE END

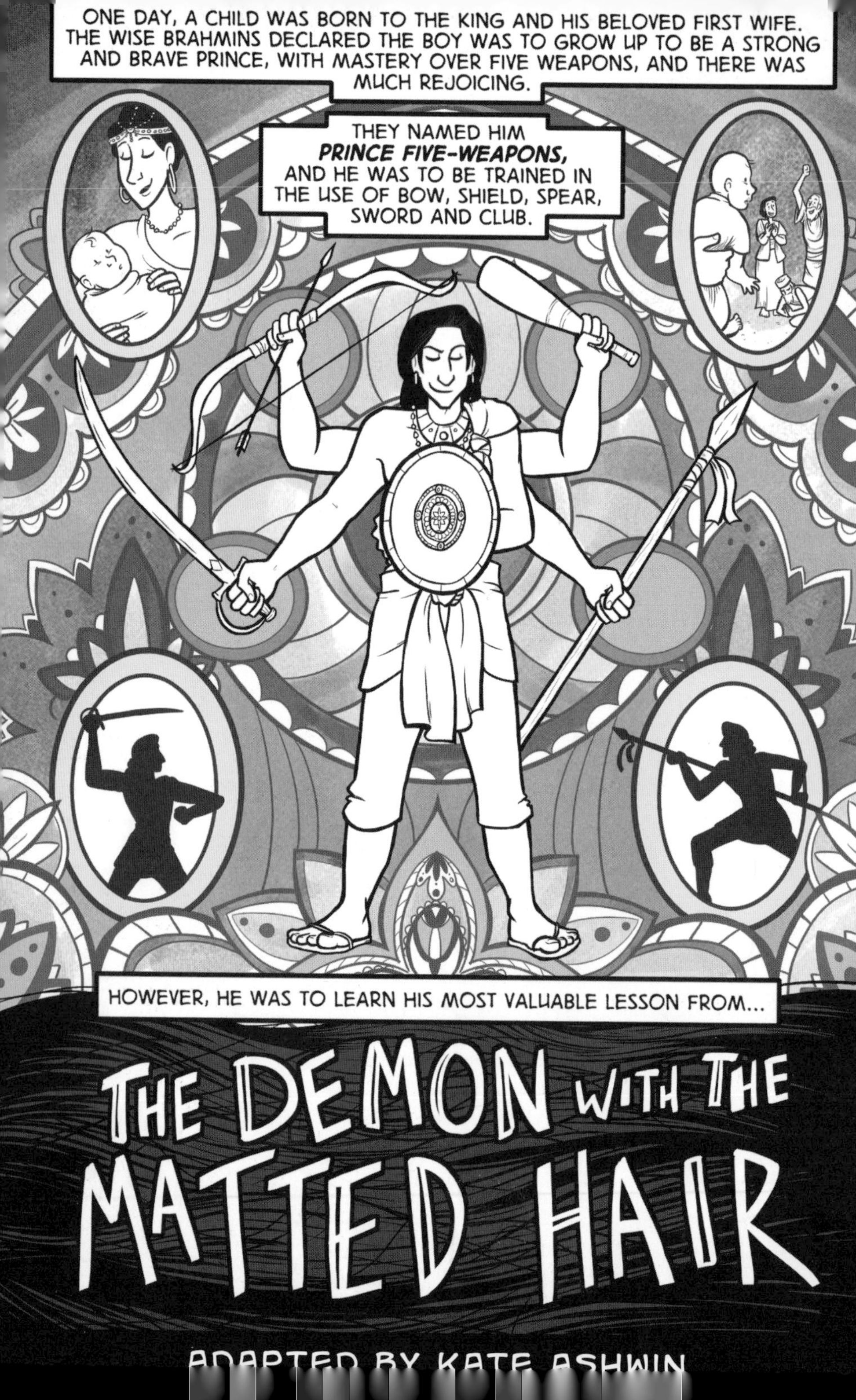
ONE DAY, A CHILD WAS BORN TO THE KING AND HIS BELOVED FIRST WIFE. THE WISE BRAHMINS DECLARED THE BOY WAS TO GROW UP TO BE A STRONG AND BRAVE PRINCE, WITH MASTERY OVER FIVE WEAPONS, AND THERE WAS MUCH REJOICING.
THEY NAMED HIM ***PRINCE FIVE-WEAPONS,*** AND HE WAS TO BE TRAINED IN THE USE OF BOW, SHIELD, SPEAR, SWORD AND CLUB.
HOWEVER, HE WAS TO LEARN HIS MOST VALUABLE LESSON FROM...
THE DEMON WITH THE MATTED HAIR
ADAPTED BY KATE ASHWIN

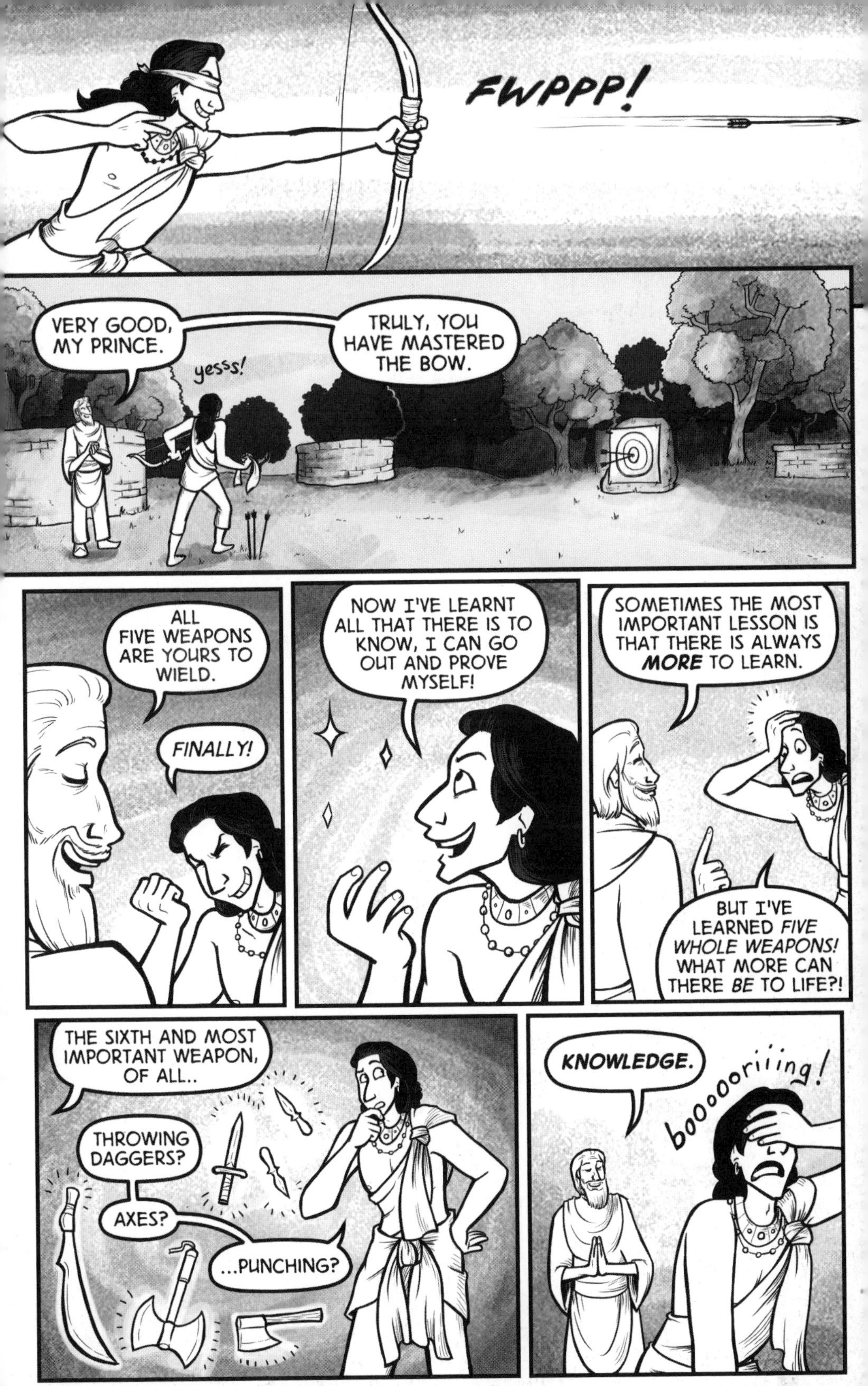
FWPPP!
VERY GOOD, MY PRINCE.
TRULY, YOU HAVE MASTERED THE BOW.
yesss!
ALL FIVE WEAPONS ARE YOURS TO WIELD.
FINALLY!
NOW I'VE LEARNT ALL THAT THERE IS TO KNOW, I CAN GO OUT AND PROVE MYSELF!
SOMETIMES THE MOST IMPORTANT LESSON IS THAT THERE IS ALWAYS *MORE* TO LEARN.
BUT I'VE LEARNED *FIVE WHOLE WEAPONS!* WHAT MORE CAN THERE *BE* TO LIFE?!
THE SIXTH AND MOST IMPORTANT WEAPON, OF ALL..
THROWING DAGGERS?
AXES?
...PUNCHING?
KNOWLEDGE.
boooooriiing!

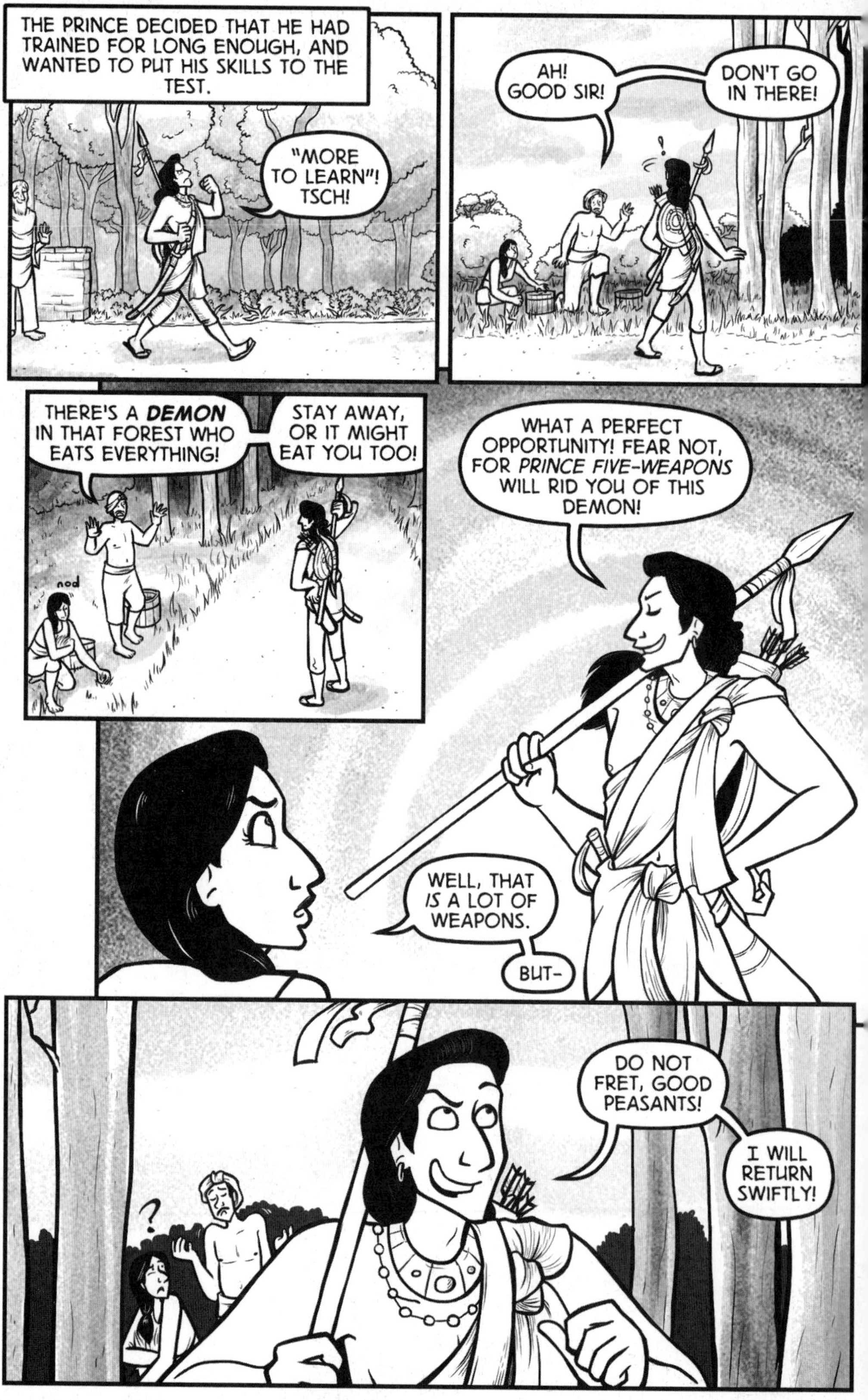
THE PRINCE DECIDED THAT HE HAD TRAINED FOR LONG ENOUGH, AND WANTED TO PUT HIS SKILLS TO THE TEST.
"MORE TO LEARN"! TSCH!
AH! GOOD SIR!
DON'T GO IN THERE!
!
THERE'S A **DEMON** IN THAT FOREST WHO EATS EVERYTHING!
STAY AWAY, OR IT MIGHT EAT YOU TOO!
nod
WHAT A PERFECT OPPORTUNITY! FEAR NOT, FOR *PRINCE FIVE-WEAPONS* WILL RID YOU OF THIS DEMON!
WELL, THAT *IS* A LOT OF WEAPONS.
BUT-
DO NOT FRET, GOOD PEASANTS!
I WILL RETURN SWIFTLY!
?

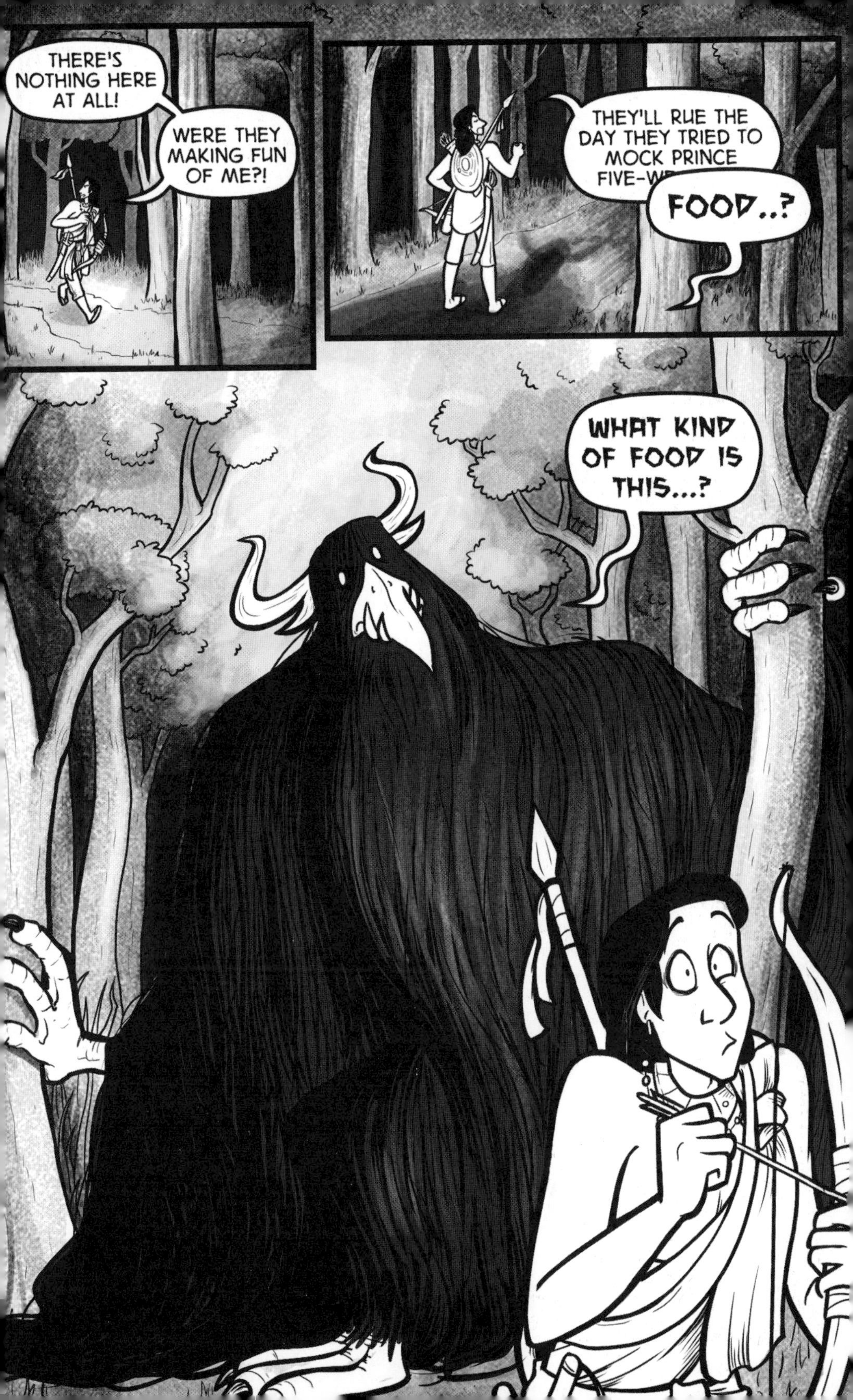

THERE'S NOTHING HERE AT ALL!
WERE THEY MAKING FUN OF ME?!
THEY'LL RUE THE DAY THEY TRIED TO MOCK PRINCE FIVE-W
FOOD..?
WHAT KIND OF FOOD IS THIS...?

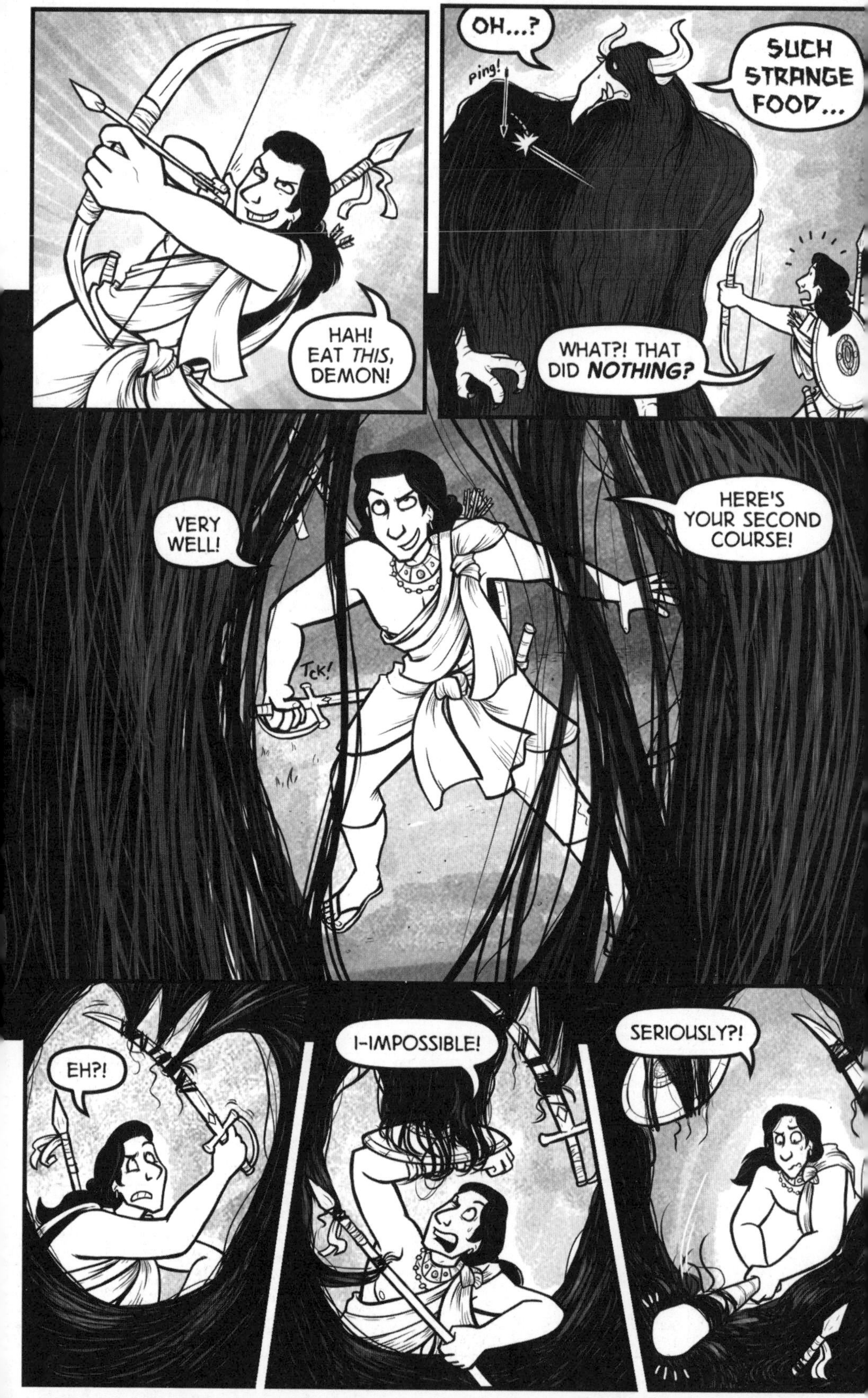
HAH! EAT *THIS*, DEMON!
OH...?
ping!
SUCH STRANGE FOOD...
WHAT?! THAT DID ***NOTHING?***
VERY WELL!
HERE'S YOUR SECOND COURSE!
TCK!
EH?!
I-IMPOSSIBLE!
SERIOUSLY?!

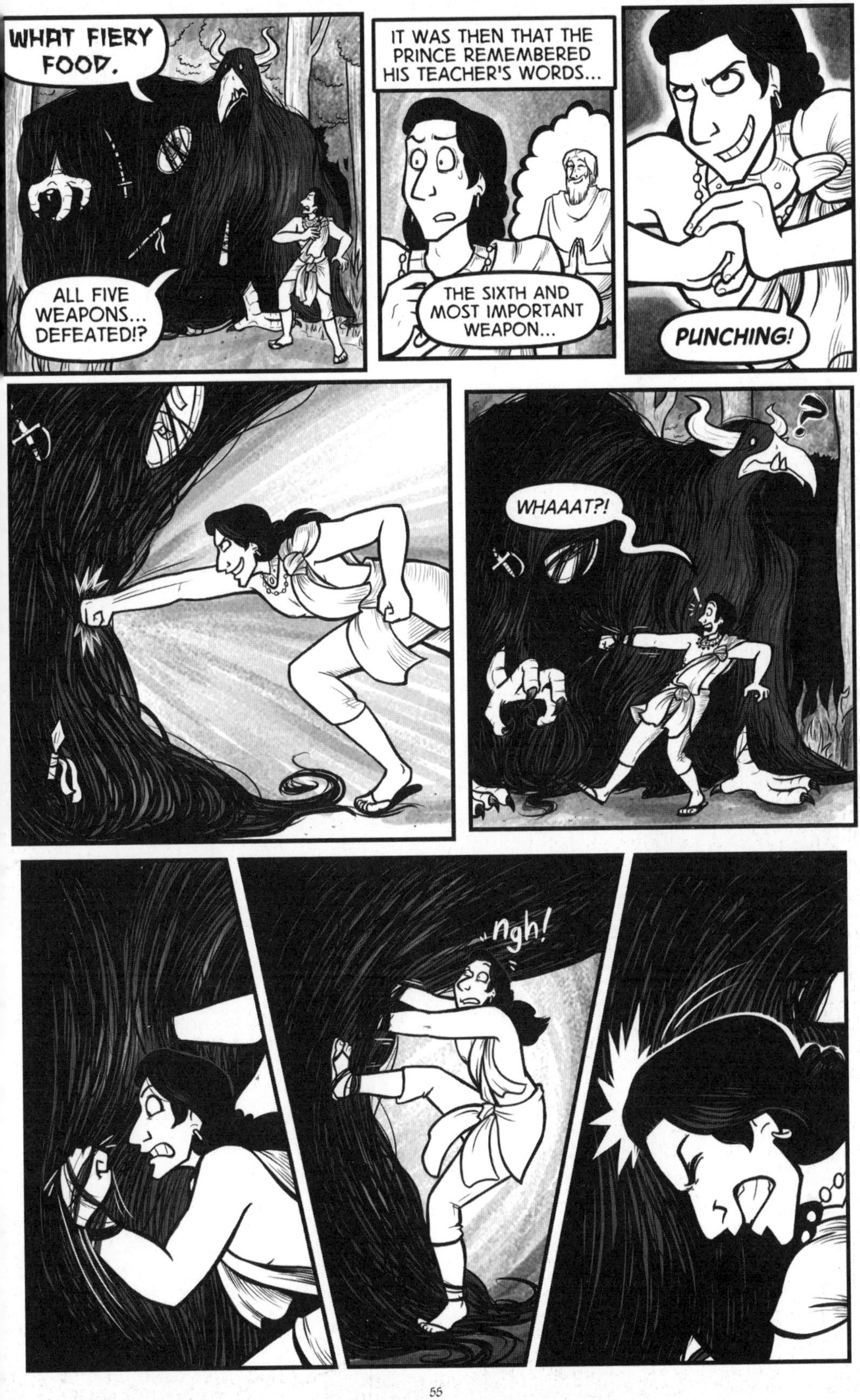
WHAT FIERY FOOD.
ALL FIVE WEAPONS... DEFEATED!?
IT WAS THEN THAT THE PRINCE REMEMBERED HIS TEACHER'S WORDS...
THE SIXTH AND MOST IMPORTANT WEAPON...
PUNCHING!
WHAAAT?!
Ngh!

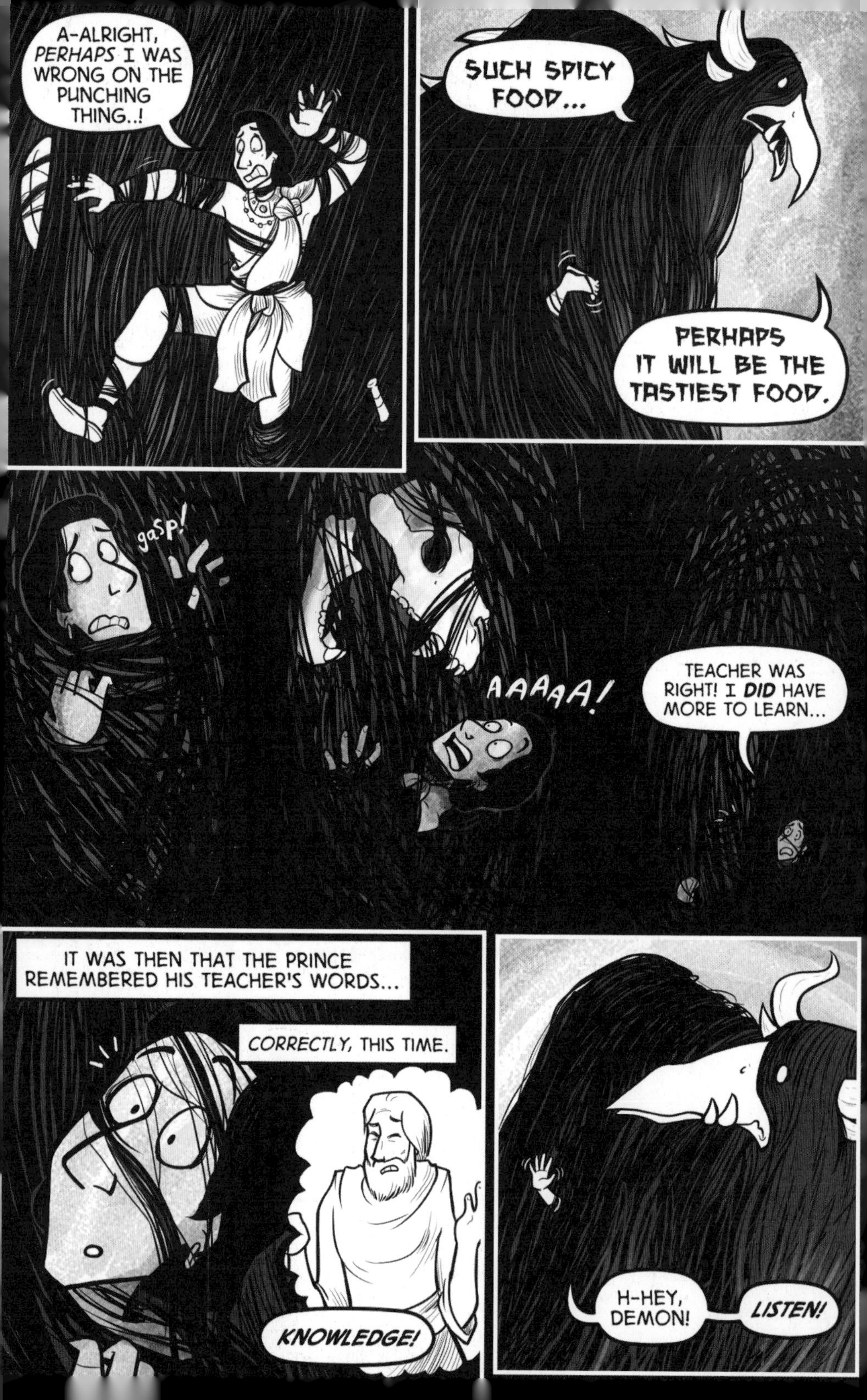
A-ALRIGHT, *PERHAPS* I WAS WRONG ON THE PUNCHING THING..!
SUCH SPICY FOOD...
PERHAPS IT WILL BE THE TASTIEST FOOD.
gasp!
AAAAA!
TEACHER WAS RIGHT! I ***DID*** HAVE MORE TO LEARN...
IT WAS THEN THAT THE PRINCE REMEMBERED HIS TEACHER'S WORDS...
CORRECTLY, THIS TIME.
KNOWLEDGE!
H-HEY, DEMON!
LISTEN!

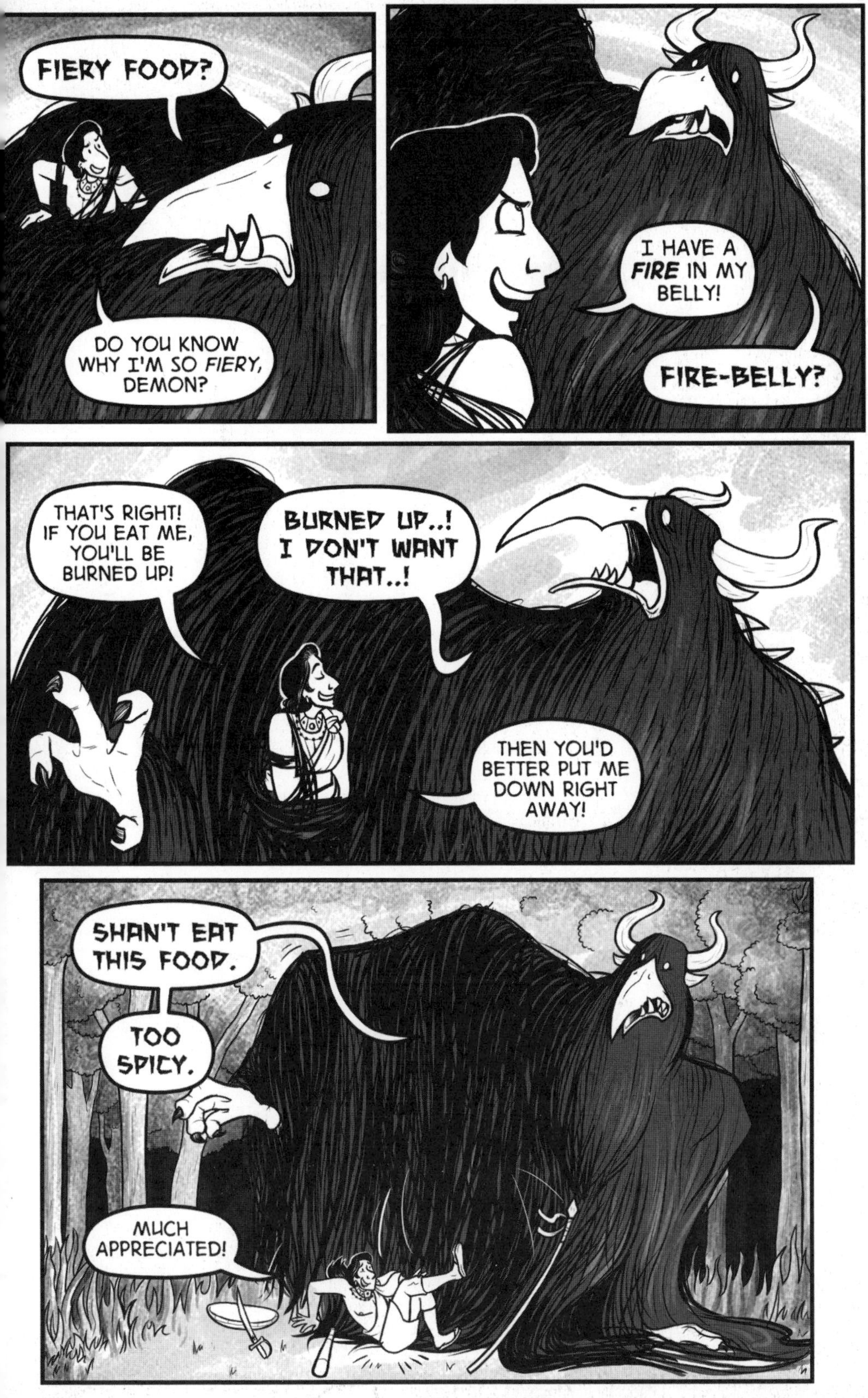
FIERY FOOD?
DO YOU KNOW WHY I'M SO *FIERY*, DEMON?
I HAVE A *FIRE* IN MY BELLY!
FIRE-BELLY?
THAT'S RIGHT! IF YOU EAT ME, YOU'LL BE BURNED UP!
BURNED UP..! I DON'T WANT THAT..!
THEN YOU'D BETTER PUT ME DOWN RIGHT AWAY!
SHAN'T EAT THIS FOOD.
TOO SPICY.
MUCH APPRECIATED!

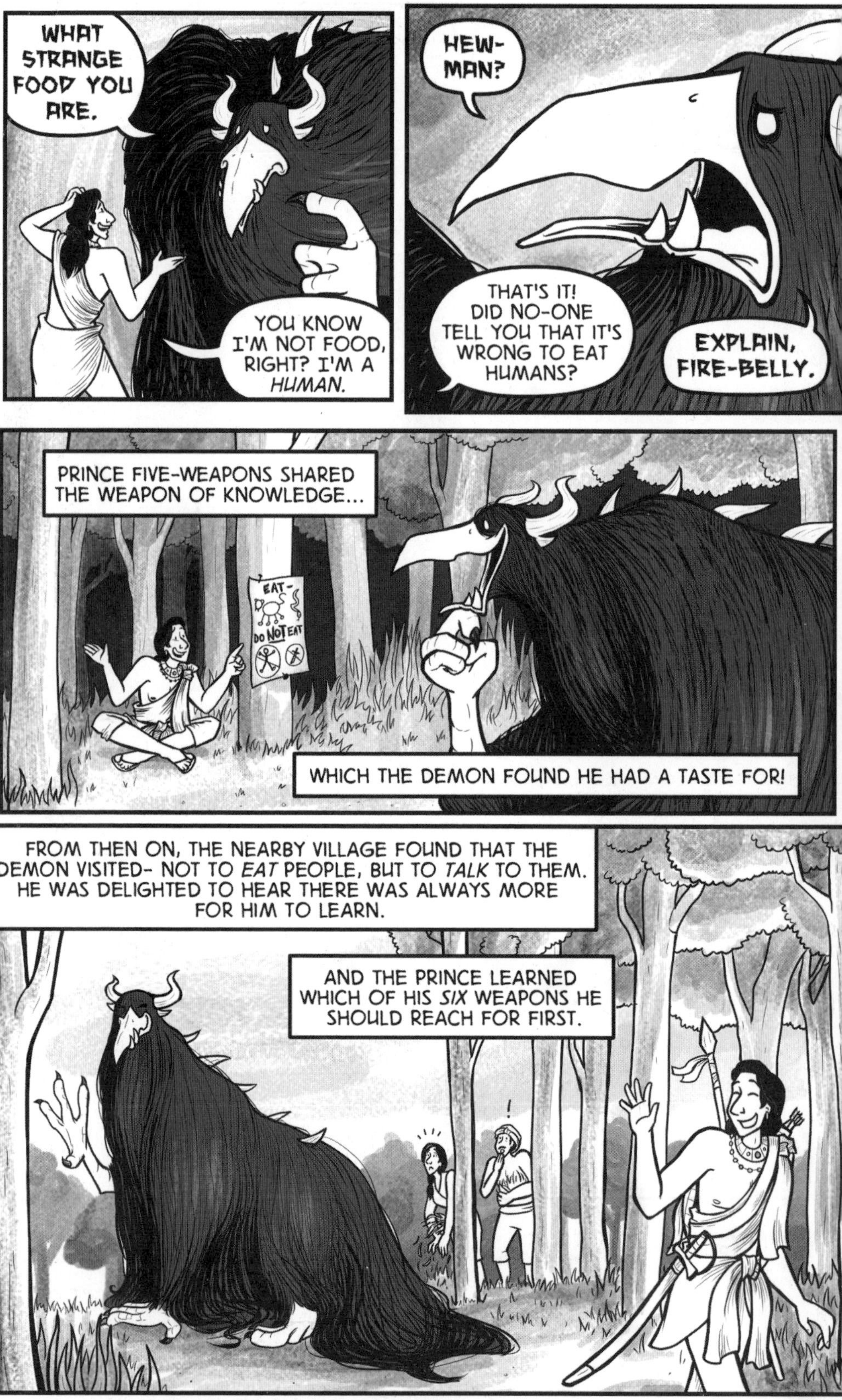
WHAT STRANGE FOOD YOU ARE.
YOU KNOW I'M NOT FOOD, RIGHT? I'M A *HUMAN.*
HEW-MAN?
THAT'S IT! DID NO-ONE TELL YOU THAT IT'S WRONG TO EAT HUMANS?
EXPLAIN, FIRE-BELLY.
PRINCE FIVE-WEAPONS SHARED THE WEAPON OF KNOWLEDGE...
EAT-
DO NOT EAT
WHICH THE DEMON FOUND HE HAD A TASTE FOR!
FROM THEN ON, THE NEARBY VILLAGE FOUND THAT THE DEMON VISITED- NOT TO *EAT* PEOPLE, BUT TO *TALK* TO THEM. HE WAS DELIGHTED TO HEAR THERE WAS ALWAYS MORE FOR HIM TO LEARN.
AND THE PRINCE LEARNED WHICH OF HIS *SIX* WEAPONS HE SHOULD REACH FOR FIRST.

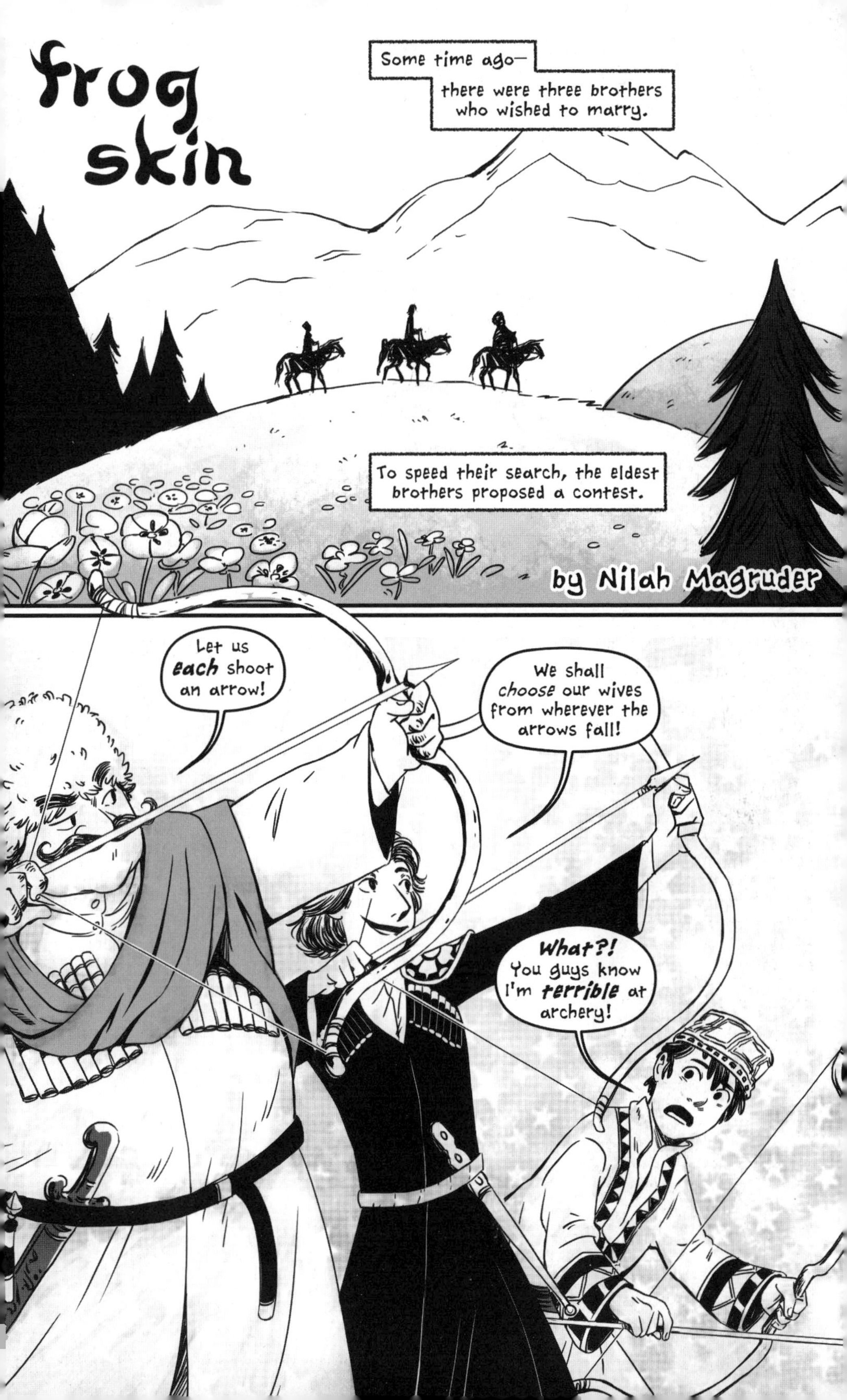
frog skin
Some time ago—
there were three brothers who wished to marry.
To speed their search, the eldest brothers proposed a contest.
by Nilah Magruder
Let us **each** shoot an arrow!
We shall *choose* our wives from wherever the arrows fall!
What?! You guys know I'm ***terrible*** at archery!

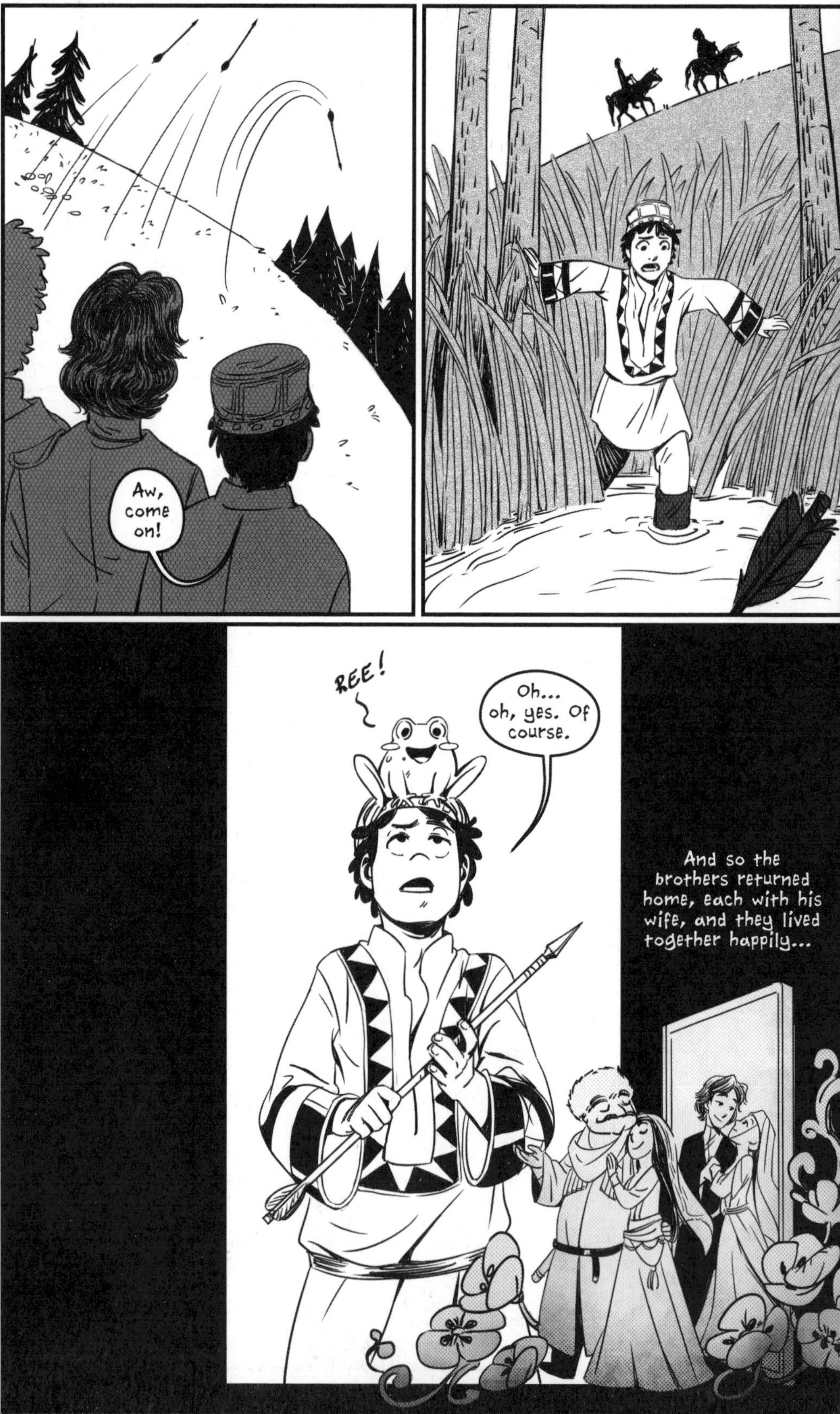
Aw, come on!
REE!
Oh... oh, yes. Of course.
And so the brothers returned home, each with his wife, and they lived together happily...

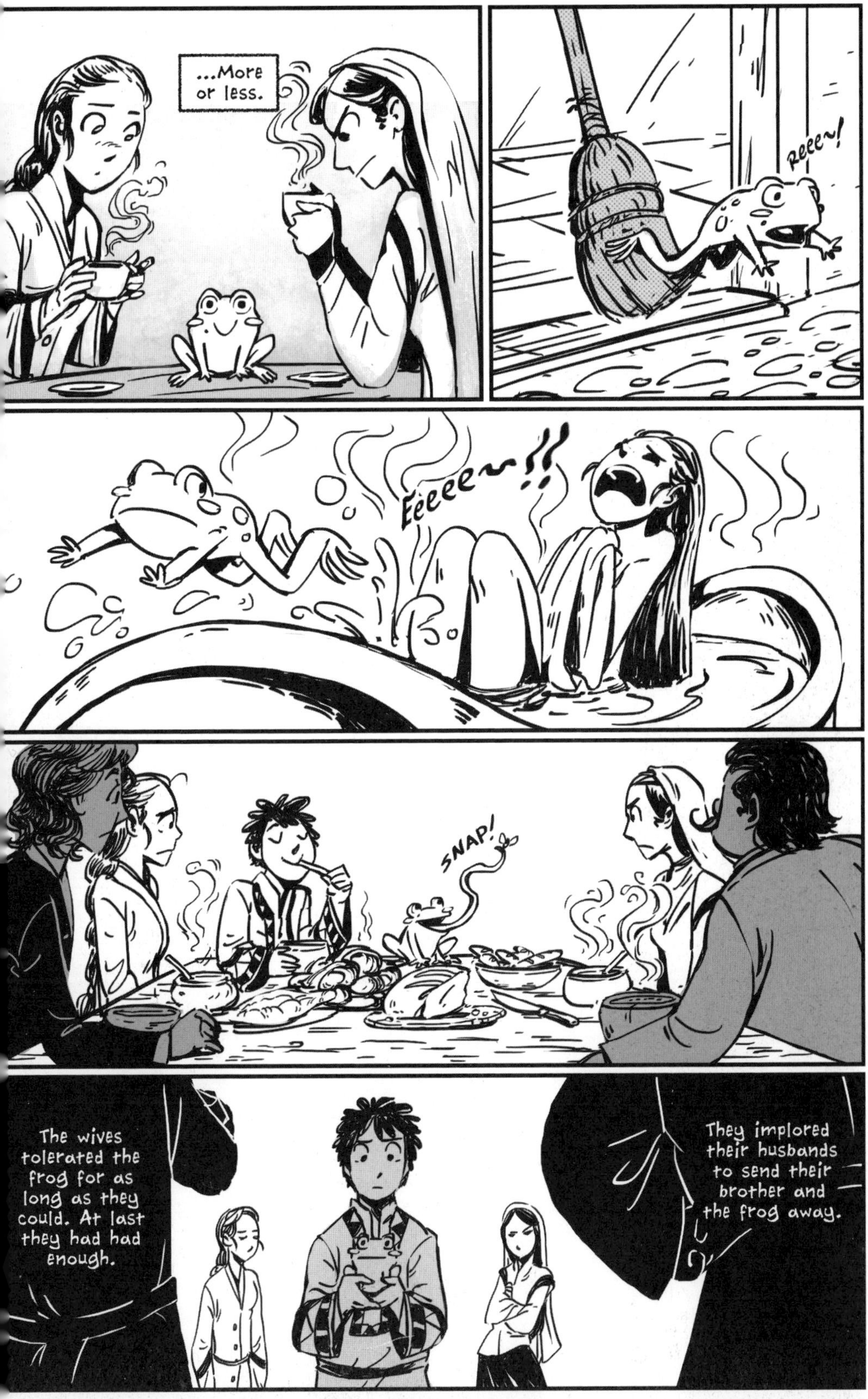
...More or less.
Reeee~!
Eeeee~!!
SNAP!
The wives tolerated the frog for as long as they could. At last they had had enough.
They implored their husbands to send their brother and the frog away.

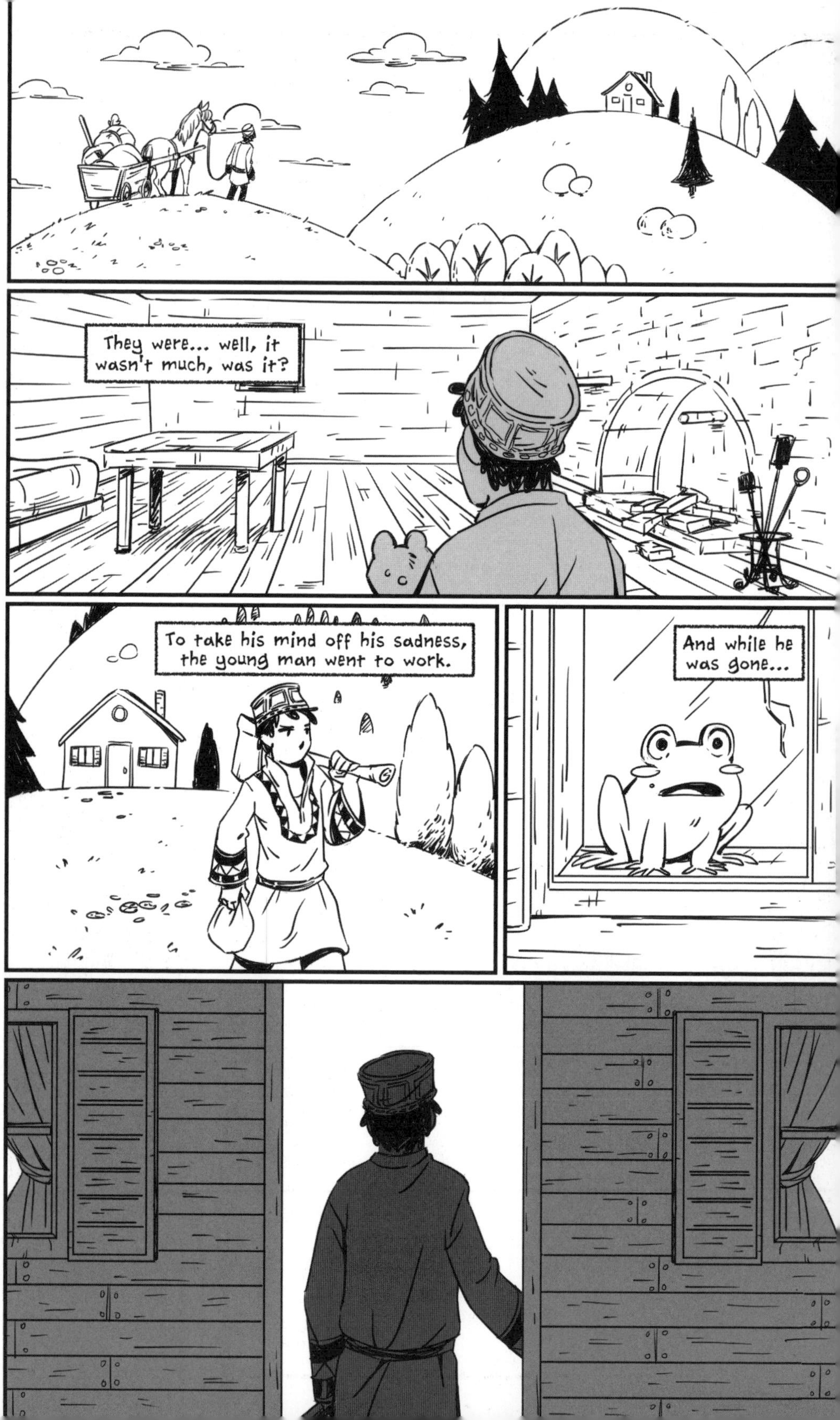
They were... well, it wasn't much, was it?
To take his mind off his sadness, the young man went to work.
And while he was gone...

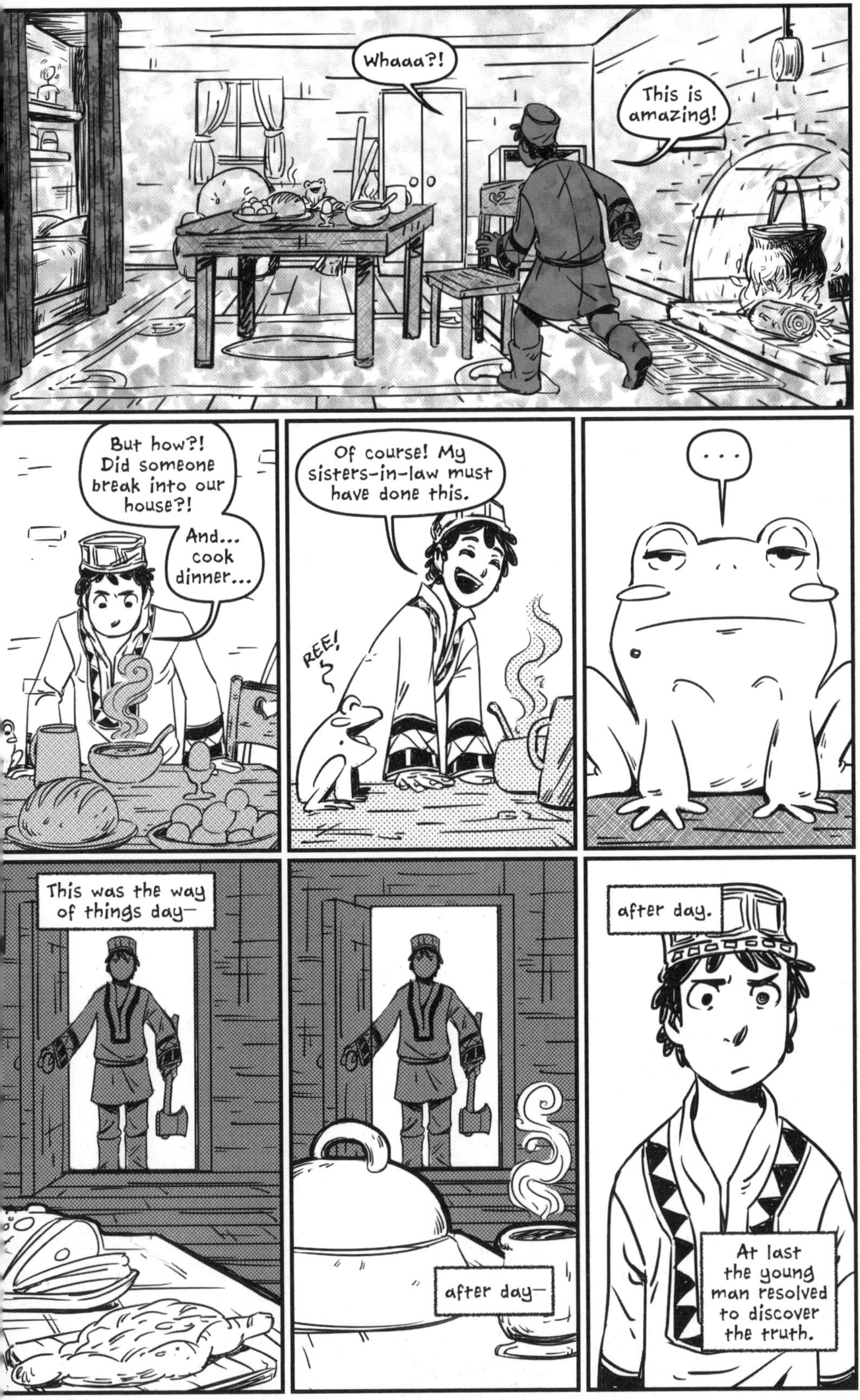
Whaaa?!
This is amazing!
But how?! Did someone break into our house?!
And... cook dinner...
Of course! My sisters-in-law must have done this.
REE!
...
This was the way of things day—
after day—
after day.
At last the young man resolved to discover the truth.

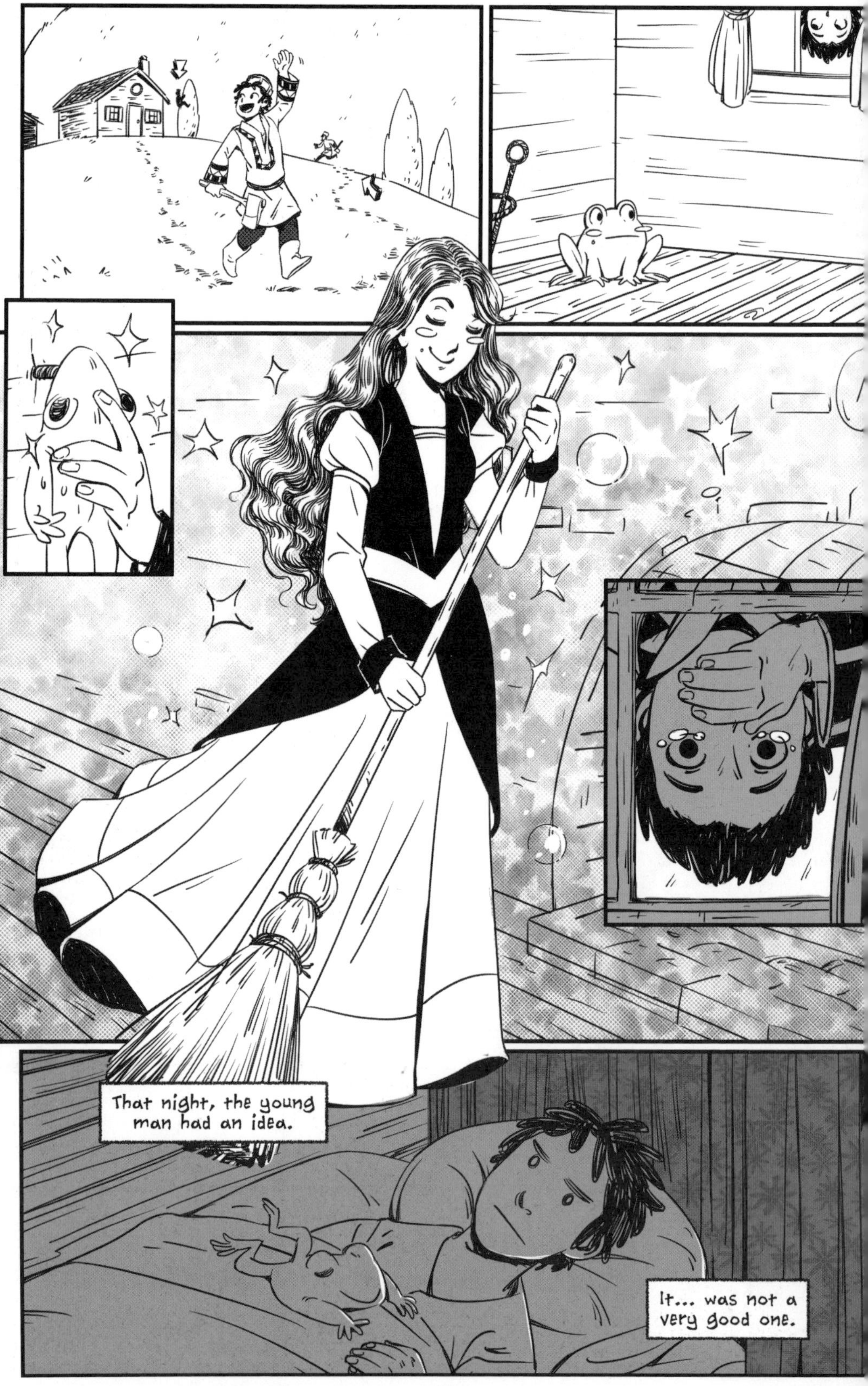
That night, the young man had an idea.
It... was not a very good one.

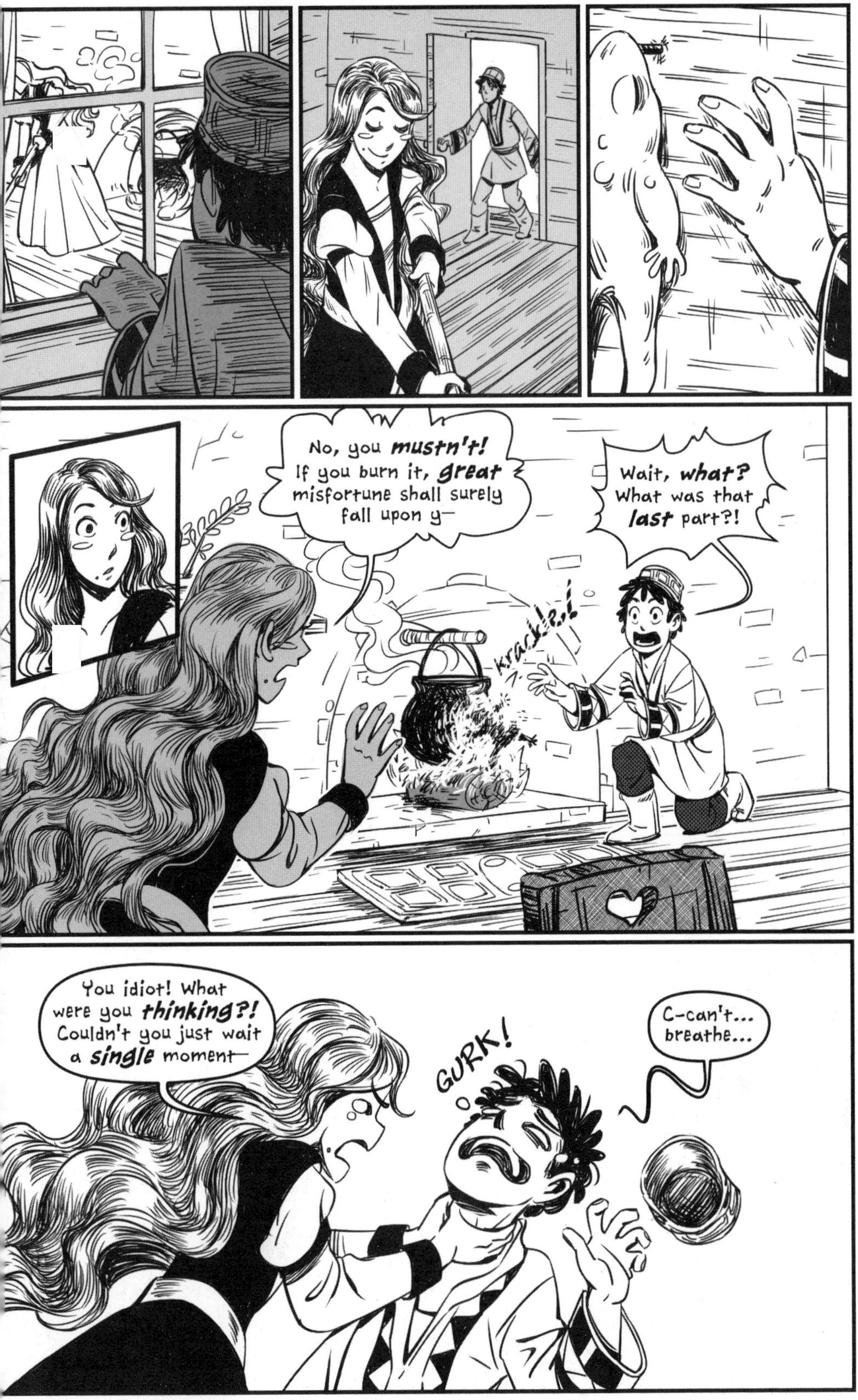
No, you mustn't! If you burn it, great misfortune shall surely fall upon y—
Wait, what? What was that last part?!
You idiot! What were you thinking?! Couldn't you just wait a single moment—
GURK!
C-can't... breathe...

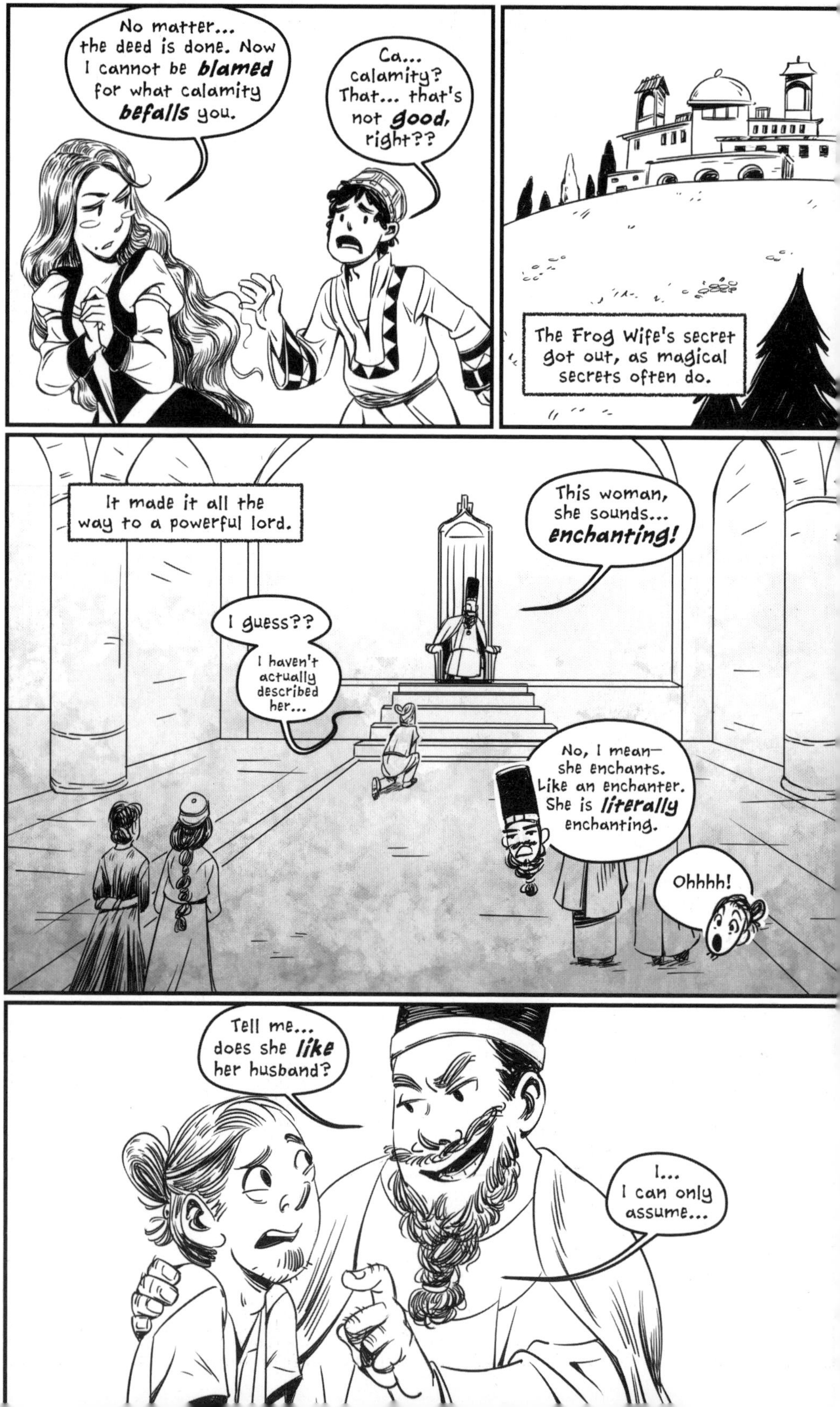
No matter... the deed is done. Now I cannot be **blamed** for what calamity **befalls** you.
Ca... calamity? That... that's not **good**, right??
The Frog Wife's secret got out, as magical secrets often do.
It made it all the way to a powerful lord.
This woman, she sounds... **enchanting!**
I guess??
I haven't actually described her...
No, I mean— she enchants. Like an enchanter. She is **literally** enchanting.
Ohhhh!
Tell me... does she **like** her husband?
I... I can only assume...

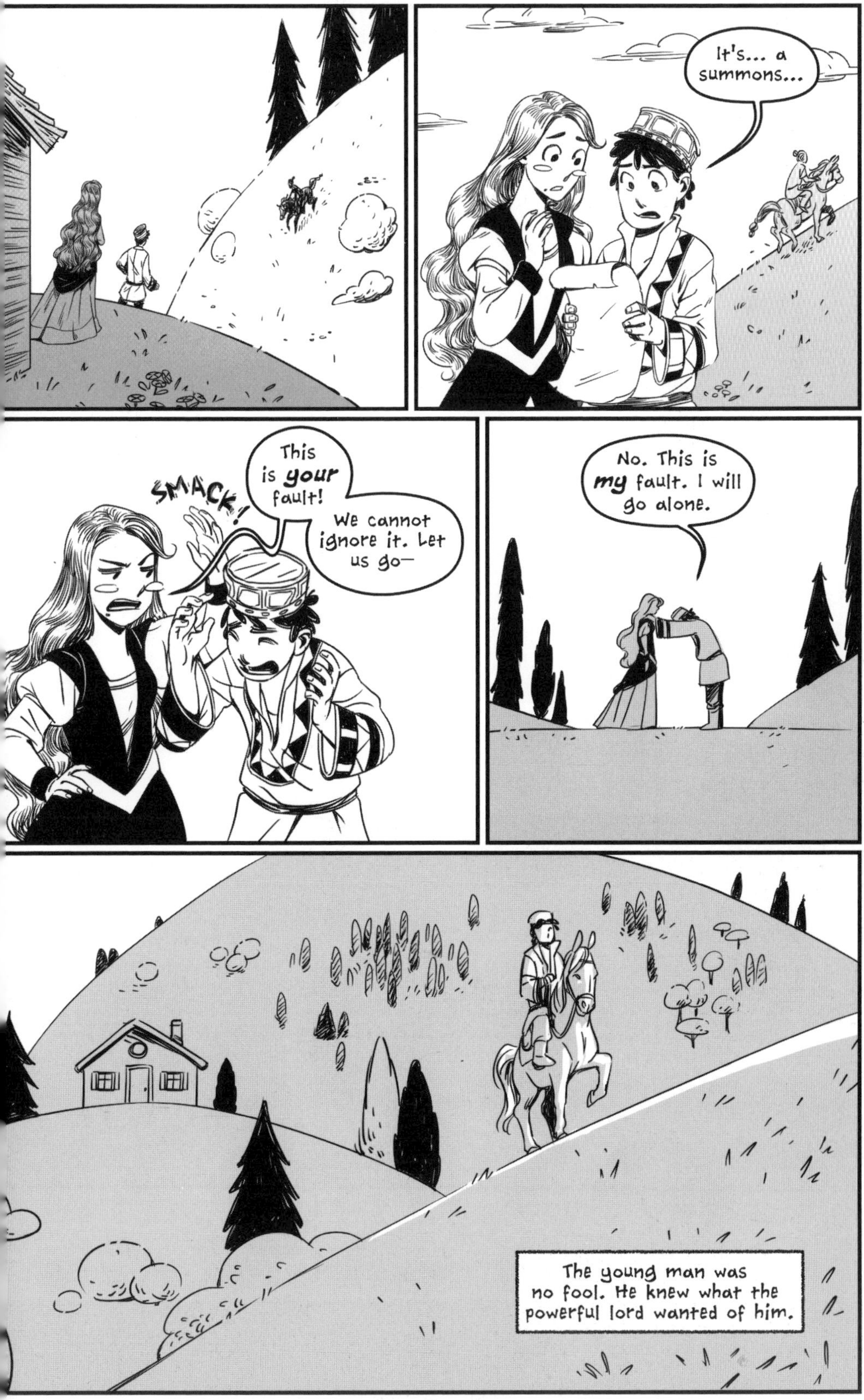
It's... a summons...
SMACK!
This is **your** fault!
We cannot ignore it. Let us go—
No. This is **my** fault. I will go alone.
The young man was no fool. He knew what the powerful lord wanted of him.

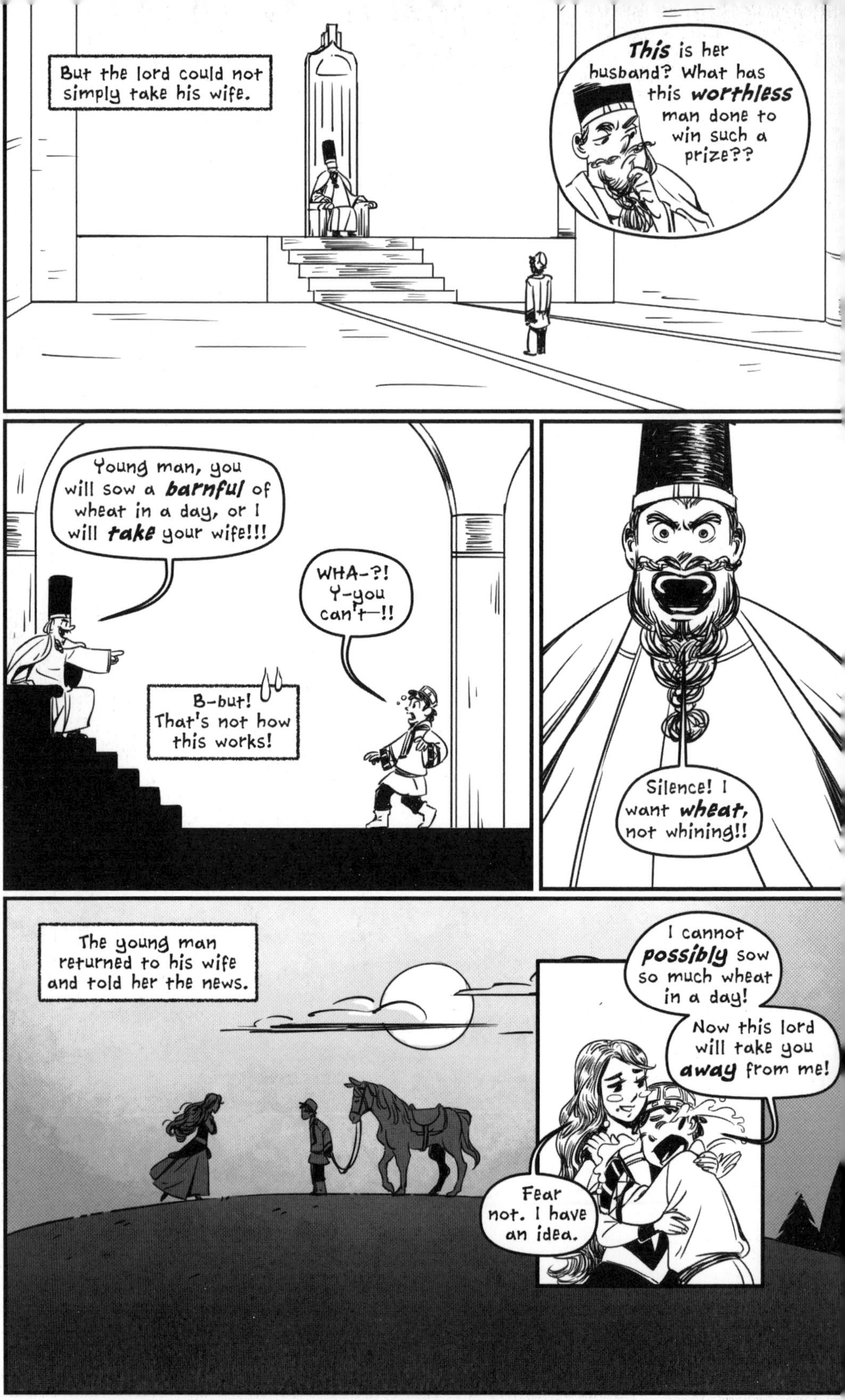
But the lord could not simply take his wife.
This is her husband? What has this worthless man done to win such a prize??
Young man, you will sow a barnful of wheat in a day, or I will take your wife!!!
WHA-?! Y-you can't—!!
B-but! That's not how this works!
Silence! I want wheat, not whining!!
The young man returned to his wife and told her the news.
I cannot possibly sow so much wheat in a day!
Now this lord will take you away from me!
Fear not. I have an idea.

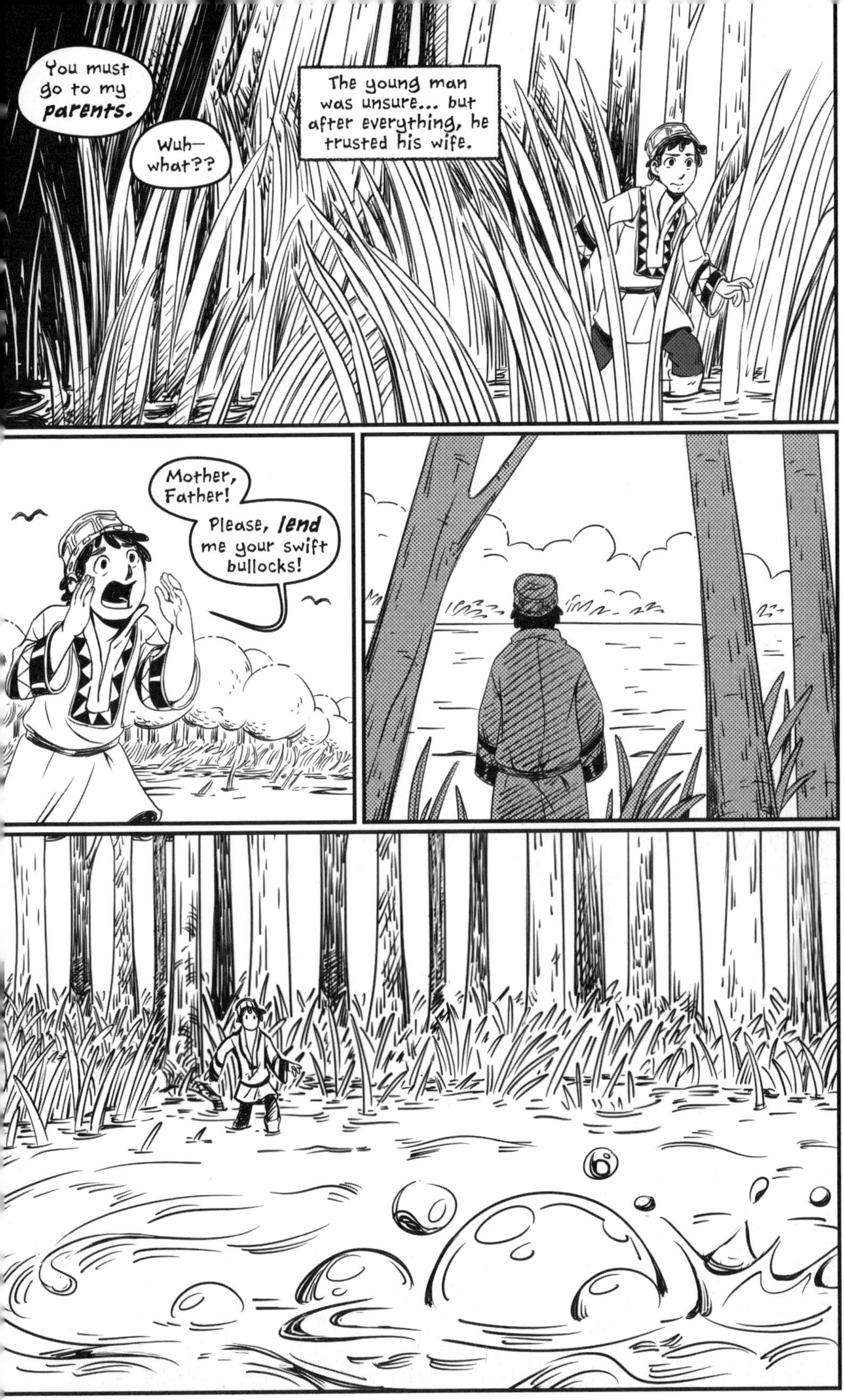
You must go to my **parents.**
Wuh—what??
The young man was unsure... but after everything, he trusted his wife.
Mother, Father!
Please, **lend** me your swift bullocks!

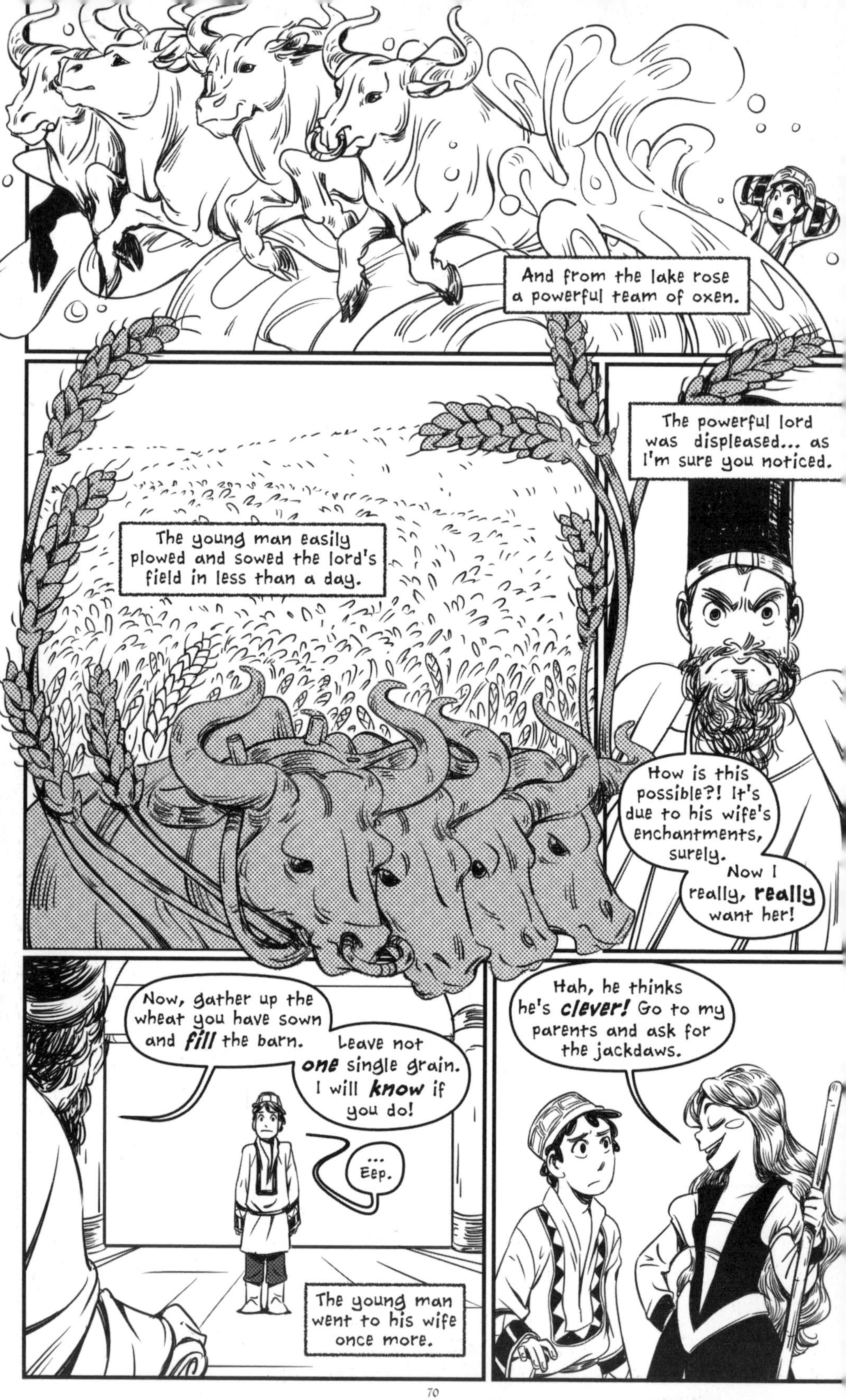

And from the lake rose a powerful team of oxen.
The young man easily plowed and sowed the lord's field in less than a day.
The powerful lord was displeased... as I'm sure you noticed.
How is this possible?! It's due to his wife's enchantments, surely.
Now I really, really want her!
Now, gather up the wheat you have sown and fill the barn.
Leave not one single grain. I will know if you do!
... Eep.
The young man went to his wife once more.
Hah, he thinks he's clever! Go to my parents and ask for the jackdaws.

Once more, the young man went to his wife's parents...

...and requested help just as she instructed.

CAW CAW CAW

CAW
CAW
CAW
CAW

What...

CAW
CAW

What is that **sound**?

CAW
CAW
CAW
CAW
CAW CAW CAW

CAW

The jackdaws harvested the wheat down to the last grain.

CAW
CAW
CAW

...Impossible.

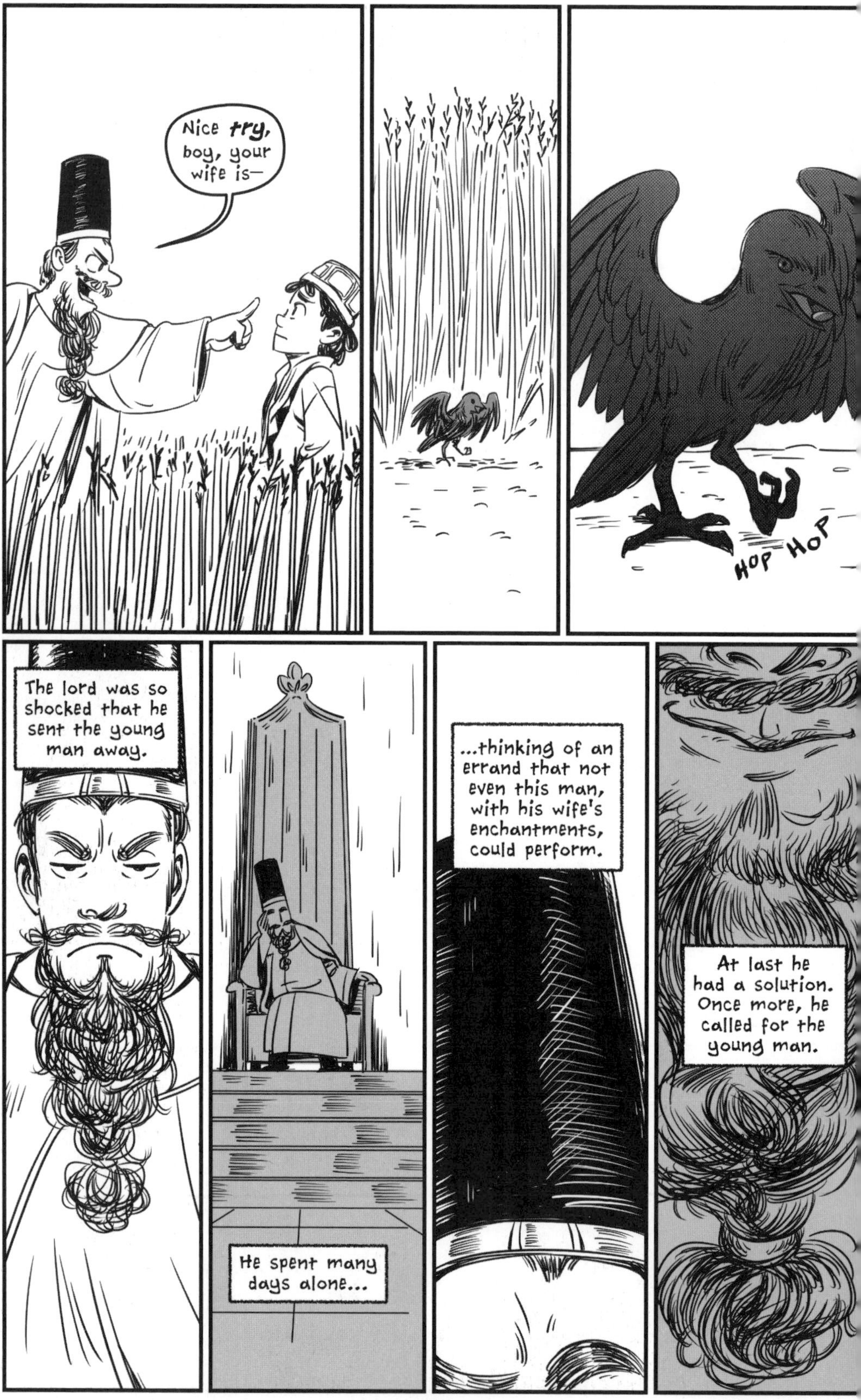
Nice *try*, boy, your wife is—
HOP HOP
The lord was so shocked that he sent the young man away.
He spent many days alone...
...thinking of an errand that not even this man, with his wife's enchantments, could perform.
At last he had a solution. Once more, he called for the young man.

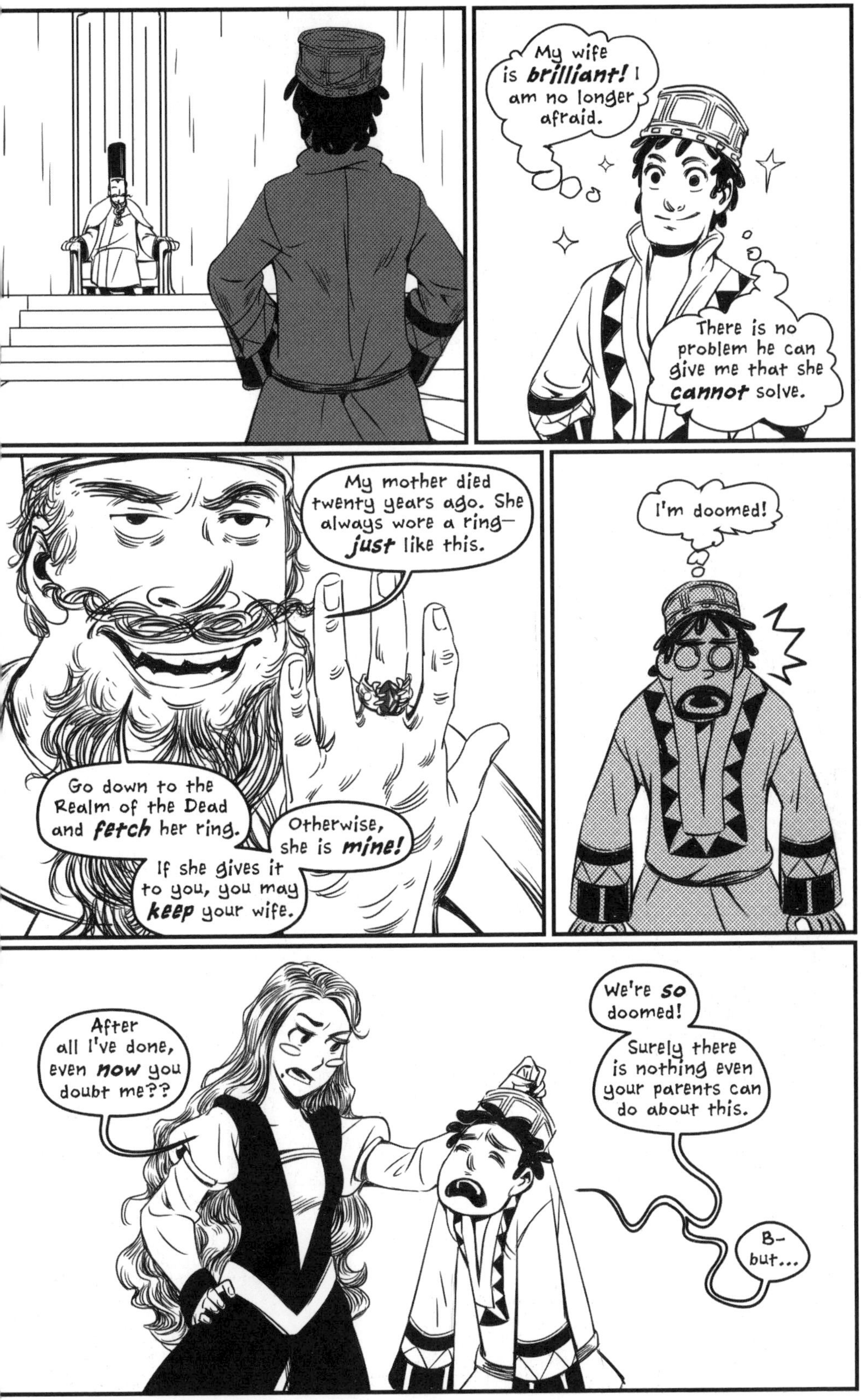
My wife is brilliant! I am no longer afraid.
There is no problem he can give me that she cannot solve.
My mother died twenty years ago. She always wore a ring—just like this.
Go down to the Realm of the Dead and fetch her ring.
If she gives it to you, you may keep your wife.
Otherwise, she is mine!
I'm doomed!
We're so doomed!
Surely there is nothing even your parents can do about this.
After all I've done, even now you doubt me??
B–but...

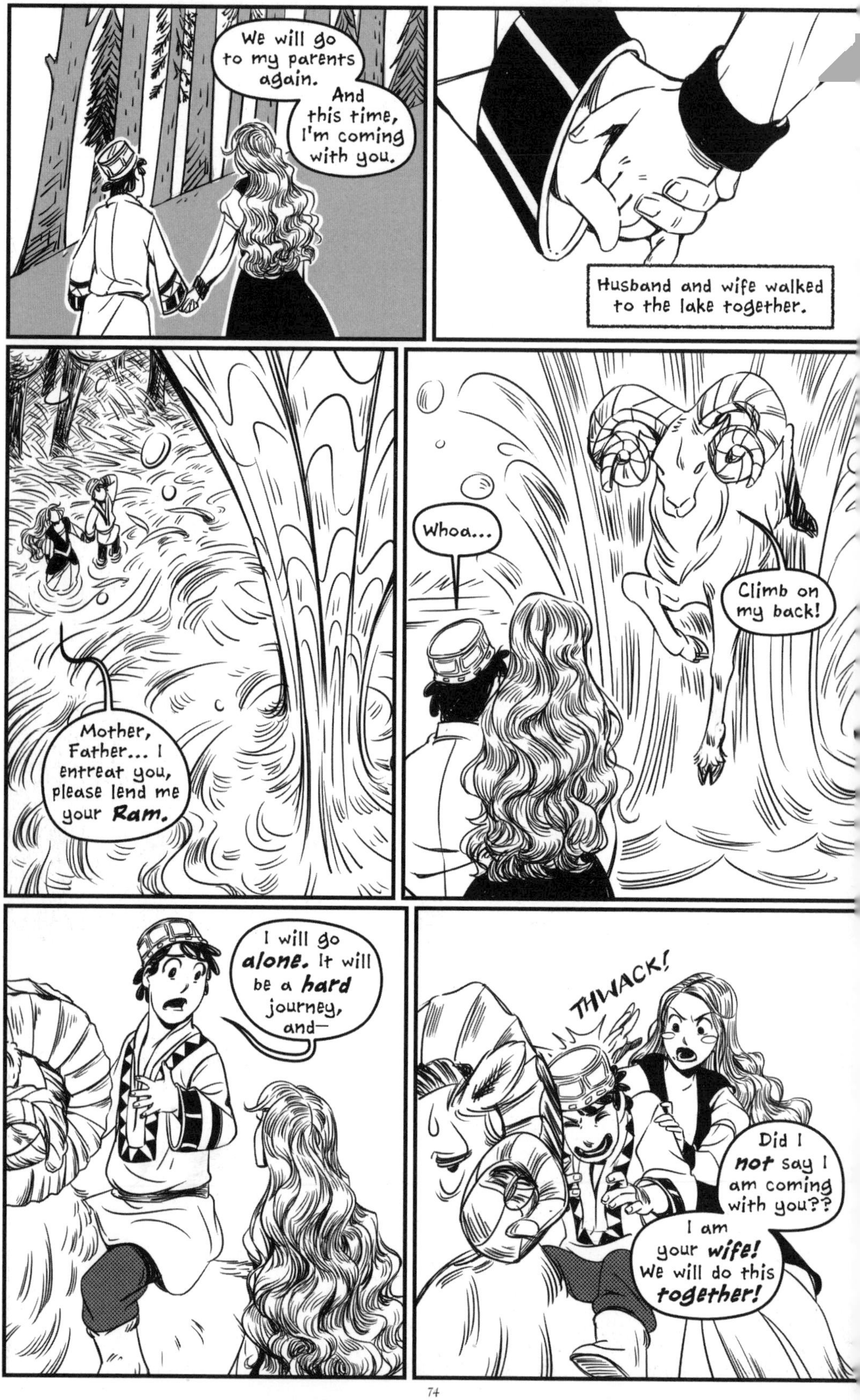
We will go to my parents again.
And this time, I'm coming with you.
Husband and wife walked to the lake together.
Mother, Father... I entreat you, please lend me your Ram.
Whoa...
Climb on my back!
I will go alone. It will be a hard journey, and—
THWACK!
Did I not say I am coming with you??
I am your wife! We will do this together!

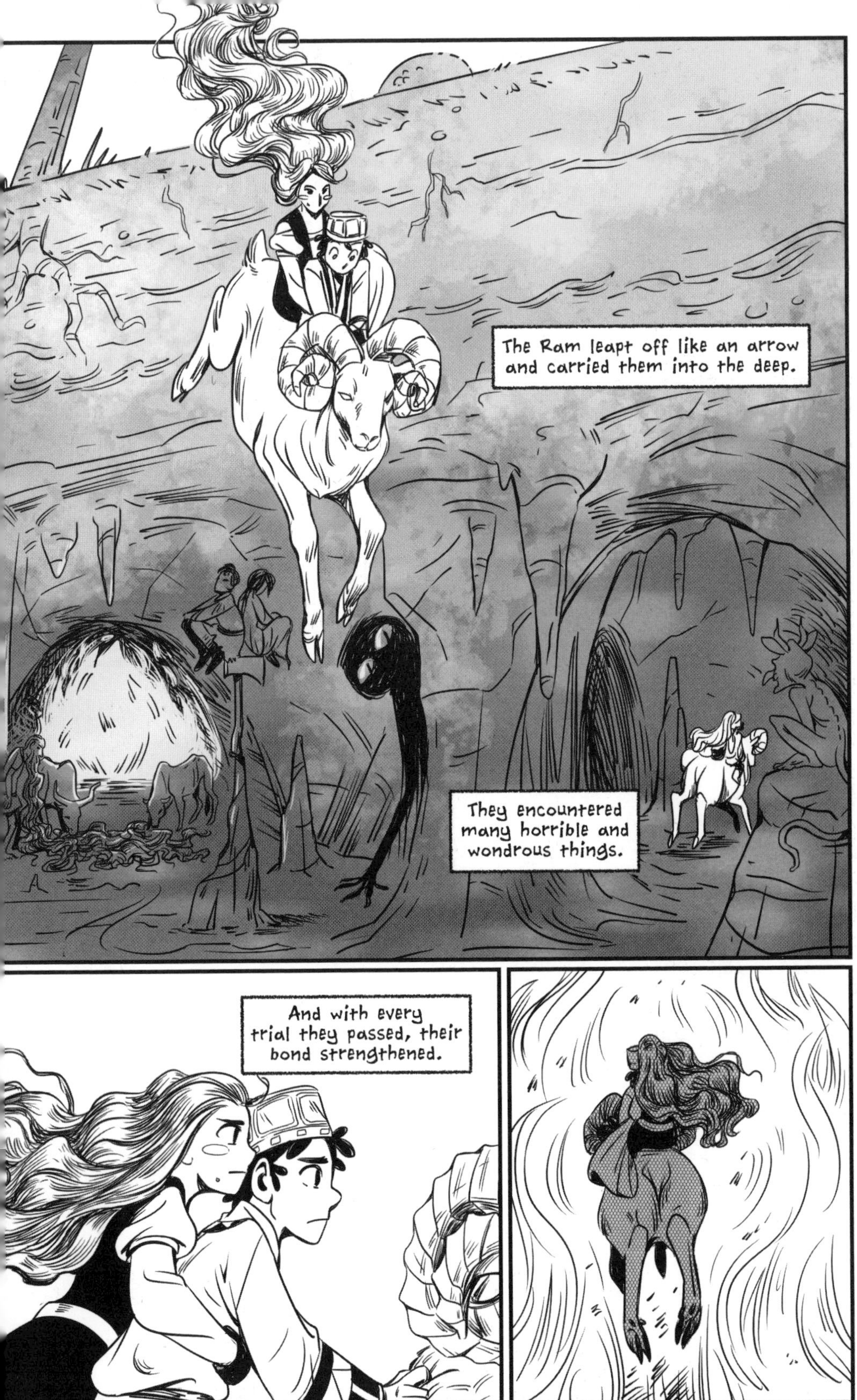

The Ram leapt off like an arrow and carried them into the deep.
They encountered many horrible and wondrous things.
And with every trial they passed, their bond strengthened.

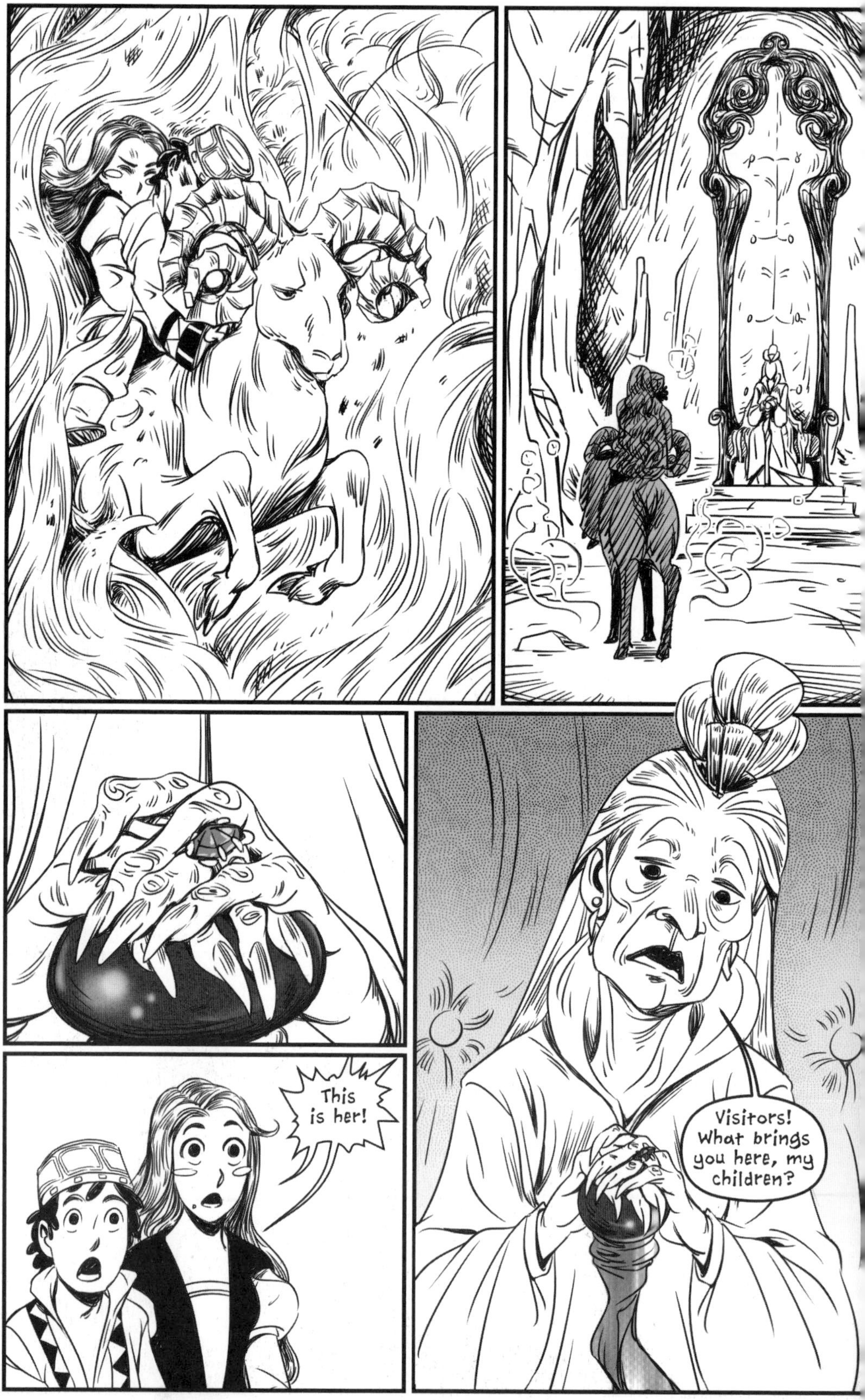
This is her!
Visitors! What brings you here, my children?

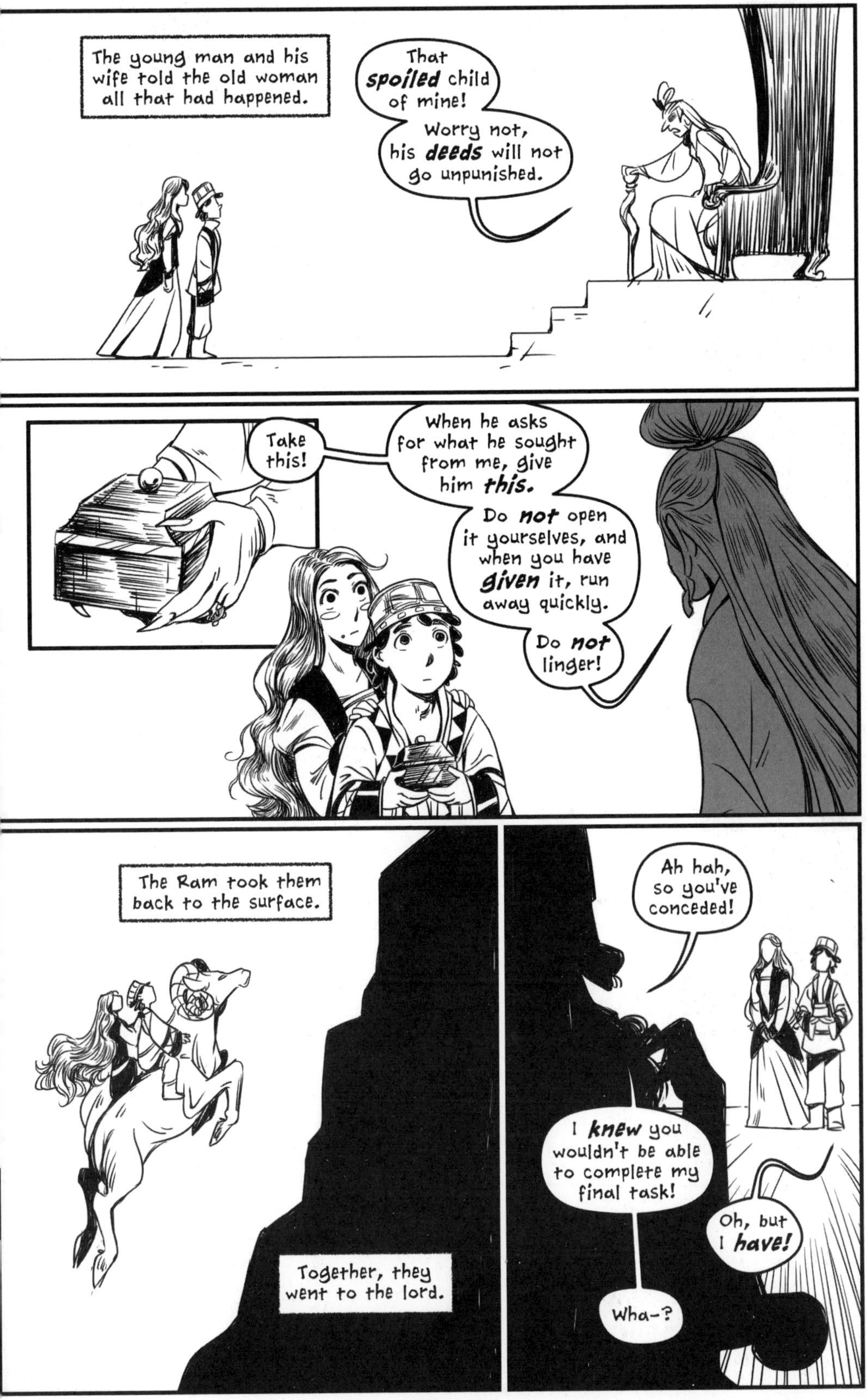
The young man and his wife told the old woman all that had happened.
That *spoiled* child of mine!
Worry not, his *deeds* will not go unpunished.
Take this!
When he asks for what he sought from me, give him *this.*
Do *not* open it yourselves, and when you have *given* it, run away quickly.
Do *not* linger!
The Ram took them back to the surface.
Together, they went to the lord.
Ah hah, so you've conceded!
I *knew* you wouldn't be able to complete my final task!
Oh, but I *have!*
Wha-?

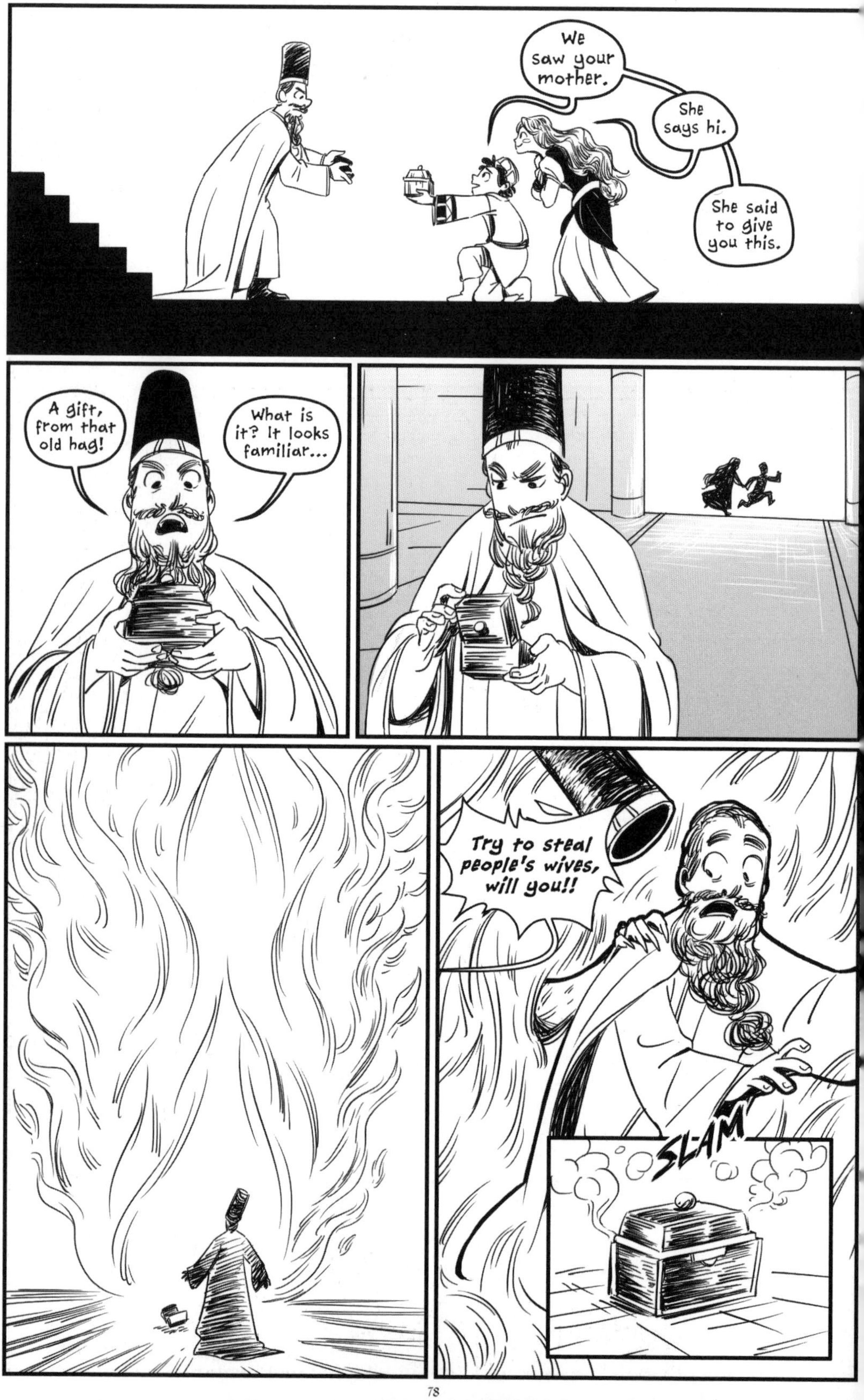
We saw your mother.
She says hi.
She said to give you this.
A gift, from that old hag!
What is it? It looks familiar...
Try to steal people's wives, will you!!
SLAM

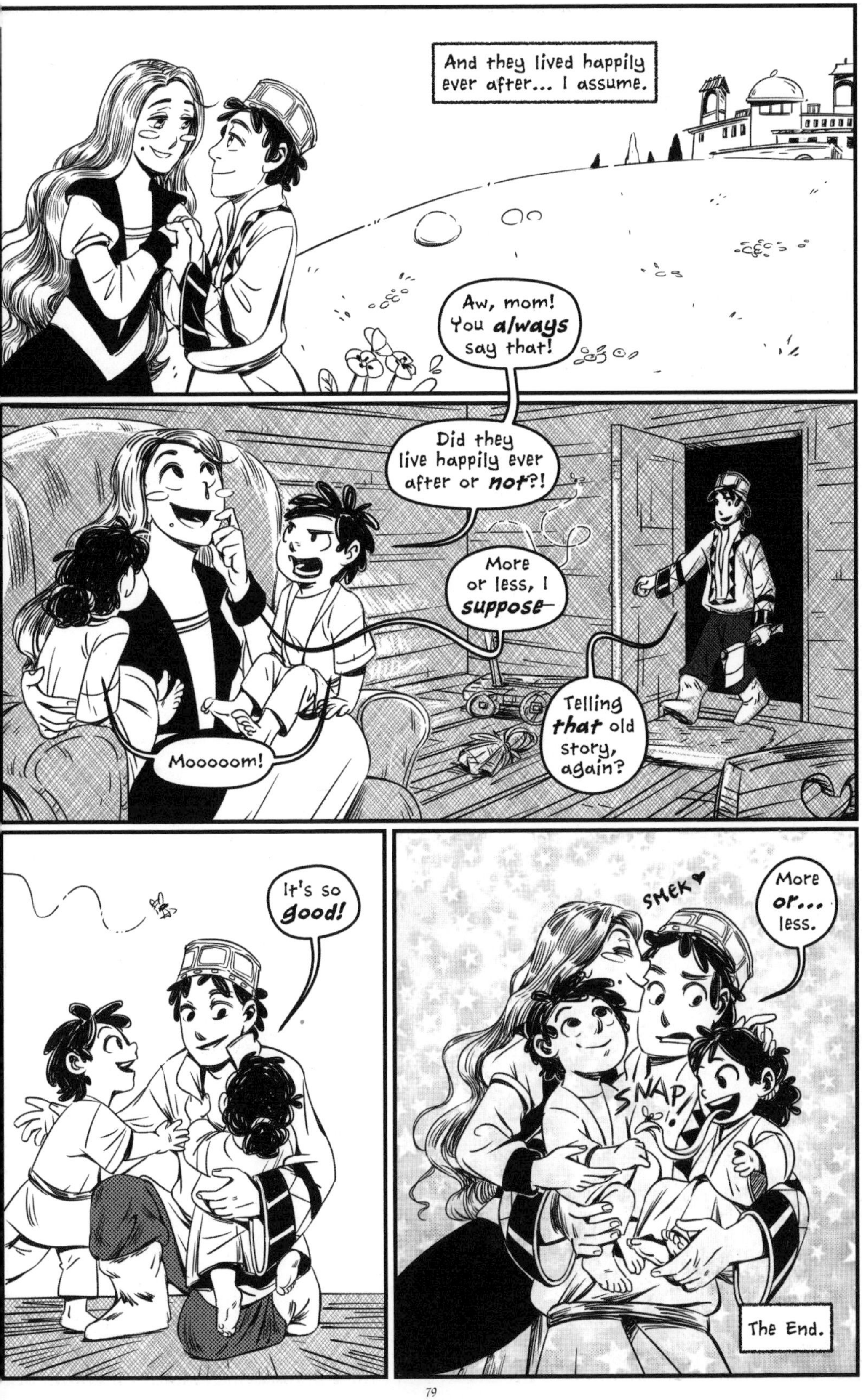
And they lived happily ever after... I assume.
Aw, mom! You always say that!
Did they live happily ever after or not?!
More or less, I suppose—
Moooom!
Telling that old story, again?
It's so good!
SMEK
More or... less.
SNAP
The End.

The Girl Who Married a Tiger

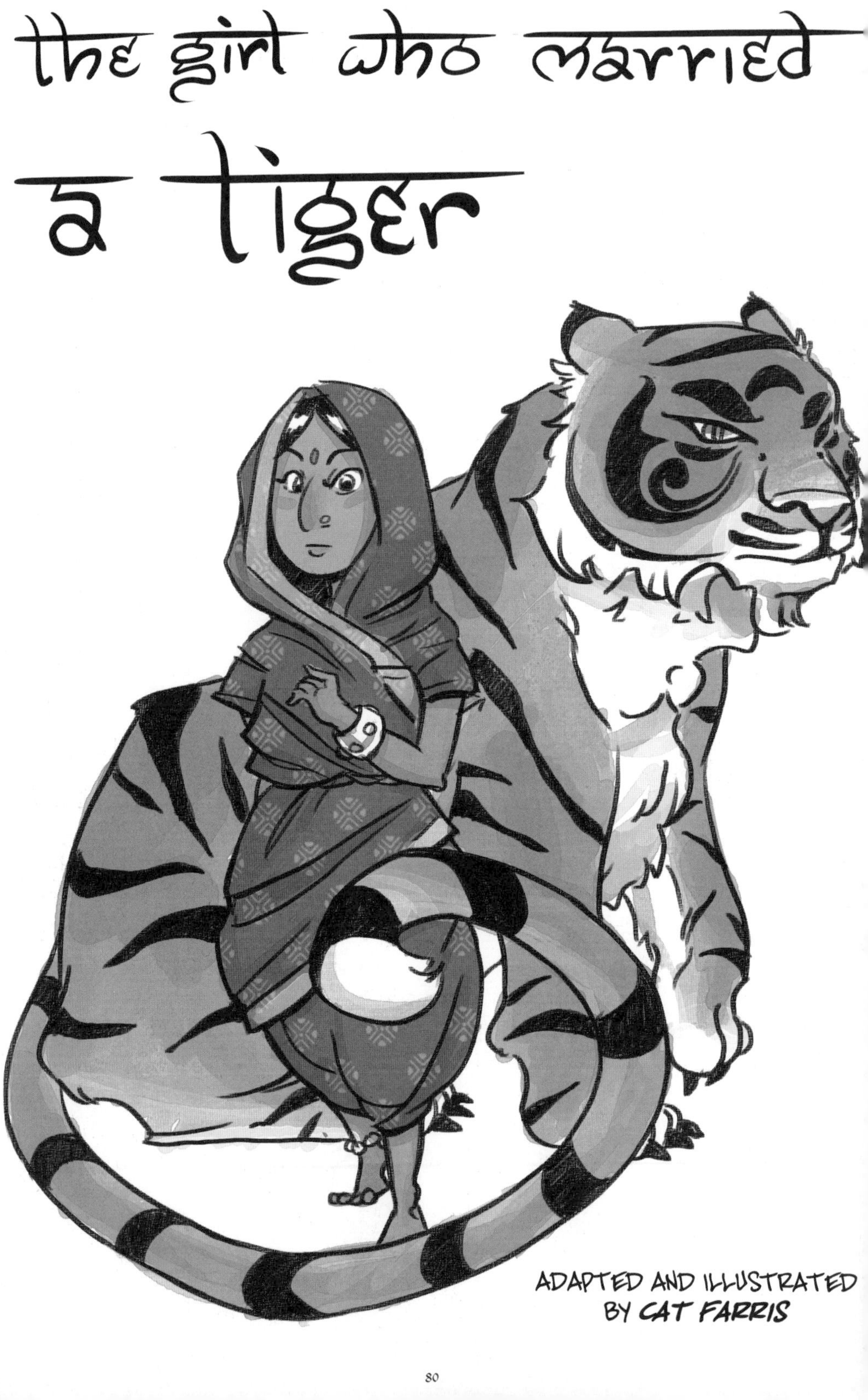

ADAPTED AND ILLUSTRATED
BY CAT FARRIS

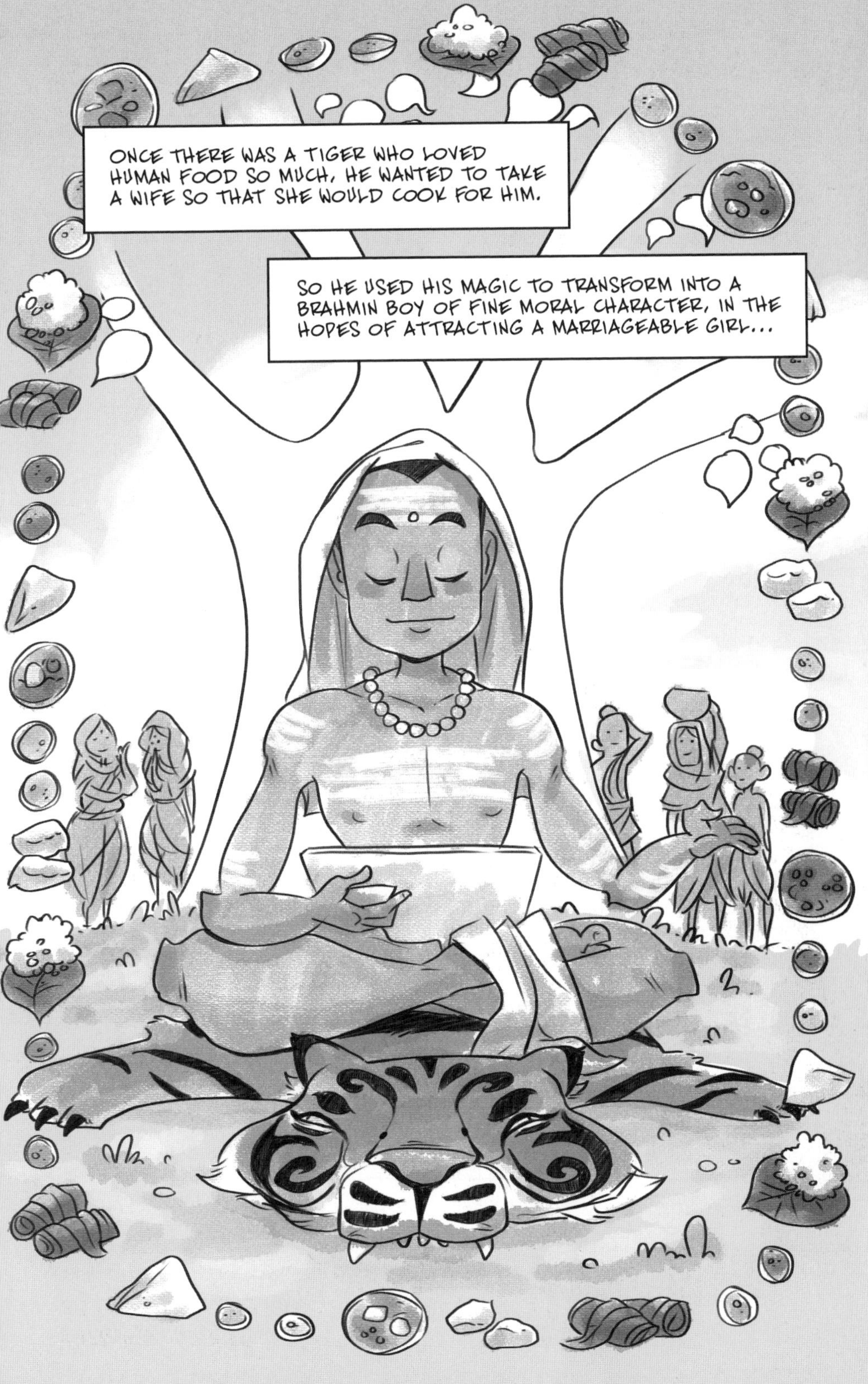
ONCE THERE WAS A TIGER WHO LOVED HUMAN FOOD SO MUCH, HE WANTED TO TAKE A WIFE SO THAT SHE WOULD COOK FOR HIM.
SO HE USED HIS MAGIC TO TRANSFORM INTO A BRAHMIN BOY OF FINE MORAL CHARACTER, IN THE HOPES OF ATTRACTING A MARRIAGEABLE GIRL...

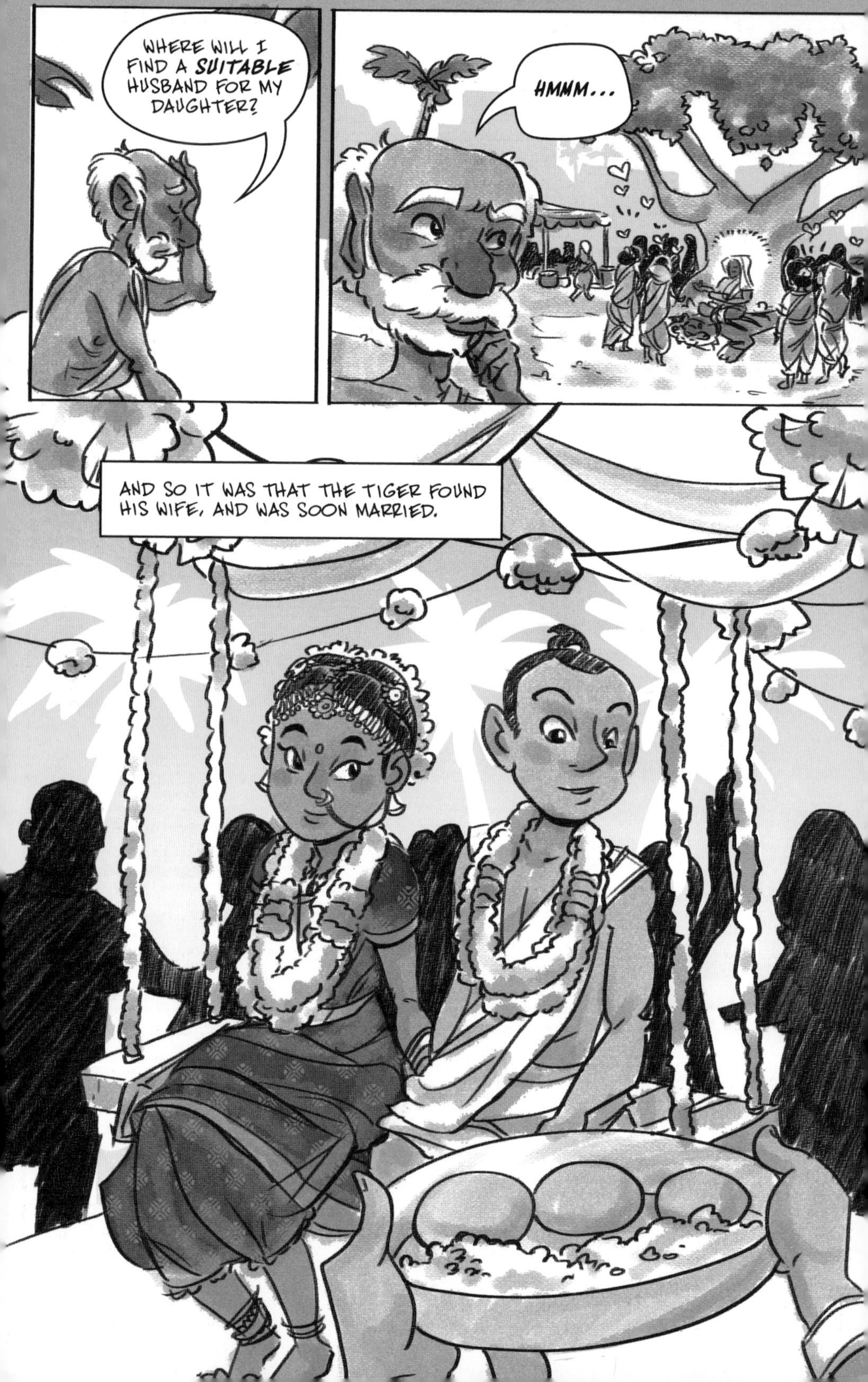
WHERE WILL I FIND A SUITABLE HUSBAND FOR MY DAUGHTER?
HMMM...
AND SO IT WAS THAT THE TIGER FOUND HIS WIFE, AND WAS SOON MARRIED.

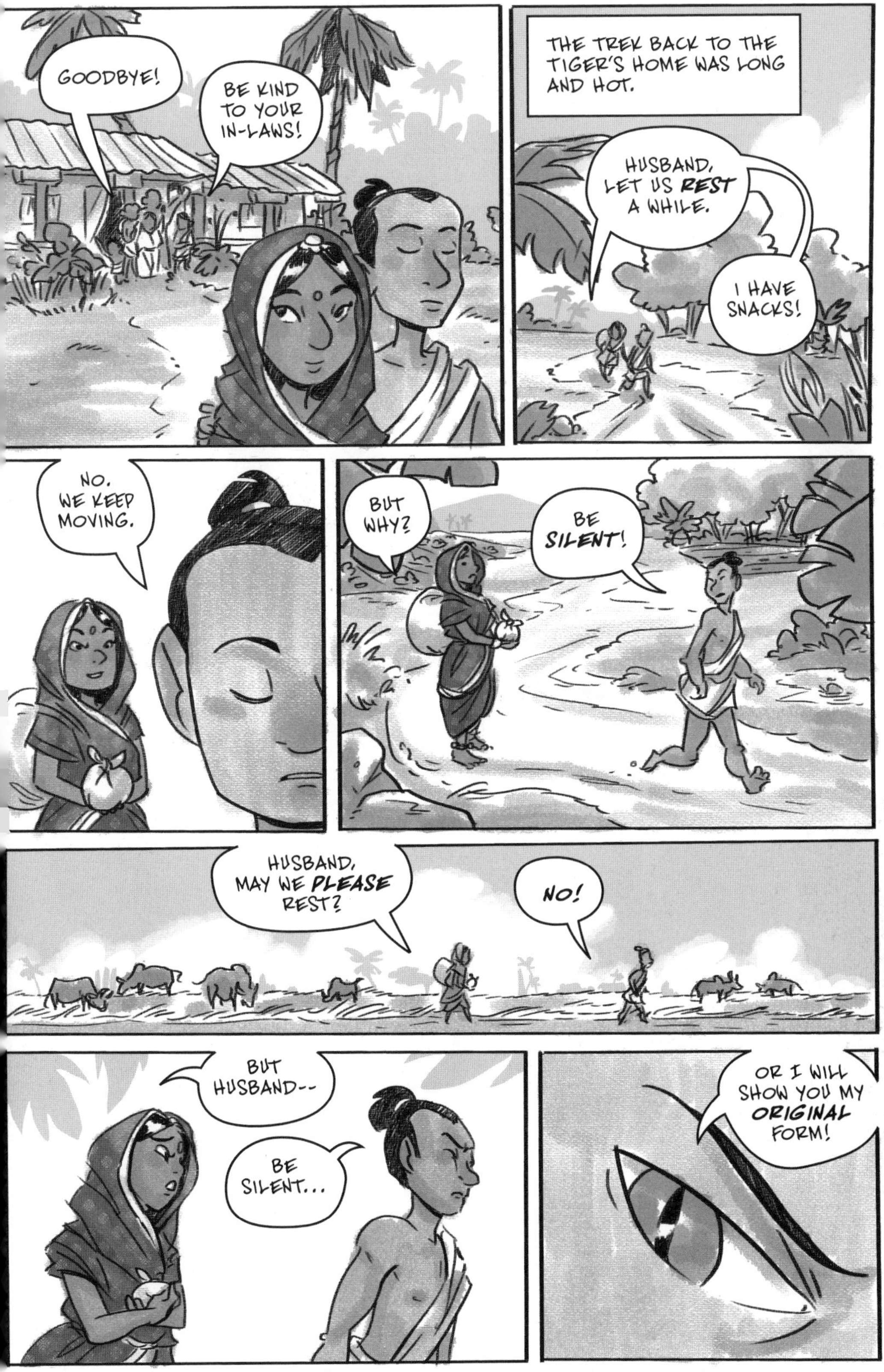
GOODBYE!
BE KIND TO YOUR IN-LAWS!
THE TREK BACK TO THE TIGER'S HOME WAS LONG AND HOT.
HUSBAND, LET US **REST** A WHILE.
I HAVE SNACKS!
NO. WE KEEP MOVING.
BUT WHY?
BE **SILENT**!
HUSBAND, MAY WE **PLEASE** REST?
NO!
BUT HUSBAND--
BE SILENT...
OR I WILL SHOW YOU MY **ORIGINAL** FORM!

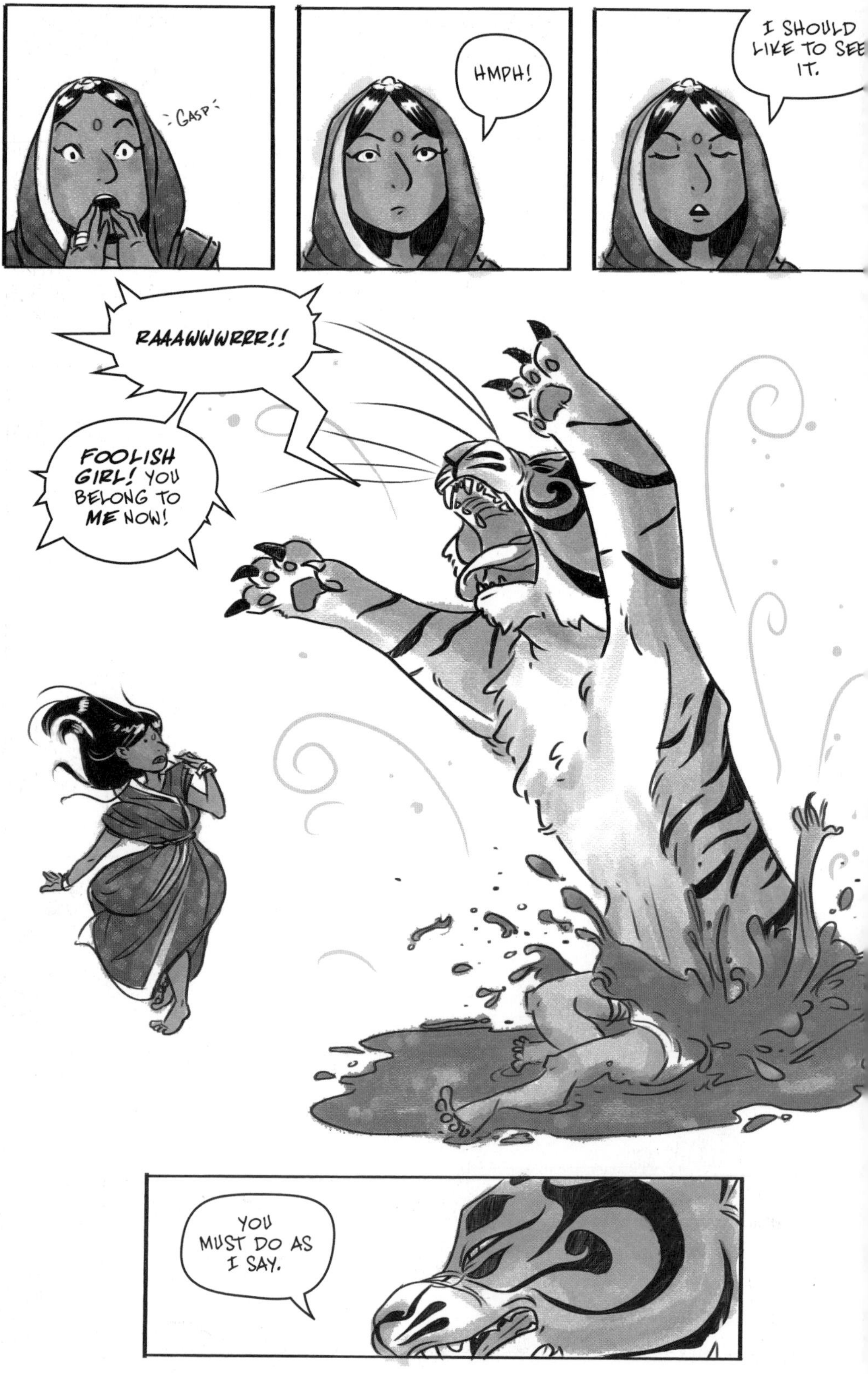
GASP
HMPH!
I SHOULD LIKE TO SEE IT.
RAAAWWWRRR!!
FOOLISH GIRL! YOU BELONG TO ME NOW!
YOU MUST DO AS I SAY.

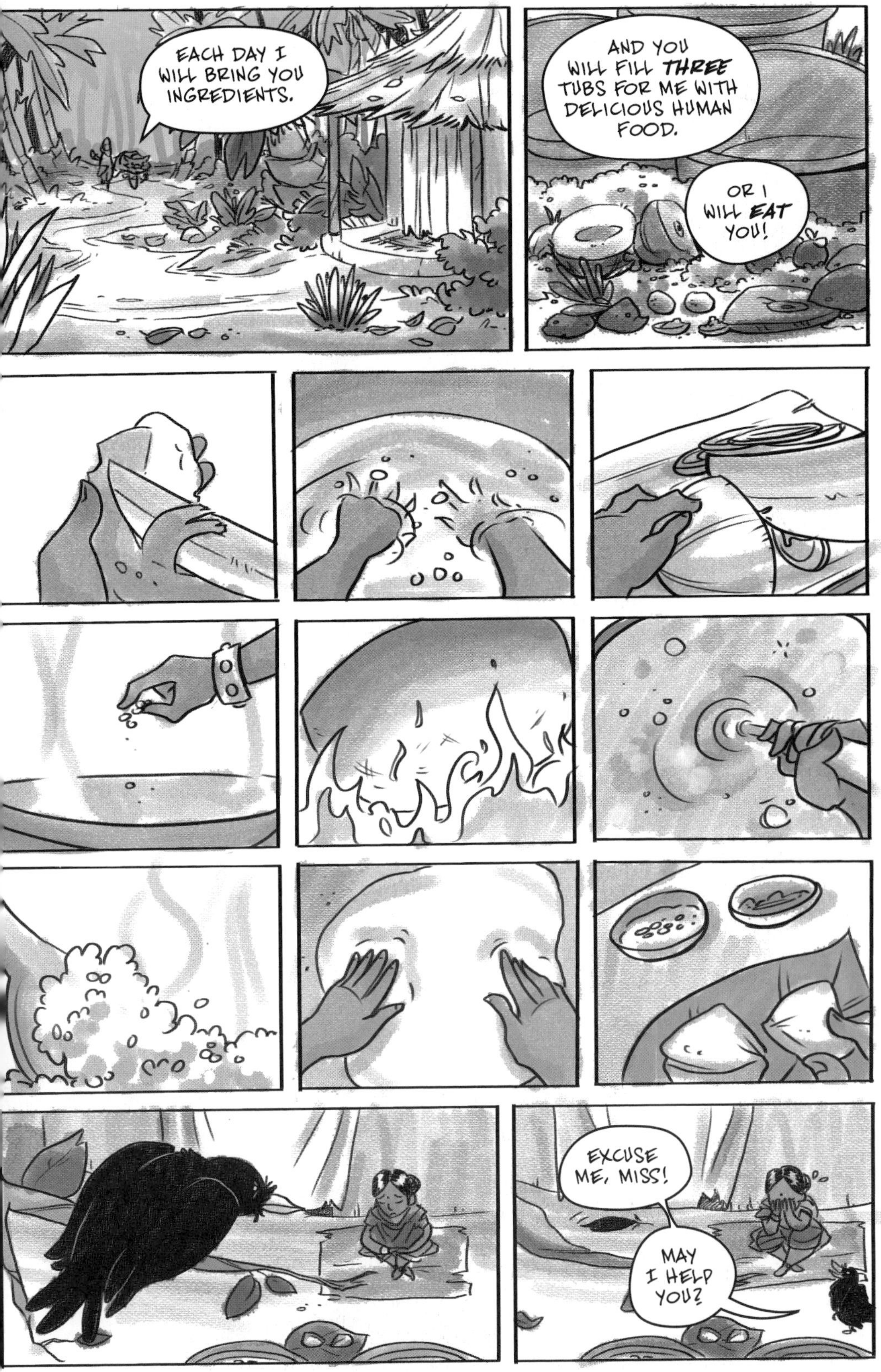
EACH DAY I WILL BRING YOU INGREDIENTS.
AND YOU WILL FILL THREE TUBS FOR ME WITH DELICIOUS HUMAN FOOD.
OR I WILL EAT YOU!
EXCUSE ME, MISS!
MAY I HELP YOU?

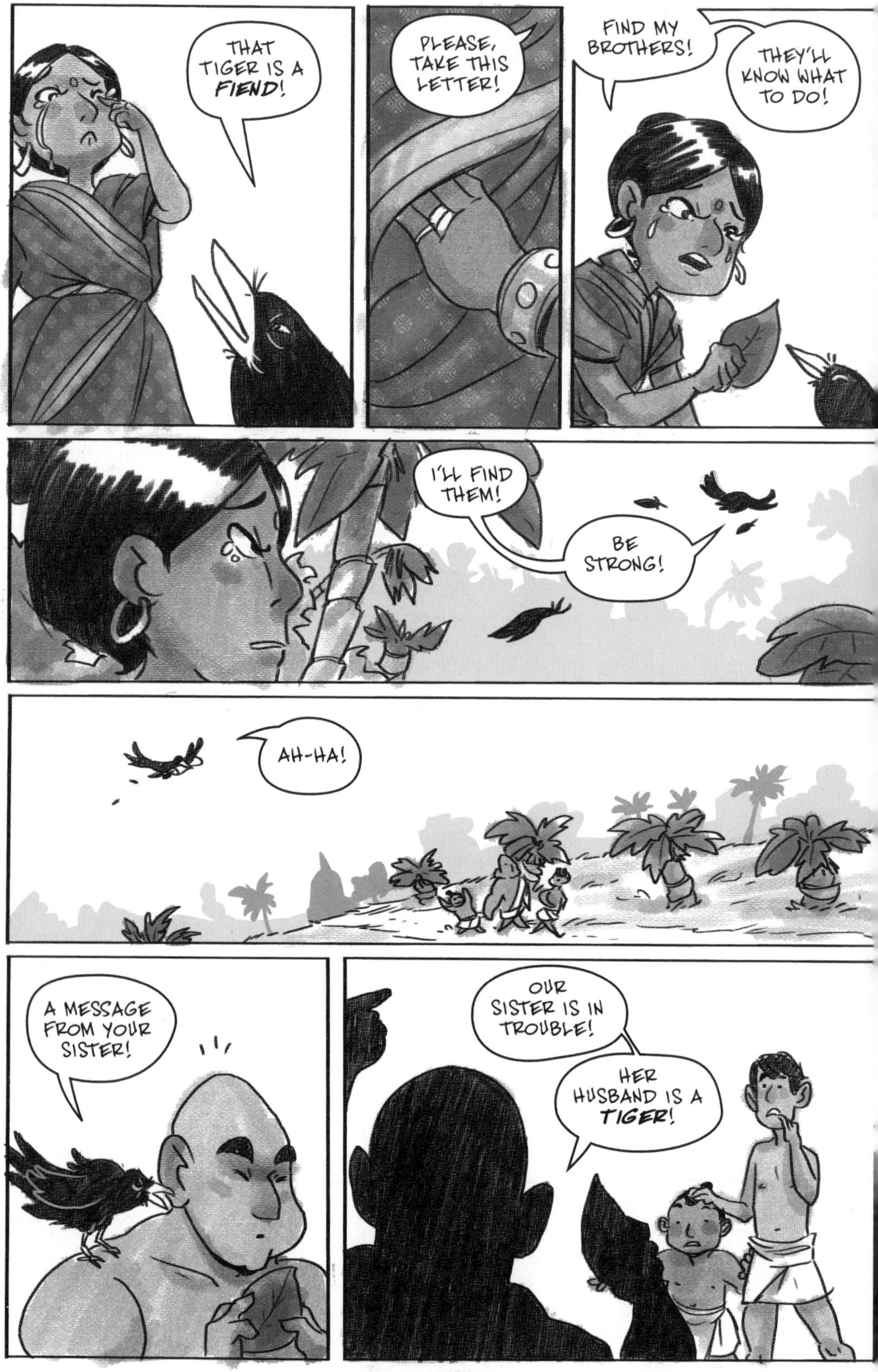
THAT TIGER IS A FIEND!
PLEASE, TAKE THIS LETTER!
FIND MY BROTHERS!
THEY'LL KNOW WHAT TO DO!
I'LL FIND THEM!
BE STRONG!
AH-HA!
A MESSAGE FROM YOUR SISTER!
OUR SISTER IS IN TROUBLE!
HER HUSBAND IS A TIGER!

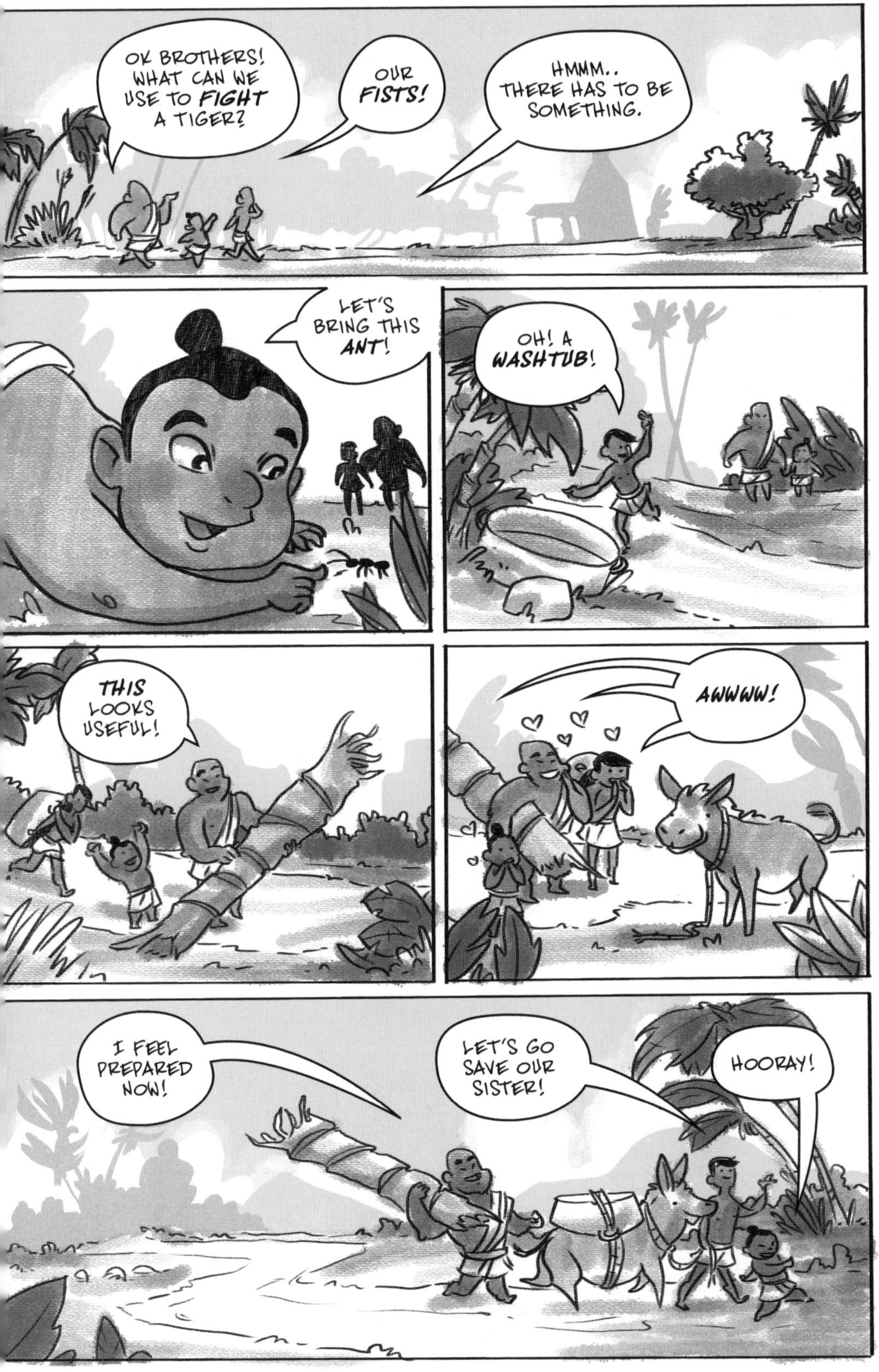
OK BROTHERS! WHAT CAN WE USE TO FIGHT A TIGER?
OUR FISTS!
HMMM.. THERE HAS TO BE SOMETHING.
LET'S BRING THIS ANT!
OH! A WASHTUB!
THIS LOOKS USEFUL!
AWWWW!
I FEEL PREPARED NOW!
LET'S GO SAVE OUR SISTER!
HOORAY!

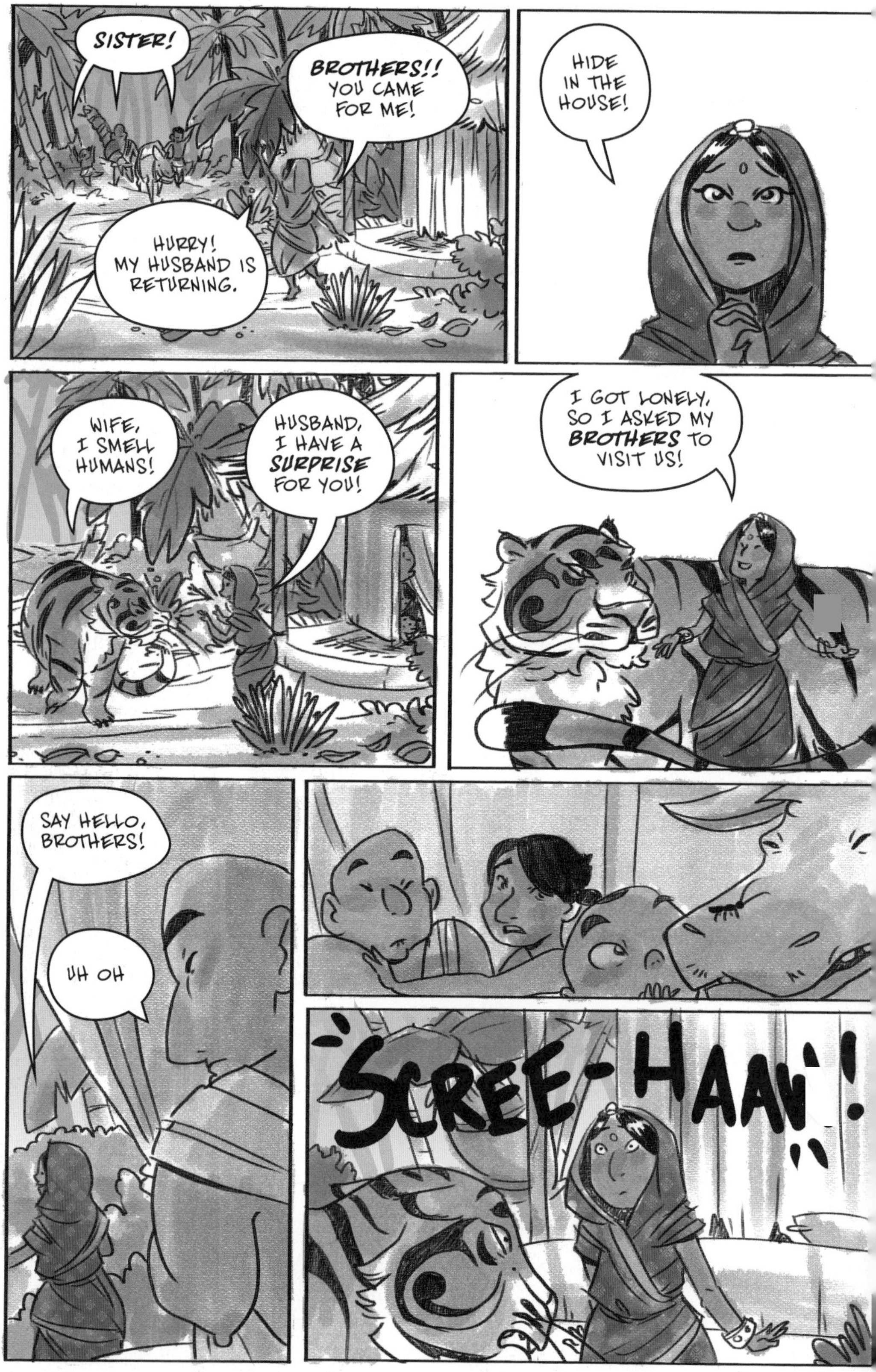
SISTER!
BROTHERS!! YOU CAME FOR ME!
HURRY! MY HUSBAND IS RETURNING.
HIDE IN THE HOUSE!
WIFE, I SMELL HUMANS!
HUSBAND, I HAVE A SURPRISE FOR YOU!
I GOT LONELY, SO I ASKED MY BROTHERS TO VISIT US!
SAY HELLO, BROTHERS!
UH OH
SCREE-HAAW!

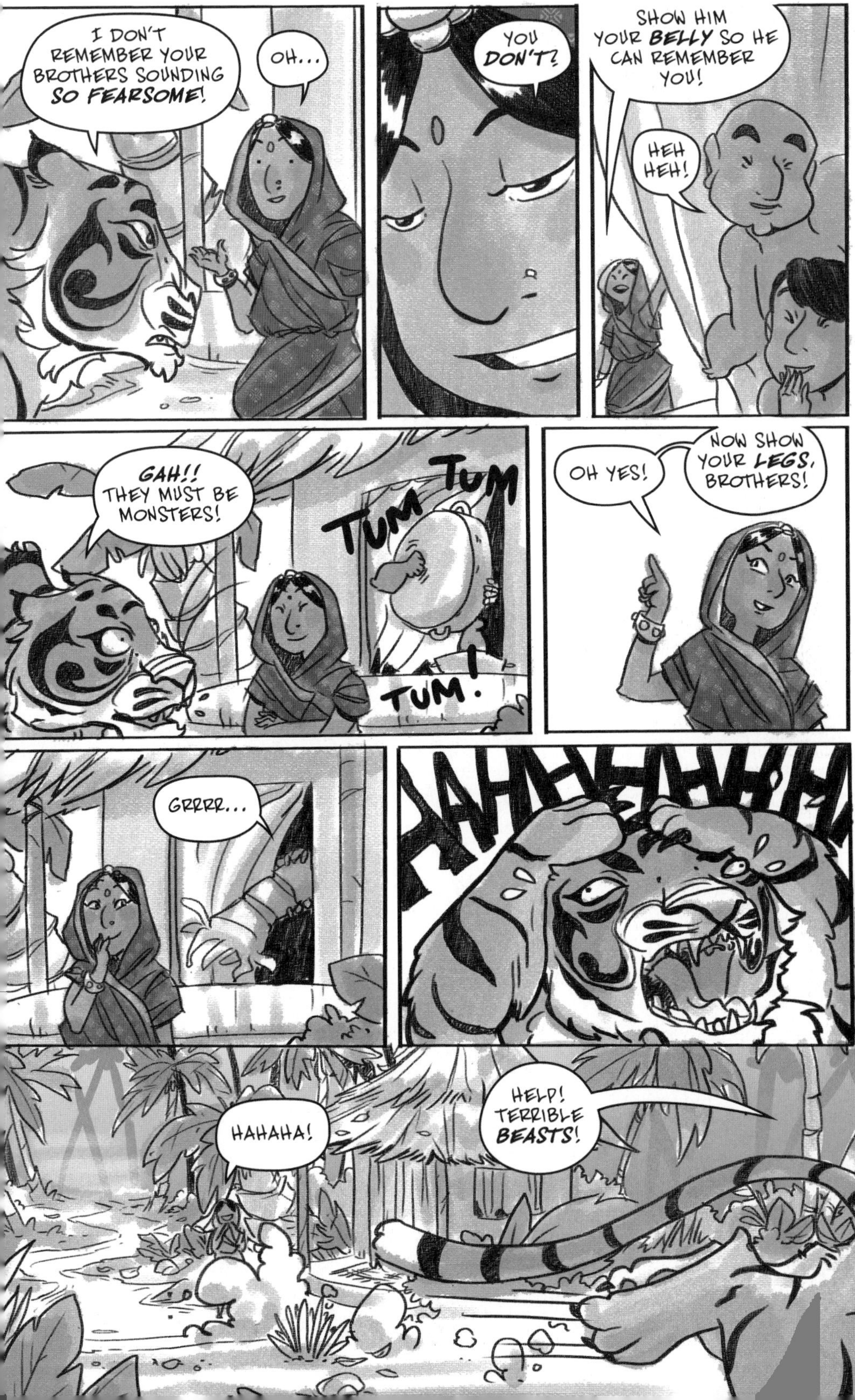

I DON'T REMEMBER YOUR BROTHERS SOUNDING SO FEARSOME!
OH...
YOU DON'T?
SHOW HIM YOUR BELLY SO HE CAN REMEMBER YOU!
HEH HEH!
GAH!! THEY MUST BE MONSTERS!
TUM TUM
TUM!
OH YES!
NOW SHOW YOUR LEGS, BROTHERS!
GRRRR...
HAHAHAHAHA
HAHAHA!
HELP! TERRIBLE BEASTS!

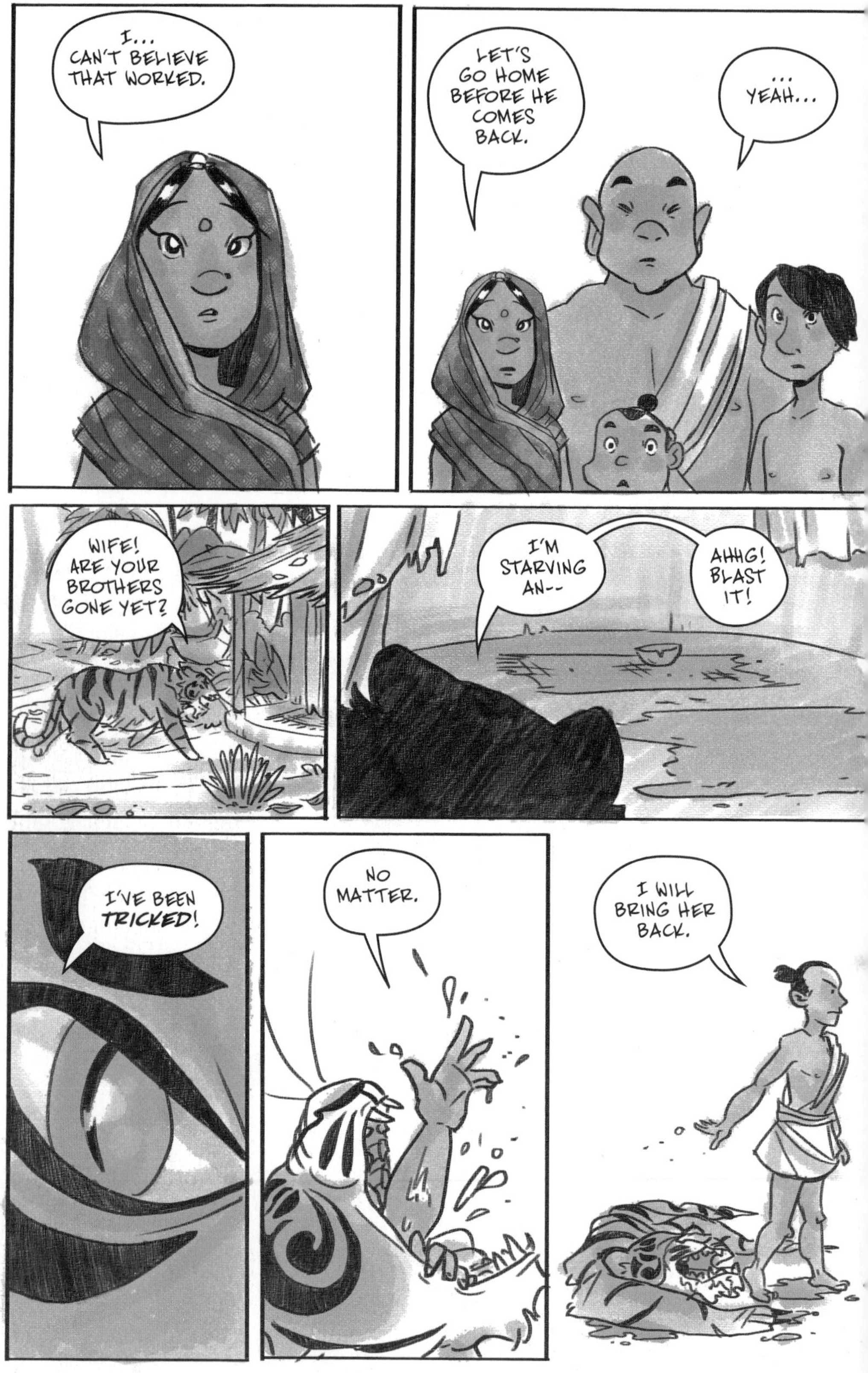
I... CAN'T BELIEVE THAT WORKED.
LET'S GO HOME BEFORE HE COMES BACK.
... YEAH...
WIFE! ARE YOUR BROTHERS GONE YET?
I'M STARVING AN--
AHHG! BLAST IT!
I'VE BEEN TRICKED!
NO MATTER.
I WILL BRING HER BACK.

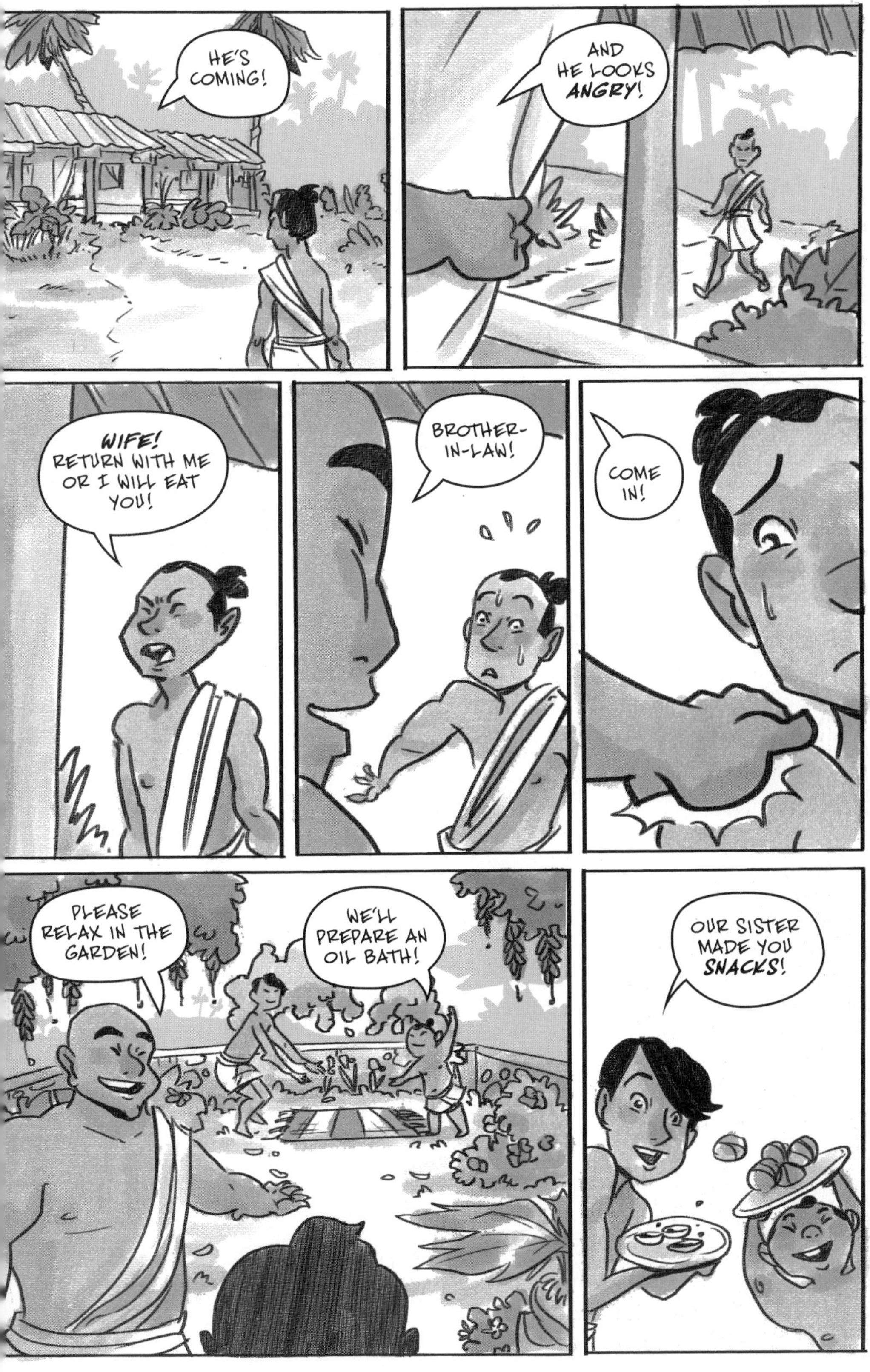
HE'S COMING!
AND HE LOOKS ANGRY!
WIFE! RETURN WITH ME OR I WILL EAT YOU!
BROTHER-IN-LAW!
COME IN!
PLEASE RELAX IN THE GARDEN!
WE'LL PREPARE AN OIL BATH!
OUR SISTER MADE YOU SNACKS!

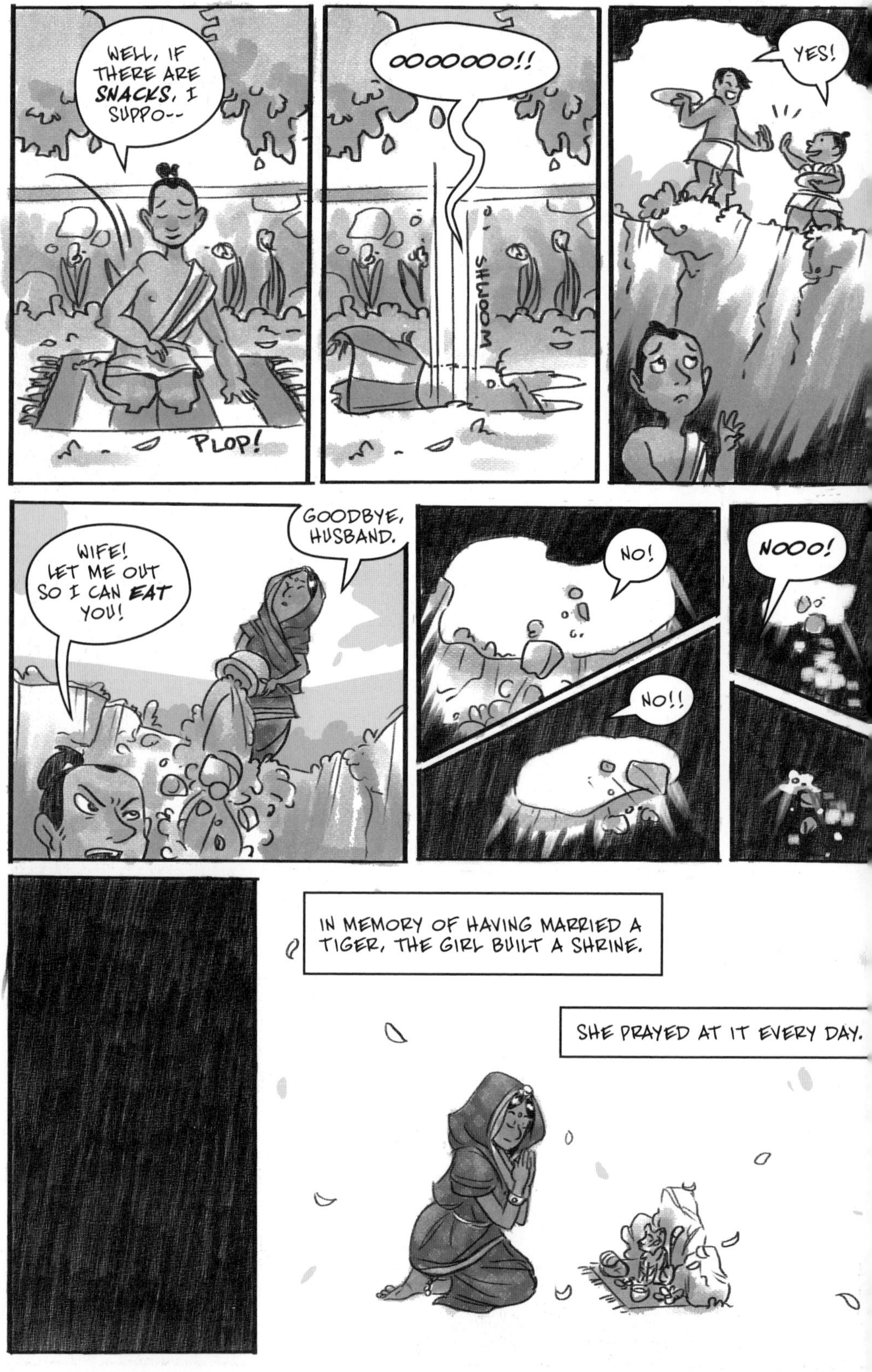
WELL, IF THERE ARE SNACKS, I SUPPO--
PLOP!
OOOOOOO!!
SHWOOM
YES!
WIFE! LET ME OUT SO I CAN EAT YOU!
GOODBYE, HUSBAND.
NO!
NO!!
NOOO!
IN MEMORY OF HAVING MARRIED A TIGER, THE GIRL BUILT A SHRINE.
SHE PRAYED AT IT EVERY DAY.

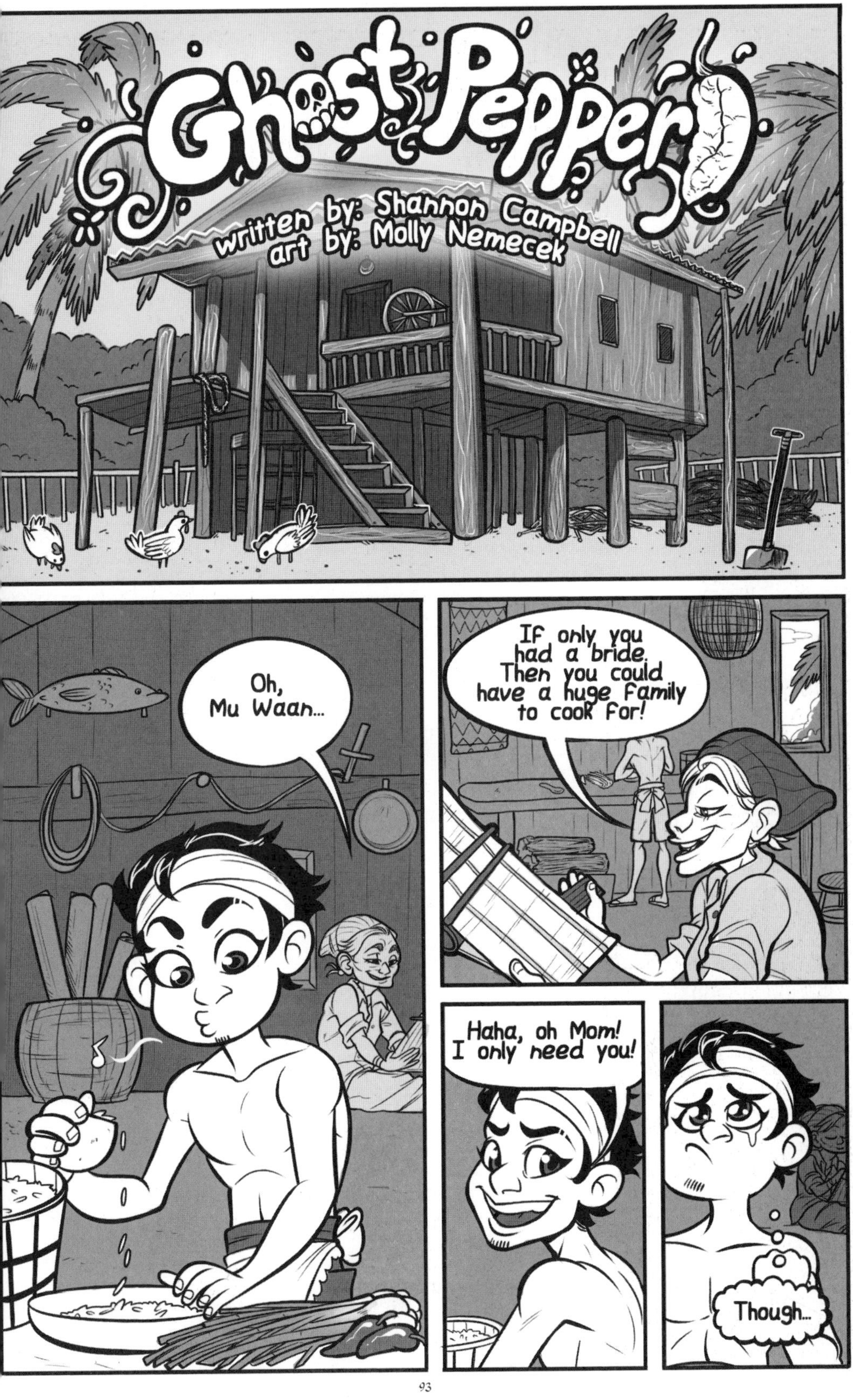
Ghost Pepper
written by: Shannon Campbell
art by: Molly Nemecek
Oh, Mu Waan...
If only you had a bride. Then you could have a huge family to cook for!
Haha, oh Mom! I only need you!
Though...

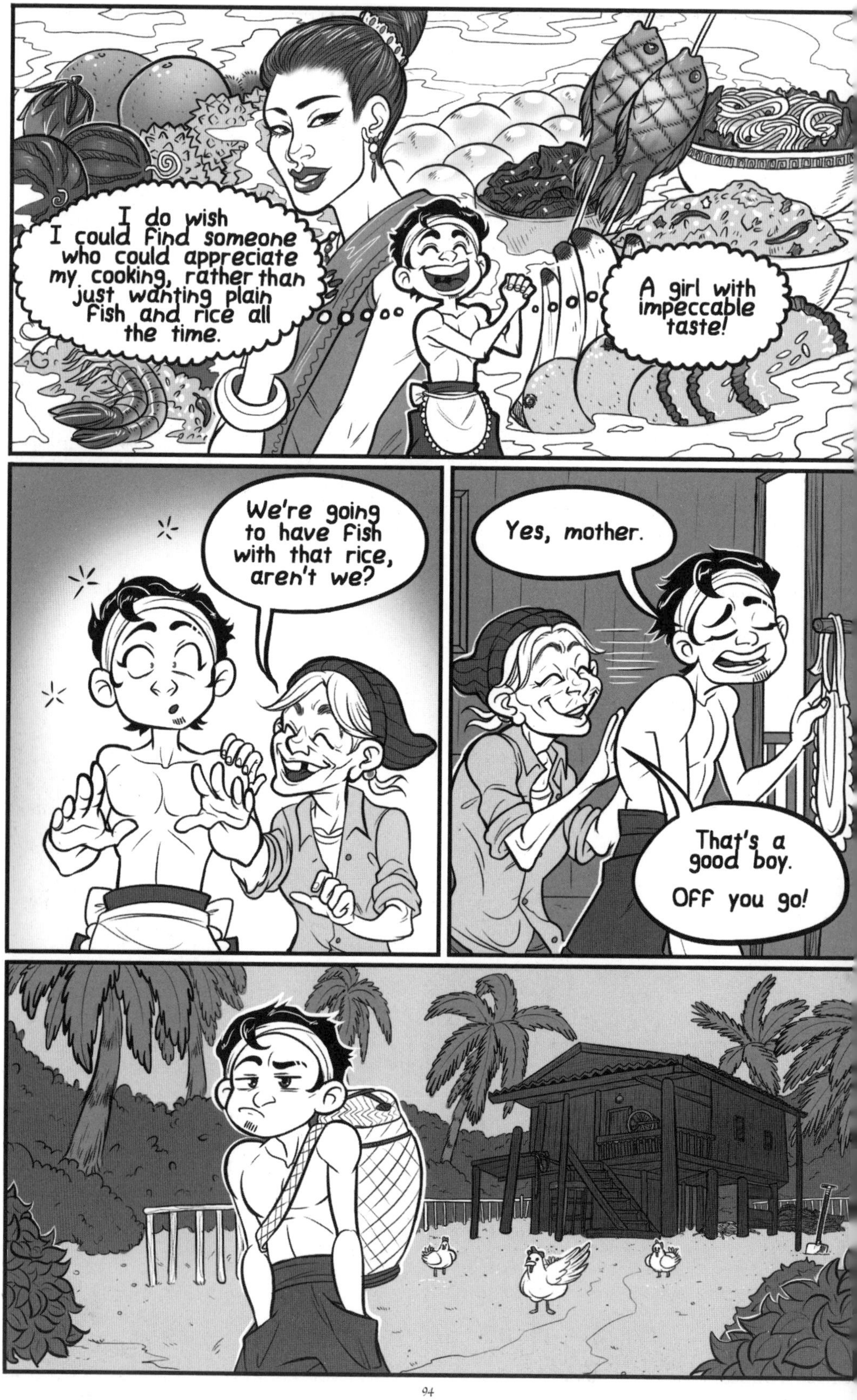
I do wish I could find someone who could appreciate my cooking, rather than just wanting plain fish and rice all the time.
A girl with impeccable taste!
We're going to have fish with that rice, aren't we?
Yes, mother.
That's a good boy.
Off you go!

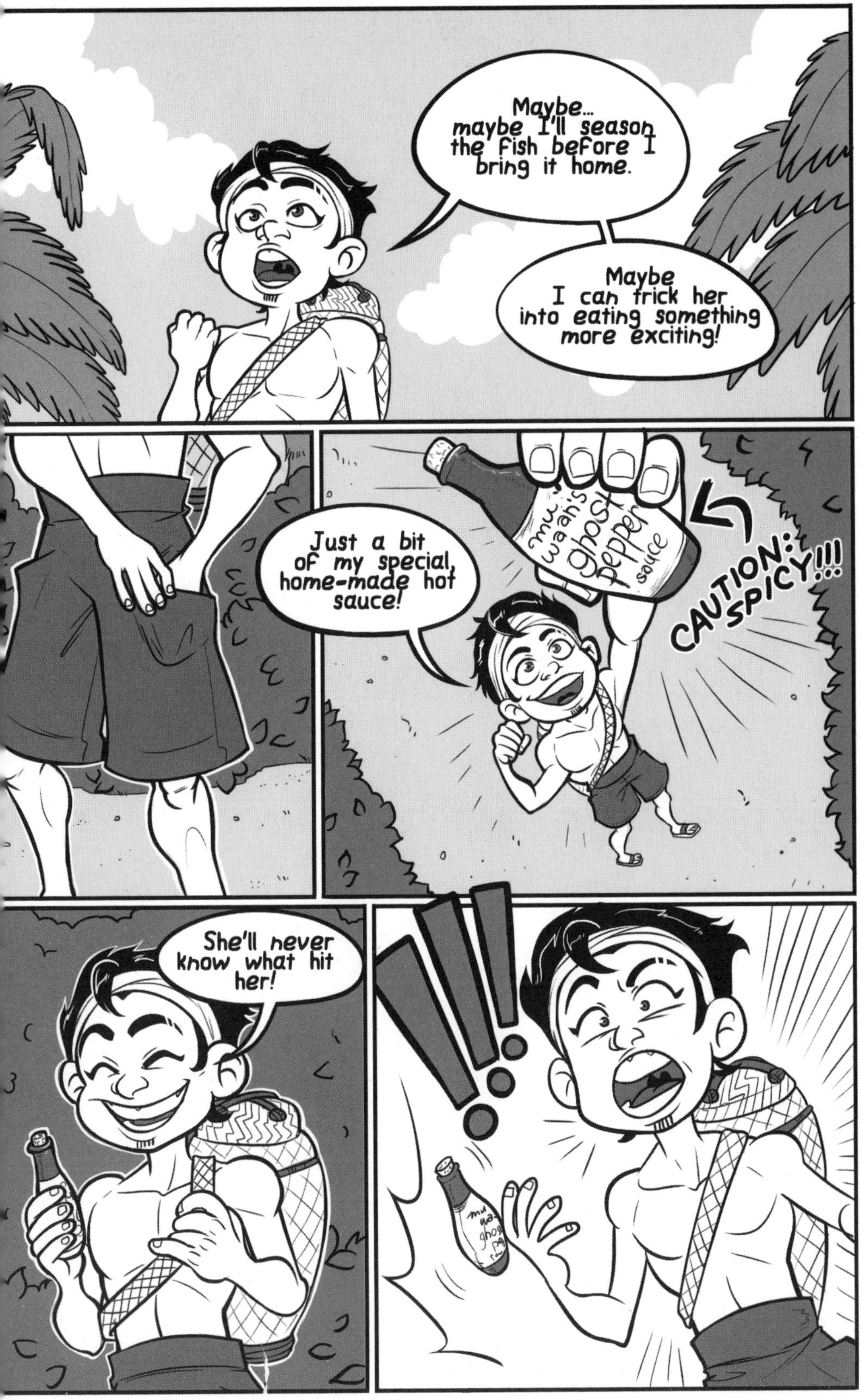
Maybe... maybe I'll season the fish before I bring it home.
Maybe I can trick her into eating something more exciting!
Just a bit of my special home-made hot sauce!
mu waah's ghost pepper sauce
CAUTION: SPICY!!!
She'll never know what hit her!

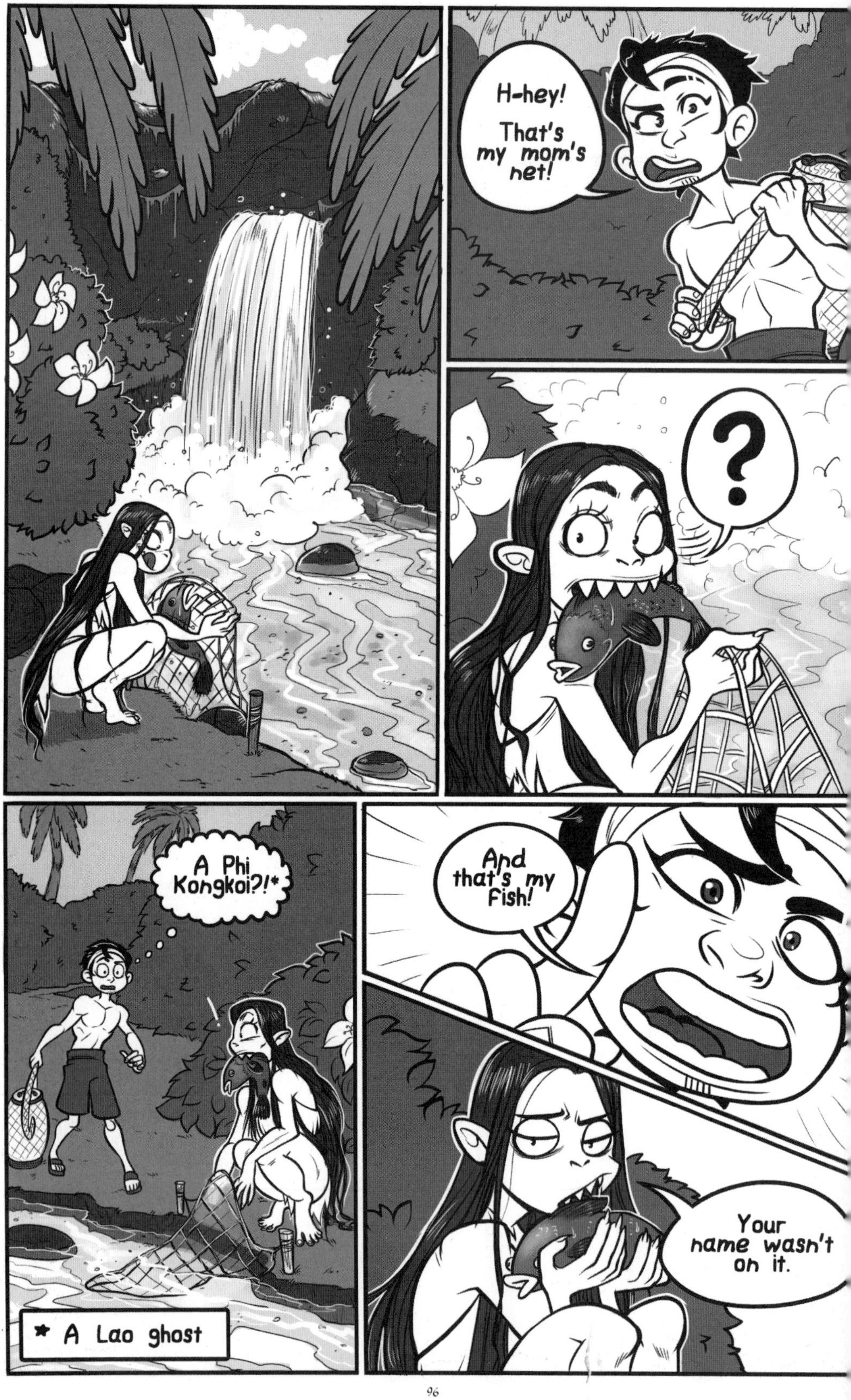
H-hey! That's my mom's net!
?
A Phi Kongkoi?!*
* A Lao ghost
And that's my fish!
Your name wasn't on it.

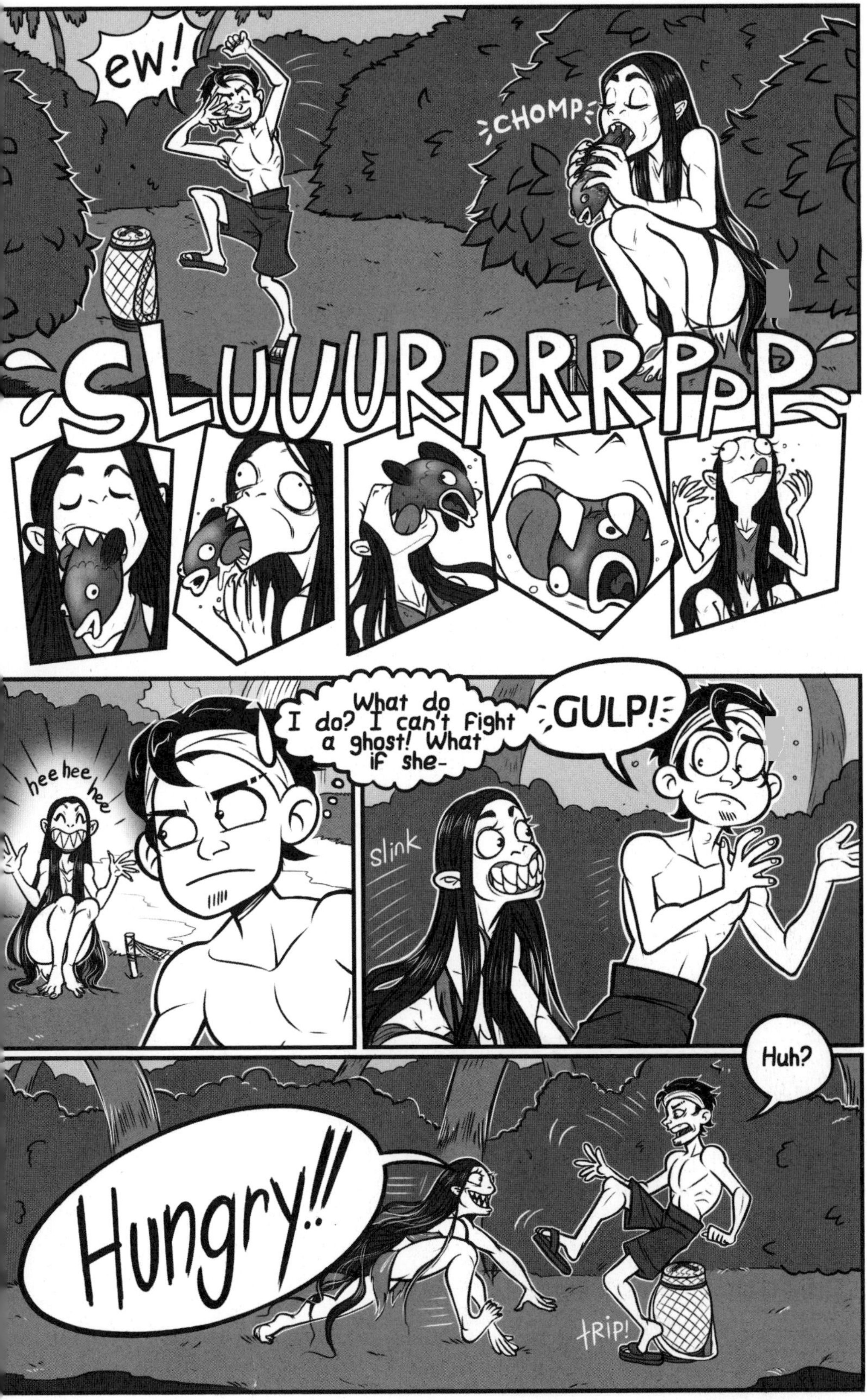
ew!
CHOMP
SLUUURRRRPPP
hee hee hee
What do I do? I can't fight a ghost! What if she-
GULP!
slink
Huh?
Hungry!!
trip!

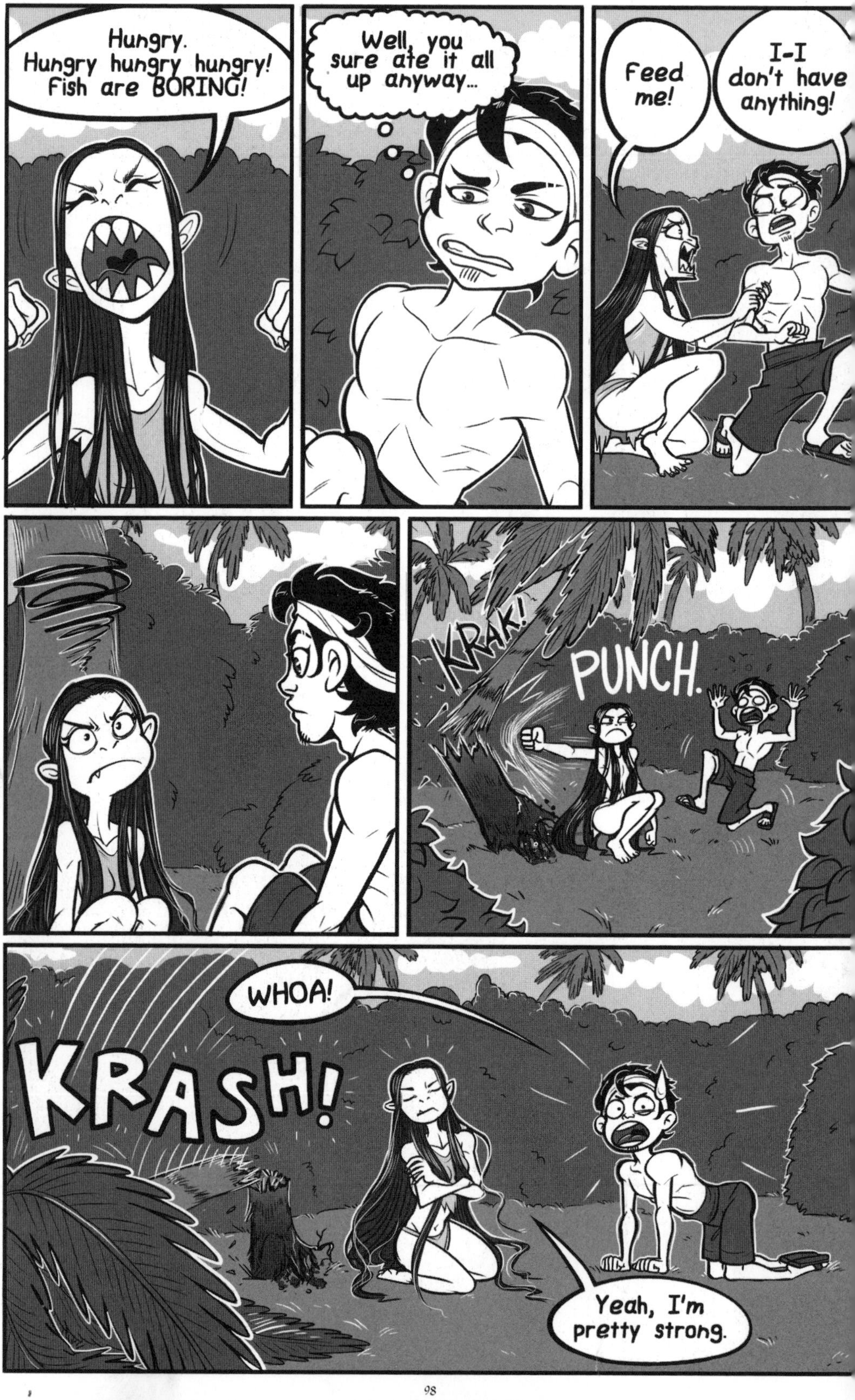
Hungry.
Hungry hungry hungry!
Fish are BORING!
Well, you sure ate it all up anyway...
Feed me!
I-I don't have anything!
KRAK!
PUNCH.
WHOA!
KRASH!
Yeah, I'm pretty strong.

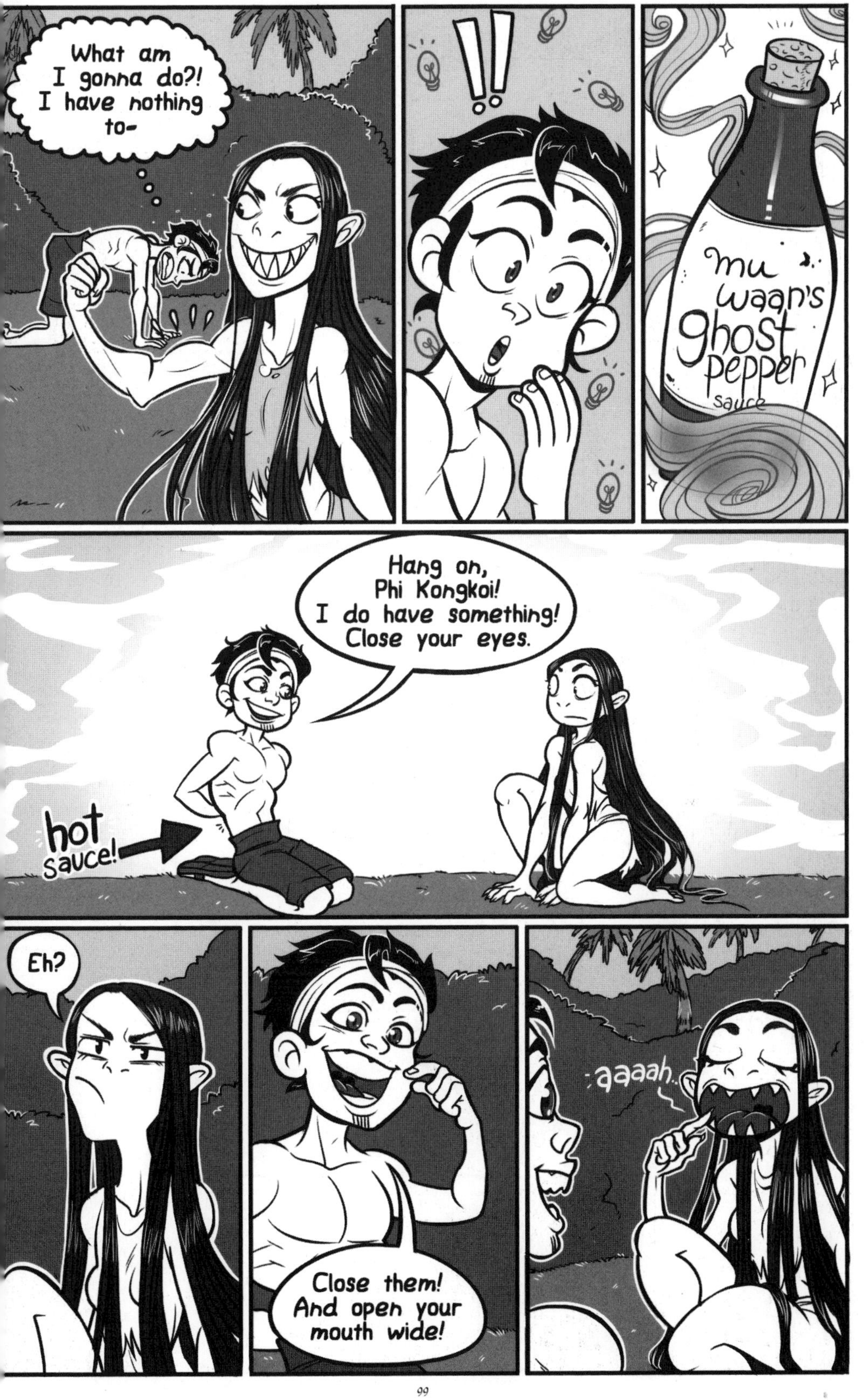

What am I gonna do?! I have nothing to-
!!
mu waan's ghost pepper sauce
Hang on, Phi Kongkoi! I do have something! Close your eyes.
hot sauce!
Eh?
Close them! And open your mouth wide!
aaaah..

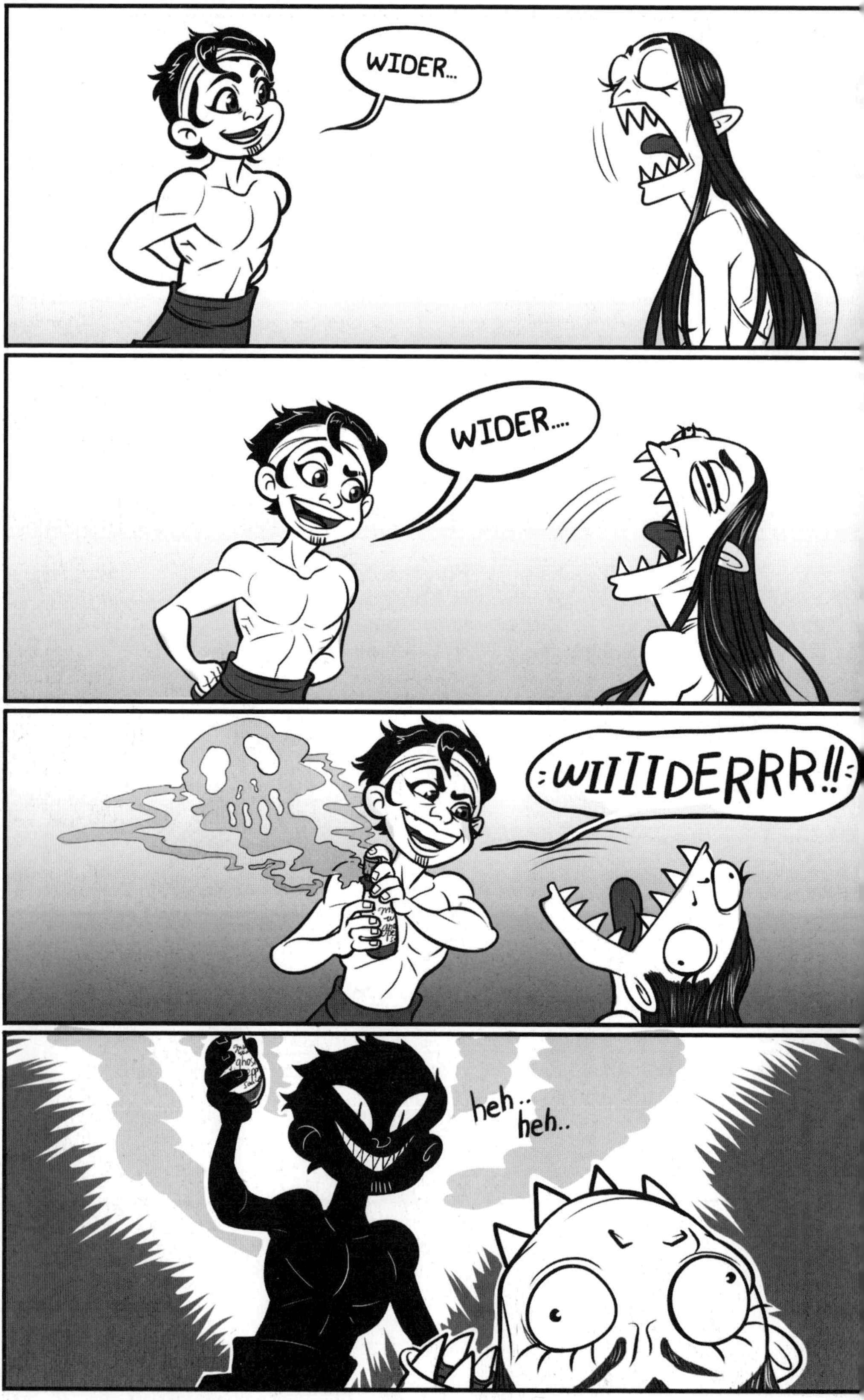
WIDER...
WIDER....
WIIIIDERRR!!
heh..
heh..

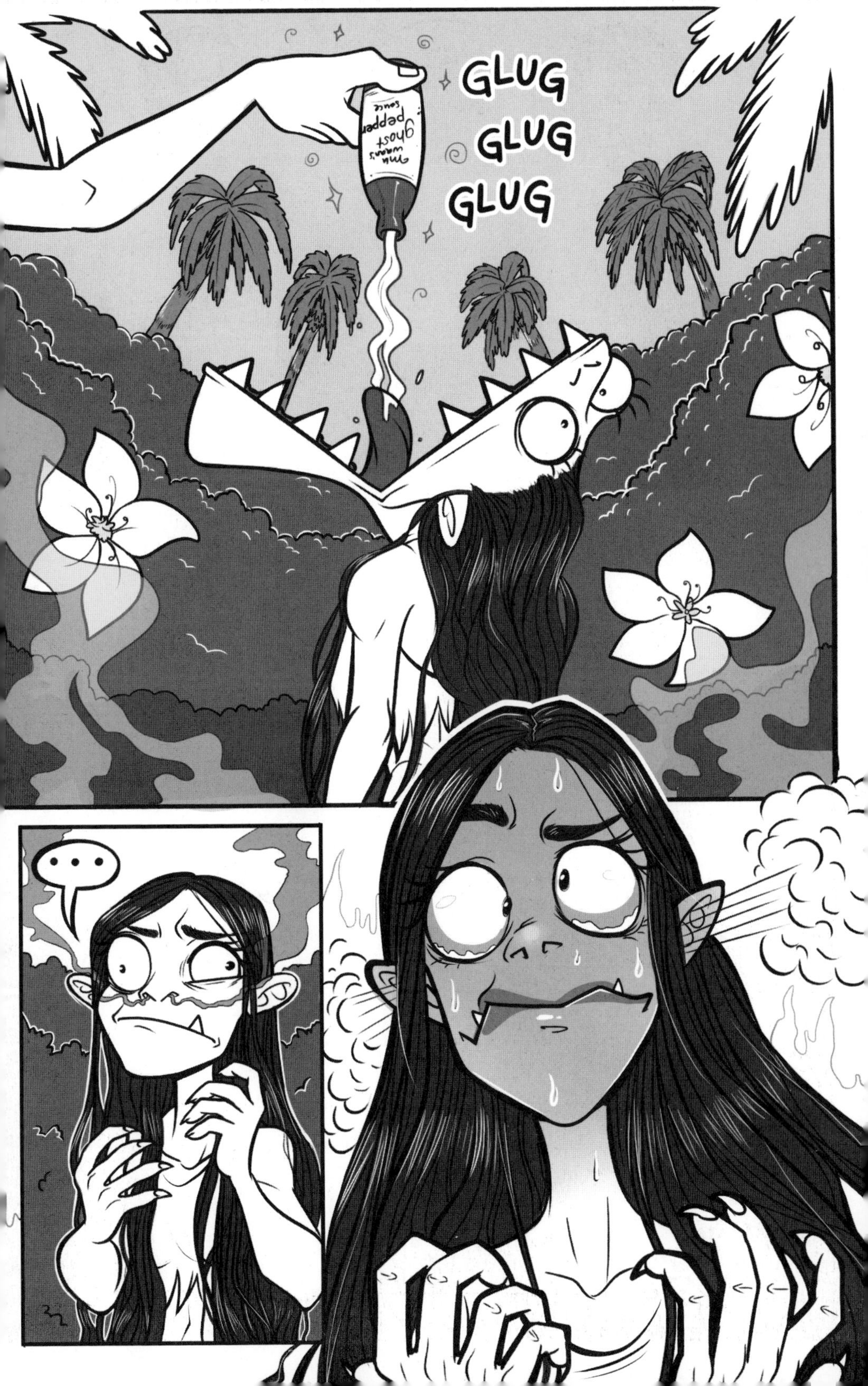
ghost pepper sauce
GLUG
GLUG
GLUG
...

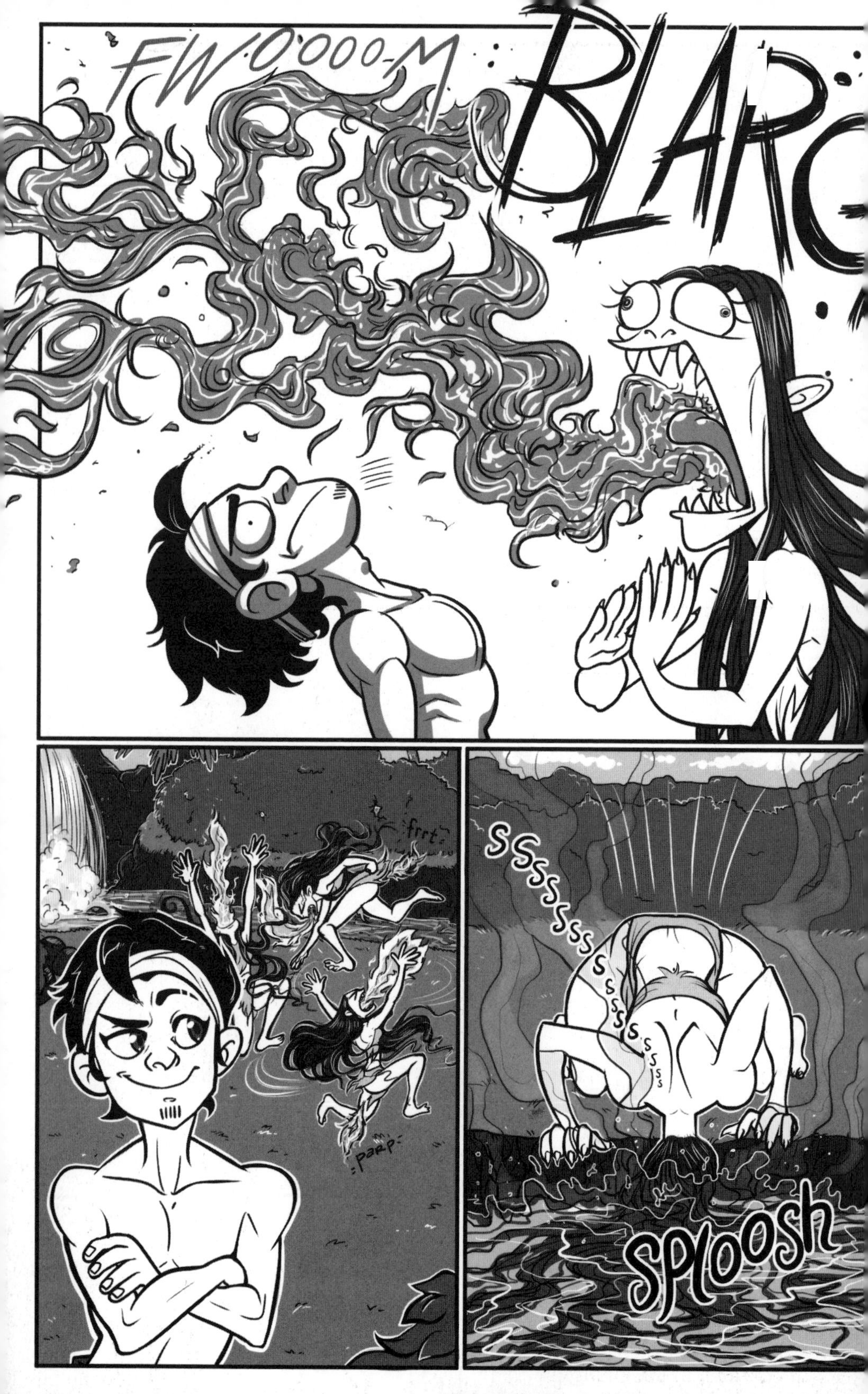
FWOOOO-M
BLARG
frrt
parp
SSSSSSSSSSSSSSSS
SPLOOSH

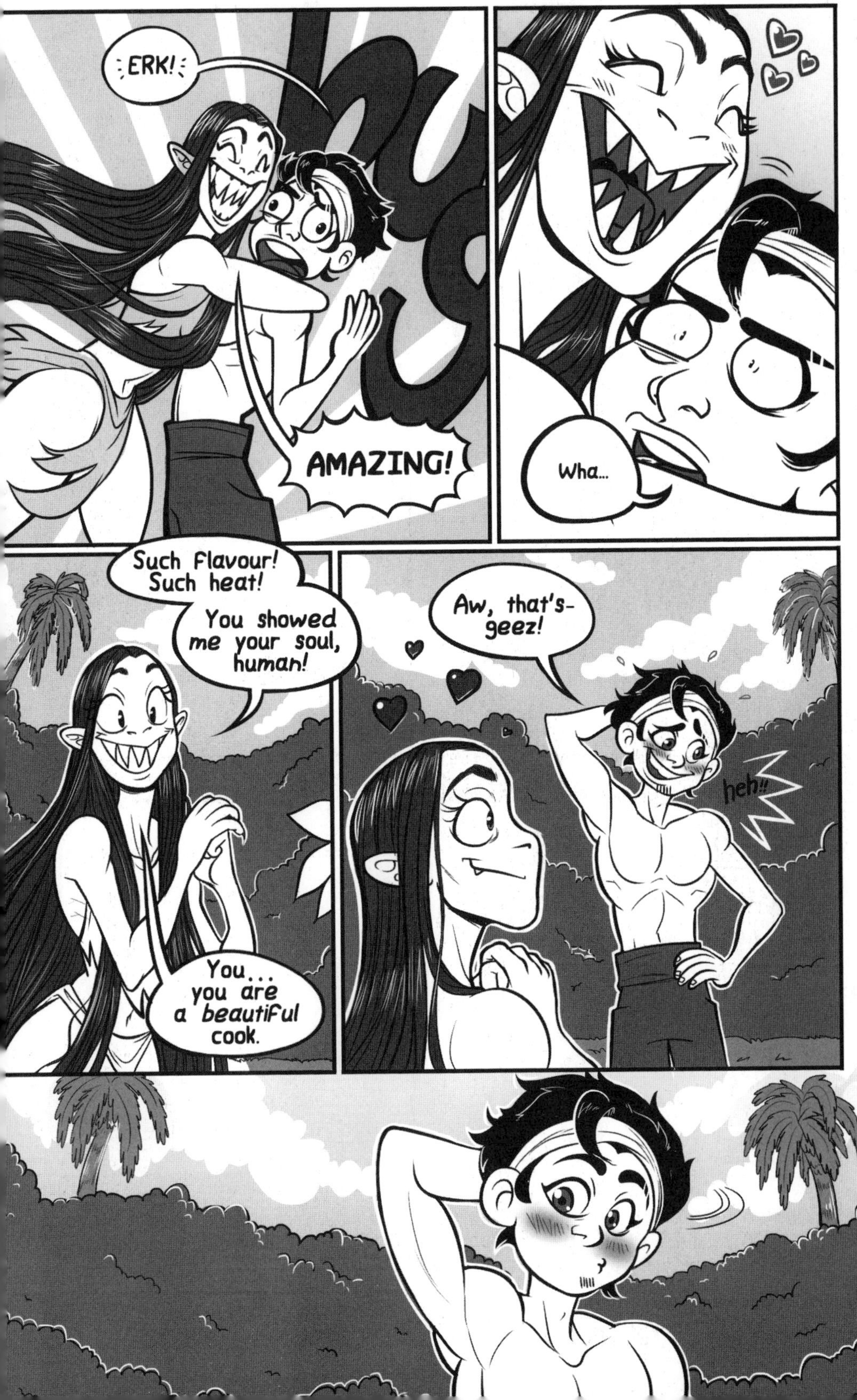
ERK!
AMAZING!
Wha...
Such flavour! Such heat!
You showed me your soul, human!
You... you are a beautiful cook.
Aw, that's- geez!
heh!!

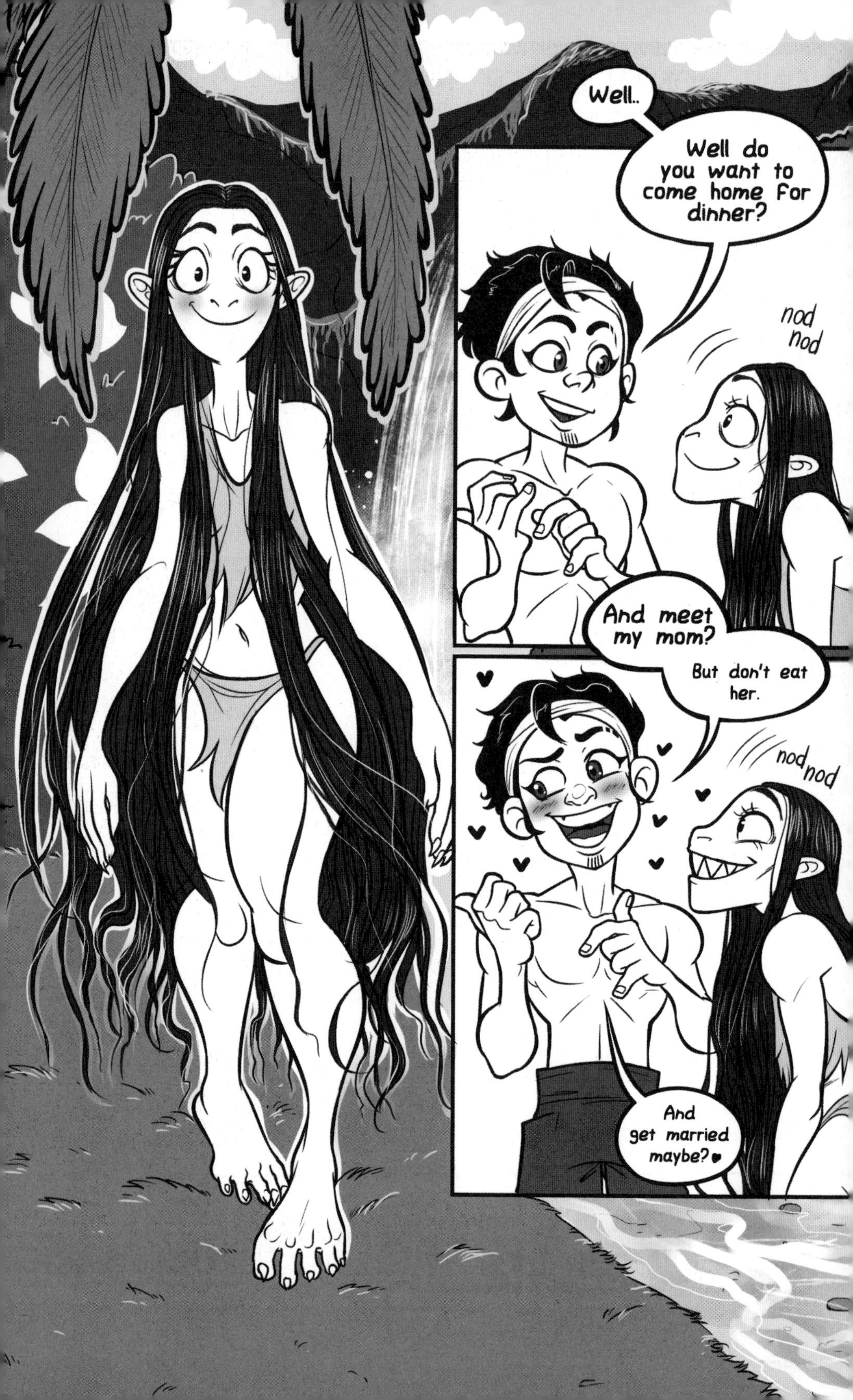
Well..
Well do you want to come home for dinner?
nod nod
And meet my mom?
But don't eat her.
nod nod
And get married maybe?

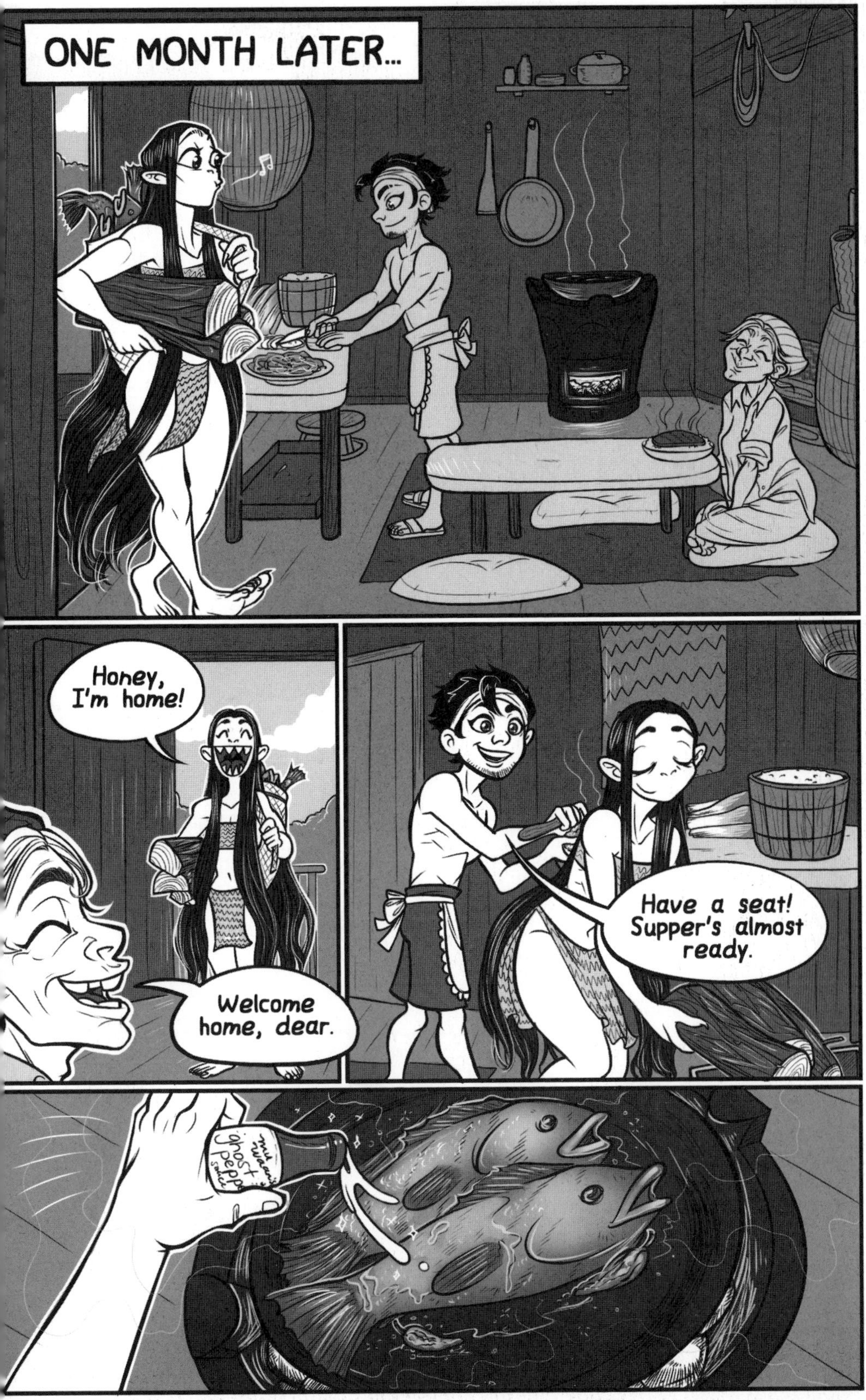
ONE MONTH LATER...
Honey, I'm home!
Welcome home, dear.
Have a seat! Supper's almost ready.

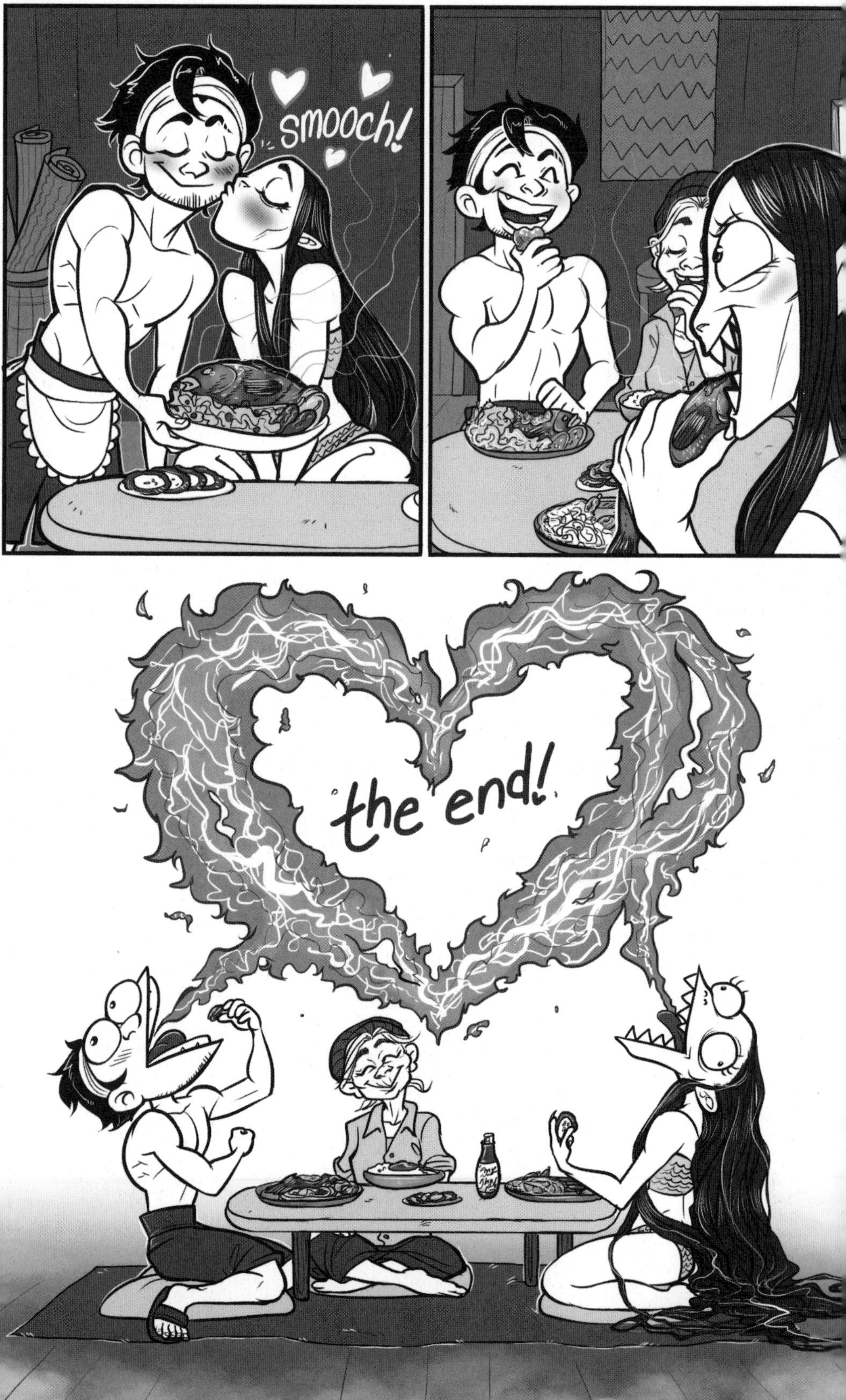
smooch!
the end!

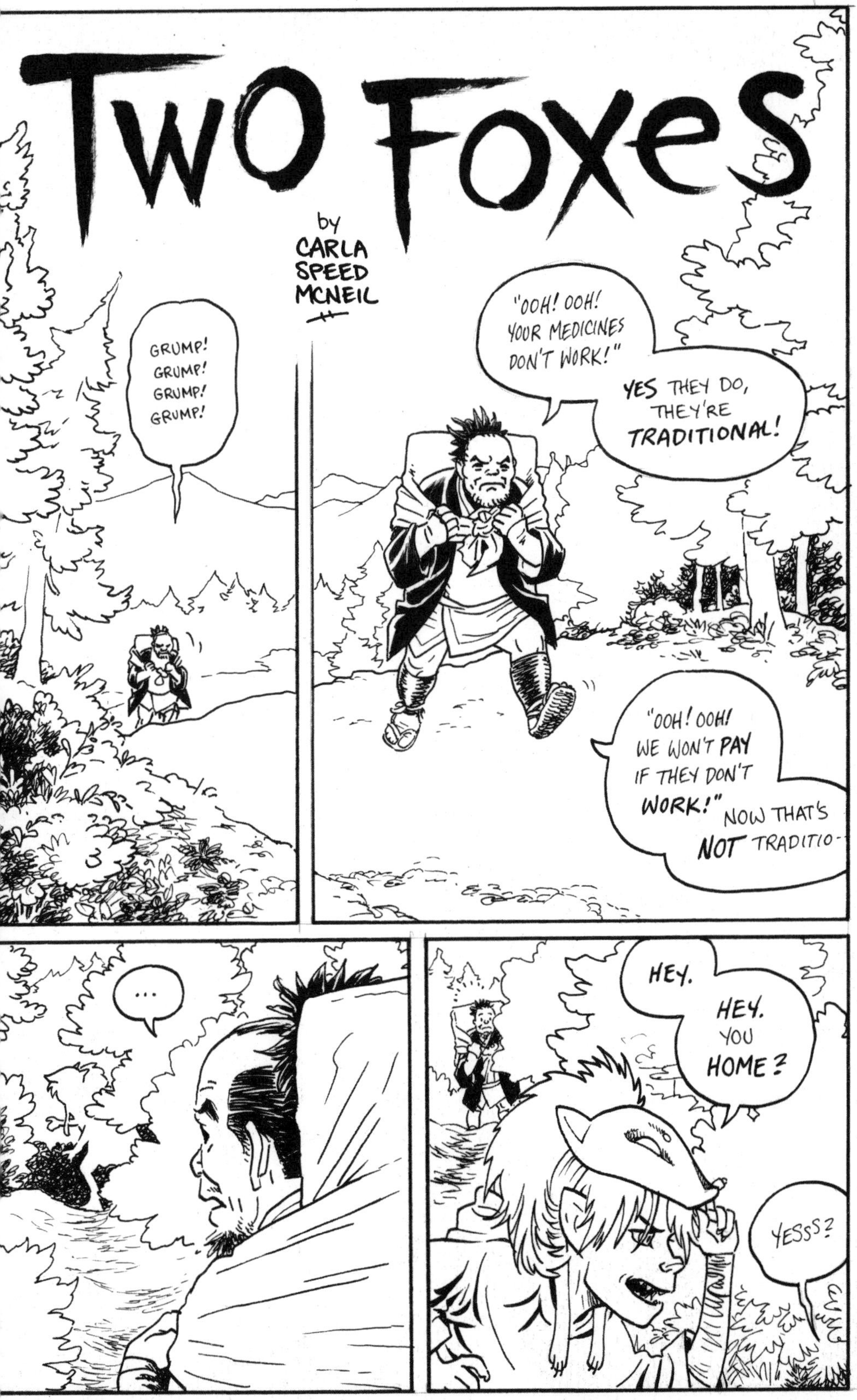

TWO FOXES
by CARLA SPEED MCNEIL
GRUMP! GRUMP! GRUMP! GRUMP!
"OOH! OOH! YOUR MEDICINES DON'T WORK!"
YES THEY DO, THEY'RE TRADITIONAL!
"OOH! OOH! WE WON'T PAY IF THEY DON'T WORK!" NOW THAT'S NOT TRADITIO-
...
HEY.
HEY. YOU HOME?
YESSS?

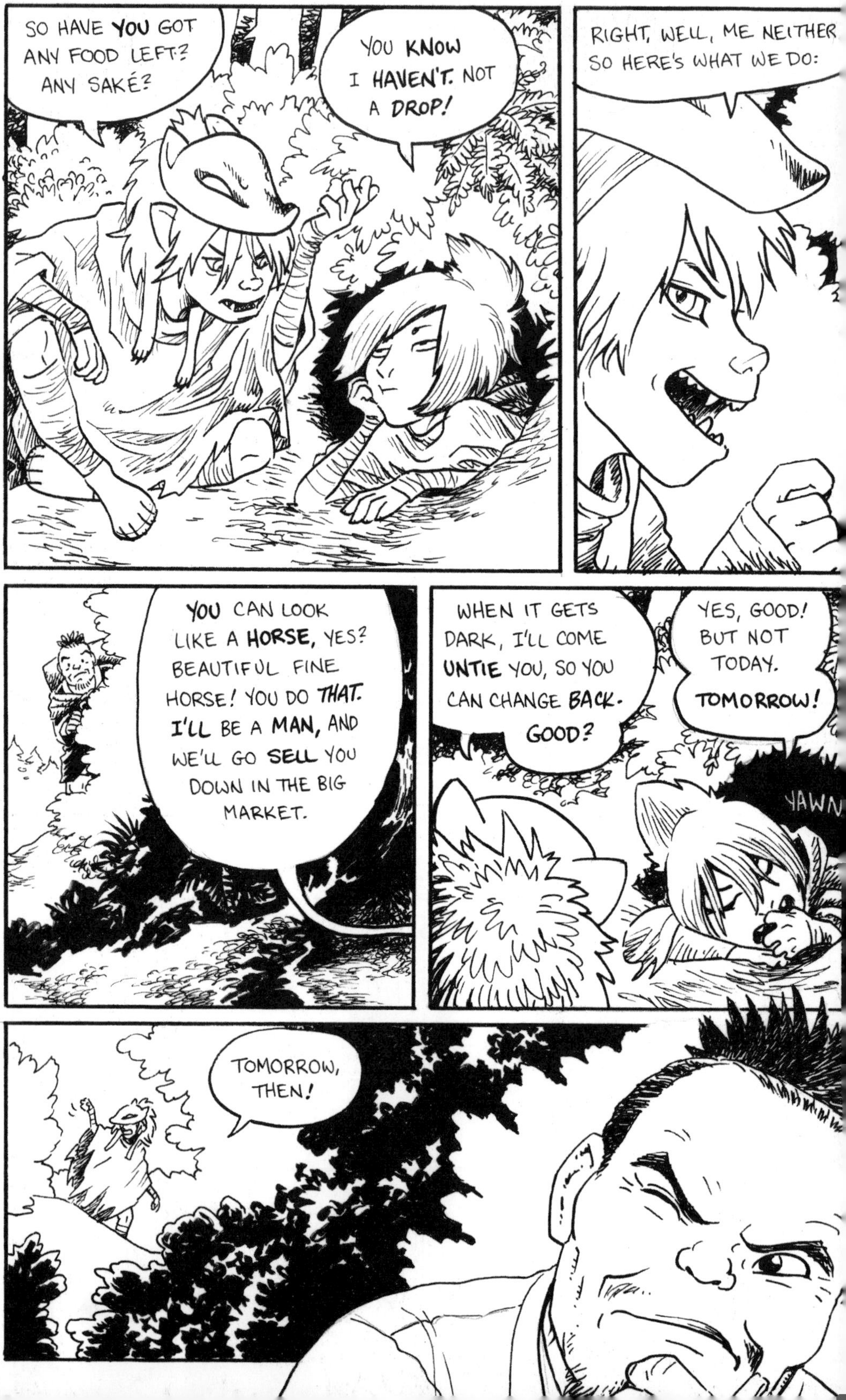
SO HAVE YOU GOT ANY FOOD LEFT? ANY SAKÉ?
YOU KNOW I HAVEN'T. NOT A DROP!
RIGHT, WELL, ME NEITHER SO HERE'S WHAT WE DO:
YOU CAN LOOK LIKE A HORSE, YES? BEAUTIFUL FINE HORSE! YOU DO THAT. I'LL BE A MAN, AND WE'LL GO SELL YOU DOWN IN THE BIG MARKET.
WHEN IT GETS DARK, I'LL COME UNTIE YOU, SO YOU CAN CHANGE BACK. GOOD?
YES, GOOD! BUT NOT TODAY. TOMORROW!
YAWN
TOMORROW, THEN!

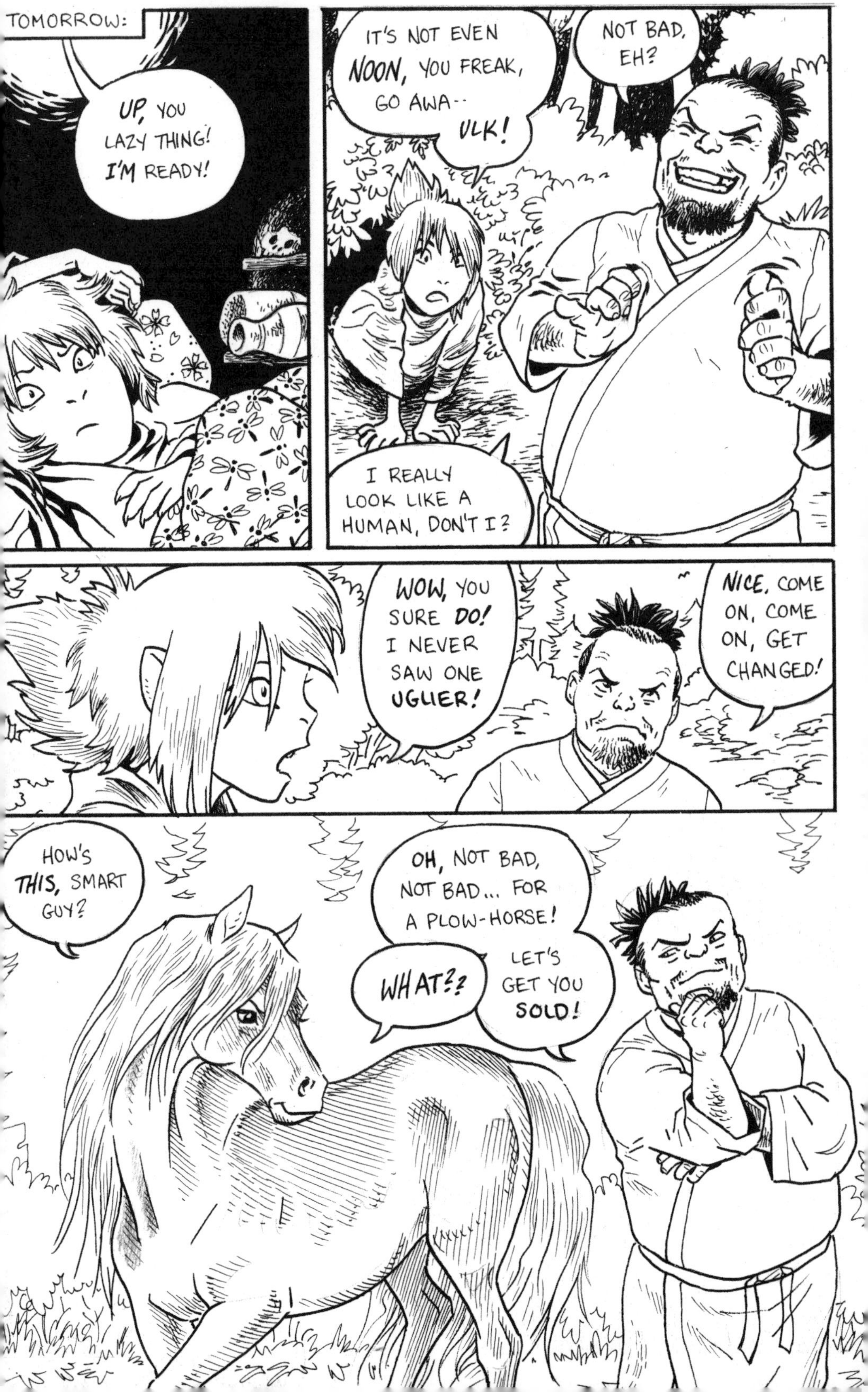
TOMORROW:
UP, YOU LAZY THING! I'M READY!
IT'S NOT EVEN NOON, YOU FREAK, GO AWA--
ULK!
NOT BAD, EH?
I REALLY LOOK LIKE A HUMAN, DON'T I?
WOW, YOU SURE DO! I NEVER SAW ONE UGLIER!
NICE. COME ON, COME ON, GET CHANGED!
HOW'S THIS, SMART GUY?
OH, NOT BAD, NOT BAD... FOR A PLOW-HORSE!
WHAT?!?
LET'S GET YOU SOLD!

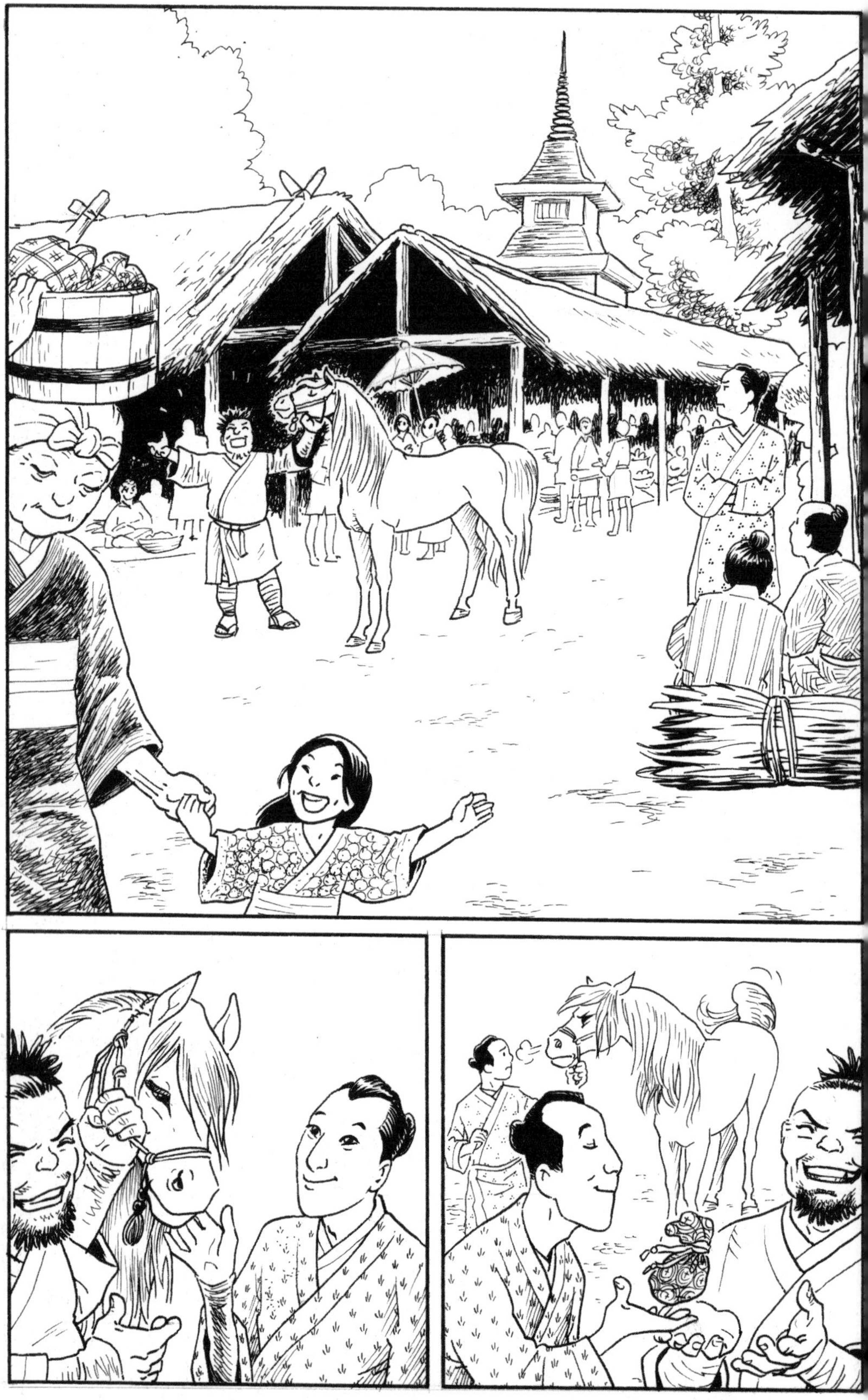

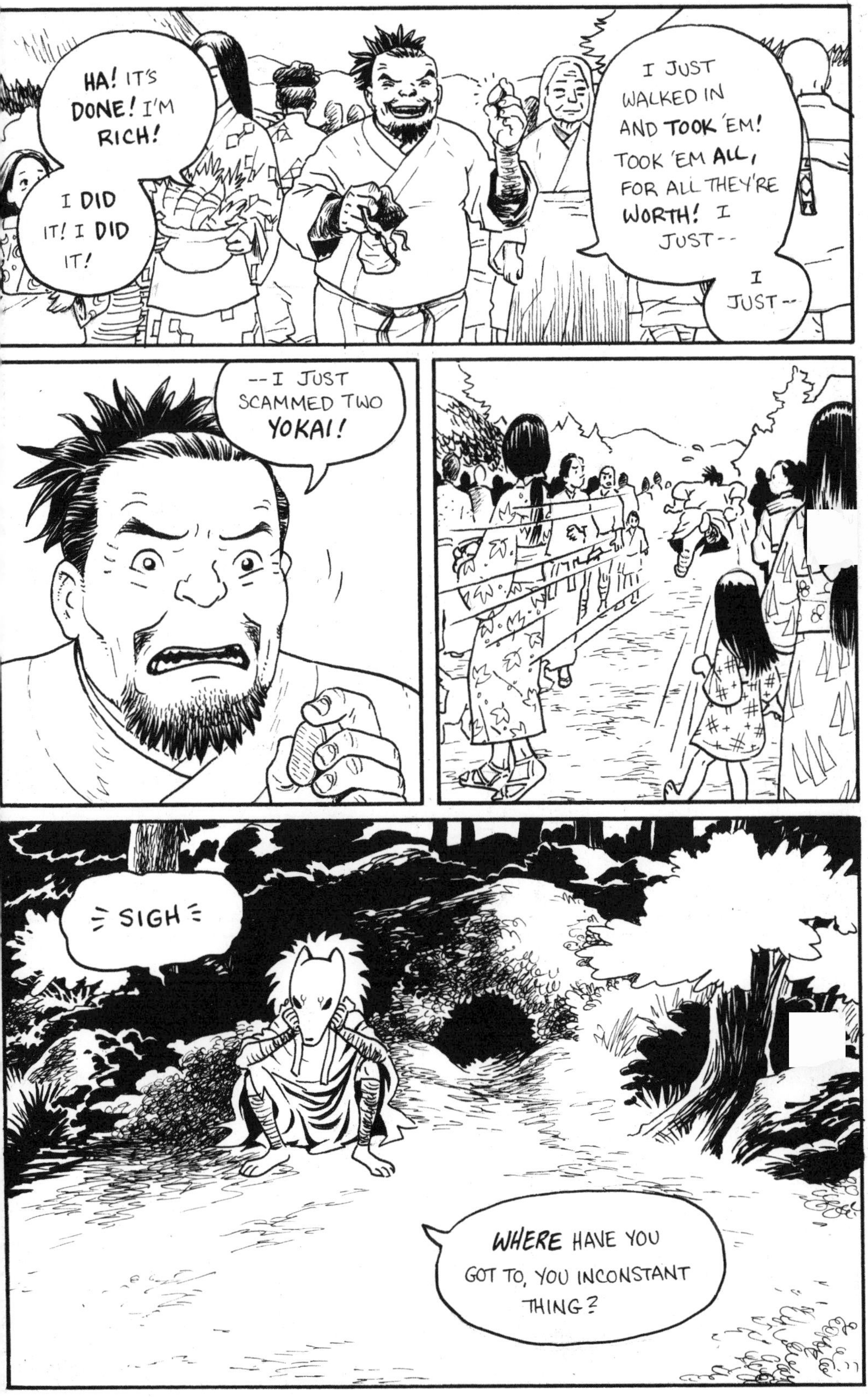
HA! IT'S DONE! I'M RICH!
I DID IT! I DID IT!
I JUST WALKED IN AND TOOK 'EM! TOOK 'EM ALL, FOR ALL THEY'RE WORTH! I JUST--
I JUST--
--I JUST SCAMMED TWO YOKAI!
SIGH
WHERE HAVE YOU GOT TO, YOU INCONSTANT THING?

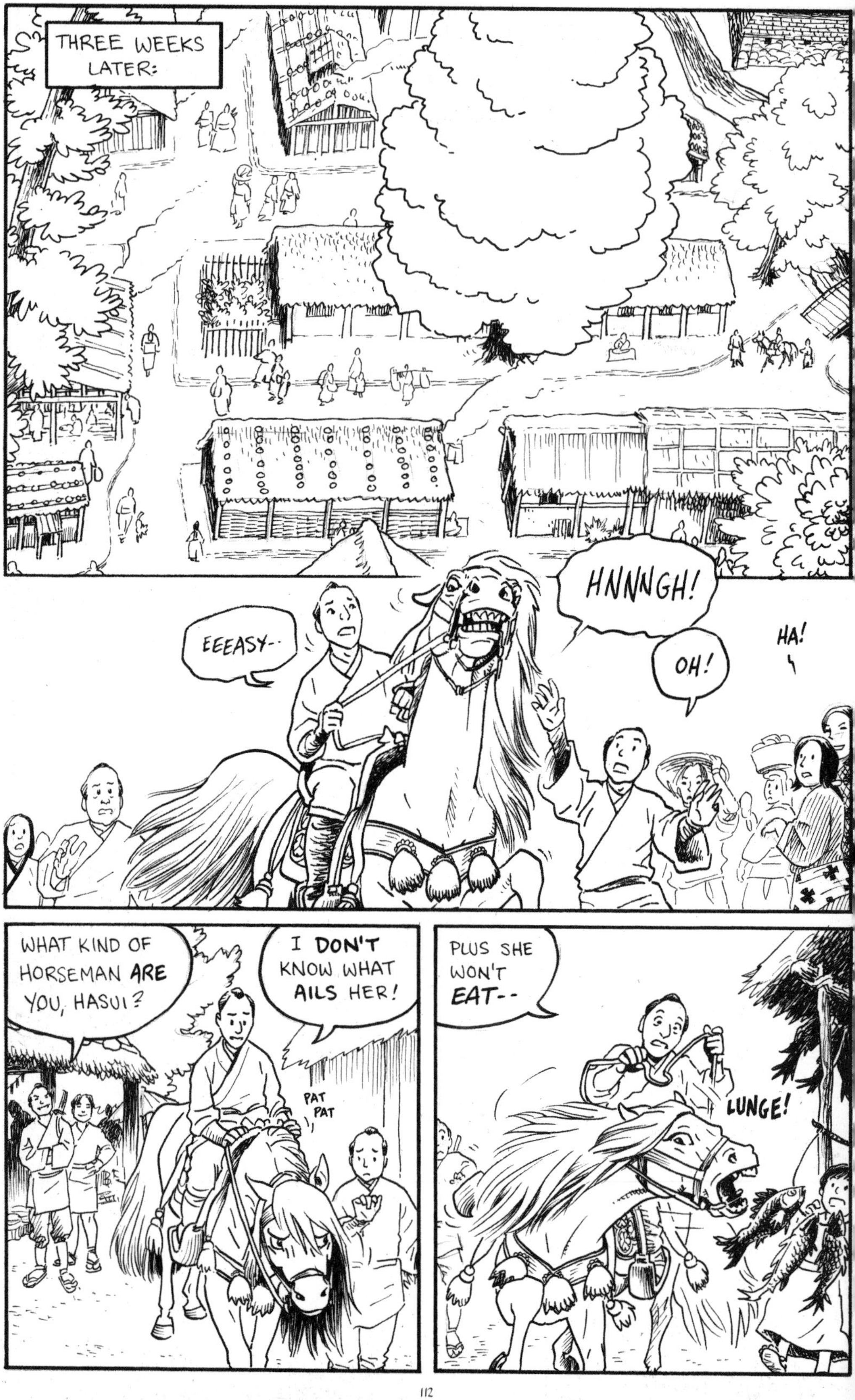
THREE WEEKS LATER:
EEEASY--
HNNNGH!
OH!
HA!
WHAT KIND OF HORSEMAN **ARE** YOU, HASUI?
I **DON'T** KNOW WHAT **AILS** HER!
PAT PAT
PLUS SHE WON'T ***EAT***--
LUNGE!

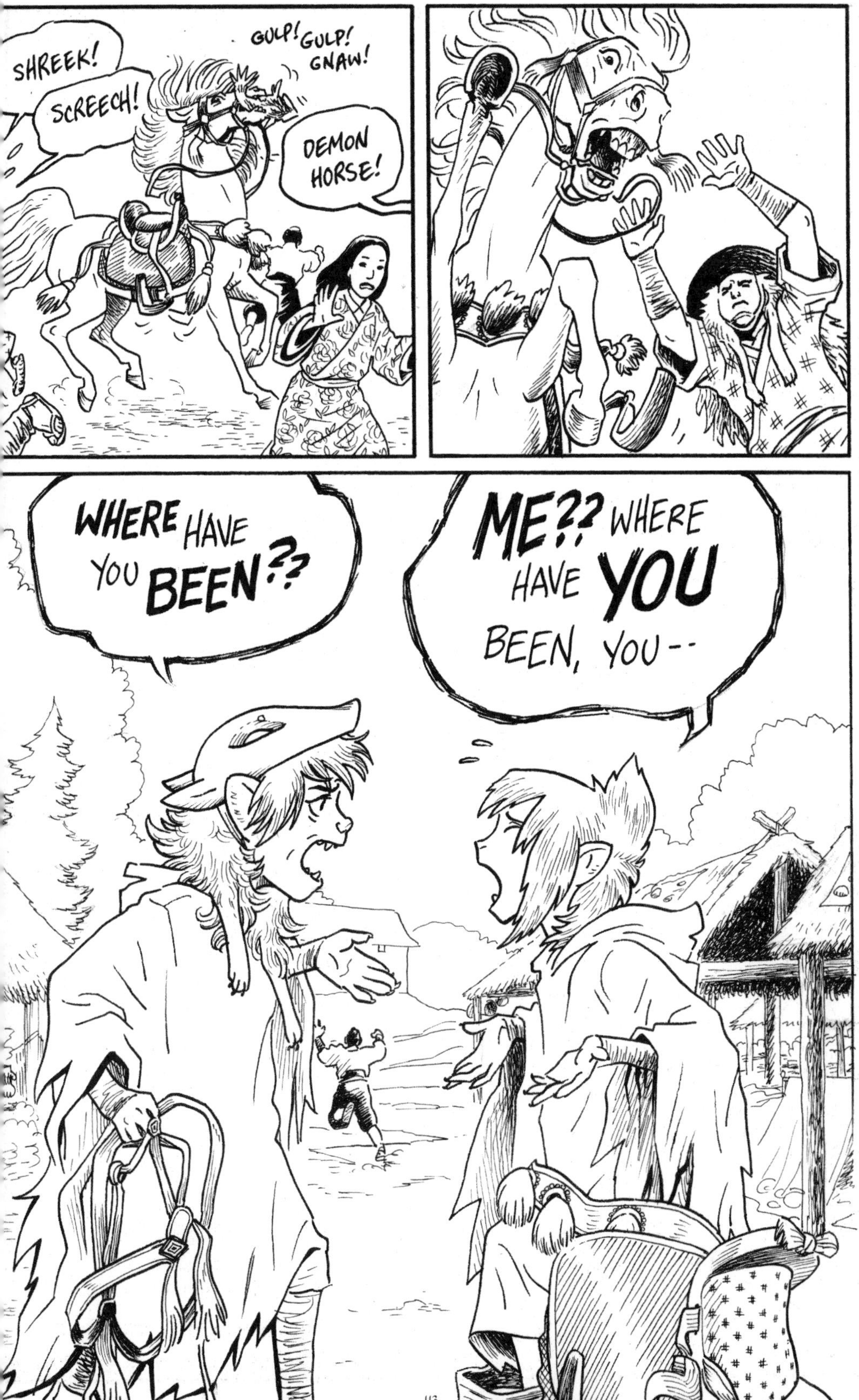
SHREEK!
SCREECH!
GULP! GULP! GNAW!
DEMON HORSE!
WHERE HAVE YOU BEEN??
ME?? WHERE HAVE YOU BEEN, YOU--

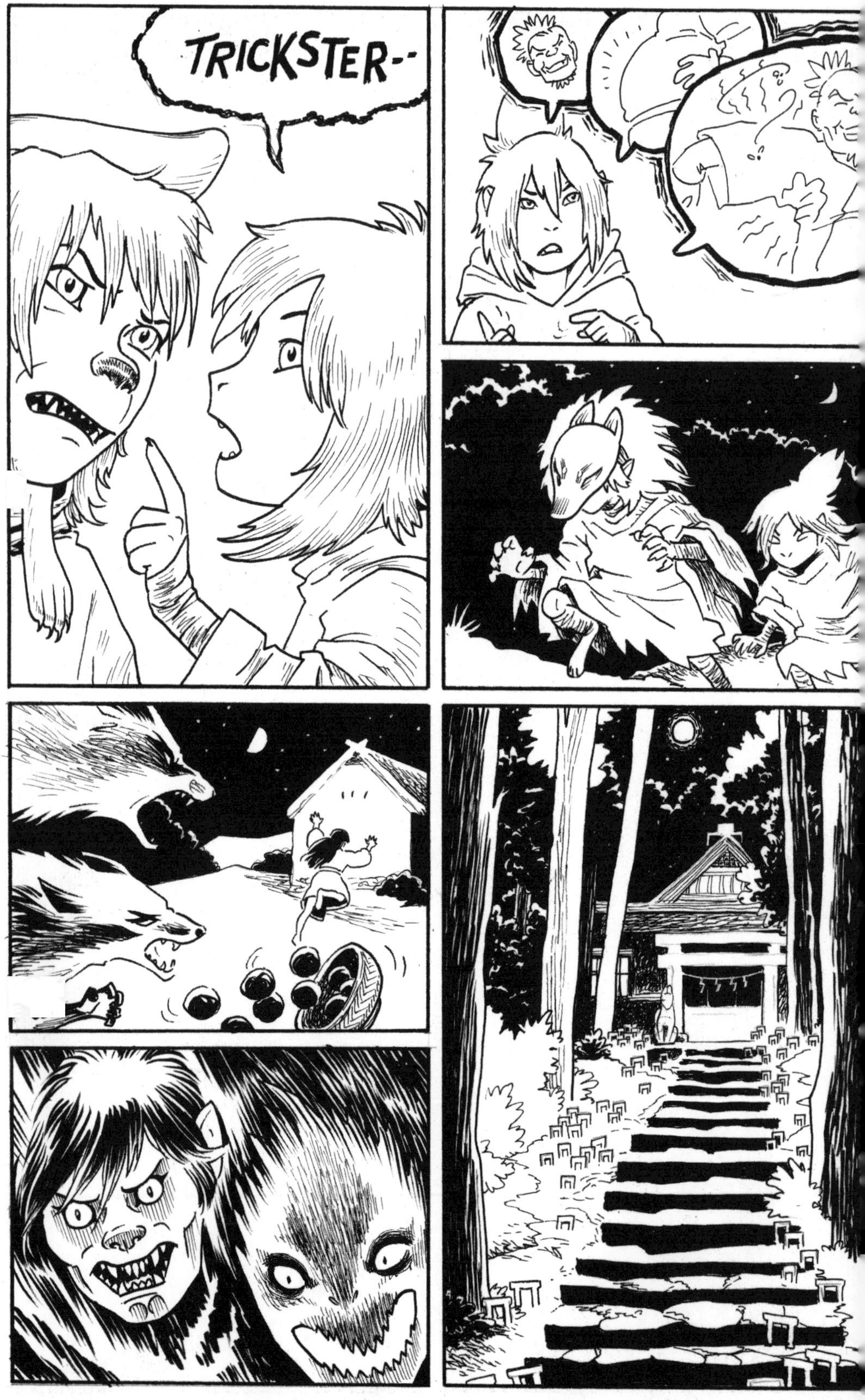
TRICKSTER--

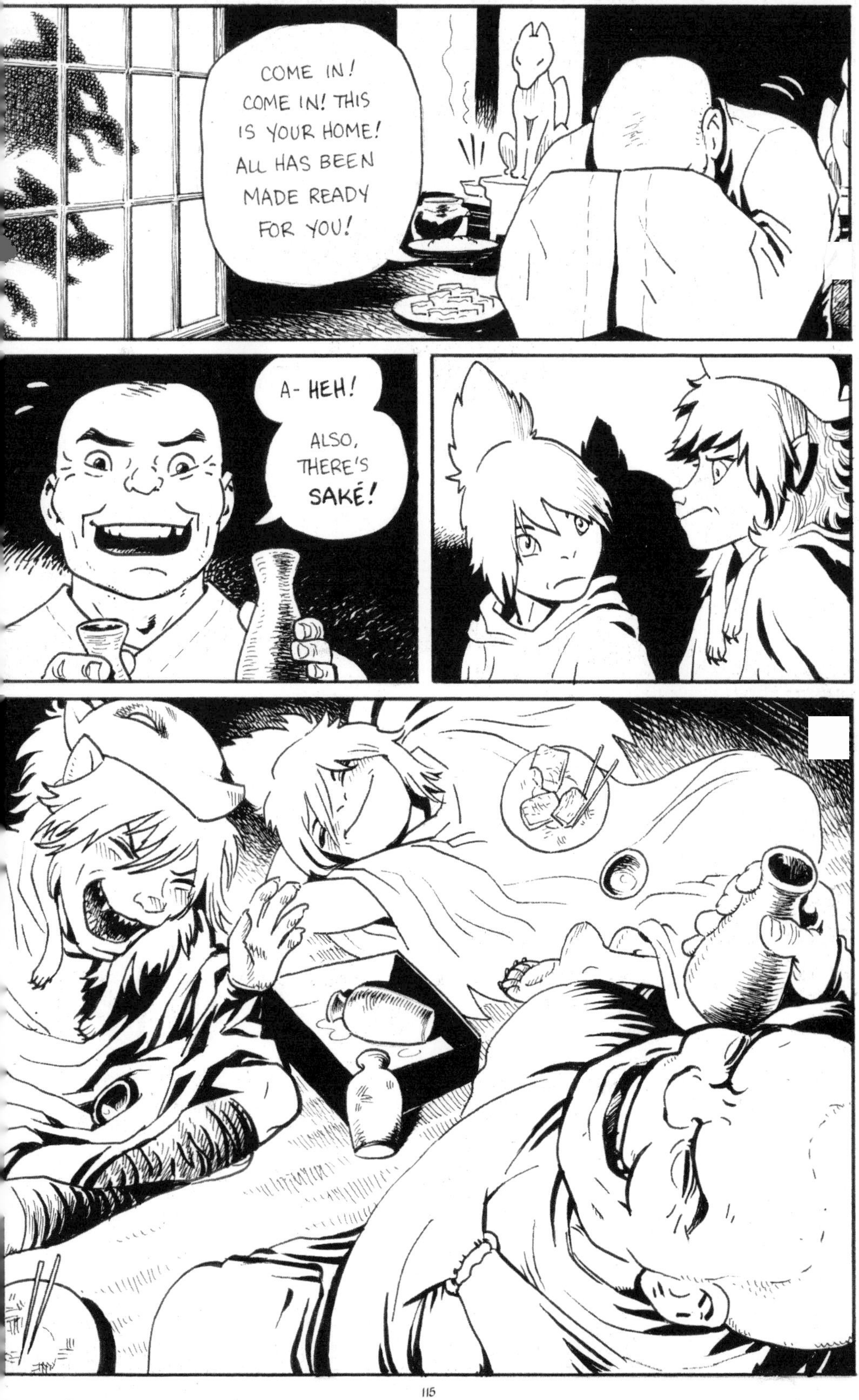
COME IN! COME IN! THIS IS YOUR HOME! ALL HAS BEEN MADE READY FOR YOU!
A- HEH!
ALSO, THERE'S SAKÉ!

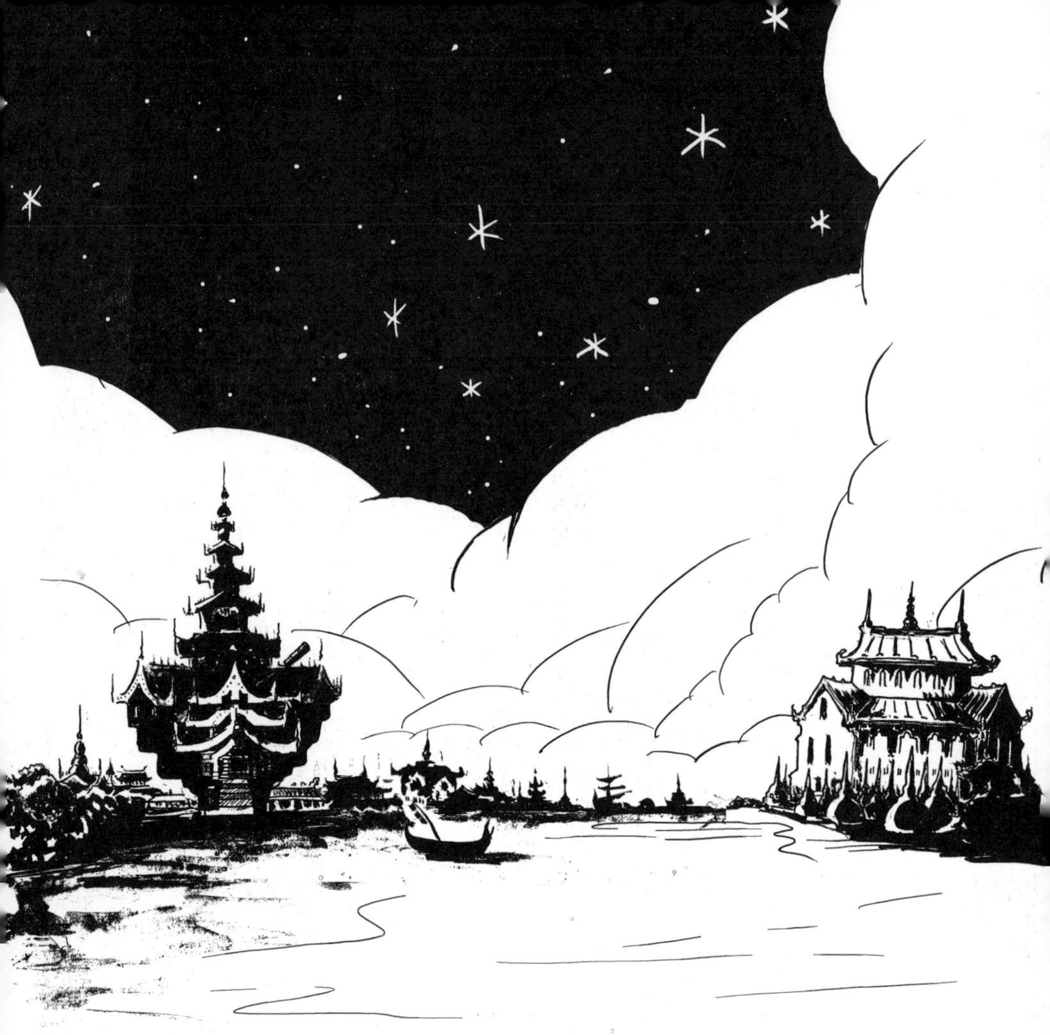

after the rain

(the origin of the rainbow)

Jose Pimienta

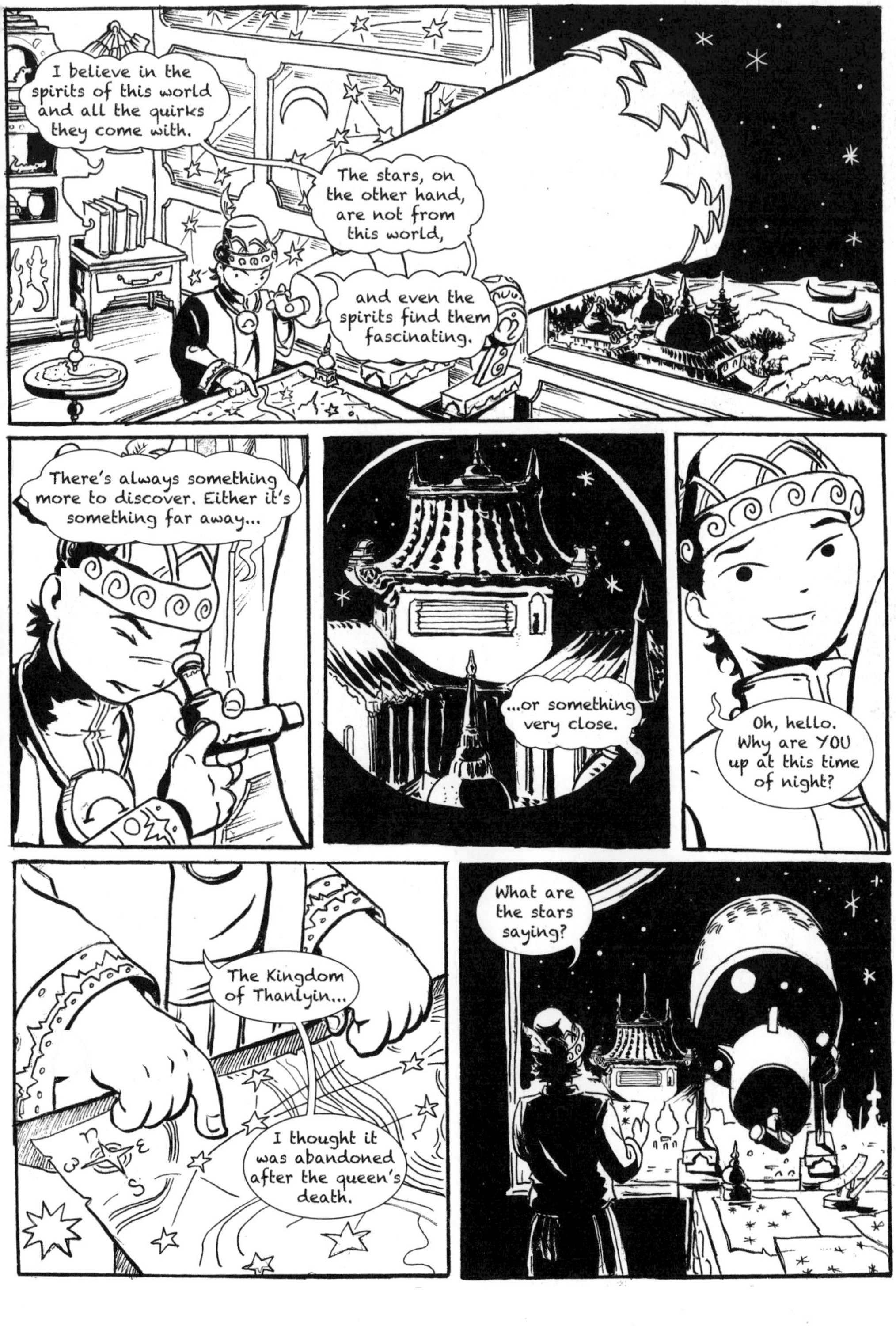
I believe in the spirits of this world and all the quirks they come with.
The stars, on the other hand, are not from this world,
and even the spirits find them fascinating.
There's always something more to discover. Either it's something far away...
...or something very close.
Oh, hello. Why are YOU up at this time of night?
The Kingdom of Thanlyin...
I thought it was abandoned after the queen's death.
What are the stars saying?

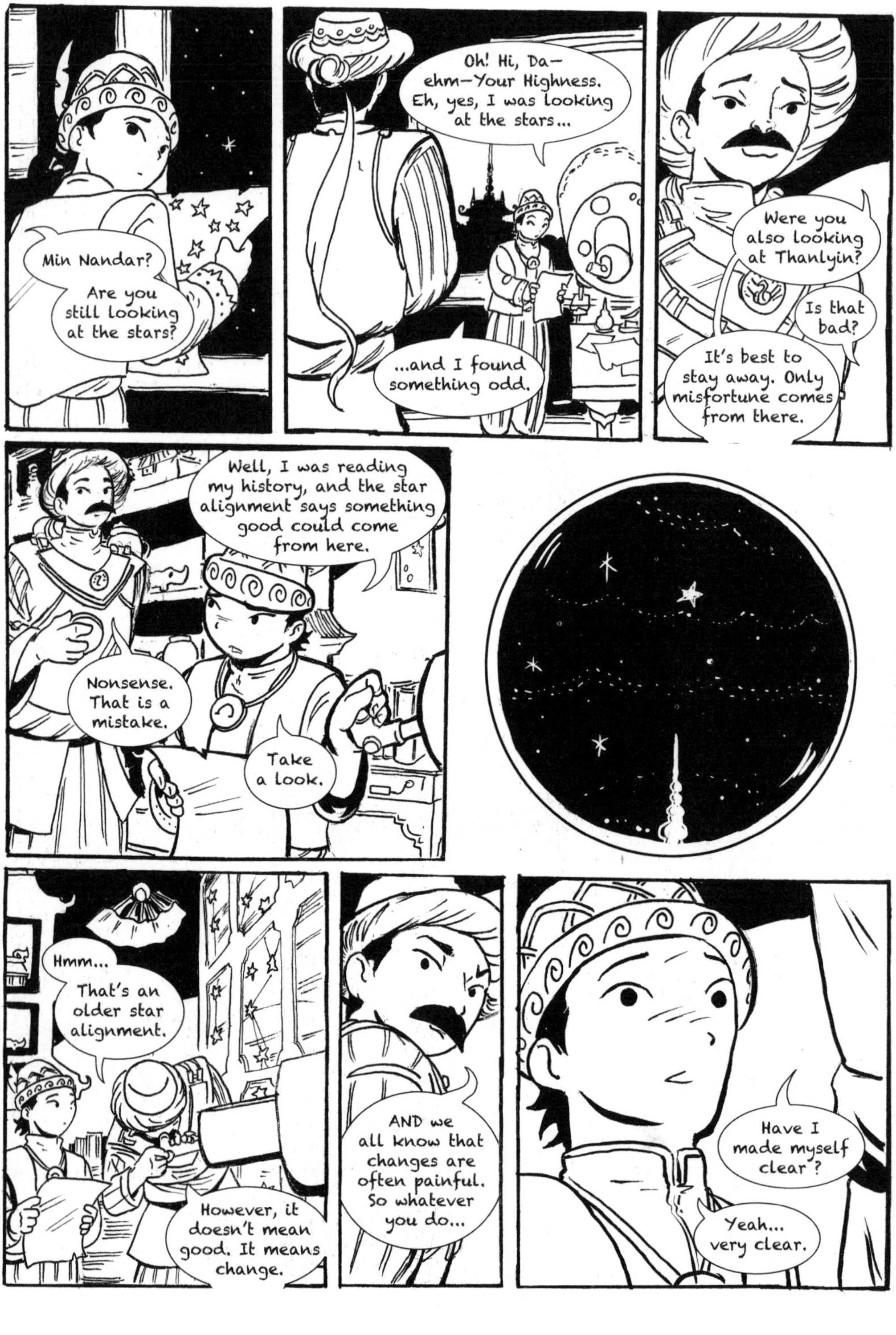
Min Nandar?
Are you still looking at the stars?
Oh! Hi, Da—ehm—Your Highness. Eh, yes, I was looking at the stars...
...and I found something odd.
Were you also looking at Thanlyin?
Is that bad?
It's best to stay away. Only misfortune comes from there.
Well, I was reading my history, and the star alignment says something good could come from here.
Nonsense. That is a mistake.
Take a look.
Hmm...
That's an older star alignment.
However, it doesn't mean good. It means change.
AND we all know that changes are often painful. So whatever you do...
Have I made myself clear?
Yeah... very clear.

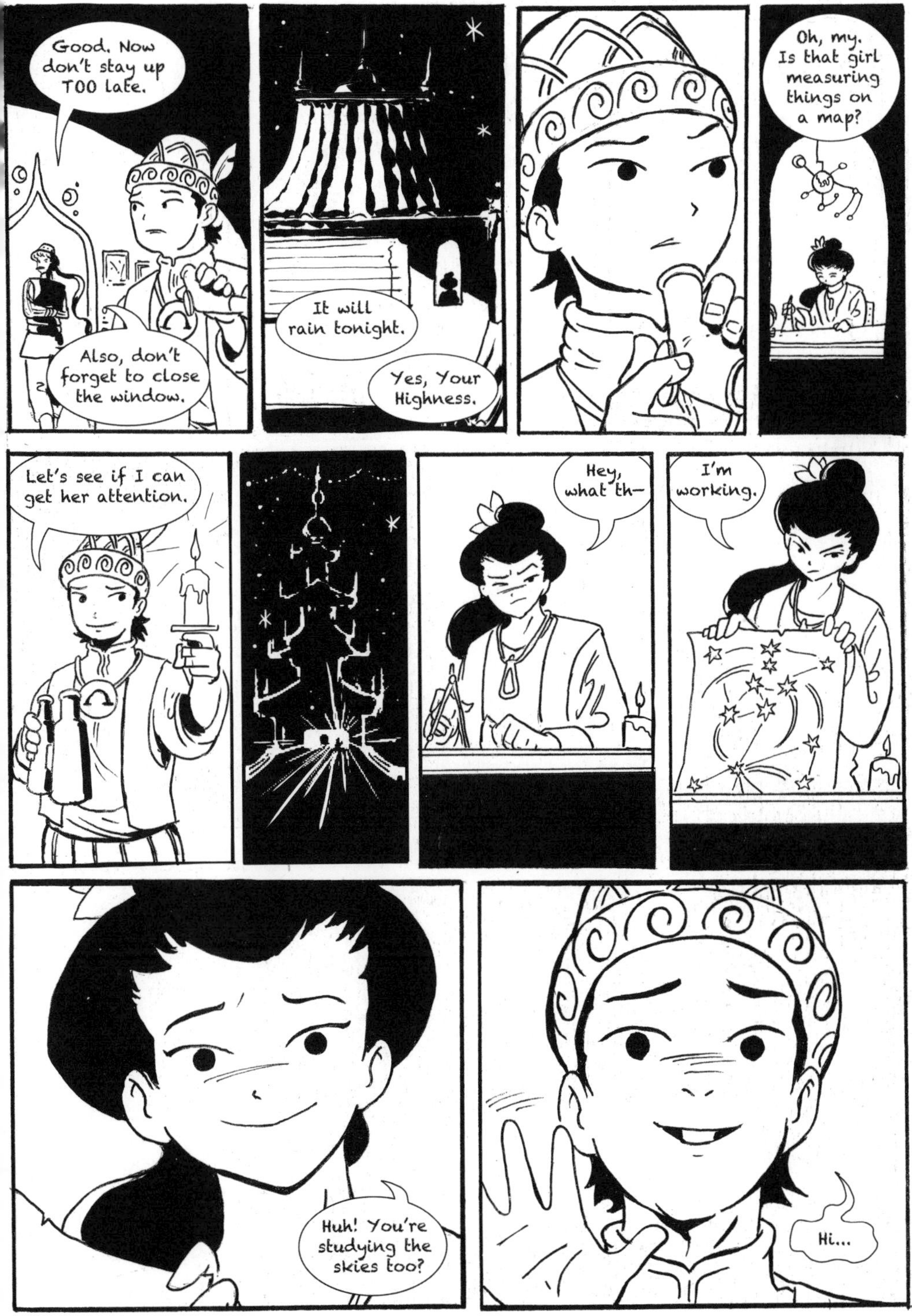
Good. Now don't stay up TOO late.
Also, don't forget to close the window.
It will rain tonight.
Yes, Your Highness.
Oh, my. Is that girl measuring things on a map?
Let's see if I can get her attention.
Hey, what th—
I'm working.
Huh! You're studying the skies too?
Hi...

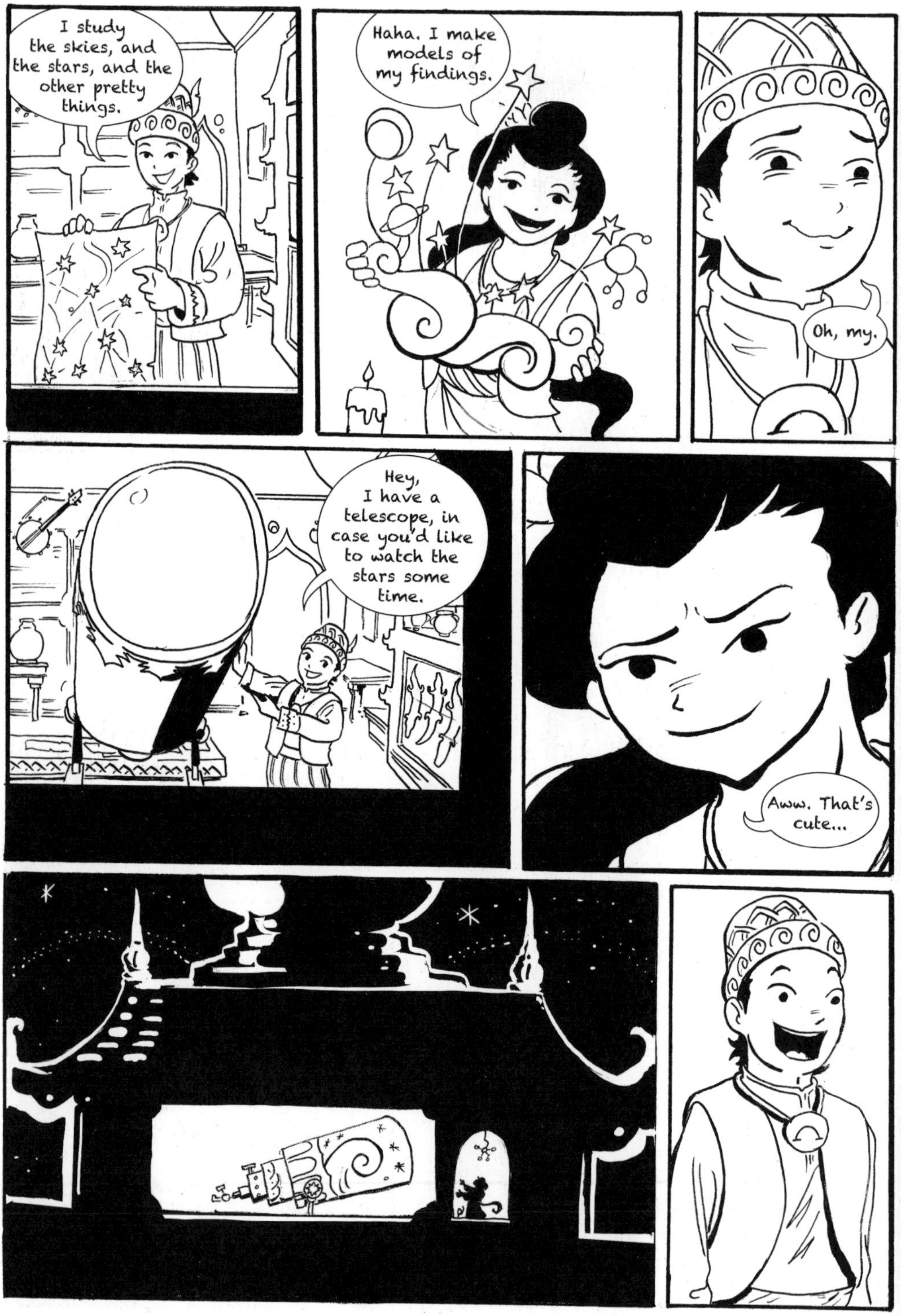
I study the skies, and the stars, and the other pretty things.
Haha. I make models of my findings.
Oh, my.
Hey, I have a telescope, in case you'd like to watch the stars some time.
Aww. That's cute...

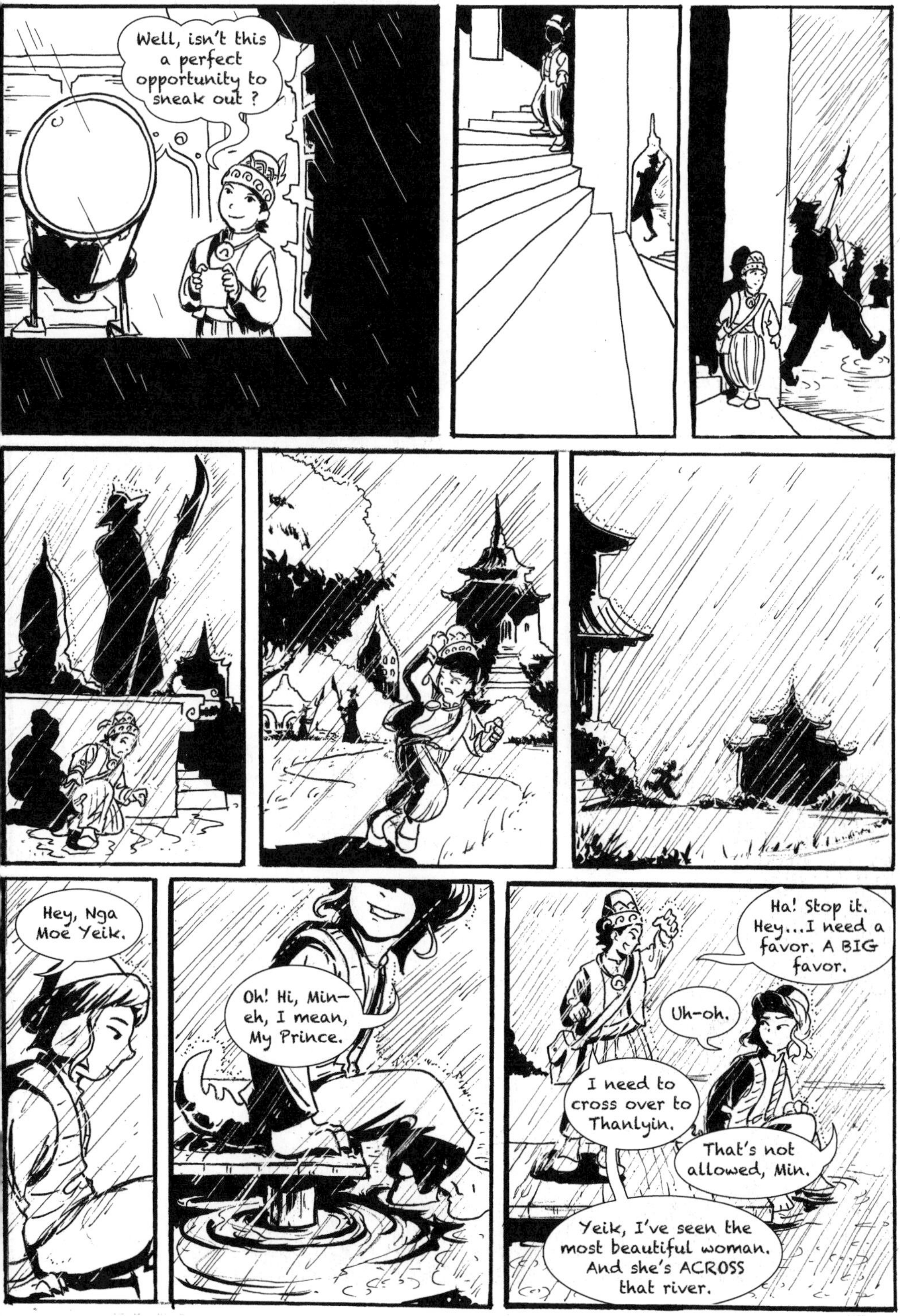
Well, isn't this a perfect opportunity to sneak out ?
Hey, Nga Moe Yeik.
Oh! Hi, Min-eh, I mean, My Prince.
Ha! Stop it. Hey...I need a favor. A BIG favor.
Uh-oh.
I need to cross over to Thanlyin.
That's not allowed, Min.
Yeik, I've seen the most beautiful woman. And she's ACROSS that river.

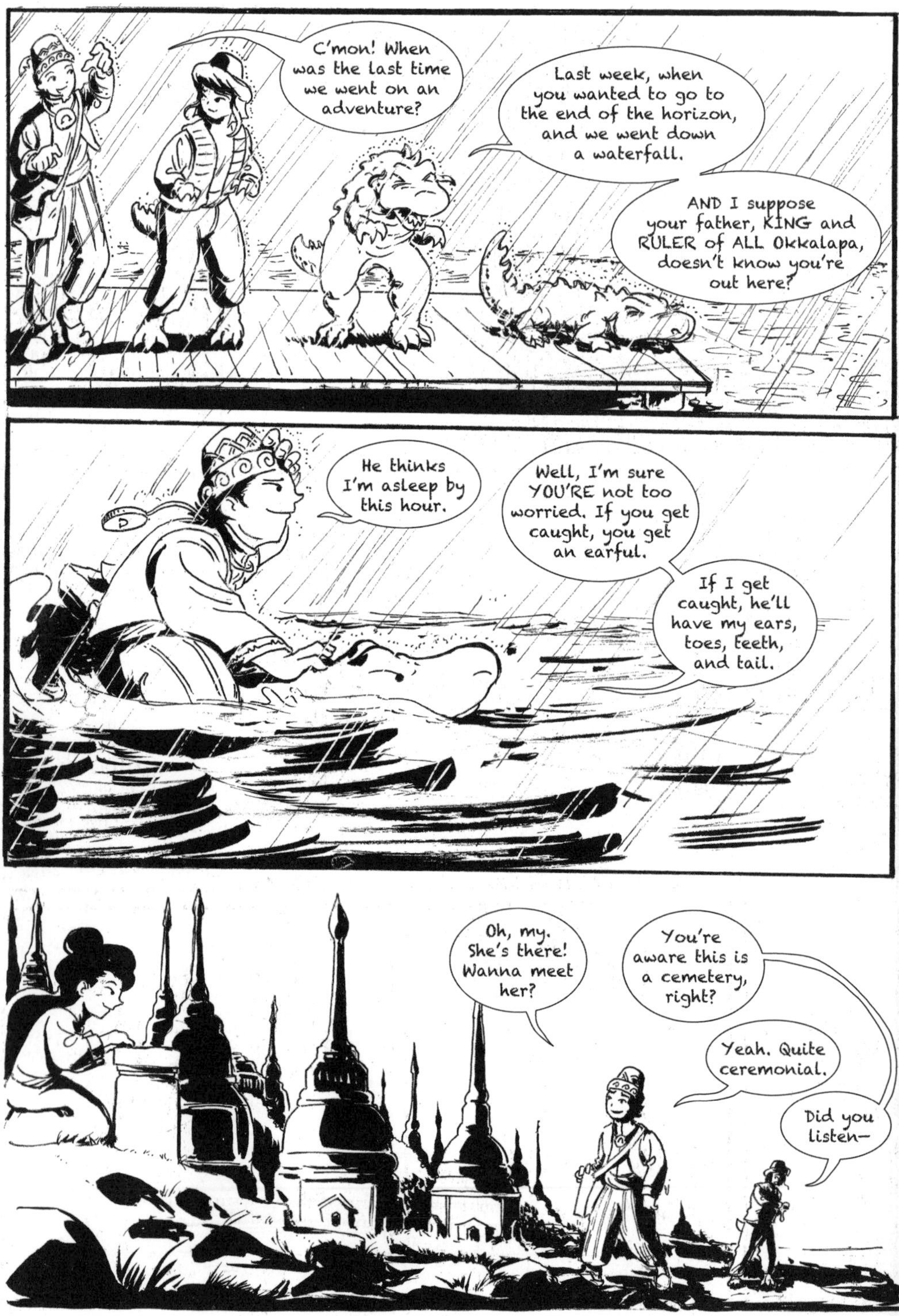
C'mon! When was the last time we went on an adventure?
Last week, when you wanted to go to the end of the horizon, and we went down a waterfall.
AND I suppose your father, KING and RULER of ALL Okkalapa, doesn't know you're out here?
He thinks I'm asleep by this hour.
Well, I'm sure YOU'RE not too worried. If you get caught, you get an earful.
If I get caught, he'll have my ears, toes, teeth, and tail.
Oh, my. She's there! Wanna meet her?
You're aware this is a cemetery, right?
Yeah. Quite ceremonial.
Did you listen—

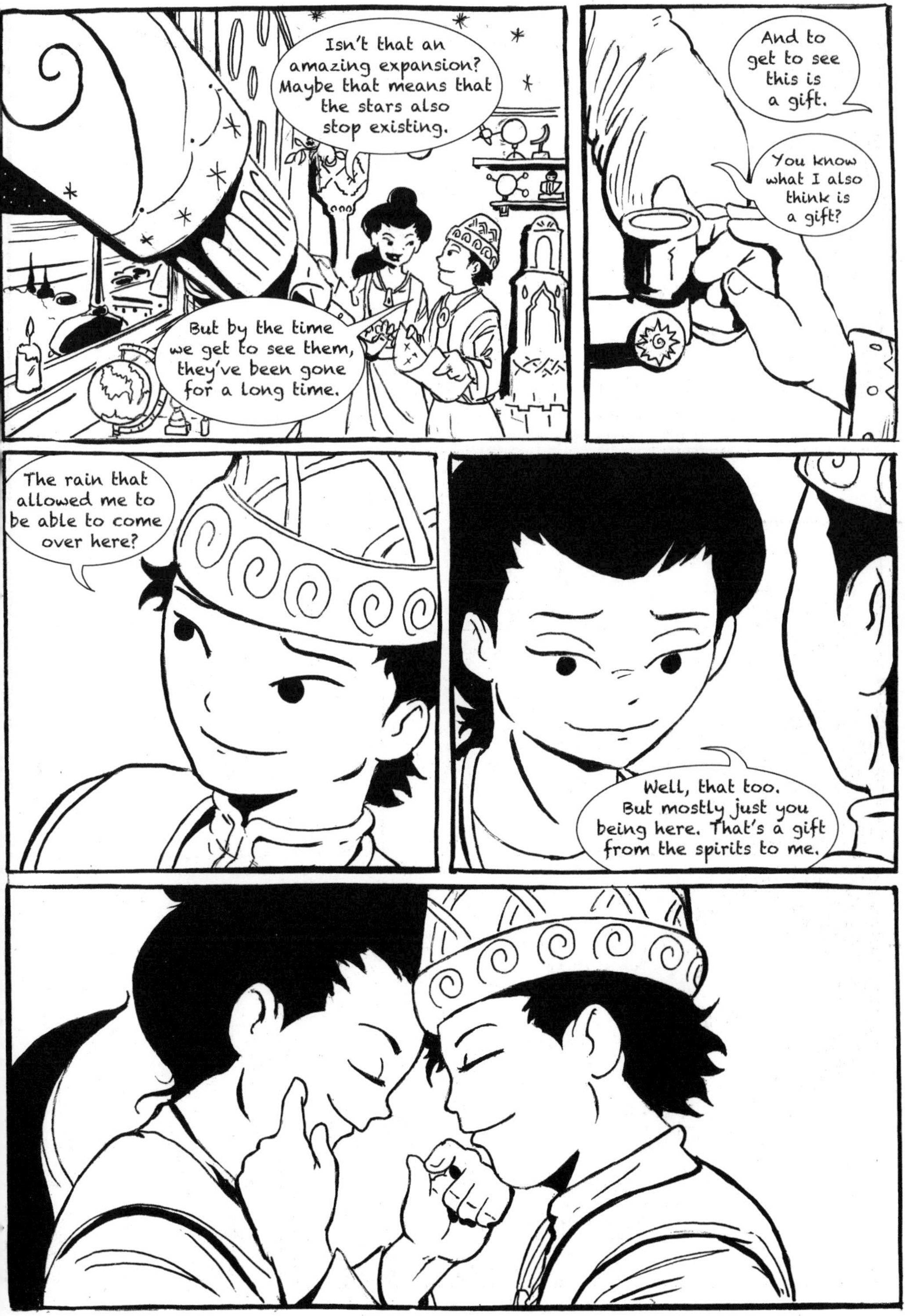
Isn't that an amazing expansion? Maybe that means that the stars also stop existing.
But by the time we get to see them, they've been gone for a long time.
And to get to see this is a gift.
You know what I also think is a gift?
The rain that allowed me to be able to come over here?
Well, that too. But mostly just you being here. That's a gift from the spirits to me.

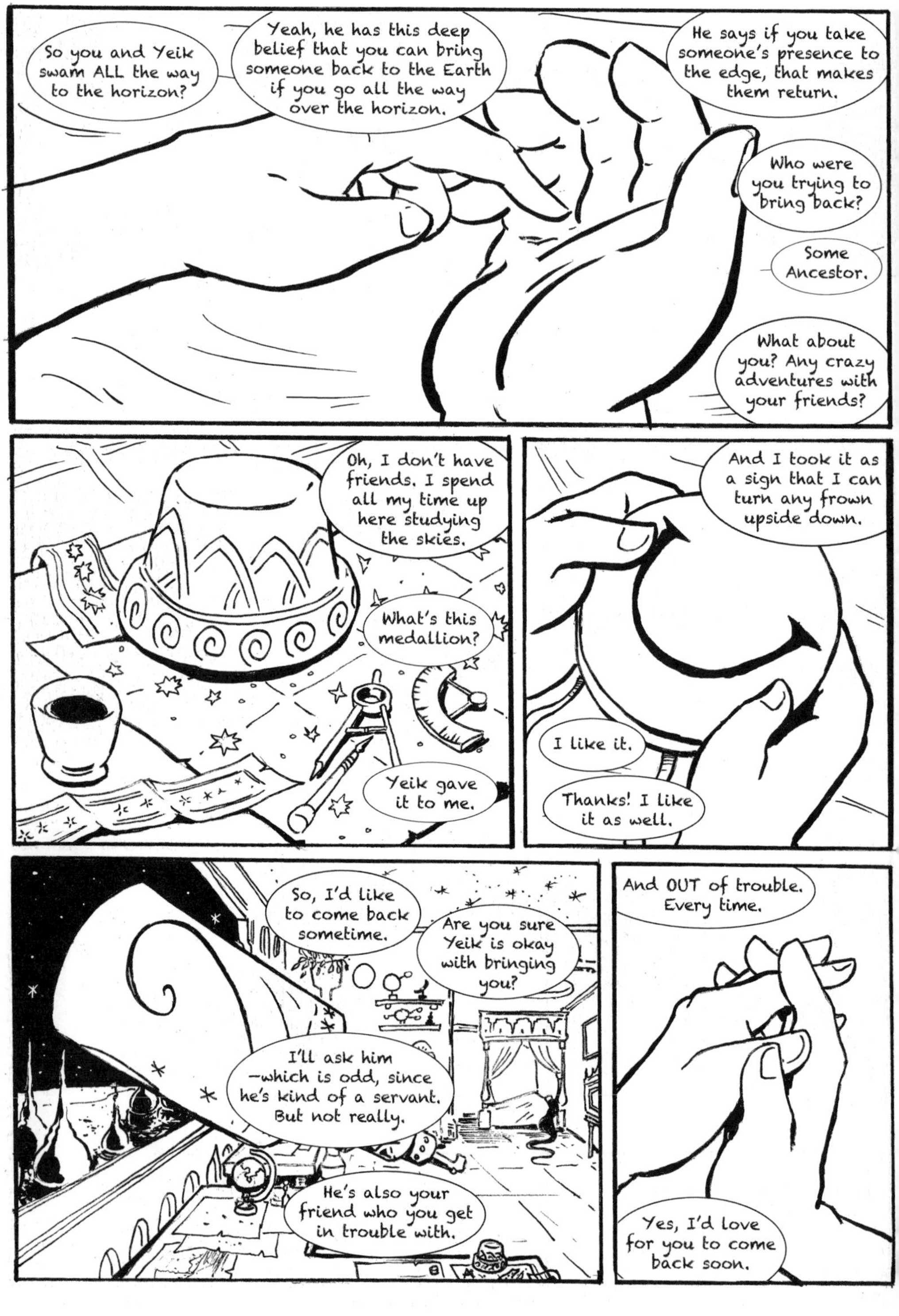
So you and Yeik swam ALL the way to the horizon?
Yeah, he has this deep belief that you can bring someone back to the Earth if you go all the way over the horizon.
He says if you take someone's presence to the edge, that makes them return.
Who were you trying to bring back?
Some Ancestor.
What about you? Any crazy adventures with your friends?
Oh, I don't have friends. I spend all my time up here studying the skies.
What's this medallion?
Yeik gave it to me.
And I took it as a sign that I can turn any frown upside down.
I like it.
Thanks! I like it as well.
So, I'd like to come back sometime.
Are you sure Yeik is okay with bringing you?
I'll ask him —which is odd, since he's kind of a servant. But not really.
He's also your friend who you get in trouble with.
And OUT of trouble. Every time.
Yes, I'd love for you to come back soon.

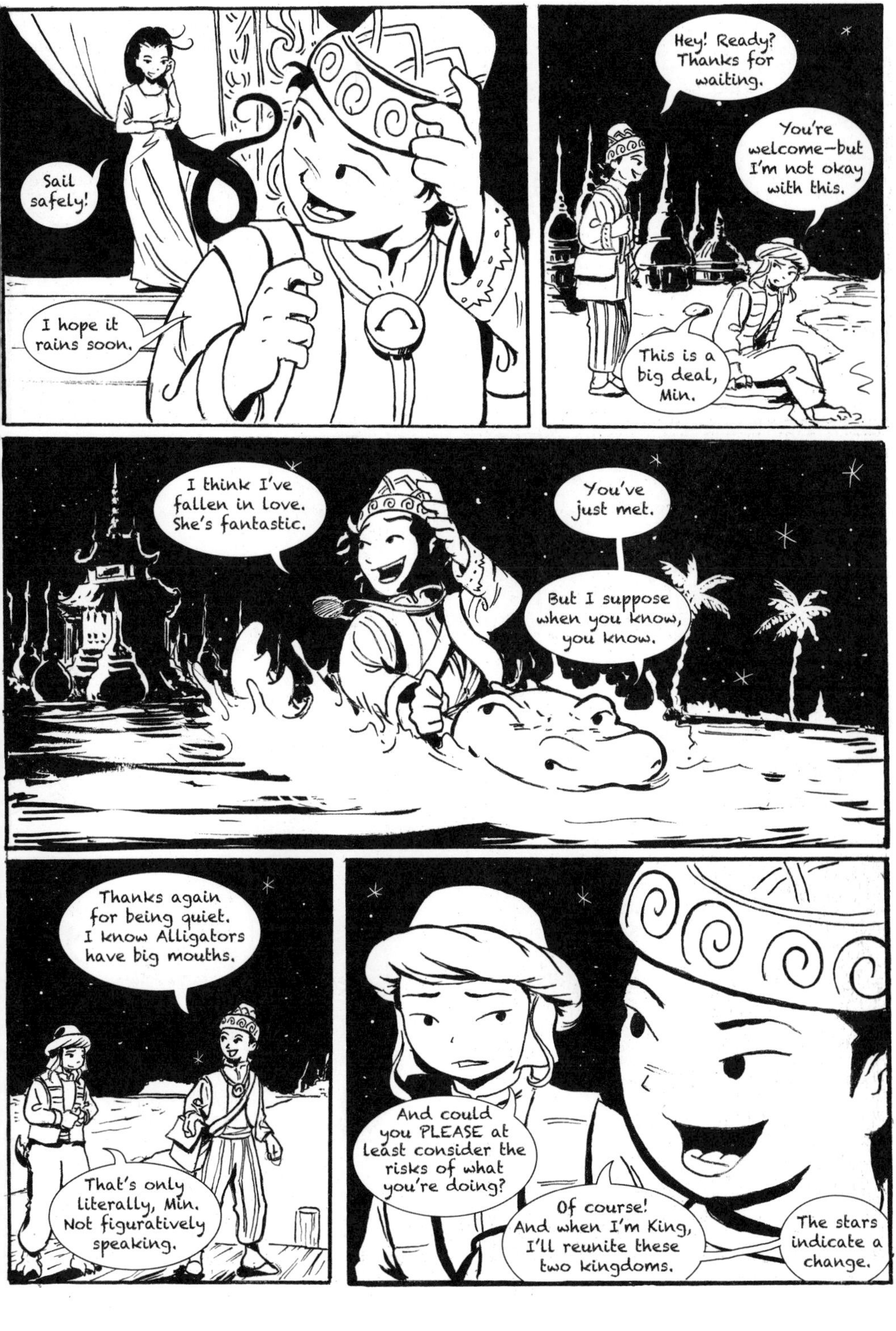
Sail safely!
I hope it rains soon.
Hey! Ready? Thanks for waiting.
You're welcome—but I'm not okay with this.
This is a big deal, Min.
I think I've fallen in love. She's fantastic.
You've just met.
But I suppose when you know, you know.
Thanks again for being quiet. I know Alligators have big mouths.
That's only literally, Min. Not figuratively speaking.
And could you PLEASE at least consider the risks of what you're doing?
Of course! And when I'm King, I'll reunite these two kingdoms.
The stars indicate a change.

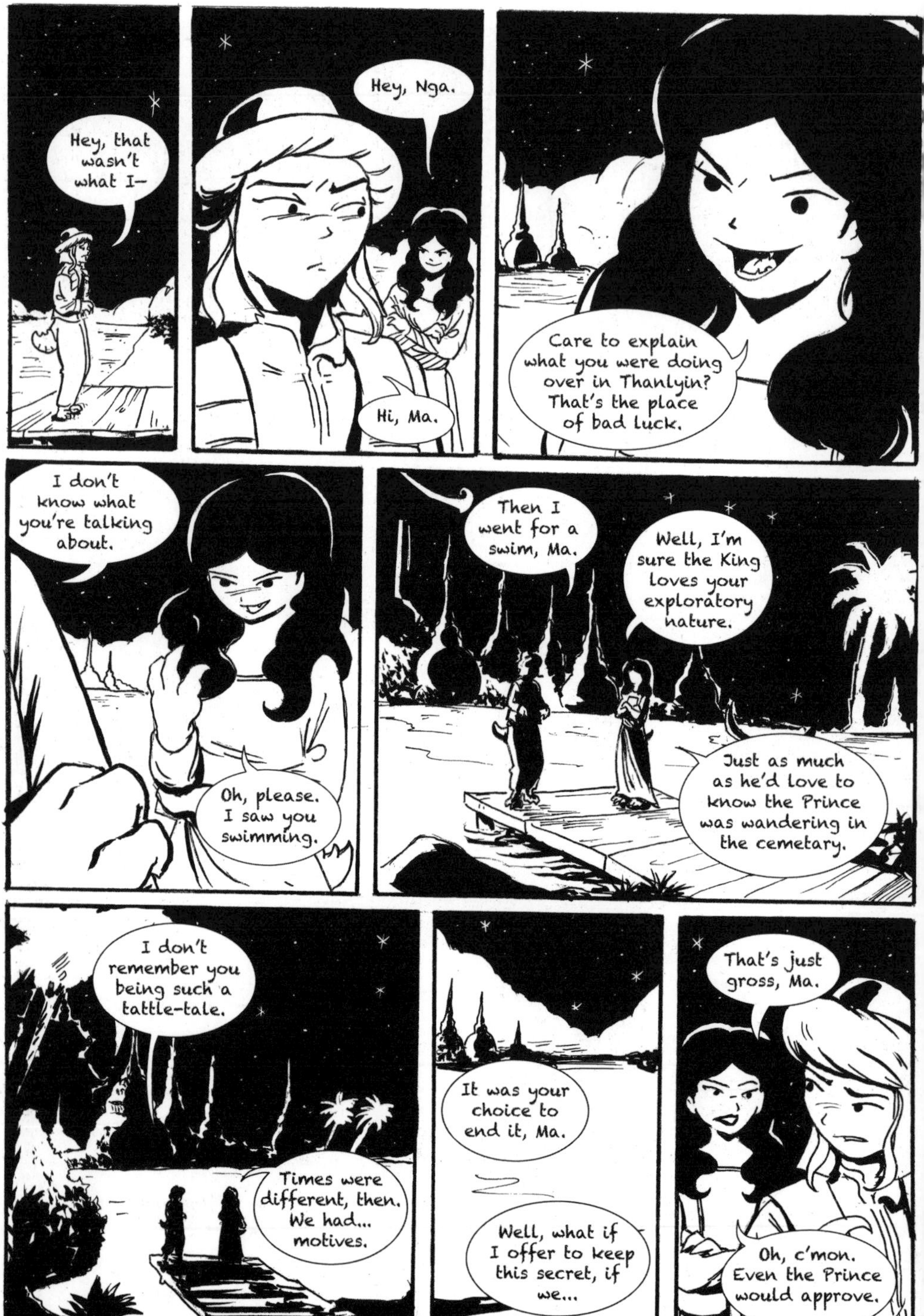
Hey, that wasn't what I—
Hey, Nga.
Hi, Ma.
Care to explain what you were doing over in Thanlyin? That's the place of bad luck.
I don't know what you're talking about.
Oh, please. I saw you swimming.
Then I went for a swim, Ma.
Well, I'm sure the King loves your exploratory nature.
Just as much as he'd love to know the Prince was wandering in the cemetary.
I don't remember you being such a tattle-tale.
Times were different, then. We had... motives.
It was your choice to end it, Ma.
Well, what if I offer to keep this secret, if we...
That's just gross, Ma.
Oh, c'mon. Even the Prince would approve.

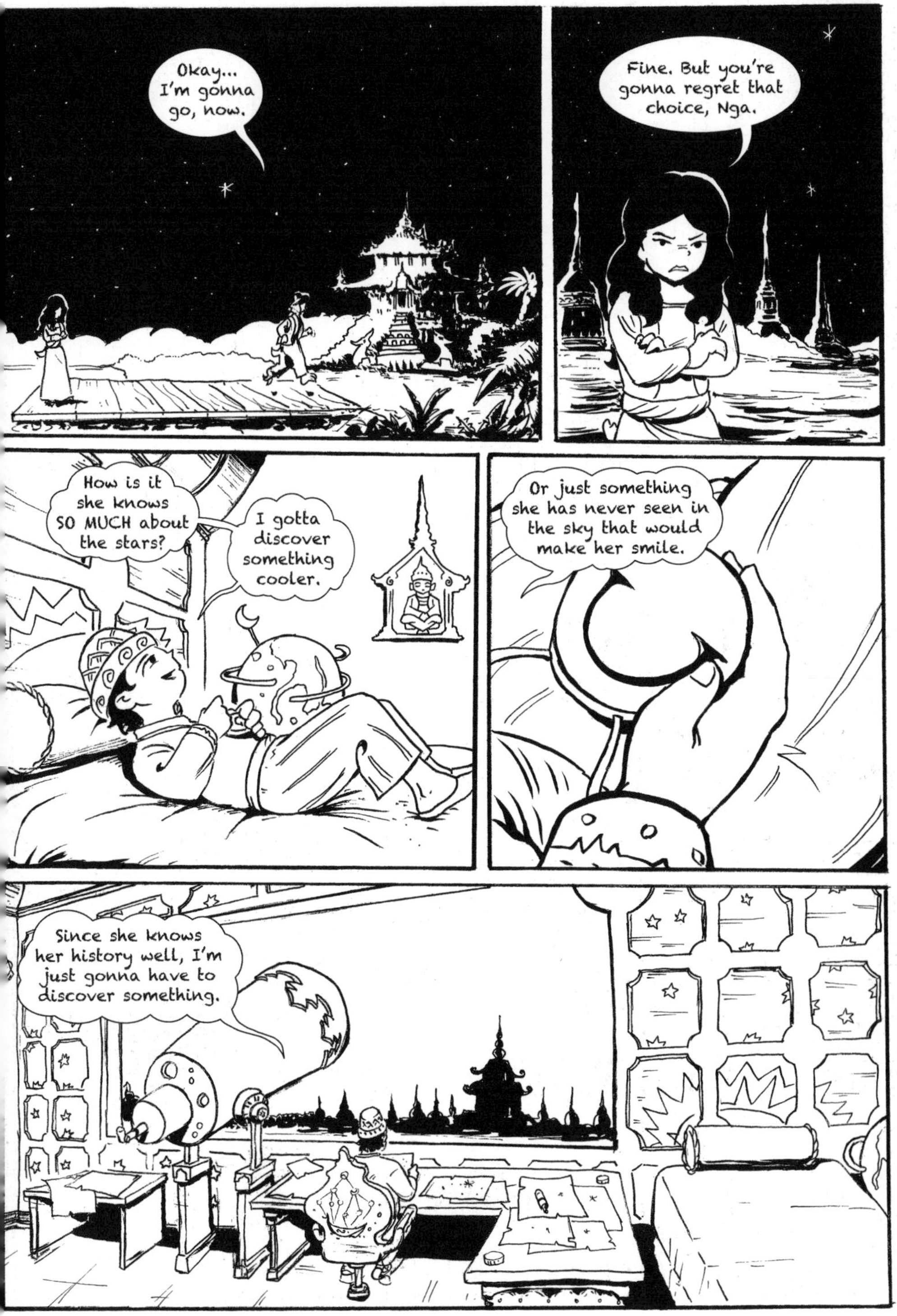

Okay... I'm gonna go, now.
Fine. But you're gonna regret that choice, Nga.
How is it she knows SO MUCH about the stars?
I gotta discover something cooler.
Or just something she has never seen in the sky that would make her smile.
Since she knows her history well, I'm just gonna have to discover something.

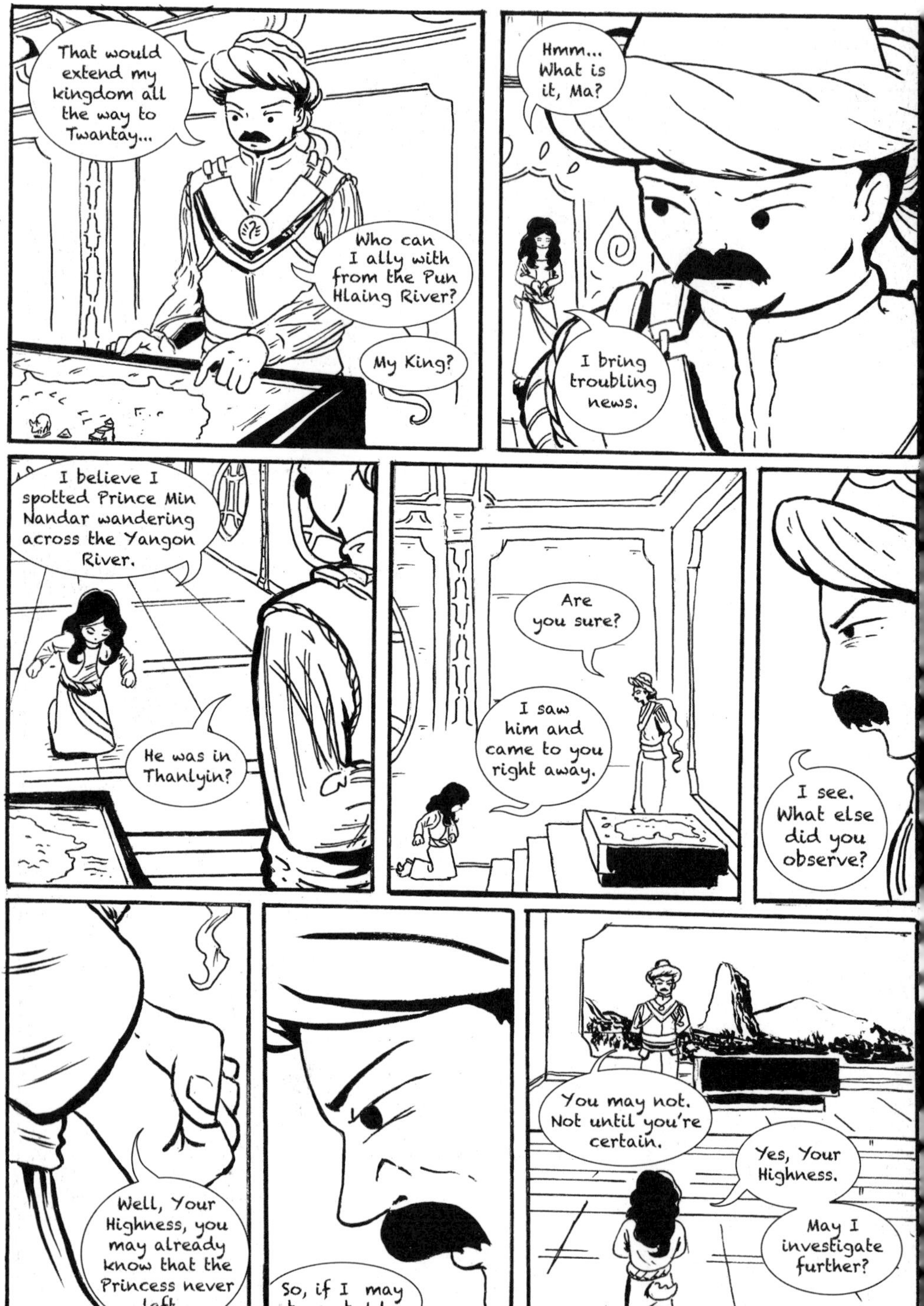
That would extend my kingdom all the way to Twantay...
Who can I ally with from the Pun Hlaing River?
My King?
Hmm... What is it, Ma?
I bring troubling news.
I believe I spotted Prince Min Nandar wandering across the Yangon River.
He was in Thanlyin?
Are you sure?
I saw him and came to you right away.
I see. What else did you observe?
Well, Your Highness, you may already know that the Princess never left...
So, if I may be so bold—
You may not. Not until you're certain.
Yes, Your Highness.
May I investigate further?

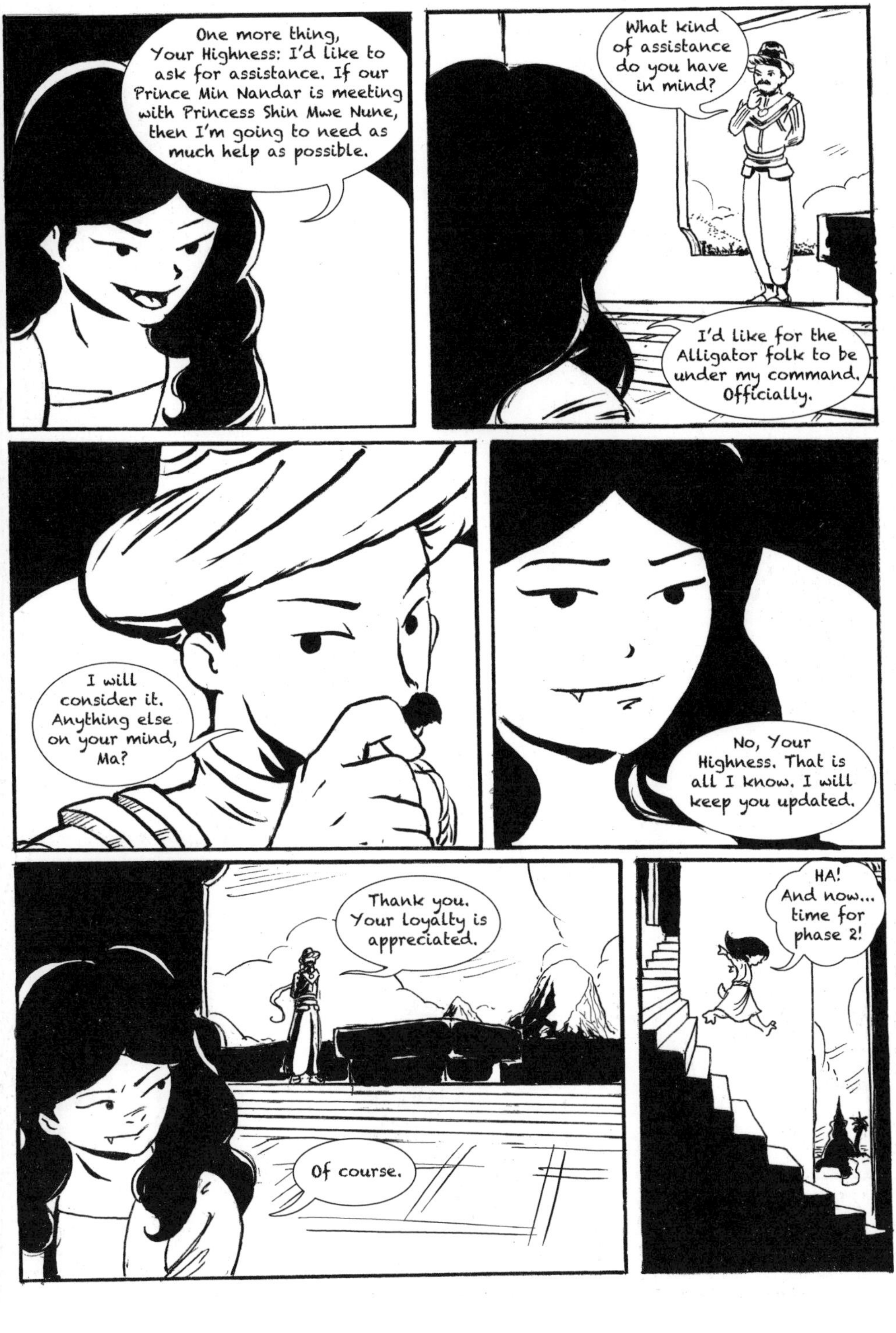
One more thing, Your Highness: I'd like to ask for assistance. If our Prince Min Nandar is meeting with Princess Shin Mwe Nune, then I'm going to need as much help as possible.
What kind of assistance do you have in mind?
I'd like for the Alligator folk to be under my command. Officially.
I will consider it. Anything else on your mind, Ma?
No, Your Highness. That is all I know. I will keep you updated.
Thank you. Your loyalty is appreciated.
Of course.
HA! And now... time for phase 2!

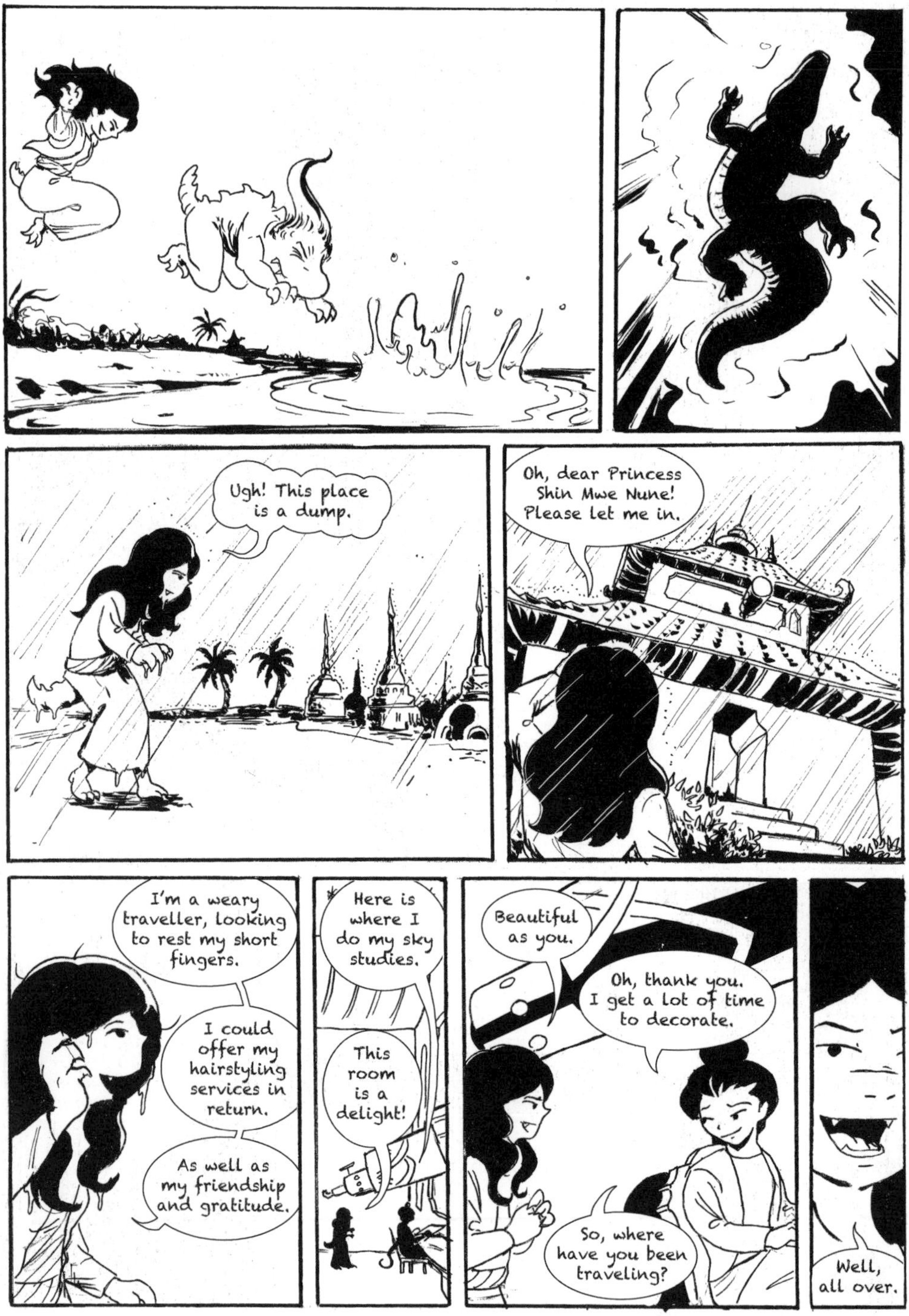
Ugh! This place is a dump.
Oh, dear Princess Shin Mwe Nune! Please let me in.
I'm a weary traveller, looking to rest my short fingers.
I could offer my hairstyling services in return.
As well as my friendship and gratitude.
Here is where I do my sky studies.
This room is a delight!
Beautiful as you.
Oh, thank you. I get a lot of time to decorate.
So, where have you been traveling?
Well, all over.

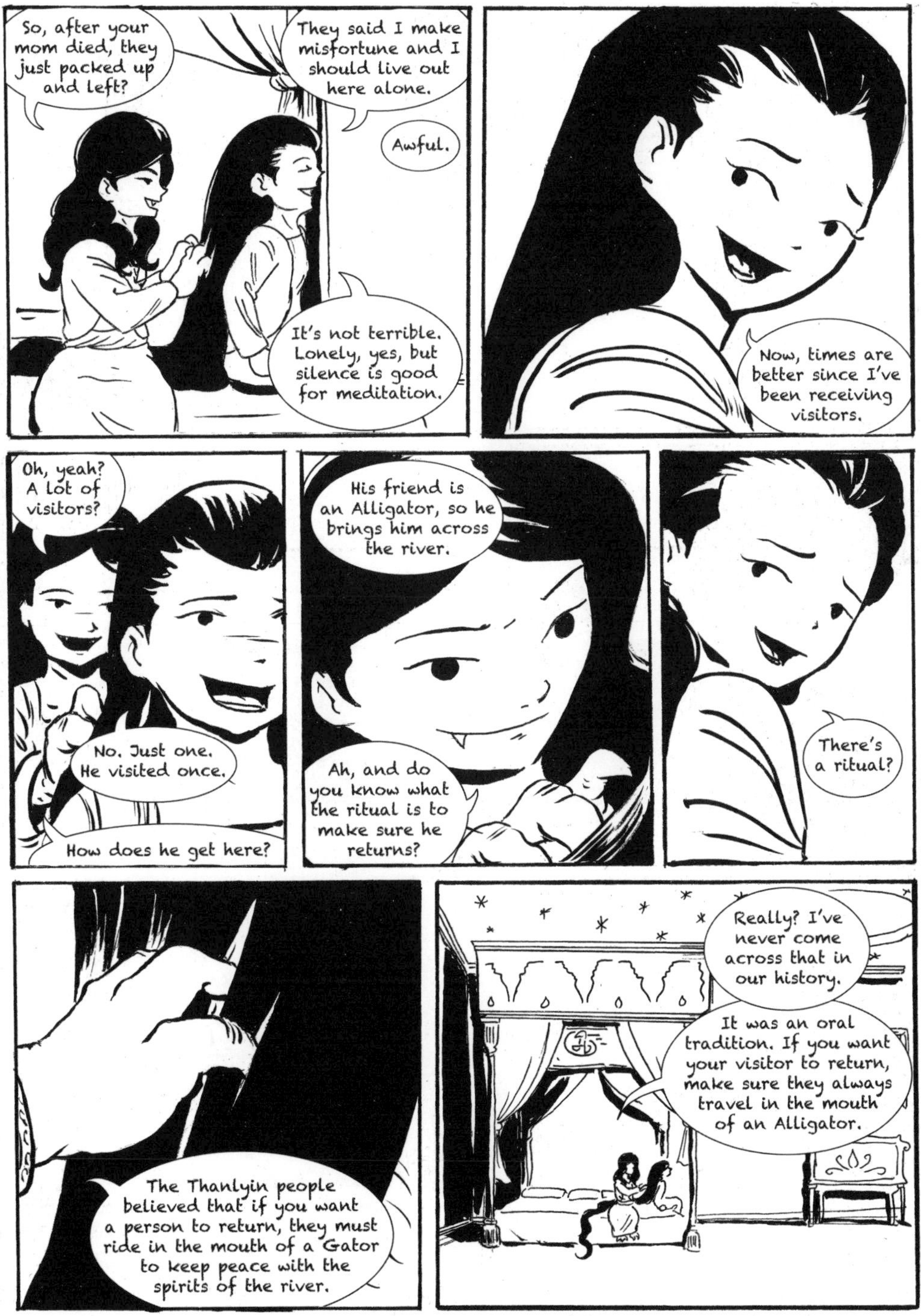
So, after your mom died, they just packed up and left?
They said I make misfortune and I should live out here alone.
Awful.
It's not terrible. Lonely, yes, but silence is good for meditation.
Now, times are better since I've been receiving visitors.
Oh, yeah? A lot of visitors?
No. Just one. He visited once.
How does he get here?
His friend is an Alligator, so he brings him across the river.
Ah, and do you know what the ritual is to make sure he returns?
There's a ritual?
The Thanlyin people believed that if you want a person to return, they must ride in the mouth of a Gator to keep peace with the spirits of the river.
Really? I've never come across that in our history.
It was an oral tradition. If you want your visitor to return, make sure they always travel in the mouth of an Alligator.

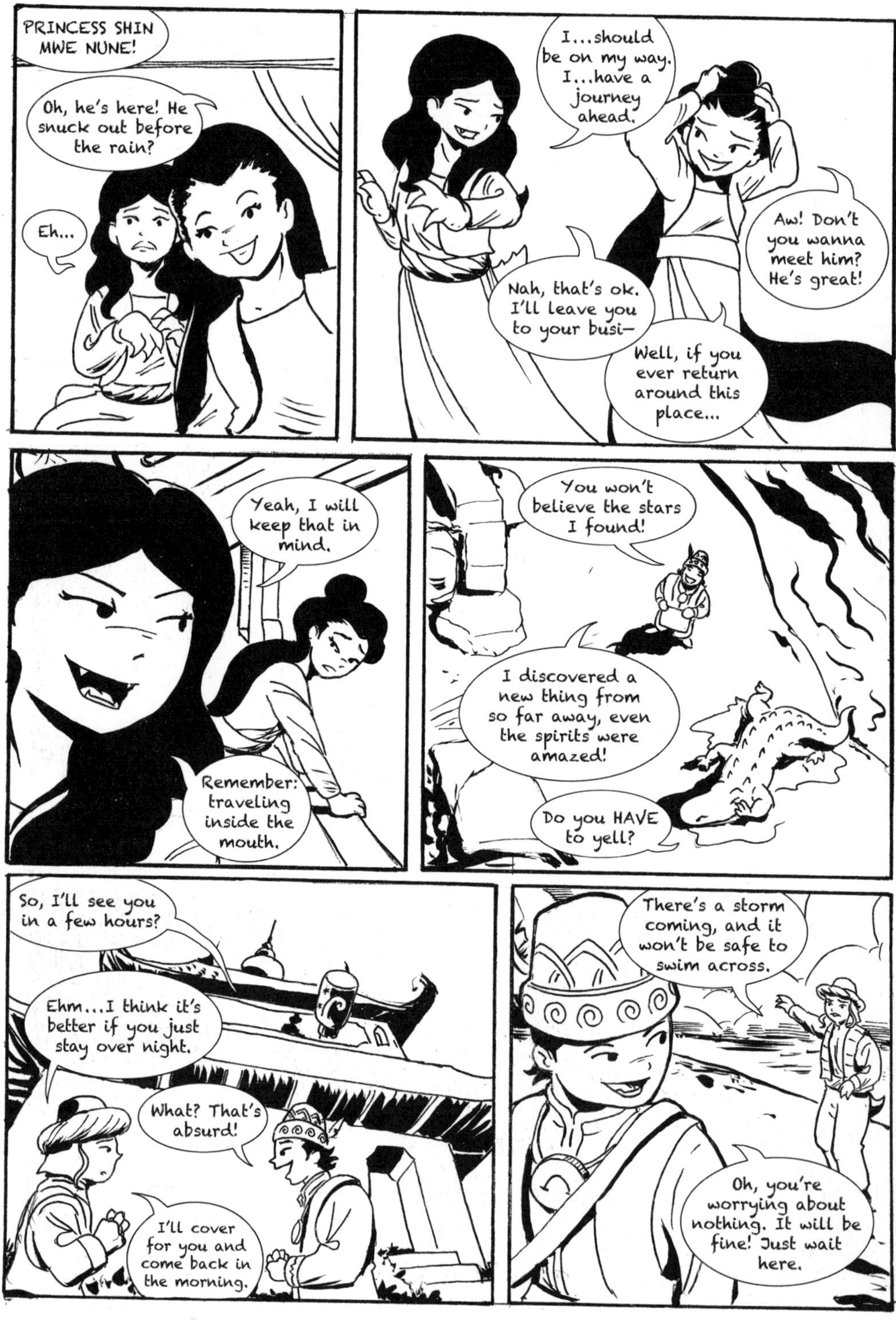
PRINCESS SHIN MWE NUNE!
Oh, he's here! He snuck out before the rain?
Eh...
I...should be on my way. I...have a journey ahead.
Aw! Don't you wanna meet him? He's great!
Nah, that's ok. I'll leave you to your busi—
Well, if you ever return around this place...
Yeah, I will keep that in mind.
Remember: traveling inside the mouth.
You won't believe the stars I found!
I discovered a new thing from so far away, even the spirits were amazed!
Do you HAVE to yell?
So, I'll see you in a few hours?
Ehm...I think it's better if you just stay over night.
What? That's absurd!
I'll cover for you and come back in the morning.
There's a storm coming, and it won't be safe to swim across.
Oh, you're worrying about nothing. It will be fine! Just wait here.

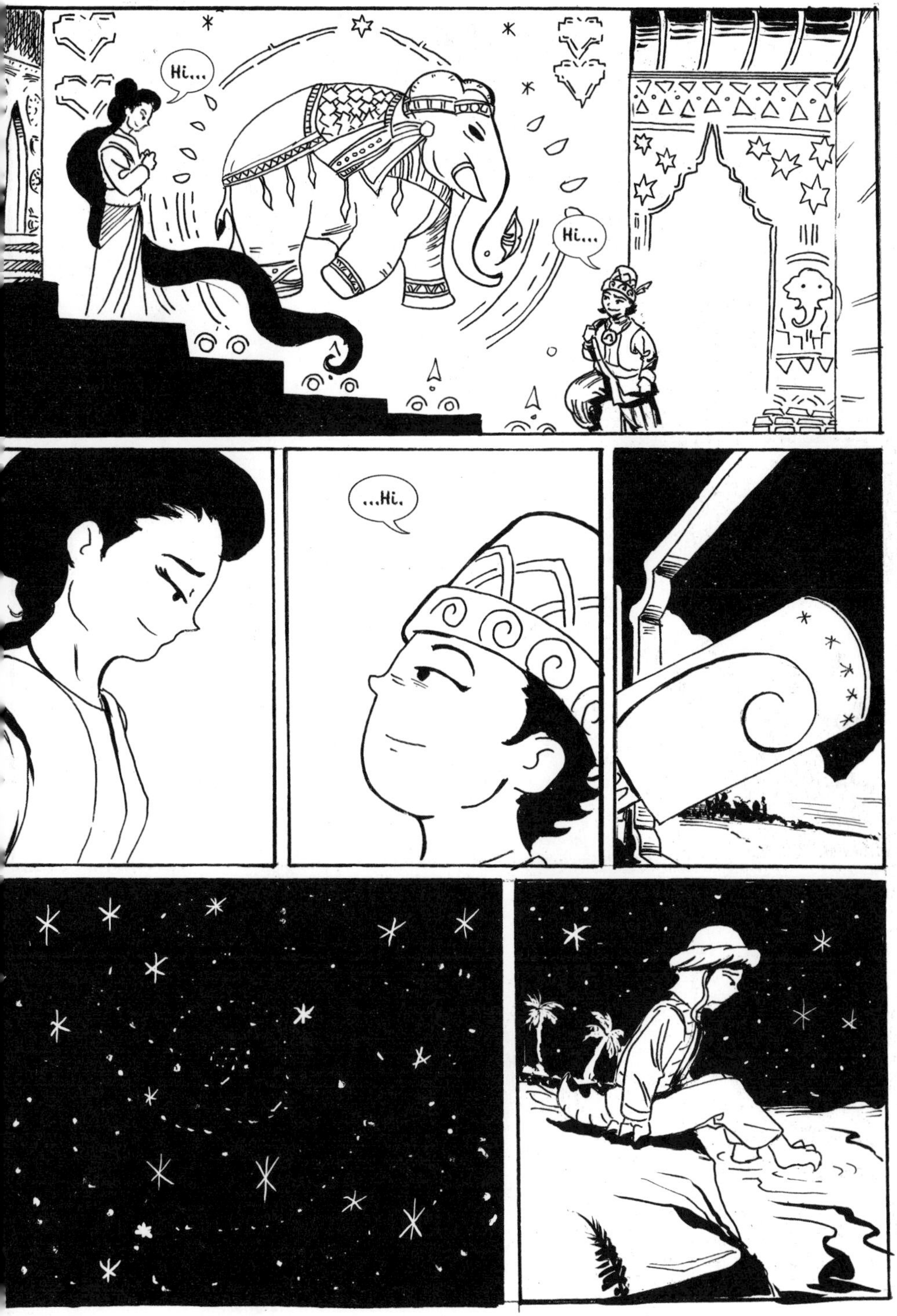
Hi...
Hi...
...Hi.

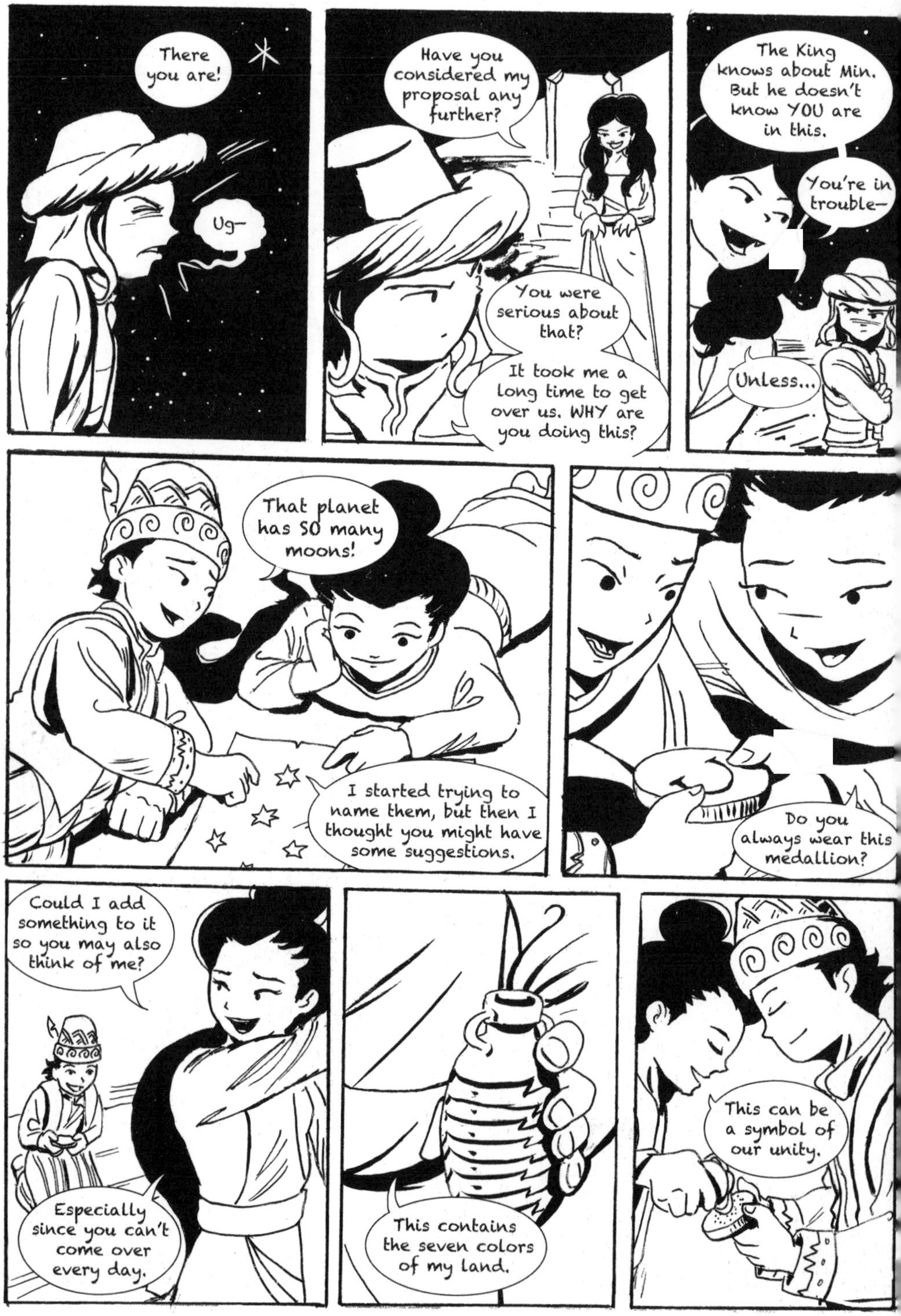
There you are!
Ug-
Have you considered my proposal any further?
You were serious about that?
It took me a long time to get over us. WHY are you doing this?
The King knows about Min. But he doesn't know YOU are in this.
You're in trouble-
Unless...
That planet has SO many moons!
I started trying to name them, but then I thought you might have some suggestions.
Do you always wear this medallion?
Could I add something to it so you may also think of me?
Especially since you can't come over every day.
This contains the seven colors of my land.
This can be a symbol of our unity.

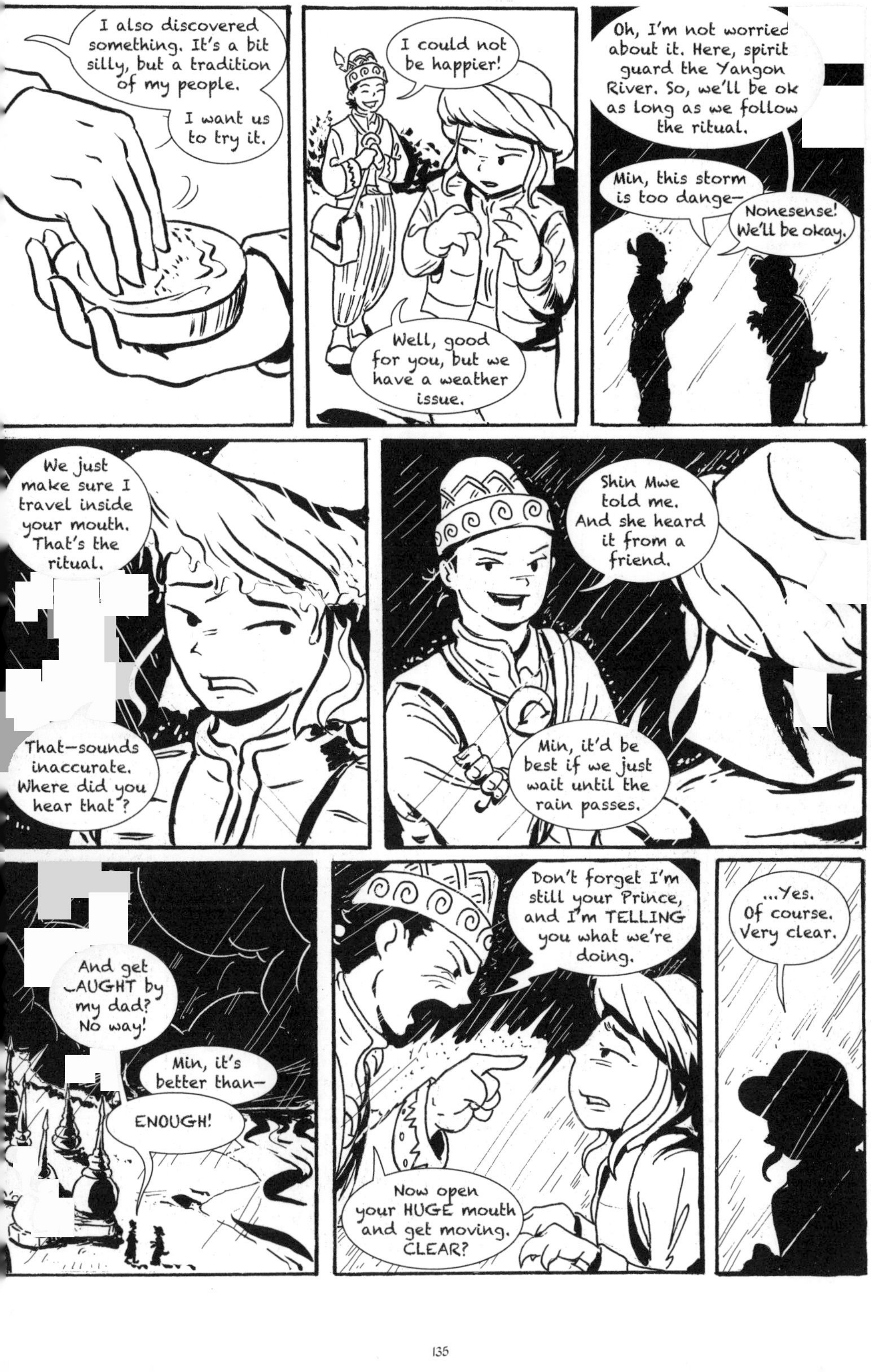
I also discovered something. It's a bit silly, but a tradition of my people.
I want us to try it.
I could not be happier!
Well, good for you, but we have a weather issue.
Oh, I'm not worried about it. Here, spirit guard the Yangon River. So, we'll be ok as long as we follow the ritual.
Min, this storm is too dange—
Nonesense! We'll be okay.
We just make sure I travel inside your mouth. That's the ritual.
That—sounds inaccurate. Where did you hear that?
Shin Mwe told me. And she heard it from a friend.
Min, it'd be best if we just wait until the rain passes.
And get AUGHT by my dad? No way!
Min, it's better than—
ENOUGH!
Don't forget I'm still your Prince, and I'm TELLING you what we're doing.
Now open your HUGE mouth and get moving. CLEAR?
...Yes. Of course. Very clear.

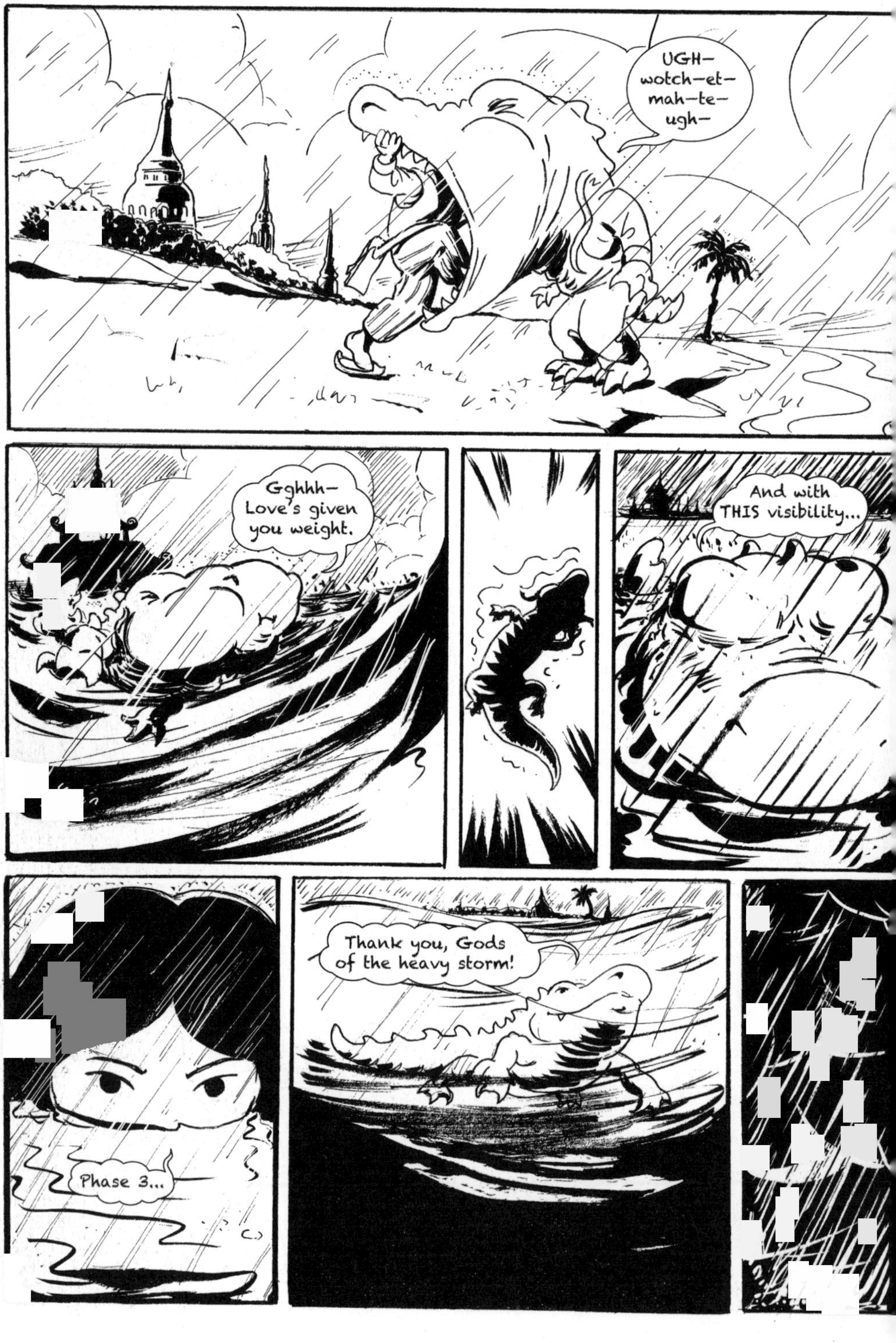
UGH—
wotch—et—
mah—te—
ugh—
Gghhh—
Love's given
you weight.
And with
THIS visibility...
Thank you, Gods
of the heavy storm!
Phase 3...

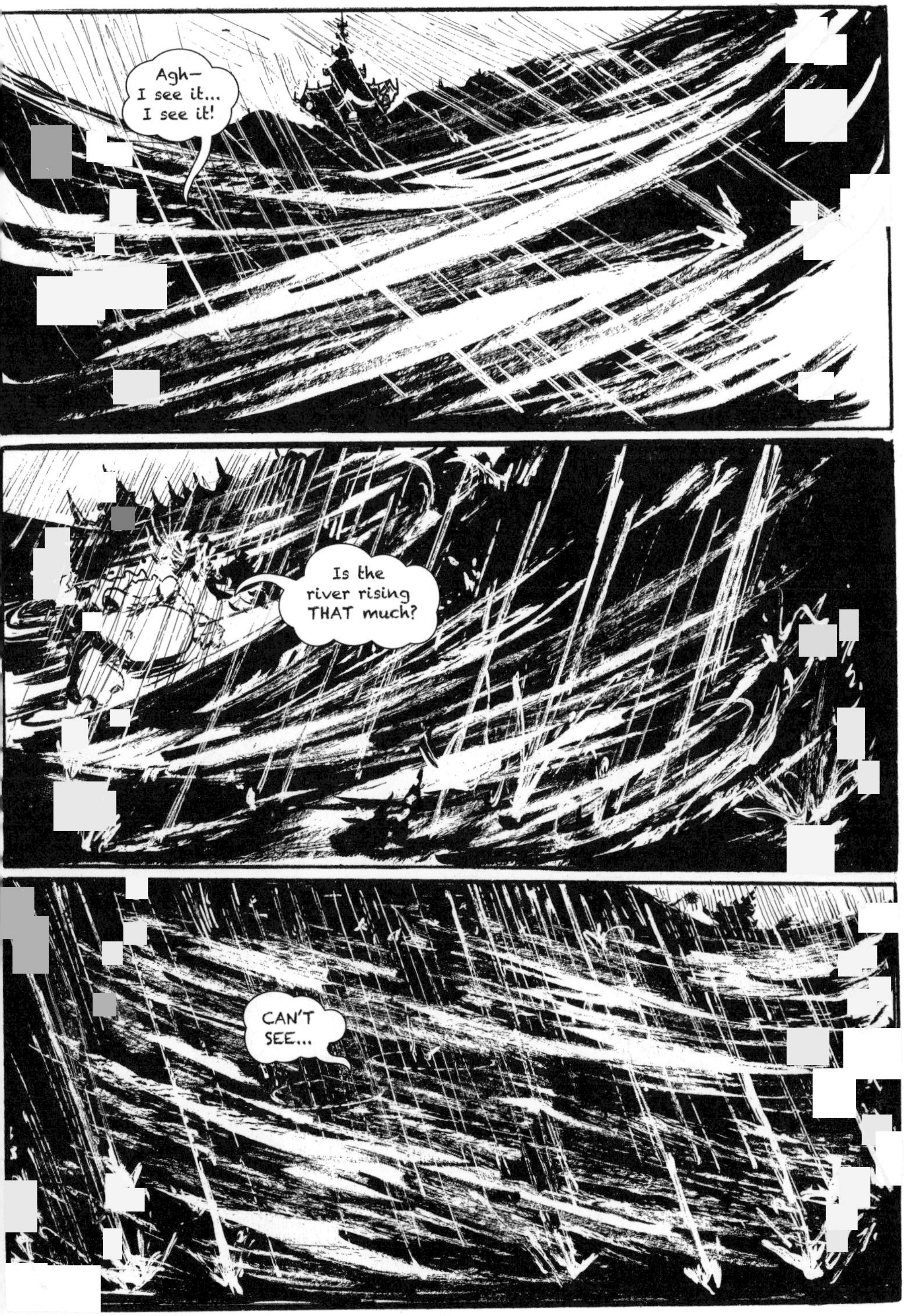
Agh— I see it... I see it!
Is the river rising THAT much?
CAN'T SEE...

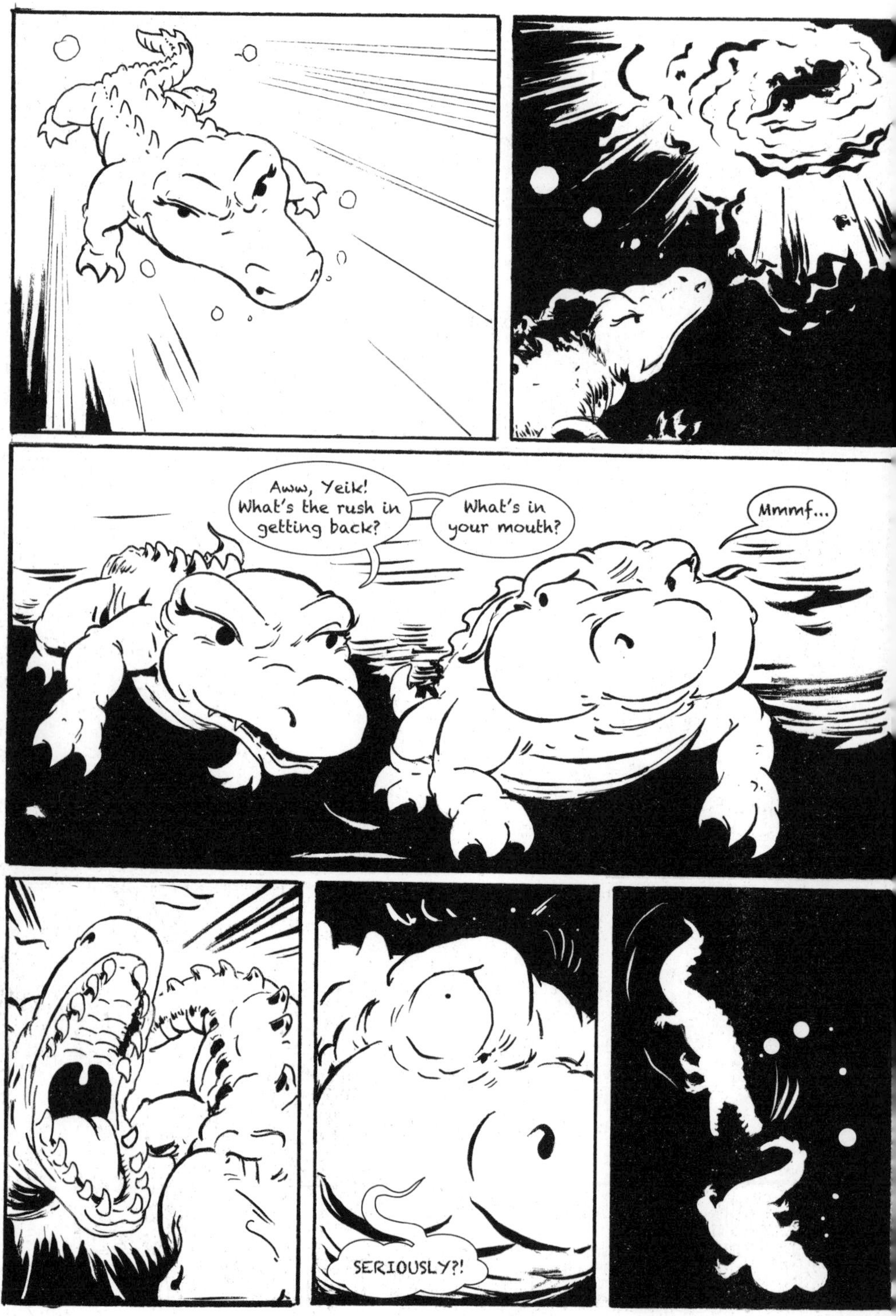

Aww, Yeik!
What's the rush in
getting back?
What's in
your mouth?
Mmmf...
SERIOUSLY?!

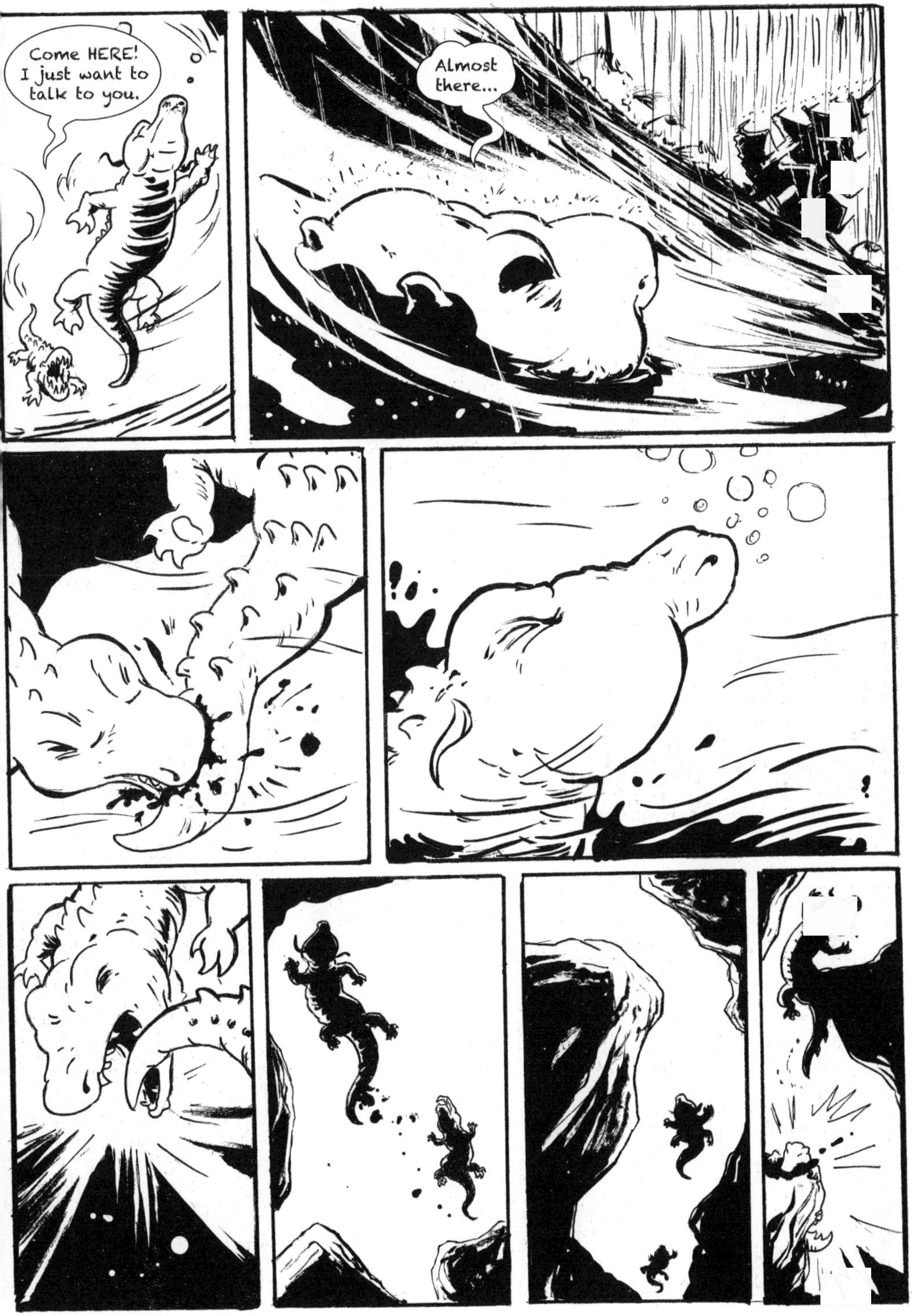
Come HERE! I just want to talk to you.
Almost there...

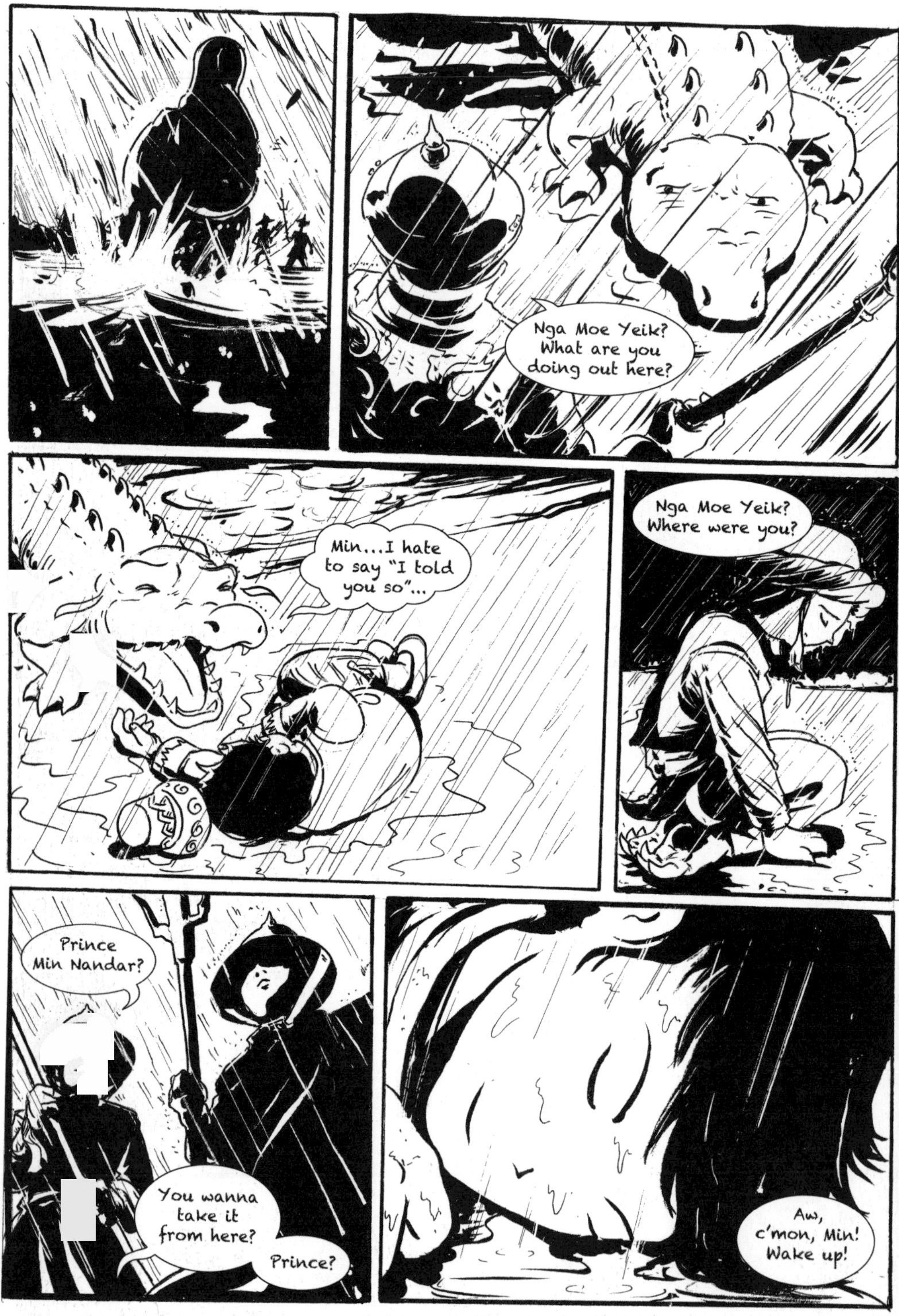
Nga Moe Yeik? What are you doing out here?
Min... I hate to say "I told you so"...
Nga Moe Yeik? Where were you?
Prince Min Nandar?
You wanna take it from here?
Prince?
Aw, c'mon, Min! Wake up!

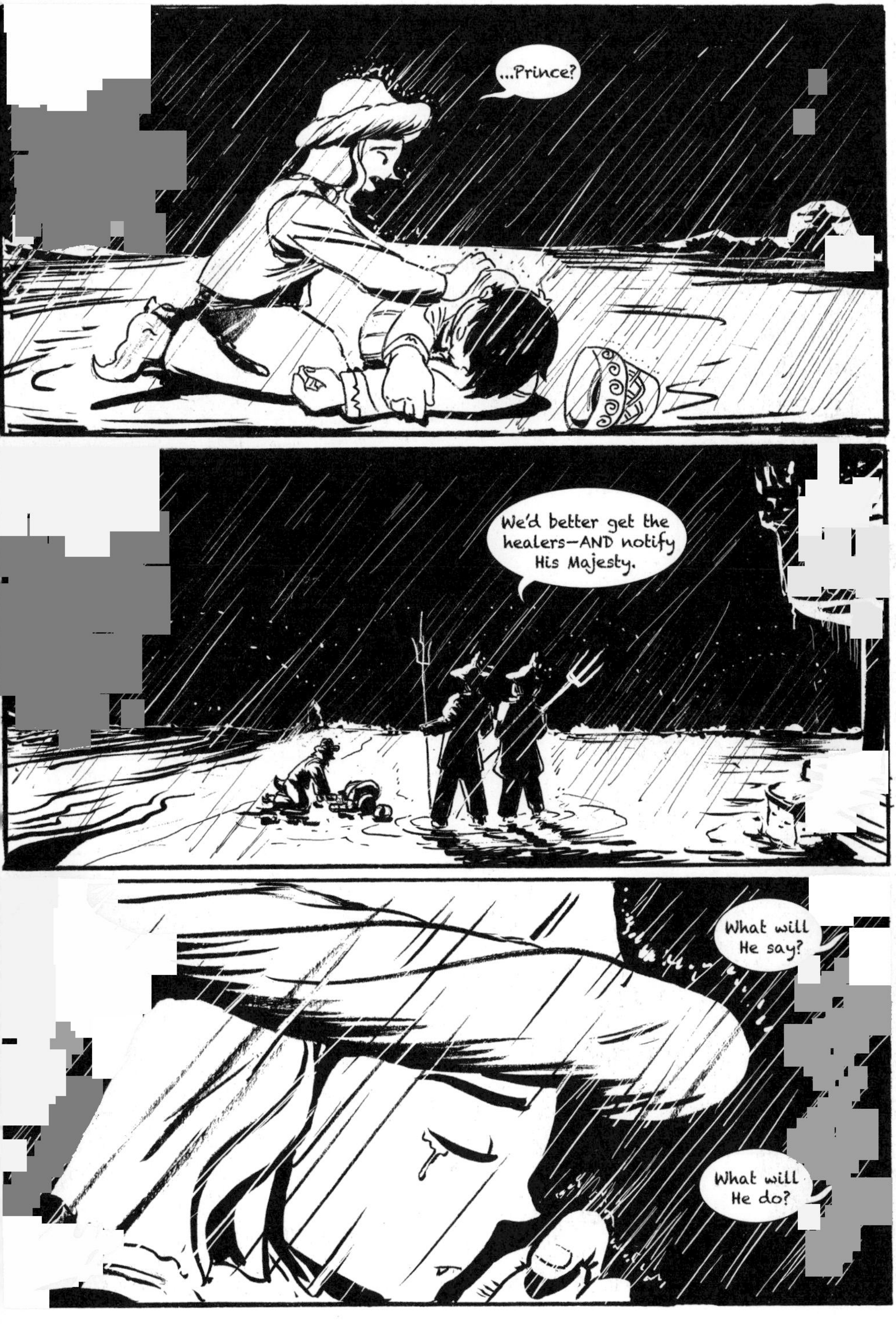
...Prince?
We'd better get the healers—AND notify His Majesty.
What will He say?
What will He do?

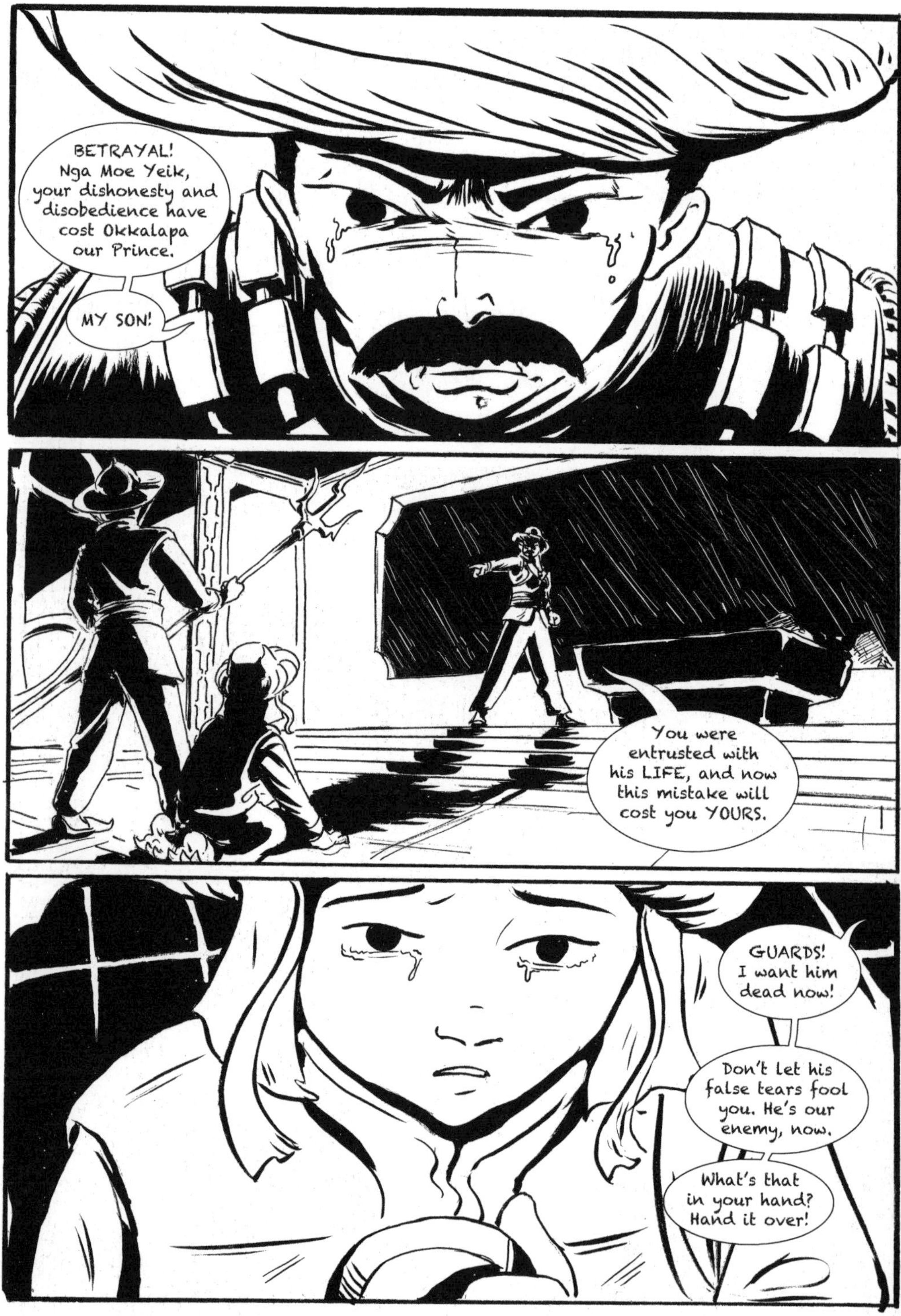
BETRAYAL! Nga Moe Yeik, your dishonesty and disobedience have cost Okkalapa our Prince.
MY SON!
You were entrusted with his LIFE, and now this mistake will cost you YOURS.
GUARDS! I want him dead now!
Don't let his false tears fool you. He's our enemy, now.
What's that in your hand? Hand it over!

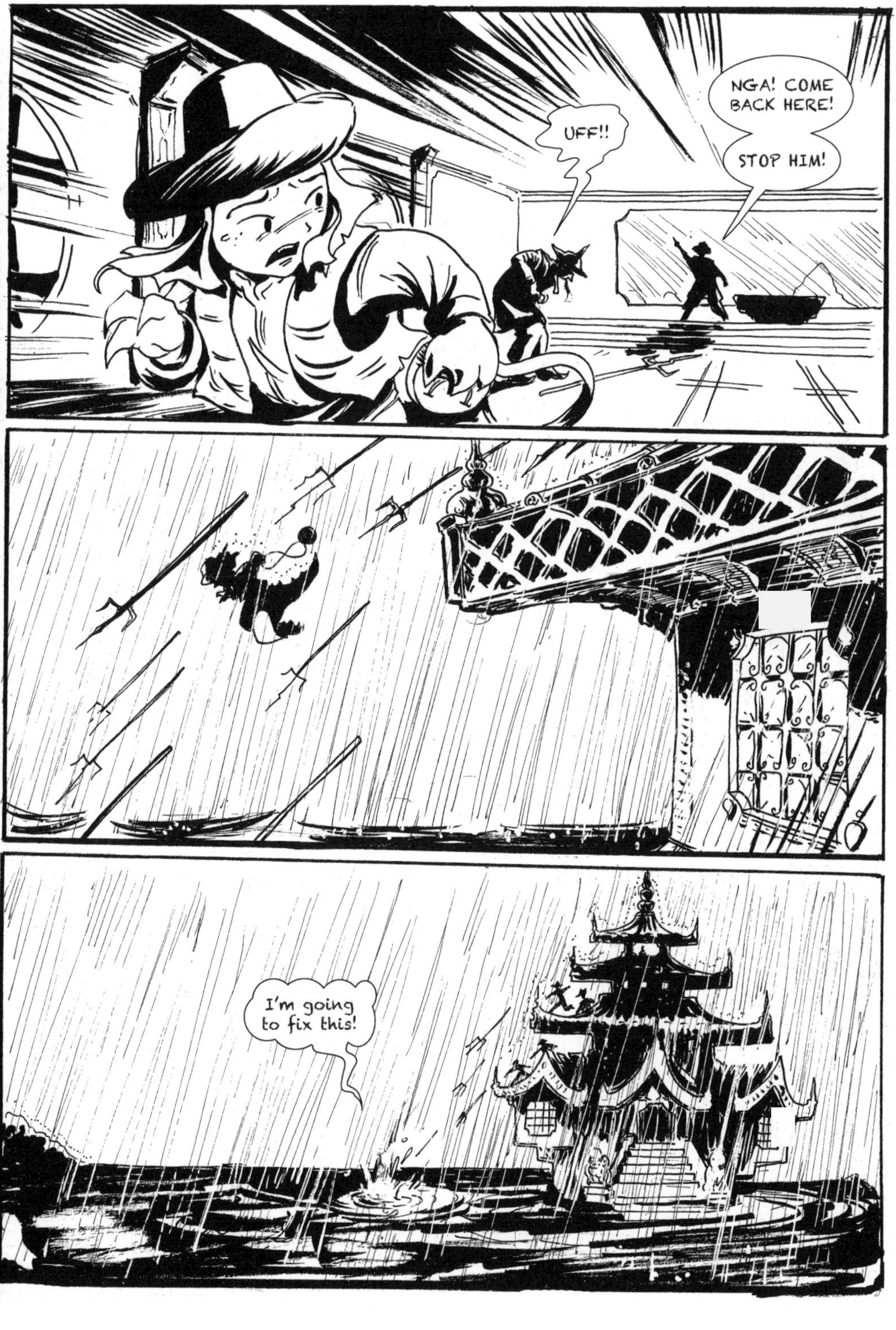
UFF!!
NGA! COME BACK HERE!
STOP HIM!
I'm going to fix this!

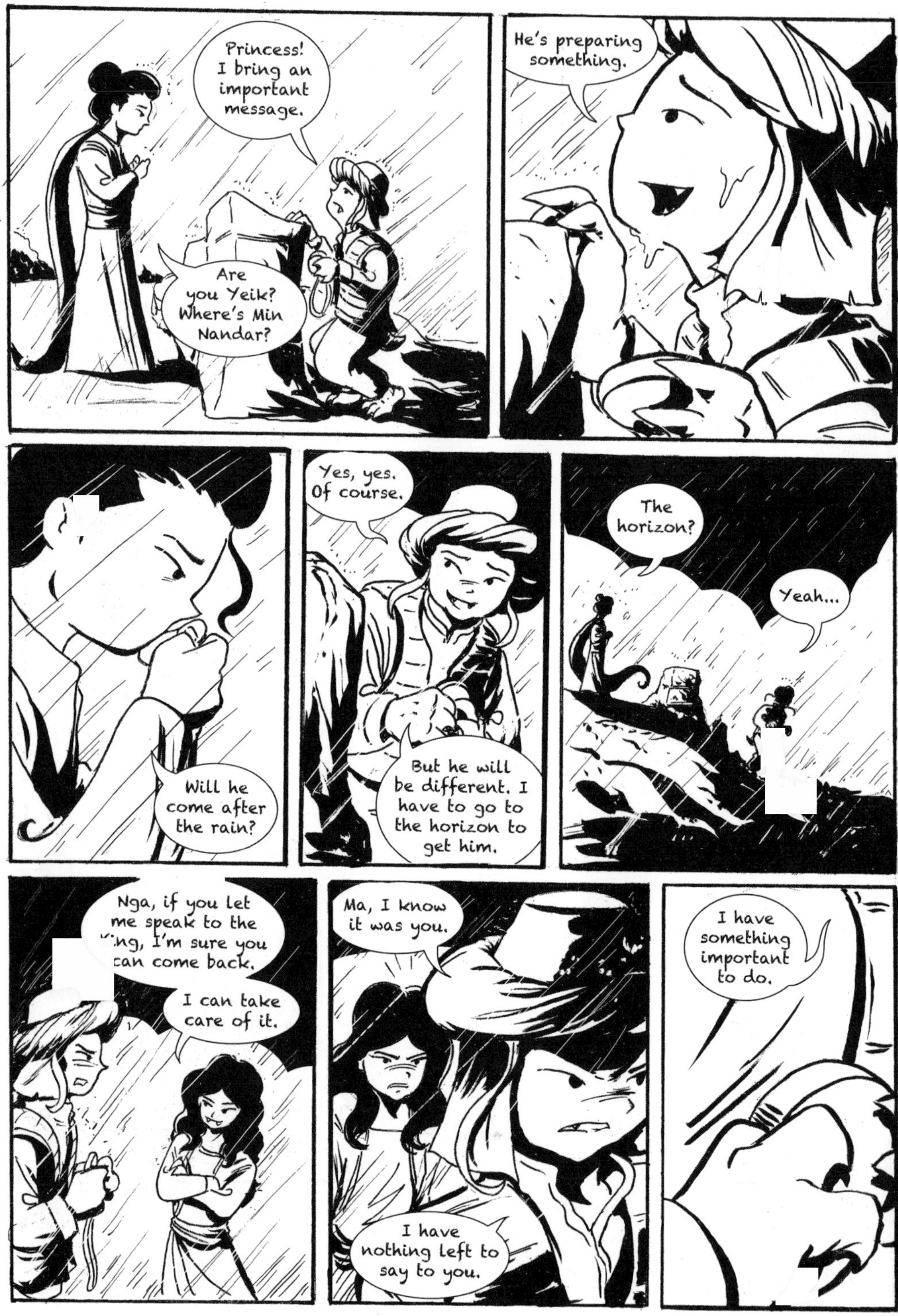

Princess! I bring an important message.
Are you Yeik? Where's Min Nandar?
He's preparing something.
Will he come after the rain?
Yes, yes. Of course.
But he will be different. I have to go to the horizon to get him.
The horizon?
Yeah...
Nga, if you let me speak to the ing, I'm sure you can come back.
I can take care of it.
Ma, I know it was you.
I have nothing left to say to you.
I have something important to do.

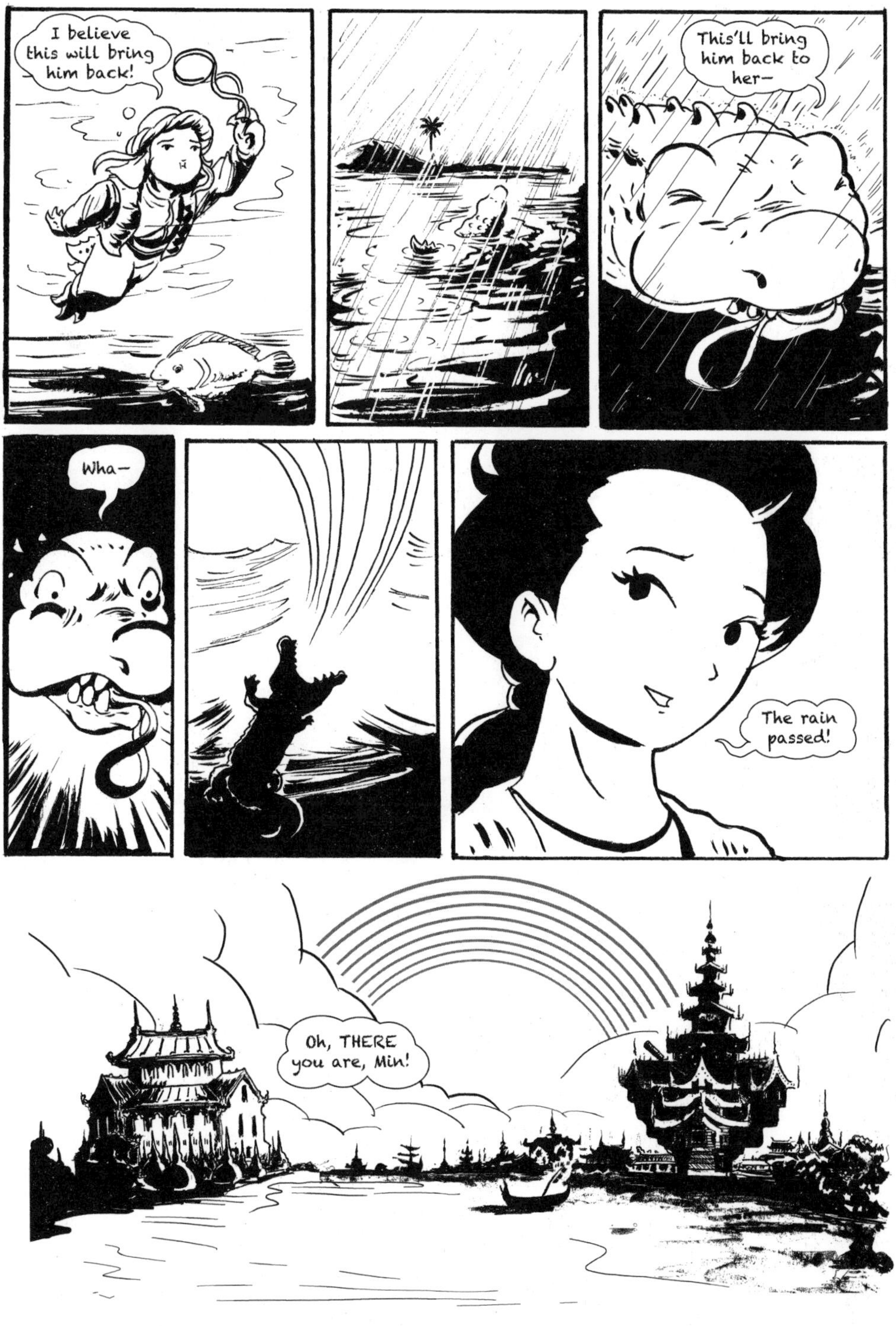
I believe this will bring him back!
This'll bring him back to her–
Wha–
The rain passed!
Oh, THERE you are, Min!

From the Journal of the Monkey King

Gene Luen Yang

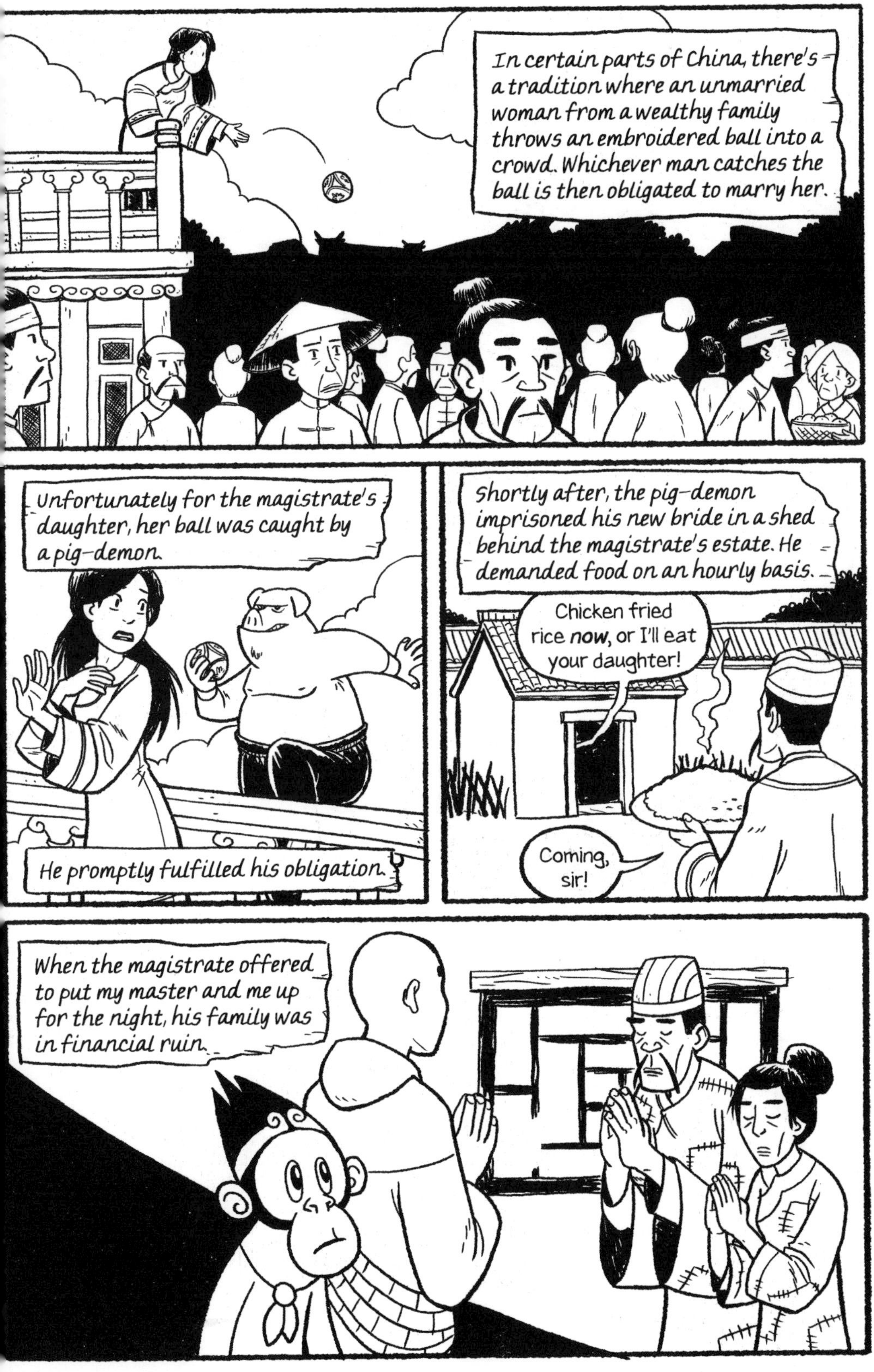
In certain parts of China, there's a tradition where an unmarried woman from a wealthy family throws an embroidered ball into a crowd. Whichever man catches the ball is then obligated to marry her.
Unfortunately for the magistrate's daughter, her ball was caught by a pig-demon.
He promptly fulfilled his obligation.
Shortly after, the pig-demon imprisoned his new bride in a shed behind the magistrate's estate. He demanded food on an hourly basis.
Chicken fried rice **now**, or I'll eat your daughter!
Coming, sir!
When the magistrate offered to put my master and me up for the night, his family was in financial ruin.

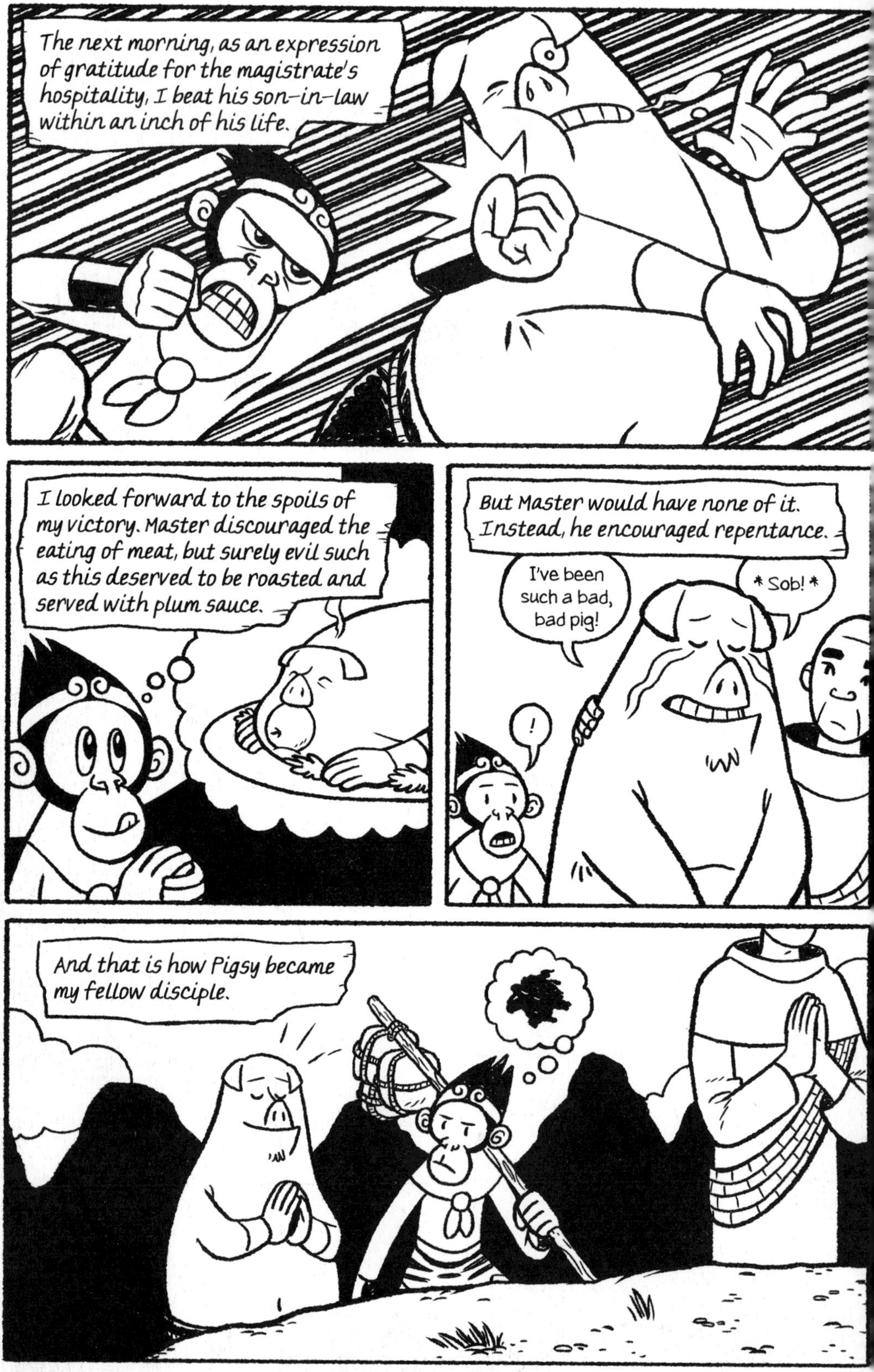

The next morning, as an expression of gratitude for the magistrate's hospitality, I beat his son-in-law within an inch of his life.
I looked forward to the spoils of my victory. Master discouraged the eating of meat, but surely evil such as this deserved to be roasted and served with plum sauce.
But Master would have none of it. Instead, he encouraged repentance.
I've been such a bad, bad pig!
* Sob! *
!
And that is how Pigsy became my fellow disciple.

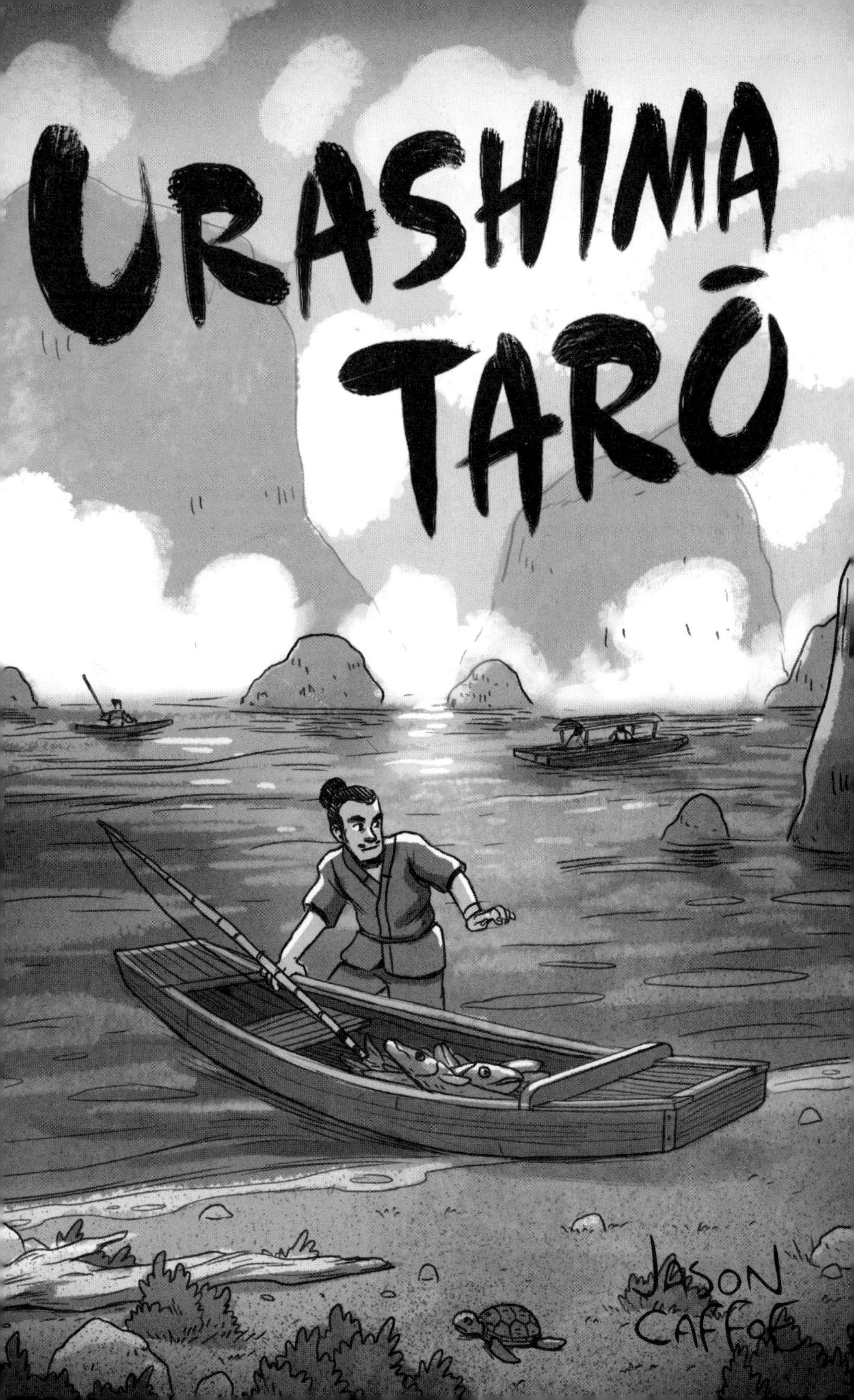
URASHIMA
TARŌ
JASON
CAFFOE

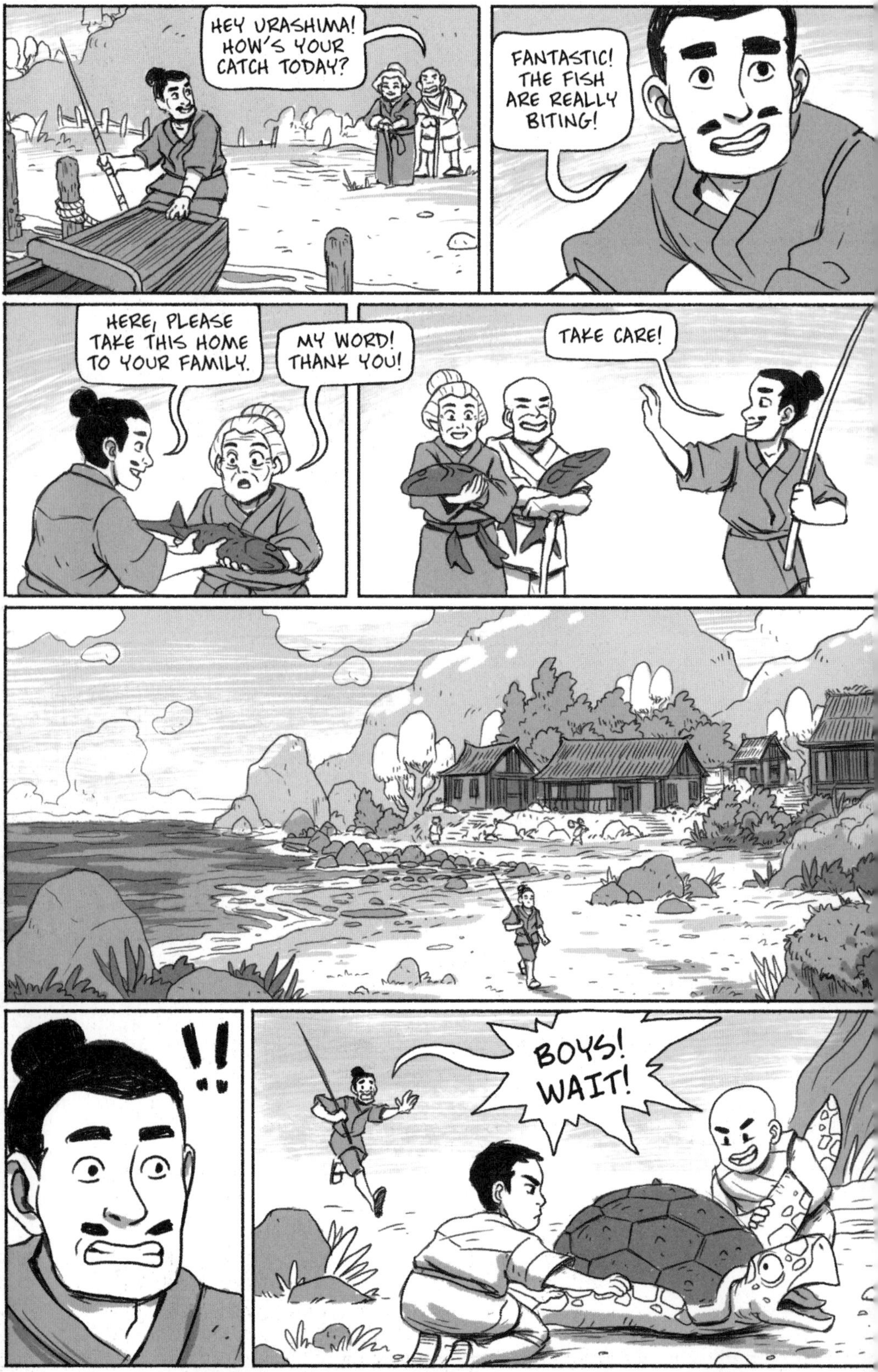
HEY URASHIMA! HOW'S YOUR CATCH TODAY?
FANTASTIC! THE FISH ARE REALLY BITING!
HERE, PLEASE TAKE THIS HOME TO YOUR FAMILY.
MY WORD! THANK YOU!
TAKE CARE!
!!
BOYS! WAIT!

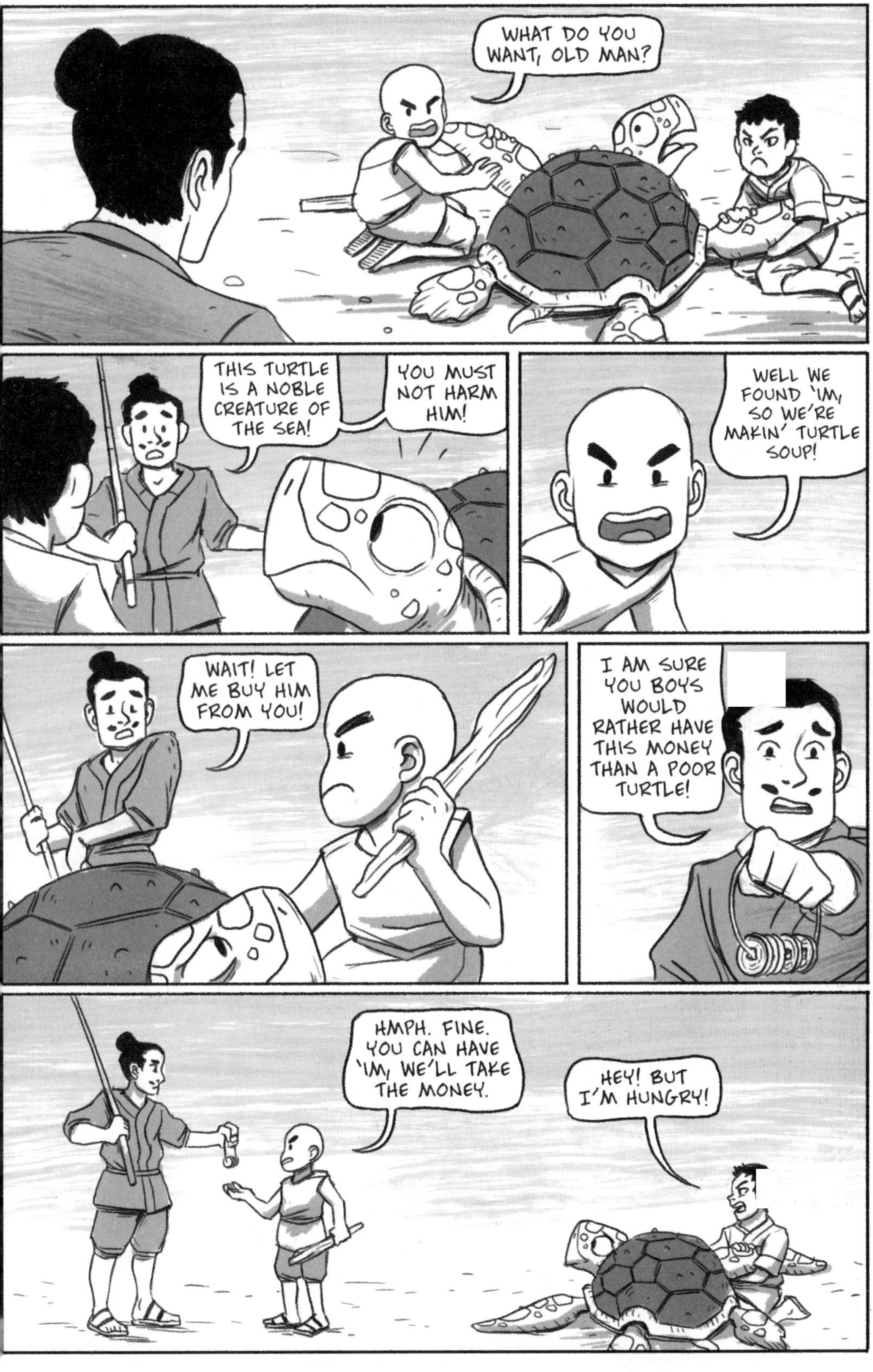
WHAT DO YOU WANT, OLD MAN?
THIS TURTLE IS A NOBLE CREATURE OF THE SEA!
YOU MUST NOT HARM HIM!
WELL WE FOUND 'IM, SO WE'RE MAKIN' TURTLE SOUP!
WAIT! LET ME BUY HIM FROM YOU!
I AM SURE YOU BOYS WOULD RATHER HAVE THIS MONEY THAN A POOR TURTLE!
HMPH. FINE. YOU CAN HAVE 'IM, WE'LL TAKE THE MONEY.
HEY! BUT I'M HUNGRY!

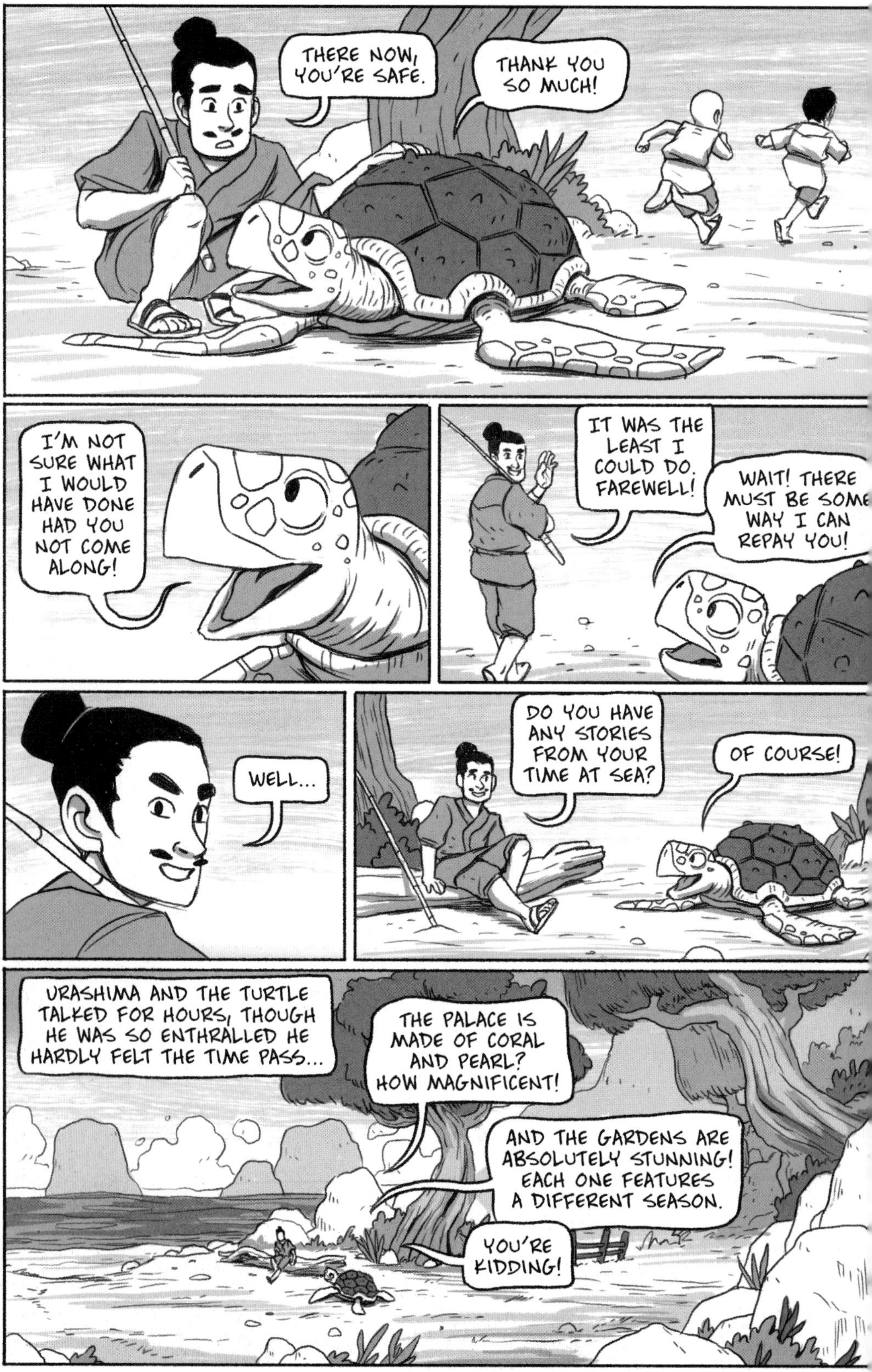
THERE NOW, YOU'RE SAFE.
THANK YOU SO MUCH!
I'M NOT SURE WHAT I WOULD HAVE DONE HAD YOU NOT COME ALONG!
IT WAS THE LEAST I COULD DO. FAREWELL!
WAIT! THERE MUST BE SOME WAY I CAN REPAY YOU!
WELL...
DO YOU HAVE ANY STORIES FROM YOUR TIME AT SEA?
OF COURSE!
URASHIMA AND THE TURTLE TALKED FOR HOURS, THOUGH HE WAS SO ENTHRALLED HE HARDLY FELT THE TIME PASS...
THE PALACE IS MADE OF CORAL AND PEARL? HOW MAGNIFICENT!
AND THE GARDENS ARE ABSOLUTELY STUNNING! EACH ONE FEATURES A DIFFERENT SEASON.
YOU'RE KIDDING!

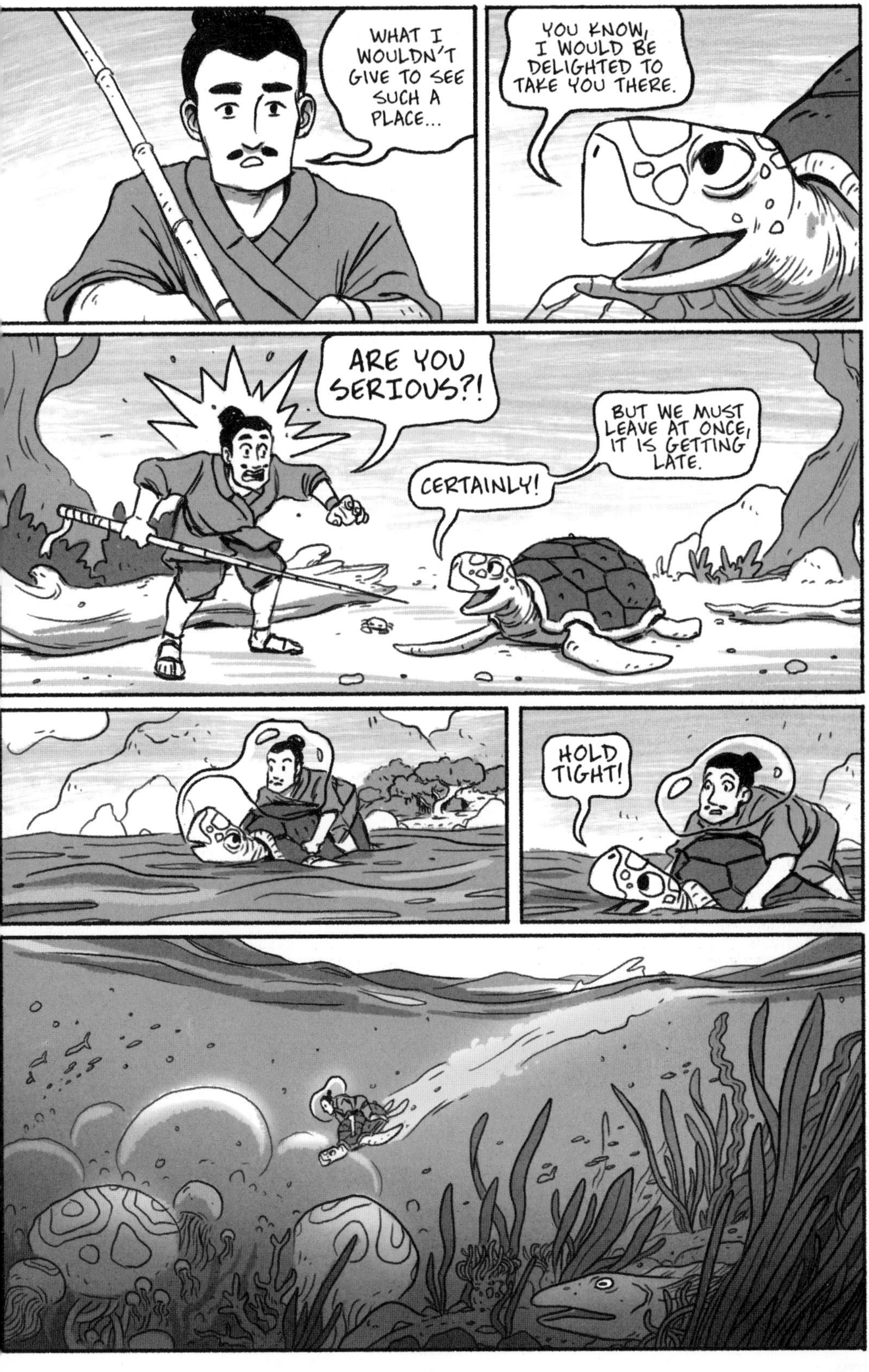
WHAT I WOULDN'T GIVE TO SEE SUCH A PLACE...
YOU KNOW, I WOULD BE DELIGHTED TO TAKE YOU THERE.
ARE YOU SERIOUS?!
CERTAINLY!
BUT WE MUST LEAVE AT ONCE, IT IS GETTING LATE.
HOLD TIGHT!

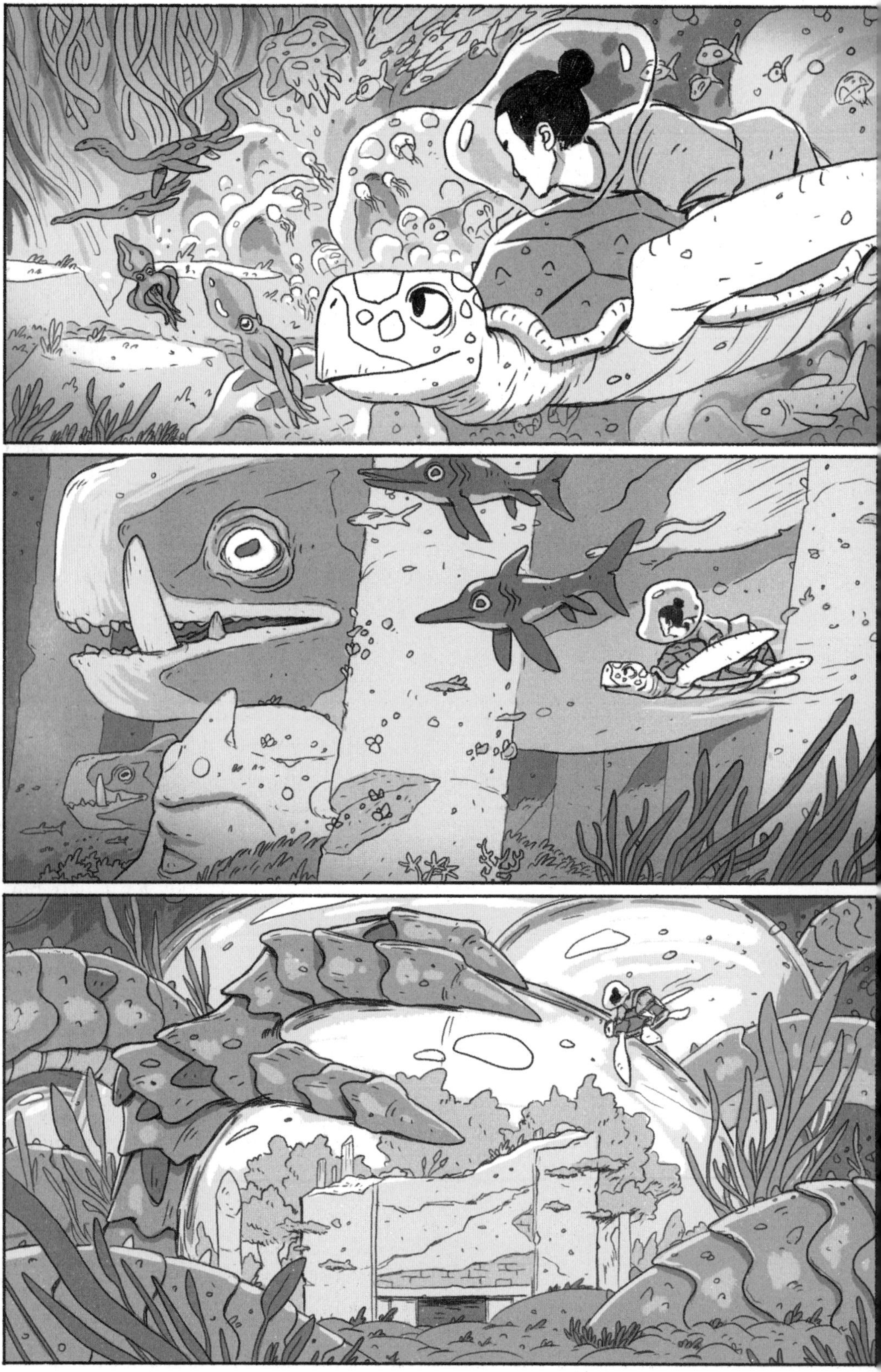

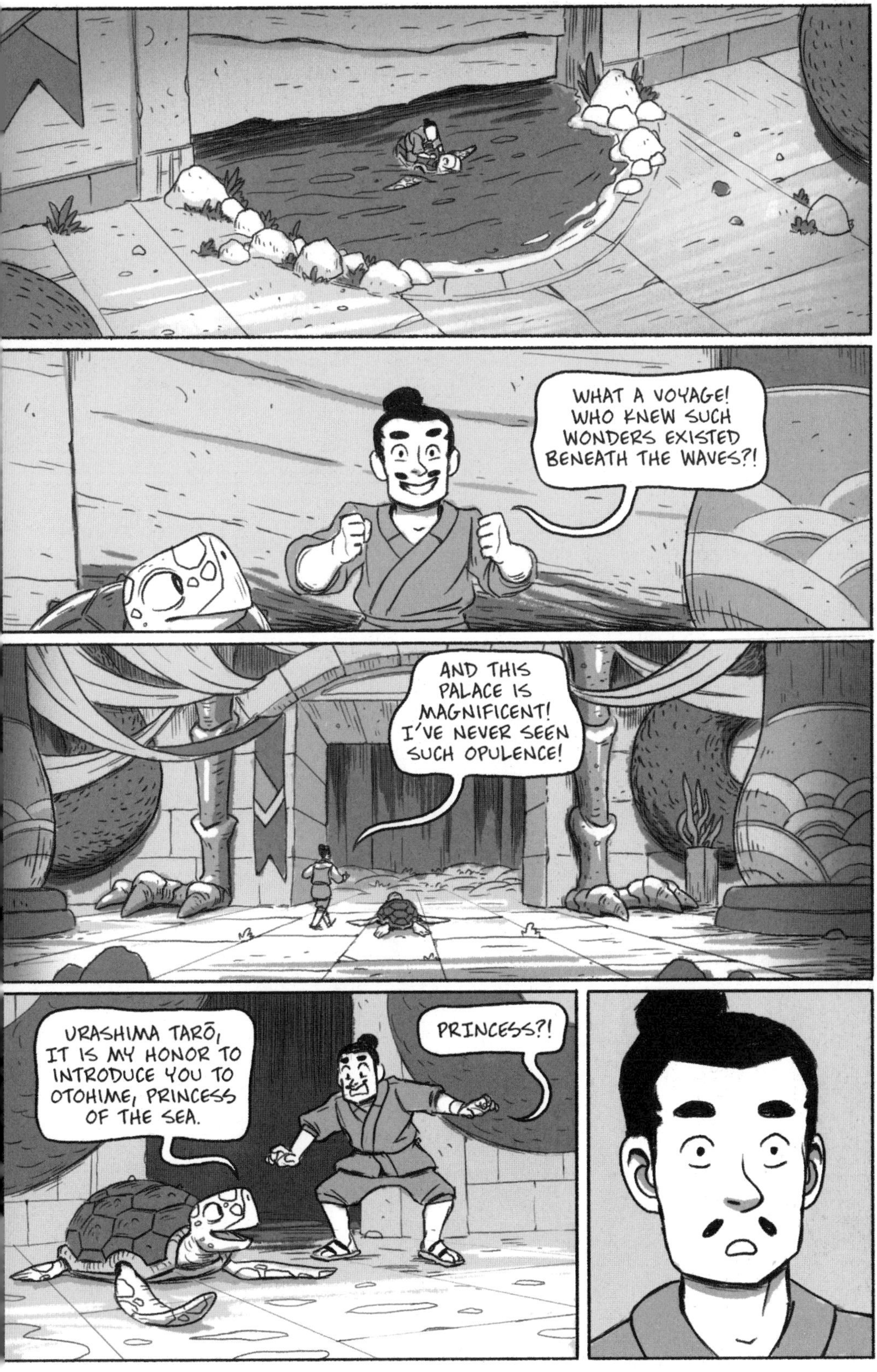
WHAT A VOYAGE! WHO KNEW SUCH WONDERS EXISTED BENEATH THE WAVES?!
AND THIS PALACE IS MAGNIFICENT! I'VE NEVER SEEN SUCH OPULENCE!
URASHIMA TARŌ, IT IS MY HONOR TO INTRODUCE YOU TO OTOHIME, PRINCESS OF THE SEA.
PRINCESS?!

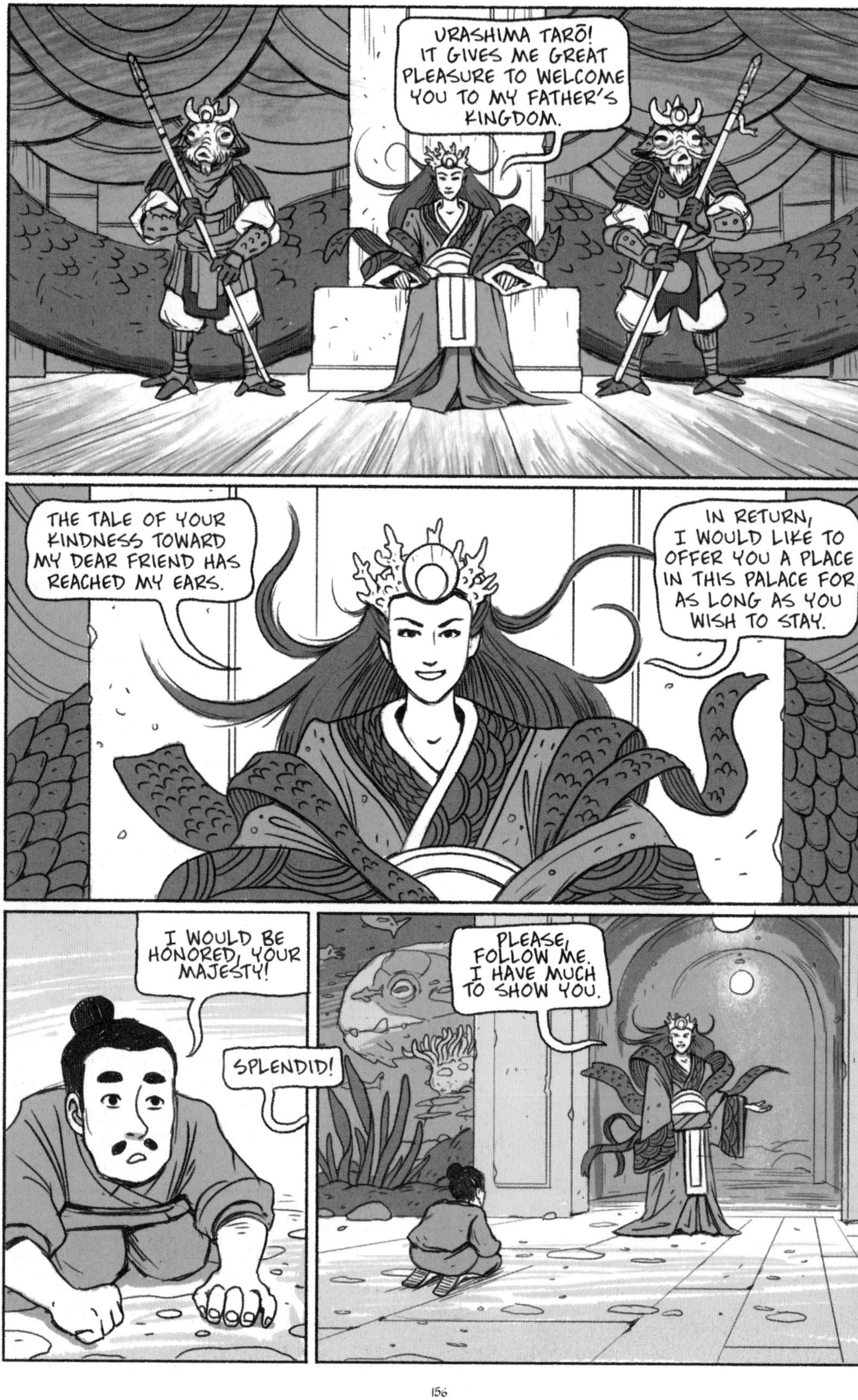
URASHIMA TARŌ! IT GIVES ME GREAT PLEASURE TO WELCOME YOU TO MY FATHER'S KINGDOM.
THE TALE OF YOUR KINDNESS TOWARD MY DEAR FRIEND HAS REACHED MY EARS.
IN RETURN, I WOULD LIKE TO OFFER YOU A PLACE IN THIS PALACE FOR AS LONG AS YOU WISH TO STAY.
I WOULD BE HONORED, YOUR MAJESTY!
SPLENDID!
PLEASE, FOLLOW ME. I HAVE MUCH TO SHOW YOU.

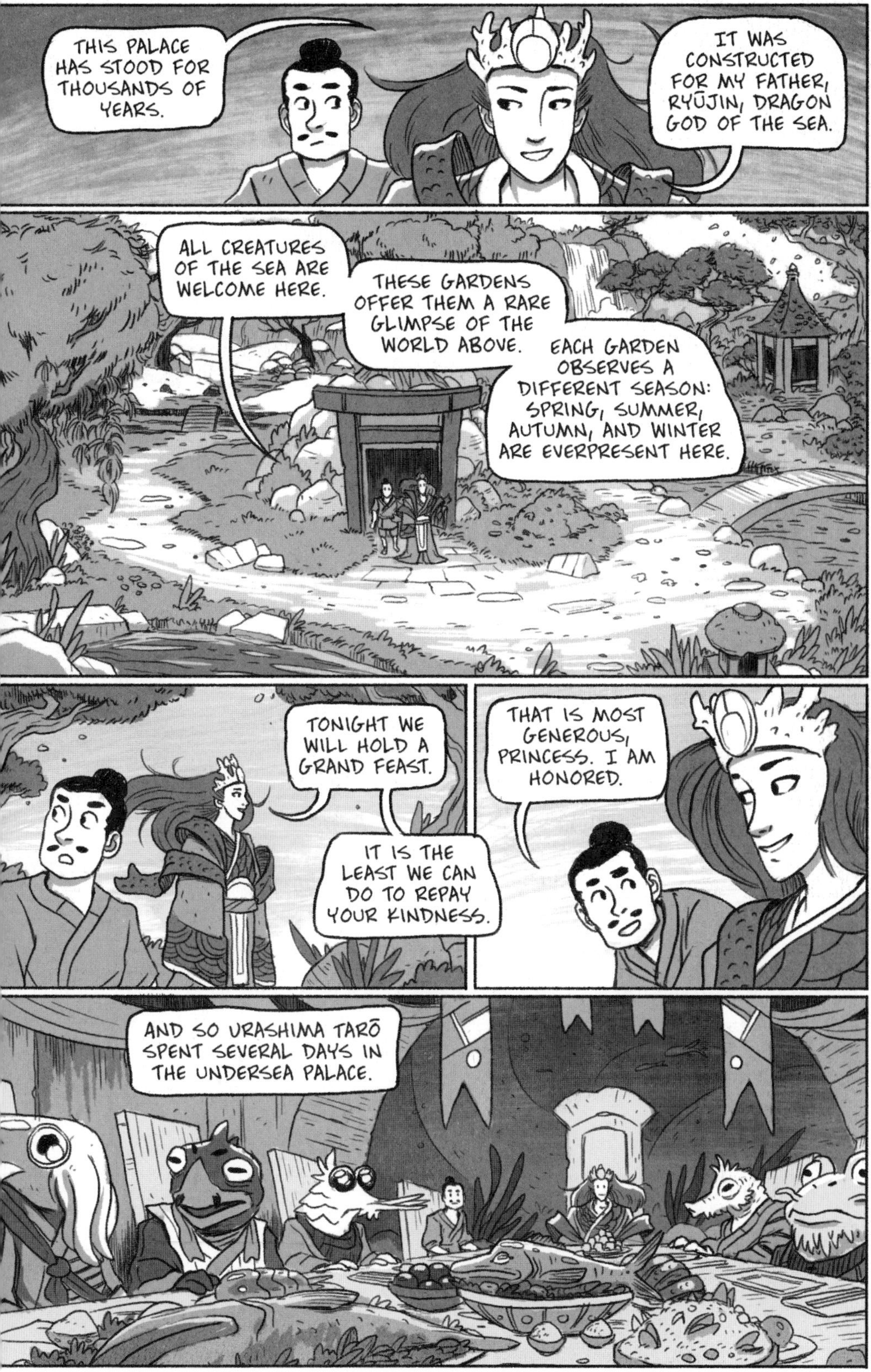
THIS PALACE HAS STOOD FOR THOUSANDS OF YEARS.
IT WAS CONSTRUCTED FOR MY FATHER, RYŪJIN, DRAGON GOD OF THE SEA.
ALL CREATURES OF THE SEA ARE WELCOME HERE.
THESE GARDENS OFFER THEM A RARE GLIMPSE OF THE WORLD ABOVE.
EACH GARDEN OBSERVES A DIFFERENT SEASON: SPRING, SUMMER, AUTUMN, AND WINTER ARE EVERPRESENT HERE.
TONIGHT WE WILL HOLD A GRAND FEAST.
IT IS THE LEAST WE CAN DO TO REPAY YOUR KINDNESS.
THAT IS MOST GENEROUS, PRINCESS. I AM HONORED.
AND SO URASHIMA TARŌ SPENT SEVERAL DAYS IN THE UNDERSEA PALACE.

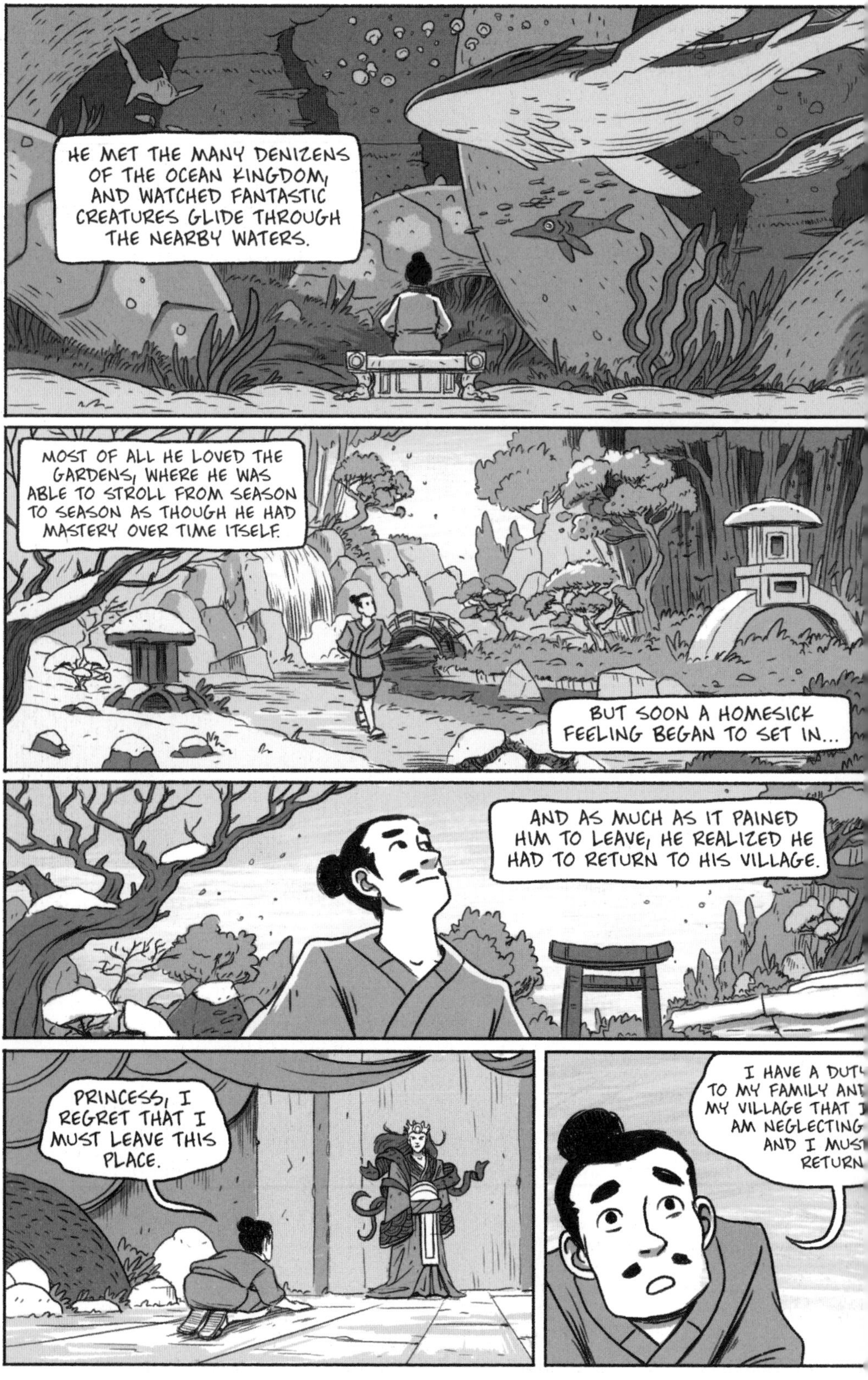
HE MET THE MANY DENIZENS OF THE OCEAN KINGDOM, AND WATCHED FANTASTIC CREATURES GLIDE THROUGH THE NEARBY WATERS.
MOST OF ALL HE LOVED THE GARDENS, WHERE HE WAS ABLE TO STROLL FROM SEASON TO SEASON AS THOUGH HE HAD MASTERY OVER TIME ITSELF.
BUT SOON A HOMESICK FEELING BEGAN TO SET IN...
AND AS MUCH AS IT PAINED HIM TO LEAVE, HE REALIZED HE HAD TO RETURN TO HIS VILLAGE.
PRINCESS, I REGRET THAT I MUST LEAVE THIS PLACE.
I HAVE A DUTY TO MY FAMILY AND MY VILLAGE THAT I AM NEGLECTING AND I MUST RETURN.

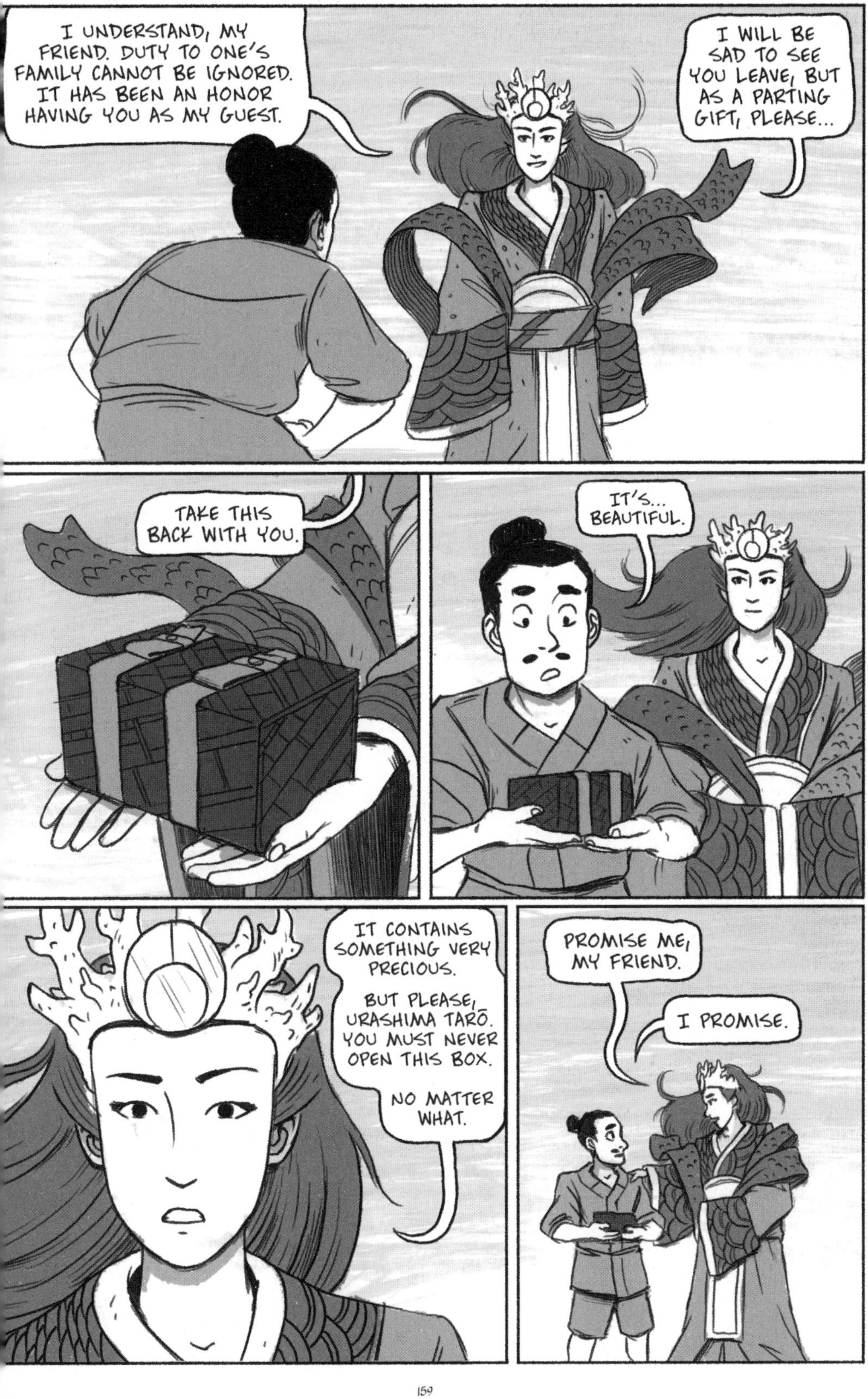
I UNDERSTAND, MY FRIEND. DUTY TO ONE'S FAMILY CANNOT BE IGNORED. IT HAS BEEN AN HONOR HAVING YOU AS MY GUEST.
I WILL BE SAD TO SEE YOU LEAVE, BUT AS A PARTING GIFT, PLEASE...
TAKE THIS BACK WITH YOU.
IT'S... BEAUTIFUL.
IT CONTAINS SOMETHING VERY PRECIOUS.
BUT PLEASE, URASHIMA TARŌ. YOU MUST NEVER OPEN THIS BOX.
NO MATTER WHAT.
PROMISE ME, MY FRIEND.
I PROMISE.

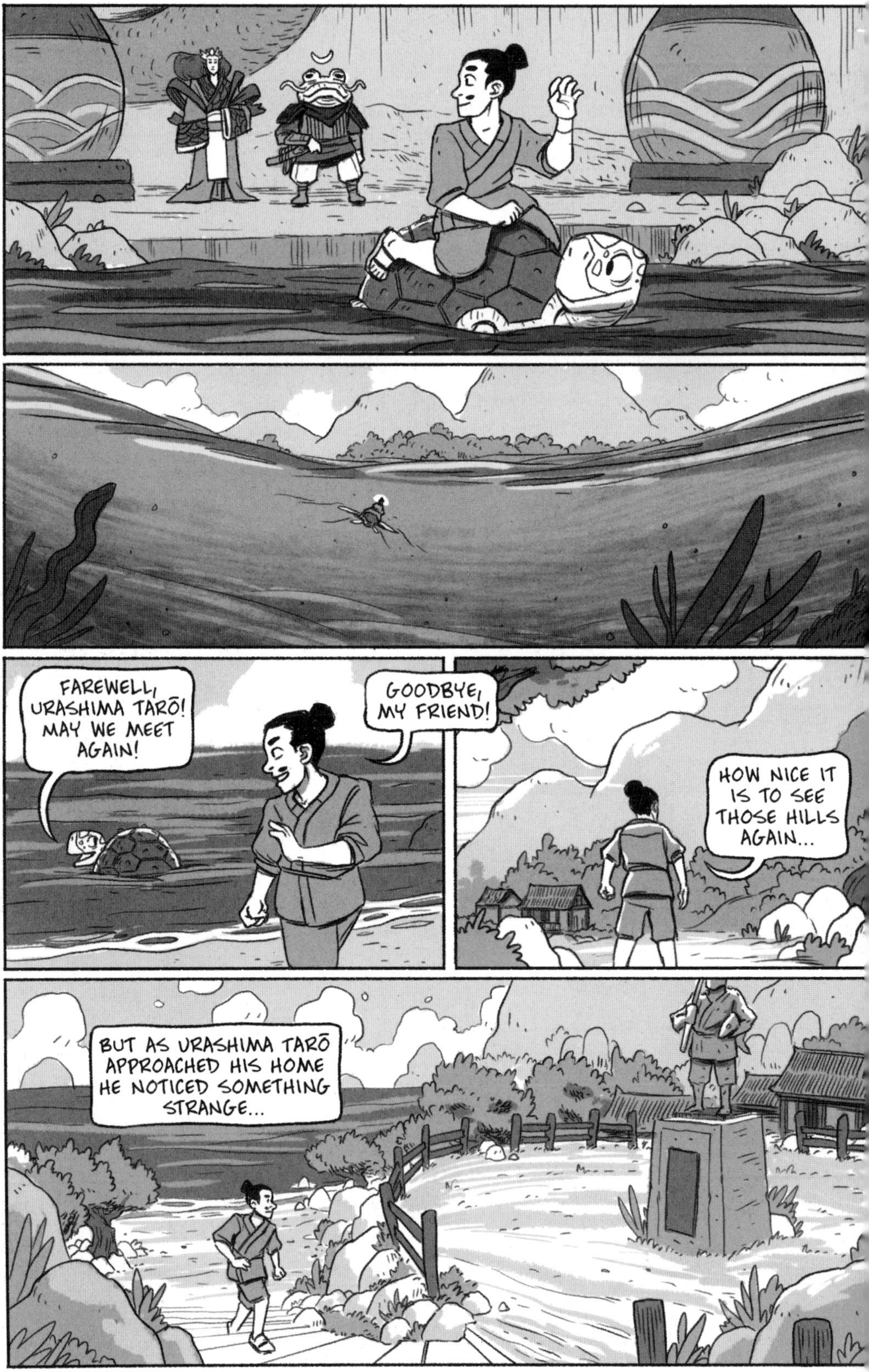
FAREWELL, URASHIMA TARŌ! MAY WE MEET AGAIN!
GOODBYE, MY FRIEND!
HOW NICE IT IS TO SEE THOSE HILLS AGAIN...
BUT AS URASHIMA TARŌ APPROACHED HIS HOME HE NOTICED SOMETHING STRANGE...

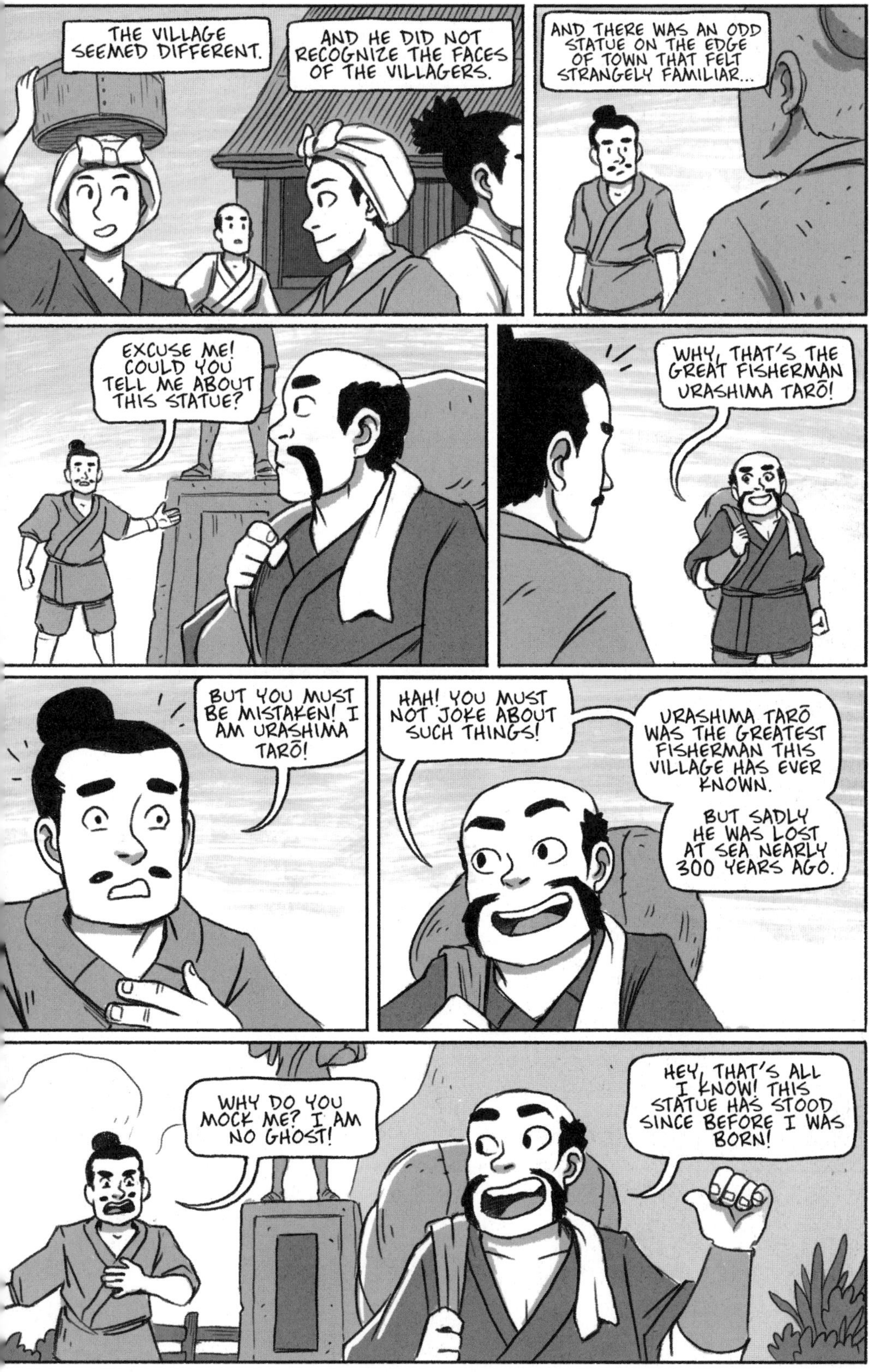
THE VILLAGE SEEMED DIFFERENT.
AND HE DID NOT RECOGNIZE THE FACES OF THE VILLAGERS.
AND THERE WAS AN ODD STATUE ON THE EDGE OF TOWN THAT FELT STRANGELY FAMILIAR...
EXCUSE ME! COULD YOU TELL ME ABOUT THIS STATUE?
WHY, THAT'S THE GREAT FISHERMAN URASHIMA TARŌ!
BUT YOU MUST BE MISTAKEN! I AM URASHIMA TARŌ!
HAH! YOU MUST NOT JOKE ABOUT SUCH THINGS!
URASHIMA TARŌ WAS THE GREATEST FISHERMAN THIS VILLAGE HAS EVER KNOWN.
BUT SADLY HE WAS LOST AT SEA NEARLY 300 YEARS AGO.
WHY DO YOU MOCK ME? I AM NO GHOST!
HEY, THAT'S ALL I KNOW! THIS STATUE HAS STOOD SINCE BEFORE I WAS BORN!

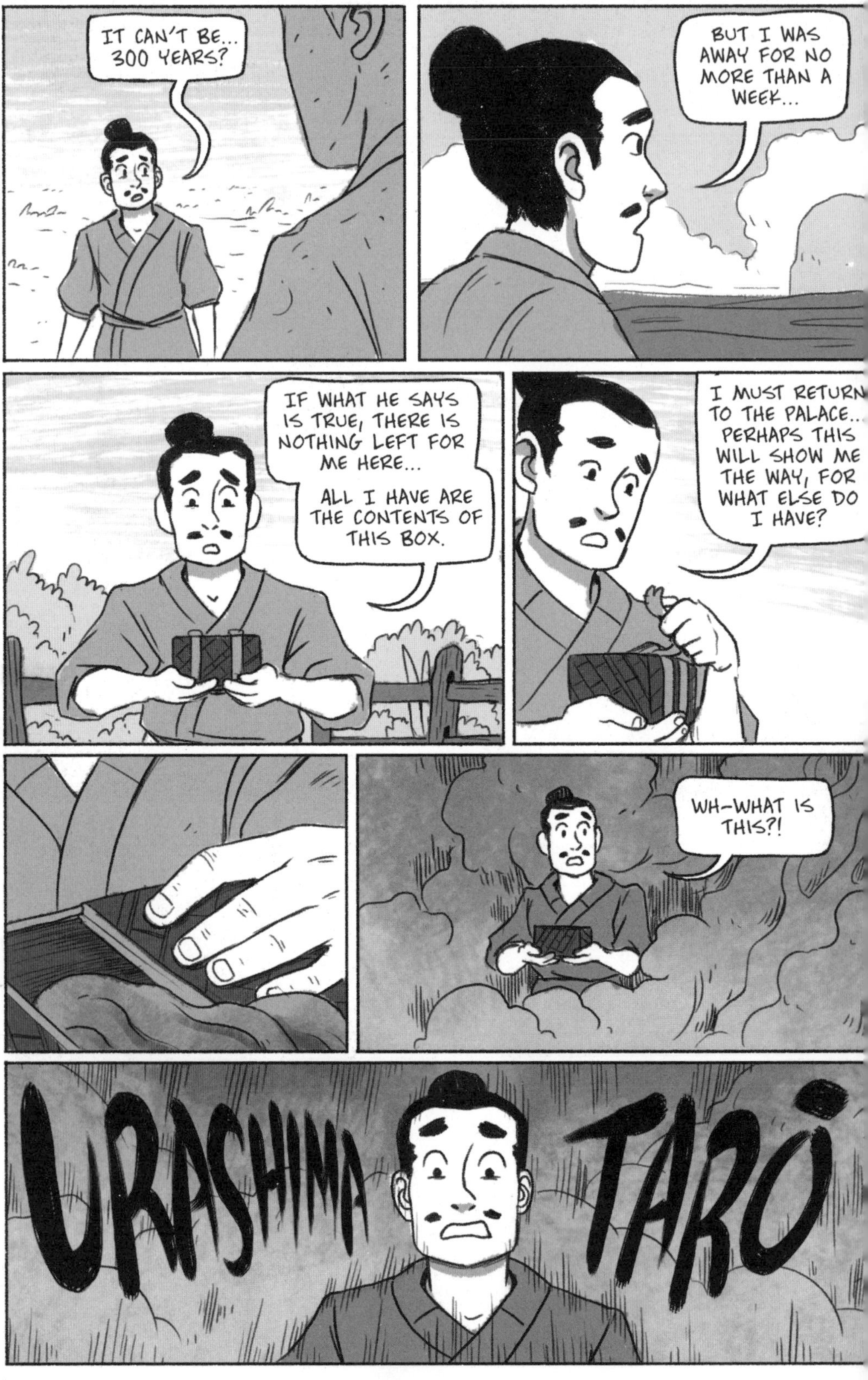
IT CAN'T BE... 300 YEARS?
BUT I WAS AWAY FOR NO MORE THAN A WEEK...
IF WHAT HE SAYS IS TRUE, THERE IS NOTHING LEFT FOR ME HERE...
ALL I HAVE ARE THE CONTENTS OF THIS BOX.
I MUST RETURN TO THE PALACE... PERHAPS THIS WILL SHOW ME THE WAY, FOR WHAT ELSE DO I HAVE?
WH-WHAT IS THIS?!
URASHIMA TARŌ

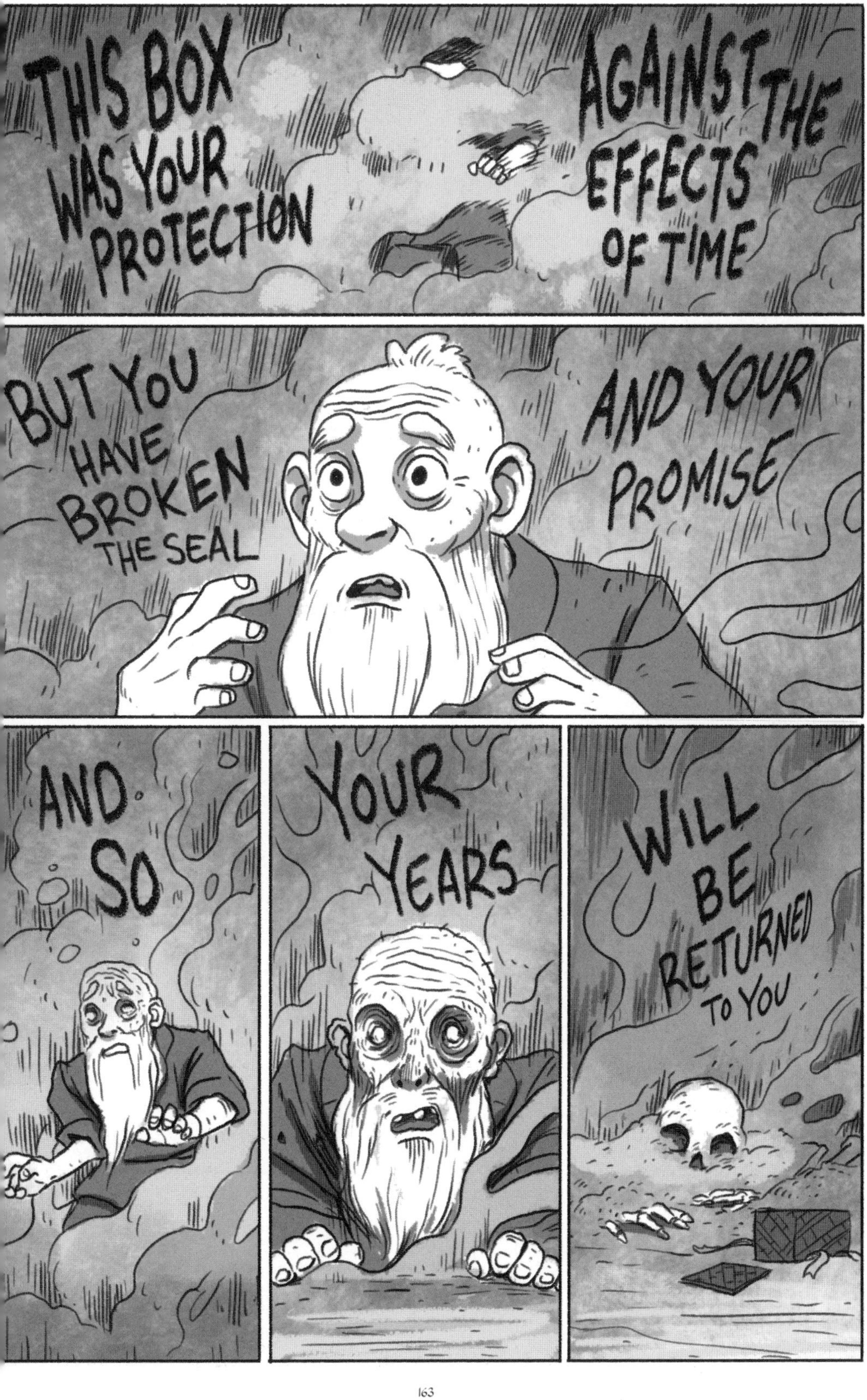
THIS BOX WAS YOUR PROTECTION
AGAINST THE EFFECTS OF TIME
BUT YOU HAVE BROKEN THE SEAL
AND YOUR PROMISE
AND SO
YOUR YEARS
WILL BE RETURNED TO YOU

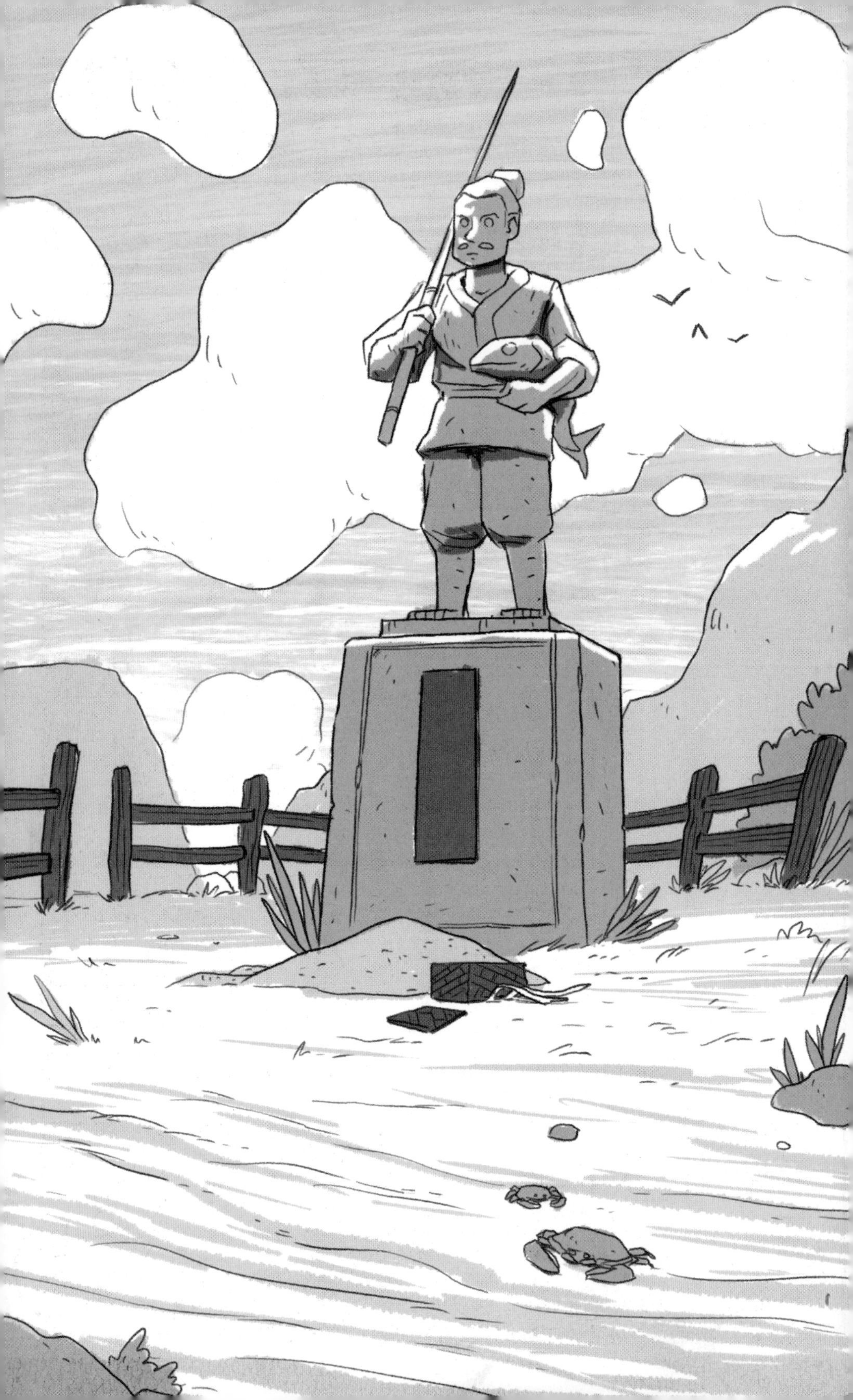

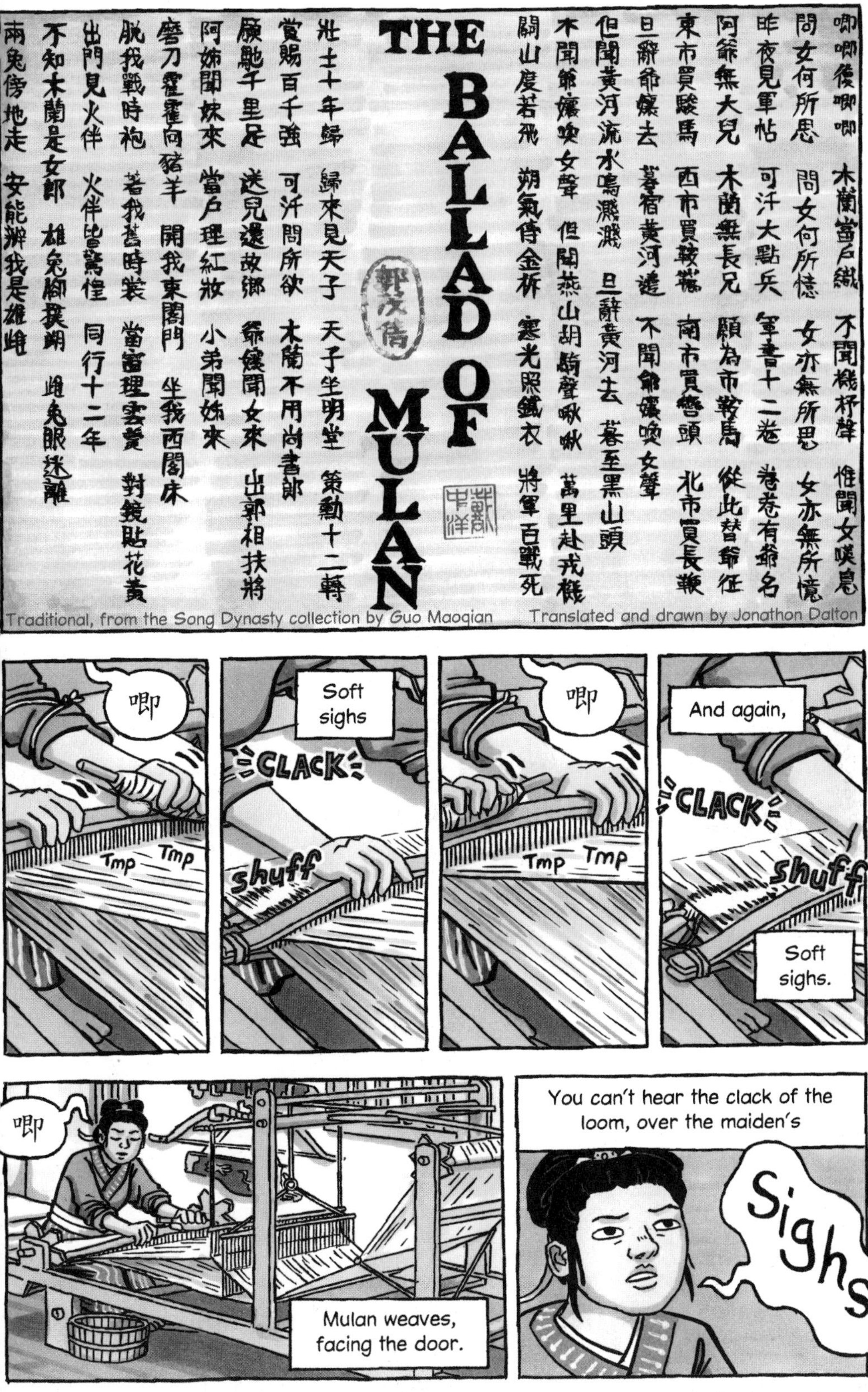

唧唧後唧唧 木蘭當戶織 不聞機杼聲 惟聞女嘆息
問女何所思 問女何所憶 女亦無所思 女亦無所憶
昨夜見軍帖 可汗大點兵 軍書十二卷 卷卷有爺名
阿爺無大兒 木蘭無長兄 願為市鞍馬 從此替爺征
東市買駿馬 西市買鞍韉 南市買轡頭 北市買長鞭
旦辭爺孃去 暮宿黃河邊 不聞爺孃喚女聲
但聞黃河流水鳴濺濺 旦辭黃河去 暮至黑山頭
不聞爺孃喚女聲 但聞燕山胡騎聲啾啾 萬里赴戎機
關山度若飛 朔氣傳金柝 寒光照鐵衣 將軍百戰死
THE BALLAD OF MULAN
壯士十年歸 歸來見天子 天子坐明堂 策勳十二轉
賞賜百千強 可汗問所欲 木蘭不用尚書郎
願馳千里足 送兒還故鄉 爺孃聞女來 出郭相扶將
阿姊聞妹來 當戶理紅妝 小弟聞姊來
磨刀霍霍向豬羊 開我東閣門 坐我西閣床
脫我戰時袍 著我舊時裳 當窗理雲鬢 對鏡貼花黃
出門見火伴 火伴皆驚惶 同行十二年
不知木蘭是女郎 雄兔腳撲朔 雌兔眼迷離
兩兔傍地走 安能辨我是雄雌
Traditional, from the Song Dynasty collection by Guo Maoqian
Translated and drawn by Jonathon Dalton
唧
Tmp Tmp
Soft sighs
CLACK
shuff
唧
Tmp Tmp
And again,
CLACK
shuff
Soft sighs.
唧
Mulan weaves, facing the door.
You can't hear the clack of the loom, over the maiden's
Sighs

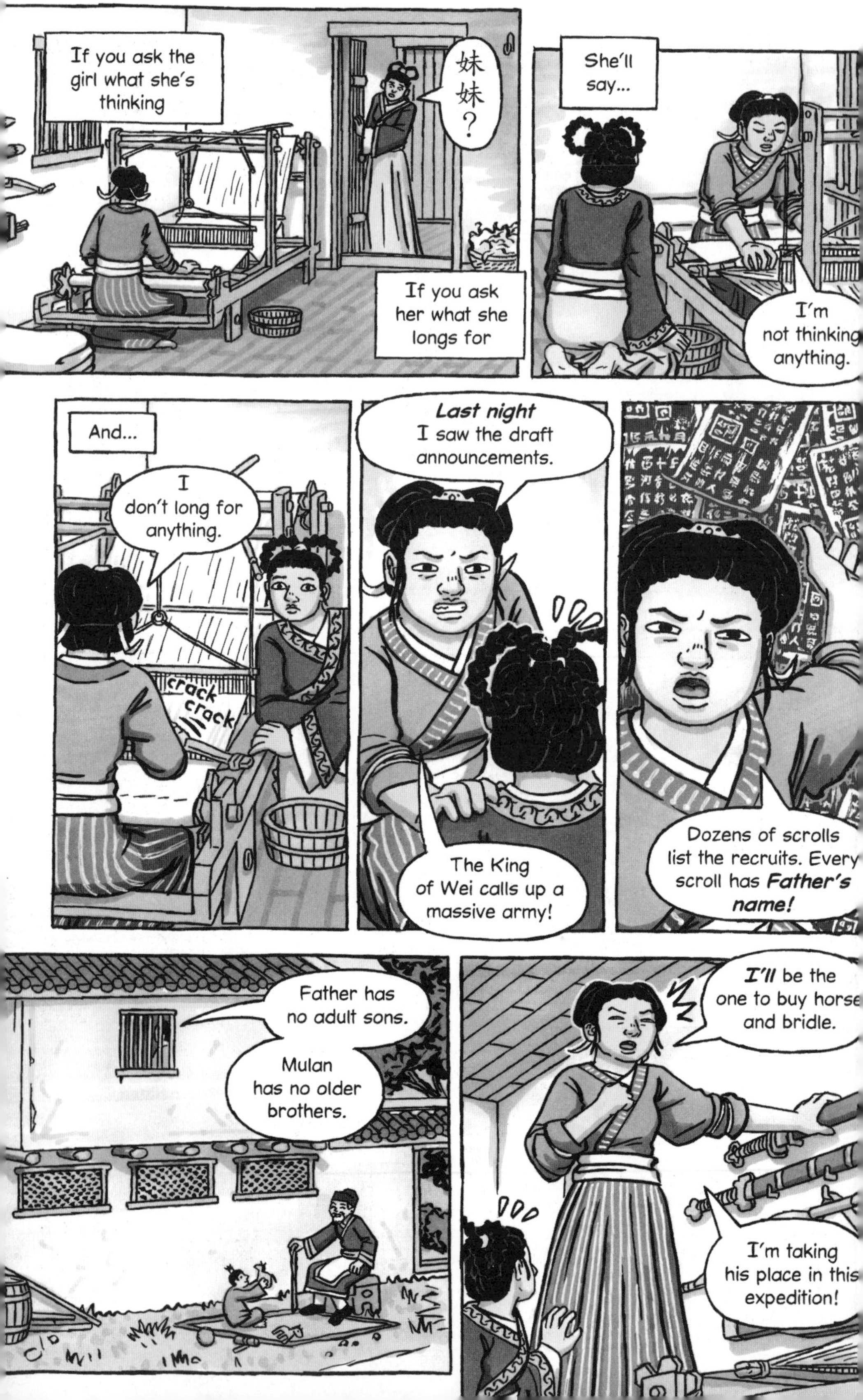
If you ask the girl what she's thinking
妹妹？
If you ask her what she longs for
She'll say...
I'm not thinking anything.
And...
I don't long for anything.
crack crack
Last night I saw the draft announcements.
The King of Wei calls up a massive army!
Dozens of scrolls list the recruits. Every scroll has ***Father's name!***
Father has no adult sons.
Mulan has no older brothers.
I'll be the one to buy horse and bridle.
I'm taking his place in this expedition!

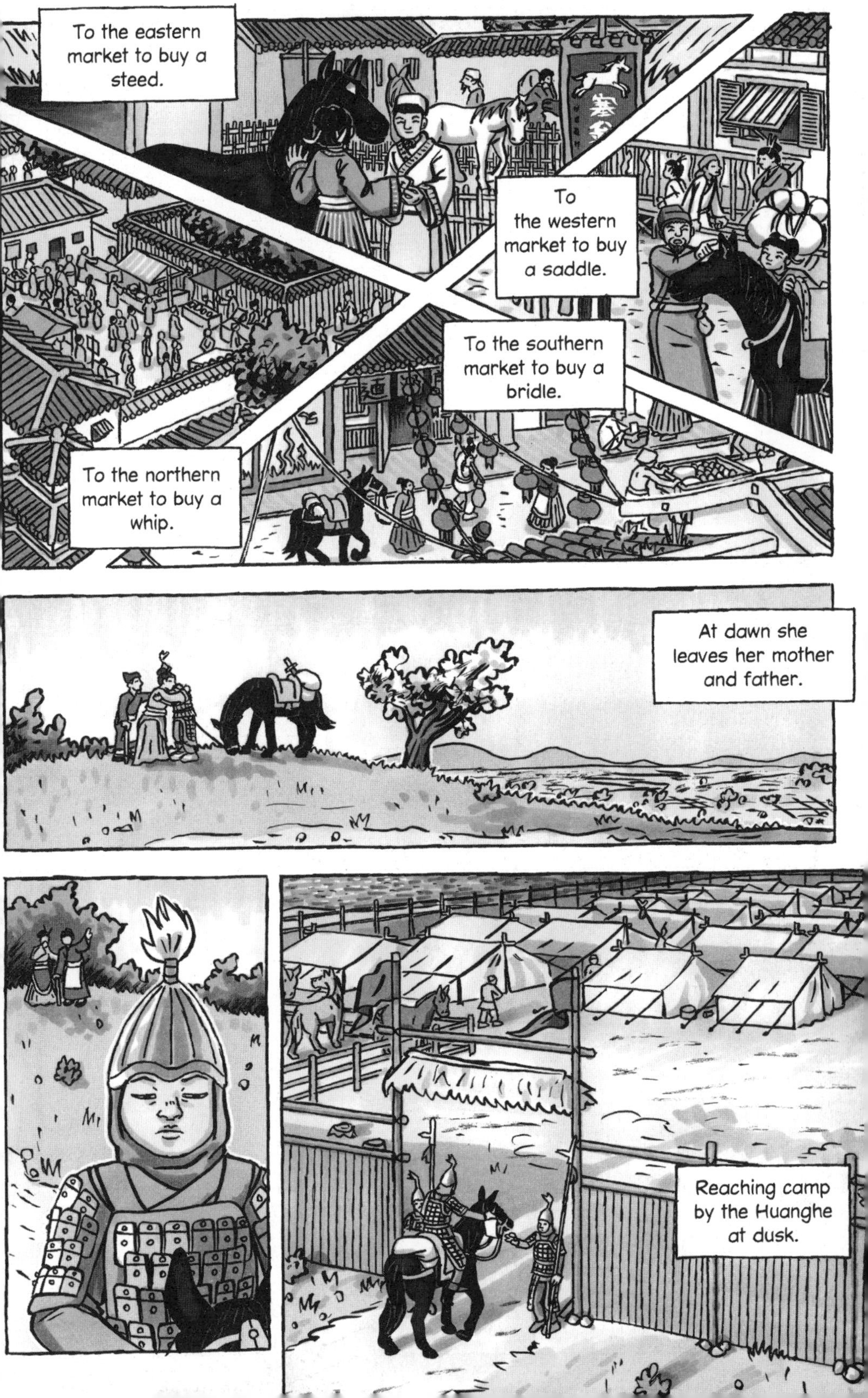
To the eastern market to buy a steed.
To the western market to buy a saddle.
To the southern market to buy a bridle.
To the northern market to buy a whip.
At dawn she leaves her mother and father.
Reaching camp by the Huanghe at dusk.

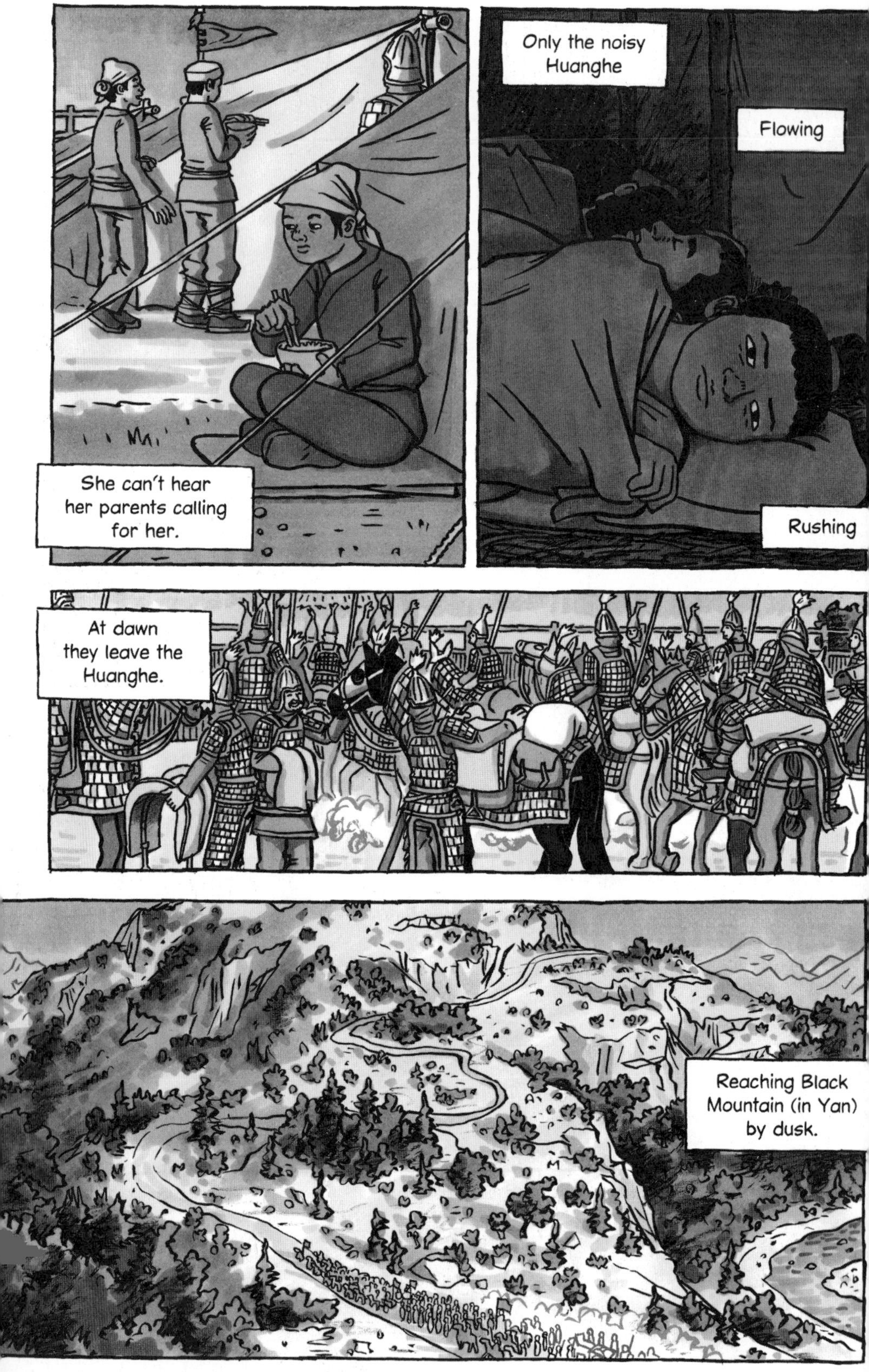
She can't hear her parents calling for her.
Only the noisy Huanghe
Flowing
Rushing
At dawn they leave the Huanghe.
Reaching Black Mountain (in Yan) by dusk.

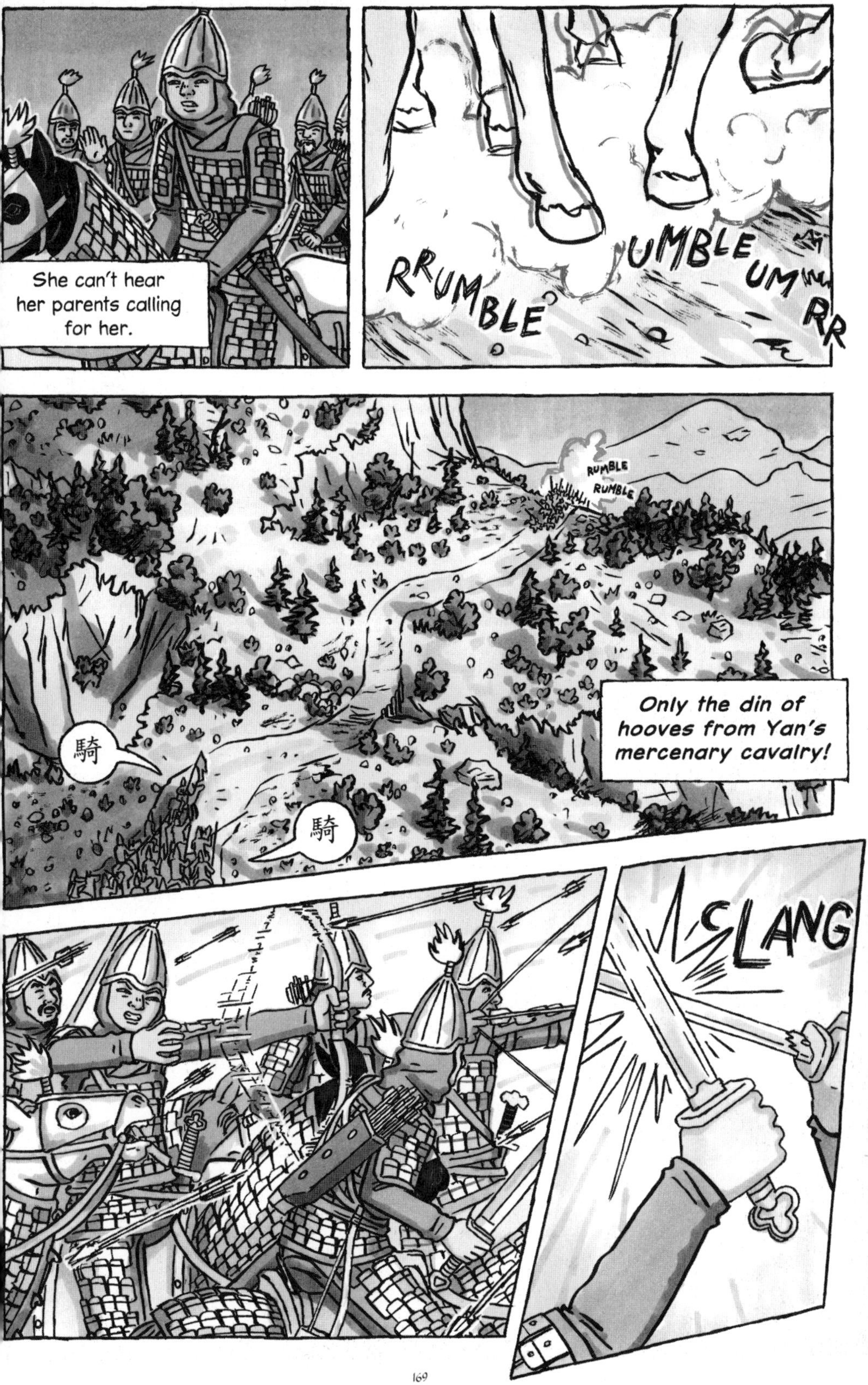
She can't hear her parents calling for her.
RRUMBLE
UMBLE UM
RR
RUMBLE
RUMBLE
Only the din of hooves from Yan's mercenary cavalry!
騎
騎
CLANG

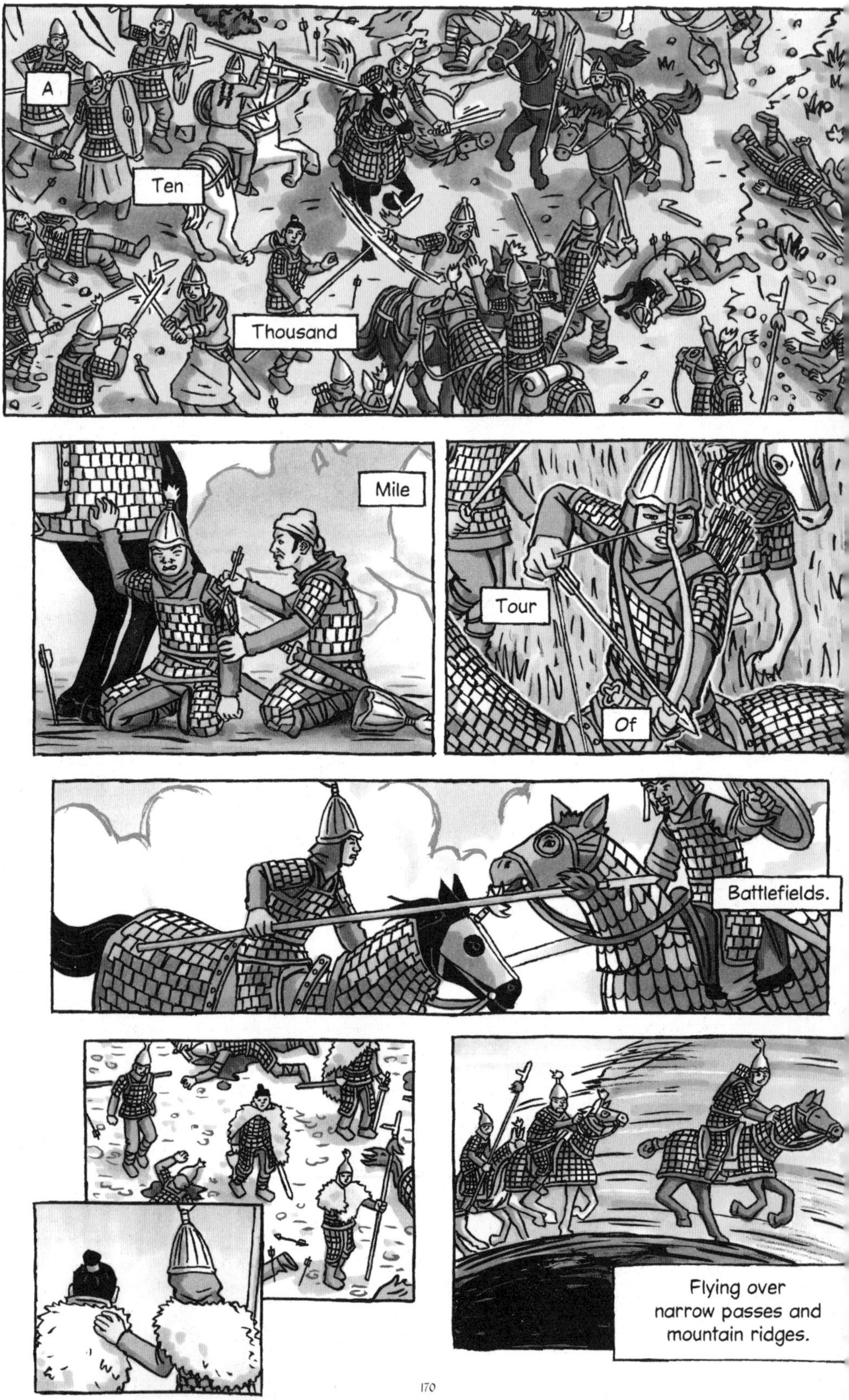
A
Ten
Thousand
Mile
Tour
Of
Battlefields.
Flying over narrow passes and mountain ridges.

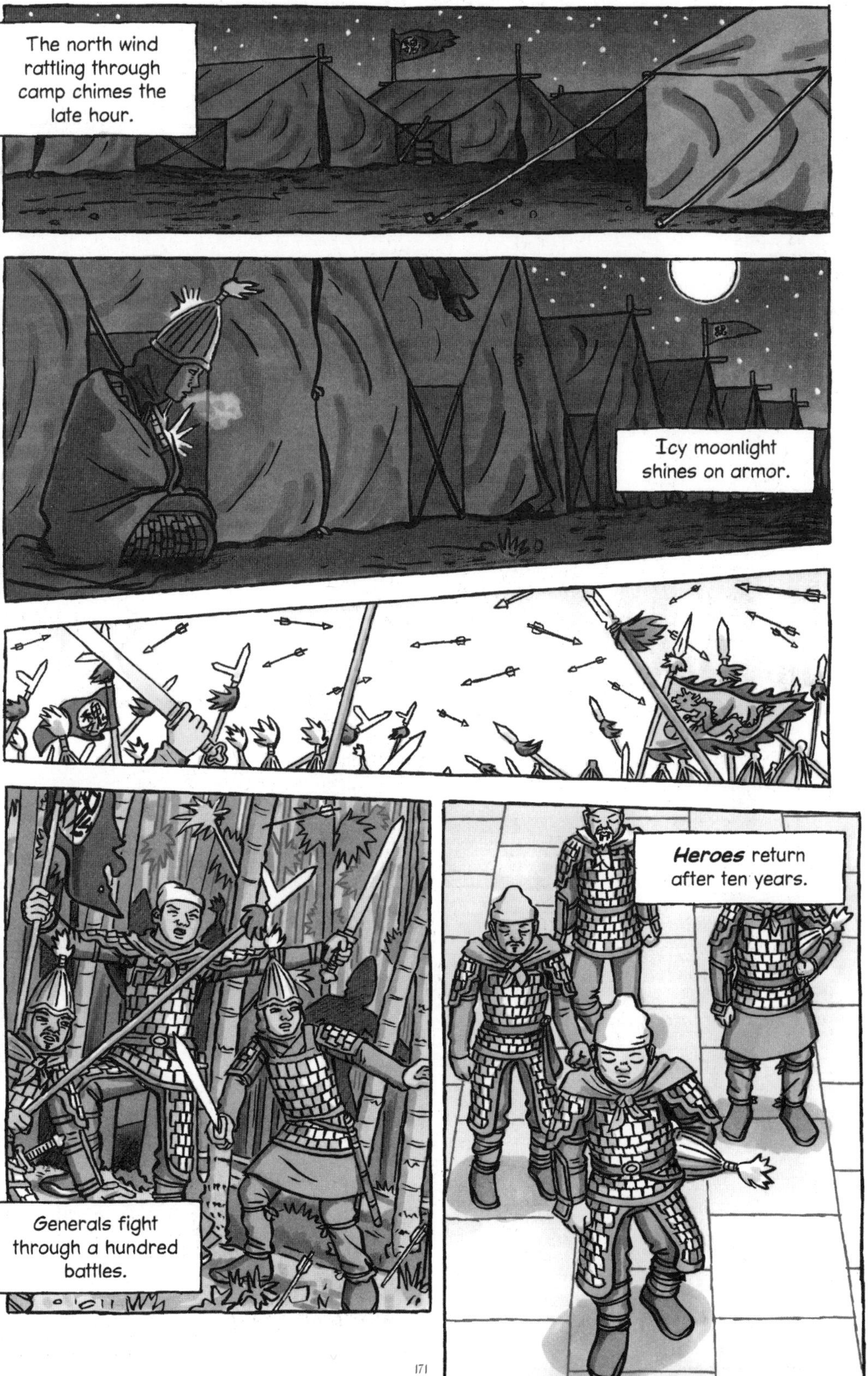
The north wind rattling through camp chimes the late hour.
Icy moonlight shines on armor.
Generals fight through a hundred battles.
Heroes return after ten years.

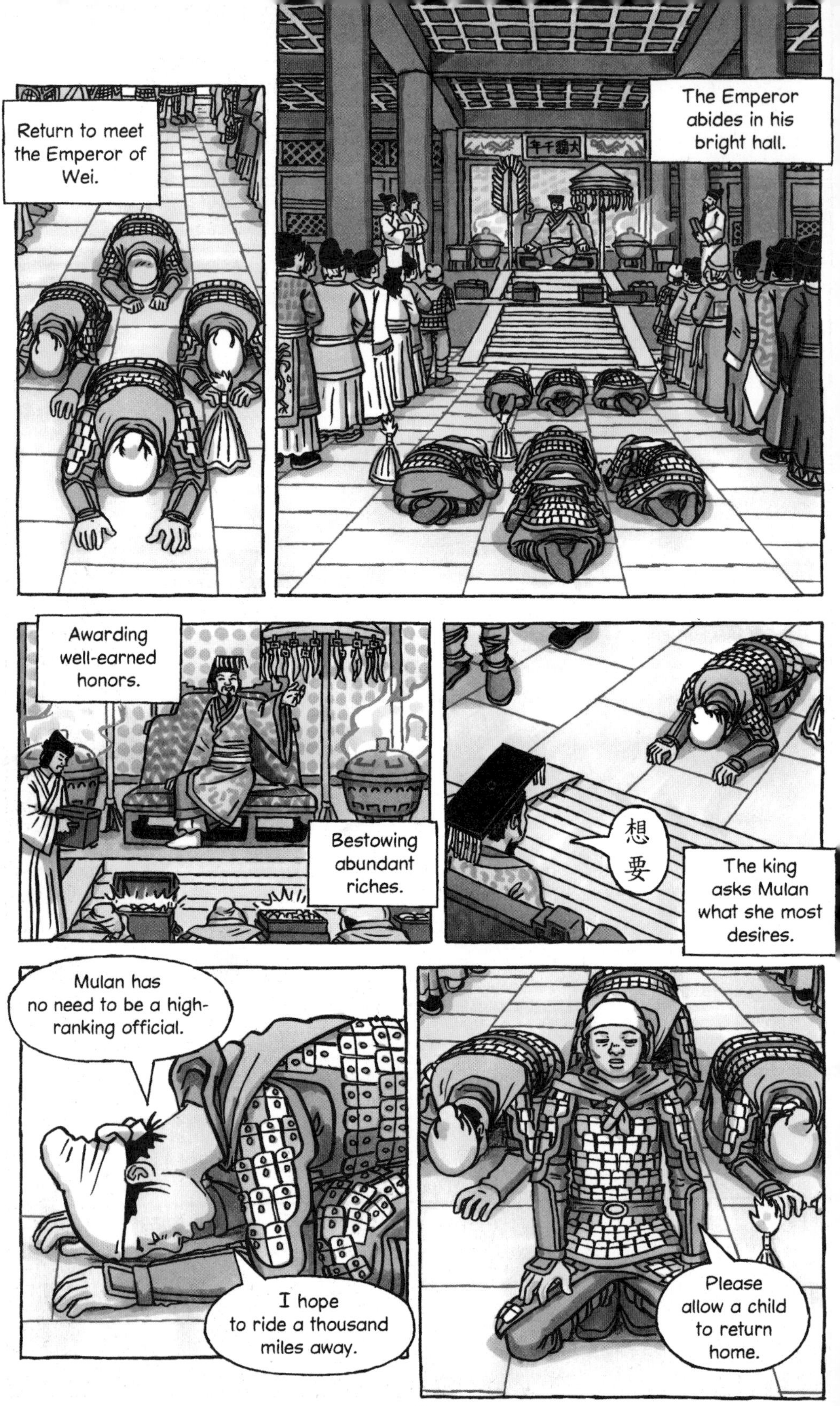

Return to meet the Emperor of Wei.
The Emperor abides in his bright hall.
Awarding well-earned honors.
Bestowing abundant riches.
想要
The king asks Mulan what she most desires.
Mulan has no need to be a high-ranking official.
I hope to ride a thousand miles away.
Please allow a child to return home.

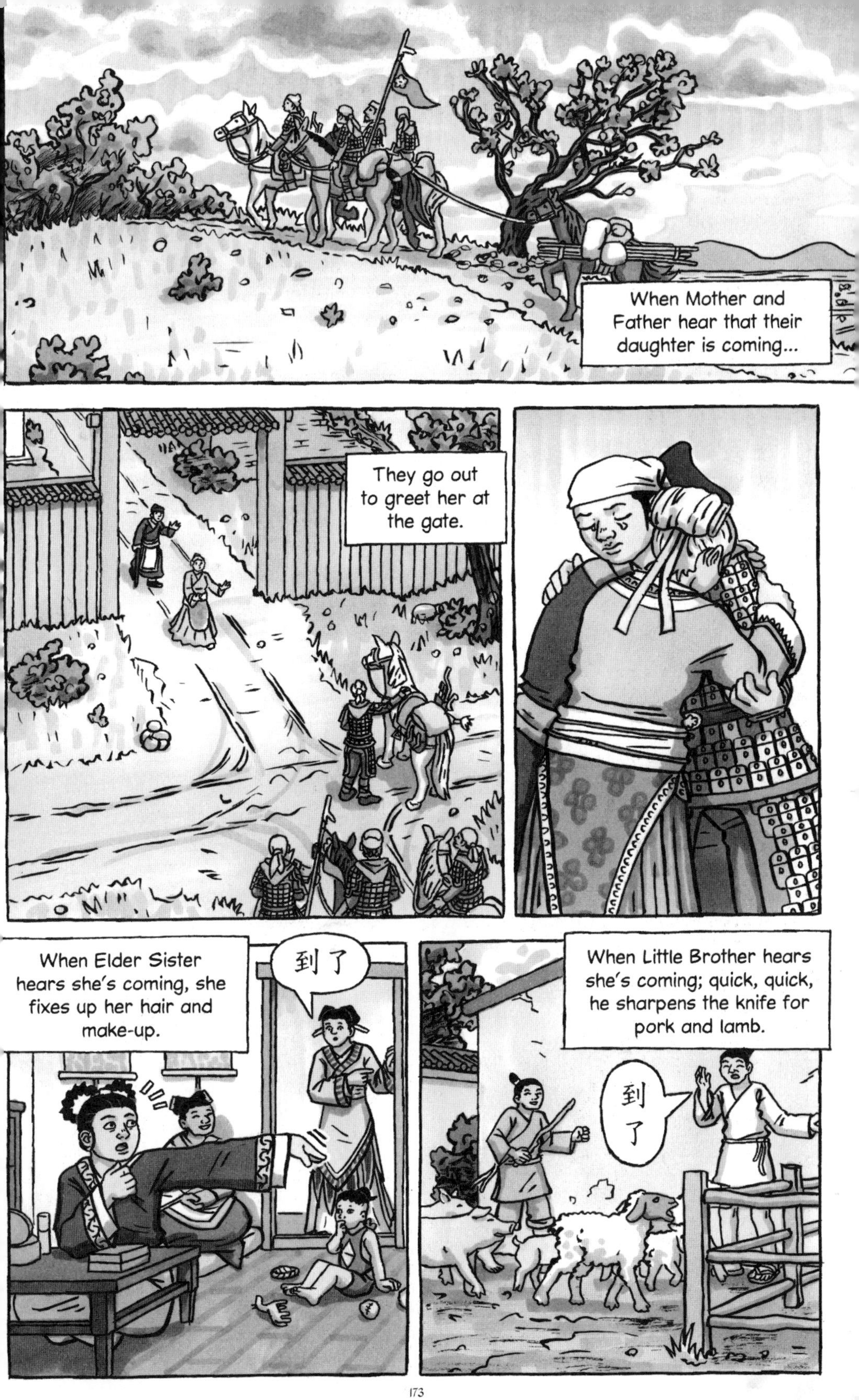
When Mother and
Father hear that their
daughter is coming...
They go out
to greet her at
the gate.
When Elder Sister
hears she's coming, she
fixes up her hair and
make-up.
到了
When Little Brother hears
she's coming; quick, quick,
he sharpens the knife for
pork and lamb.
到了

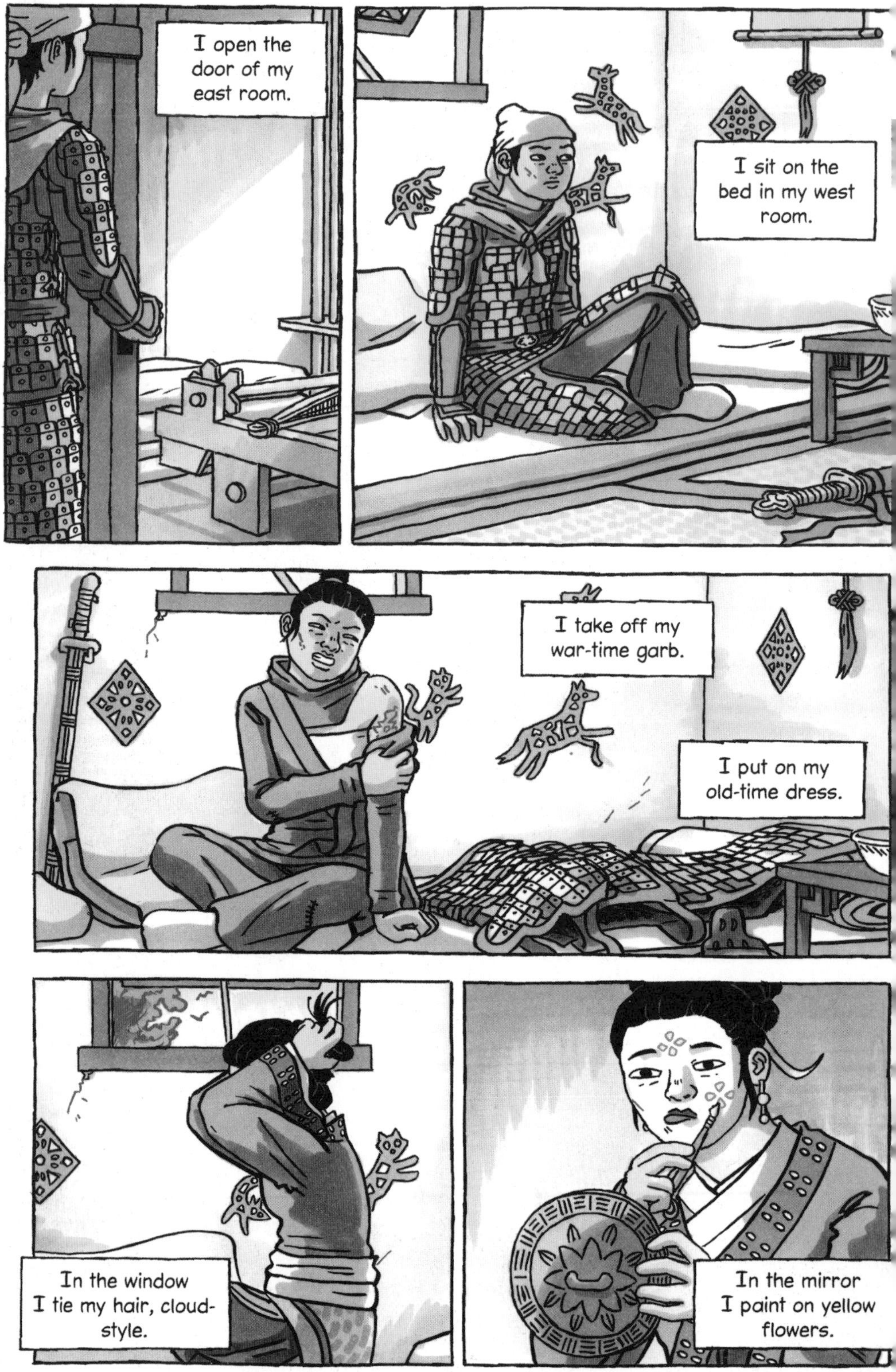
I open the door of my east room.
I sit on the bed in my west room.
I take off my war-time garb.
I put on my old-time dress.
In the window I tie my hair, cloud-style.
In the mirror I paint on yellow flowers.

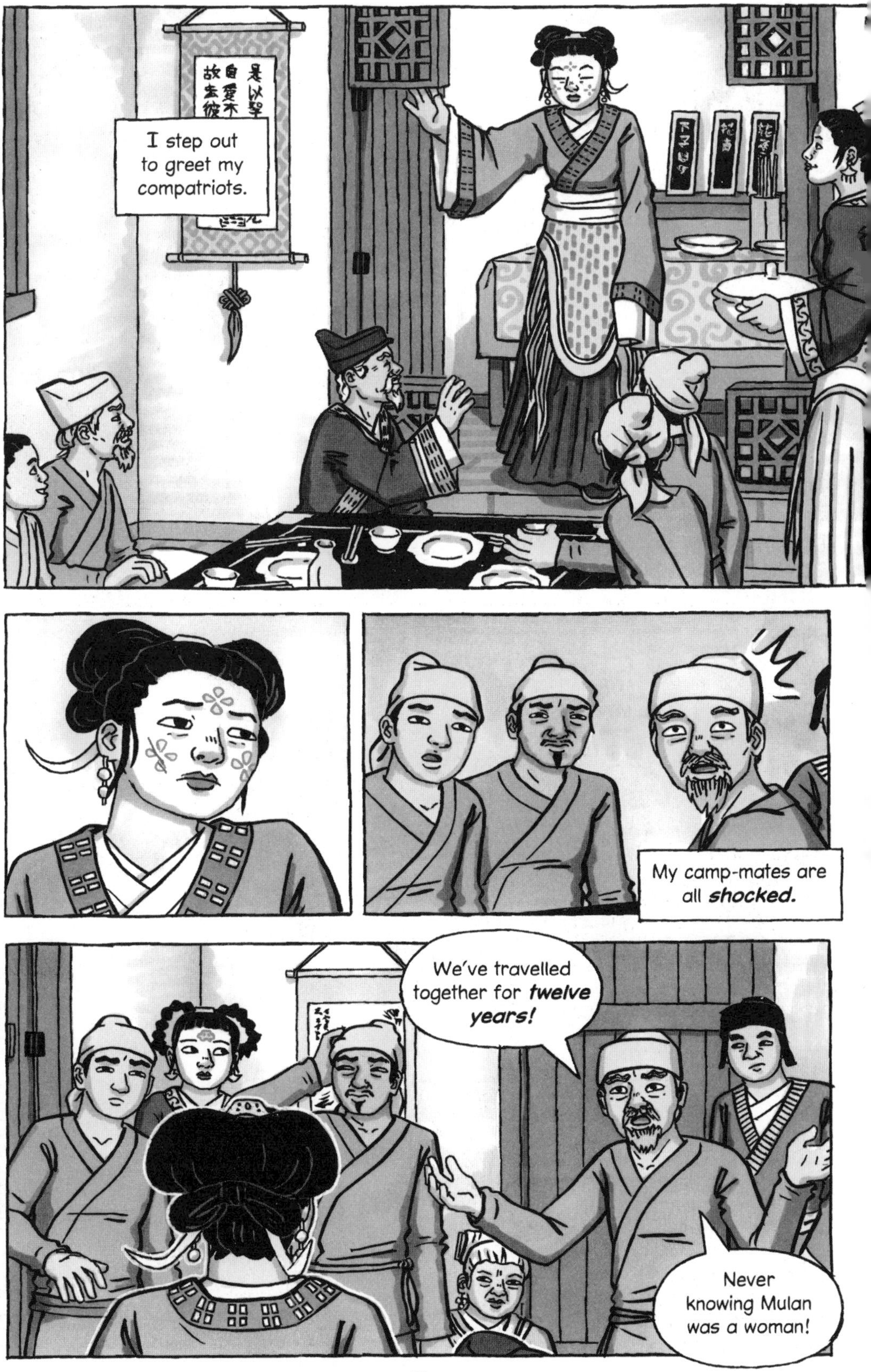
I step out to greet my compatriots.
My camp-mates are all ***shocked.***
We've travelled together for ***twelve years!***
Never knowing Mulan was a woman!

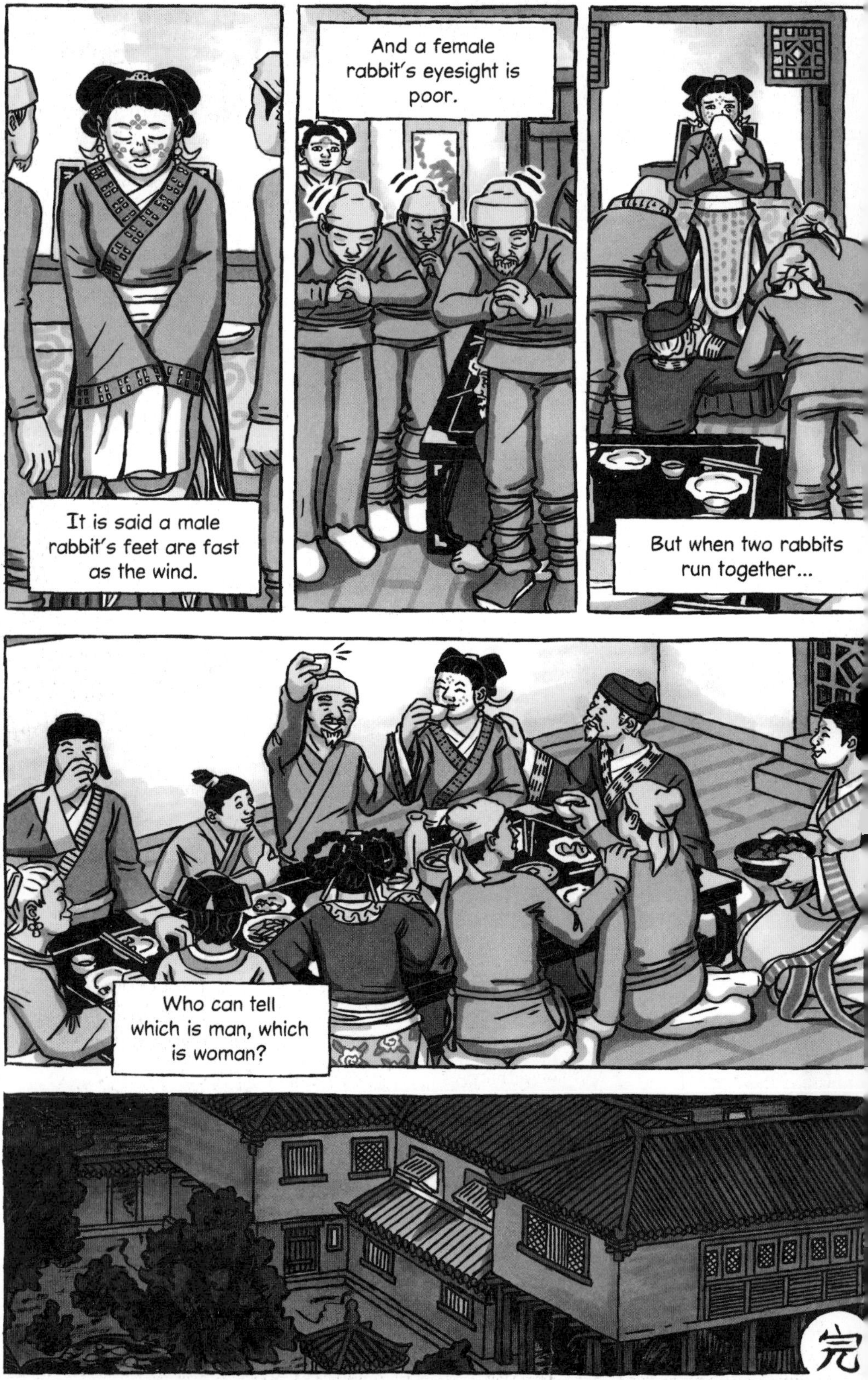
It is said a male rabbit's feet are fast as the wind.
And a female rabbit's eyesight is poor.
But when two rabbits run together...
Who can tell which is man, which is woman?
完

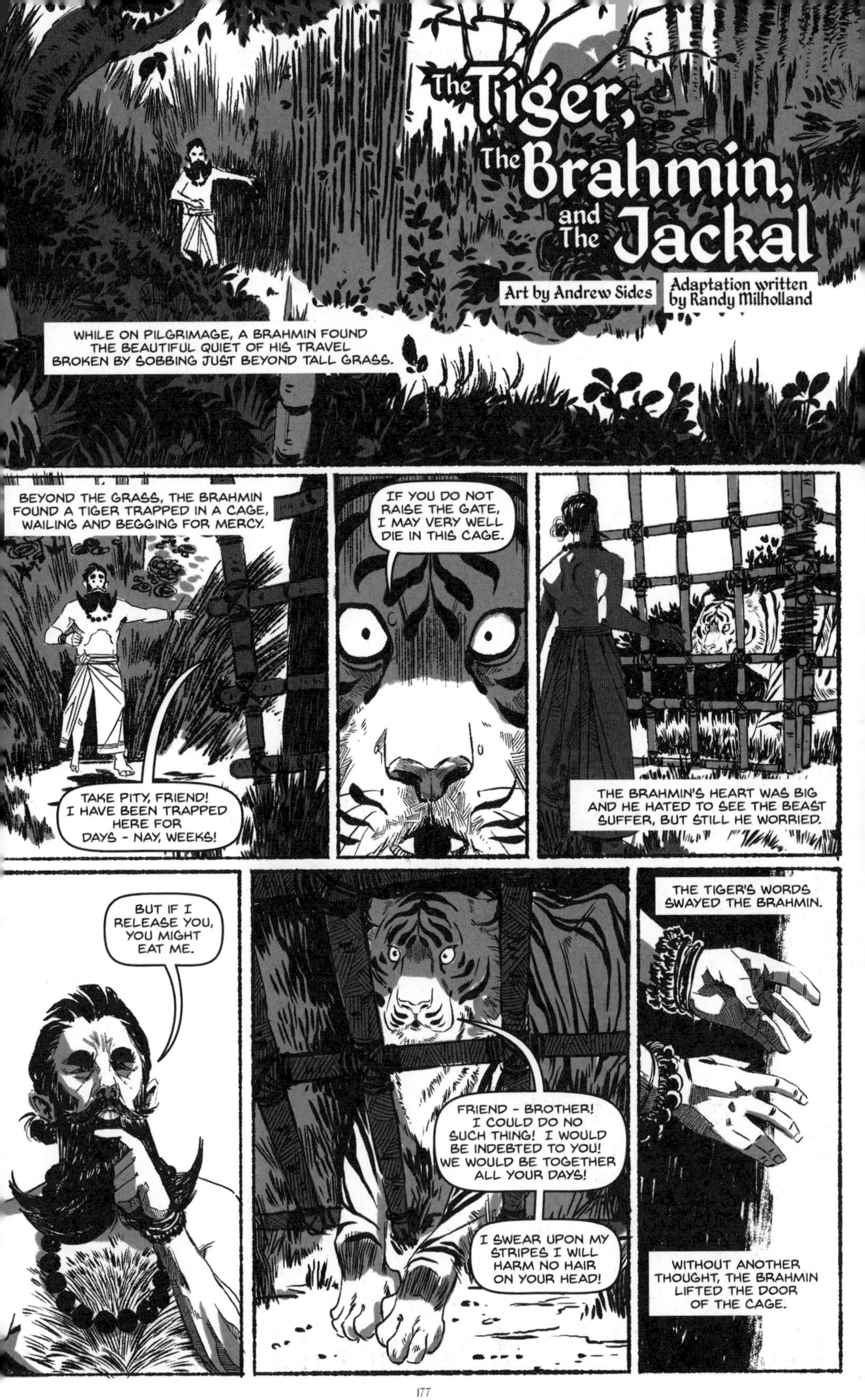
The Tiger, The Brahmin, and The Jackal
Art by Andrew Sides
Adaptation written by Randy Milholland
WHILE ON PILGRIMAGE, A BRAHMIN FOUND THE BEAUTIFUL QUIET OF HIS TRAVEL BROKEN BY SOBBING JUST BEYOND TALL GRASS.
BEYOND THE GRASS, THE BRAHMIN FOUND A TIGER TRAPPED IN A CAGE, WAILING AND BEGGING FOR MERCY.
TAKE PITY, FRIEND! I HAVE BEEN TRAPPED HERE FOR DAYS - NAY, WEEKS!
IF YOU DO NOT RAISE THE GATE, I MAY VERY WELL DIE IN THIS CAGE.
THE BRAHMIN'S HEART WAS BIG AND HE HATED TO SEE THE BEAST SUFFER, BUT STILL HE WORRIED.
BUT IF I RELEASE YOU, YOU MIGHT EAT ME.
FRIEND - BROTHER! I COULD DO NO SUCH THING! I WOULD BE INDEBTED TO YOU! WE WOULD BE TOGETHER ALL YOUR DAYS!
I SWEAR UPON MY STRIPES I WILL HARM NO HAIR ON YOUR HEAD!
THE TIGER'S WORDS SWAYED THE BRAHMIN.
WITHOUT ANOTHER THOUGHT, THE BRAHMIN LIFTED THE DOOR OF THE CAGE.

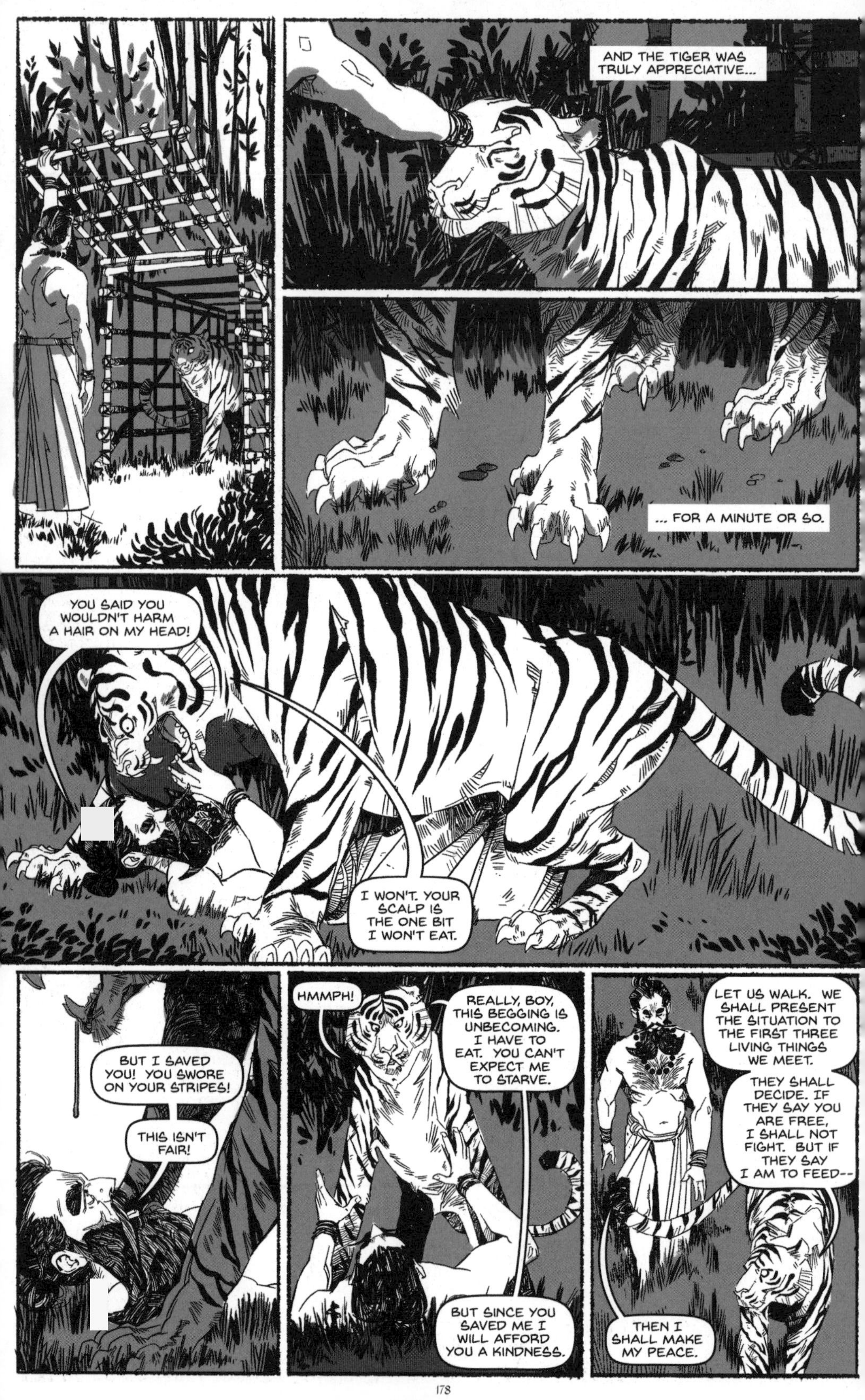
AND THE TIGER WAS TRULY APPRECIATIVE...
... FOR A MINUTE OR SO.
YOU SAID YOU WOULDN'T HARM A HAIR ON MY HEAD!
I WON'T. YOUR SCALP IS THE ONE BIT I WON'T EAT.
BUT I SAVED YOU! YOU SWORE ON YOUR STRIPES!
THIS ISN'T FAIR!
HMMPH!
REALLY, BOY, THIS BEGGING IS UNBECOMING. I HAVE TO EAT. YOU CAN'T EXPECT ME TO STARVE.
BUT SINCE YOU SAVED ME I WILL AFFORD YOU A KINDNESS.
LET US WALK. WE SHALL PRESENT THE SITUATION TO THE FIRST THREE LIVING THINGS WE MEET.
THEY SHALL DECIDE. IF THEY SAY YOU ARE FREE, I SHALL NOT FIGHT. BUT IF THEY SAY I AM TO FEED--
THEN I SHALL MAKE MY PEACE.

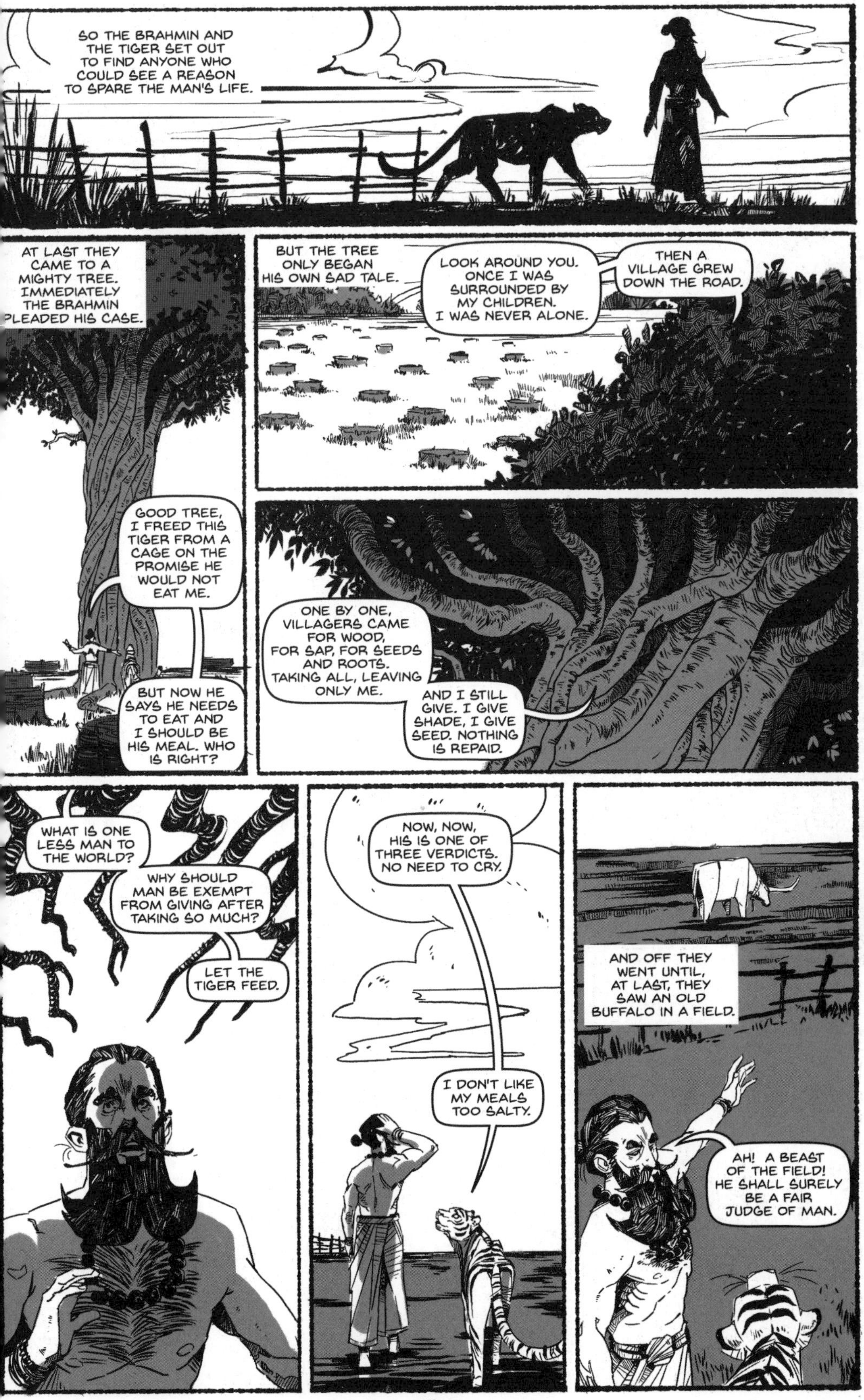
SO THE BRAHMIN AND THE TIGER SET OUT TO FIND ANYONE WHO COULD SEE A REASON TO SPARE THE MAN'S LIFE.
AT LAST THEY CAME TO A MIGHTY TREE. IMMEDIATELY THE BRAHMIN PLEADED HIS CASE.
GOOD TREE, I FREED THIS TIGER FROM A CAGE ON THE PROMISE HE WOULD NOT EAT ME.
BUT NOW HE SAYS HE NEEDS TO EAT AND I SHOULD BE HIS MEAL. WHO IS RIGHT?
BUT THE TREE ONLY BEGAN HIS OWN SAD TALE.
LOOK AROUND YOU. ONCE I WAS SURROUNDED BY MY CHILDREN. I WAS NEVER ALONE.
THEN A VILLAGE GREW DOWN THE ROAD.
ONE BY ONE, VILLAGERS CAME FOR WOOD, FOR SAP, FOR SEEDS AND ROOTS. TAKING ALL, LEAVING ONLY ME.
AND I STILL GIVE. I GIVE SHADE, I GIVE SEED. NOTHING IS REPAID.
WHAT IS ONE LESS MAN TO THE WORLD?
WHY SHOULD MAN BE EXEMPT FROM GIVING AFTER TAKING SO MUCH?
LET THE TIGER FEED.
NOW, NOW, HIS IS ONE OF THREE VERDICTS. NO NEED TO CRY.
I DON'T LIKE MY MEALS TOO SALTY.
AND OFF THEY WENT UNTIL, AT LAST, THEY SAW AN OLD BUFFALO IN A FIELD.
AH! A BEAST OF THE FIELD! HE SHALL SURELY BE A FAIR JUDGE OF MAN.

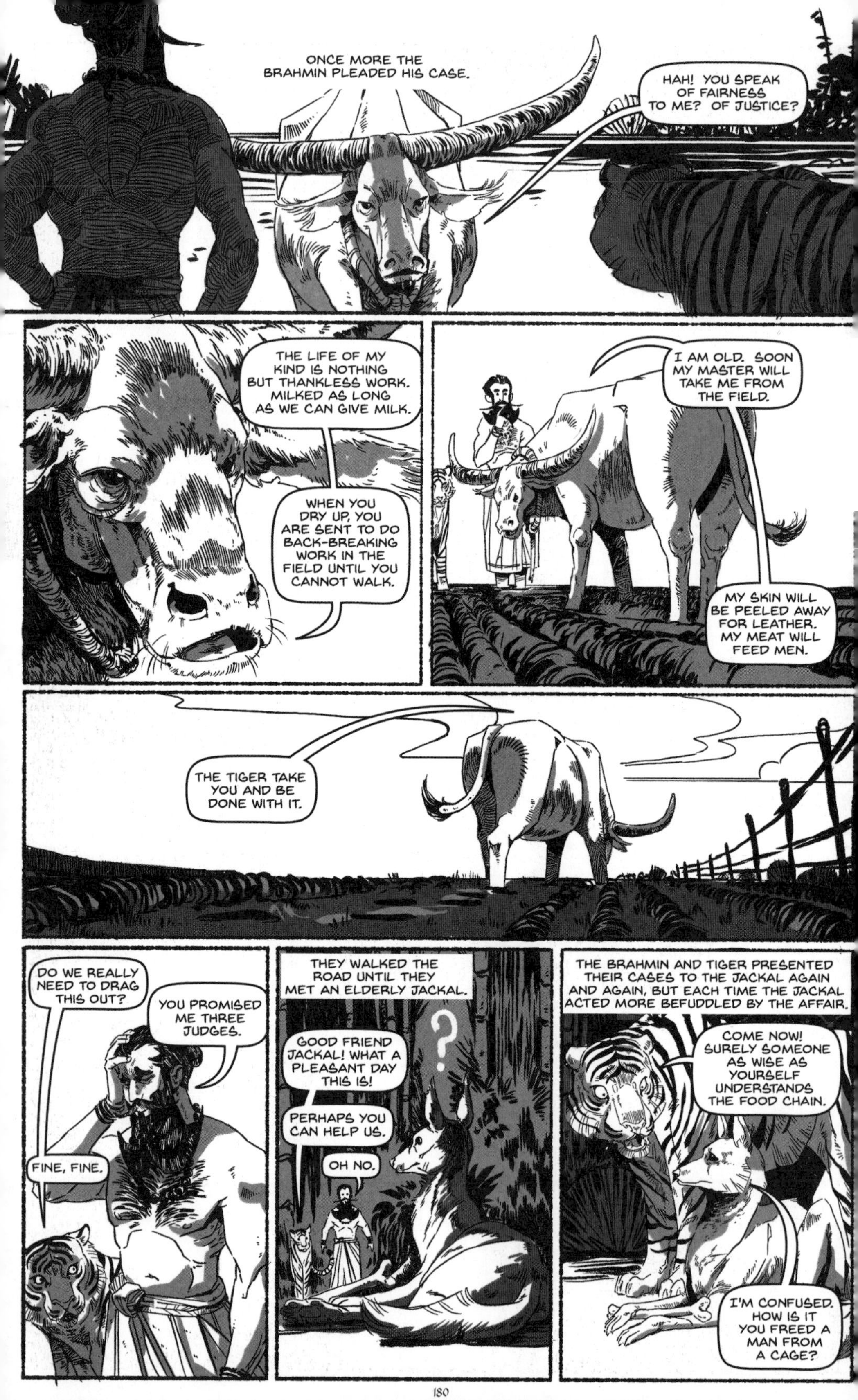
ONCE MORE THE BRAHMIN PLEADED HIS CASE.
HAH! YOU SPEAK OF FAIRNESS TO ME? OF JUSTICE?
THE LIFE OF MY KIND IS NOTHING BUT THANKLESS WORK. MILKED AS LONG AS WE CAN GIVE MILK.
WHEN YOU DRY UP, YOU ARE SENT TO DO BACK-BREAKING WORK IN THE FIELD UNTIL YOU CANNOT WALK.
I AM OLD. SOON MY MASTER WILL TAKE ME FROM THE FIELD.
MY SKIN WILL BE PEELED AWAY FOR LEATHER. MY MEAT WILL FEED MEN.
THE TIGER TAKE YOU AND BE DONE WITH IT.
DO WE REALLY NEED TO DRAG THIS OUT?
YOU PROMISED ME THREE JUDGES.
FINE, FINE.
THEY WALKED THE ROAD UNTIL THEY MET AN ELDERLY JACKAL.
?
GOOD FRIEND JACKAL! WHAT A PLEASANT DAY THIS IS!
PERHAPS YOU CAN HELP US.
OH NO.
THE BRAHMIN AND TIGER PRESENTED THEIR CASES TO THE JACKAL AGAIN AND AGAIN, BUT EACH TIME THE JACKAL ACTED MORE BEFUDDLED BY THE AFFAIR.
COME NOW! SURELY SOMEONE AS WISE AS YOURSELF UNDERSTANDS THE FOOD CHAIN.
I'M CONFUSED. HOW IS IT YOU FREED A MAN FROM A CAGE?

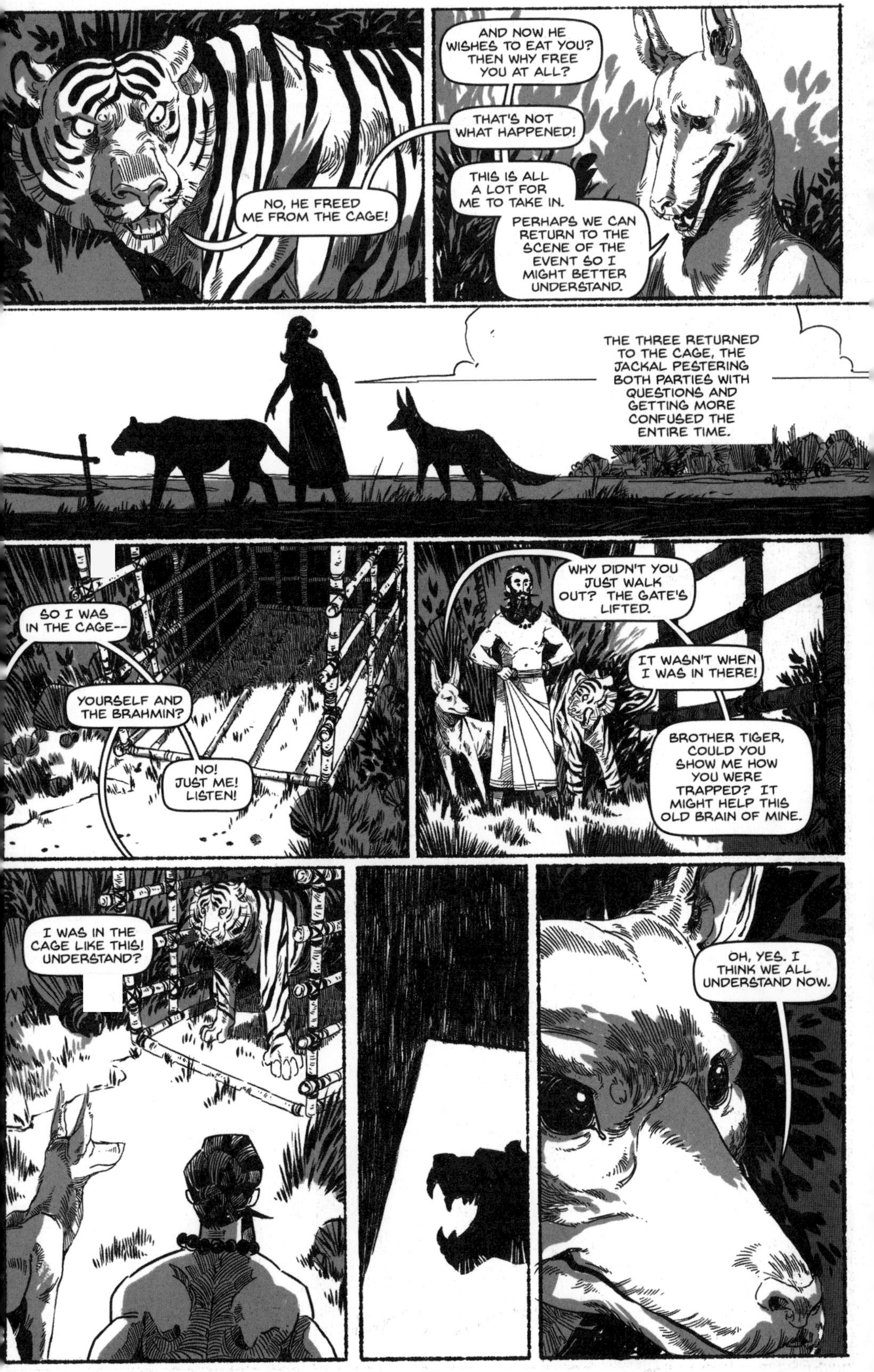
AND NOW HE WISHES TO EAT YOU? THEN WHY FREE YOU AT ALL?
NO, HE FREED ME FROM THE CAGE!
THAT'S NOT WHAT HAPPENED!
THIS IS ALL A LOT FOR ME TO TAKE IN.
PERHAPS WE CAN RETURN TO THE SCENE OF THE EVENT SO I MIGHT BETTER UNDERSTAND.
THE THREE RETURNED TO THE CAGE, THE JACKAL PESTERING BOTH PARTIES WITH QUESTIONS AND GETTING MORE CONFUSED THE ENTIRE TIME.
SO I WAS IN THE CAGE--
YOURSELF AND THE BRAHMIN?
NO! JUST ME! LISTEN!
WHY DIDN'T YOU JUST WALK OUT? THE GATE'S LIFTED.
IT WASN'T WHEN I WAS IN THERE!
BROTHER TIGER, COULD YOU SHOW ME HOW YOU WERE TRAPPED? IT MIGHT HELP THIS OLD BRAIN OF MINE.
I WAS IN THE CAGE LIKE THIS! UNDERSTAND?
OH, YES. I THINK WE ALL UNDERSTAND NOW.

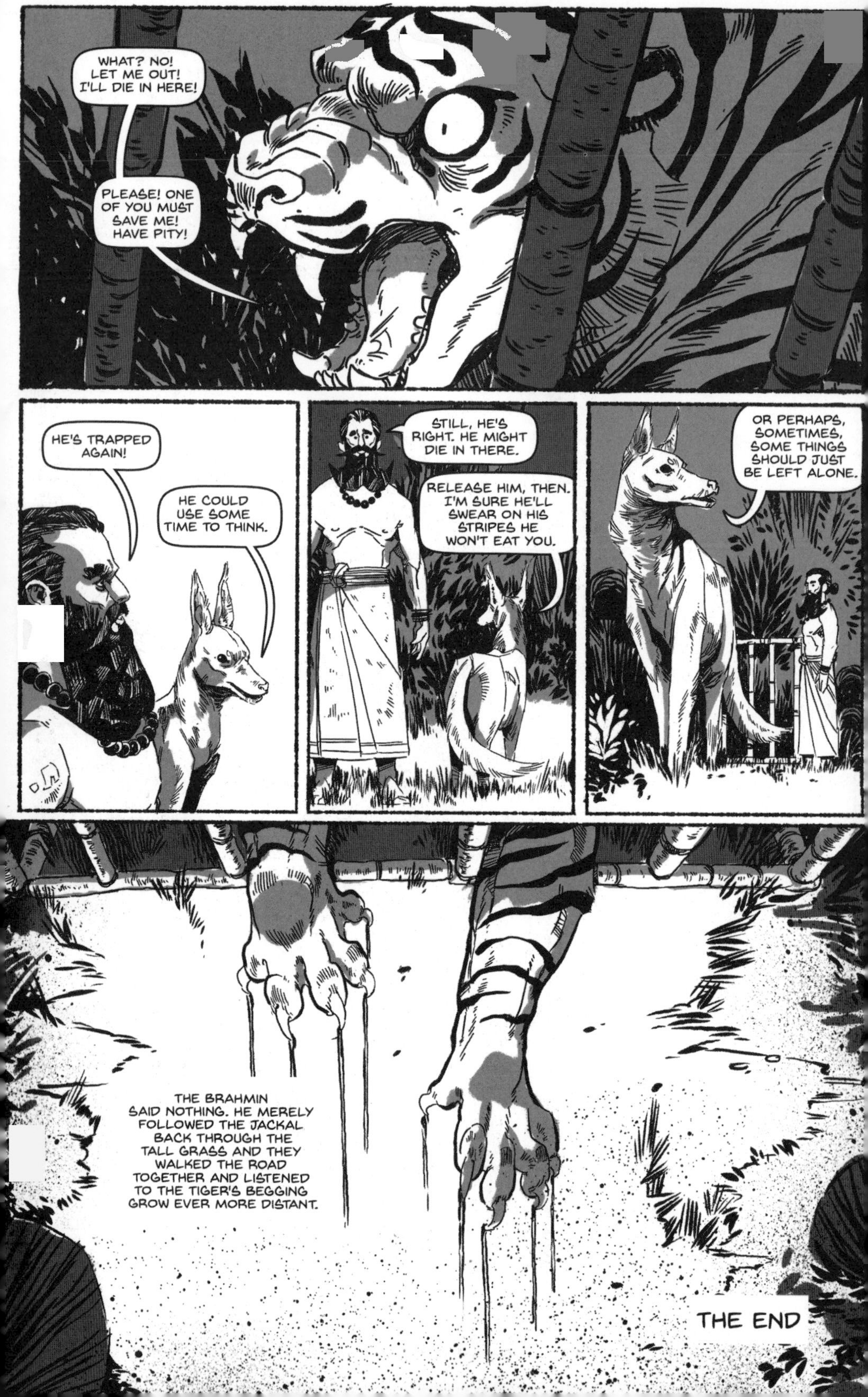
WHAT? NO! LET ME OUT! I'LL DIE IN HERE!
PLEASE! ONE OF YOU MUST SAVE ME! HAVE PITY!
HE'S TRAPPED AGAIN!
HE COULD USE SOME TIME TO THINK.
STILL, HE'S RIGHT. HE MIGHT DIE IN THERE.
RELEASE HIM, THEN. I'M SURE HE'LL SWEAR ON HIS STRIPES HE WON'T EAT YOU.
OR PERHAPS, SOMETIMES, SOME THINGS SHOULD JUST BE LEFT ALONE.
THE BRAHMIN SAID NOTHING. HE MERELY FOLLOWED THE JACKAL BACK THROUGH THE TALL GRASS AND THEY WALKED THE ROAD TOGETHER AND LISTENED TO THE TIGER'S BEGGING GROW EVER MORE DISTANT.
THE END

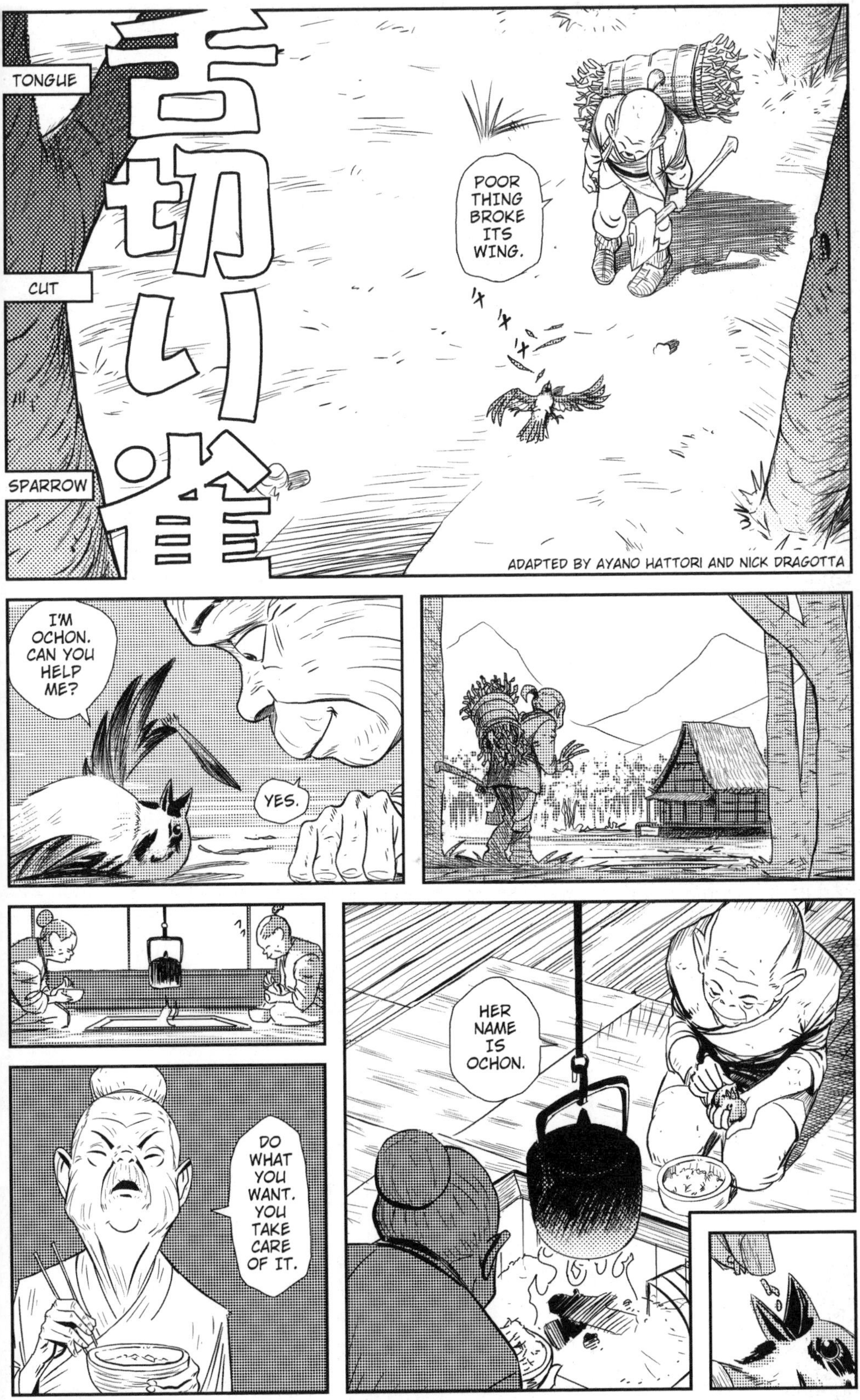

舌切り雀
TONGUE
CUT
SPARROW
ADAPTED BY AYANO HATTORI AND NICK DRAGOTTA
POOR THING BROKE ITS WING.
I'M OCHON. CAN YOU HELP ME?
YES.
HER NAME IS OCHON.
DO WHAT YOU WANT. YOU TAKE CARE OF IT.

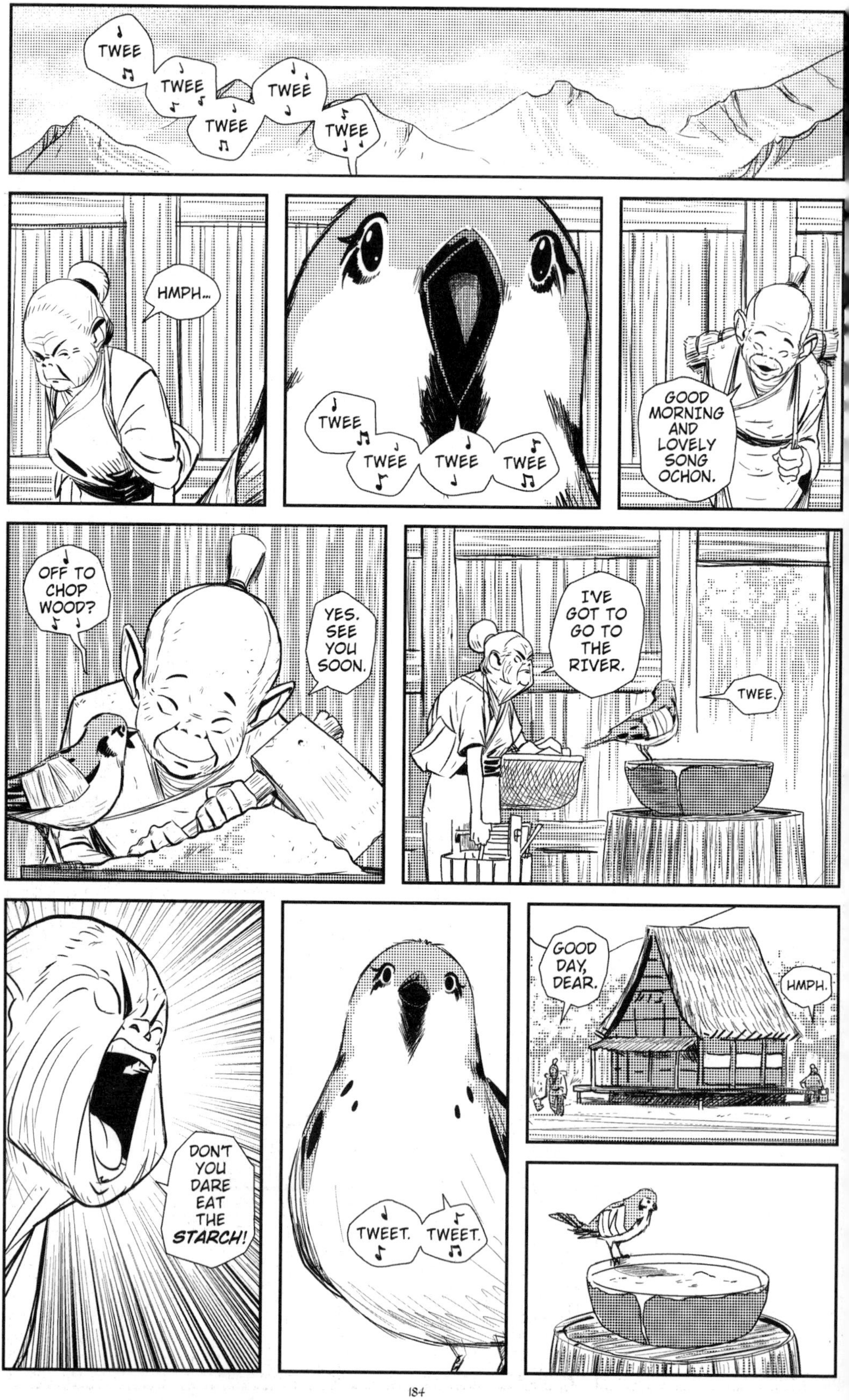
TWEE
TWEE
TWEE
TWEE
TWEE
HMPH...
TWEE
TWEE
TWEE
TWEE
GOOD MORNING AND LOVELY SONG OCHON.
OFF TO CHOP WOOD?
YES. SEE YOU SOON.
I'VE GOT TO GO TO THE RIVER.
TWEE.
DON'T YOU DARE EAT THE STARCH!
TWEET.
TWEET.
GOOD DAY, DEAR.
HMPH.

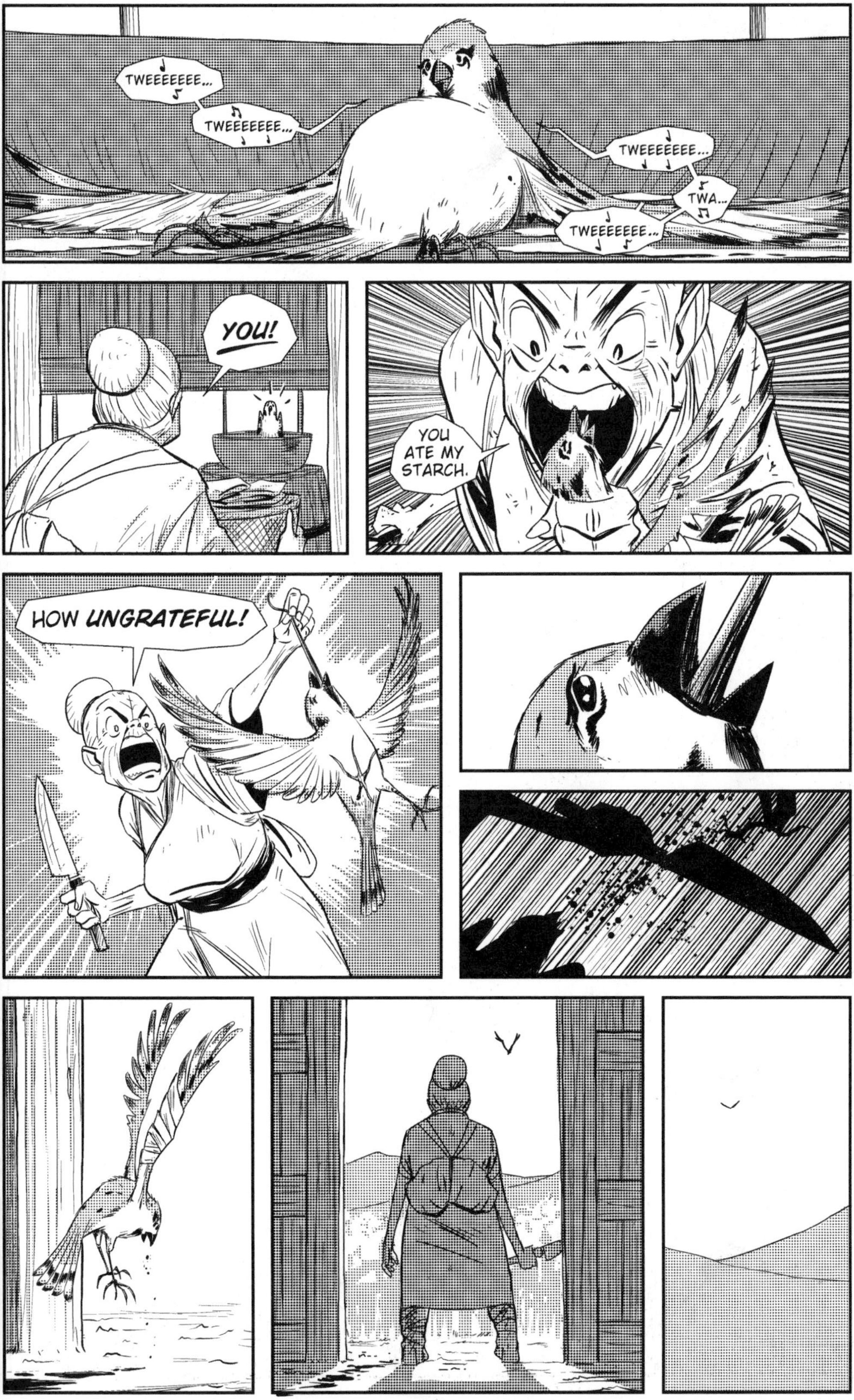
TWEEEEEEE...
TWEEEEEEE...
TWEEEEEEE...
TWA...
TWEEEEEEE...
YOU!
YOU ATE MY STARCH.
HOW UNGRATEFUL!

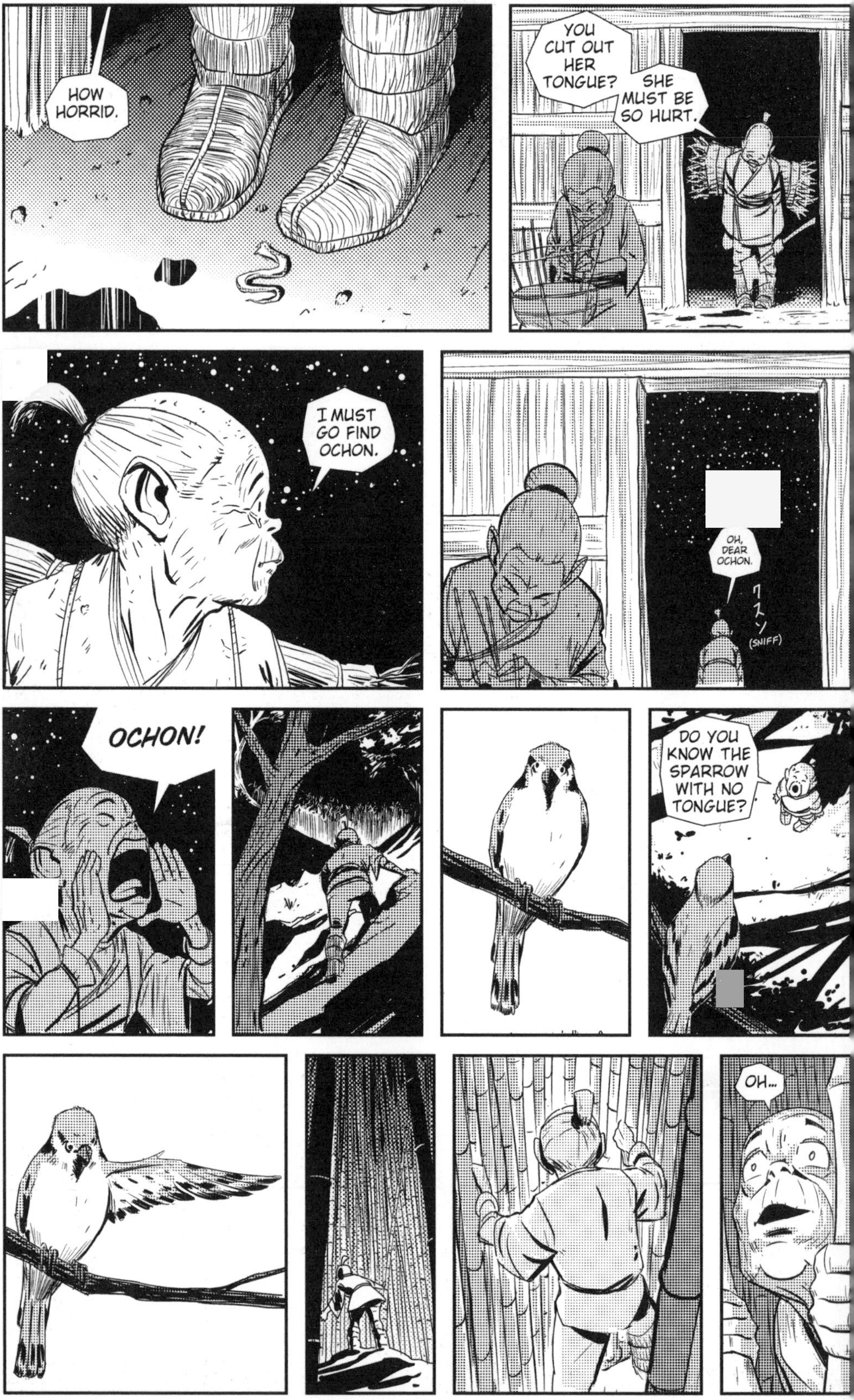
HOW HORRID.
YOU CUT OUT HER TONGUE?
SHE MUST BE SO HURT.
I MUST GO FIND OCHON.
OH, DEAR OCHON.
クスン
(SNIFF)
OCHON!
DO YOU KNOW THE SPARROW WITH NO TONGUE?
OH...

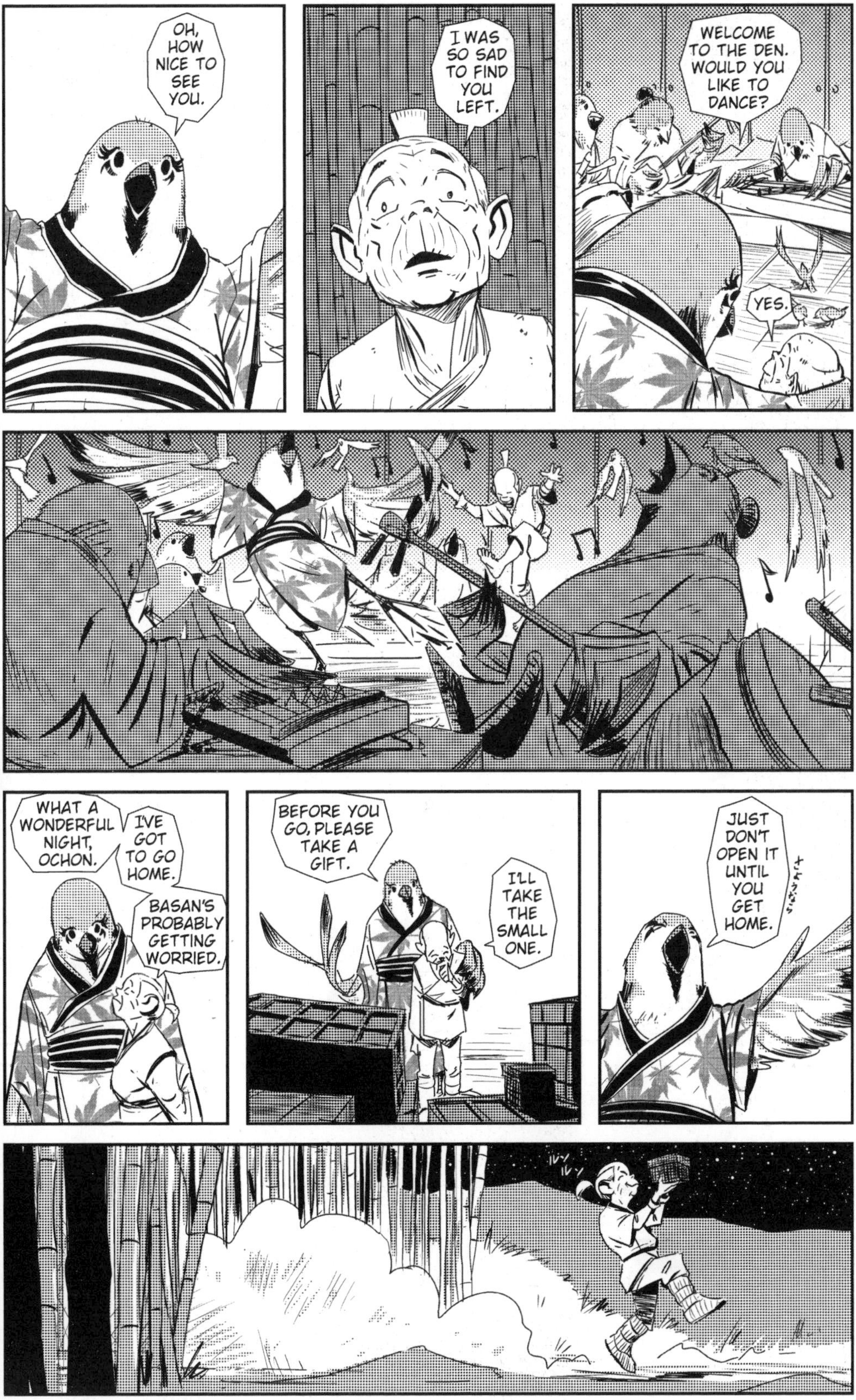
OH, HOW NICE TO SEE YOU.
I WAS SO SAD TO FIND YOU LEFT.
WELCOME TO THE DEN. WOULD YOU LIKE TO DANCE?
YES.
WHAT A WONDERFUL NIGHT, OCHON.
I'VE GOT TO GO HOME.
BASAN'S PROBABLY GETTING WORRIED.
BEFORE YOU GO, PLEASE TAKE A GIFT.
I'LL TAKE THE SMALL ONE.
JUST DON'T OPEN IT UNTIL YOU GET HOME.
さようなら
ルンルン

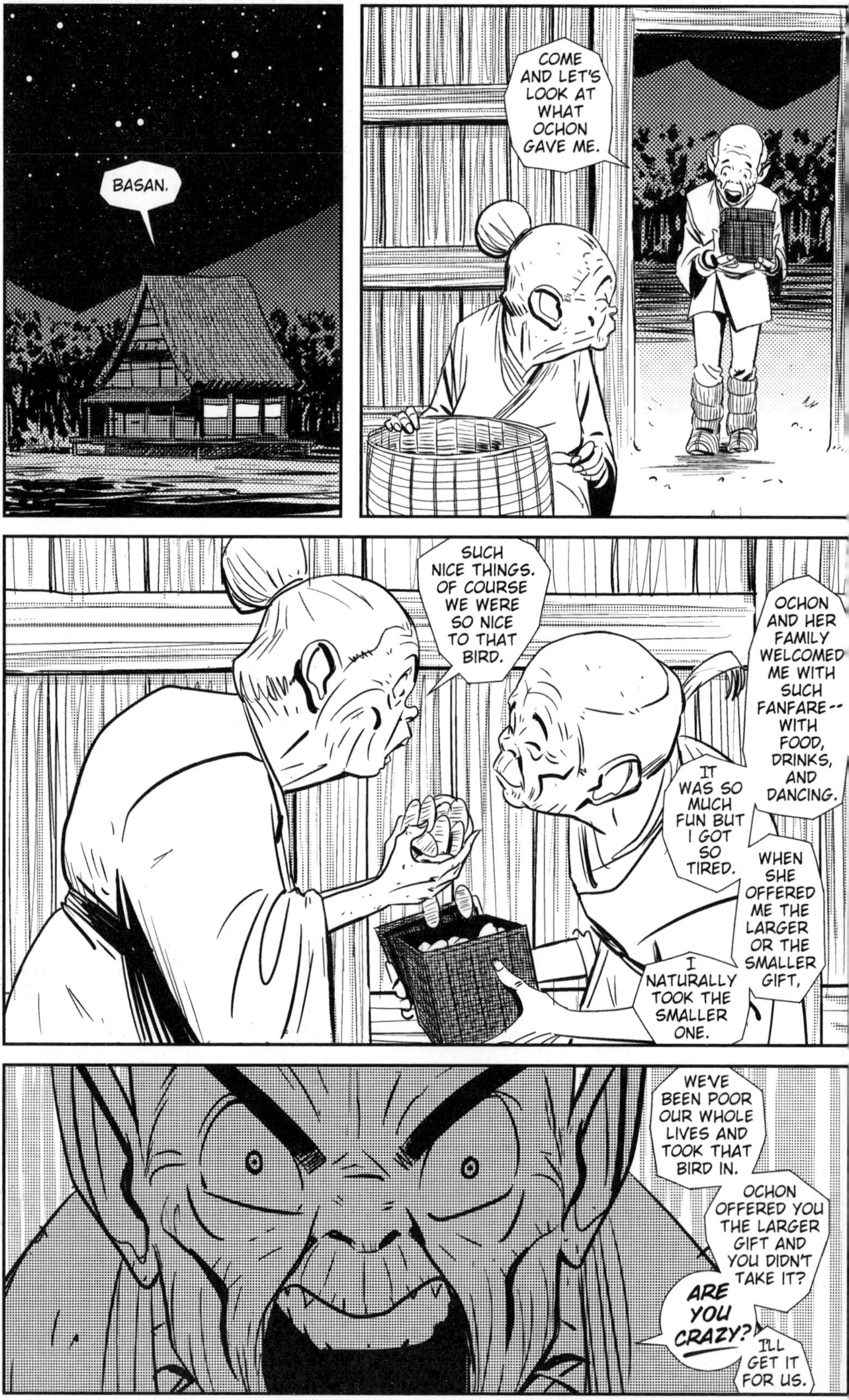
BASAN.
COME AND LET'S LOOK AT WHAT OCHON GAVE ME.
SUCH NICE THINGS. OF COURSE WE WERE SO NICE TO THAT BIRD.
OCHON AND HER FAMILY WELCOMED ME WITH SUCH FANFARE-- WITH FOOD, DRINKS, AND DANCING.
IT WAS SO MUCH FUN BUT I GOT SO TIRED.
WHEN SHE OFFERED ME THE LARGER OR THE SMALLER GIFT,
I NATURALLY TOOK THE SMALLER ONE.
WE'VE BEEN POOR OUR WHOLE LIVES AND TOOK THAT BIRD IN.
OCHON OFFERED YOU THE LARGER GIFT AND YOU DIDN'T TAKE IT?
ARE YOU CRAZY?
I'LL GET IT FOR US.

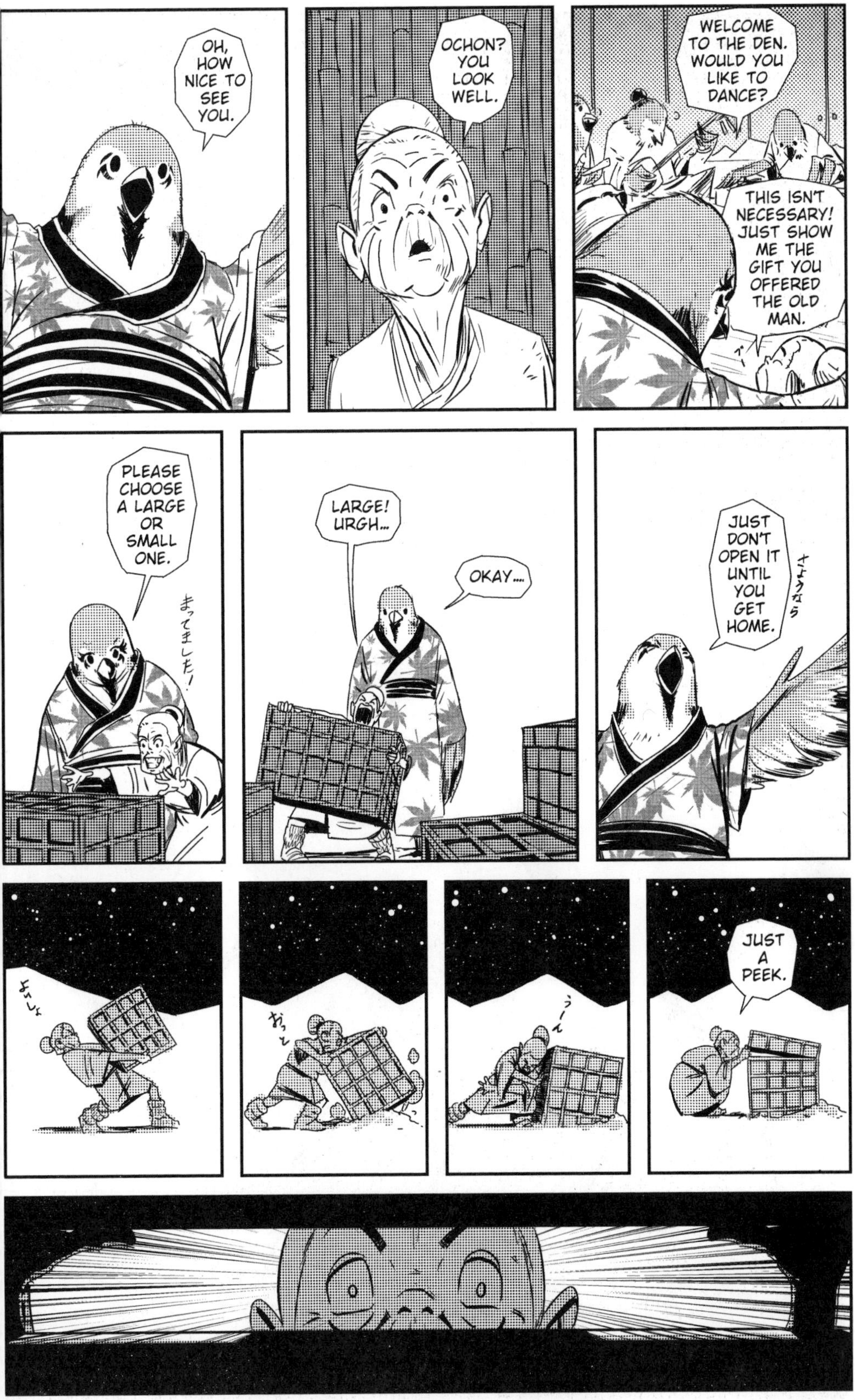
OH, HOW NICE TO SEE YOU.
OCHON? YOU LOOK WELL.
WELCOME TO THE DEN. WOULD YOU LIKE TO DANCE?
THIS ISN'T NECESSARY! JUST SHOW ME THE GIFT YOU OFFERED THE OLD MAN.
PLEASE CHOOSE A LARGE OR SMALL ONE.
まってました!
LARGE! URGH...
OKAY....
JUST DON'T OPEN IT UNTIL YOU GET HOME.
さようなら
よいしょ
おっと
うーん
JUST A PEEK.

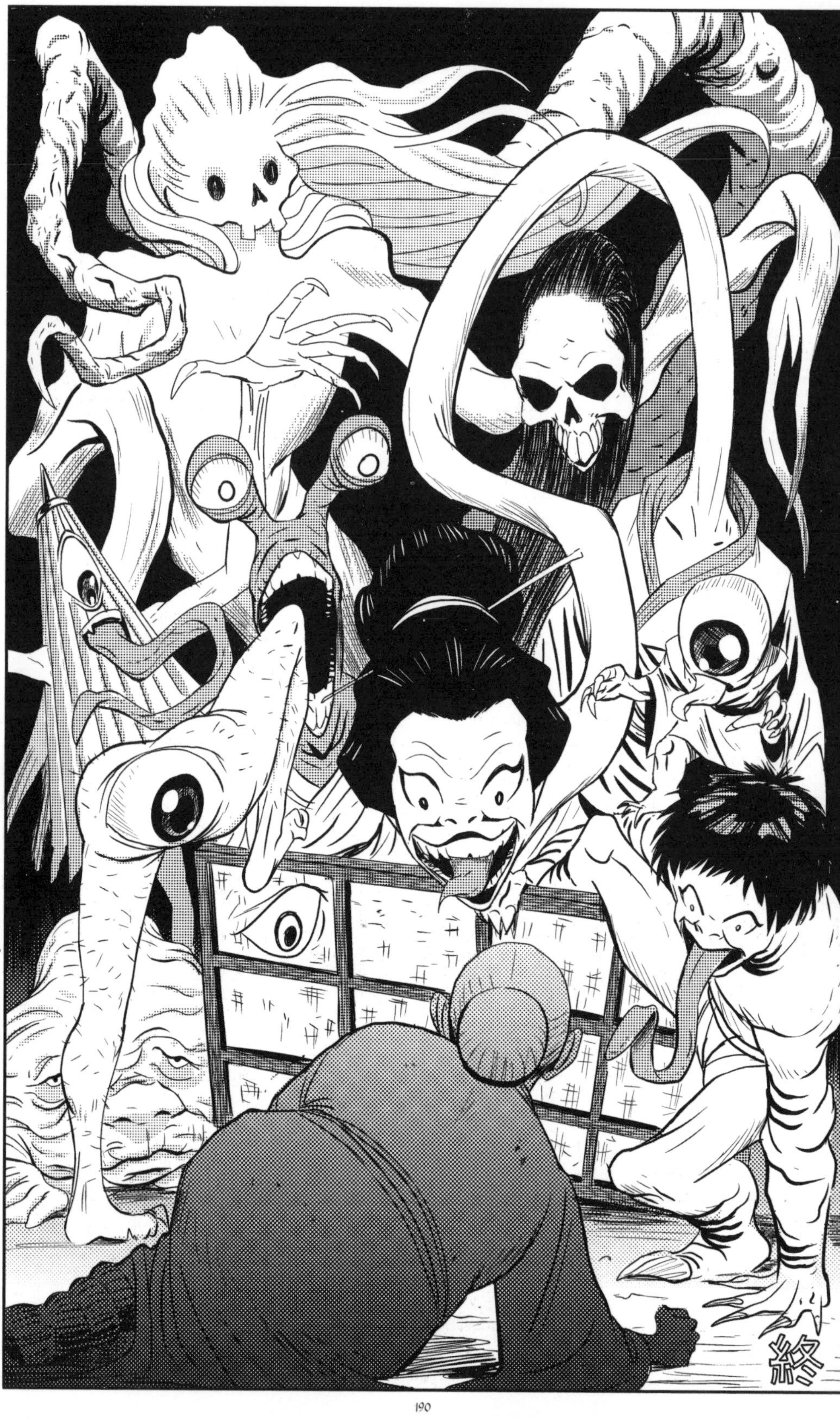
終

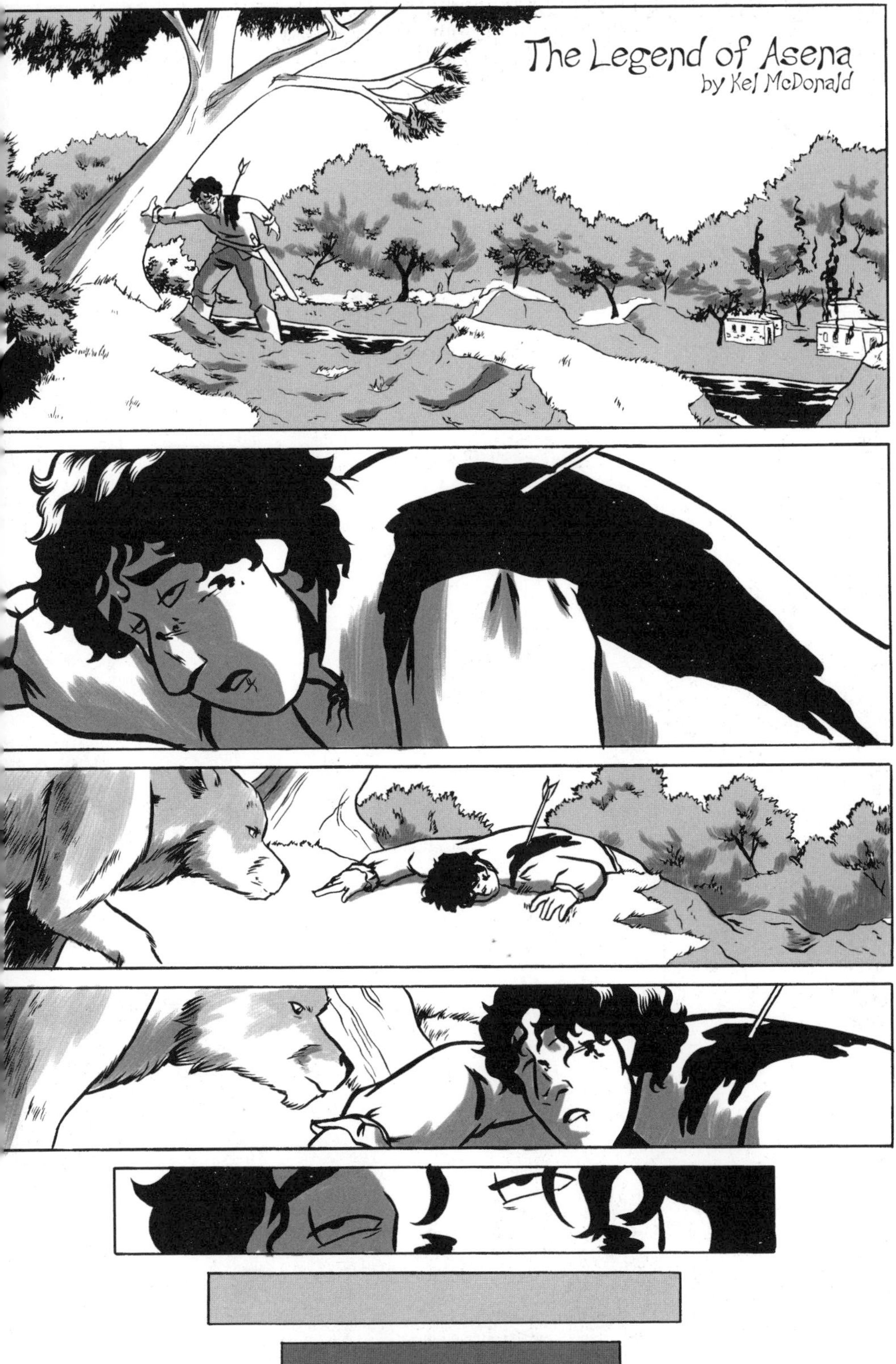
The Legend of Asena
by Kel McDonald

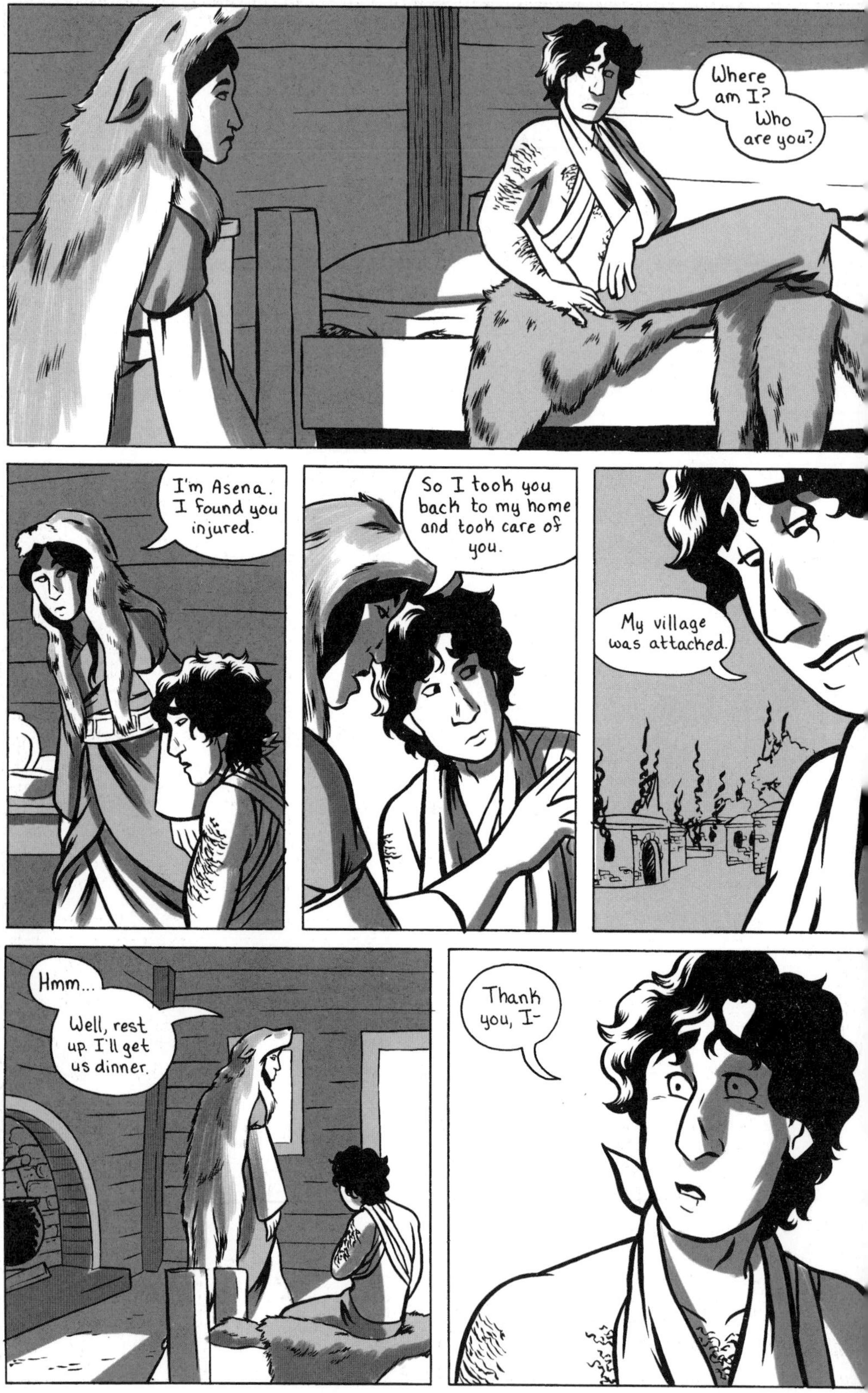
Where am I? Who are you?
I'm Asena. I found you injured.
So I took you back to my home and took care of you.
My village was attacked.
Hmm...
Well, rest up. I'll get us dinner.
Thank you, I-

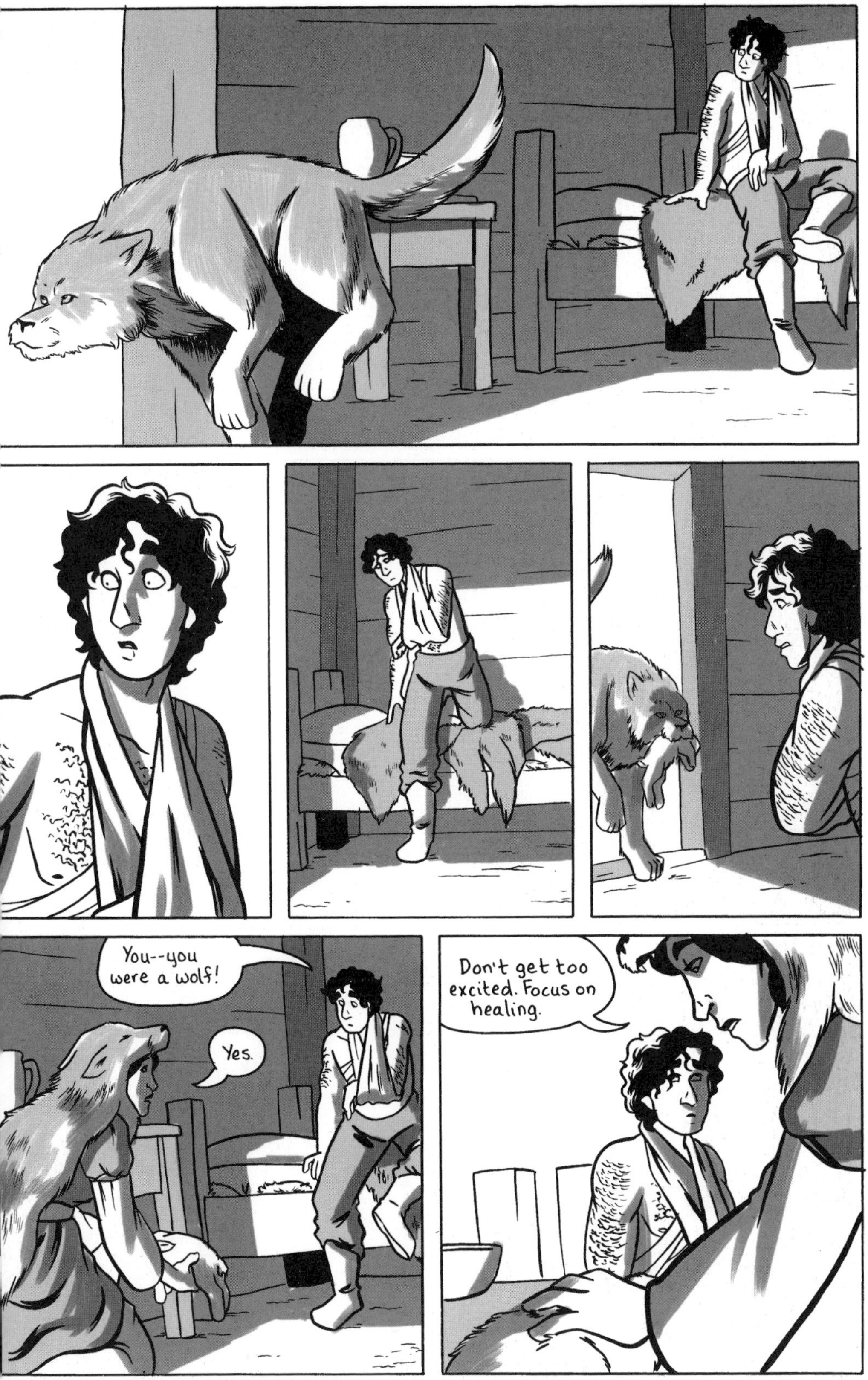
You--you were a wolf!
Yes.
Don't get too excited. Focus on healing.

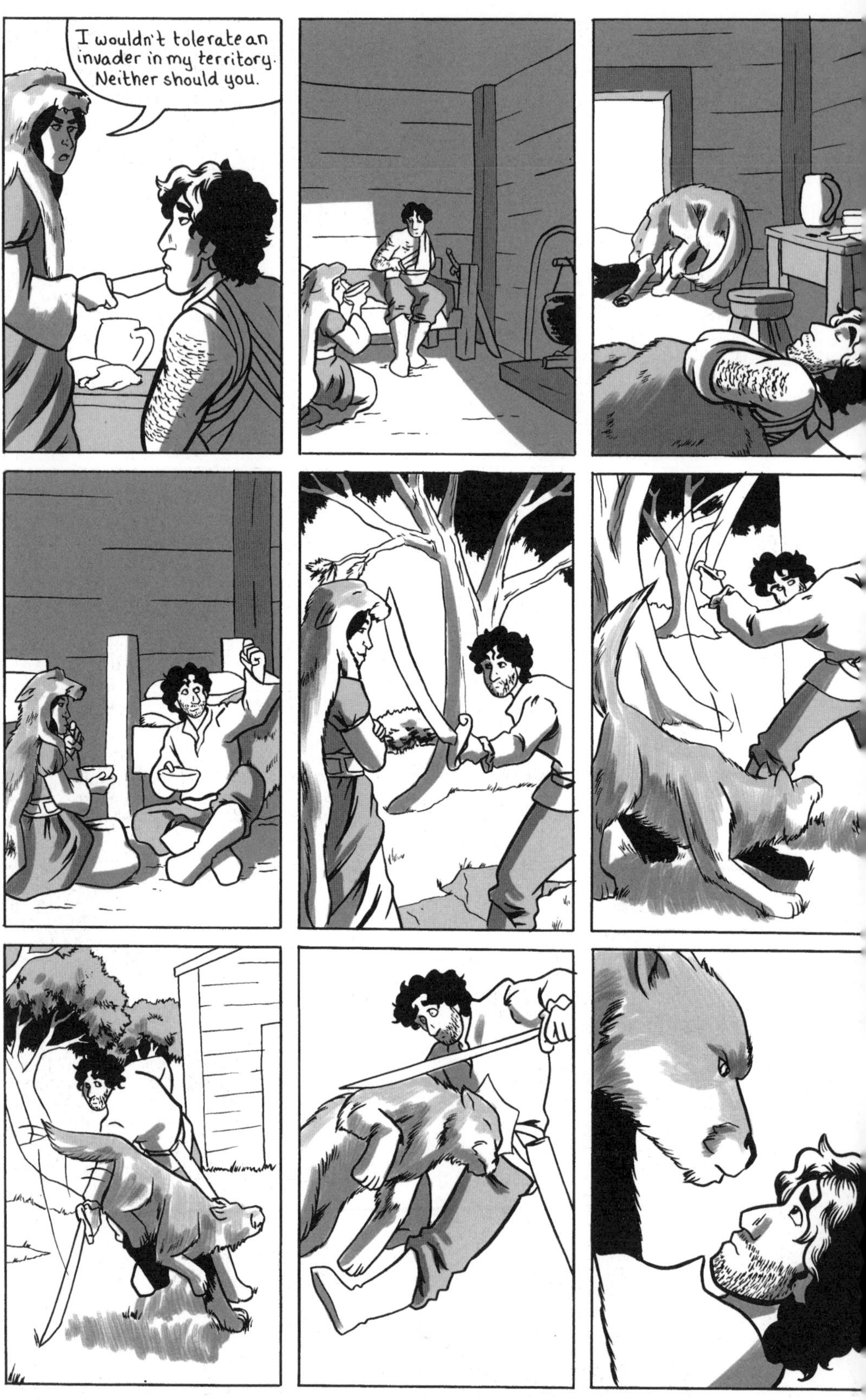
I wouldn't tolerate an invader in my territory. Neither should you.

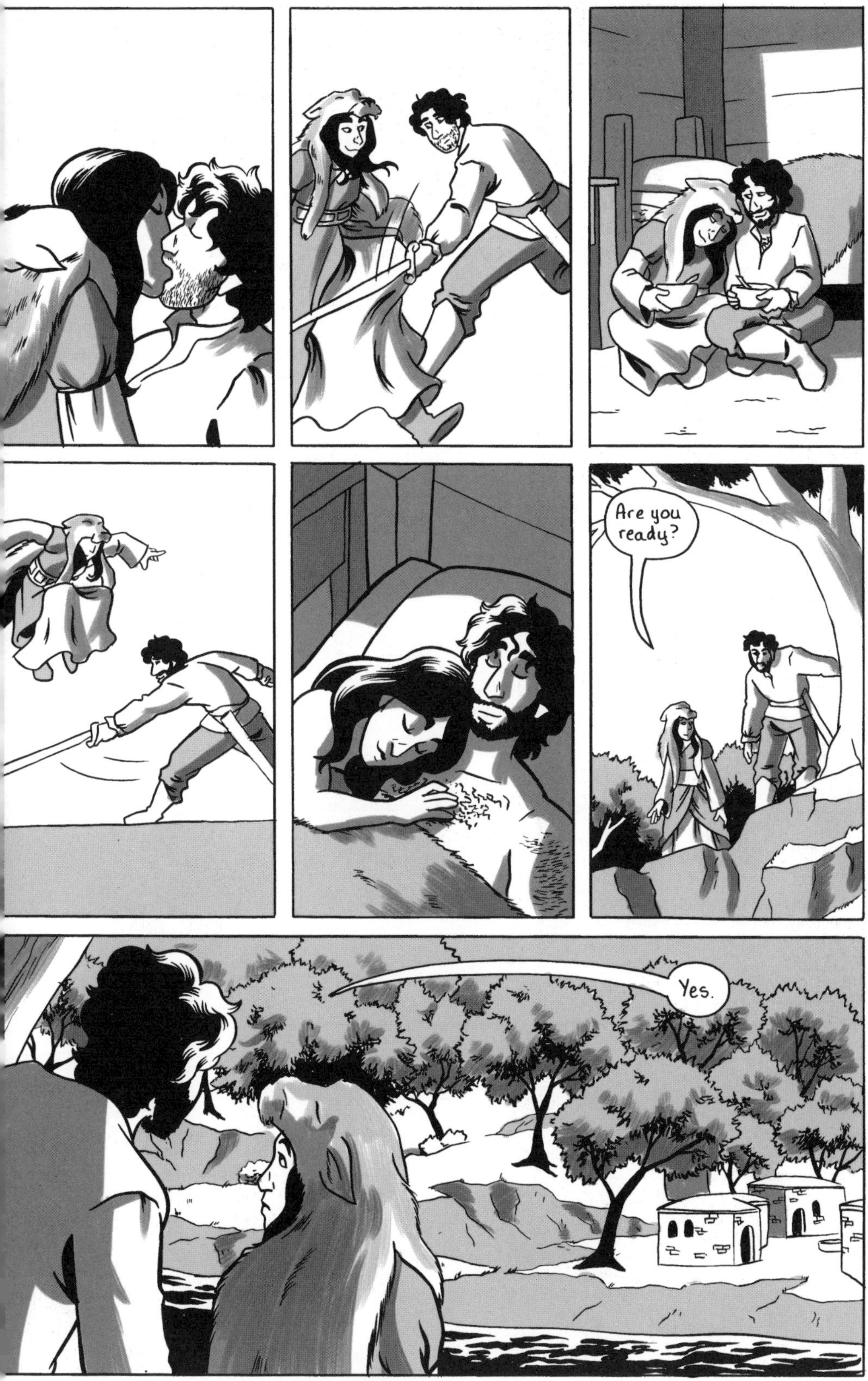
Are you ready?
Yes.

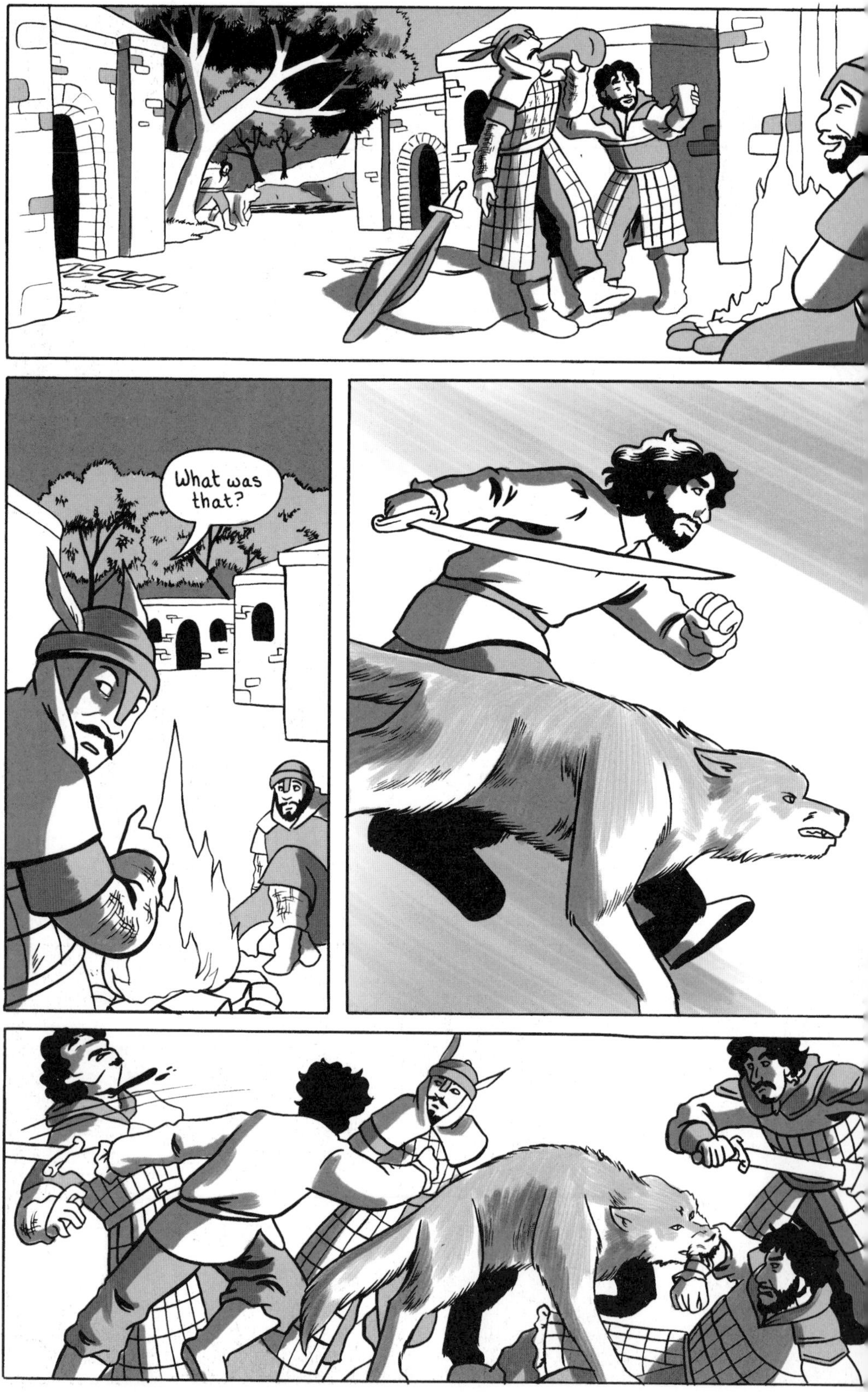
What was that?

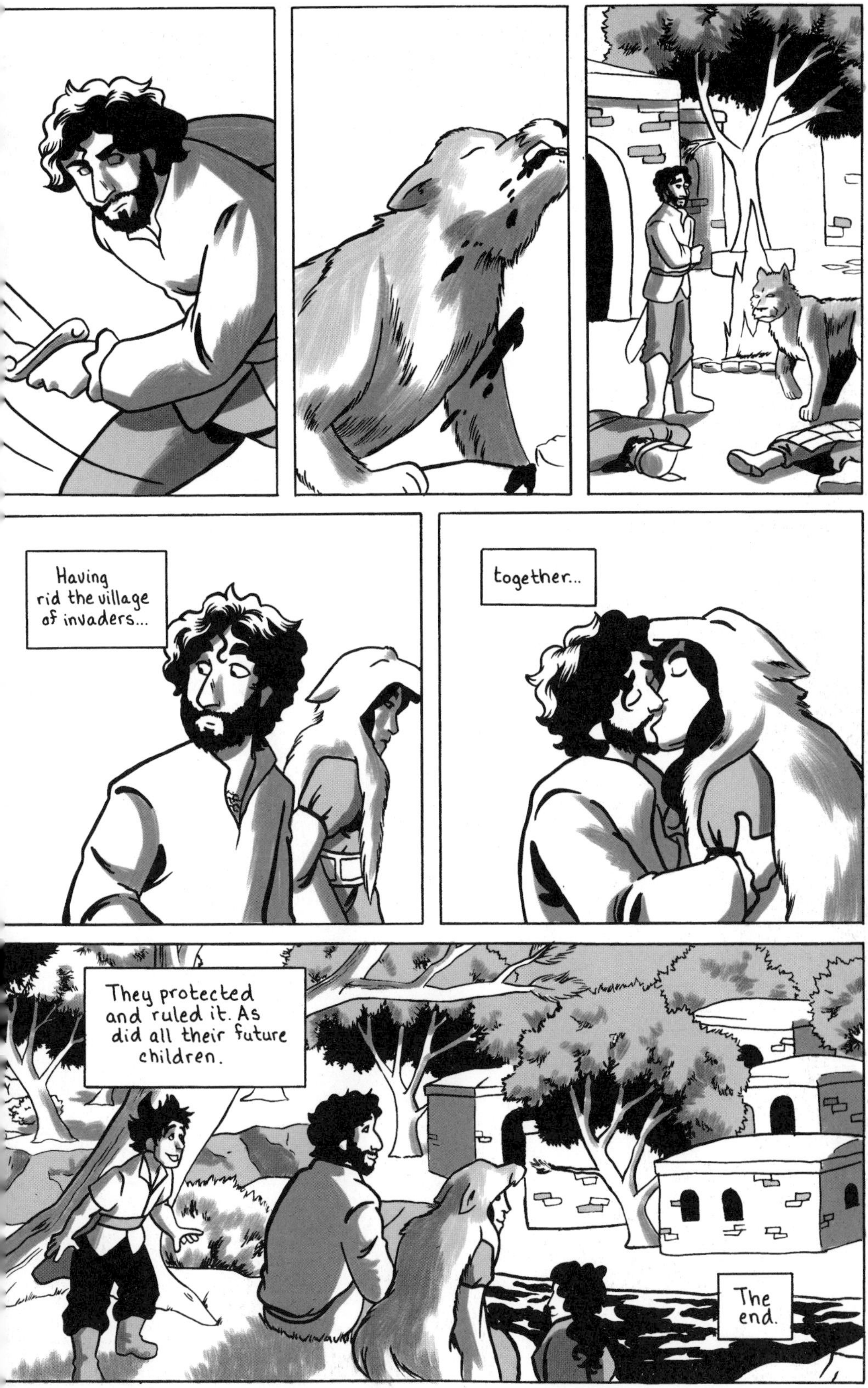
Having rid the village of invaders...
together...
They protected and ruled it. As did all their future children.
The end.

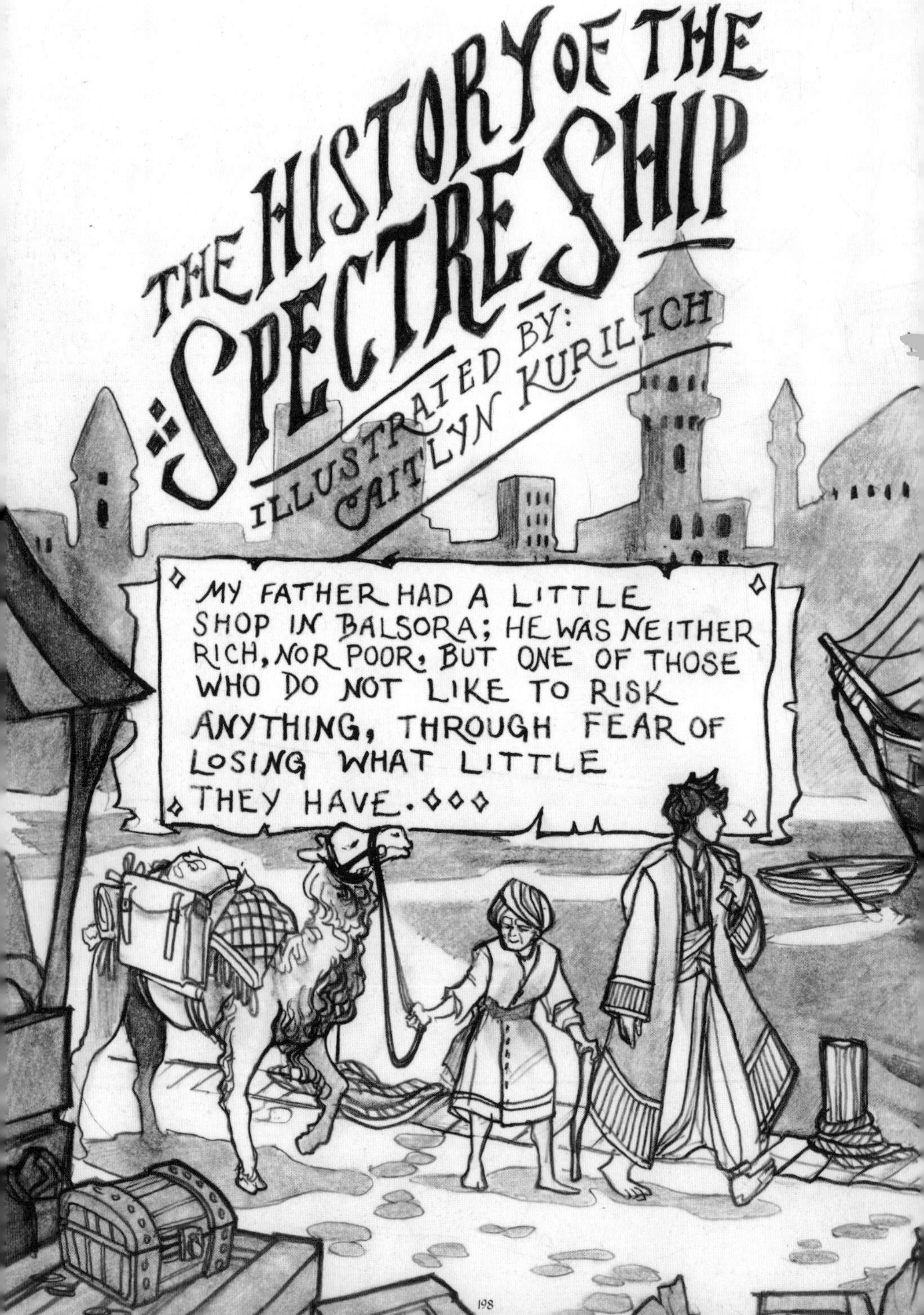
THE HISTORY OF THE SPECTRE SHIP
ILLUSTRATED BY: CAITLYN KURILICH
MY FATHER HAD A LITTLE SHOP IN BALSORA; HE WAS NEITHER RICH, NOR POOR, BUT ONE OF THOSE WHO DO NOT LIKE TO RISK ANYTHING, THROUGH FEAR OF LOSING WHAT LITTLE THEY HAVE.

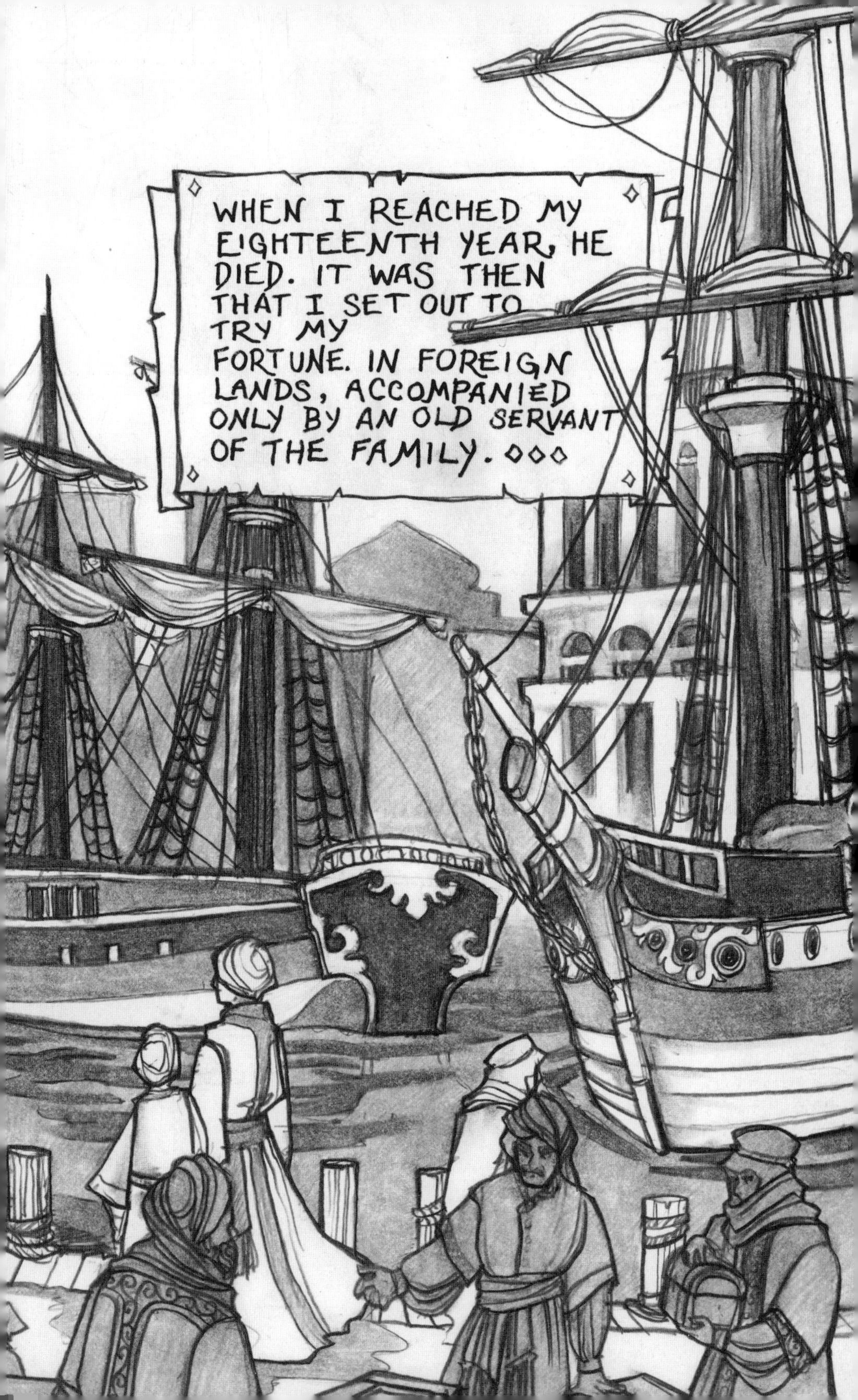
WHEN I REACHED MY EIGHTEENTH YEAR, HE DIED. IT WAS THEN THAT I SET OUT TO TRY MY FORTUNE. IN FOREIGN LANDS, ACCOMPANIED ONLY BY AN OLD SERVANT OF THE FAMILY. ...

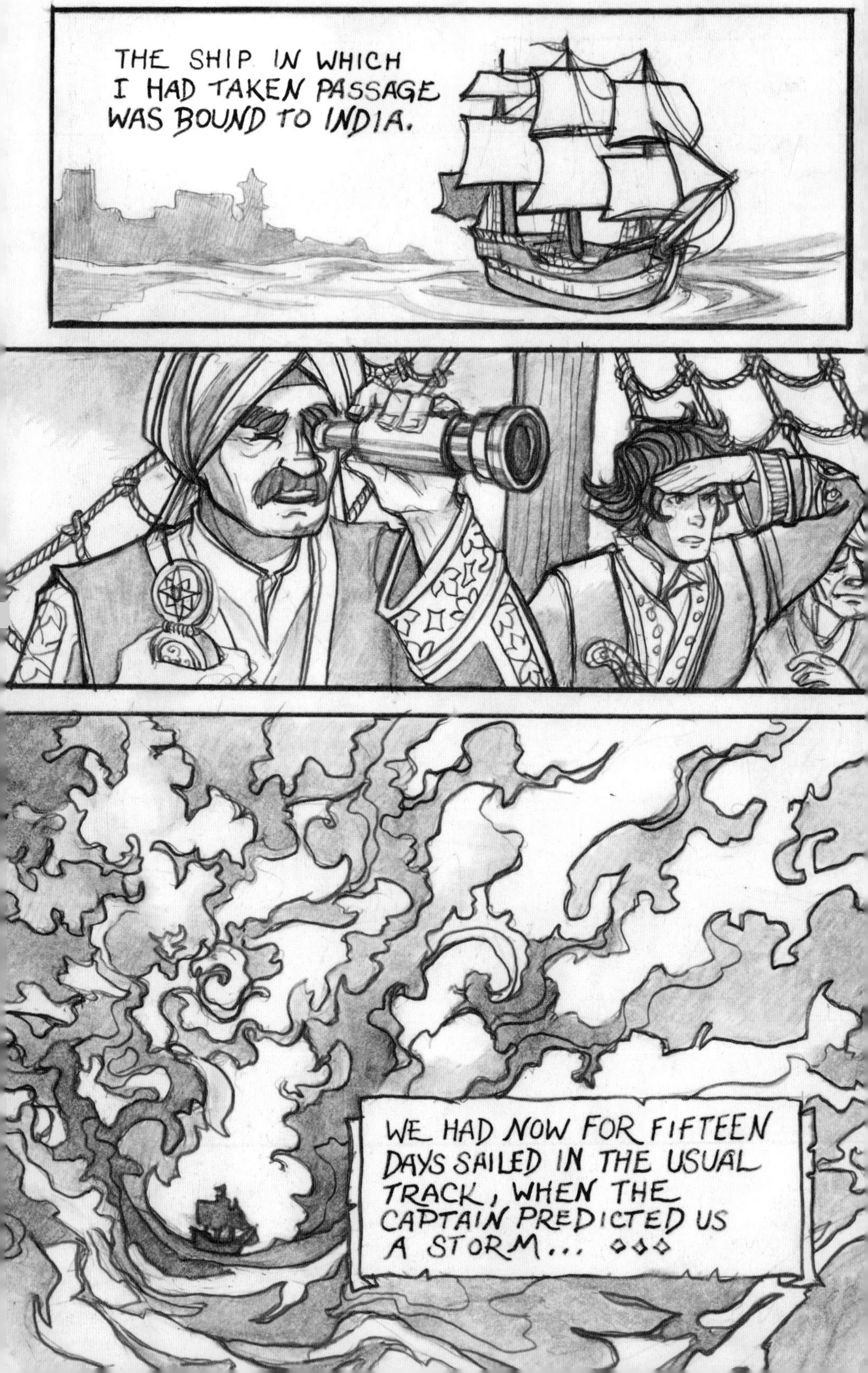
THE SHIP IN WHICH I HAD TAKEN PASSAGE WAS BOUND TO INDIA.
WE HAD NOW FOR FIFTEEN DAYS SAILED IN THE USUAL TRACK, WHEN THE CAPTAIN PREDICTED US A STORM...

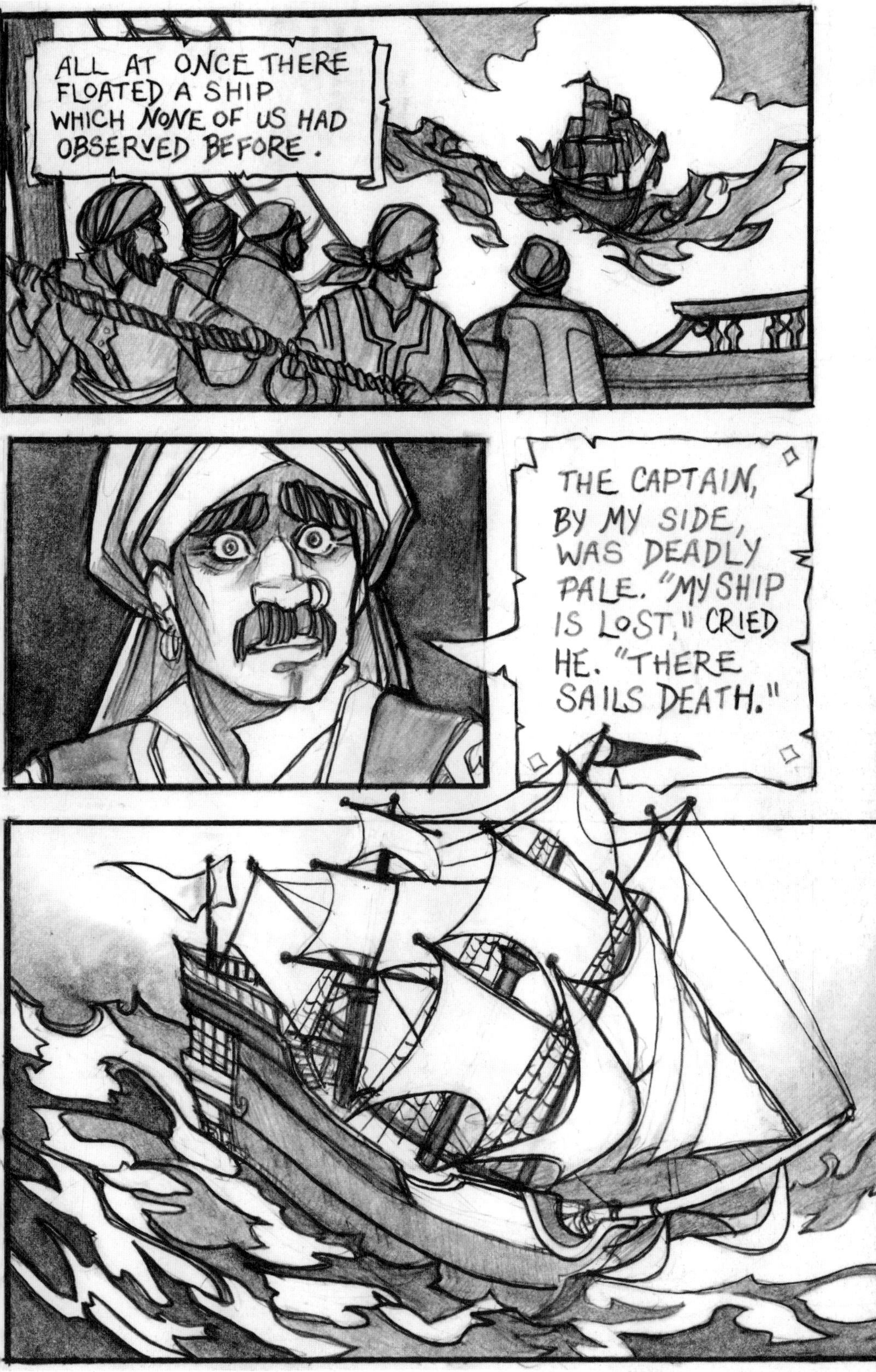
ALL AT ONCE THERE FLOATED A SHIP WHICH NONE OF US HAD OBSERVED BEFORE.
THE CAPTAIN, BY MY SIDE, WAS DEADLY PALE. "MY SHIP IS LOST," CRIED HE. "THERE SAILS DEATH."

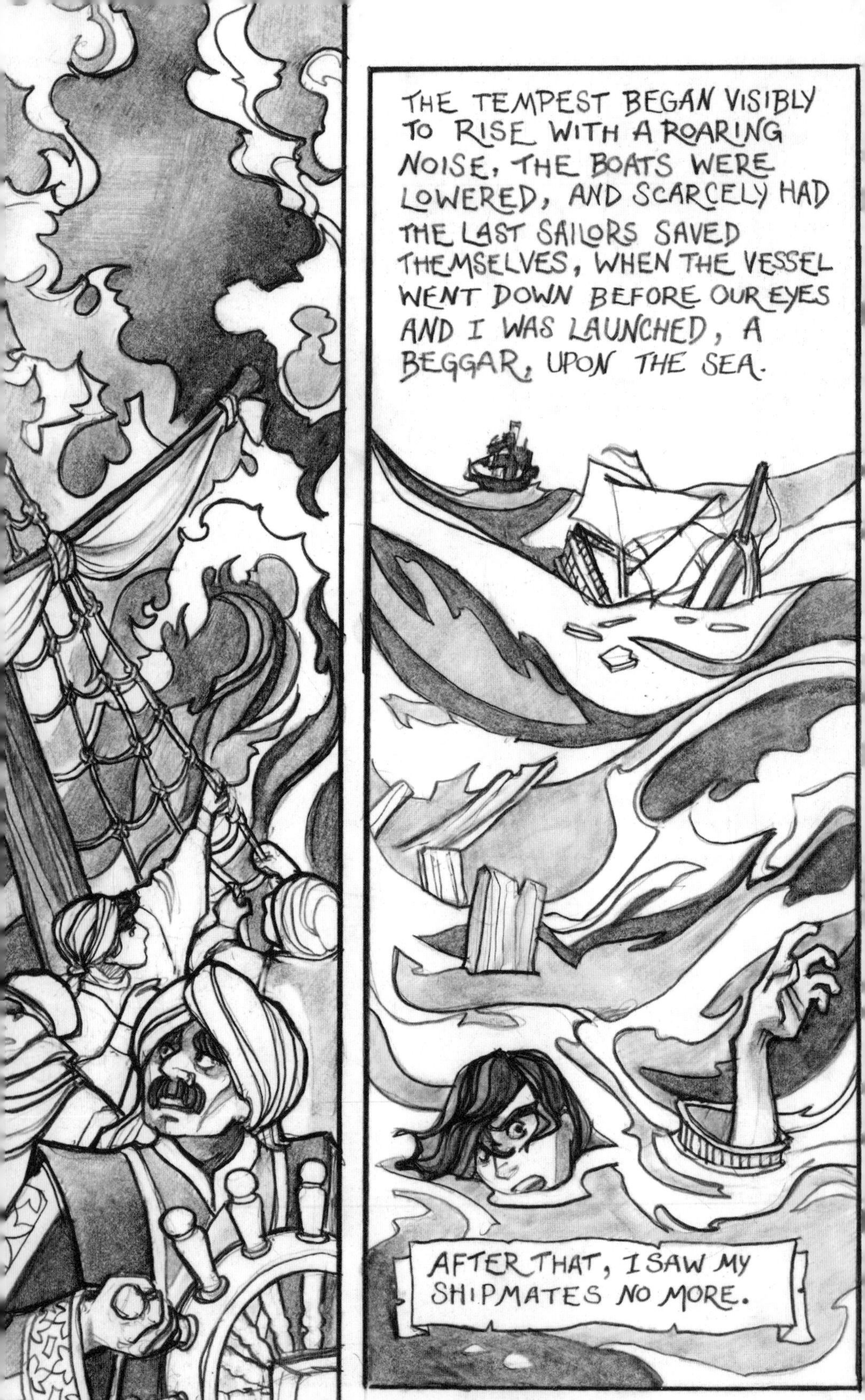
THE TEMPEST BEGAN VISIBLY TO RISE WITH A ROARING NOISE, THE BOATS WERE LOWERED, AND SCARCELY HAD THE LAST SAILORS SAVED THEMSELVES, WHEN THE VESSEL WENT DOWN BEFORE OUR EYES AND I WAS LAUNCHED, A BEGGAR, UPON THE SEA.
AFTER THAT, I SAW MY SHIPMATES NO MORE.

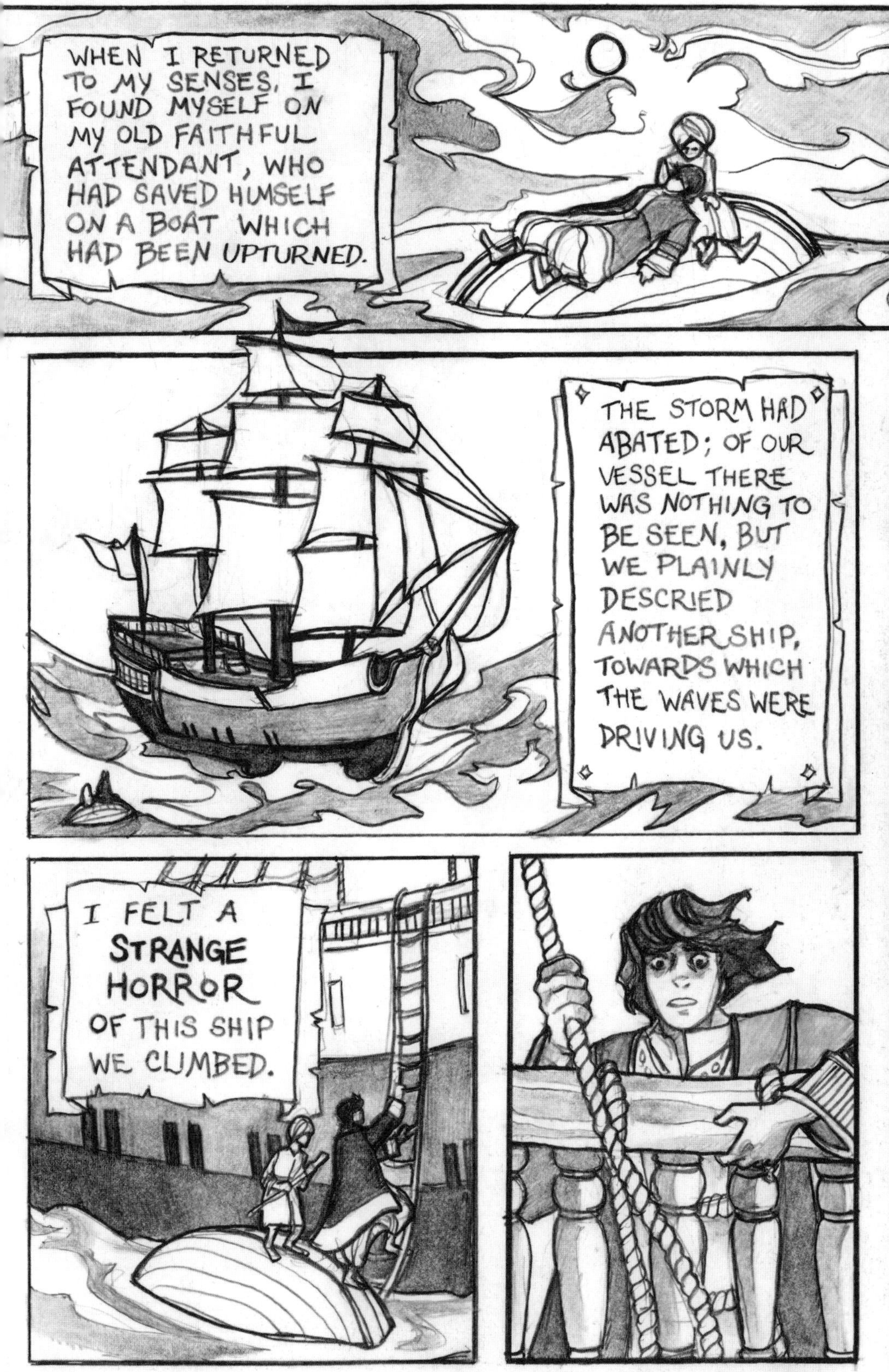
WHEN I RETURNED TO MY SENSES, I FOUND MYSELF ON MY OLD FAITHFUL ATTENDANT, WHO HAD SAVED HIMSELF ON A BOAT WHICH HAD BEEN UPTURNED.
THE STORM HAD ABATED; OF OUR VESSEL THERE WAS NOTHING TO BE SEEN, BUT WE PLAINLY DESCRIED ANOTHER SHIP, TOWARDS WHICH THE WAVES WERE DRIVING US.
I FELT A STRANGE HORROR OF THIS SHIP WE CLIMBED.

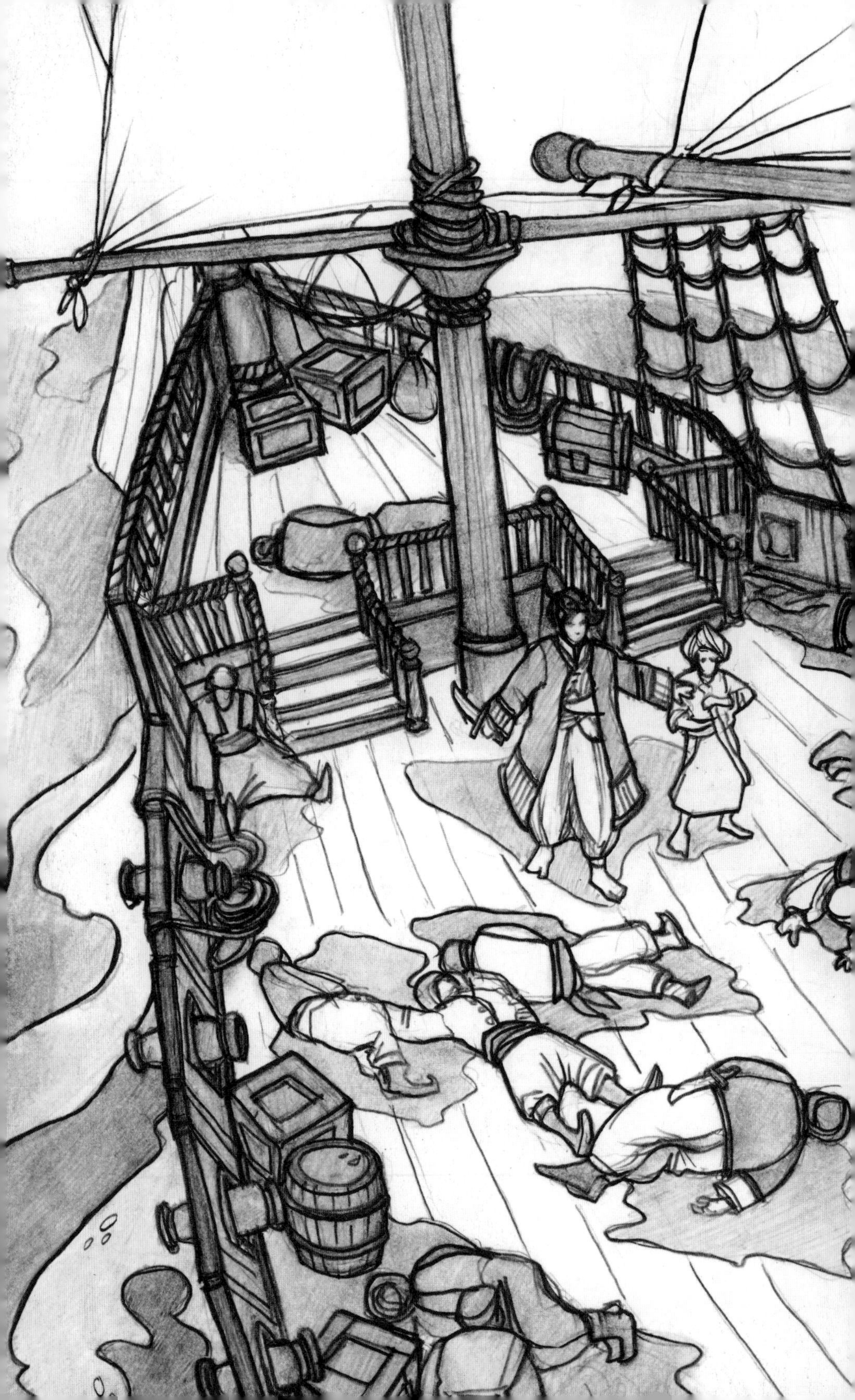

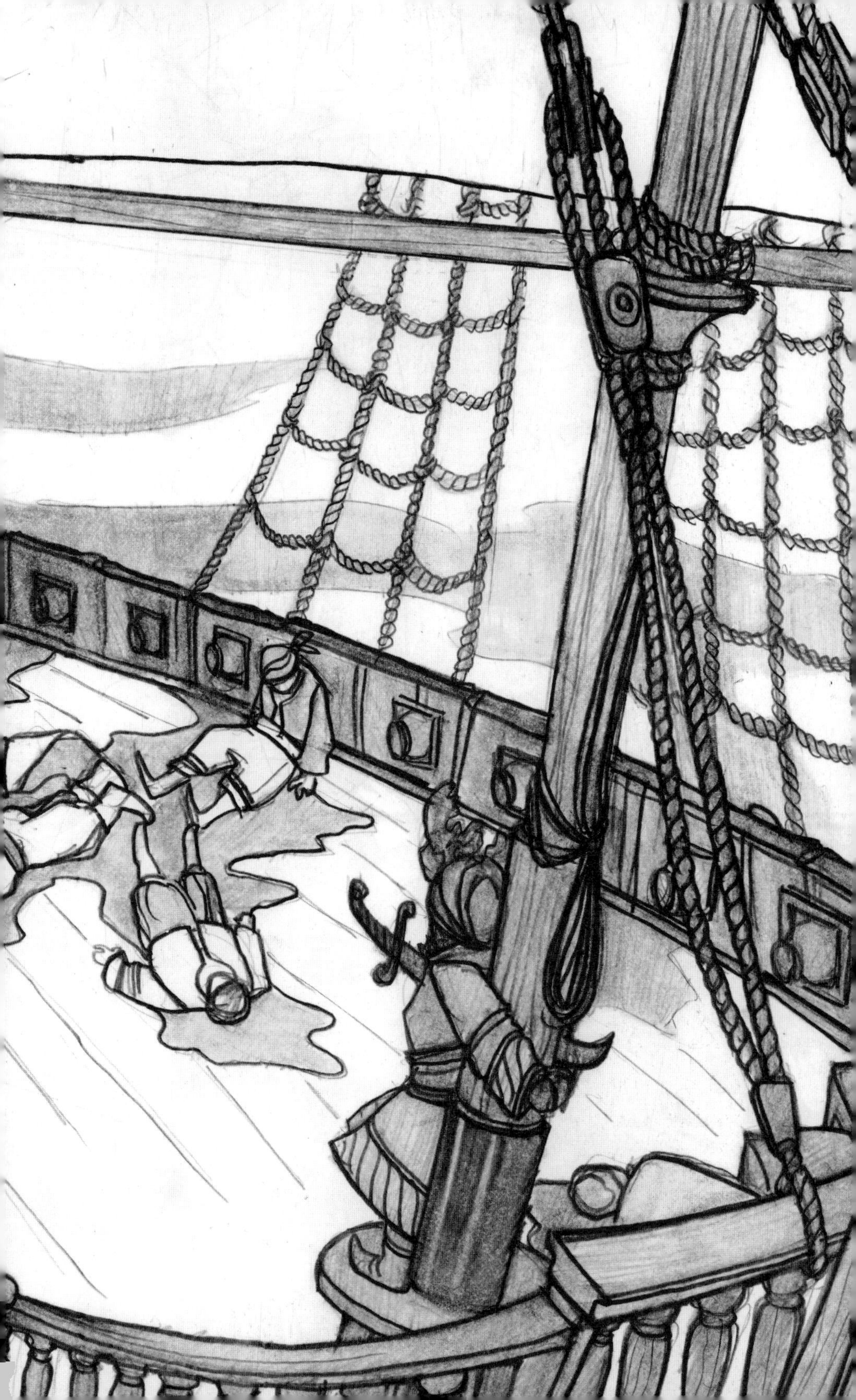

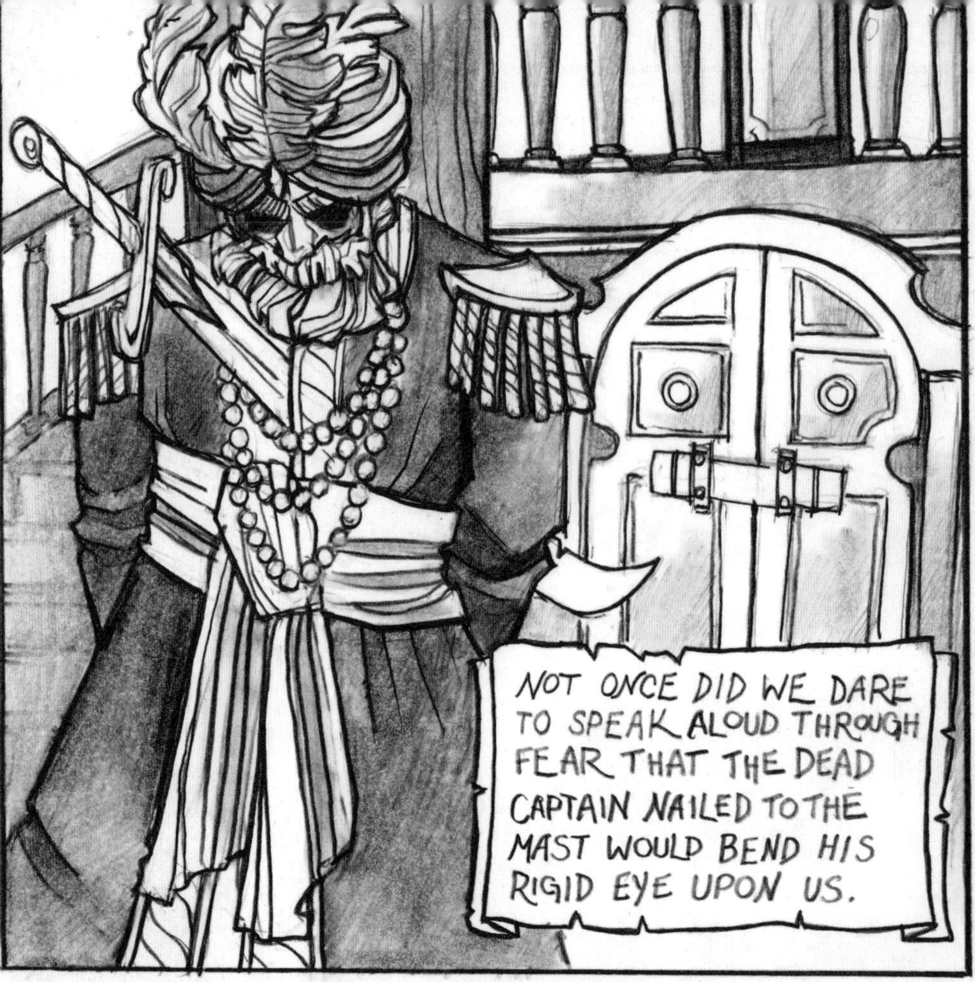
NOT ONCE DID WE DARE TO SPEAK ALOUD THROUGH FEAR THAT THE DEAD CAPTAIN NAILED TO THE MAST WOULD BEND HIS RIGID EYE UPON US.

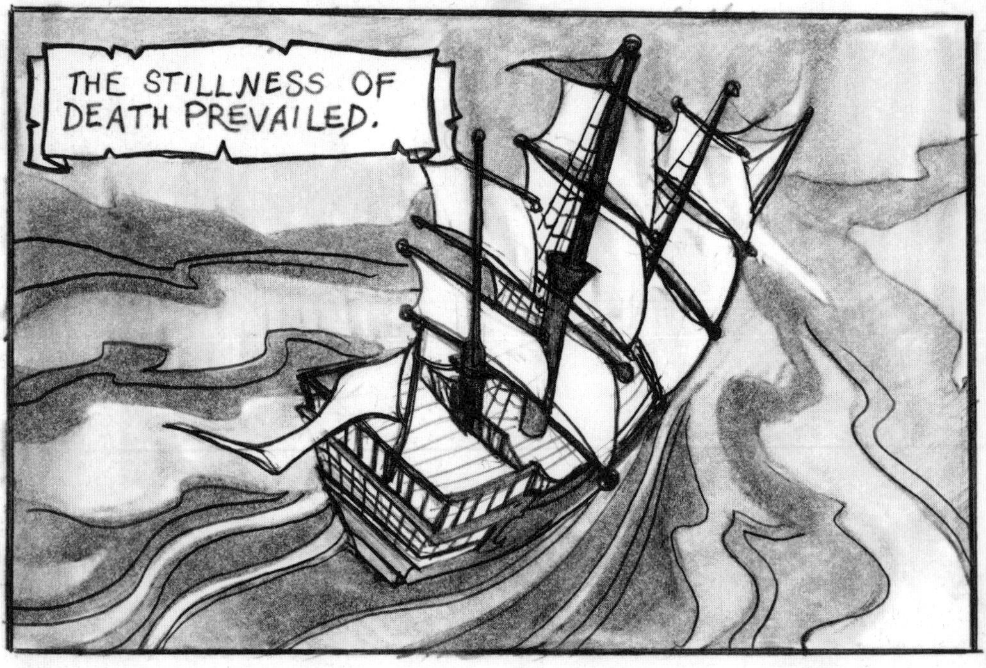
THE STILLNESS OF DEATH PREVAILED.

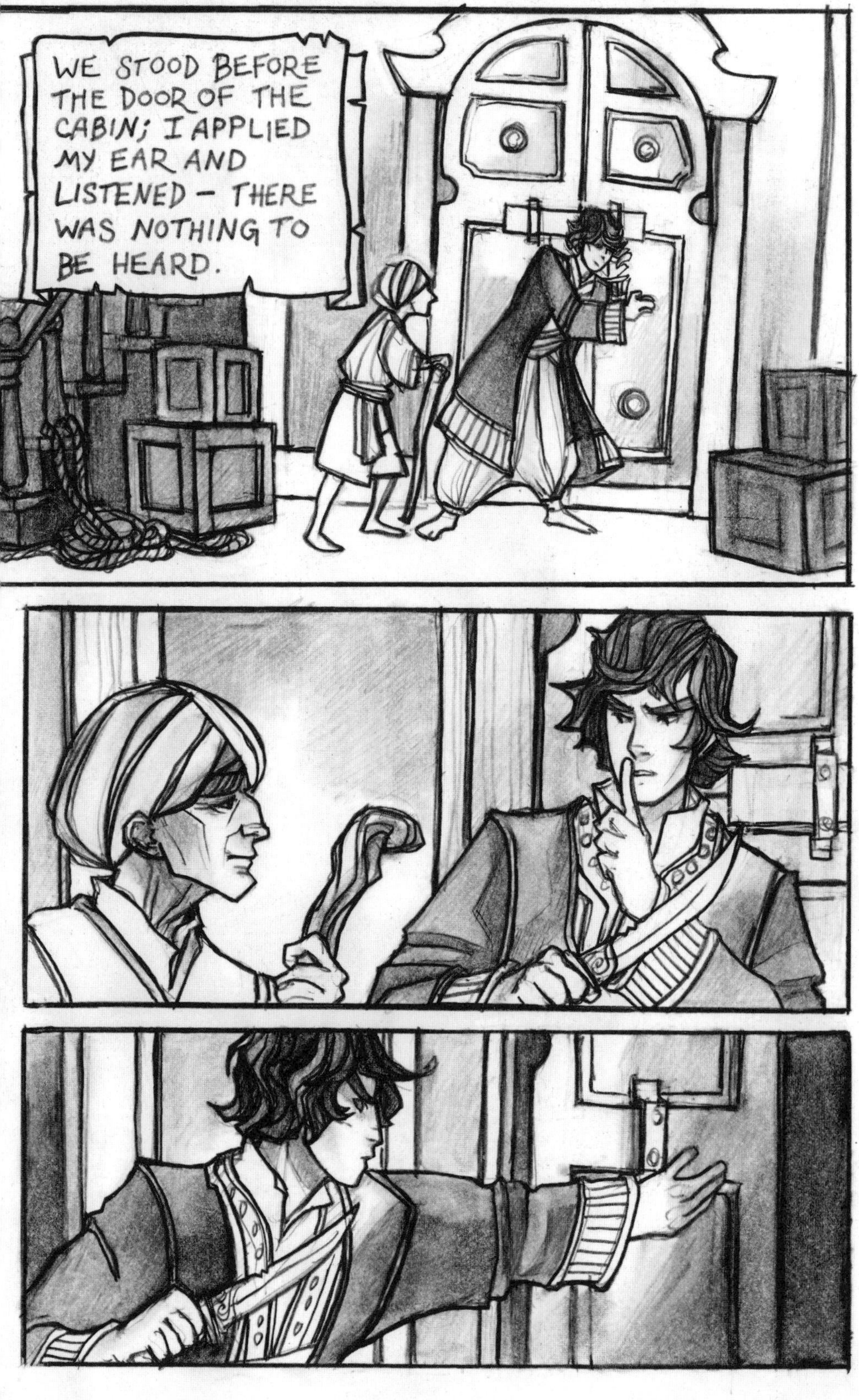
WE STOOD BEFORE THE DOOR OF THE CABIN; I APPLIED MY EAR AND LISTENED - THERE WAS NOTHING TO BE HEARD.

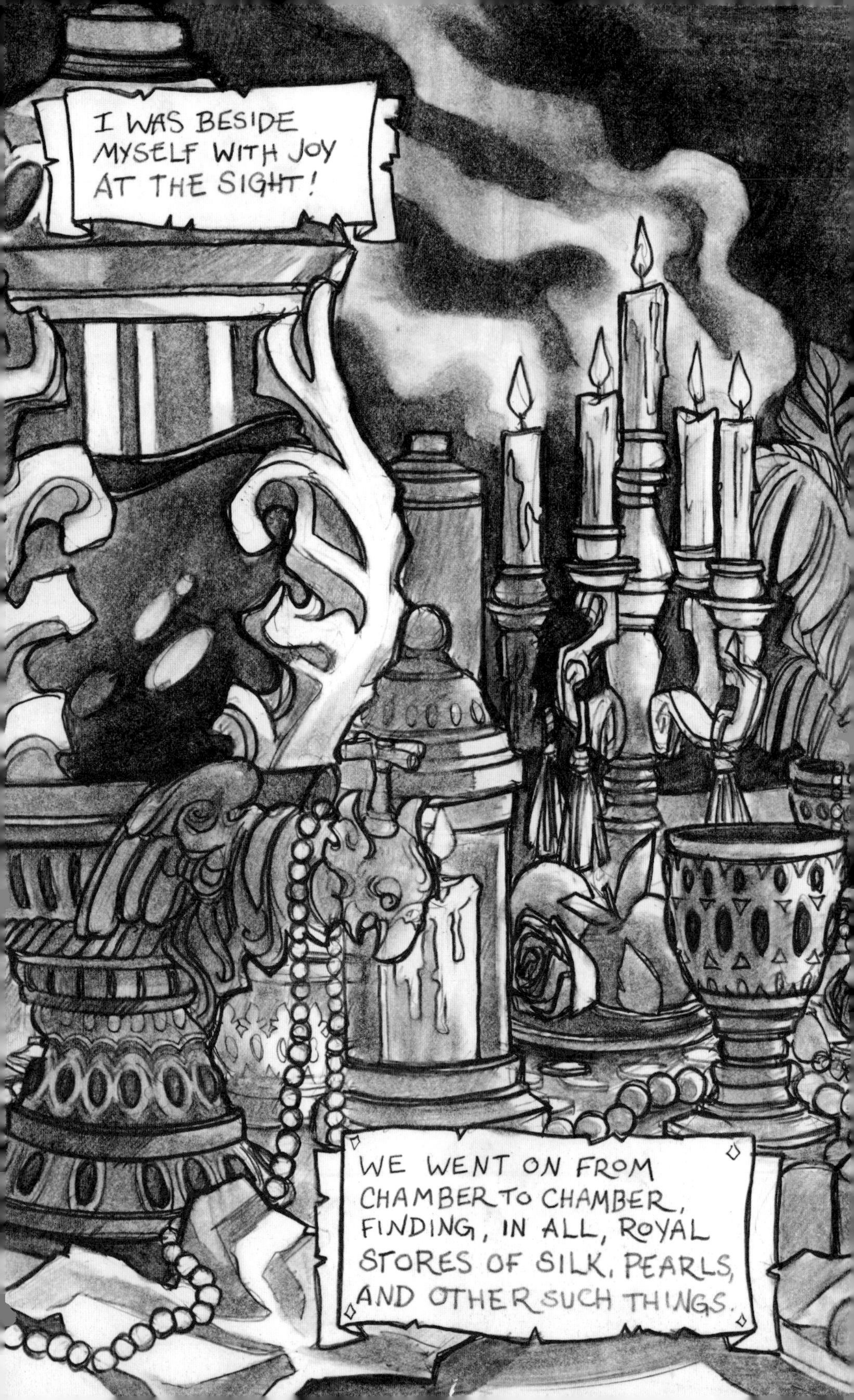
I WAS BESIDE MYSELF WITH JOY AT THE SIGHT!
WE WENT ON FROM CHAMBER TO CHAMBER, FINDING, IN ALL, ROYAL STORES OF SILK, PEARLS, AND OTHER SUCH THINGS.

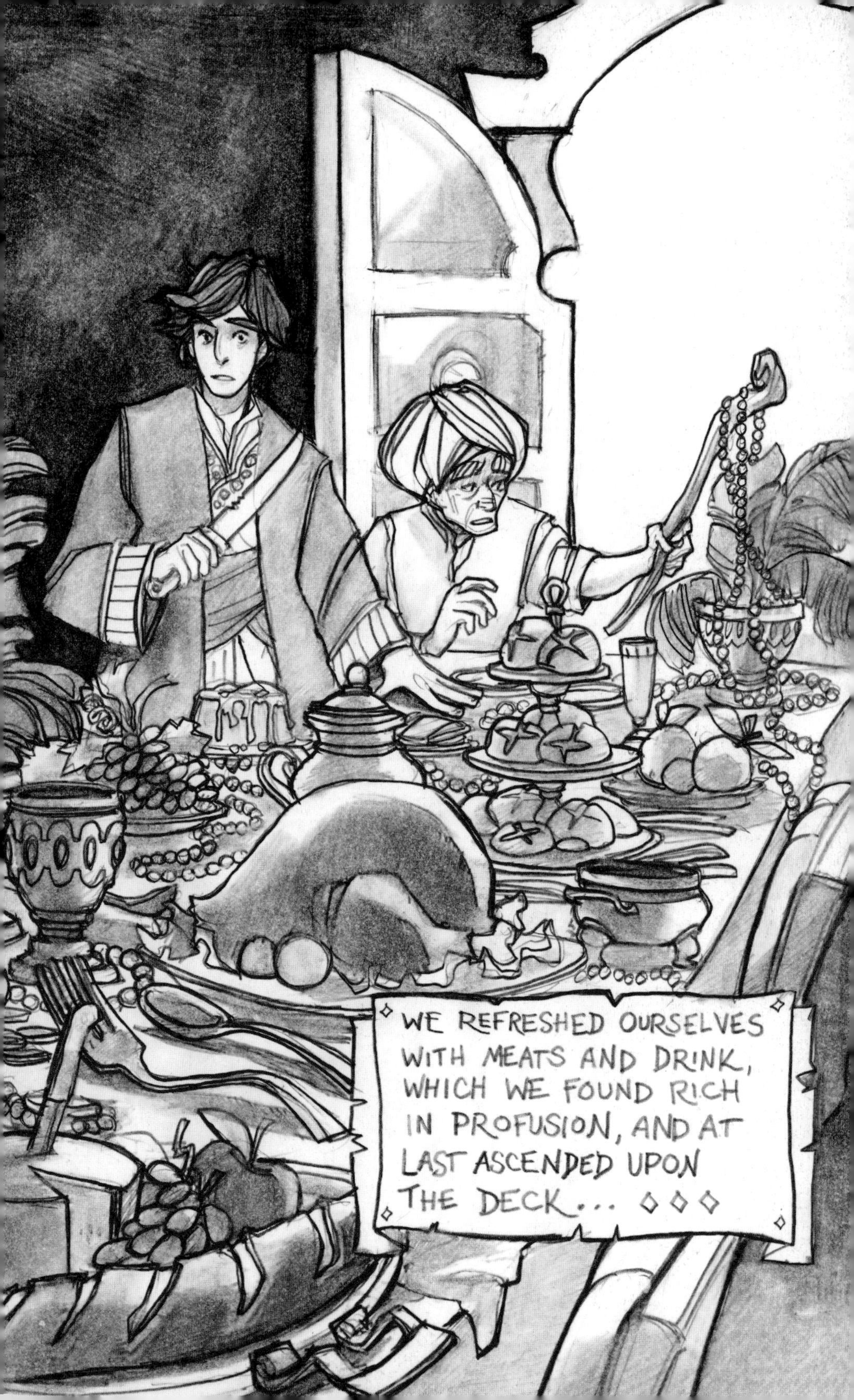
WE REFRESHED OURSELVES WITH MEATS AND DRINK, WHICH WE FOUND RICH IN PROFUSION, AND AT LAST ASCENDED UPON THE DECK...

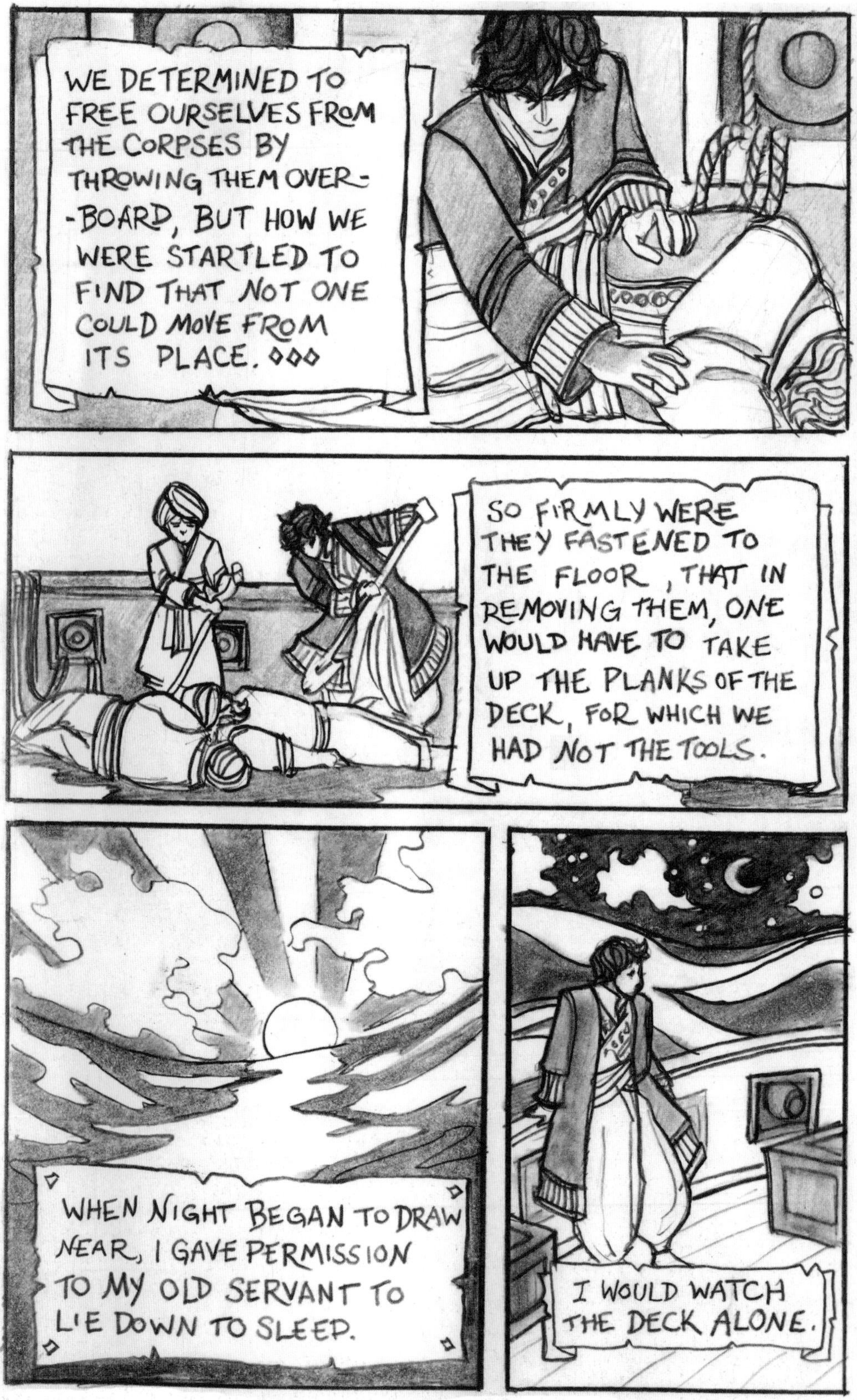
WE DETERMINED TO FREE OURSELVES FROM THE CORPSES BY THROWING THEM OVER--BOARD, BUT HOW WE WERE STARTLED TO FIND THAT NOT ONE COULD MOVE FROM ITS PLACE. ◊◊◊
SO FIRMLY WERE THEY FASTENED TO THE FLOOR, THAT IN REMOVING THEM, ONE WOULD HAVE TO TAKE UP THE PLANKS OF THE DECK, FOR WHICH WE HAD NOT THE TOOLS.
WHEN NIGHT BEGAN TO DRAW NEAR, I GAVE PERMISSION TO MY OLD SERVANT TO LIE DOWN TO SLEEP.
I WOULD WATCH THE DECK ALONE.

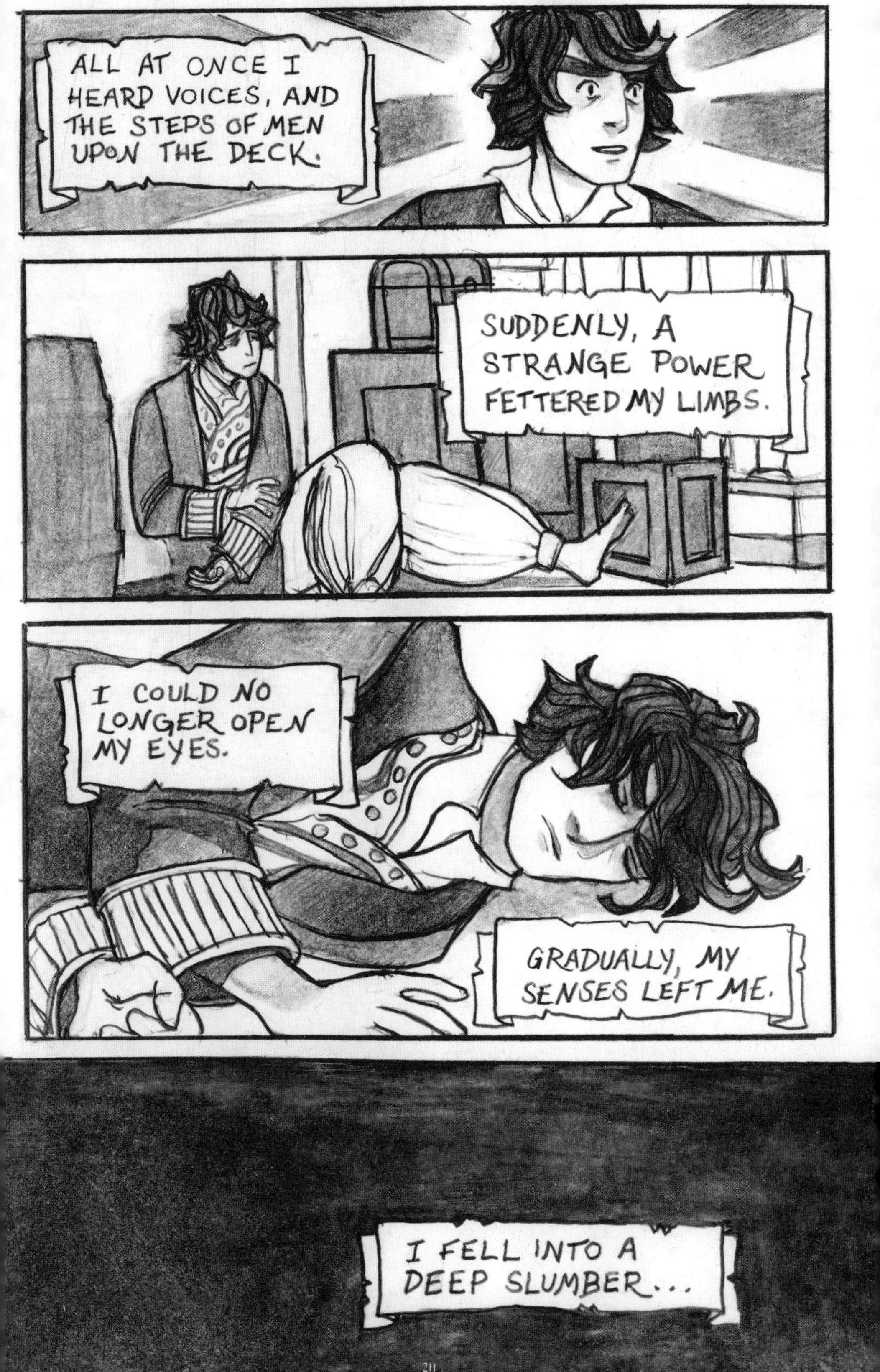
ALL AT ONCE I HEARD VOICES, AND THE STEPS OF MEN UPON THE DECK.
SUDDENLY, A STRANGE POWER FETTERED MY LIMBS.
I COULD NO LONGER OPEN MY EYES.
GRADUALLY, MY SENSES LEFT ME.
I FELL INTO A DEEP SLUMBER...

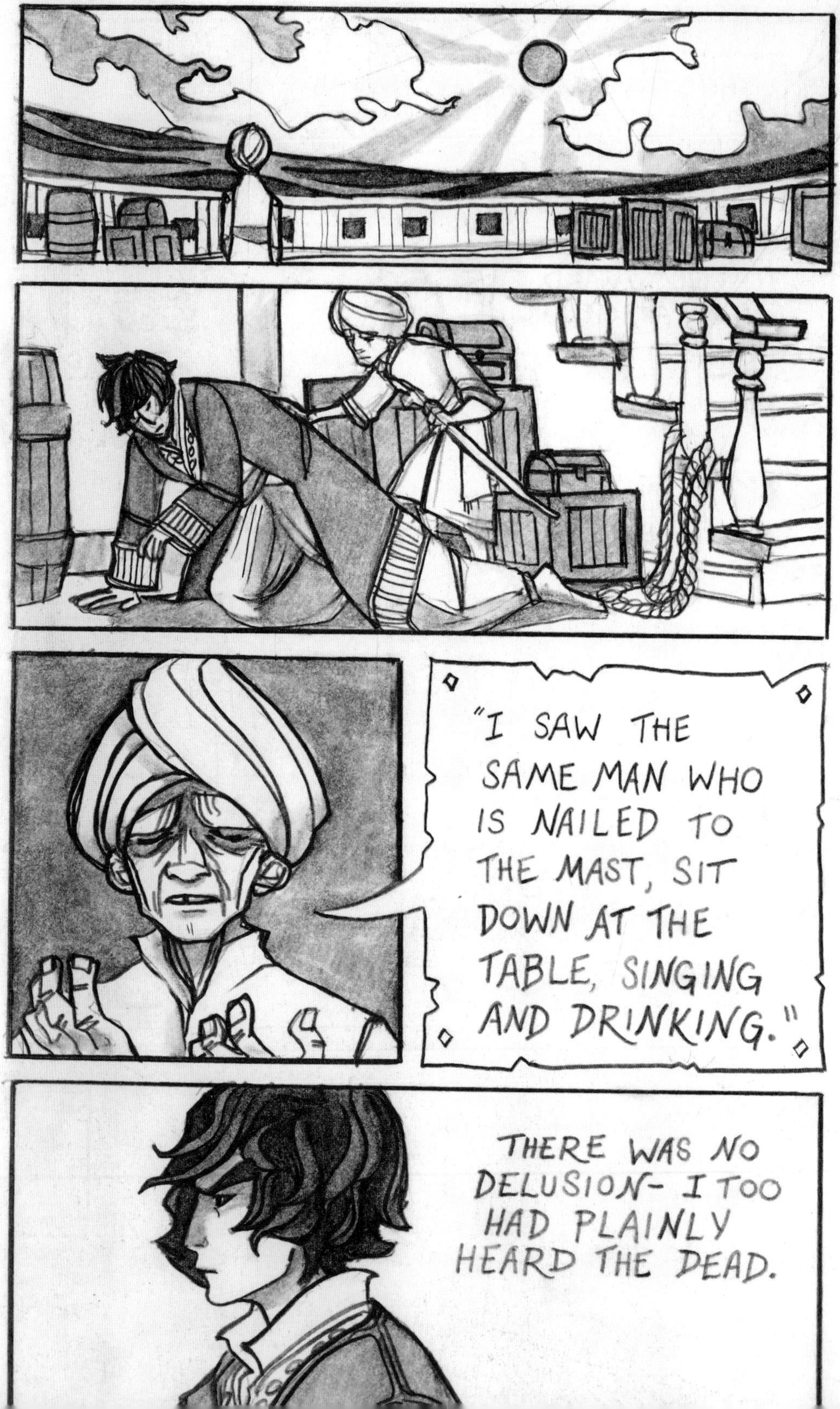
"I SAW THE SAME MAN WHO IS NAILED TO THE MAST, SIT DOWN AT THE TABLE, SINGING AND DRINKING."
THERE WAS NO DELUSION- I TOO HAD PLAINLY HEARD THE DEAD.

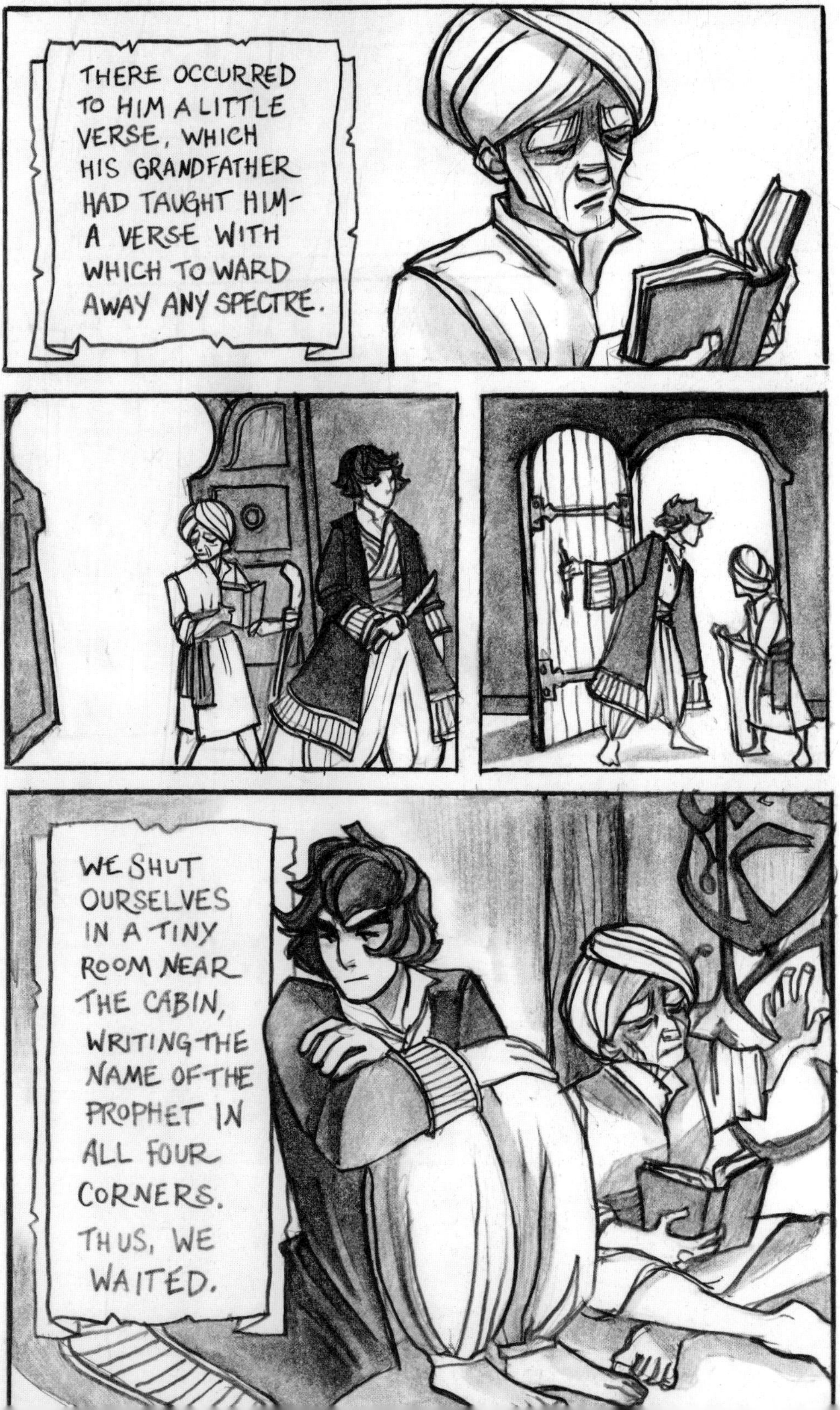
THERE OCCURRED TO HIM A LITTLE VERSE, WHICH HIS GRANDFATHER HAD TAUGHT HIM- A VERSE WITH WHICH TO WARD AWAY ANY SPECTRE.
WE SHUT OURSELVES IN A TINY ROOM NEAR THE CABIN, WRITING THE NAME OF THE PROPHET IN ALL FOUR CORNERS. THUS, WE WAITED.

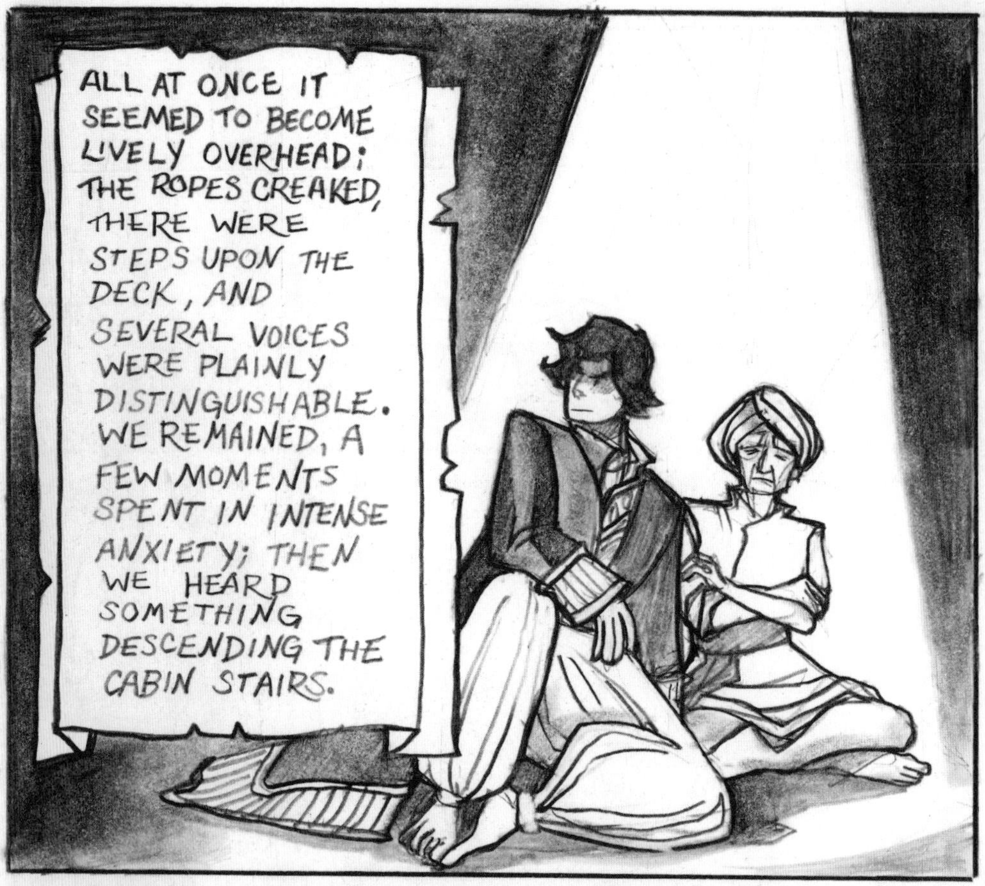
ALL AT ONCE IT SEEMED TO BECOME LIVELY OVERHEAD; THE ROPES CREAKED, THERE WERE STEPS UPON THE DECK, AND SEVERAL VOICES WERE PLAINLY DISTINGUISHABLE. WE REMAINED, A FEW MOMENTS SPENT IN INTENSE ANXIETY; THEN WE HEARD SOMETHING DESCENDING THE CABIN STAIRS.

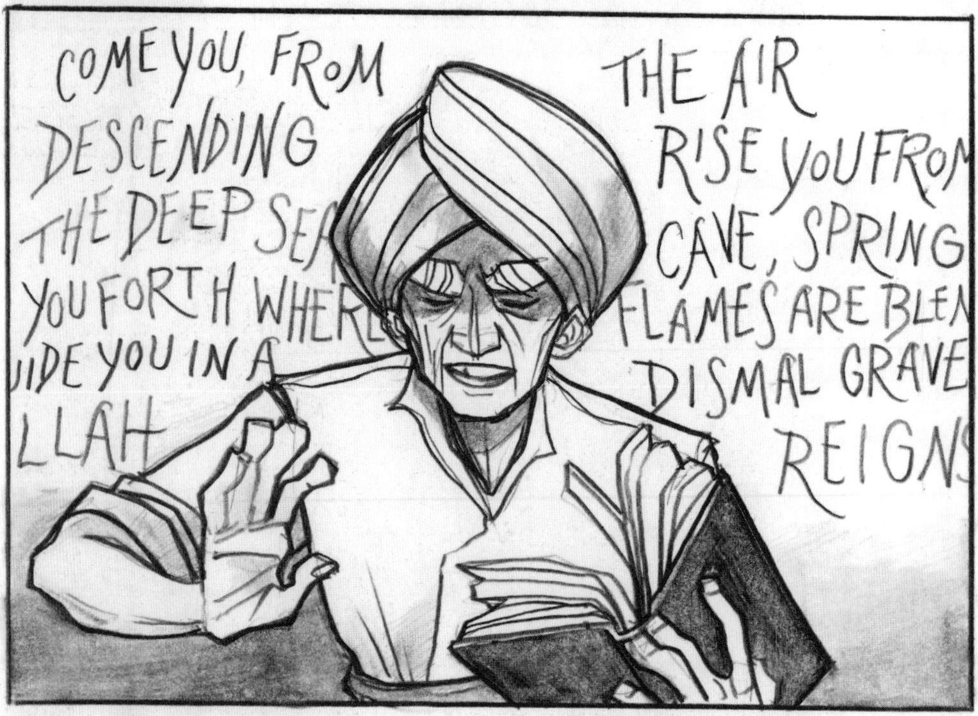
COME YOU, FROM
DESCENDING
THE DEEP SEA
YOU FORTH WHERE
IDE YOU IN A
LLAH
THE AIR
RISE YOU FROM
CAVE, SPRING
FLAMES ARE BLEN
DISMAL GRAVE
REIGNS

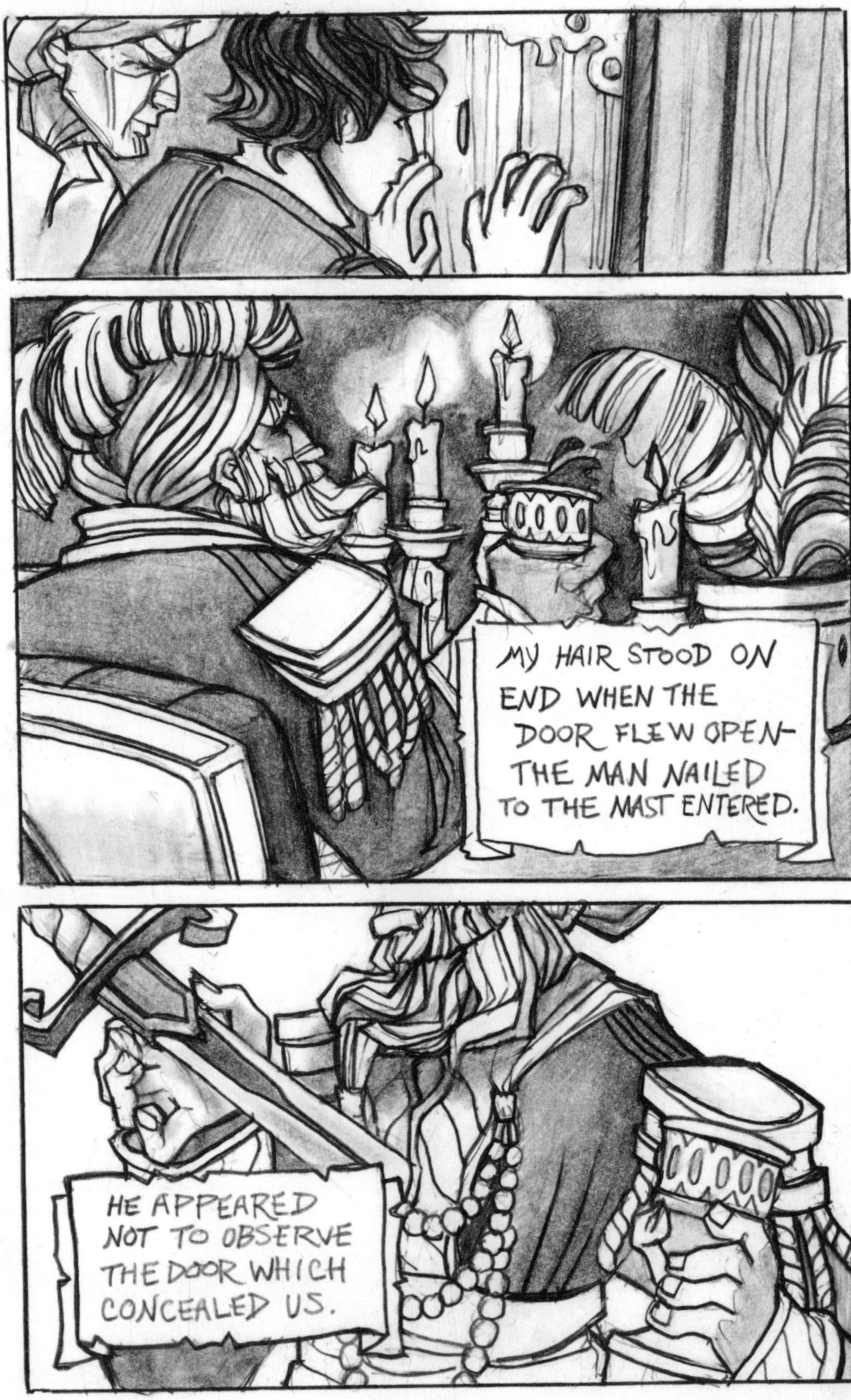
MY HAIR STOOD ON END WHEN THE DOOR FLEW OPEN—THE MAN NAILED TO THE MAST ENTERED.
HE APPEARED NOT TO OBSERVE THE DOOR WHICH CONCEALED US.

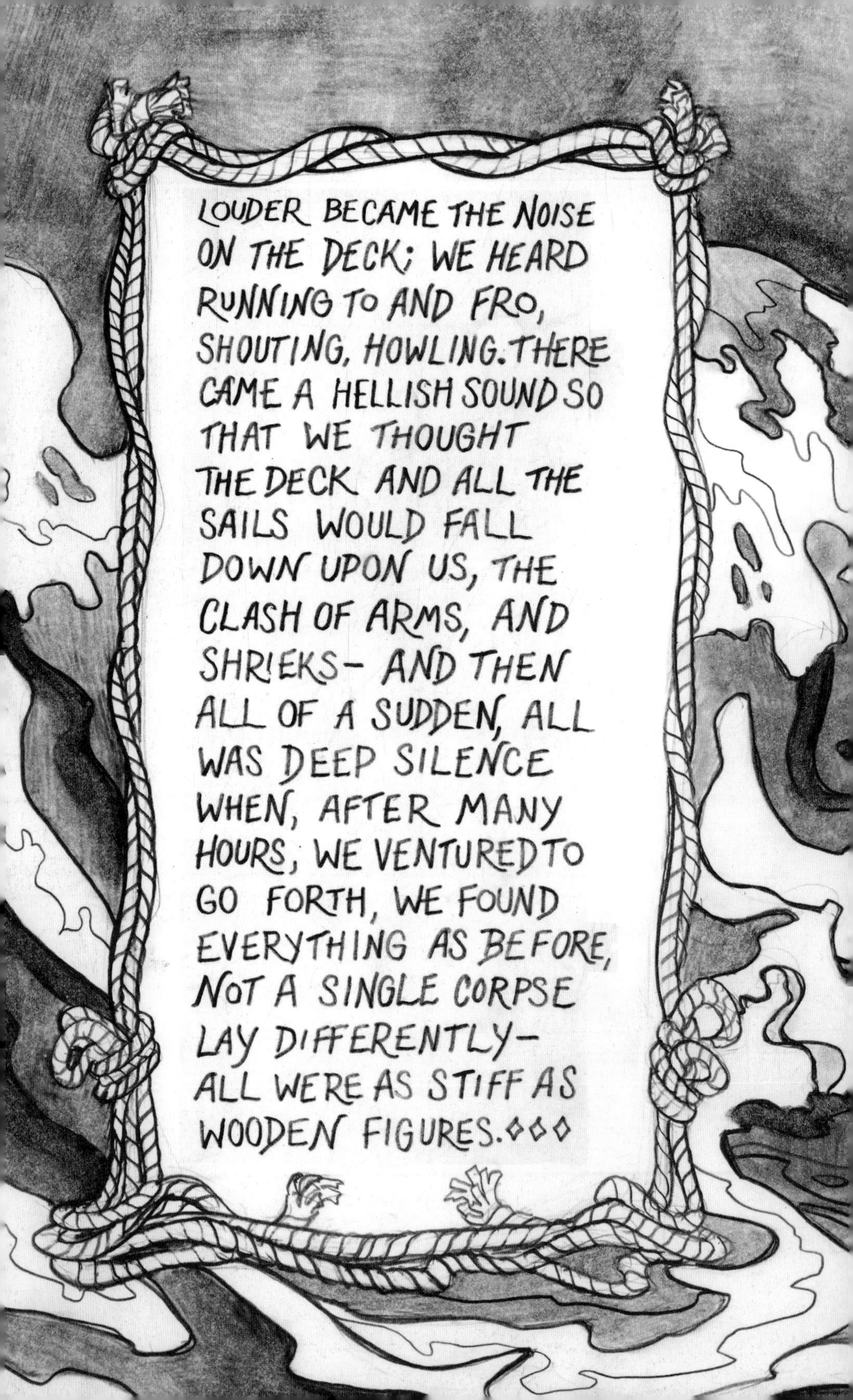
LOUDER BECAME THE NOISE ON THE DECK; WE HEARD RUNNING TO AND FRO, SHOUTING, HOWLING. THERE CAME A HELLISH SOUND SO THAT WE THOUGHT THE DECK AND ALL THE SAILS WOULD FALL DOWN UPON US, THE CLASH OF ARMS, AND SHRIEKS– AND THEN ALL OF A SUDDEN, ALL WAS DEEP SILENCE WHEN, AFTER MANY HOURS, WE VENTURED TO GO FORTH, WE FOUND EVERYTHING AS BEFORE, NOT A SINGLE CORPSE LAY DIFFERENTLY– ALL WERE AS STIFF AS WOODEN FIGURES.

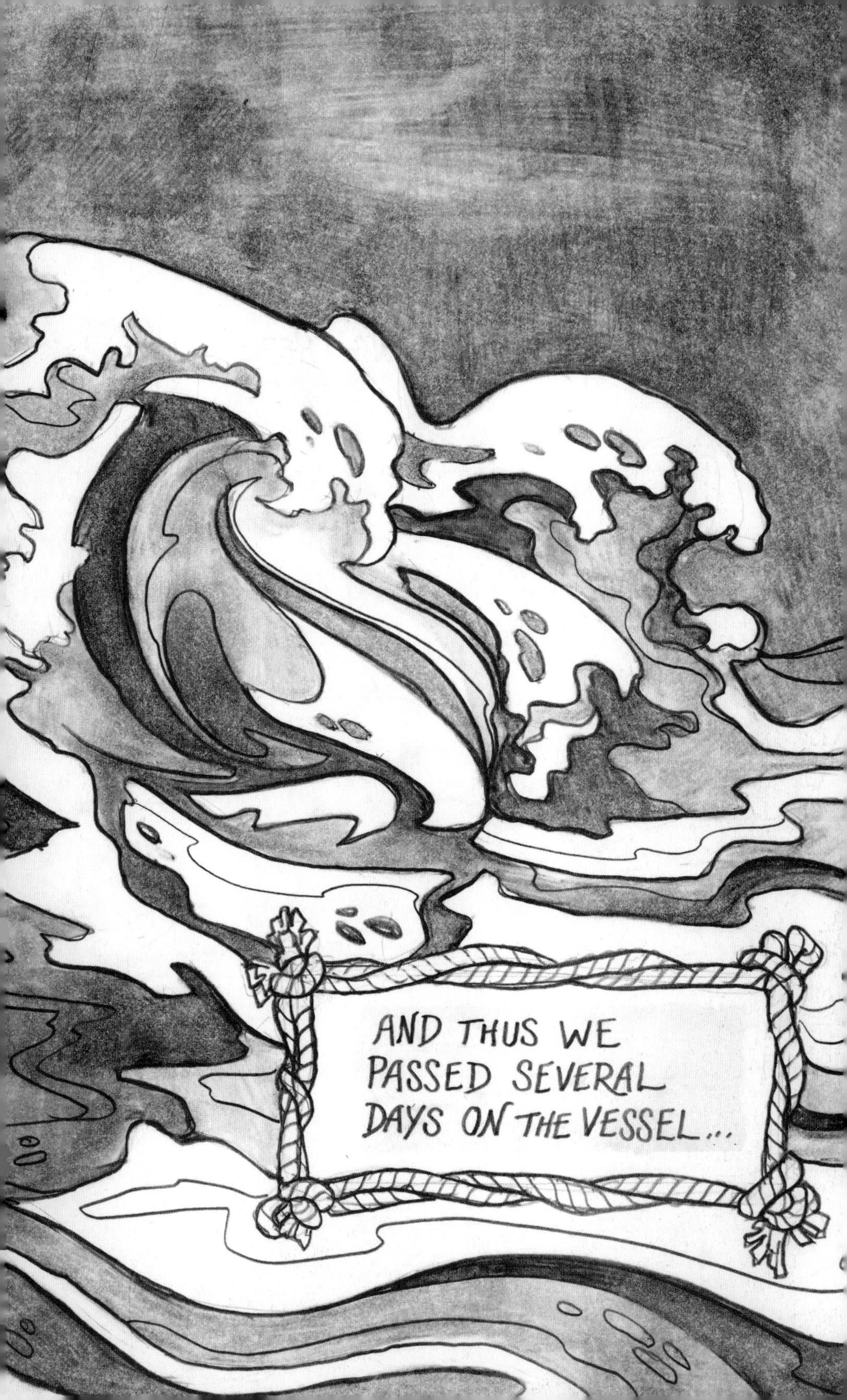
AND THUS WE PASSED SEVERAL DAYS ON THE VESSEL...

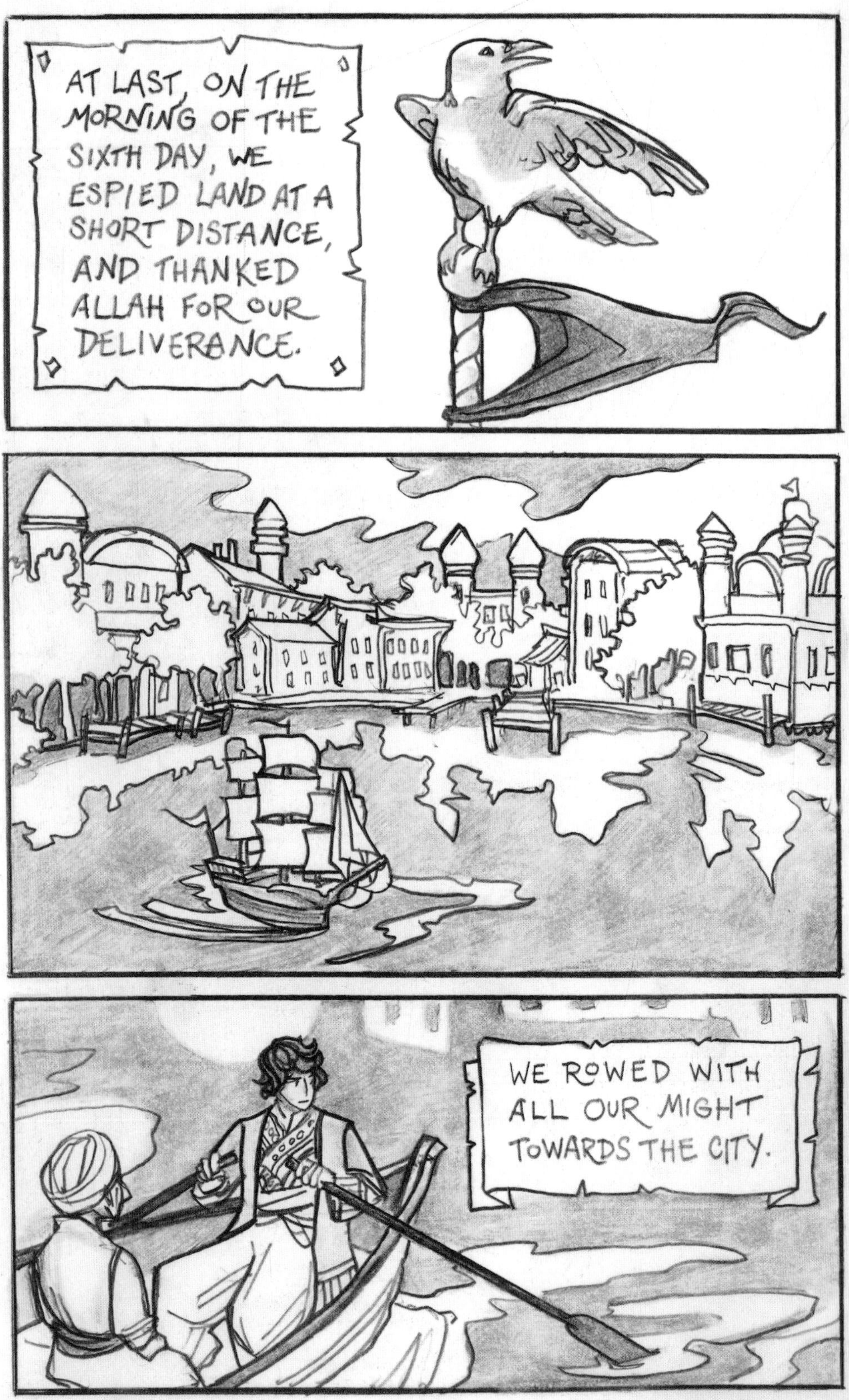
AT LAST, ON THE MORNING OF THE SIXTH DAY, WE ESPIED LAND AT A SHORT DISTANCE, AND THANKED ALLAH FOR OUR DELIVERANCE.
WE ROWED WITH ALL OUR MIGHT TOWARDS THE CITY.

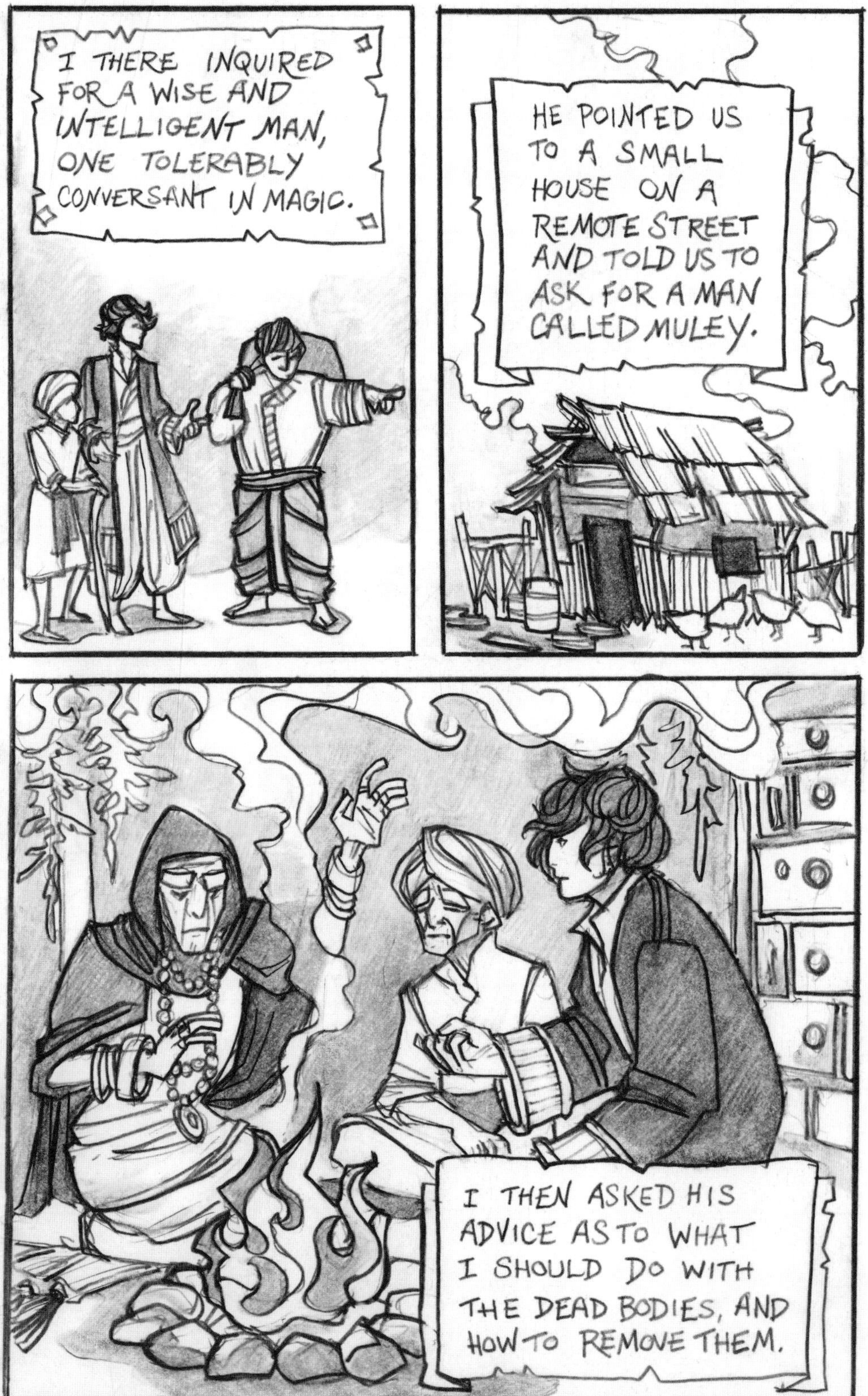
I THERE INQUIRED FOR A WISE AND INTELLIGENT MAN, ONE TOLERABLY CONVERSANT IN MAGIC.
HE POINTED US TO A SMALL HOUSE ON A REMOTE STREET AND TOLD US TO ASK FOR A MAN CALLED MULEY.
I THEN ASKED HIS ADVICE AS TO WHAT I SHOULD DO WITH THE DEAD BODIES, AND HOW TO REMOVE THEM.

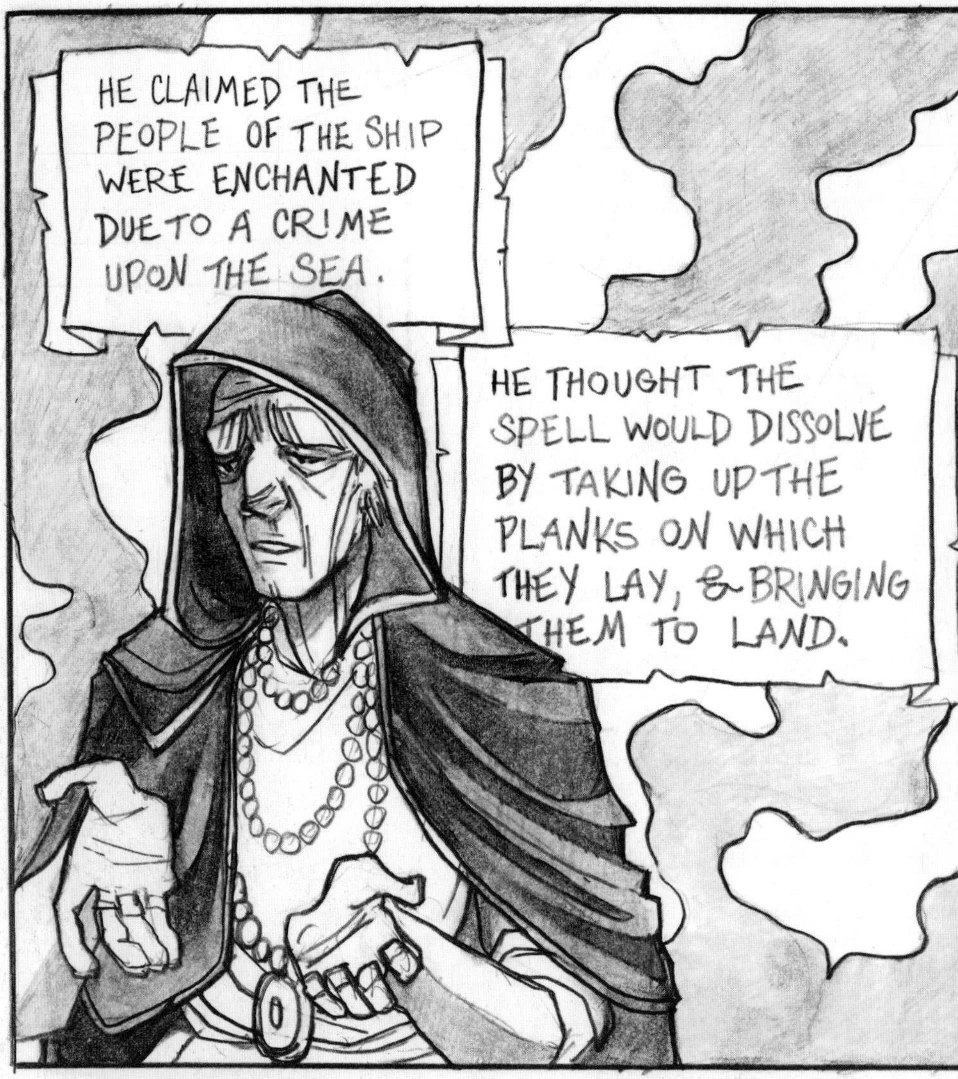
HE CLAIMED THE PEOPLE OF THE SHIP WERE ENCHANTED DUE TO A CRIME UPON THE SEA.
HE THOUGHT THE SPELL WOULD DISSOLVE BY TAKING UP THE PLANKS ON WHICH THEY LAY, & BRINGING THEM TO LAND.

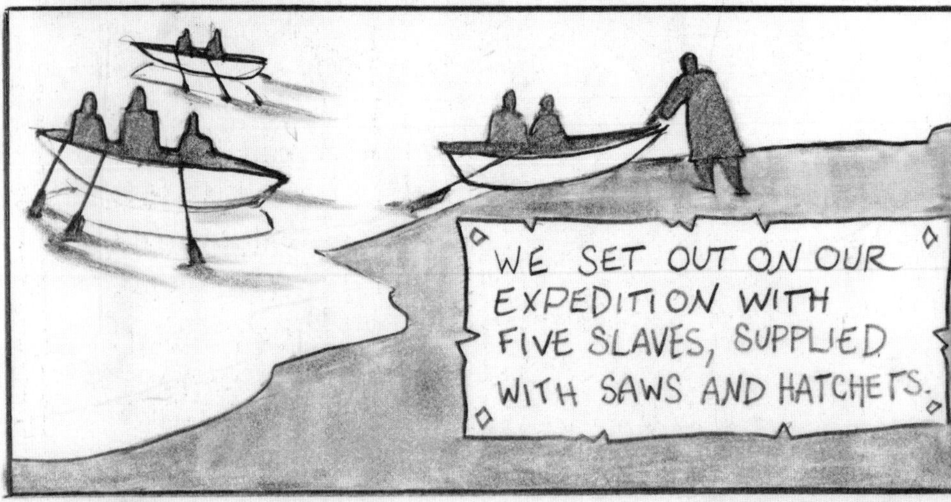
WE SET OUT ON OUR EXPEDITION WITH FIVE SLAVES, SUPPLIED WITH SAWS AND HATCHETS.

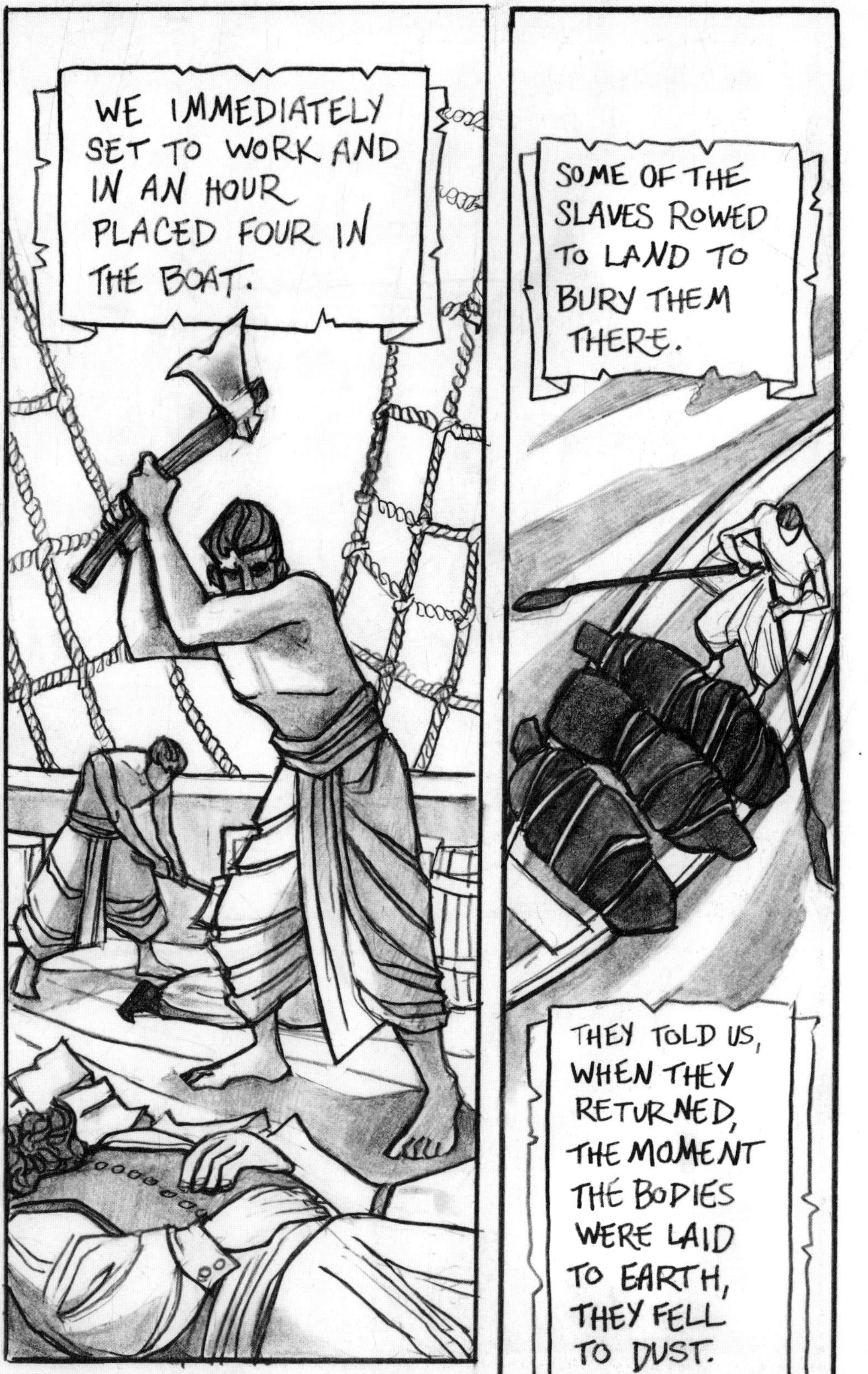
WE IMMEDIATELY SET TO WORK AND IN AN HOUR PLACED FOUR IN THE BOAT.
SOME OF THE SLAVES ROWED TO LAND TO BURY THEM THERE.
THEY TOLD US, WHEN THEY RETURNED, THE MOMENT THE BODIES WERE LAID TO EARTH, THEY FELL TO DUST.

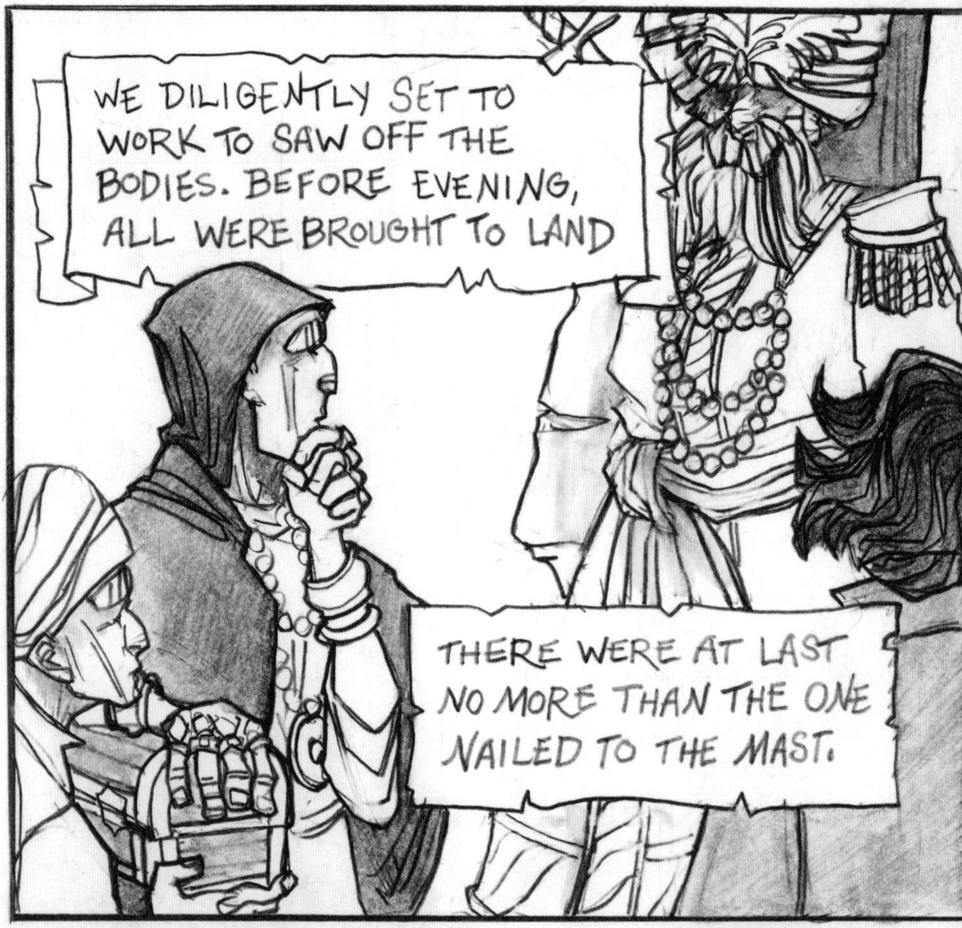
WE DILIGENTLY SET TO WORK TO SAW OFF THE BODIES. BEFORE EVENING, ALL WERE BROUGHT TO LAND
THERE WERE AT LAST NO MORE THAN THE ONE NAILED TO THE MAST.

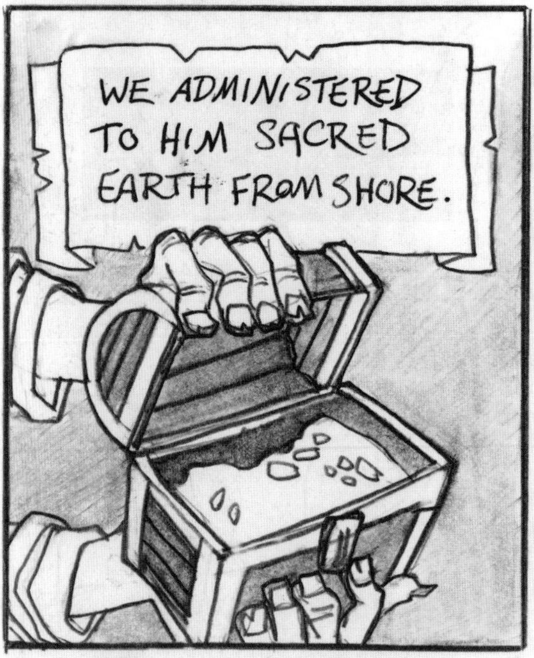
WE ADMINISTERED TO HIM SACRED EARTH FROM SHORE.

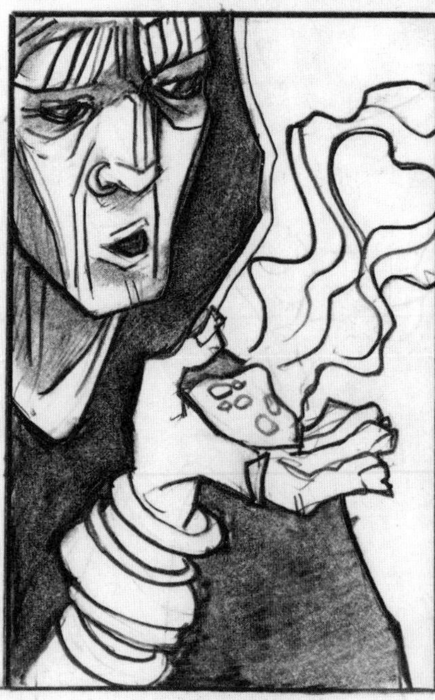

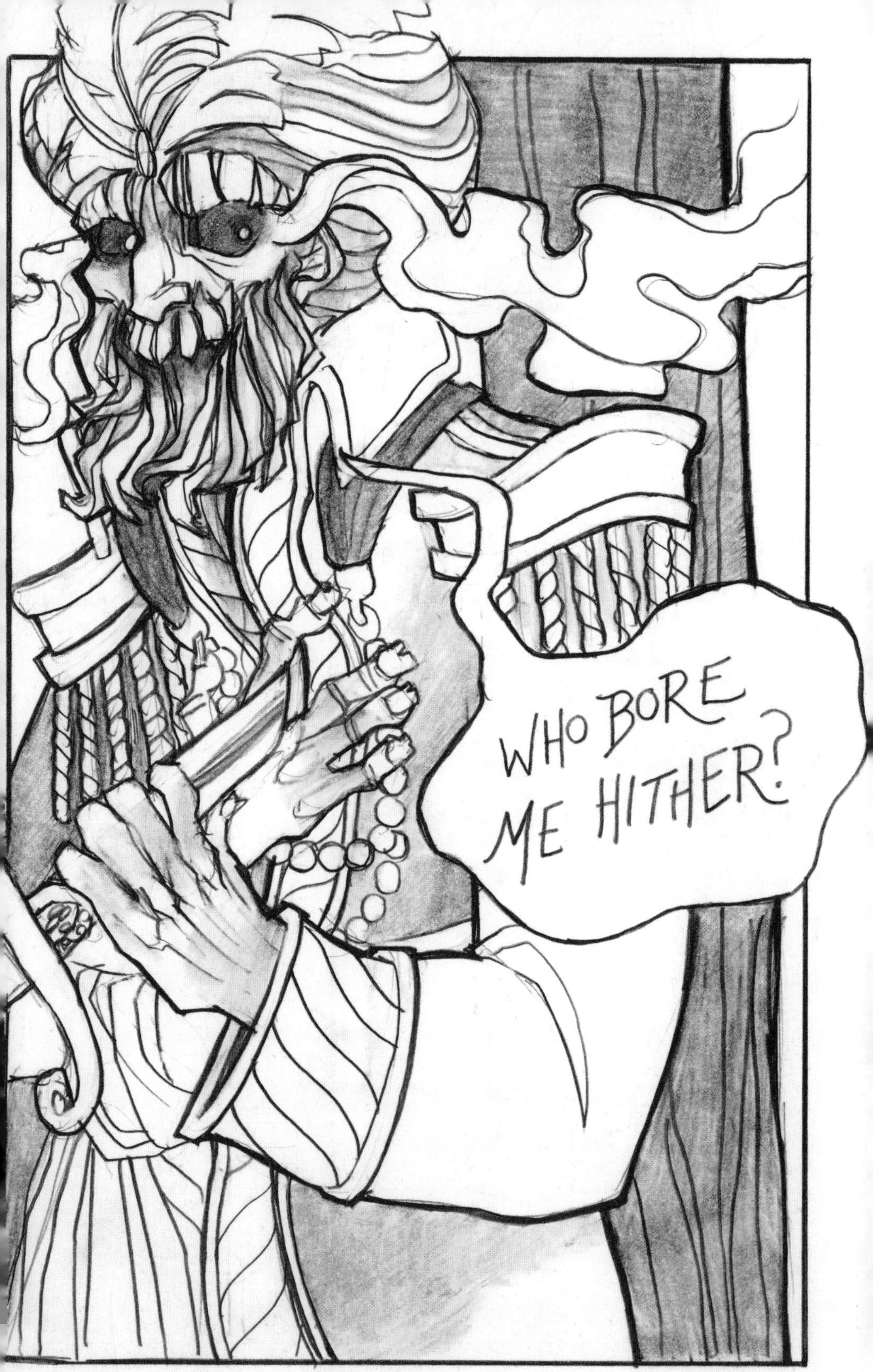
WHO BORE ME HITHER?

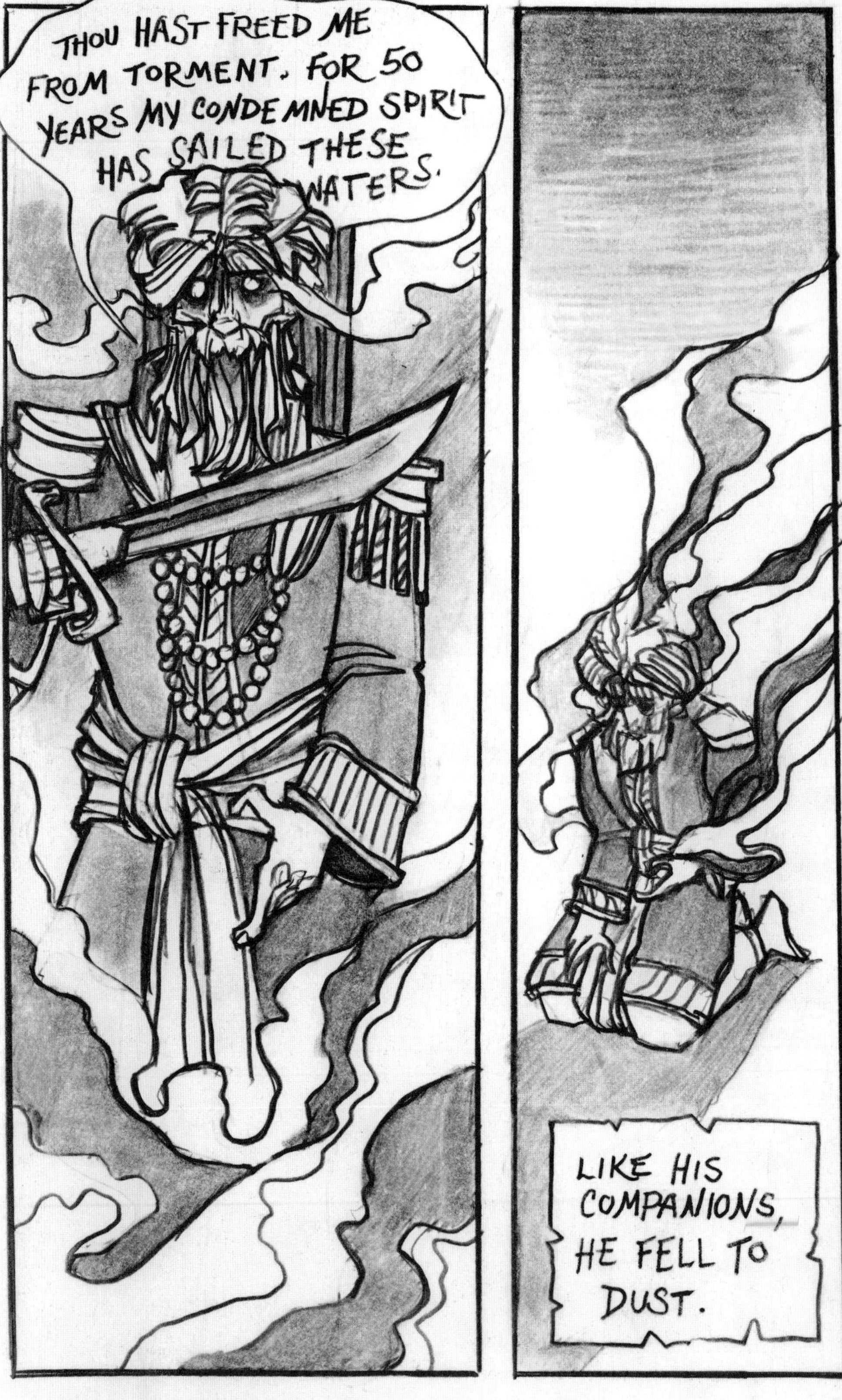
THOU HAST FREED ME FROM TORMENT. FOR 50 YEARS MY CONDEMNED SPIRIT HAS SAILED THESE WATERS.
LIKE HIS COMPANIONS, HE FELL TO DUST.

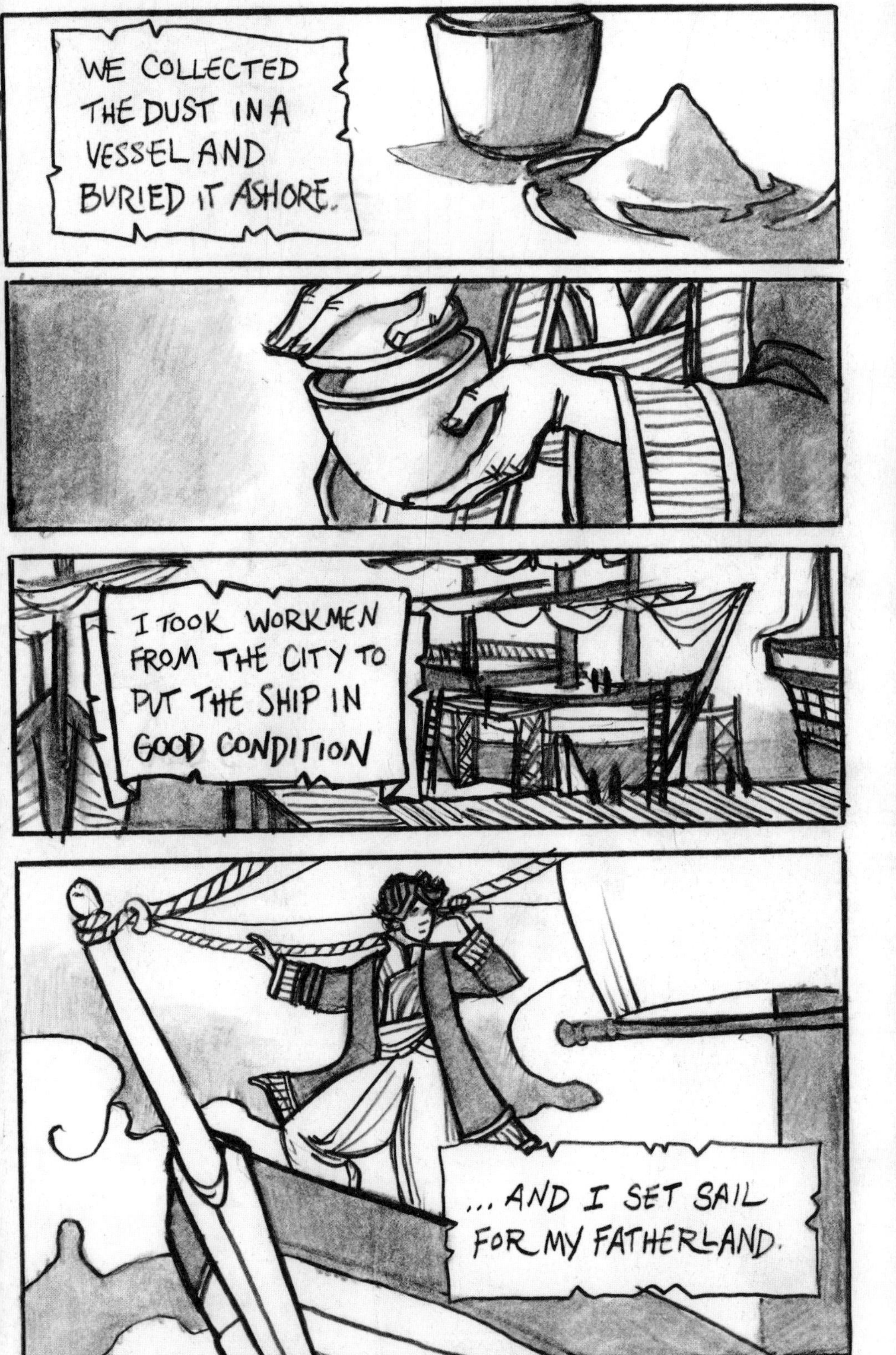
WE COLLECTED THE DUST IN A VESSEL AND BURIED IT ASHORE.
I TOOK WORKMEN FROM THE CITY TO PUT THE SHIP IN GOOD CONDITION
... AND I SET SAIL FOR MY FATHERLAND.

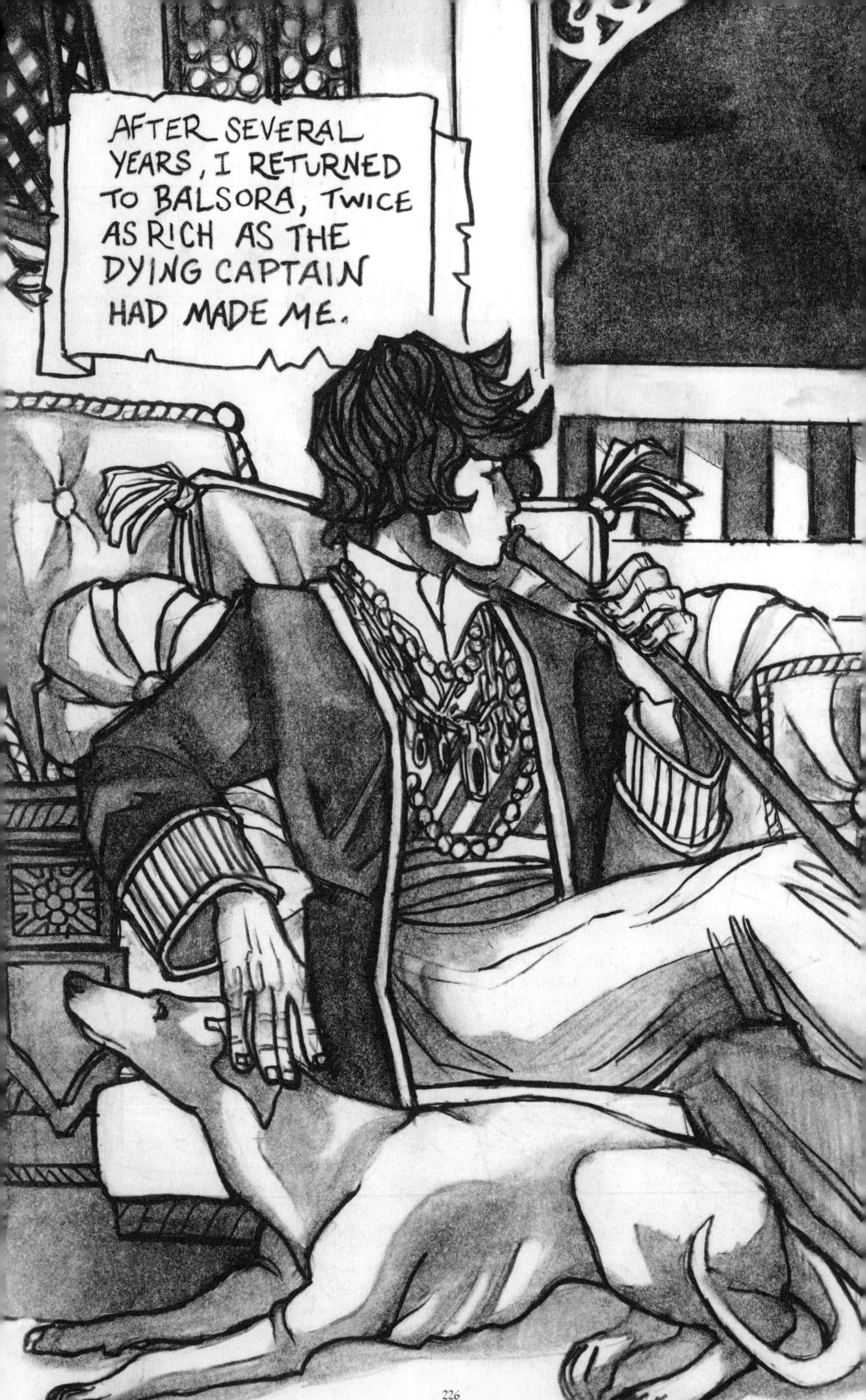
AFTER SEVERAL YEARS, I RETURNED TO BALSORA, TWICE AS RICH AS THE DYING CAPTAIN HAD MADE ME.

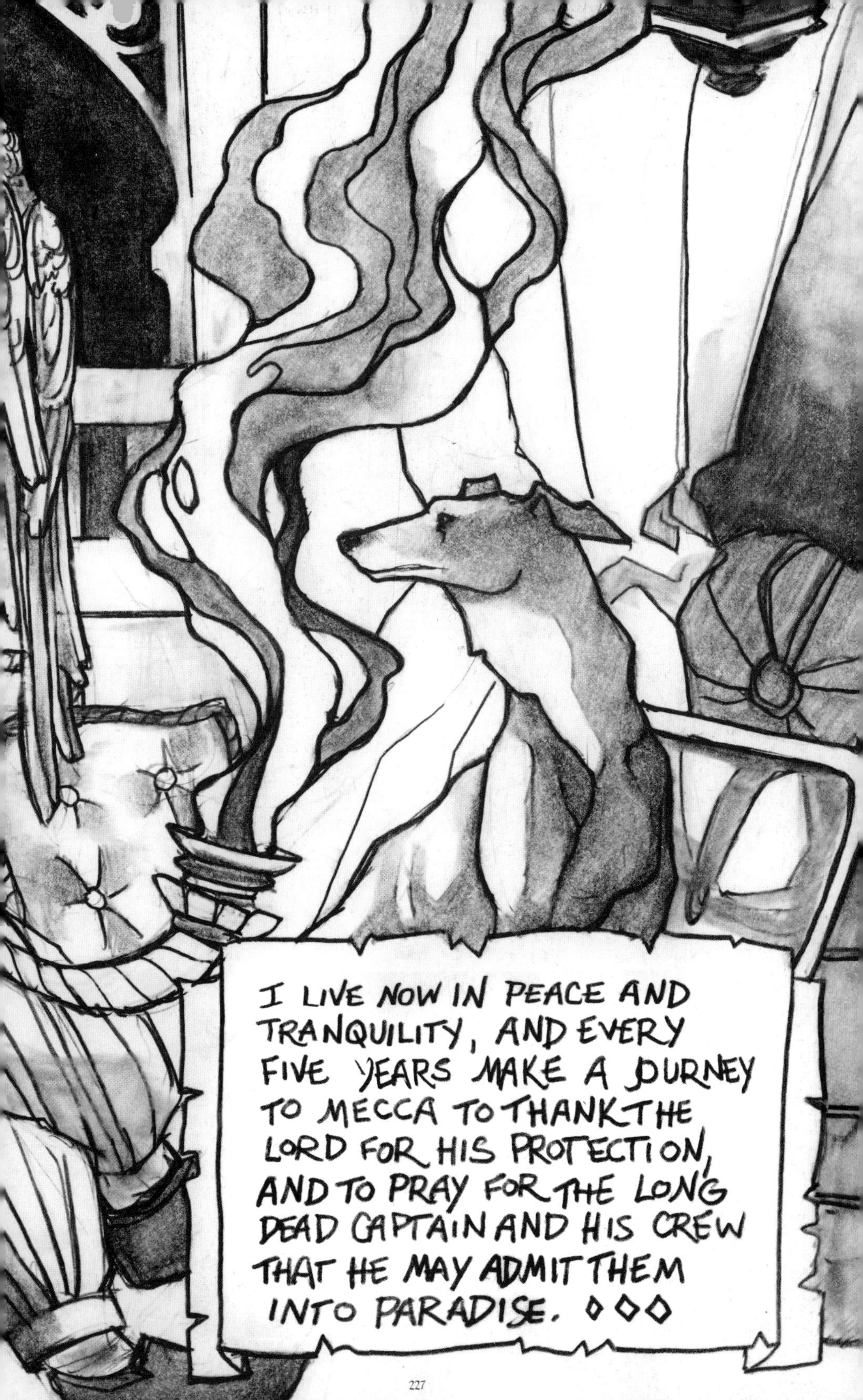
I LIVE NOW IN PEACE AND TRANQUILITY, AND EVERY FIVE YEARS MAKE A JOURNEY TO MECCA TO THANK THE LORD FOR HIS PROTECTION, AND TO PRAY FOR THE LONG DEAD CAPTAIN AND HIS CREW THAT HE MAY ADMIT THEM INTO PARADISE. ◊◊◊

TAMAMO
the fox maiden

by Terry Blas

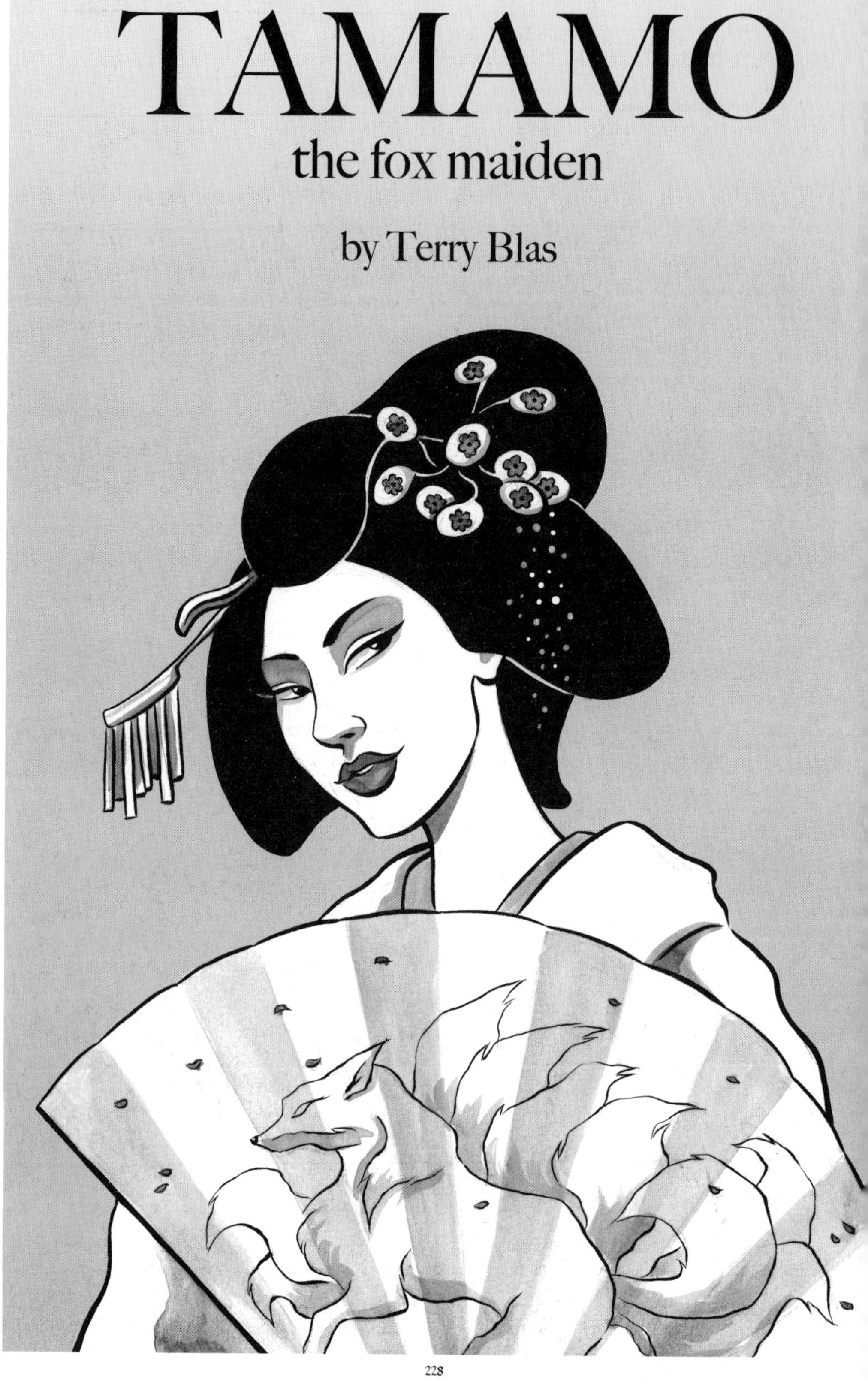

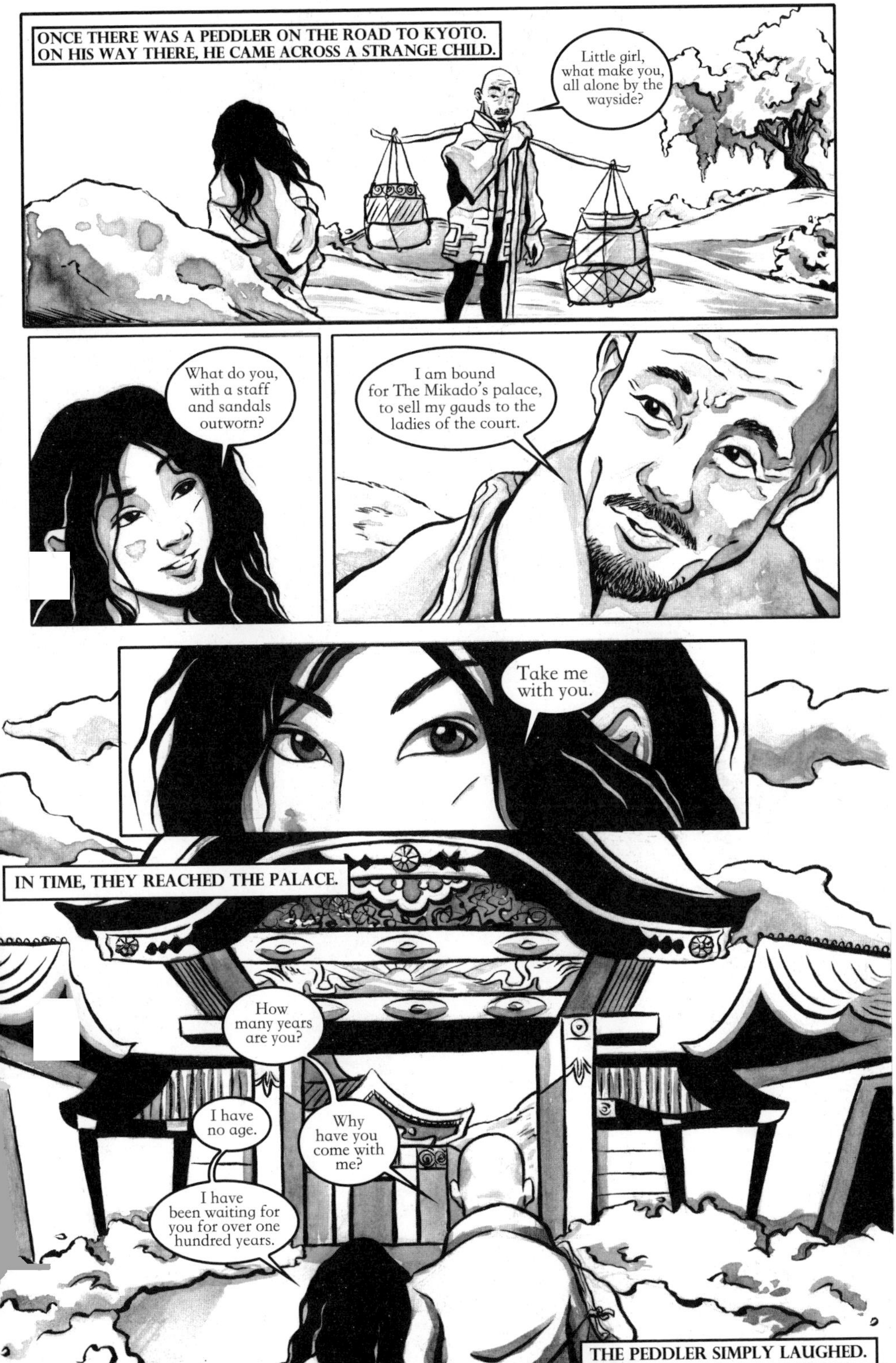
ONCE THERE WAS A PEDDLER ON THE ROAD TO KYOTO. ON HIS WAY THERE, HE CAME ACROSS A STRANGE CHILD.
Little girl, what make you, all alone by the wayside?
What do you, with a staff and sandals outworn?
I am bound for The Mikado's palace, to sell my gauds to the ladies of the court.
Take me with you.
IN TIME, THEY REACHED THE PALACE.
How many years are you?
I have no age.
Why have you come with me?
I have been waiting for you for over one hundred years.
THE PEDDLER SIMPLY LAUGHED.

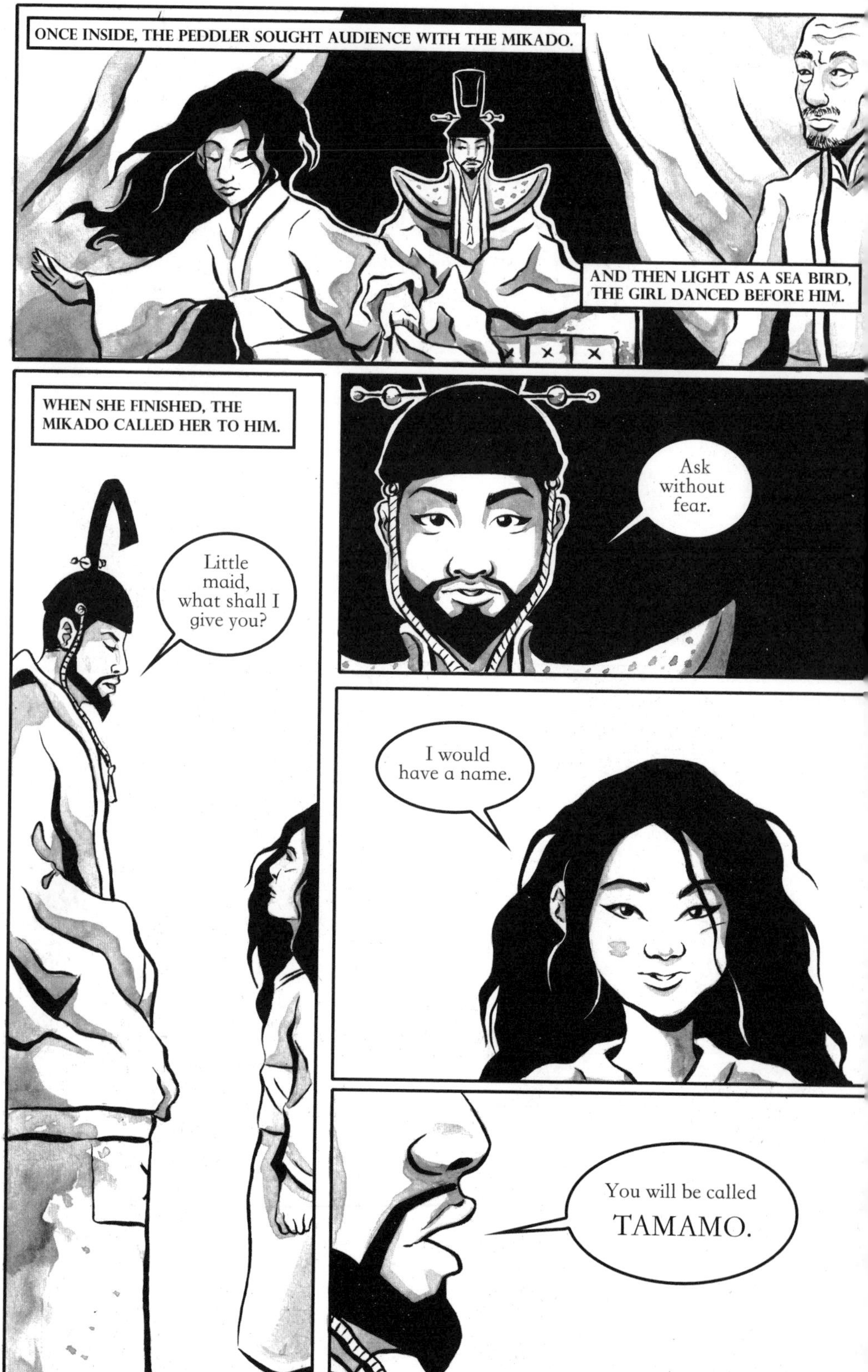
ONCE INSIDE, THE PEDDLER SOUGHT AUDIENCE WITH THE MIKADO.
AND THEN LIGHT AS A SEA BIRD, THE GIRL DANCED BEFORE HIM.
WHEN SHE FINISHED, THE MIKADO CALLED HER TO HIM.
Little maid, what shall I give you?
Ask without fear.
I would have a name.
You will be called TAMAMO.

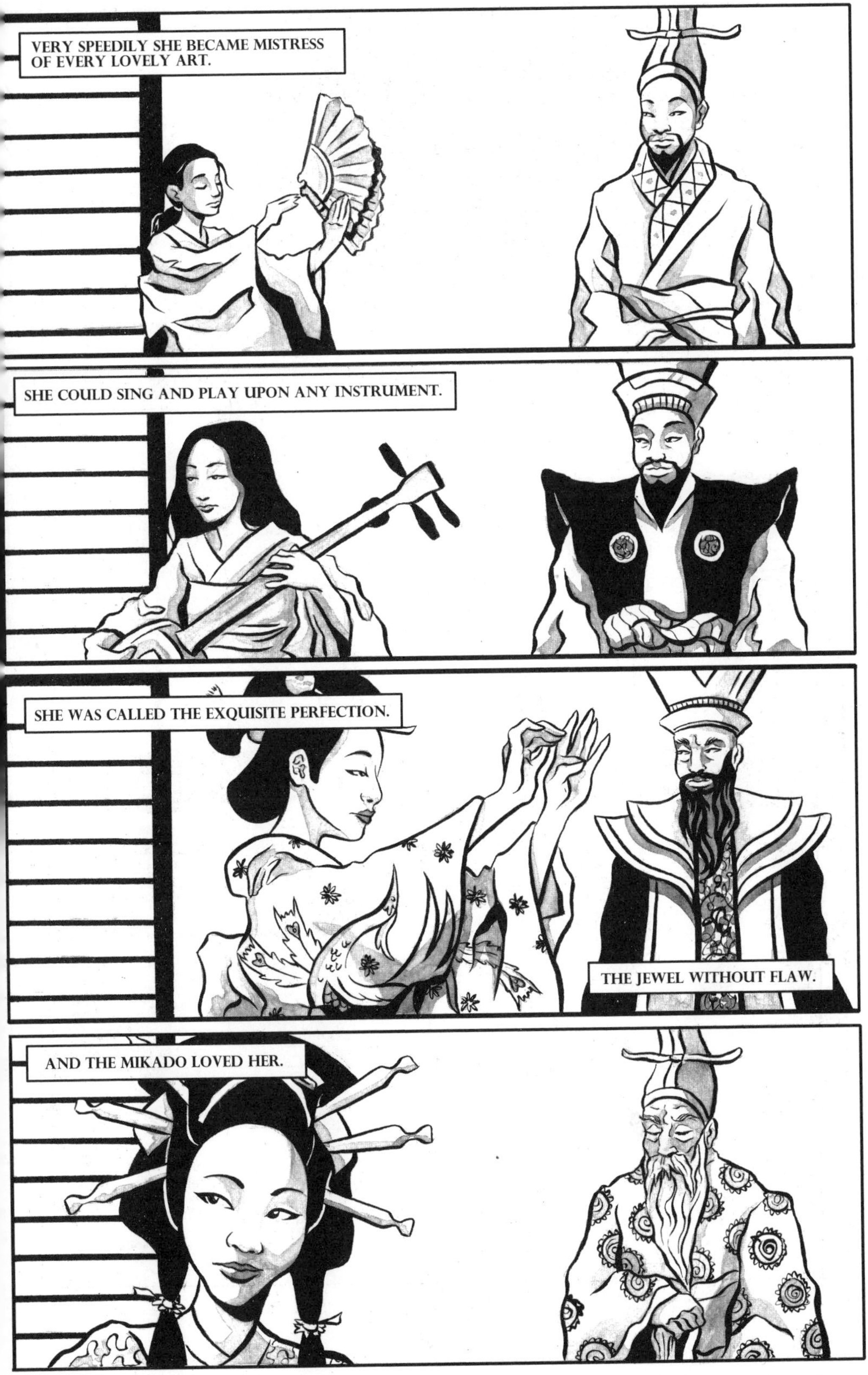
VERY SPEEDILY SHE BECAME MISTRESS OF EVERY LOVELY ART.
SHE COULD SING AND PLAY UPON ANY INSTRUMENT.
SHE WAS CALLED THE EXQUISITE PERFECTION.
THE JEWEL WITHOUT FLAW.
AND THE MIKADO LOVED HER.

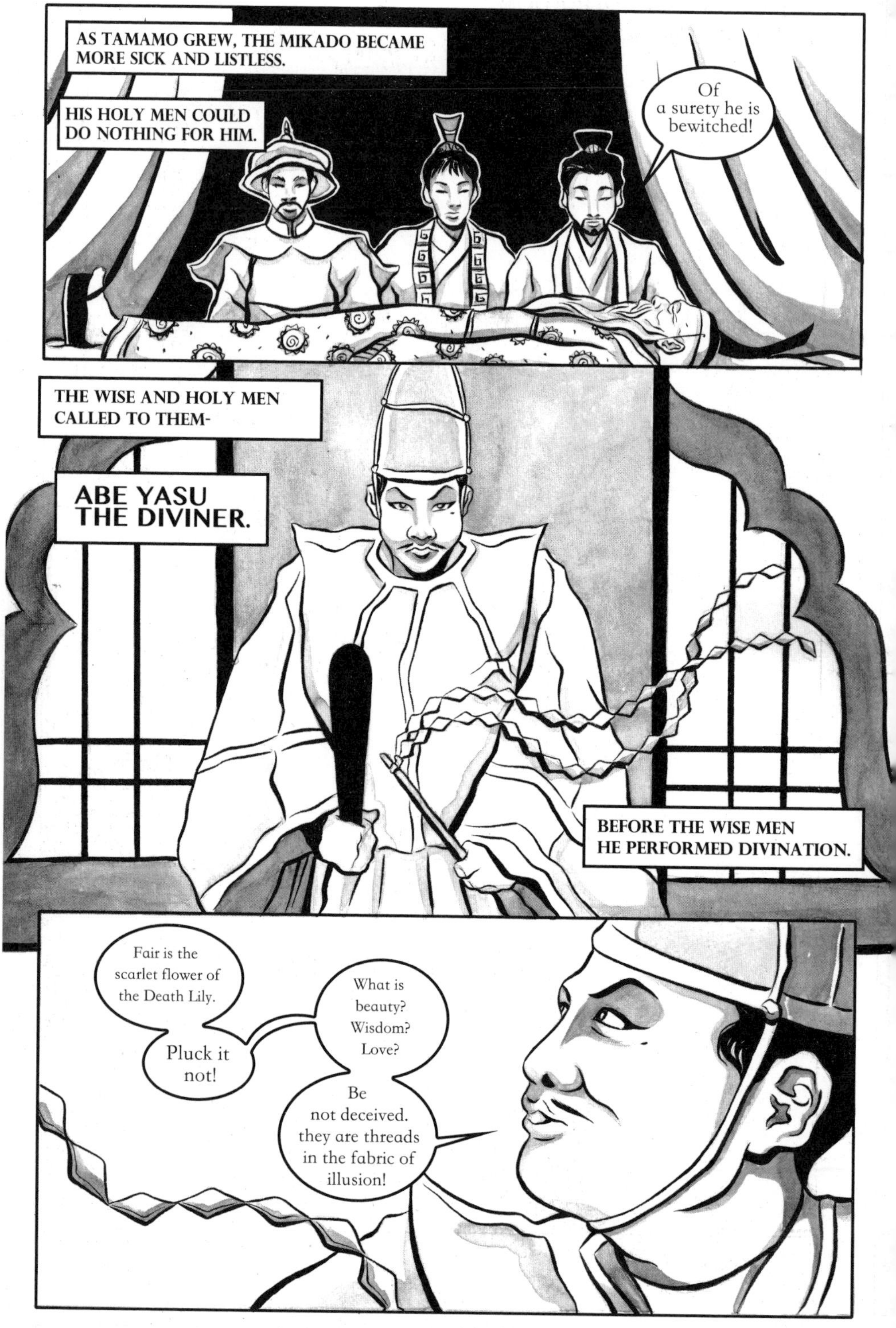

AS TAMAMO GREW, THE MIKADO BECAME MORE SICK AND LISTLESS.
HIS HOLY MEN COULD DO NOTHING FOR HIM.
Of a surety he is bewitched!
THE WISE AND HOLY MEN CALLED TO THEM-
ABE YASU THE DIVINER.
BEFORE THE WISE MEN HE PERFORMED DIVINATION.
Fair is the scarlet flower of the Death Lily.
Pluck it not!
What is beauty? Wisdom? Love?
Be not deceived. they are threads in the fabric of illusion!

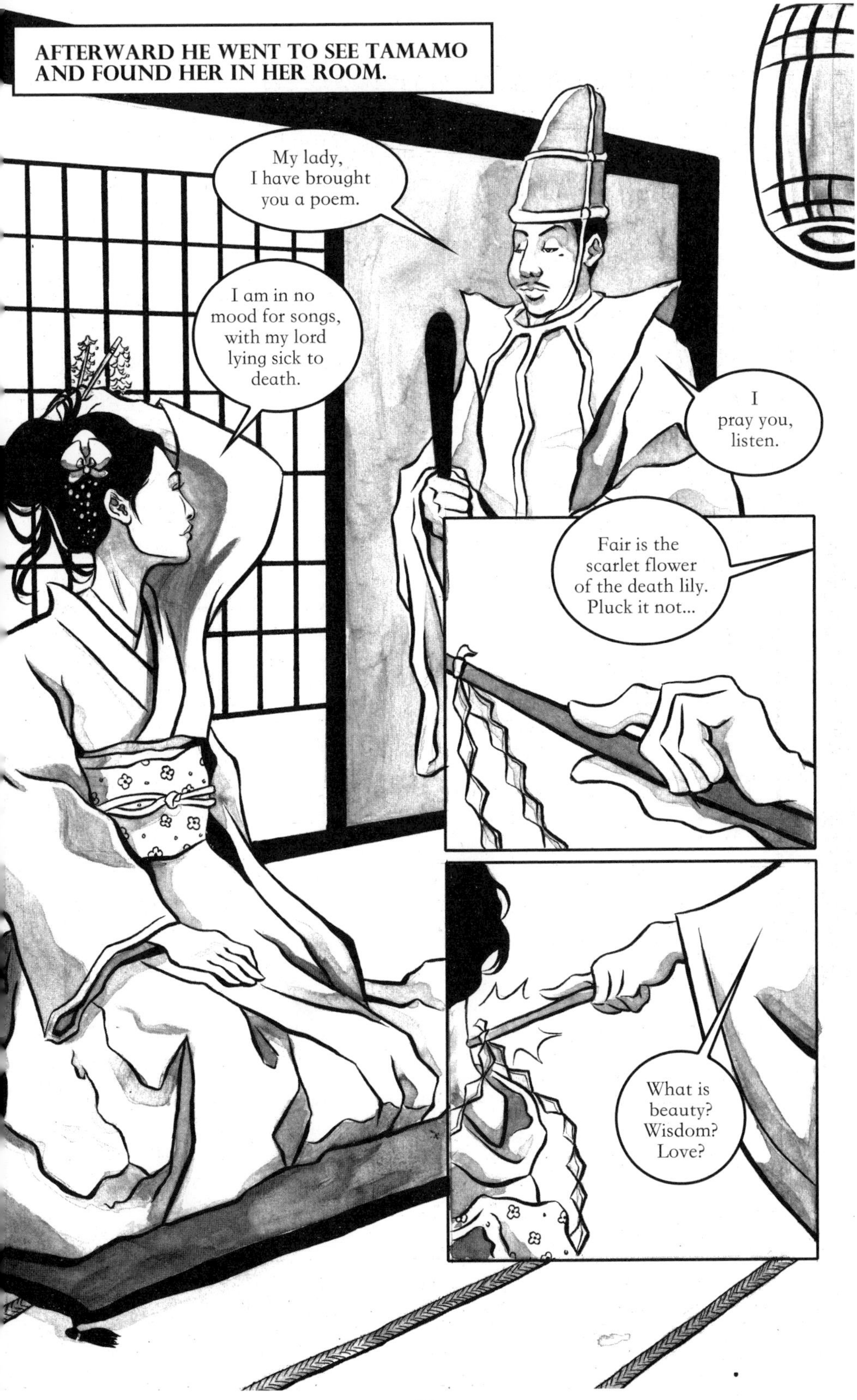
AFTERWARD HE WENT TO SEE TAMAMO AND FOUND HER IN HER ROOM.
My lady, I have brought you a poem.
I am in no mood for songs, with my lord lying sick to death.
I pray you, listen.
Fair is the scarlet flower of the death lily. Pluck it not...
What is beauty? Wisdom? Love?

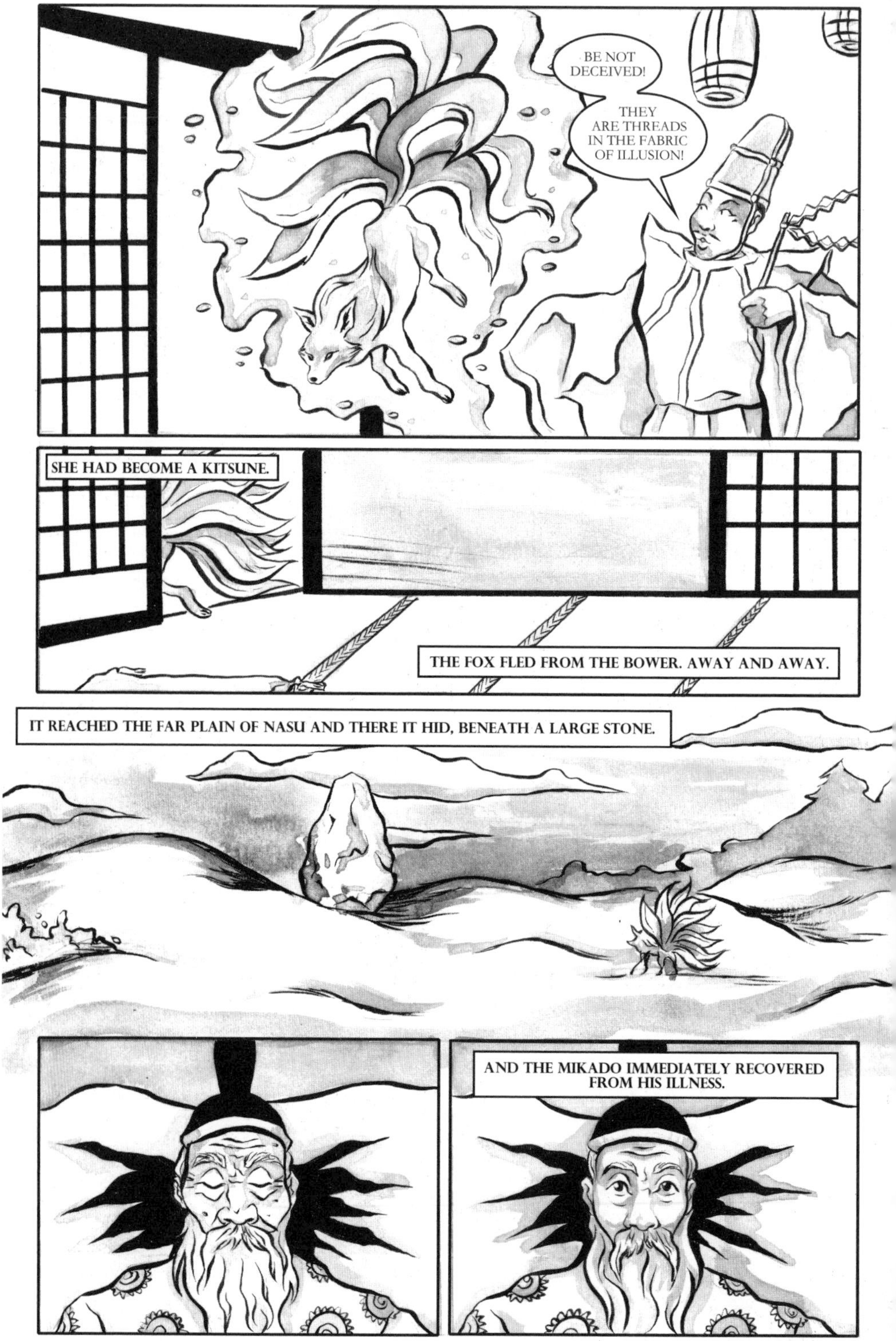
BE NOT DECEIVED!
THEY ARE THREADS IN THE FABRIC OF ILLUSION!
SHE HAD BECOME A KITSUNE.
THE FOX FLED FROM THE BOWER. AWAY AND AWAY.
IT REACHED THE FAR PLAIN OF NASU AND THERE IT HID, BENEATH A LARGE STONE.
AND THE MIKADO IMMEDIATELY RECOVERED FROM HIS ILLNESS.

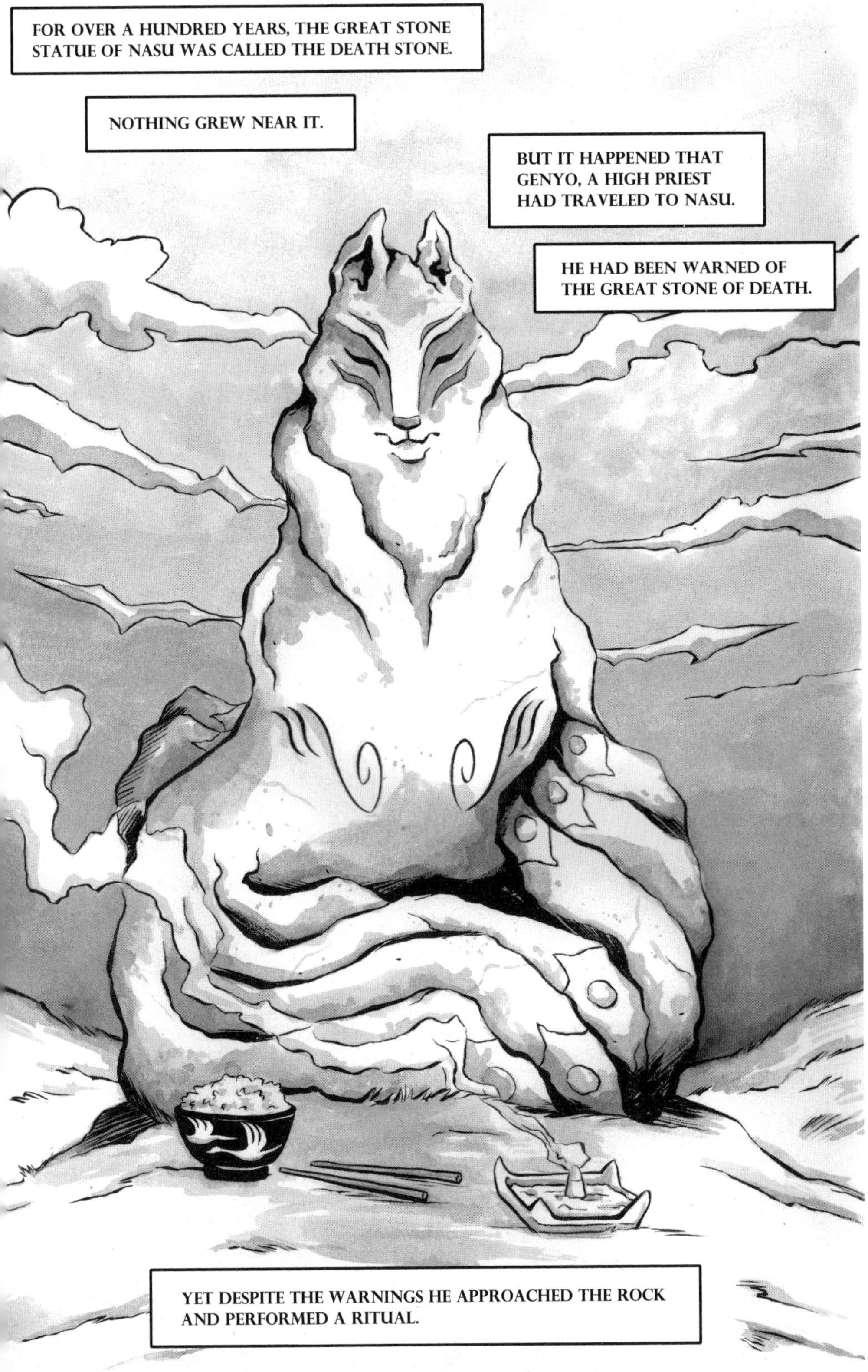
FOR OVER A HUNDRED YEARS, THE GREAT STONE STATUE OF NASU WAS CALLED THE DEATH STONE.
NOTHING GREW NEAR IT.
BUT IT HAPPENED THAT GENYO, A HIGH PRIEST HAD TRAVELED TO NASU.
HE HAD BEEN WARNED OF THE GREAT STONE OF DEATH.
YET DESPITE THE WARNINGS HE APPROACHED THE ROCK AND PERFORMED A RITUAL.

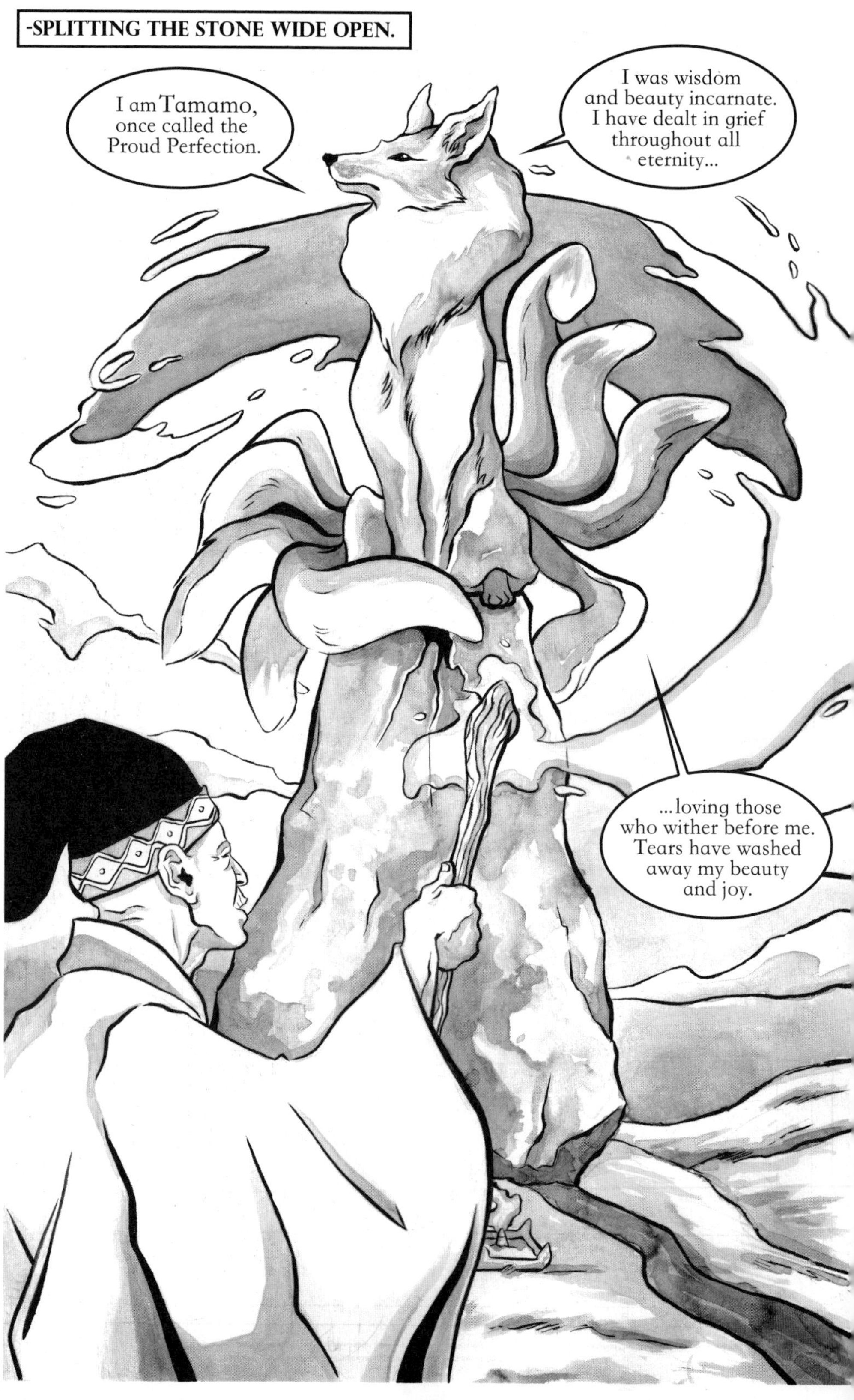
-SPLITTING THE STONE WIDE OPEN.
I am Tamamo, once called the Proud Perfection.
I was wisdom and beauty incarnate. I have dealt in grief throughout all eternity...
...loving those who wither before me. Tears have washed away my beauty and joy.

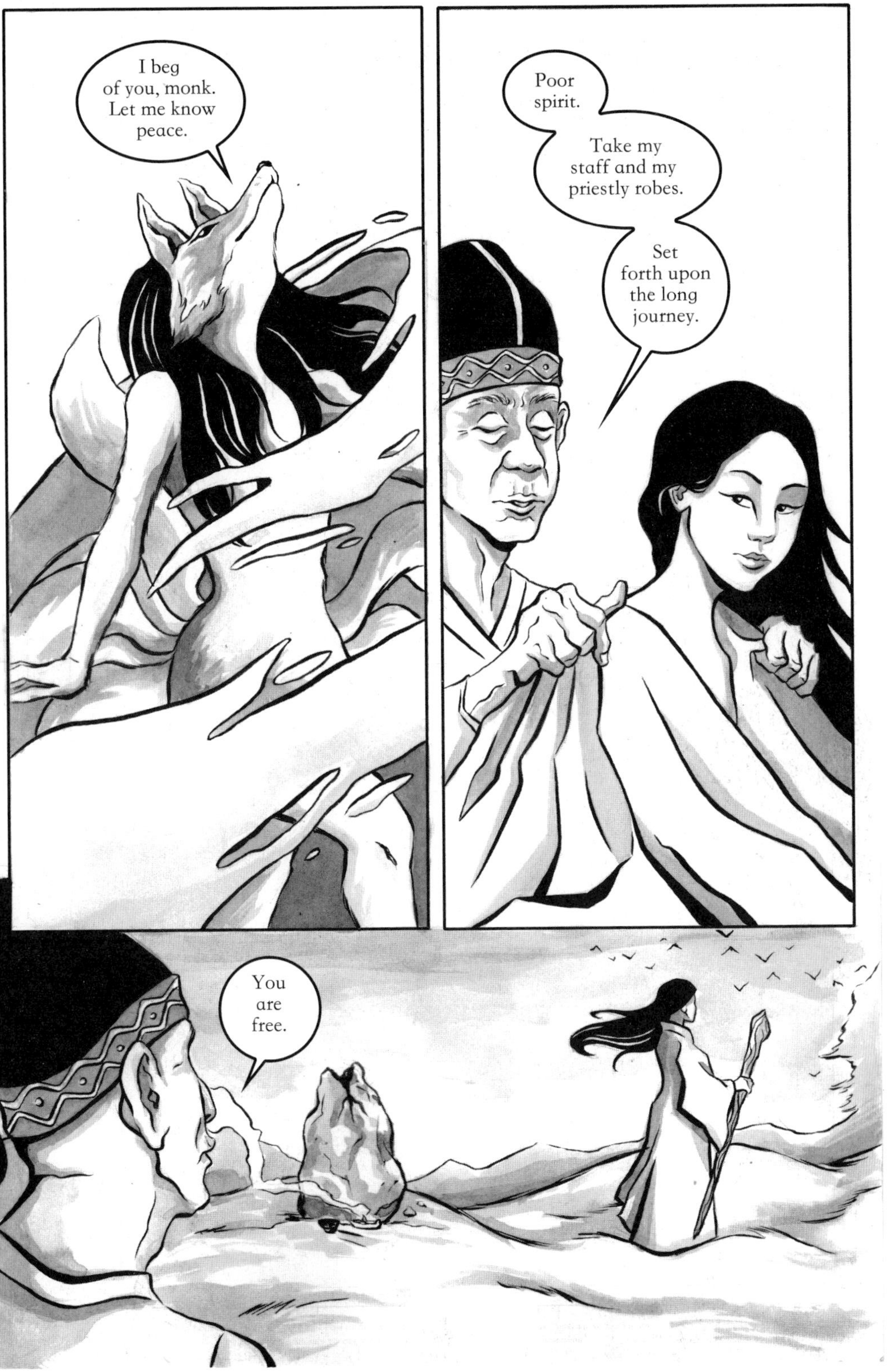
I beg of you, monk. Let me know peace.
Poor spirit.
Take my staff and my priestly robes.
Set forth upon the long journey.
You are free.

THE THREE RHYMESTERS

ONCE THERE WERE THREE DAUGHTERS
AND TO THEM EACH A HUSBAND

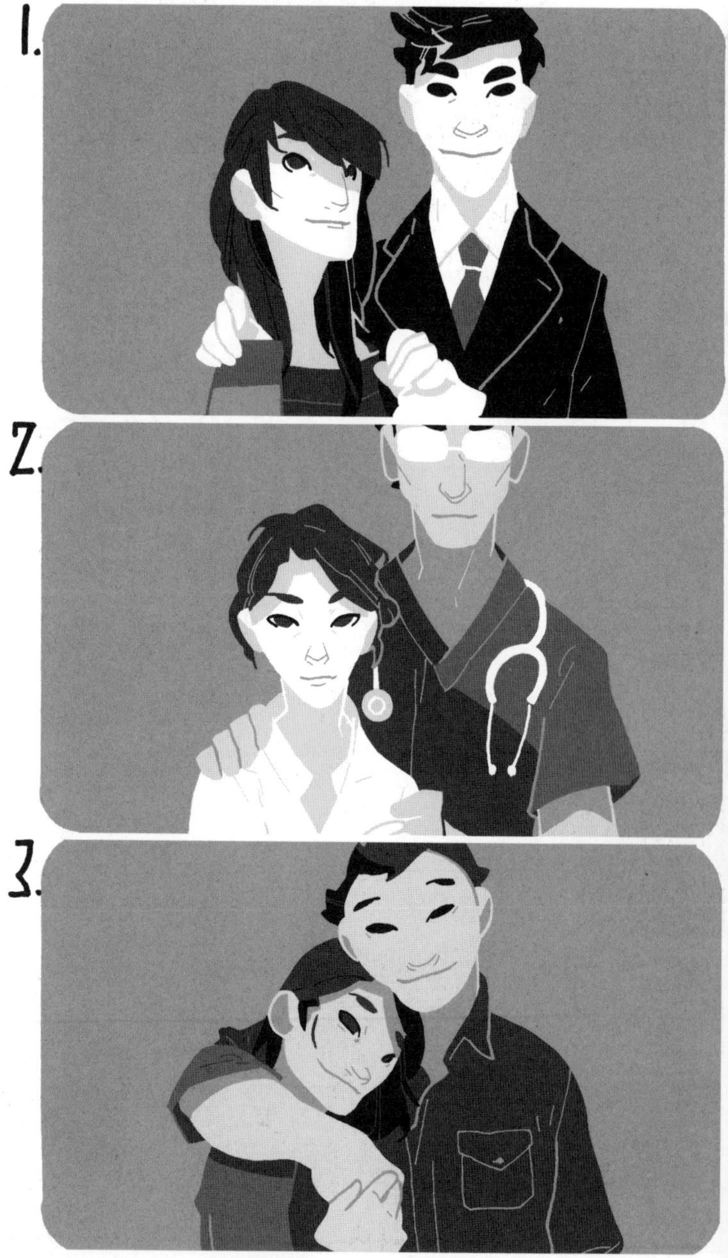
1.
2.
3.

adapted by
meredith mcclaren

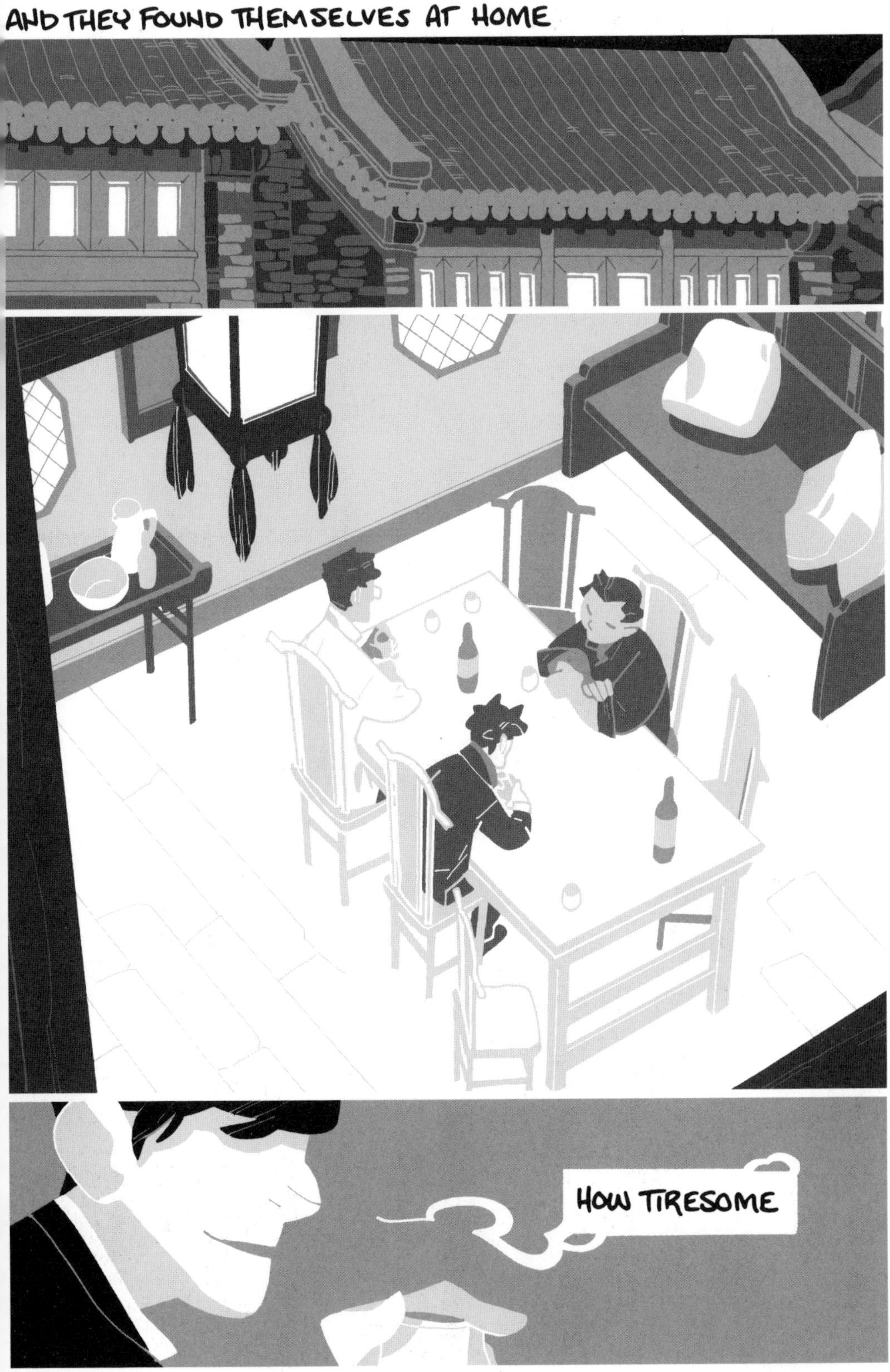
AND THEY FOUND THEMSELVES AT HOME
HOW TIRESOME

LET US HAVE A GAME
EACH OF US MUST INVENT A VERSE
THAT RHYMES AND MAKES SENSE
ON THE WORDS—
   IN THE SKY

          ON THE EARTH

                    AT THE TABLE

                              IN THE ROOM

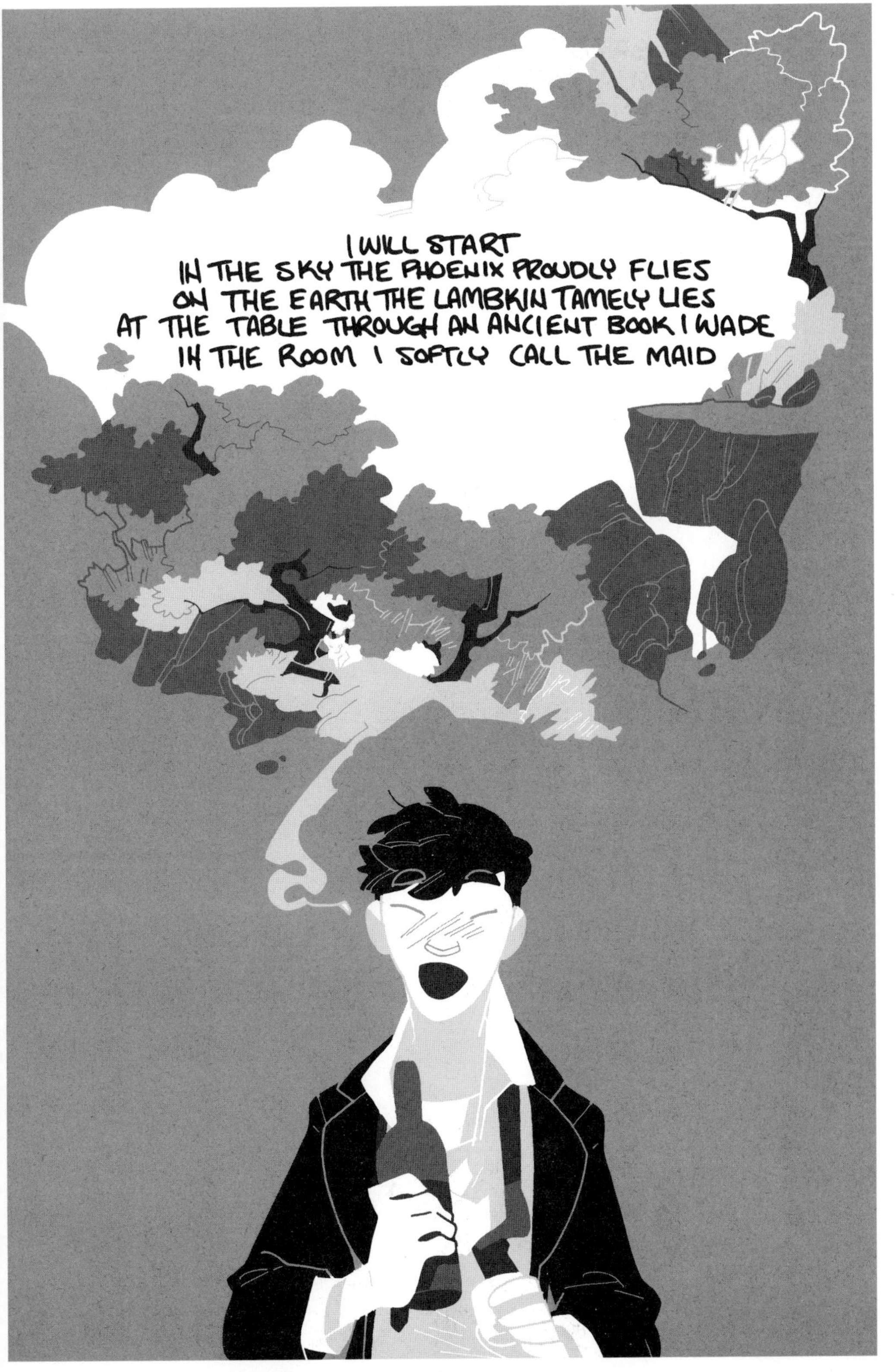
I WILL START
IN THE SKY THE PHOENIX PROUDLY FLIES
ON THE EARTH THE LAMBKIN TAMELY LIES
AT THE TABLE THROUGH AN ANCIENT BOOK I WADE
IN THE ROOM I SOFTLY CALL THE MAID

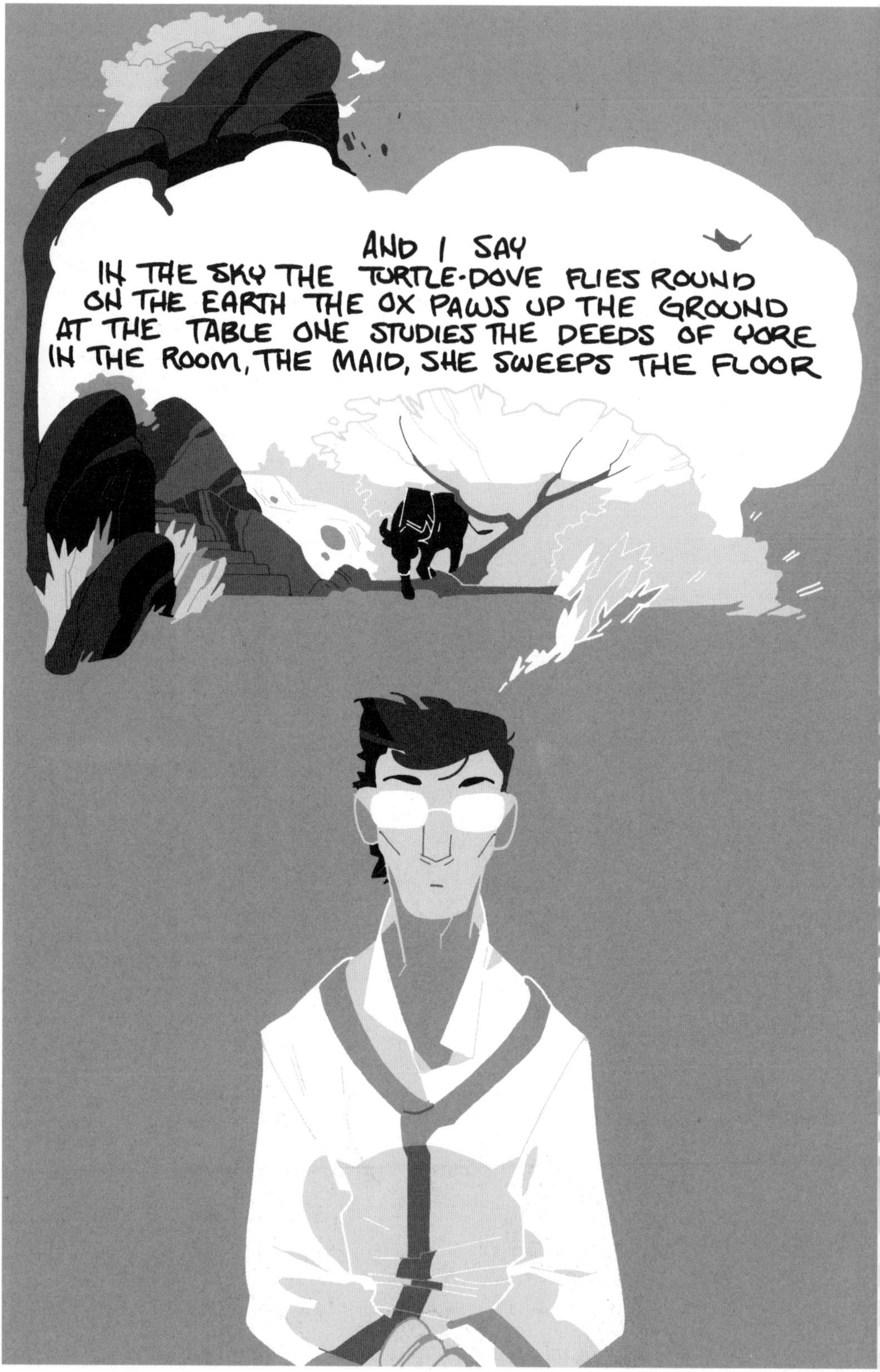
AND I SAY
IN THE SKY THE TURTLE-DOVE FLIES ROUND
ON THE EARTH THE OX PAWS UP THE GROUND
AT THE TABLE ONE STUDIES THE DEEDS OF YORE
IN THE ROOM, THE MAID, SHE SWEEPS THE FLOOR

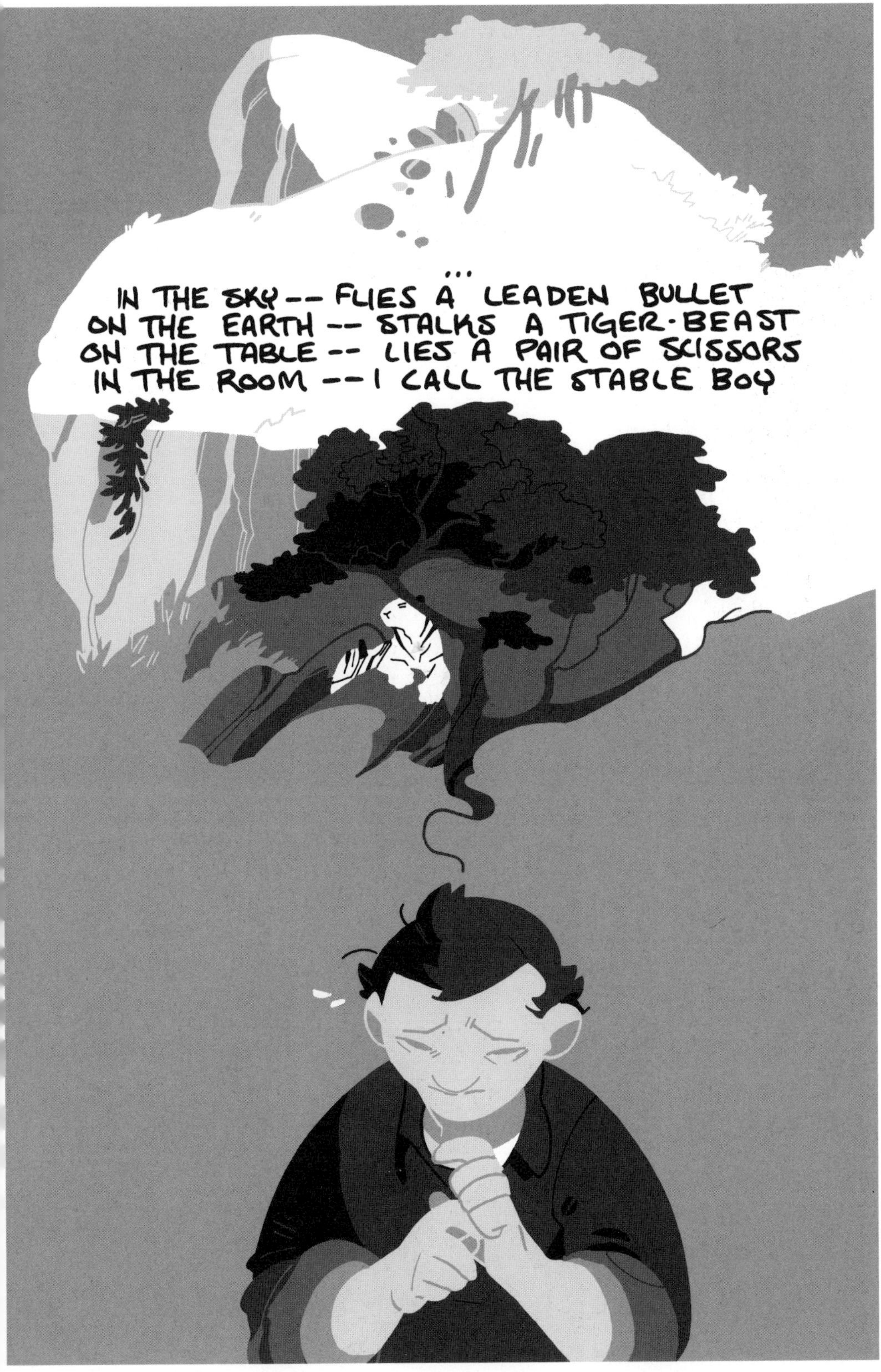
...
IN THE SKY -- FLIES A LEADEN BULLET
ON THE EARTH -- STALKS A TIGER-BEAST
ON THE TABLE -- LIES A PAIR OF SCISSORS
IN THE ROOM -- I CALL THE STABLE BOY

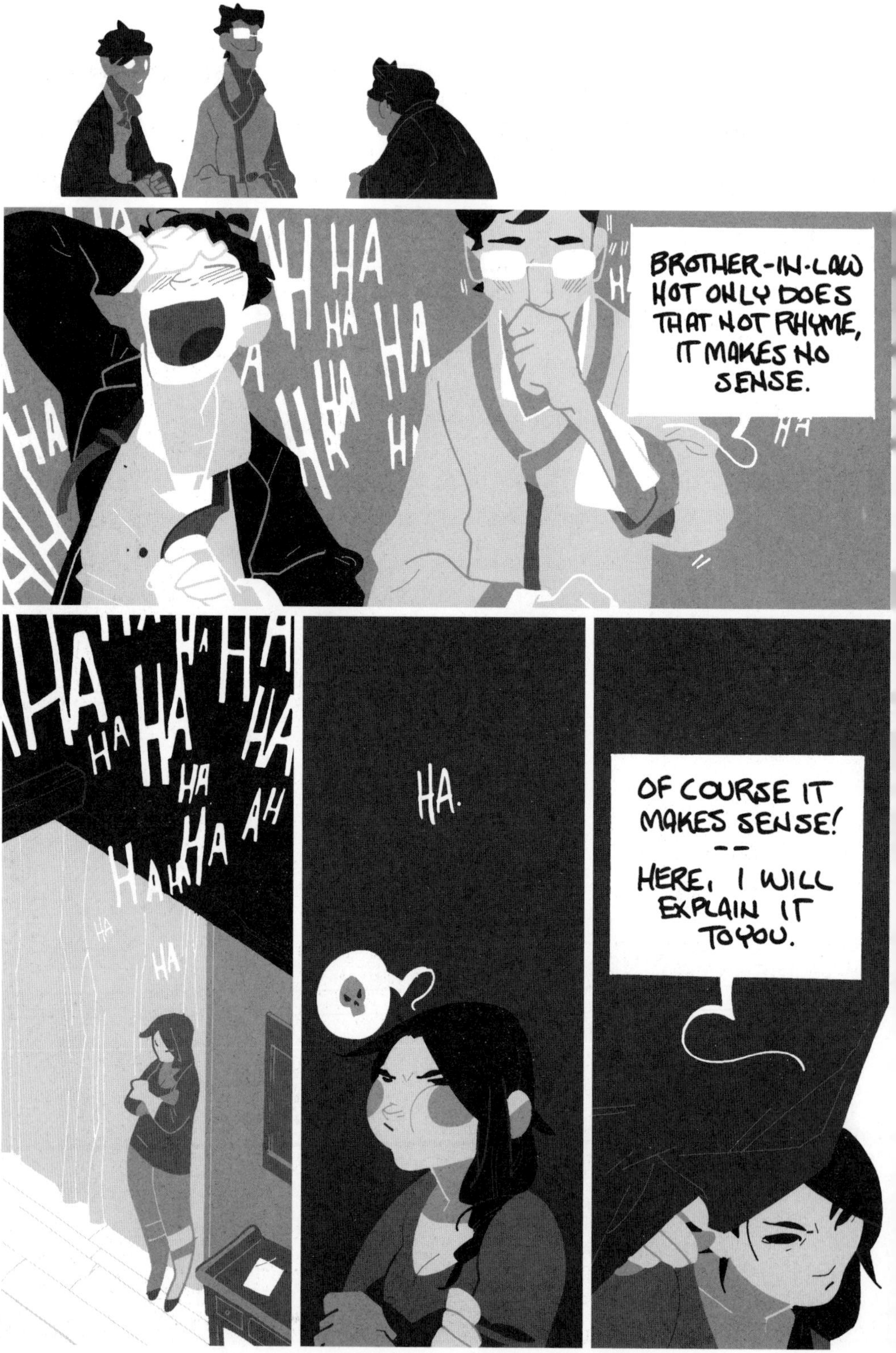
HA HA HA HA HA HA HA
BROTHER-IN-LAW NOT ONLY DOES THAT NOT RHYME, IT MAKES NO SENSE.
HA HA HA HA HA HA HA HA HA
HA.
OF COURSE IT MAKES SENSE! -- HERE, I WILL EXPLAIN IT TOYOU.

IN THE SKY OUR LEADEN BULLET WILL SHOOT YOUR PHOENIX AND YOUR TURTLE-DOVE
ON THE EARTH OUR TIGER-BEAST WILL DEVOUR YOUR SHEEP AND YOUR OX
ON THE TABLE OUR PAIR OF SCISSORS WILL CUT UP ALL YOUR BOOKS
AND FINALLY, IN THE ROOM-- WELL, THE STABLE BOY CAN MARRY YOUR MAID.'

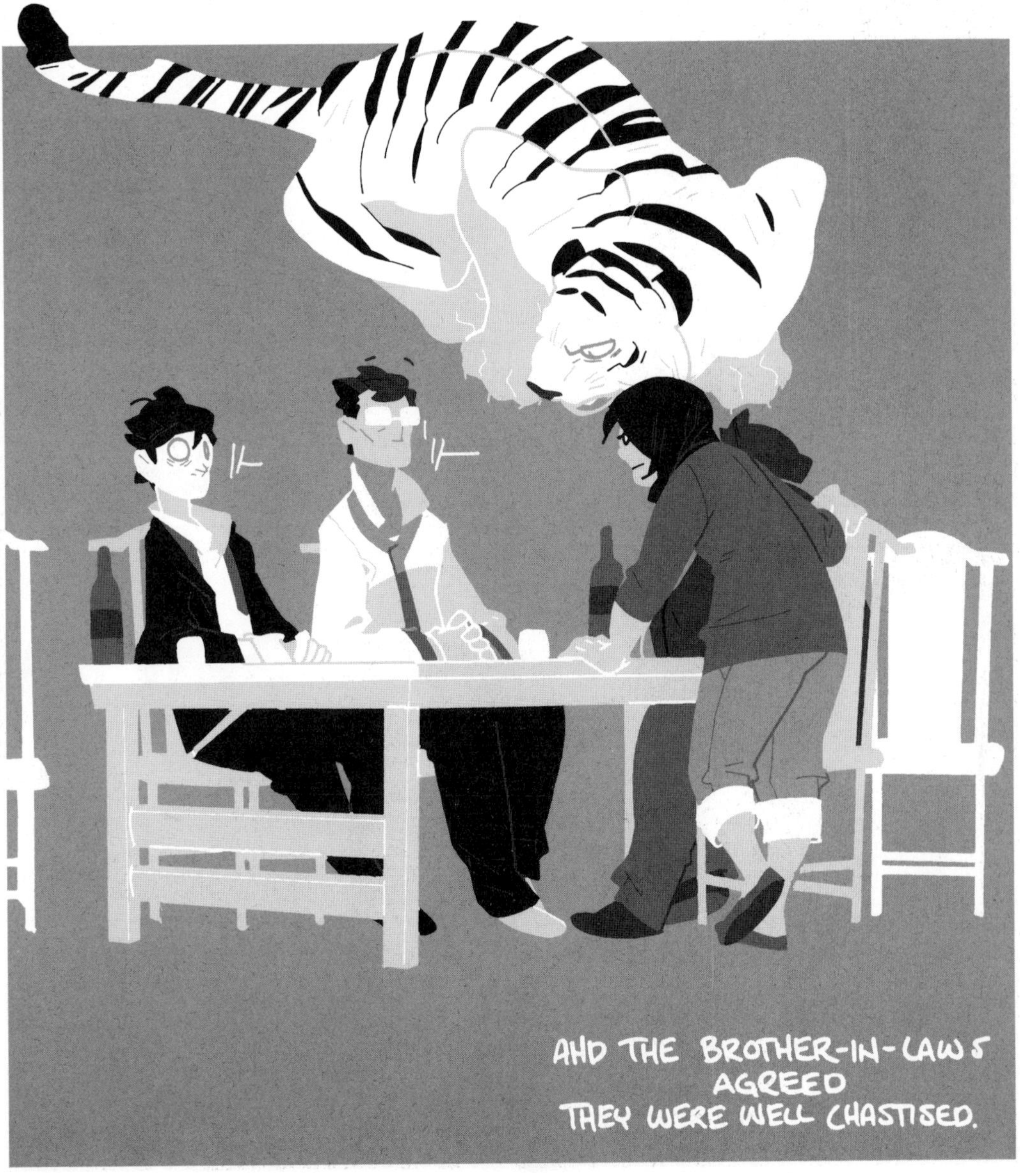
AND THE BROTHER-IN-LAWS AGREED
THEY WERE WELL CHASTISED.

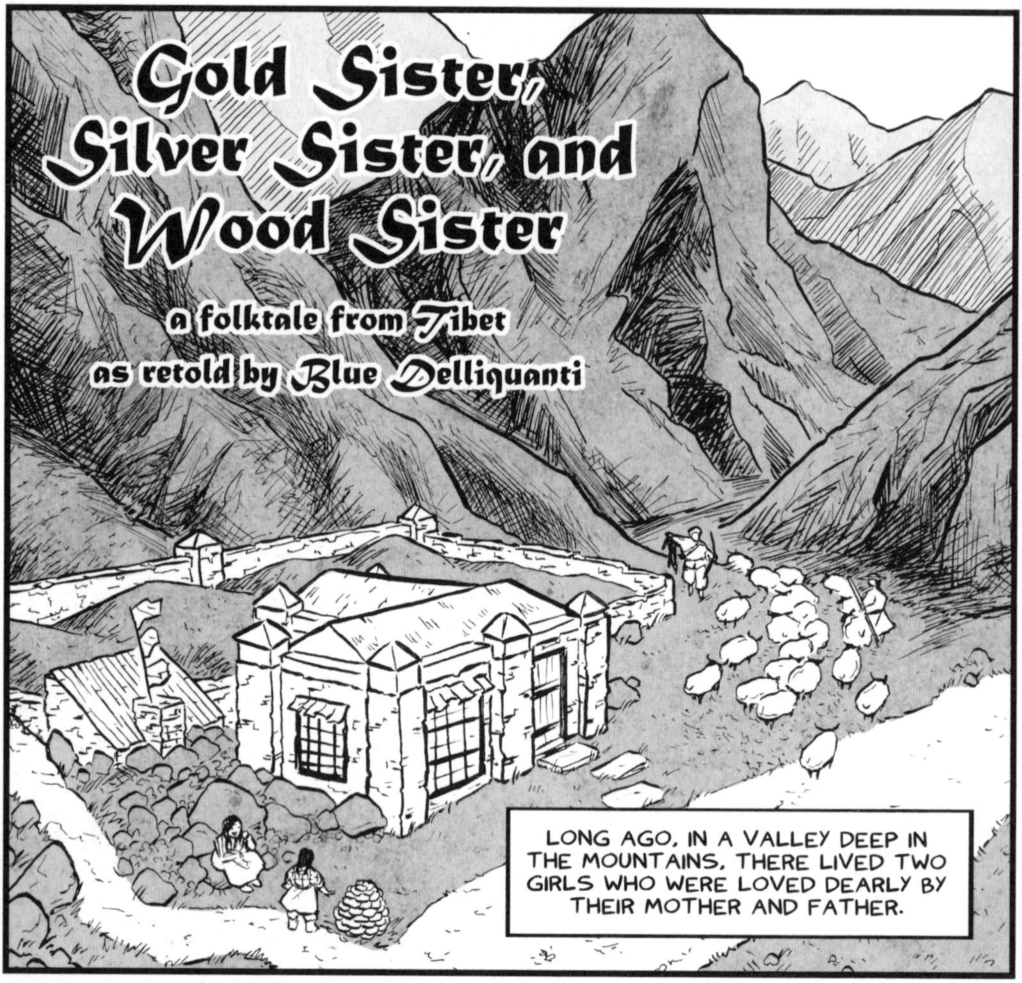
Gold Sister, Silver Sister, and Wood Sister
a folktale from Tibet
as retold by Blue Delliquanti
LONG AGO, IN A VALLEY DEEP IN THE MOUNTAINS, THERE LIVED TWO GIRLS WHO WERE LOVED DEARLY BY THEIR MOTHER AND FATHER.

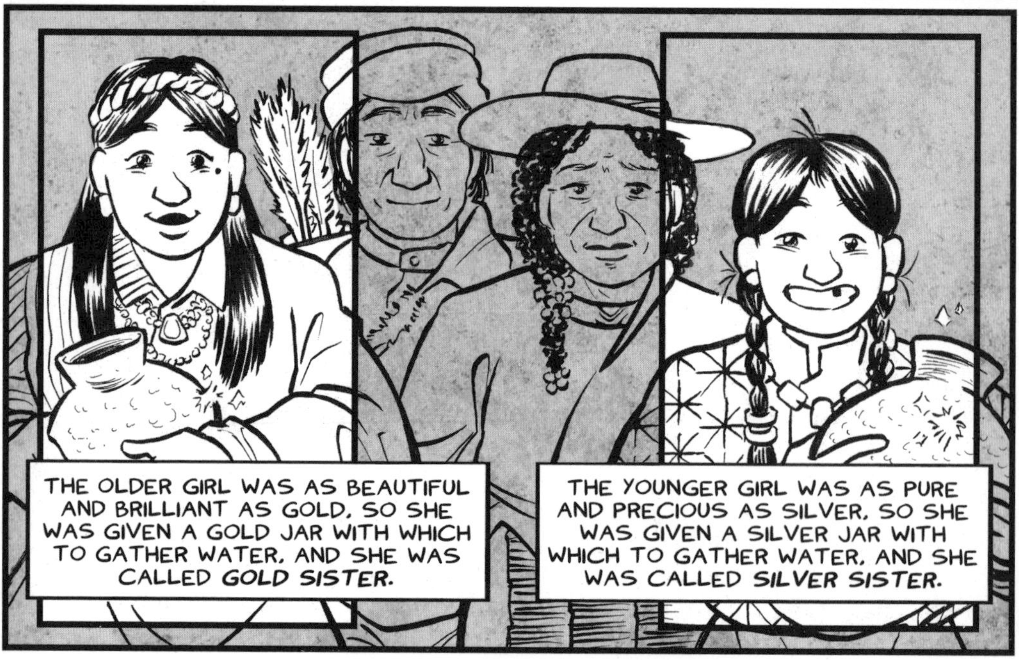
THE OLDER GIRL WAS AS BEAUTIFUL AND BRILLIANT AS GOLD, SO SHE WAS GIVEN A GOLD JAR WITH WHICH TO GATHER WATER, AND SHE WAS CALLED GOLD SISTER.
THE YOUNGER GIRL WAS AS PURE AND PRECIOUS AS SILVER, SO SHE WAS GIVEN A SILVER JAR WITH WHICH TO GATHER WATER, AND SHE WAS CALLED SILVER SISTER.

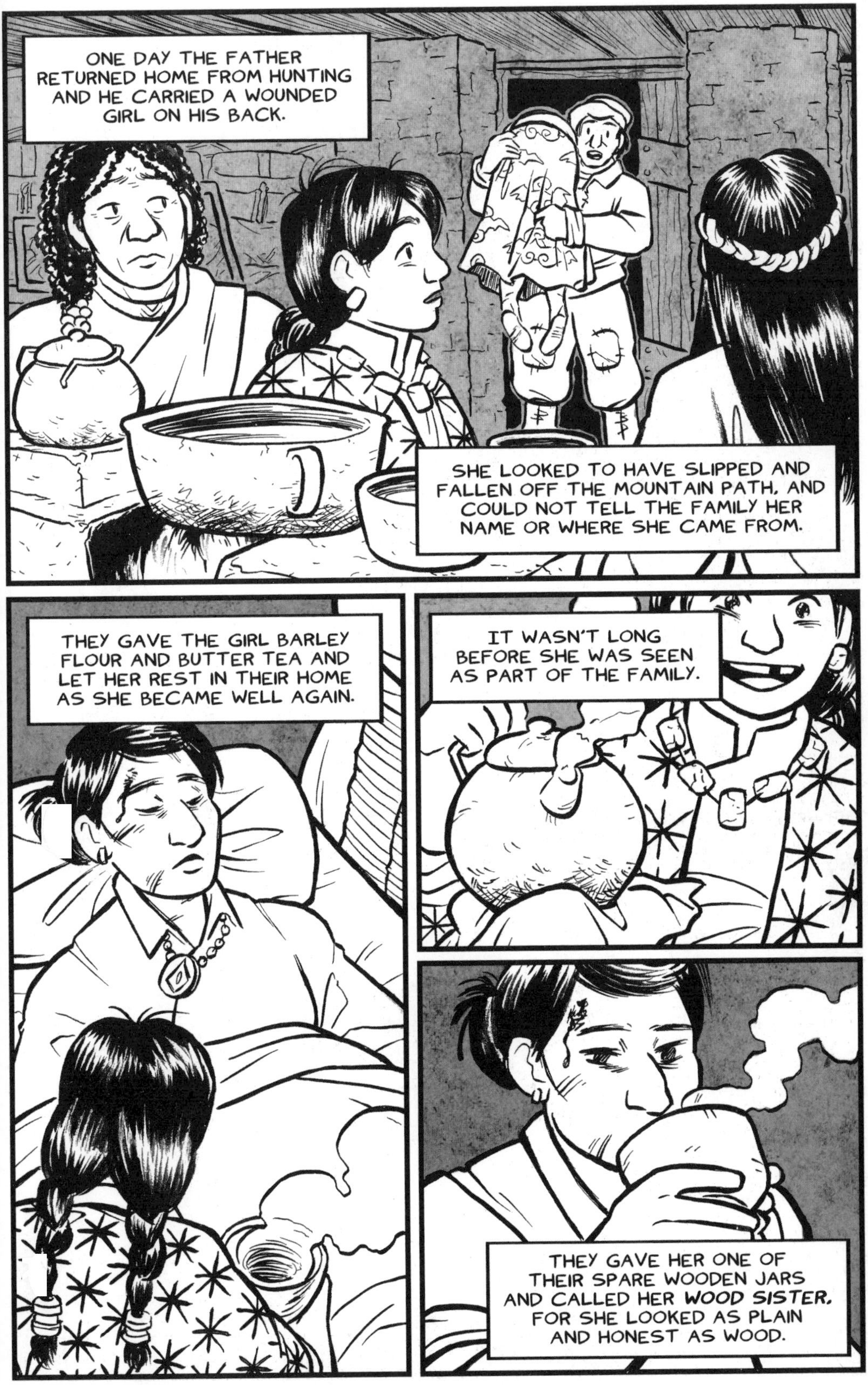
ONE DAY THE FATHER RETURNED HOME FROM HUNTING AND HE CARRIED A WOUNDED GIRL ON HIS BACK.
SHE LOOKED TO HAVE SLIPPED AND FALLEN OFF THE MOUNTAIN PATH, AND COULD NOT TELL THE FAMILY HER NAME OR WHERE SHE CAME FROM.
THEY GAVE THE GIRL BARLEY FLOUR AND BUTTER TEA AND LET HER REST IN THEIR HOME AS SHE BECAME WELL AGAIN.
IT WASN'T LONG BEFORE SHE WAS SEEN AS PART OF THE FAMILY.
THEY GAVE HER ONE OF THEIR SPARE WOODEN JARS AND CALLED HER WOOD SISTER, FOR SHE LOOKED AS PLAIN AND HONEST AS WOOD.

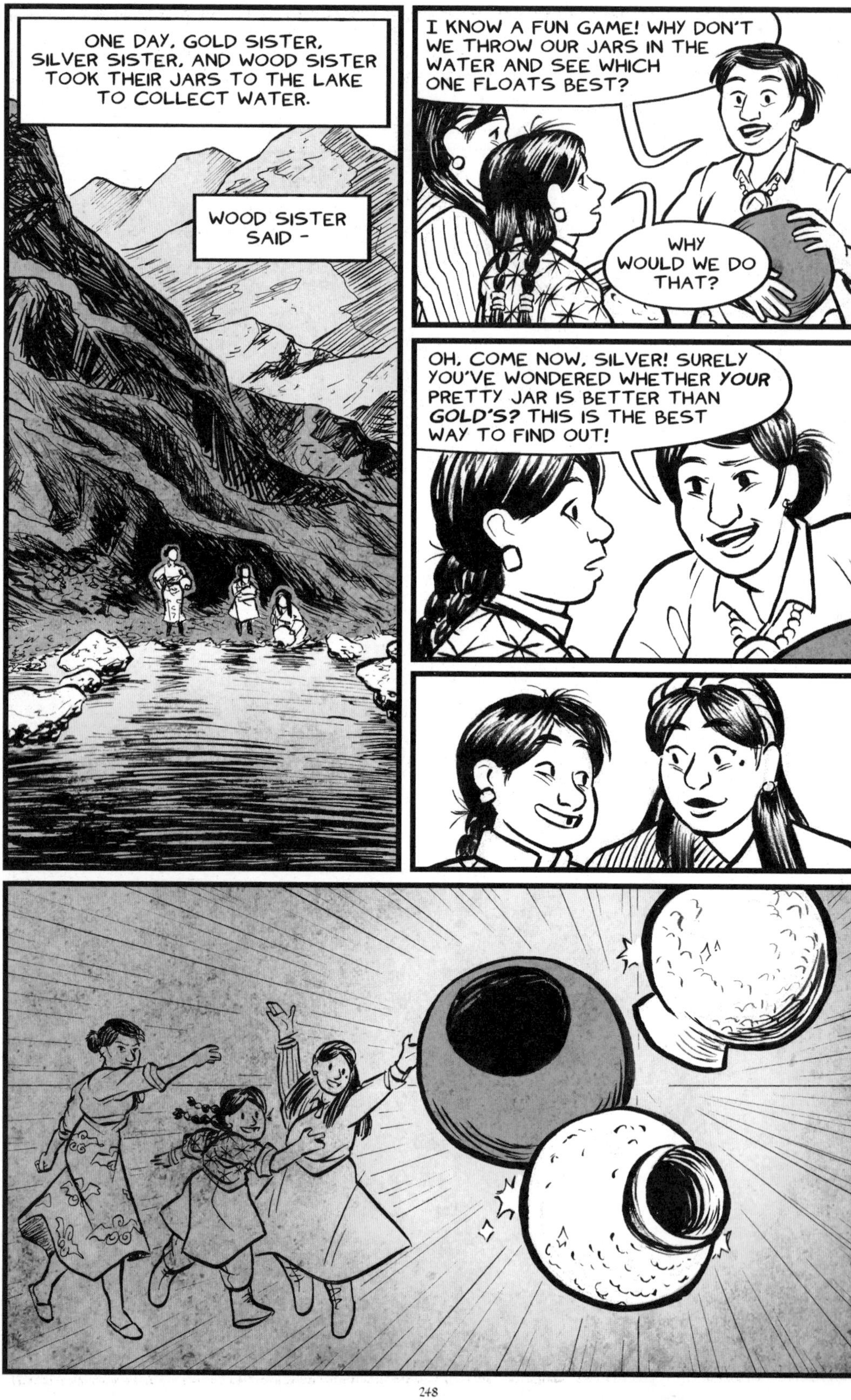
ONE DAY, GOLD SISTER, SILVER SISTER, AND WOOD SISTER TOOK THEIR JARS TO THE LAKE TO COLLECT WATER.
WOOD SISTER SAID -
I KNOW A FUN GAME! WHY DON'T WE THROW OUR JARS IN THE WATER AND SEE WHICH ONE FLOATS BEST?
WHY WOULD WE DO THAT?
OH, COME NOW, SILVER! SURELY YOU'VE WONDERED WHETHER *YOUR* PRETTY JAR IS BETTER THAN *GOLD'S?* THIS IS THE BEST WAY TO FIND OUT!

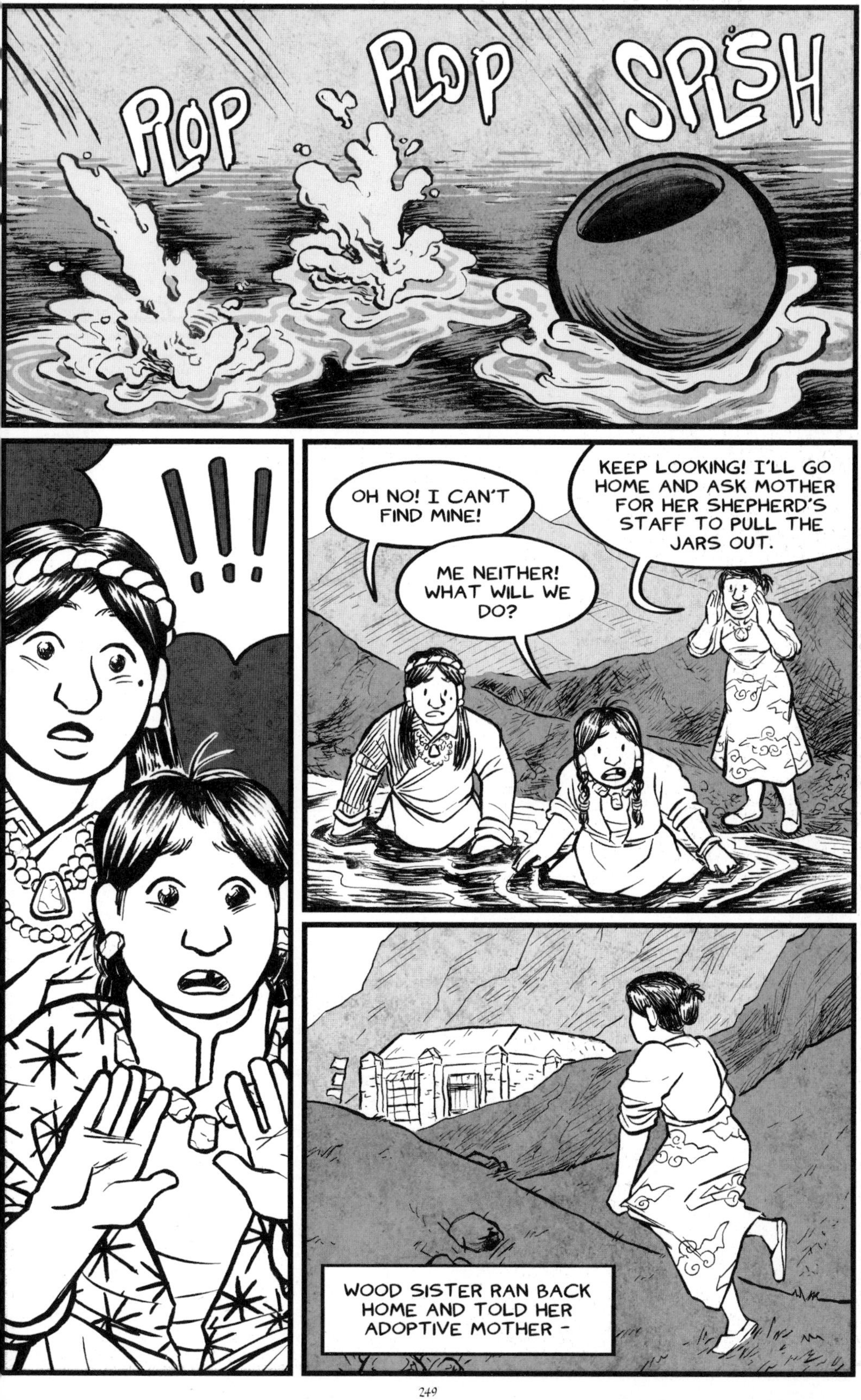
PLOP
PLOP
SPLSH
!!!
OH NO! I CAN'T FIND MINE!
ME NEITHER! WHAT WILL WE DO?
KEEP LOOKING! I'LL GO HOME AND ASK MOTHER FOR HER SHEPHERD'S STAFF TO PULL THE JARS OUT.
WOOD SISTER RAN BACK HOME AND TOLD HER ADOPTIVE MOTHER -

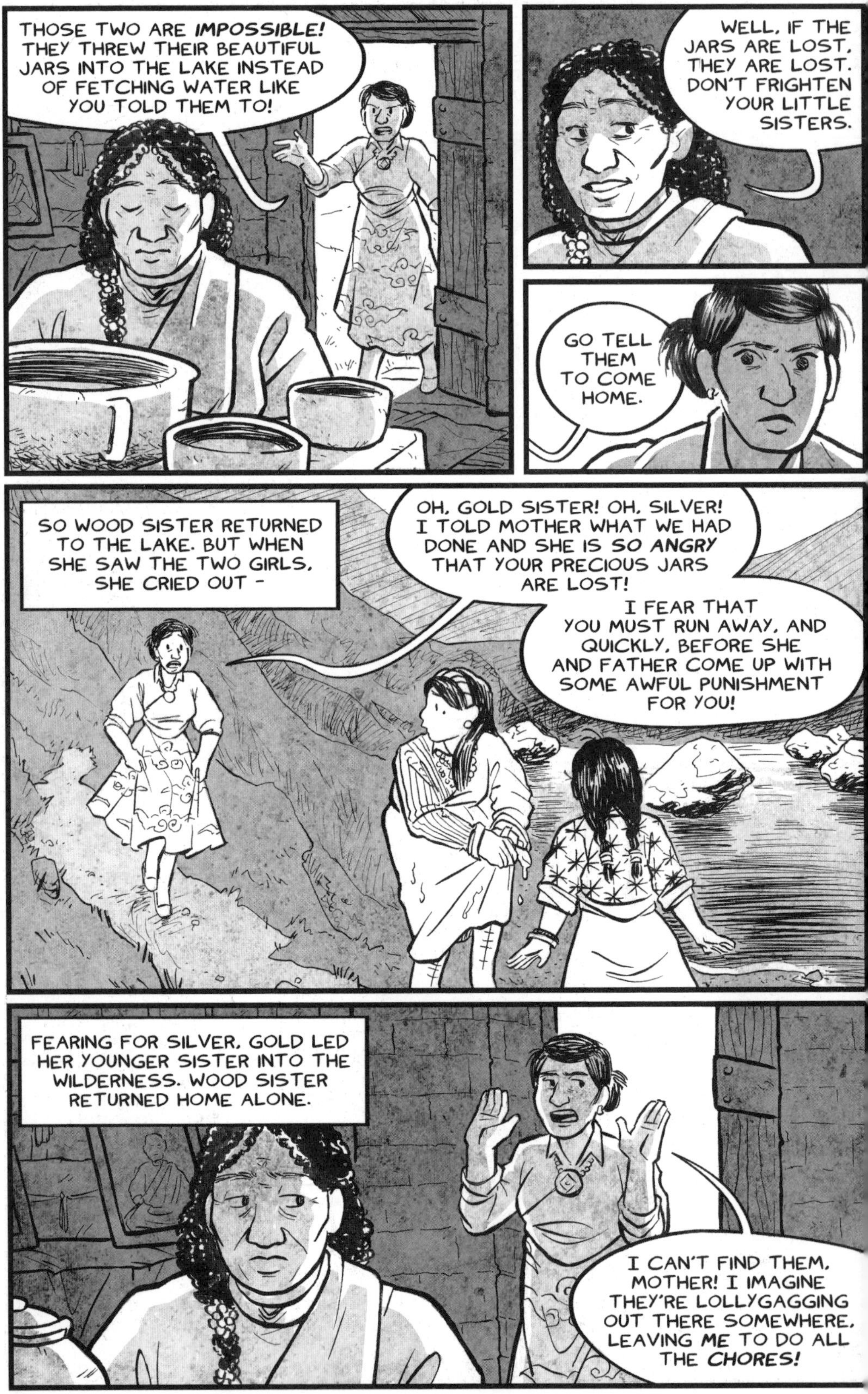
THOSE TWO ARE IMPOSSIBLE! THEY THREW THEIR BEAUTIFUL JARS INTO THE LAKE INSTEAD OF FETCHING WATER LIKE YOU TOLD THEM TO!
WELL, IF THE JARS ARE LOST, THEY ARE LOST. DON'T FRIGHTEN YOUR LITTLE SISTERS.
GO TELL THEM TO COME HOME.
SO WOOD SISTER RETURNED TO THE LAKE. BUT WHEN SHE SAW THE TWO GIRLS, SHE CRIED OUT –
OH, GOLD SISTER! OH, SILVER! I TOLD MOTHER WHAT WE HAD DONE AND SHE IS SO ANGRY THAT YOUR PRECIOUS JARS ARE LOST!
I FEAR THAT YOU MUST RUN AWAY, AND QUICKLY, BEFORE SHE AND FATHER COME UP WITH SOME AWFUL PUNISHMENT FOR YOU!
FEARING FOR SILVER, GOLD LED HER YOUNGER SISTER INTO THE WILDERNESS. WOOD SISTER RETURNED HOME ALONE.
I CAN'T FIND THEM, MOTHER! I IMAGINE THEY'RE LOLLYGAGGING OUT THERE SOMEWHERE, LEAVING ME TO DO ALL THE CHORES!

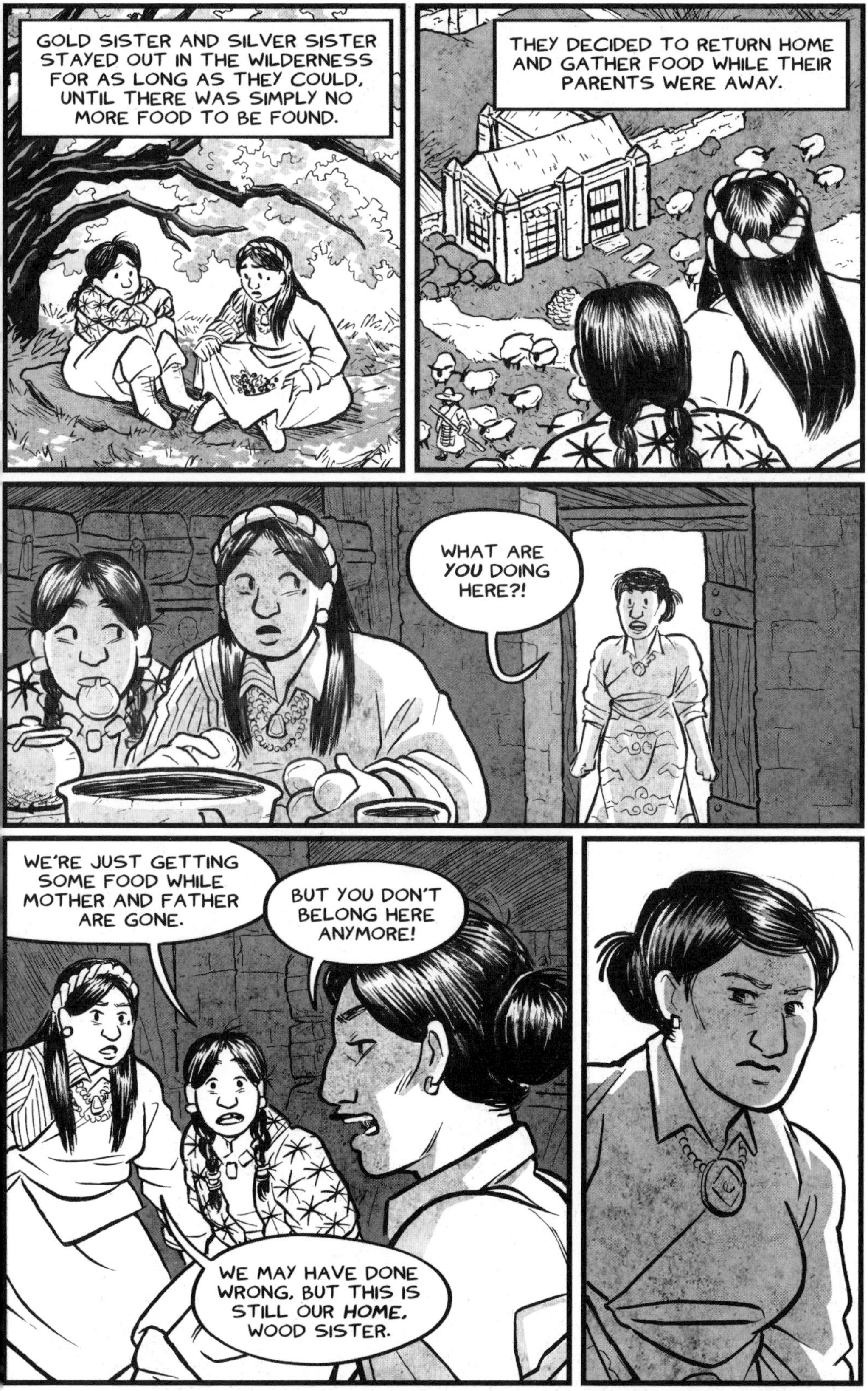
GOLD SISTER AND SILVER SISTER STAYED OUT IN THE WILDERNESS FOR AS LONG AS THEY COULD, UNTIL THERE WAS SIMPLY NO MORE FOOD TO BE FOUND.
THEY DECIDED TO RETURN HOME AND GATHER FOOD WHILE THEIR PARENTS WERE AWAY.
WHAT ARE *YOU* DOING HERE?!
WE'RE JUST GETTING SOME FOOD WHILE MOTHER AND FATHER ARE GONE.
BUT YOU DON'T BELONG HERE ANYMORE!
WE MAY HAVE DONE WRONG, BUT THIS IS STILL OUR *HOME*, WOOD SISTER.

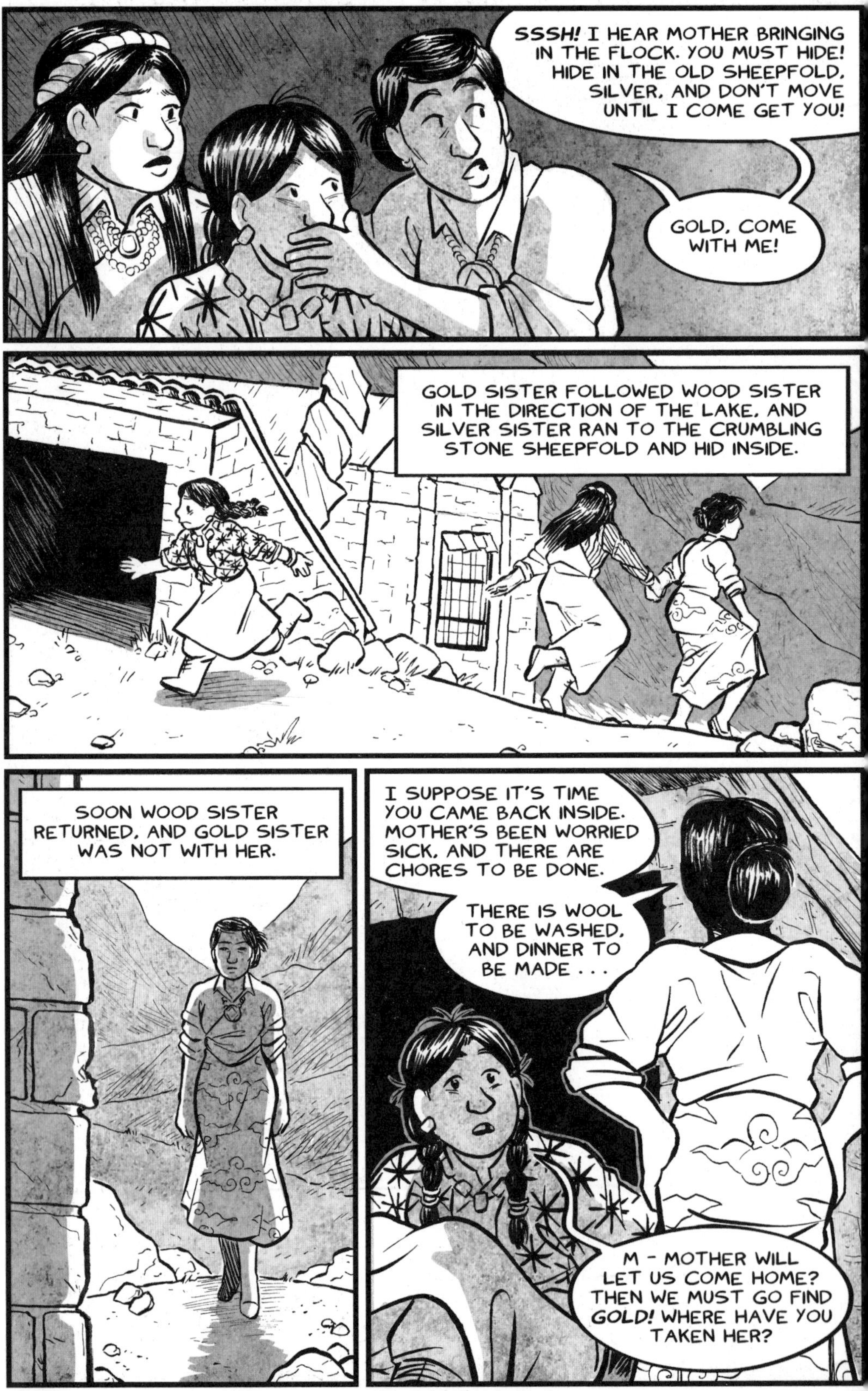
SSSH! I HEAR MOTHER BRINGING IN THE FLOCK. YOU MUST HIDE! HIDE IN THE OLD SHEEPFOLD, SILVER, AND DON'T MOVE UNTIL I COME GET YOU!
GOLD, COME WITH ME!
GOLD SISTER FOLLOWED WOOD SISTER IN THE DIRECTION OF THE LAKE, AND SILVER SISTER RAN TO THE CRUMBLING STONE SHEEPFOLD AND HID INSIDE.
SOON WOOD SISTER RETURNED, AND GOLD SISTER WAS NOT WITH HER.
I SUPPOSE IT'S TIME YOU CAME BACK INSIDE. MOTHER'S BEEN WORRIED SICK, AND THERE ARE CHORES TO BE DONE.
THERE IS WOOL TO BE WASHED, AND DINNER TO BE MADE . . .
M - MOTHER WILL LET US COME HOME? THEN WE MUST GO FIND GOLD! WHERE HAVE YOU TAKEN HER?

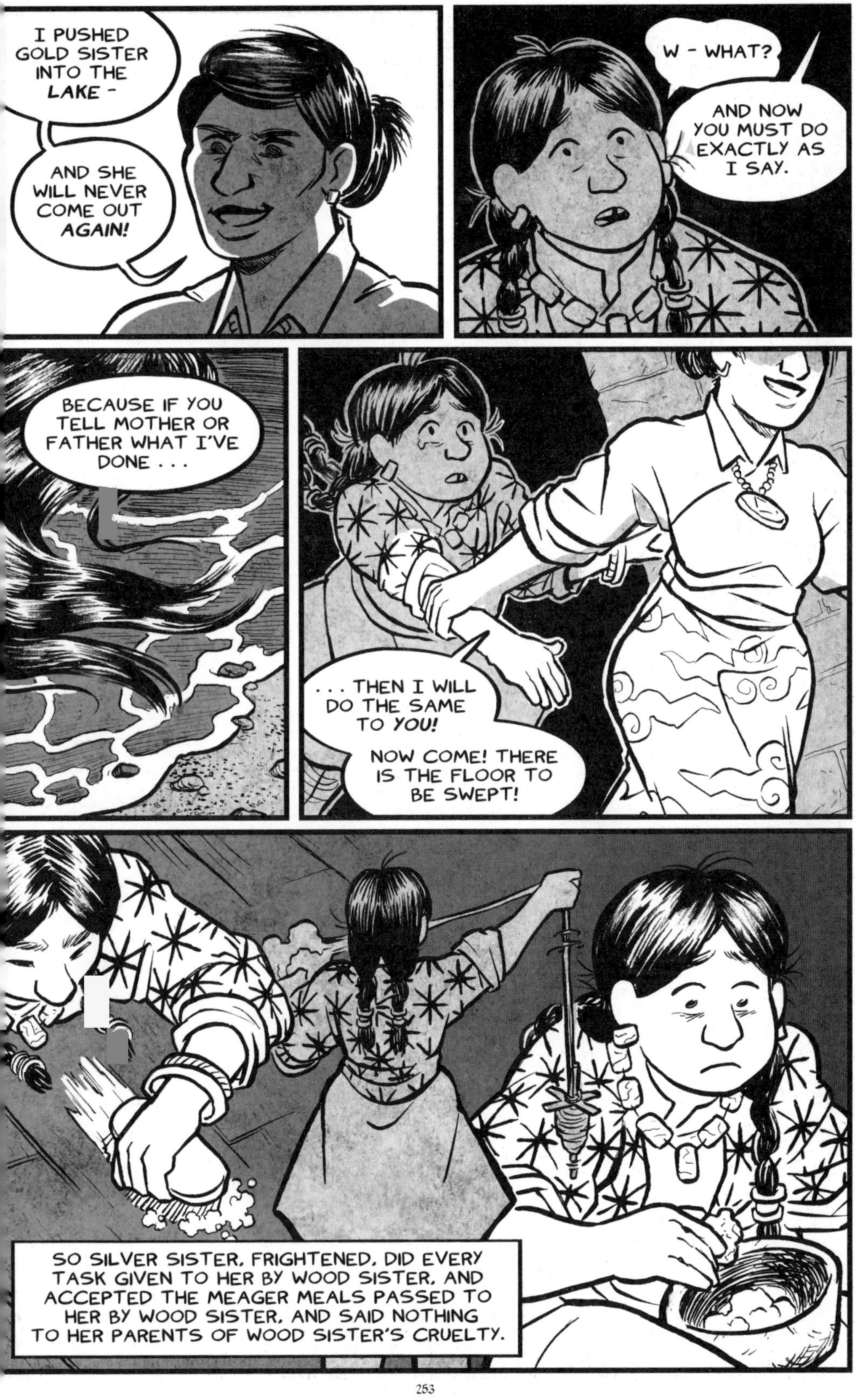
I PUSHED GOLD SISTER INTO THE LAKE -
AND SHE WILL NEVER COME OUT AGAIN!
W - WHAT?
AND NOW YOU MUST DO EXACTLY AS I SAY.
BECAUSE IF YOU TELL MOTHER OR FATHER WHAT I'VE DONE . . .
. . . THEN I WILL DO THE SAME TO YOU!
NOW COME! THERE IS THE FLOOR TO BE SWEPT!
SO SILVER SISTER, FRIGHTENED, DID EVERY TASK GIVEN TO HER BY WOOD SISTER, AND ACCEPTED THE MEAGER MEALS PASSED TO HER BY WOOD SISTER, AND SAID NOTHING TO HER PARENTS OF WOOD SISTER'S CRUELTY.

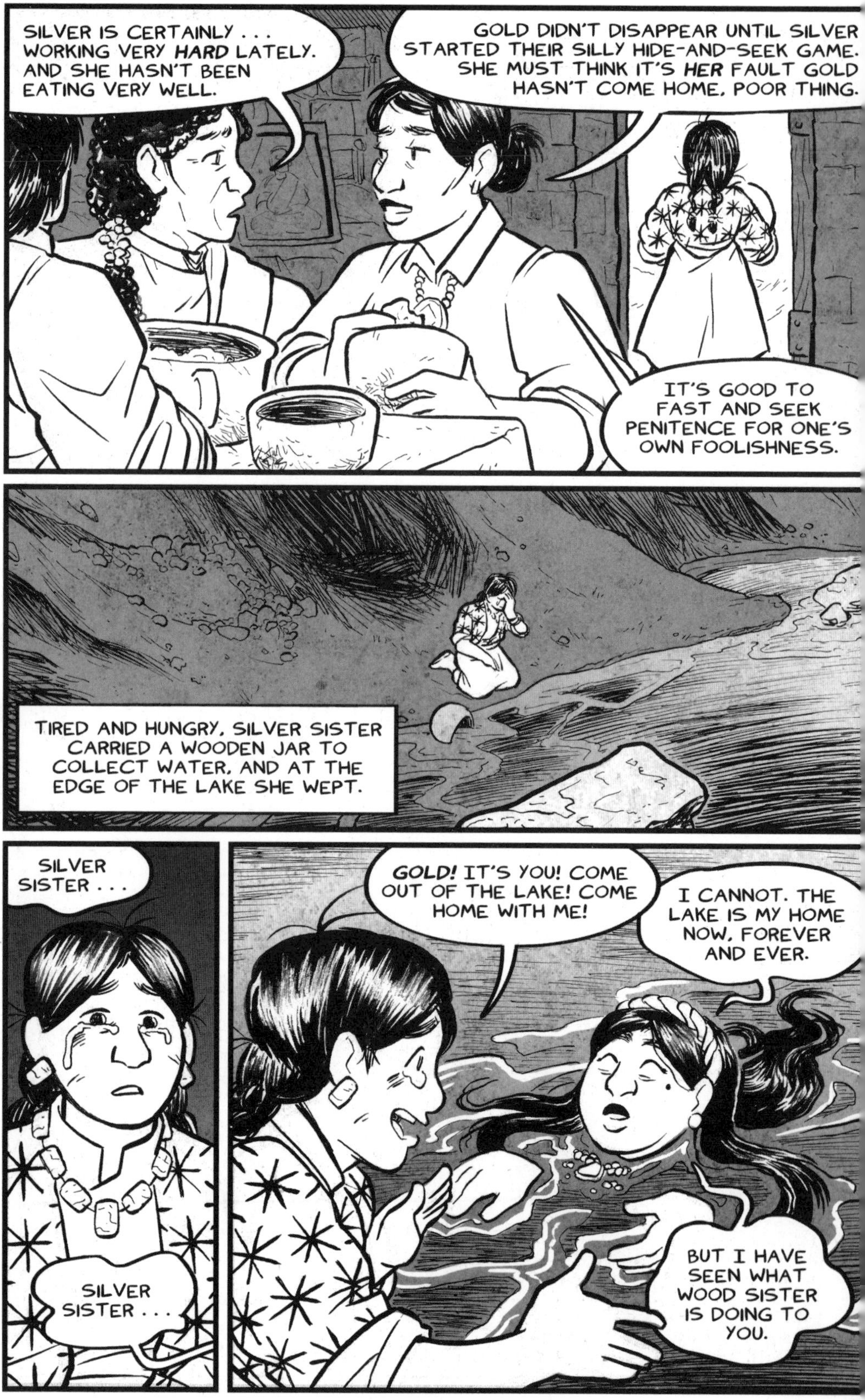
SILVER IS CERTAINLY . . . WORKING VERY HARD LATELY. AND SHE HASN'T BEEN EATING VERY WELL.
GOLD DIDN'T DISAPPEAR UNTIL SILVER STARTED THEIR SILLY HIDE-AND-SEEK GAME. SHE MUST THINK IT'S HER FAULT GOLD HASN'T COME HOME, POOR THING.
IT'S GOOD TO FAST AND SEEK PENITENCE FOR ONE'S OWN FOOLISHNESS.
TIRED AND HUNGRY, SILVER SISTER CARRIED A WOODEN JAR TO COLLECT WATER, AND AT THE EDGE OF THE LAKE SHE WEPT.
SILVER SISTER . . .
SILVER SISTER . . .
GOLD! IT'S YOU! COME OUT OF THE LAKE! COME HOME WITH ME!
I CANNOT. THE LAKE IS MY HOME NOW, FOREVER AND EVER.
BUT I HAVE SEEN WHAT WOOD SISTER IS DOING TO YOU.

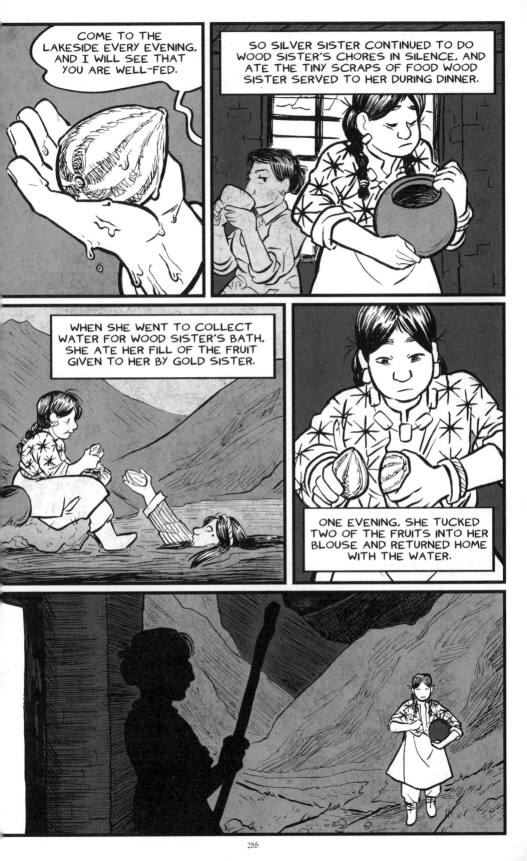

COME TO THE LAKESIDE EVERY EVENING, AND I WILL SEE THAT YOU ARE WELL-FED.

SO SILVER SISTER CONTINUED TO DO WOOD SISTER'S CHORES IN SILENCE, AND ATE THE TINY SCRAPS OF FOOD WOOD SISTER SERVED TO HER DURING DINNER.

WHEN SHE WENT TO COLLECT WATER FOR WOOD SISTER'S BATH, SHE ATE HER FILL OF THE FRUIT GIVEN TO HER BY GOLD SISTER.

ONE EVENING, SHE TUCKED TWO OF THE FRUITS INTO HER BLOUSE AND RETURNED HOME WITH THE WATER.

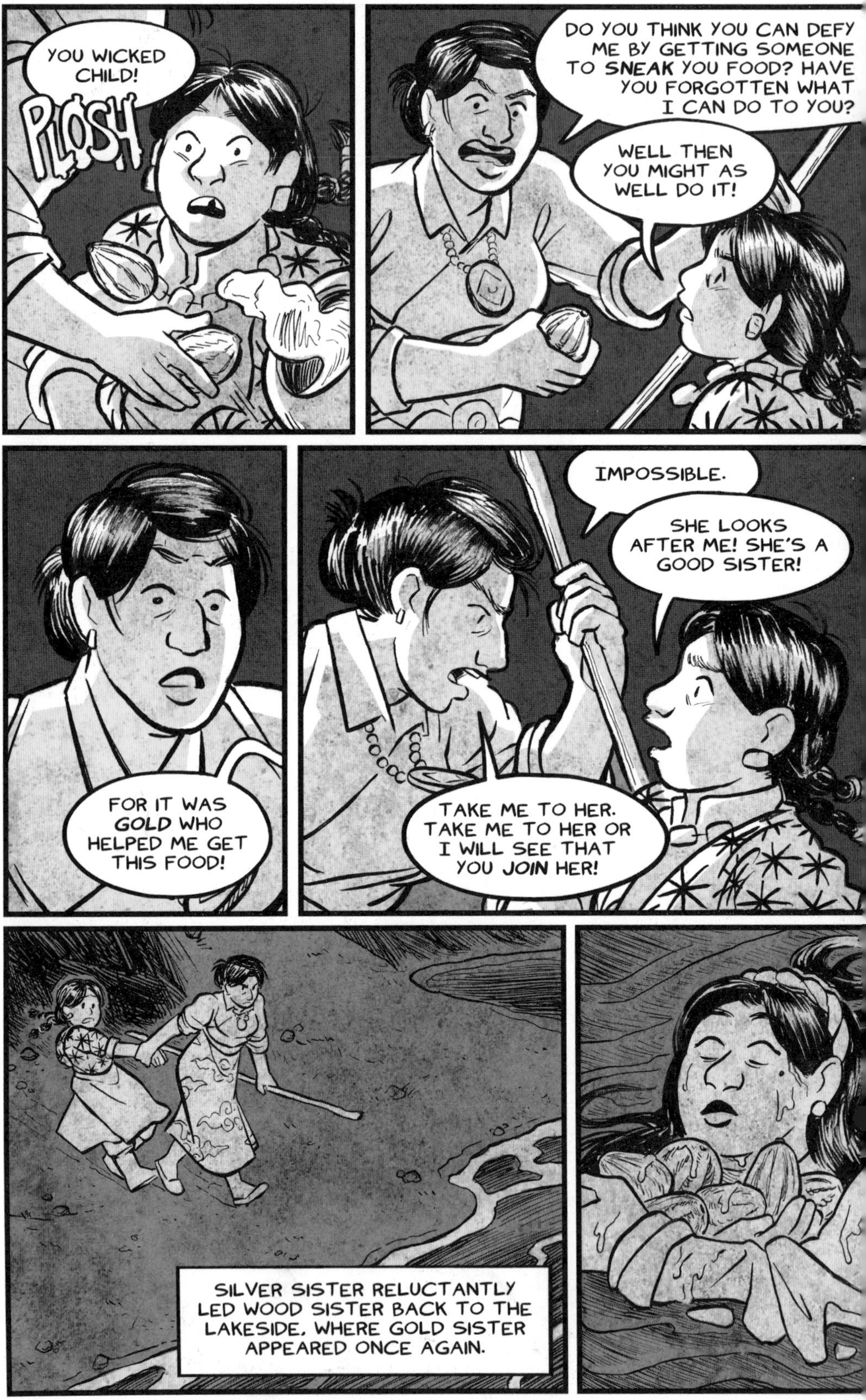
YOU WICKED CHILD!
PLOSH
DO YOU THINK YOU CAN DEFY ME BY GETTING SOMEONE TO SNEAK YOU FOOD? HAVE YOU FORGOTTEN WHAT I CAN DO TO YOU?
WELL THEN YOU MIGHT AS WELL DO IT!
FOR IT WAS GOLD WHO HELPED ME GET THIS FOOD!
IMPOSSIBLE.
SHE LOOKS AFTER ME! SHE'S A GOOD SISTER!
TAKE ME TO HER. TAKE ME TO HER OR I WILL SEE THAT YOU JOIN HER!
SILVER SISTER RELUCTANTLY LED WOOD SISTER BACK TO THE LAKESIDE, WHERE GOLD SISTER APPEARED ONCE AGAIN.

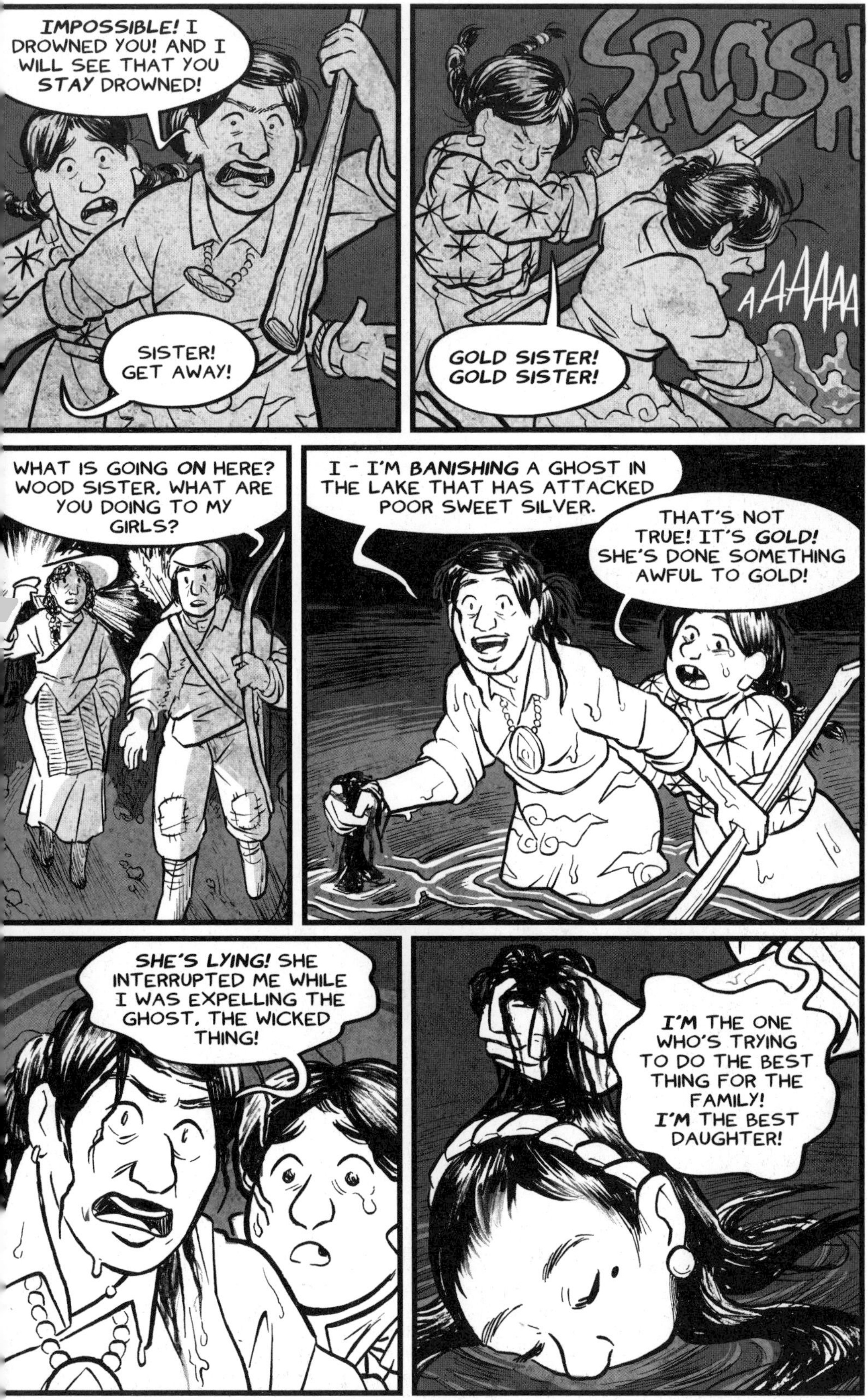
IMPOSSIBLE! I DROWNED YOU! AND I WILL SEE THAT YOU STAY DROWNED!
SISTER! GET AWAY!
SPLOSH
AAAAAA
GOLD SISTER! GOLD SISTER!
WHAT IS GOING ON HERE? WOOD SISTER, WHAT ARE YOU DOING TO MY GIRLS?
I - I'M BANISHING A GHOST IN THE LAKE THAT HAS ATTACKED POOR SWEET SILVER.
THAT'S NOT TRUE! IT'S GOLD! SHE'S DONE SOMETHING AWFUL TO GOLD!
SHE'S LYING! SHE INTERRUPTED ME WHILE I WAS EXPELLING THE GHOST, THE WICKED THING!
I'M THE ONE WHO'S TRYING TO DO THE BEST THING FOR THE FAMILY! I'M THE BEST DAUGHTER!

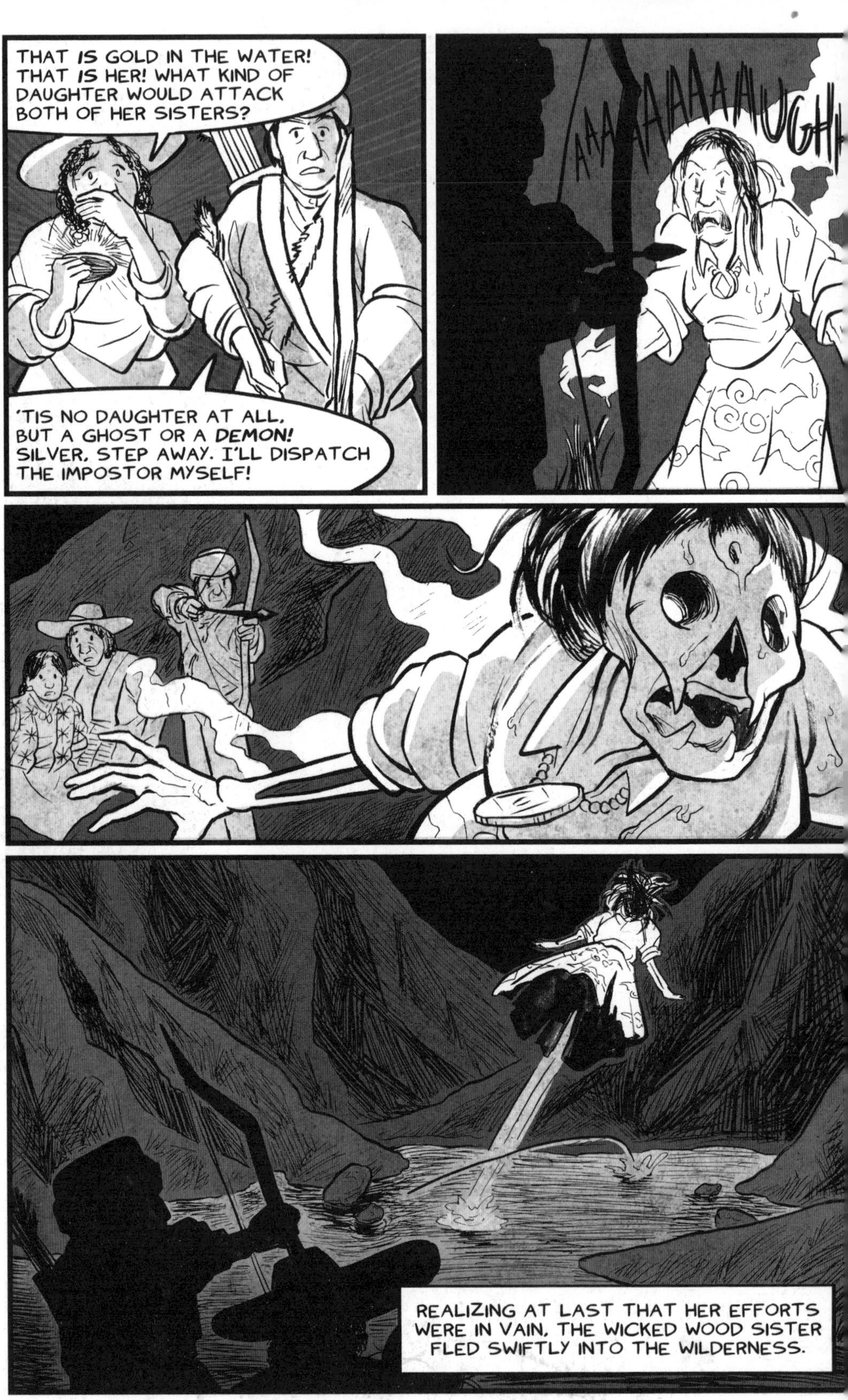
THAT *IS* GOLD IN THE WATER! THAT *IS* HER! WHAT KIND OF DAUGHTER WOULD ATTACK BOTH OF HER SISTERS?
'TIS NO DAUGHTER AT ALL, BUT A GHOST OR A **DEMON!** SILVER, STEP AWAY. I'LL DISPATCH THE IMPOSTOR MYSELF!
AAAAAAAAAAAUGH!
REALIZING AT LAST THAT HER EFFORTS WERE IN VAIN, THE WICKED WOOD SISTER FLED SWIFTLY INTO THE WILDERNESS.

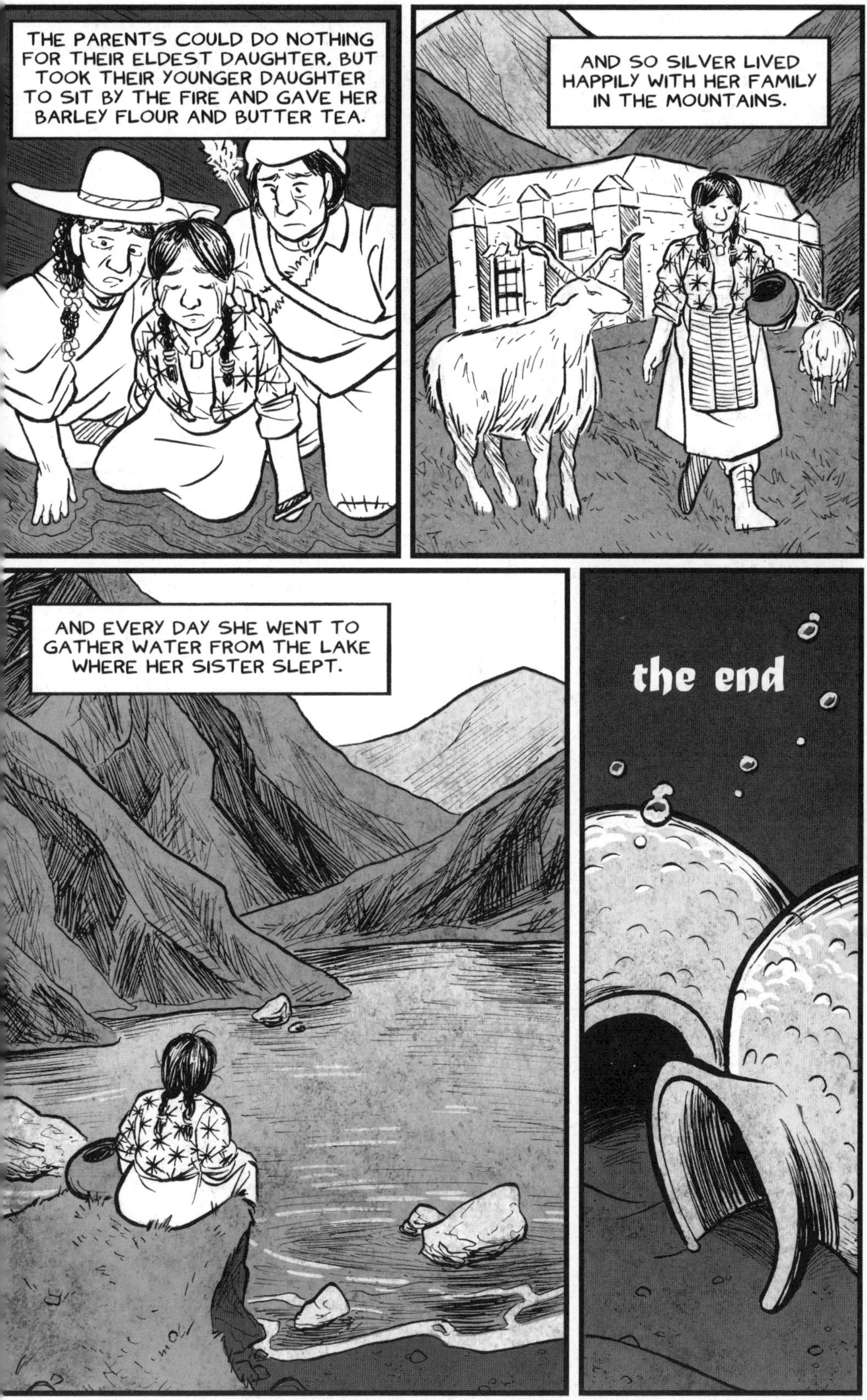
THE PARENTS COULD DO NOTHING FOR THEIR ELDEST DAUGHTER, BUT TOOK THEIR YOUNGER DAUGHTER TO SIT BY THE FIRE AND GAVE HER BARLEY FLOUR AND BUTTER TEA.
AND SO SILVER LIVED HAPPILY WITH HER FAMILY IN THE MOUNTAINS.
AND EVERY DAY SHE WENT TO GATHER WATER FROM THE LAKE WHERE HER SISTER SLEPT.
the end

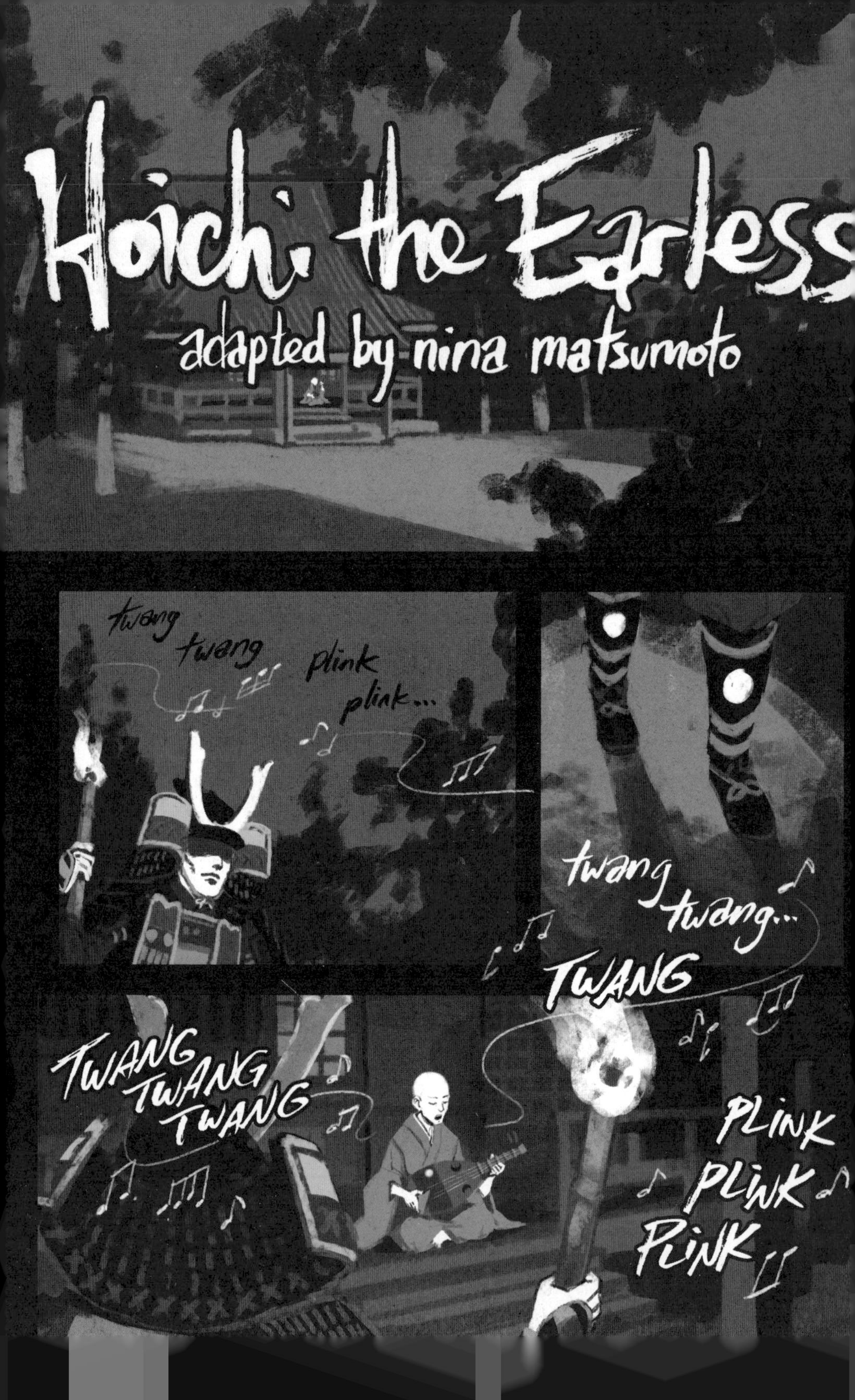

Hoichi the Earless
adapted by nina matsumoto
twang
twang
plink
plink...
twang
twang...
TWANG
TWANG
TWANG
TWANG
PLINK
PLINK
PLINK

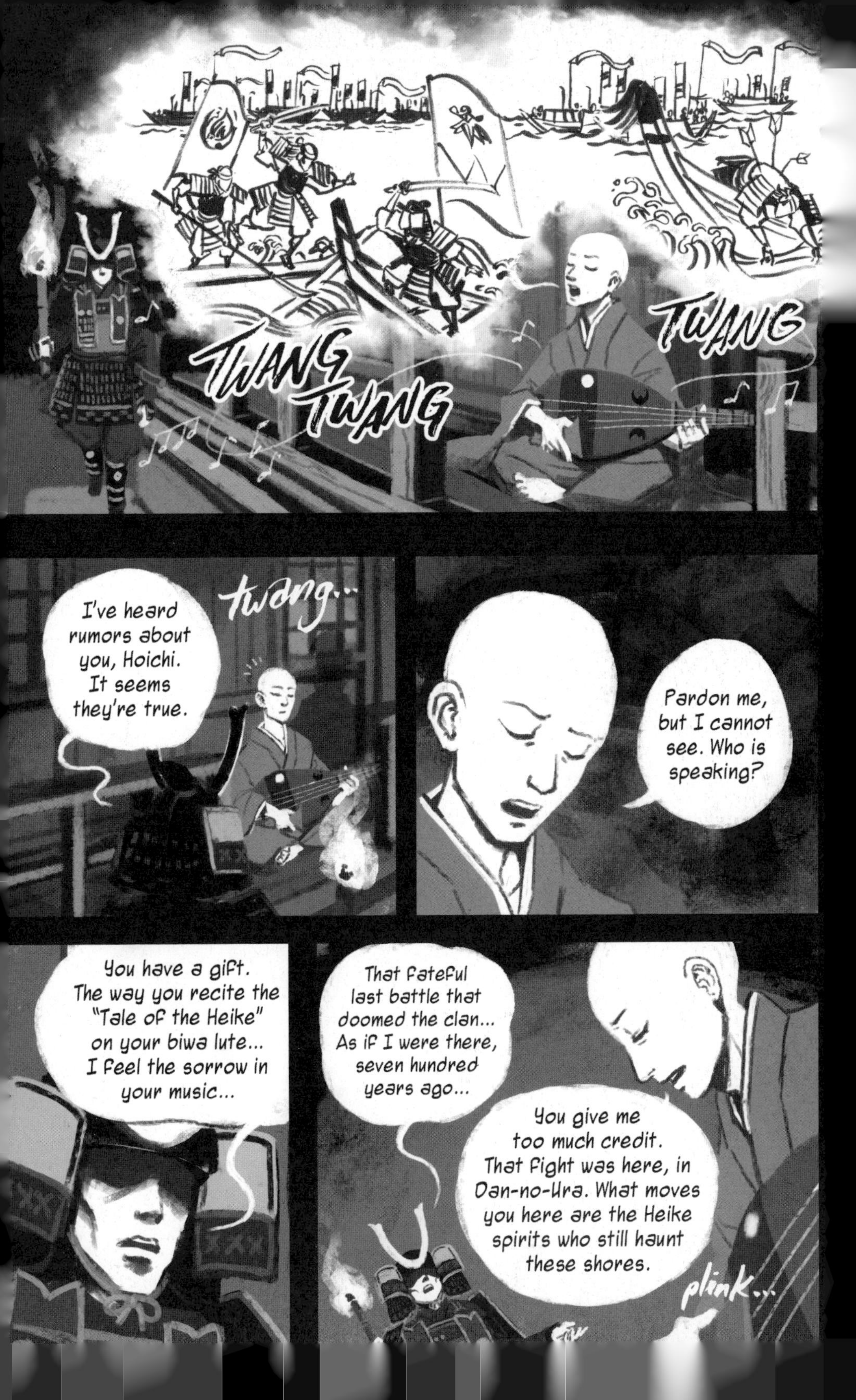
TWANG
TWANG
TWANG
twang...
I've heard rumors about you, Hoichi. It seems they're true.
Pardon me, but I cannot see. Who is speaking?
You have a gift. The way you recite the "Tale of the Heike" on your biwa lute... I feel the sorrow in your music...
That fateful last battle that doomed the clan... As if I were there, seven hundred years ago...
You give me too much credit. That fight was here, in Dan-no-Ura. What moves you here are the Heike spirits who still haunt these shores.
plink...

The war...it fascinates my lord. He travels with his attendants to view the battleground.
He requests your presence... He would hear the great Hoichi's performance.
...I cannot refuse such an honorable request.
Indeed.
crunch...
crunch...
crunch...

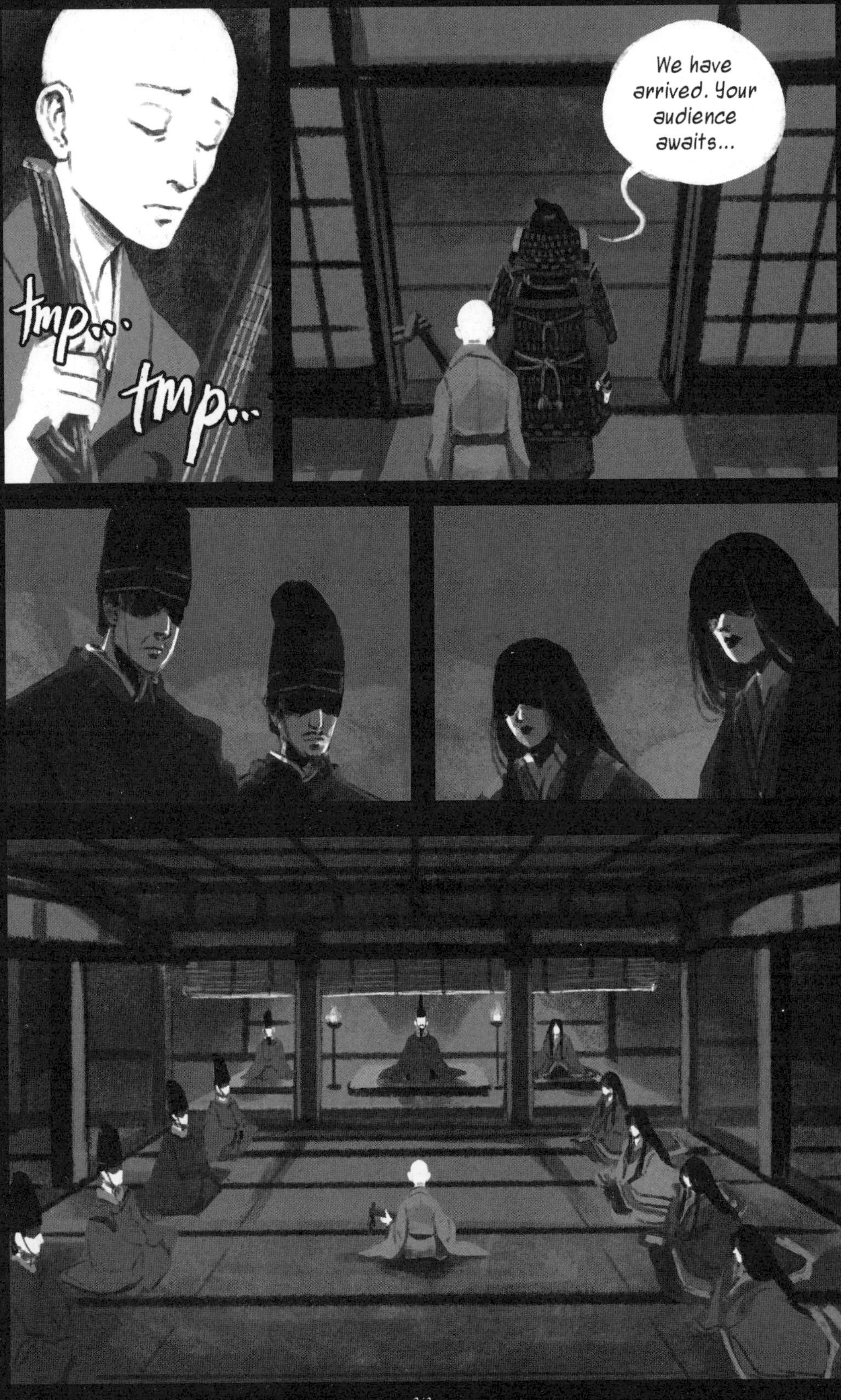
tmp...
tmp...
We have arrived. Your audience awaits...

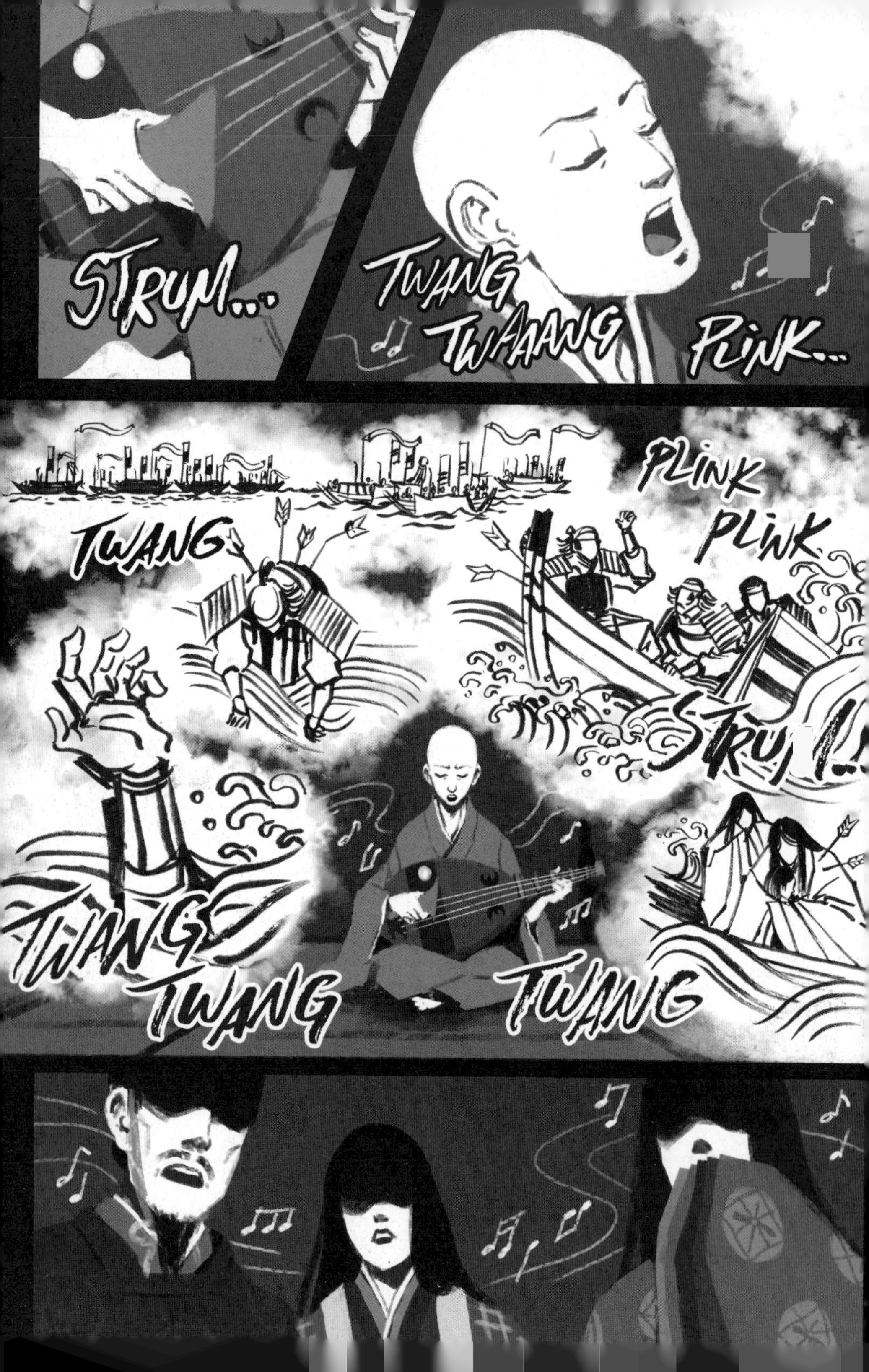
STRUM...
TWANG
TWAAANG
PLINK...
TWANG
PLINK
PLINK
STRU
TWANG
TWANG
TWANG

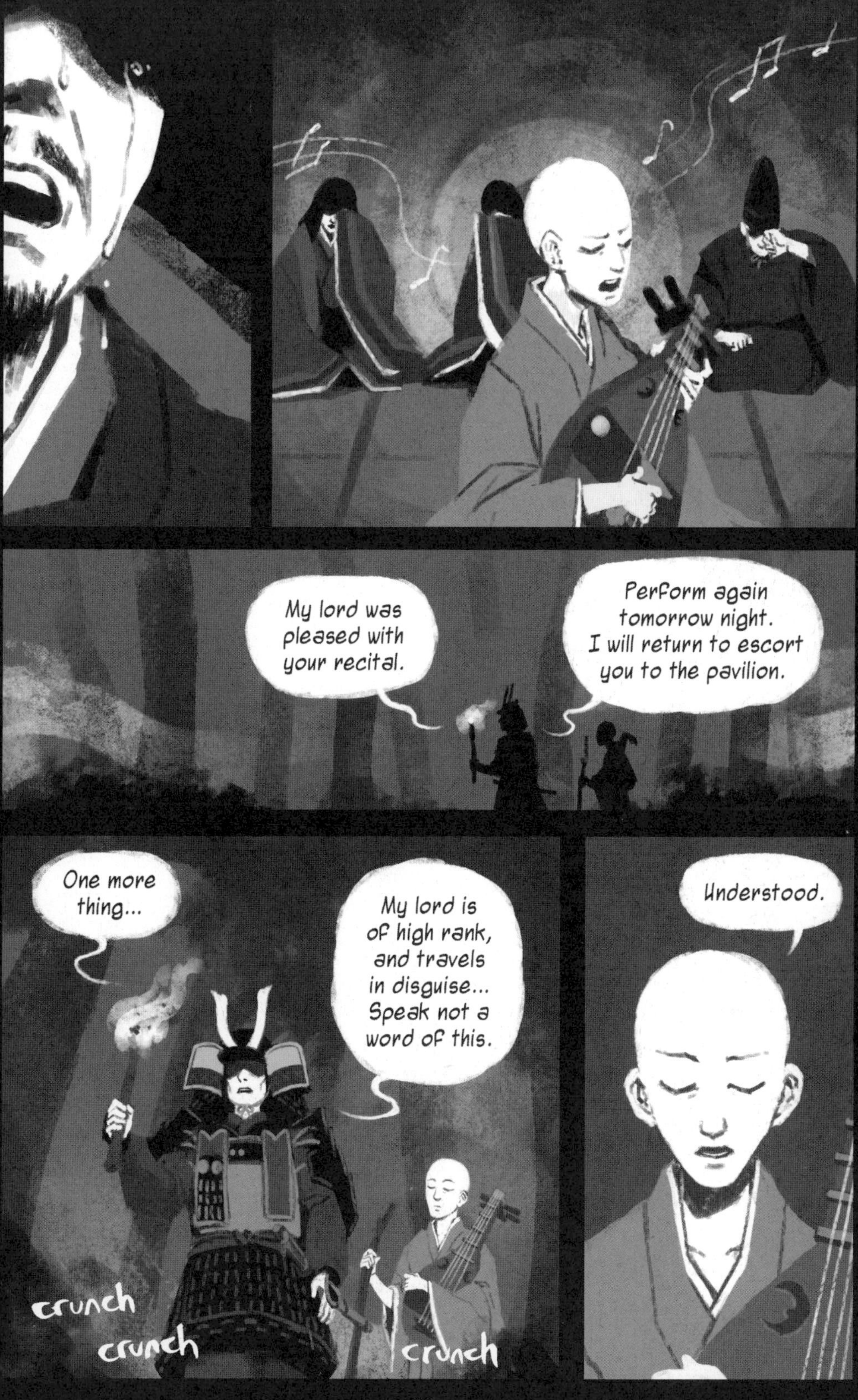
My lord was pleased with your recital.
Perform again tomorrow night. I will return to escort you to the pavilion.
One more thing...
My lord is of high rank, and travels in disguise... Speak not a word of this.
crunch
crunch
crunch
Understood.

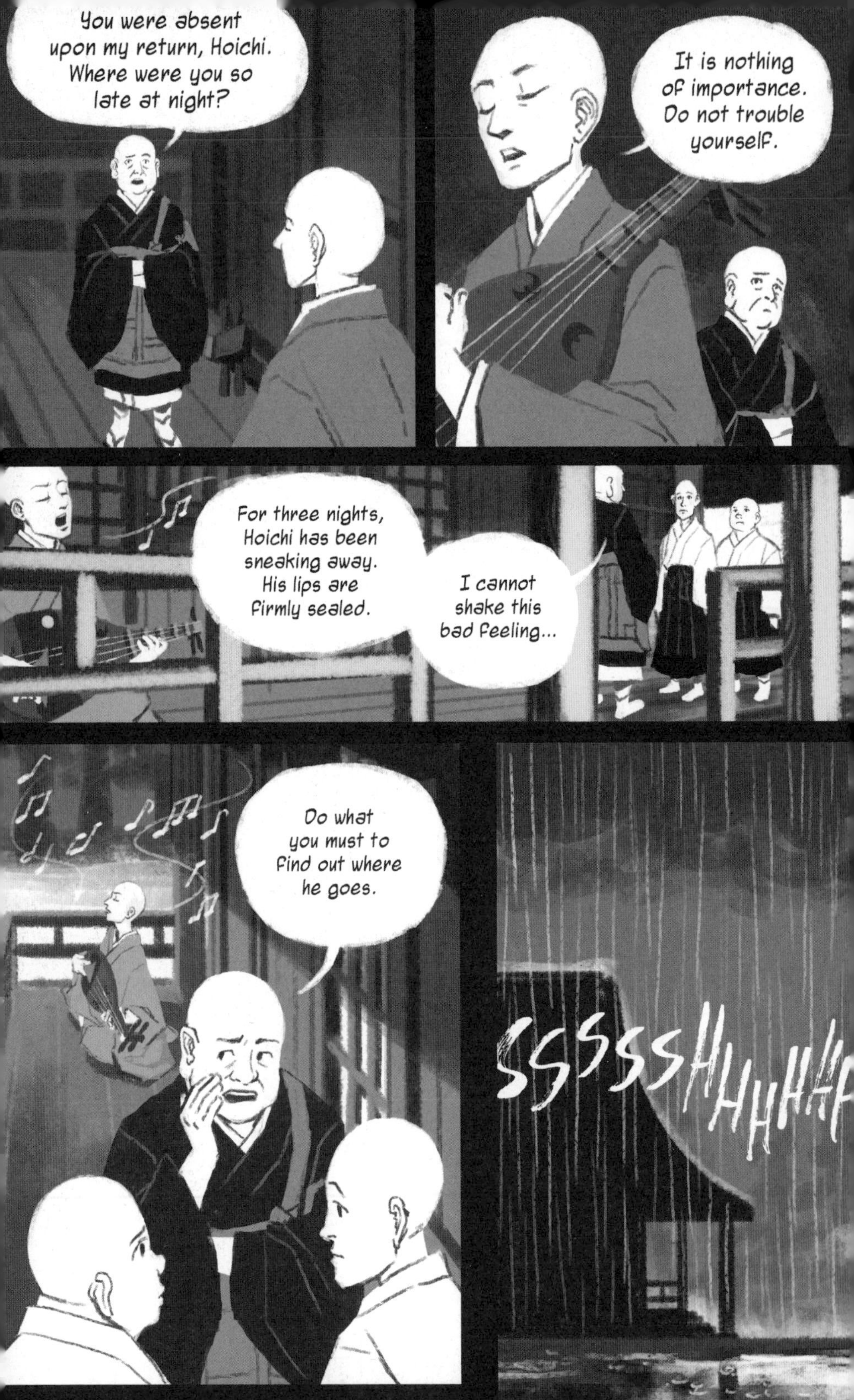
You were absent upon my return, Hoichi. Where were you so late at night?
It is nothing of importance. Do not trouble yourself.
For three nights, Hoichi has been sneaking away. His lips are firmly sealed.
I cannot shake this bad feeling...
Do what you must to find out where he goes.
SSSSSHHHHHH

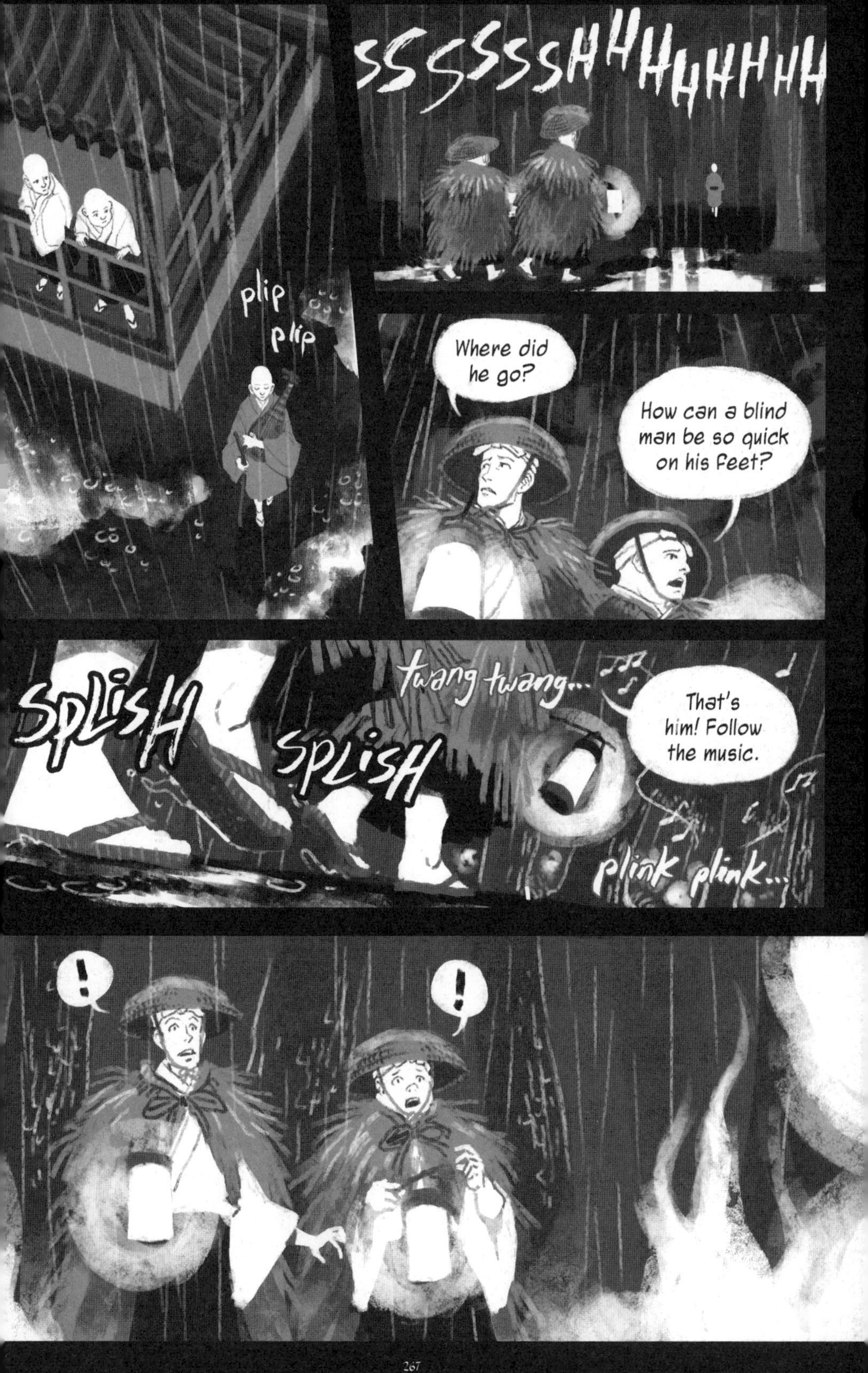
plip
plip
SSSSSSSHHHHHHHHH
Where did he go?
How can a blind man be so quick on his feet?
SPLISH
SPLISH
twang twang...
That's him! Follow the music.
plink plink...
!
!

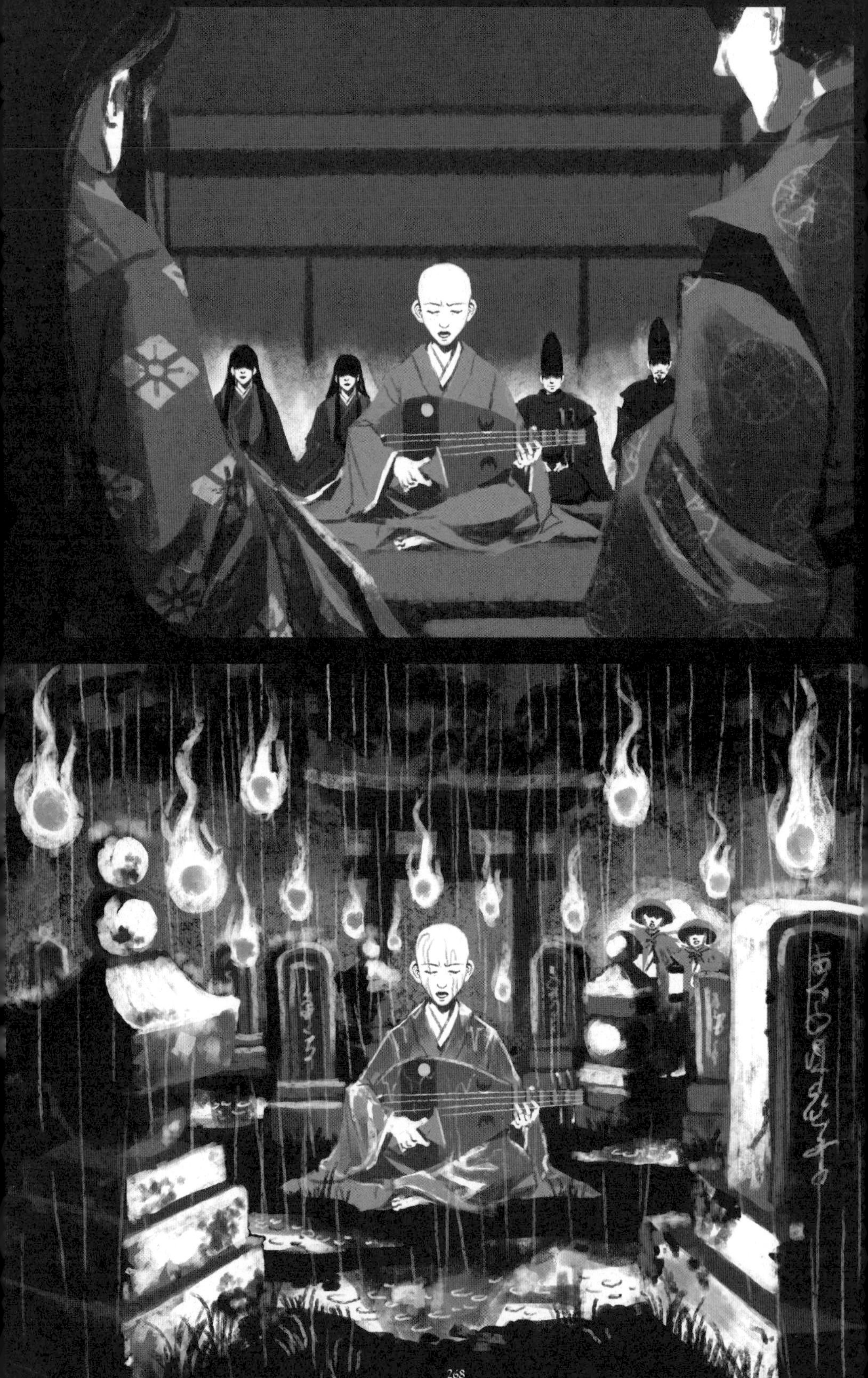

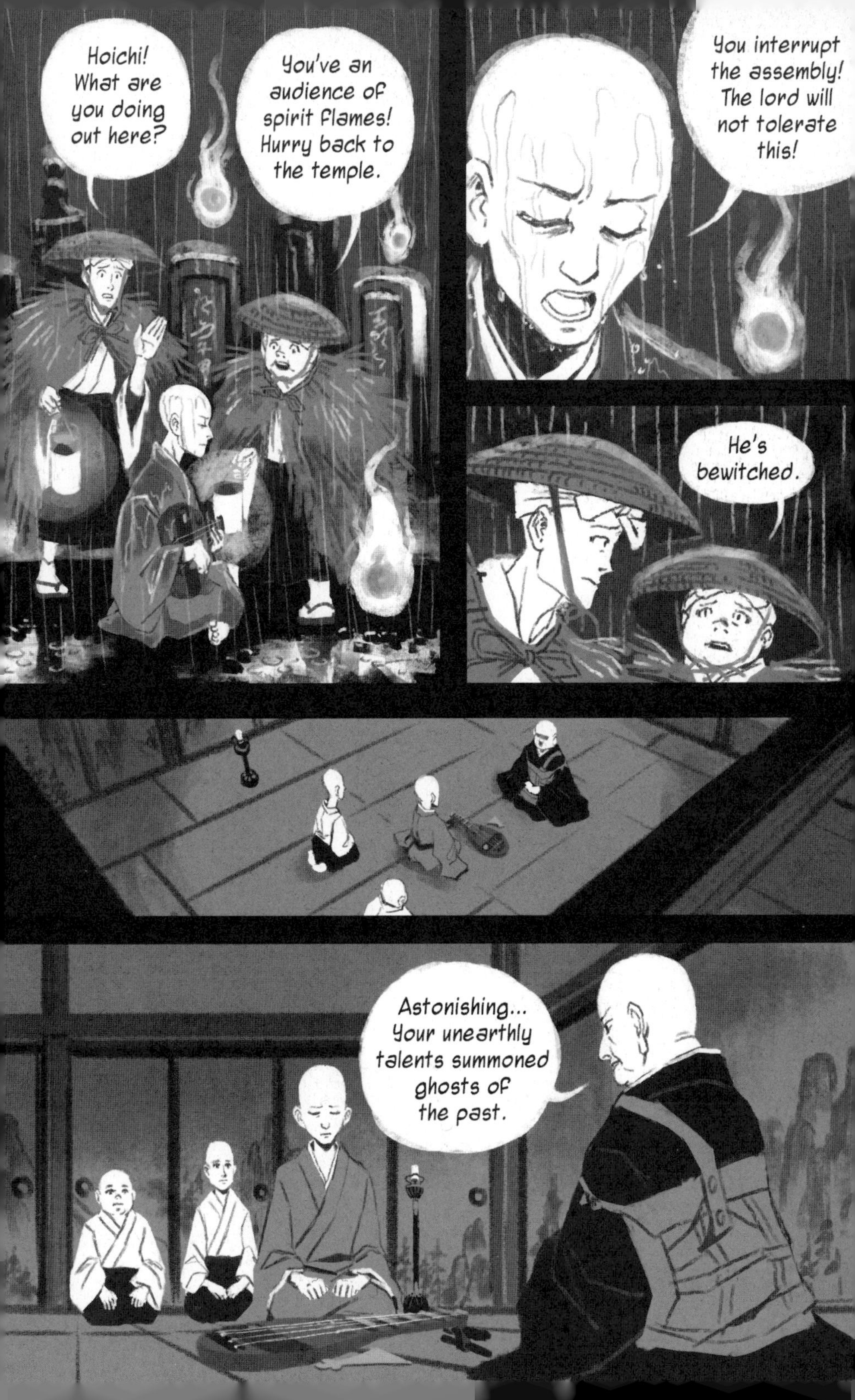
Hoichi! What are you doing out here?
You've an audience of spirit flames! Hurry back to the temple.
You interrupt the assembly! The lord will not tolerate this!
He's bewitched.
Astonishing... Your unearthly talents summoned ghosts of the past.

Had we not found you, you would have been whisked away to the cemetery every night until they consumed your body and soul.
I will do what I can to provide protection...
This sutra will conceal you from their eyes.

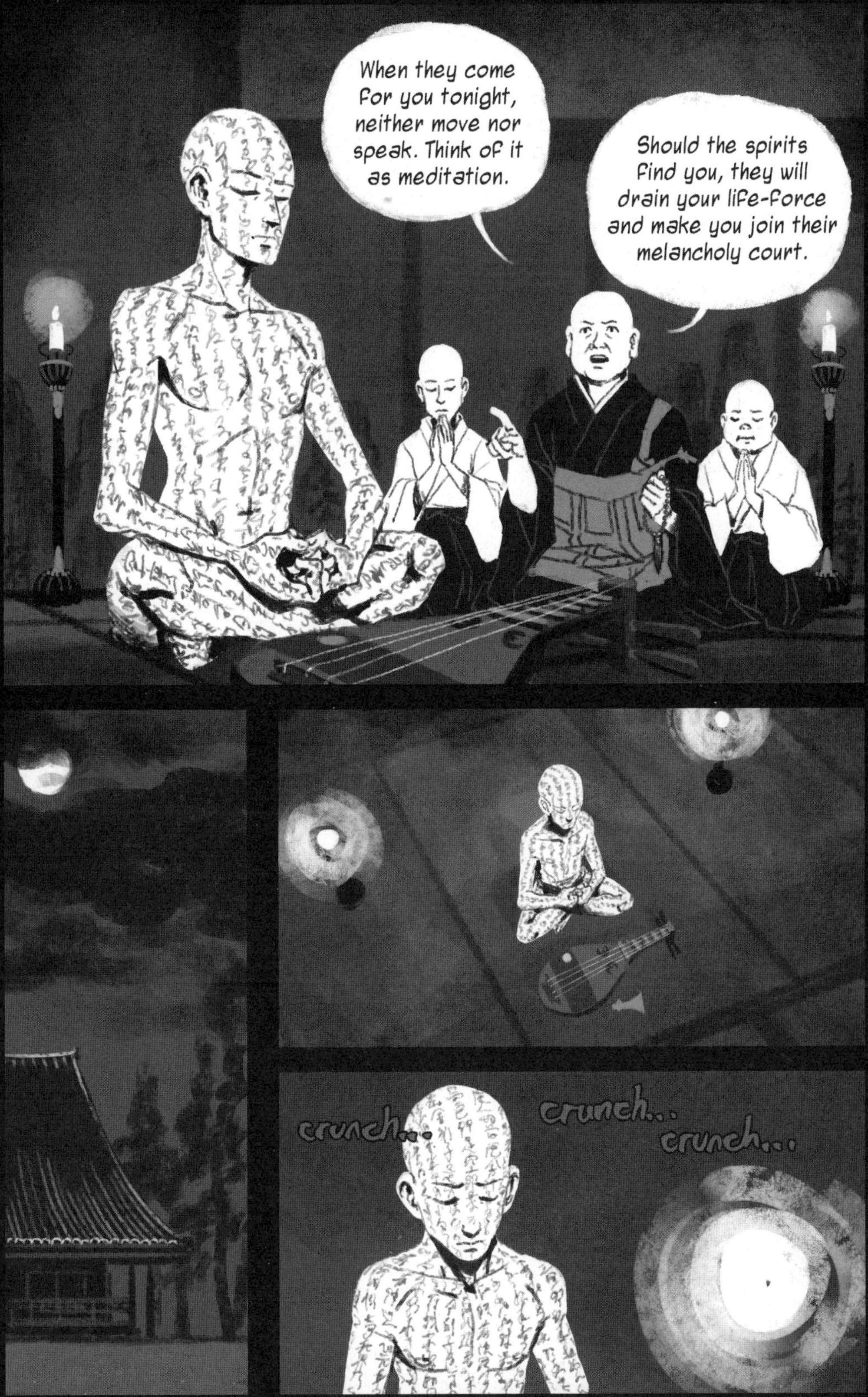
When they come for you tonight, neither move nor speak. Think of it as meditation.
Should the spirits find you, they will drain your life-force and make you join their melancholy court.
crunch...
crunch...
crunch...

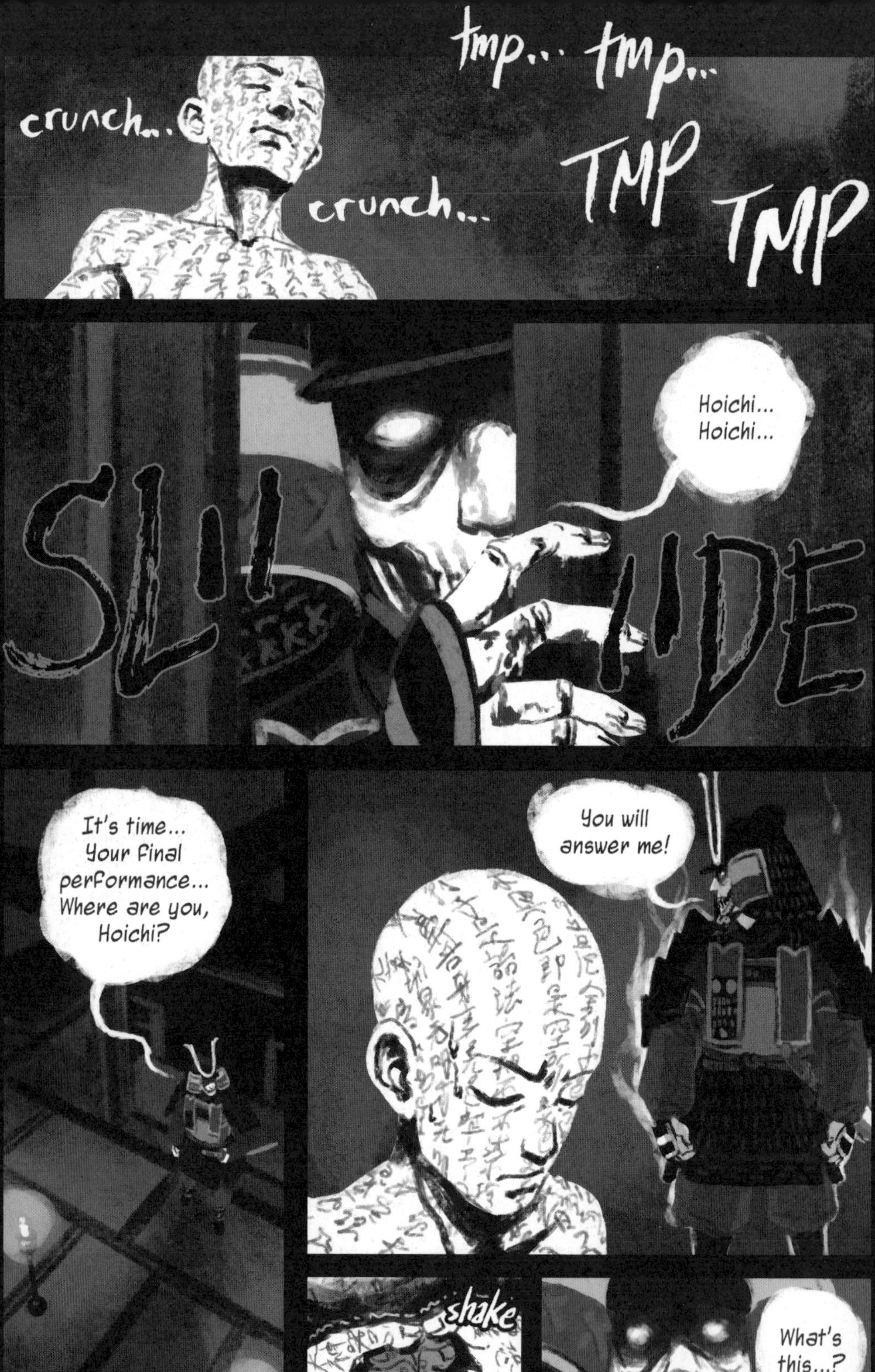

tmp... tmp...
crunch...
crunch...
TMP
TMP
Hoichi... Hoichi...
SLIIIDE
It's time... Your final performance... Where are you, Hoichi?
You will answer me!
shake
shake
What's this...?

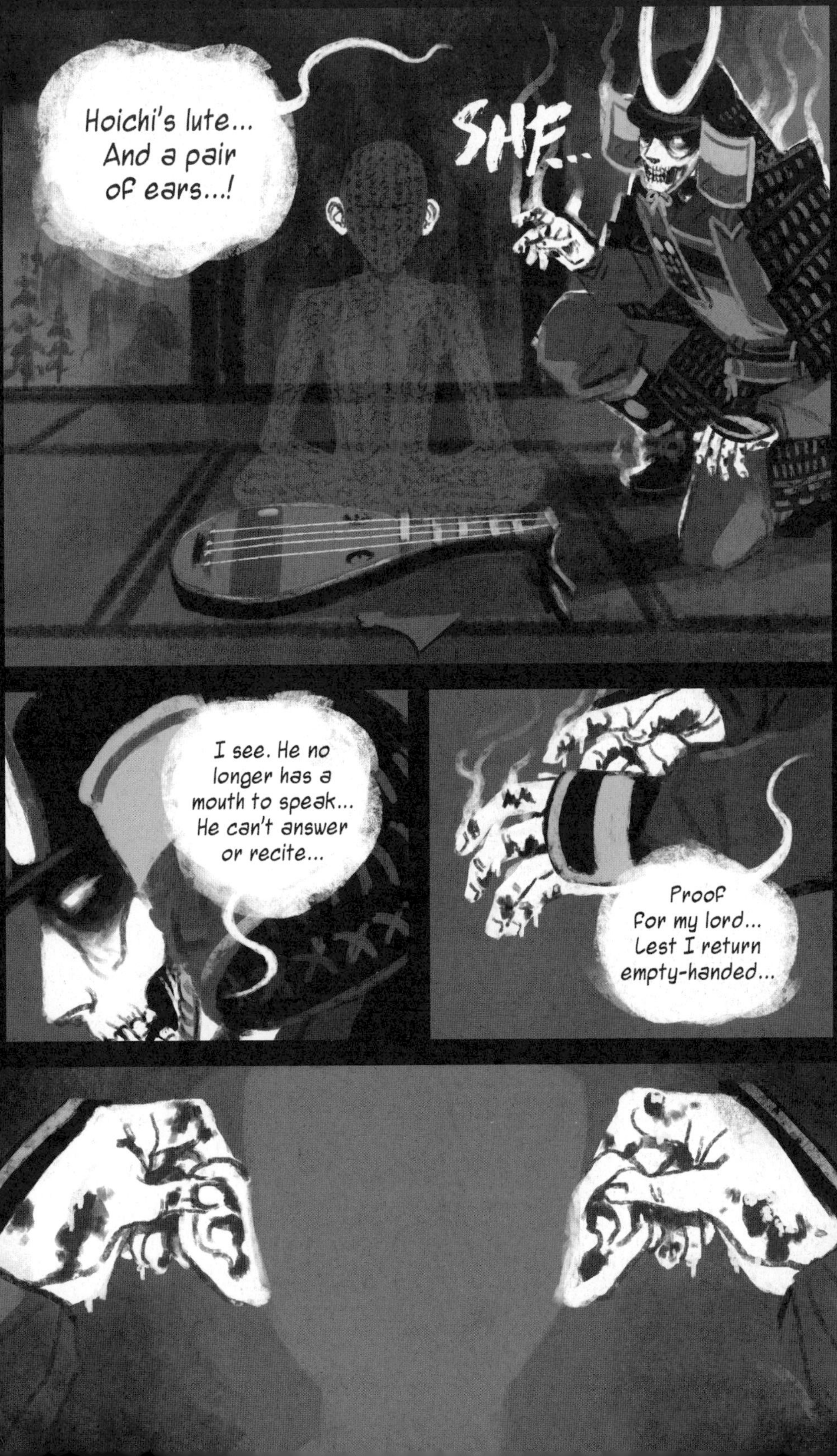
Hoichi's lute... And a pair of ears...!
SHF...
I see. He no longer has a mouth to speak... He can't answer or recite...
Proof for my lord... Lest I return empty-handed...

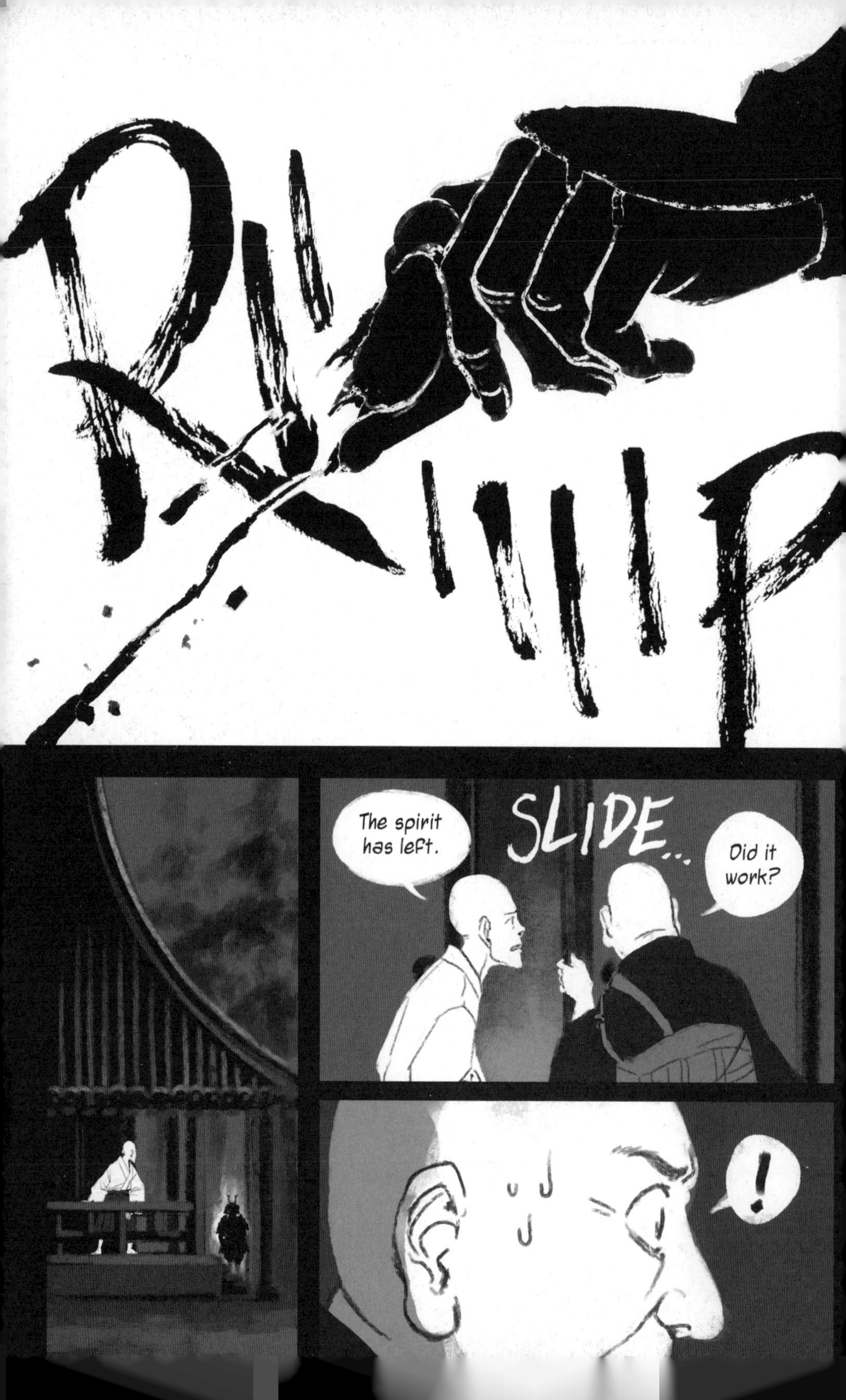
RRIIIP
The spirit has left.
SLIDE...
Did it work?
!

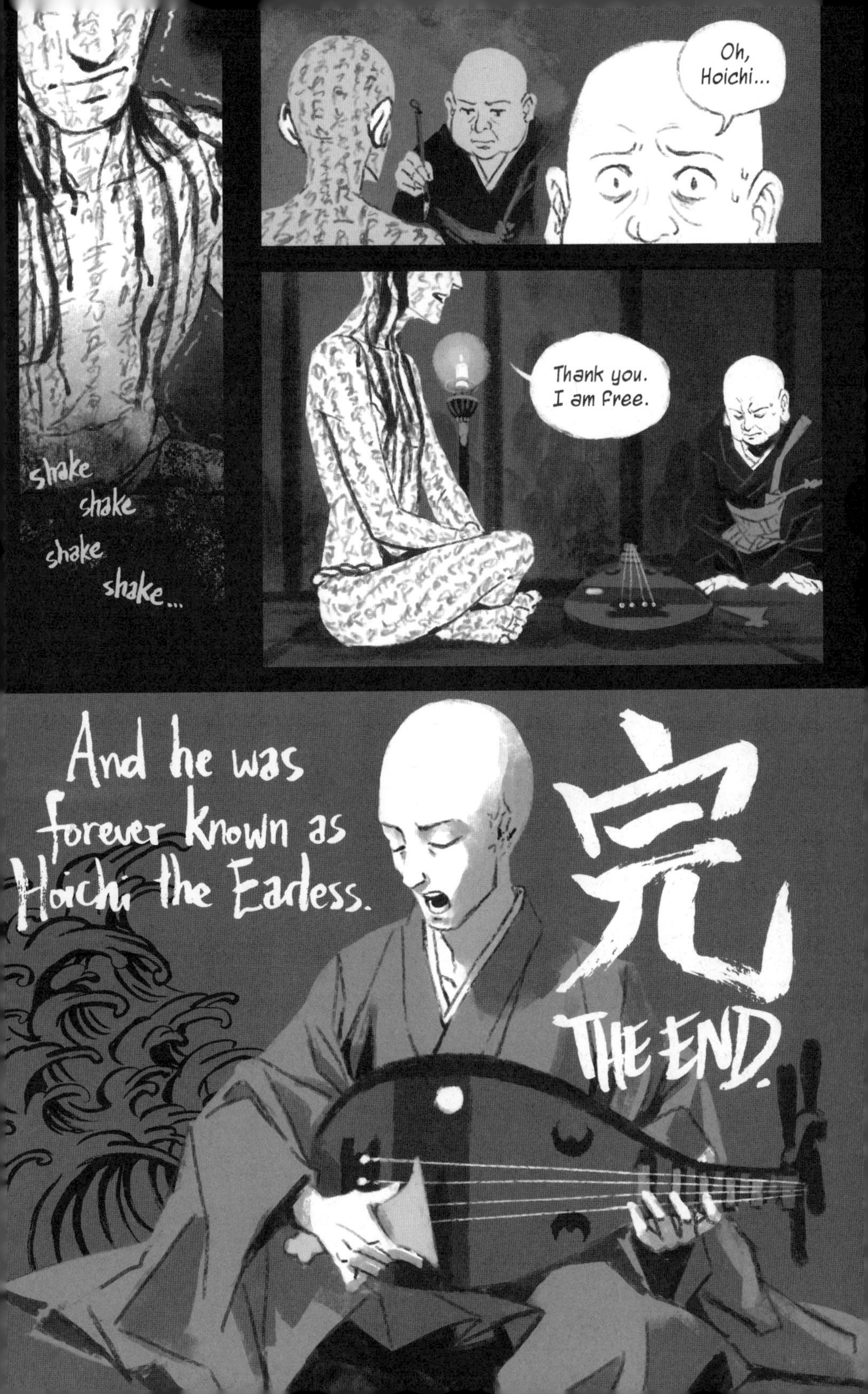
shake
shake
shake
shake...
Oh, Hoichi...
Thank you. I am free.
And he was forever known as Hoichi the Earless.
完
THE END.

The Flying Ogre

Adapted by Ron Chan

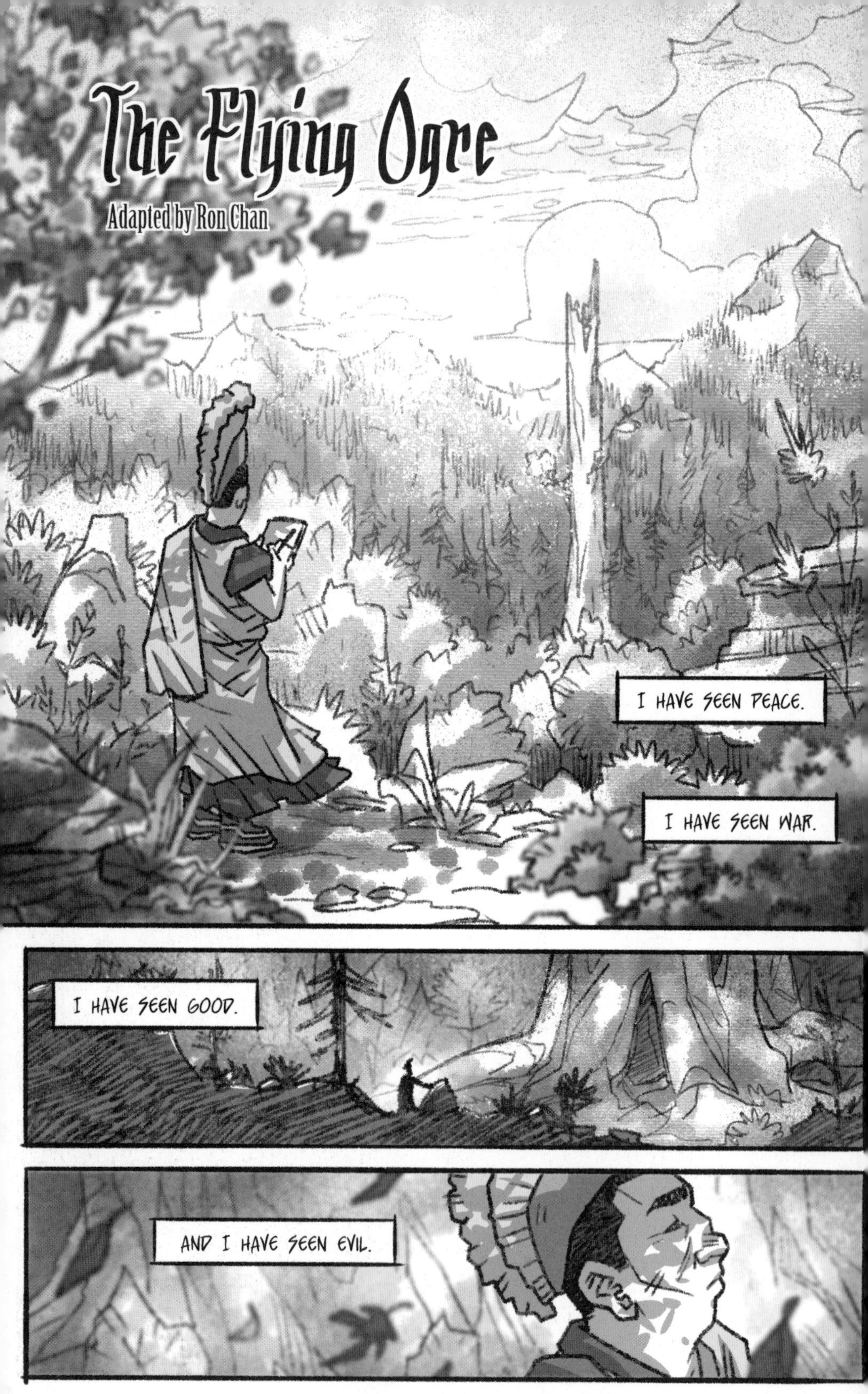
I HAVE SEEN PEACE.
I HAVE SEEN WAR.
I HAVE SEEN GOOD.
AND I HAVE SEEN EVIL.

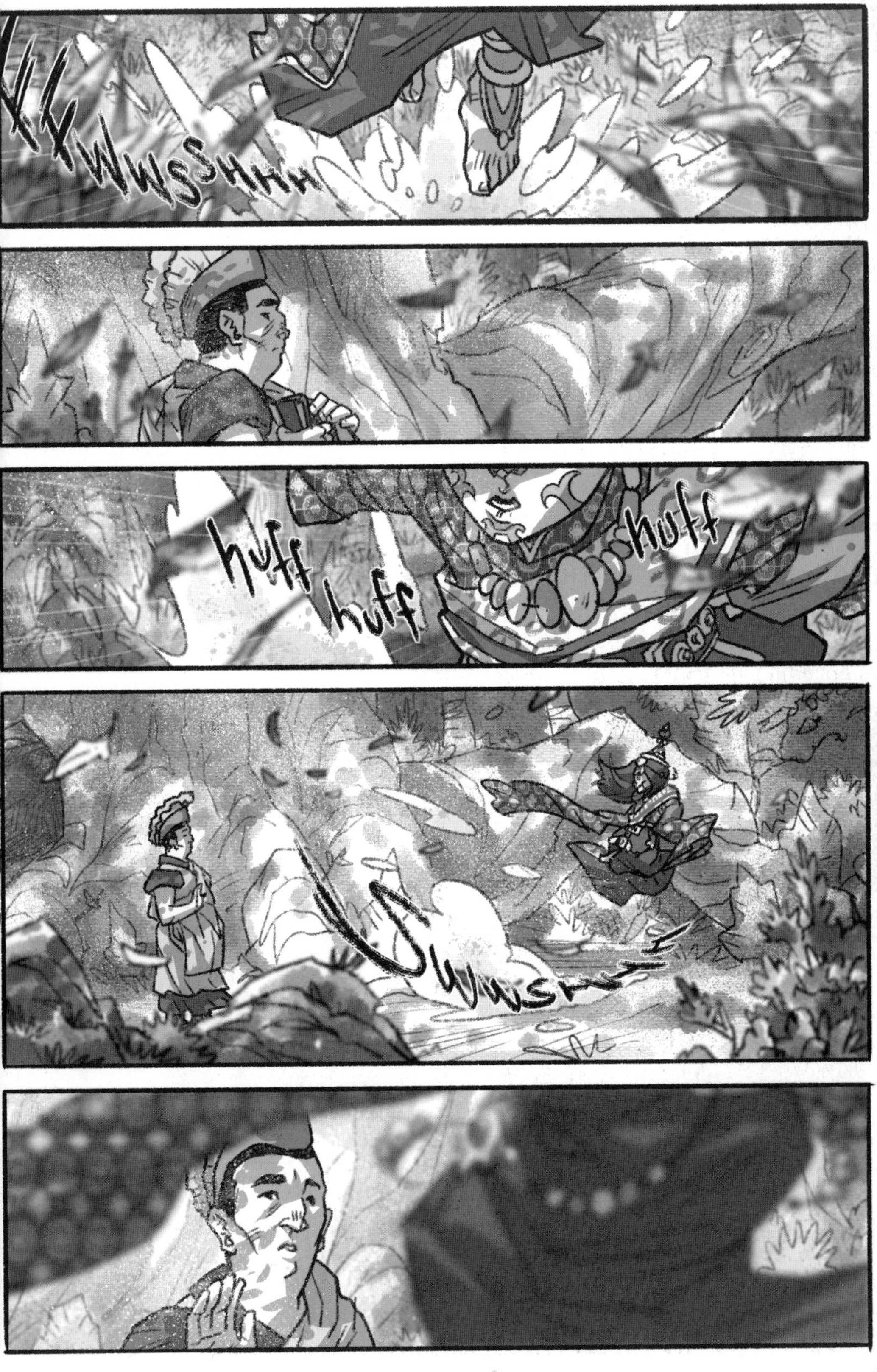
FFWWSHHH
huff
huff
huff
WWSHHH

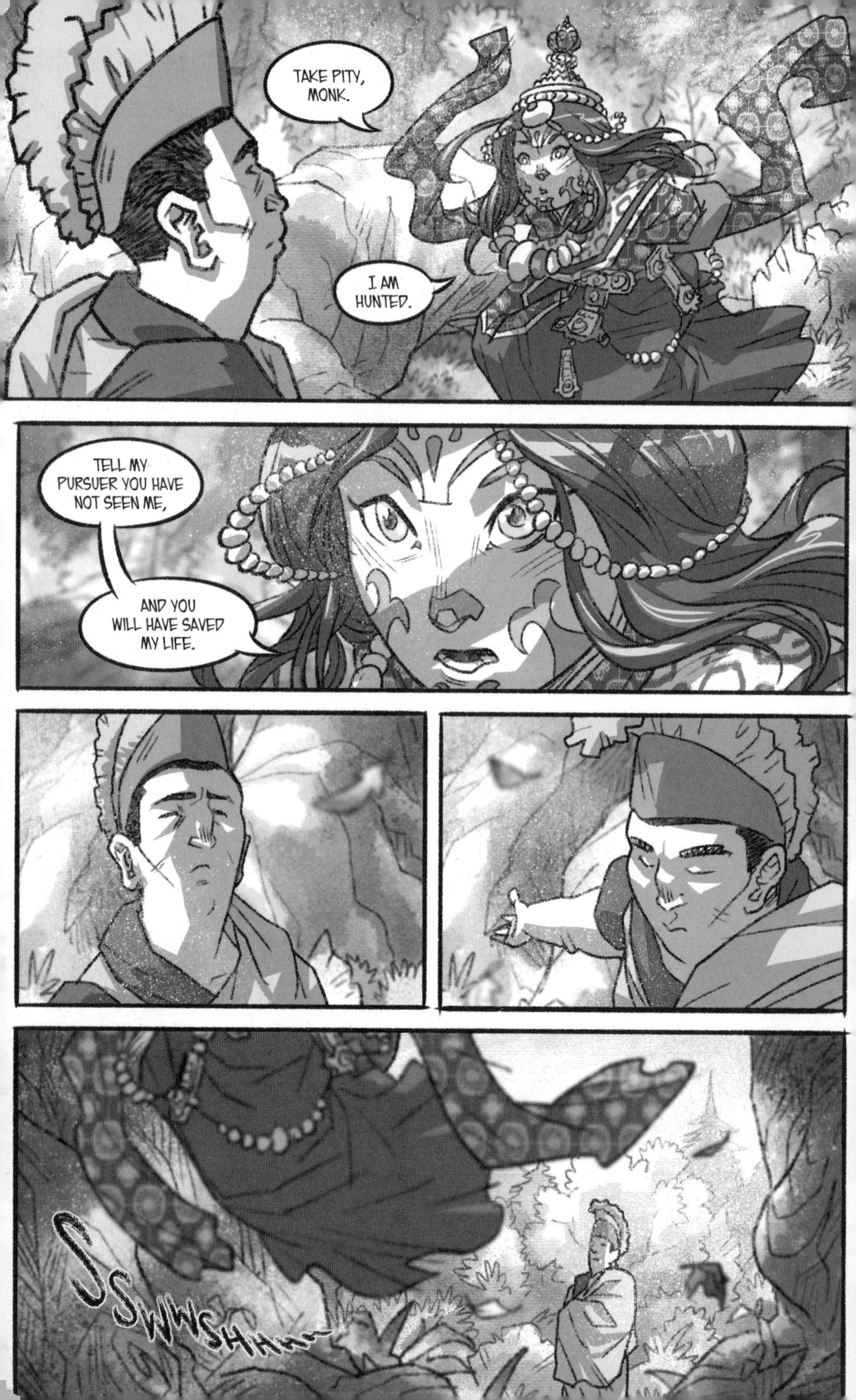
TAKE PITY, MONK.
I AM HUNTED.
TELL MY PURSUER YOU HAVE NOT SEEN ME,
AND YOU WILL HAVE SAVED MY LIFE.
SSWWSHH

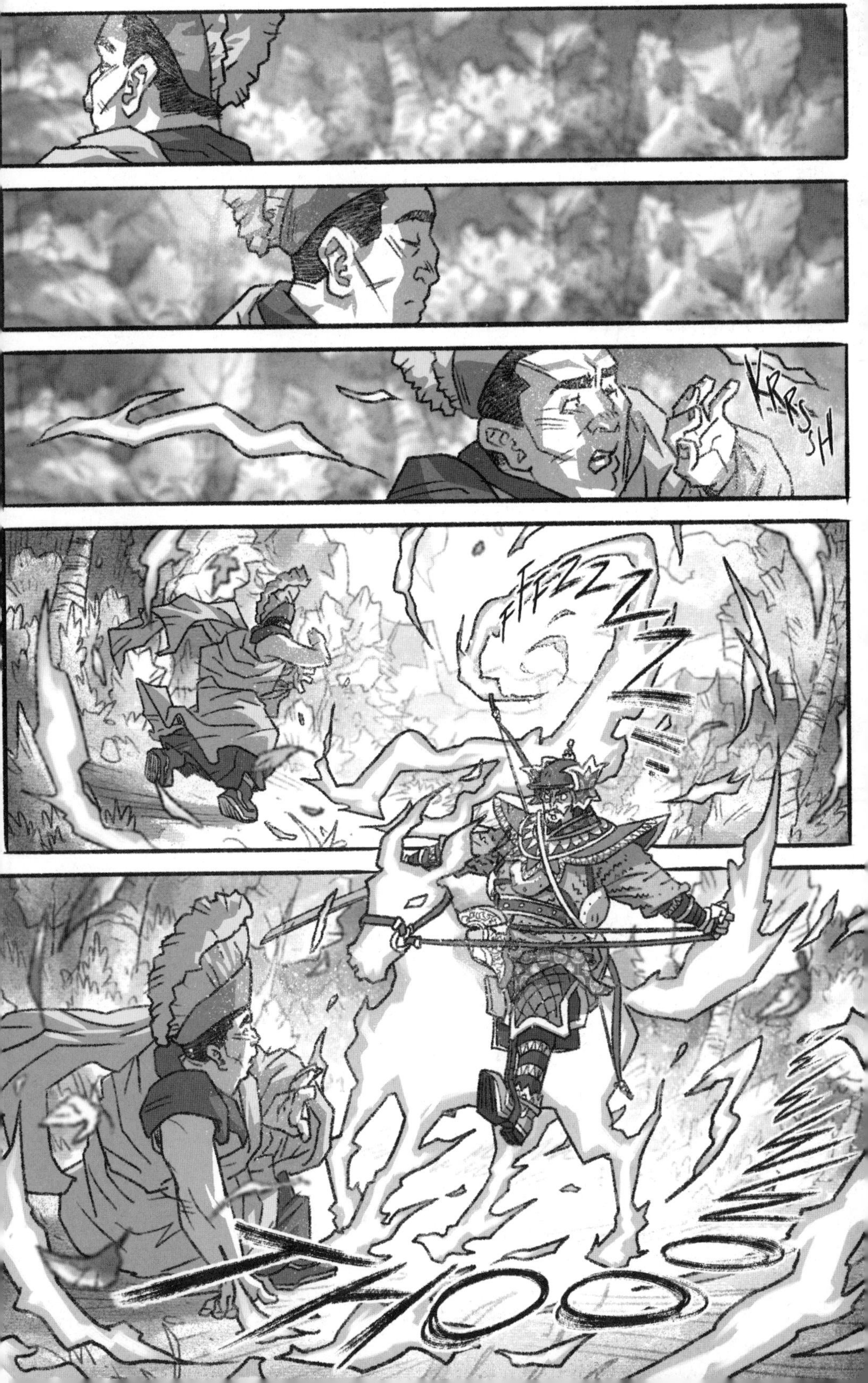
KRRRSSH
FFFZZZ
THOOOO

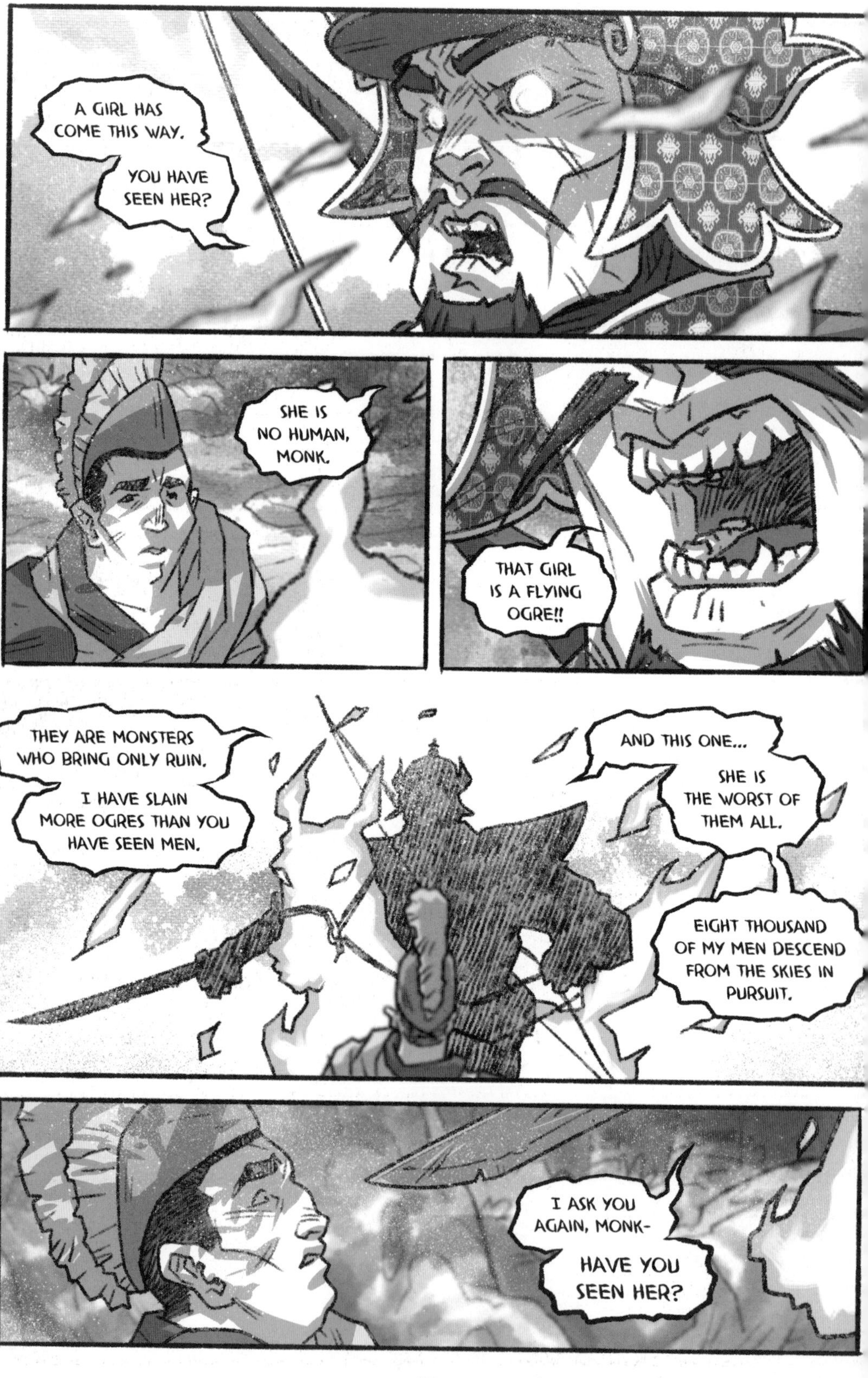
A GIRL HAS COME THIS WAY.
YOU HAVE SEEN HER?
SHE IS NO HUMAN, MONK.
THAT GIRL IS A FLYING OGRE!!
THEY ARE MONSTERS WHO BRING ONLY RUIN.
I HAVE SLAIN MORE OGRES THAN YOU HAVE SEEN MEN.
AND THIS ONE...
SHE IS THE WORST OF THEM ALL.
EIGHT THOUSAND OF MY MEN DESCEND FROM THE SKIES IN PURSUIT.
I ASK YOU AGAIN, MONK-
HAVE YOU SEEN HER?

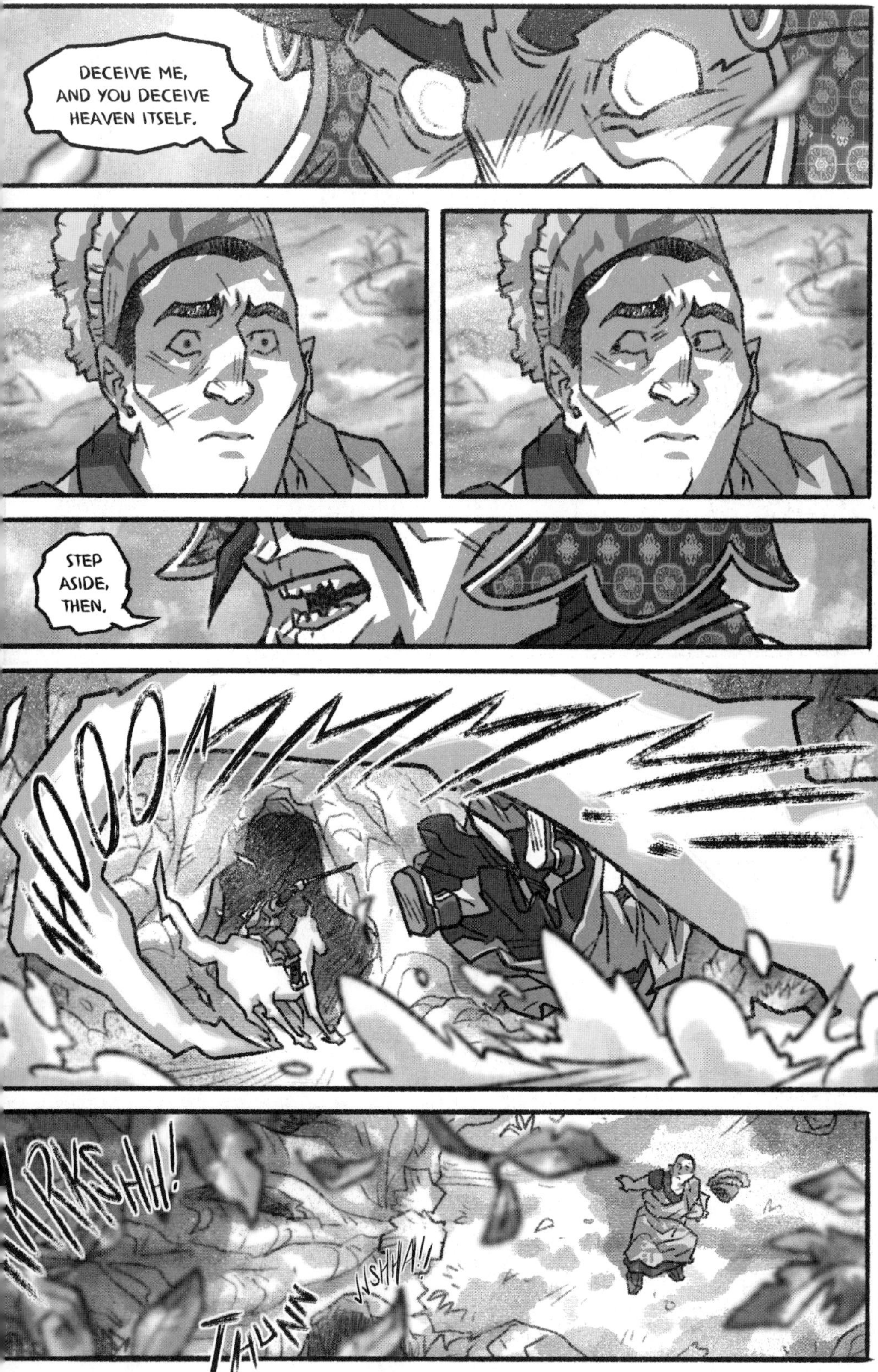
DECEIVE ME, AND YOU DECEIVE HEAVEN ITSELF.
STEP ASIDE, THEN.
WHOOOM
WHRKSHH!
THUNN
JJSHHA!!

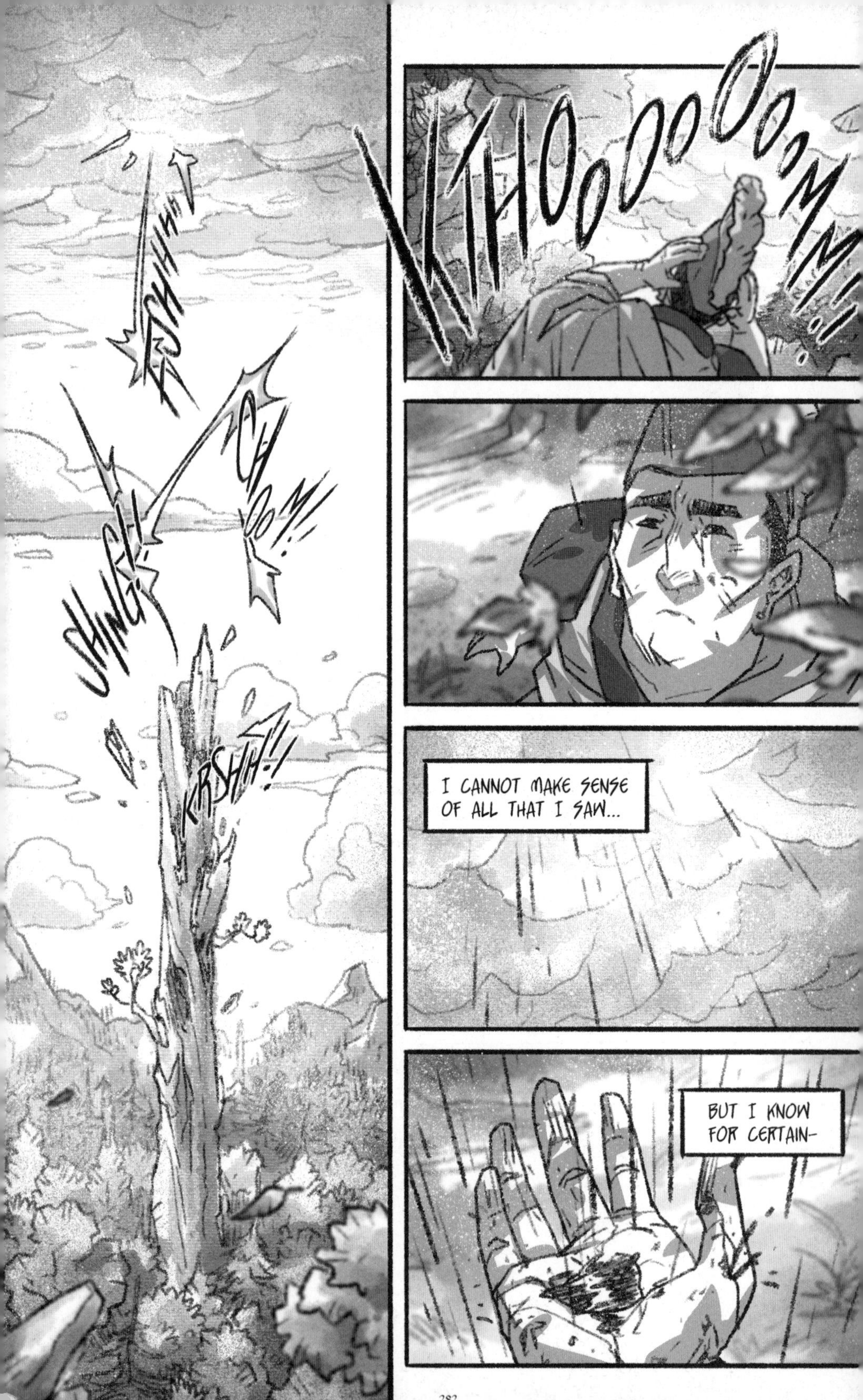
FSHHH
CHING!!
CHOOM!!
KRSHH!!
KTHOOOOOOOM!!
I CANNOT MAKE SENSE OF ALL THAT I SAW...
BUT I KNOW FOR CERTAIN-

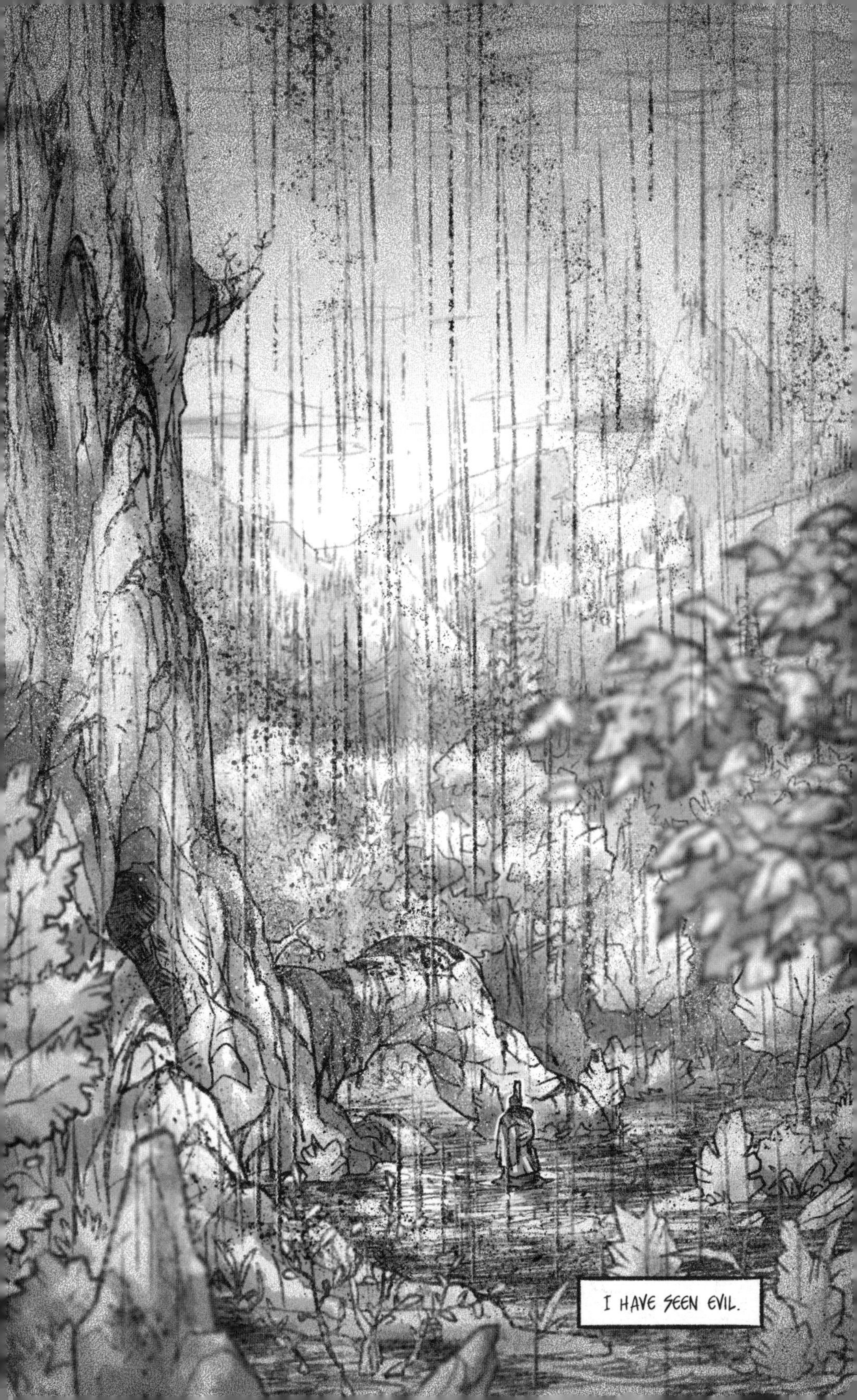
I HAVE SEEN EVIL.

About the Artists

Kate Ashwin has been writing and drawing online comics for over a decade, and has enjoyed every minute of it so far. Her completed fantasy epic **Darken** can be found online at darkencomic.com, and her ongoing Victorian-era adventure tale **Widdershins**, at widdershinscomic.com. She lives in the north of England with her husband and loud cats.

Lucy Bellwood is a nautical cartoonist working out of Periscope Studio in Portland, Oregon. When not writing and drawing her autobiographical, educational series **Baggywrinkles**, she contributes regularly to the all-ages fantasy series **Cartozia Tales**. Find more of her work at lucybellwood.com or on Twitter as @LuBellWoo.

Terry Blas is the illustrator and writer behind the ongoing web series **Briar Hollow**. His work has appeared on comic book covers for **Bravest Warriors**, **Regular Show**, **The Amazing World of Gumball**, **Adventure Time** with BOOM! Studios and **The Legend of Bold Riley** with Northwest Press. As the host of **The Gnerd Podcast**, he runs a weekly pop culture examination show. He is a member of Portland's own Periscope Studio, a collective of award-winning illustrators, cartoonists, and writers. His latest project is an original graphic novel called **Dead Weight**—a murder mystery set at a fat camp, co-written with Molly Muldoon and published by Oni Press. Recently, his auto-bio mini-comic, **You Say Latino**, was featured on NPR, OPB, Vox.com and Cosmo.com.

Jason Caffoe is the colorist and background artist for the bestselling graphic novel series **Amulet**, published by Scholastic. You can find more of his work at jcaffoe.com.

Shannon Campbell is a video game and comics writer from Vancouver, BC. She has written stories for Namco, Boom Studios, and many anthologies, and shares her positive opinions on video games, dogs, and feminism on her Twitter: @wordweasel.

Ron Chan is a comic book and storyboard artist from Portland, OR. He has worked on comics for Dark Horse, Marvel, and Image comics, and is most recently known for his work on the **Plants vs Zombies** comic. In his free time, he likes to play video games, draw fan art, and occasionally get his butt kicked taking jiu jitsu classes. Reach him at ronchan.net.

Nicole Chartrand is a concept artist by day and a comic artist by every other waking moment. She writes and draws the fantasy webcomic **Fey Winds** (which you can read at feywinds.com), drinks a lot of coffee, and has a lot of feelings about books, cartoons, and video games.

Sabrina Cotugno writes and draws stories. She graduated from Calarts in 2012 and presently works as a storyboard artist at Disney Television Animation. In her free time, she creates the webcomic **The Glass Scientists** and wishes she had more time to cook.

Jonathon Dalton lives just outside Vancouver, Canada. His past comics include the self-published graphic novels **A Mad Tea-Party** and the Xeric-winning **Lords of Death and Life**, as well as short comics for **New World**, Leia Weathington's **The Legend of Bold Riley**, and various anthologies from Cloudscape Comics. He has a lot of opinions about Hua Mulan. Reach him at lostcitycomics.com.

Blue Delliquanti is a cartoonist based out of Minneapolis and the creator of the science fiction webcomic **O Human Star**. Her work has also appeared in multiple comic anthologies, including **Beyond** and **Womanthology**. She enjoys riding trains and eating unusual foods.

Nick Dragotta is the co-creator and artist of both **Howtoons** and **East of West**, published by Image Comics.

Cat Farris is a rare Portland, OR native. She is also is the creator of the minicomic series **Flaccid Badger**, and the webcomic **The Last Diplomat**. An illustrator with an animation influence, Farris is best known for her cute and lively cartooning.

Based out of the San Francisco Bay area, **Ayano Hattori** is a freelance translator with a specialty in art and architecture. She holds a Bachelor of Arts in Japanese and Architecture from UC Berkeley. Her passion for manga started young with an introduction by a visiting family friend and, in hindsight, played a crucial part in learning the Japanese language and culture. This further propelled her interest in American comics and other arts.

Caitlyn Kurilich is a fantasy illustrator with a penchant for lady-knights, historical costuming, and tea-time. Sometimes she can be caught doodling unsuspecting strangers in cafes and gardens around Los Angeles, where she currently lives and works.

Stu Livingston is a cartoonist and storyboard artist living in Los Angeles. Creator of **The Table** and the **Spam Eggs & Rice** series, his comics have appeared in anthologies including **Flight** and **Explorer**. As a storyboard artist, his work has appeared on such shows as **Futurama**, **Steven Universe**, and **Clarence**. He has also taught Life Drawing at Calarts and The Concept Design Academy.

By day, **Nilah Magruder** is a storyboard artist in Los Angeles. By night she creates comics, children's books, and the occasional batch of chocolate chip cookies. Her webcomic, **M.F.K.**, won the inaugural Dwayne McDuffie Award for Diversity in 2015, and her first picture book, **How to Find a Fox**, was published in 2016 by Feiwel & Friends. When she is not drawing or writing,

Nilah is reading fantasy novels, watching movies, rollerskating, and fighting her cat for control of her desk chair.

Nina Matsumoto is a first generation Japanese-Canadian and Eisner-Award-winning artist who pencils for Bongo Comics (**Simpson Comics, Bart Simpson Comics**). Some of her favorite tales are kaidan—ghost stories. Her original English manga, **Yokaiden**, features Japanese spirits and monsters. When she's not drawing comics, she's designing T-shirts for video game apparel companies. Her art can also be seen in Japan on merchandise for the hit TV series **Game Center CX**. See more of her work at spacecoyote.com.

Meredith McClaren is an illustrator and cartoonist who has no business doing either. Rumor has it she's done work for Oni Press and BOOM! Studios in addition to her own webcomic series: **Hinges**. She may yet do more. Supposedly, she has a postal code in Arizona, but really she could be anywhere.

Kel McDonald draws comics all day, every day. She puts all these comics on her **Sorcery 101** site, sorcery101.net. Her main comics are **Misfits of Avalon** for Dark Horse Comics and her webcomic, **Sorcery 101**.

Carla Speed McNeil is best known for her Eisner award-winning science fiction series **Finder**, which she writes and draws. Originally from Louisiana, she now lives in Maryland with her husband and two kids, who love folktales.

Randy Milholland was born in Texas, briefly escaped to Massachusetts, and then was pulled back into his home state. He draws the comic **Something Positive** (found at somethingpositive.net) and his work has appeared in the anthology **Sleep of Reason** and the card game **Munchkin** (two cards, but that still counts). Like most people on the internet, he will tell you about his cats without provocation.

Molly "Jakface" Nemecek draws an ongoing urban fantasy webcomic called **Woo Hoo!** and inks another called **Even Death May Die!**, both of which she works on with writer J.R. Boos. She has been in the anthologies **Fujosports**, **TamaGotCheese**, **The Devastator: Otaku**, **Cry to the Moon**, **Mega Fauna**, **Purity**, and ECCC's **Monsters and Dames**. She's also done work for The Mary Sue. She occasionally draws pictures of cute booties and plays video games for inspiration. Her goal in life = bring laughter into the world by drawing fun things! She resides somewhere in BC, Canada secretly crushing on her new PM.

Jose Pimienta is a comic and storyboard artist raised in Mexicali, Mexico. His love for music, animation, and movies drove him to study comics in Georgia and hang out with other storytellers and other artists. In 2009, he moved to LA, where he currently lives, drawing, making music, and walking daily with a mug of coffee. In 2010, he had his two major books published: **A Friendly Game** and **From Scratch**. In 2014, his following book **The Leg** was out into the world and since then, he continues to storyboard commercials and do other comic work. He also has a thing for hats.

Andrew Sides is a freelance illustrator who lives in Orlando, FL. He attended Savannah College of Art and Design to study Sequential Art, and now spends his time split between studying online at the Watts Atelier, drawing fantastical illustrations, and sculpting dinosaurs. He loves learning and creating new things, but hates puns with the passion of a thousand burning suns.

Gene Luen Yang's 2006 book **American Born Chinese** was the first graphic novel to be nominated for a National Book Award and the first to win the American Library Association's Michael L. Printz Award. His 2013 two-volume graphic novel **Boxers & Saints** was also nominated for a National Book Award and won the L.A. Times Book Prize. Gene currently writes Dark Horse Comics' **Avatar: The Last Airbender** and DC Comics' **Superman**.